MEN OF GOOD WILL

THE EARTH TREMBLES

MEN OF GOOD WILL

Volume Five

Book IX. FLOOD WARNING

Book X. THE POWERS THAT BE

Translated from the French for the first time, by **GERARD HOPKINS**

THE EARTH TREMBLES

by Jules Romains

Alfred A. Knopf · New York · 1936

Originally published as
LES HOMMES DE BONNE VOLONTÉ
IX. *Montée des périls*
X. *Les Pouvoirs*

Copyright 1935 by Ernest Flammarion

Contents

9. FLOOD WARNING

Contents

10. THE POWERS THAT BE

BOOK NINE:

FLOOD WARNING

Chapter

THE NORTHERN SUBURBS

The very small hours of the 31st of October, eve of All Saints', showed a very different face in the flat industrial suburbs to the north, and in Paris proper.

At the city's centre, even in the relatively outlying districts, a few great thoroughfares, it is true, already echoed to the footsteps of early workers, or to the sound of trucks headed for the open country, but such streams as there were flowed between vast areas still silent and undisturbed. All about the hastening pedestrians thousands of their fellows yet dozed in peace, though to their senses, caught in the soft web of dreams, the noise of emptying ash-cans and the rattle of early milk-carts brought a vague consciousness of time.

But far away to the north the day's business was already in full swing. Noise and movement filled the streets. Here and there great windows, brightly lit, showed warm against the frozen pallor of the sky. Not a corner but resounded to the throb and whirr of wheels. The very earth seemed to tremble like the floor of a factory to the vibration of countless machines, each driving blindly on, intent on secret purposes. There was a quality of fierceness in the siren's shriek, even in the ears of the overalled workmen who heard it as a daily summons, telling of the last five minutes before the gates would close. Elsewhere the rhythm of the daily task was fully set; indeed, it was difficult to believe that it had ever stopped, even during the hours of night.

Narrow lanes like cracks led between walls of hollow bricks standing on flimsy foundations of rust-roughened girders. At the bottom, mud had collected which nothing but the frosts of winter or the drying warmth of spring would dissipate. It was as though the very blackness of night had joined with the waterlogged soil to produce this particular quality of filth, and now hung still about it, loth to take flight. Clogs made a sucking noise in the sticky mixture, and skidding bicycle tires left in their wake a criss-cross of seemingly capricious knots and tangles.

In addition to these narrow thoroughfares a few main avenues, vast and pallid, pierced the quarter. Between their sidewalks of beaten earth, adorned with sickly trees and iron posts, they were wide enough to accommodate two lines of street-car rails and four trucks abreast. For minutes together they were empty save for a solitary cyclist or pedestrian, and at such times the noise of factories, swelling to a roar on every hand, took on the character of some monstrous force of nature. Such moments of rare solitude, forcing on the passer-by the sense that he and all around him were caught and crushed in the steel jaws of the modern world, made the dawn seem greyer and set the teeth a-chattering in the gusty cold.

For a hundred years this northern fringe has been growing. As far as possible it has avoided all contact with earlier villages. The locality of its choice was the waste land of the low and wind-swept levels, avoided by older settlers and unattractive to those later pioneers who set out from Paris in the innocent hope of finding near at hand the freedom of the open country. For that very reason it seemed ideal as an area for industrial expansion. What Big Business needed was cheap land, and enough of it to be thought of in terms of acres rather than of yards: and it preferred converting old refuse-dumps or, at the worst, turnip-fields, to demolishing and clearing a lot of suburban villas.

Development, however, proceeded in obedience to certain perfectly definite laws. Low-priced sites were not the only consideration. Other advantages, both positive and negative, difficult to find in the immediate neighbourhood of a city like Paris, here offered themselves in abundance.

Not the least of these was the absence of hills. For the petty tradesman, seeking some site on which to build himself a chalet which should evoke the rocky charms of Switzerland, the district was clearly unsuitable. But this very flatness became an asset in the eyes of men intent on the rapid construction of factories, on the erection of rows of uniform workshops, with the roadways and court-yards necessary for convenient access. A level locality simplified the problem of transport and diminished the number of horses needed for heavy traffic.

Then it was an advantage to be within easy reach of the city's business centre while, at the same time, avoiding the embarrassment of toll dues and the inconvenience of police regulations. It was es-sential for new enterprises to have access to the railways serving the industrial provinces, and convenient to be able to make use of river and canal facilities for the reception and dispatch of heavy mer-chandise.

These various considerations combined to turn the low plain which extends northwards from Paris as far as the loop of the Seine into the city's main industrial suburb. Little by little the district was fated to become a place of huge and melancholy buildings, the home of an ever-increasing, active, pullulating proletariat: a world of steel and energy where life was lived close to the stark realities. Historic Paris, the Paris of luxury and fine monuments, of green and shady avenues, made pretence of ignoring the upstart. But, for all that, it could not but realize the alien growth there at its very gates, admit its necessity, and feel its threatening presence.

Nevertheless, this suburb, type of the new age, dedicated to the god of the machines, did not spring fully grown from the soil. It began to emerge at the beginning of the nineteenth century, at first retaining some of the simplicity, some of the unexpectedness, of an earlier dispensation, and setting itself to supply the age-old demands of the city or responding to local conditions, much as the older vil-lages which it absorbed had done.

Long before, while Paris still remained bounded by the defences of 1846, a centrifugal movement had begun, stimulated by the fact that certain aspects of the city's life, dirty and unsightly, such as sewage farms, cemeteries, slaughter-houses, depots of wood and coal, by being banished to the outer fringe, had sown the seed of later suburban growth. Soon came freight stations, railway sheds, gas-works, a conglomeration of various enterprises, each within its own walled enclosure, bounded by interminable streets, shaken with noise or hushed in frightening silence, stinking and miserable.

It needed but one further stage in this movement of decentralization, a stressing of the city's contemptuous indifference, to bring into being, on the open ground between these village settlements, a second outlying growth, a definite suburban development beyond the ramparts. In the close proximity of Paris or in demands arising in their own immediate neighbourhood, these villages soon found or created sufficient justification for their continued existence, with the result, that, little by little, for good or for ill, they found themselves becoming merged in the new rash of habitations which was slowly emerging on the outskirts of the city.

At Pantin there was a rapid increase of plaster-works owing to the accessibility of the Romainville quarries. Sugar-refineries sprang up at Aubervilliers because of the neighbouring fields and stores of beets which pervade the whole north-east of the Île-de-France with their sickening stench. Later still the erection of factories for artificial manures, for chemical products and synthetic perfumes brought an even richer variety of smells to the district, complicating the existing mixture with sewage exhalations and sulphur fumes. Aubervilliers soon became a sort of plague-spot, smothering with its fetid breath the central or the eastern districts of the city, according to the direction of the wind. It was soon the source of what those who live north of the river have become accustomed to call "the country smells," a feature of Paris life which, however unpleasant, has certain engaging features, since the wind that brings the smell is always the herald of fine weather.

Saint-Denis set itself to the fabrication of soda, chemical products, and lead plates and became the port of destination of great barges loaded with heavy goods from the provinces, taking its place as a sort of Picard or Flemish port attached to the capital. At Clichy arose, side by side, laundries of ever increasing capacity and drug-factories. Production of printed calico became the feature of Puteaux, distilleries of Neuilly. In proportion as industry felt its way towards the west, winning ground inch by inch from its more prosperous neighbours, the quality of the articles became progressively lighter and more elegant.

At a still later date the great metallurgical enterprises, with their massive plants, foundries, rolling-mills, boiler-works, began the era of their development. Machine-shops made their appearance, auto-mobile-works, and, with them, factories for the production of paint, varnishes, and shoe-polishes. This was the period of huge woodwork establishments with their subsidiary services, lumber-yards, coal-depots, steel-works, reservoirs of heavy oil and gasolene—the period of giant gas-tanks, ranged in rows like herds of elephants, squadrons of battle-cruisers, mountain systems; the period of centralized power-houses, dominating the plain with their lighted windows, shaking the earth and walls with a mysterious throbbing that made itself heard even above the noise of the traffic.

For a whole century the energy and vitality of this suburb has been growing. More and more important has it become for Paris, more and more has the capital grown to depend upon it. The city is its exacting taskmaster, setting upon its back, with hardly a thought, the burden of a harsh servitude. It has become the home of all those gross, irksome, ill-smelling, deafening, and humiliating activities which its neighbour seeks to keep hidden from the light of day and to forget, but which less and less can it do without; the slave of a thousand hands, yet master too, just because it is there, just because without it existence in the modern world has become impossible.

Little by little, without intending it, without even foreseeing it, these northern suburbs have got a stranglehold on the daily life of Paris, slowly concentrating within their grasp the power, the resources, and the means without which the city can neither continue as an agglomeration of human beings nor function as a capital.

Parallel to this increase in production, there has emerged from within the army of individuals assembled to serve it an entirely new orientation of the collective energy, of the collective will, a regrouping of spiritual factors unlike any previous reality, a hierarchy of control, the growth of which has proceeded, to some extent, surreptitiously. A new class discipline, born of the workers themselves, has developed alongside the factory discipline imposed by the employers, not at first openly hostile to it, but watchful and suspicious. Making no attempt to interfere with the daily routine of work, with the purely technical control of resources exercised by the management, it has reserved to itself the right of taking considered action, even if such action should be nothing beyond a negative resistance, whenever a situation might arise involving the whole social system; when, for instance, the day shall come for the leaders of the proletariat to exploit a revolutionary situation.

To the purely material development of industrialism has been added a trade-union movement which has penetrated into the remotest interstices of the system and followed its every ramification. An indissoluble bond has been forged between the two organizations.

As a result, Paris has found itself faced by a new social *fact,* no less strong for being invisible, and destined to be of the greatest significance for the country as a whole. But at first neither ministers, politicians, nor even the leaders of the proletariat had the faintest idea of the exact nature of what had thus come into being.

What really had happened was that two polar systems had arisen, two definite concentrations of power and material resources, ranged in mutual opposition, neither wholly ignorant of the fact, but neither as yet sure of itself or of the relationship subsisting between them. Contradictory in their respective essences, they stood at bay across a few miles of seething humanity.

To the south, in the district of the Palais-Bourbon, the Élysée, and the government offices, where the Seine, after flowing through the heart of Paris, turns left, lay the forces of legality, entrenched behind the breastworks of representative democracy and strong in the accumulated political tradition of centuries.

To the north, in the flat lands contained within the very next bend made by the river, had arisen a new authority of *fact,* as yet imperfectly organized, unsure of itself, equipped with untried weapons, but convinced that the future was its own, and already the prey of violent temptation.

It is true that in theory at least it took its orders from a general staff situated elsewhere, in the rue Grange-aux-Belles and at trade-union headquarters. But organized labour is governed at closer range than the traditional State. Decisions are taken and instructions issued in contact with the rank and file. Despite all efforts to establish a formal hierarchy, the workers have kept clear of abstractions. The system which they have forged never moves far from the mass from which it derives its sanctions, and it reflects in its nature certain characteristics of the crowd whose movements it registers direct. Its officers are not yet firmly enough seated in the saddle to separate themselves from the living forces they claim to control. When need for action arises, decisions are taken on the spot, within the confines of the northern suburbs, where this new proletariat, with the machines it serves, works out its daily life.

Chapter

2

OCTOBER STORM

For these ranged and contrasted Powers the month of October 1910 had been profoundly significant. Till then they had faced one another at a respectful distance, two massive and self-contained wholes. Unequal in strength they might be, but to what extent nobody as yet was in a position positively to state. Each had its own degree of radiation, of heat, of density, of tension. They were like two stars of different colour, weight, and age, upon the opposition and eventual clash of which much of the future was seen to depend.

The general strike, so often prophesied by the far-seeing or relegated by theorists to an exciting world of make-believe, had now become a matter of practical politics, and when it came, it came with the force of a hurricane. It had been prepared since the summer by a number of local strikes and heralded from still further back by a series of movements inspired by the trade-union organization, and quite definitely revolutionary in intention. The most important of these had been the postal strike of March 1909 and the seamen's strike of April and May 1910. From an industrial sky thus charged with thunder the storm burst with a violence which seemed to increase with every hour, shaking the whole fabric of society to its foundations and giving to those who lived within it a sense of insecurity unlike anything they had so far experienced.

It began on the 10th with the operatives of the Northern Railway and extended in the course of the next two days to all the other systems. By the 15th it had become so far general as to involve most of the services on which the capital depended for its existence.

For the first time in history the two Powers, till then confronting each other in a condition of armed truce, had actually joined battle. The younger of the two had determined to put to the test, if nothing more, the means by which it might rid itself of the domination of the older. The trade-union leaders, without, perhaps, intending to enter on the "final struggle" foretold by their prophets, and without going so far as to declare that war on society which, like every other war, commits the aggressor to a final trial of strength that can end only with the destruction of himself or his opponent, had taken the first step in their program by mobilizing the proletariat. It was not yet open revolution, but it was a dress rehearsal which might eventually turn out to be the first act. Should conditions seem favourable, should the movement, once initiated, develop of itself in a revolutionary direction, it was unlikely that its instigators would make any great efforts to check its momentum. They had not deliberately planned to go the whole hog, but they considered themselves free to be determined by the event. And, indeed, the new technique of revolution encouraged a policy of drifting, a policy to be determined by the natural tendency of results to outstrip intentions, since it consisted, essentially, not in taking the strongholds of the established order by a series of costly frontal attacks, but rather in waiting patiently for the surrender of the besieged.

Official Paris was suddenly forced to realize the presence and the pressure of the northern suburbs as an appalling reality in face of which it was helpless. It was borne in upon it that orders issued by government were no longer valid beyond the walls of the ministries, that at the distance of a few miles they dropped powerless and dead. It was as though some huge animal was lying athwart the lines that connected the central authority with its distant agents of administration. No need for the beast to move or to destroy. The mere weight of its body brought everything to a standstill, and the weight seemed to increase from day to day. Wider and wider grew the extent of its influence, more and more lines became involved. The strike, beginning with the railways, soon spread to the whole transport system and then to the power-plants. Directly or indirectly the distribution of food was affected. There was a shortage of bread and of milk as well as of light.

Paris, accustomed through its long history to an older type of revolution which had been fought out in the streets, was as much surprised as terrified to find that this new power on its outskirts, strong in its control of machinery, this new agglomeration which it had seen grow without thought or fear, was asserting its authority not to the traditional accompaniment of mob violence, but by the simpler method of suffocation. Such an enemy was hard to fight —in fact, there was no fight at all, no rising to suppress. No charge of dragoons will set dynamos going nor put the trains in motion.

On their side, too, the forces of the north were amazed by the extent of the results which they had been led to achieve by sheer inactivity. The strike is essentially a negative weapon, a suspension of work, a paralysis of effort, and as such it can hope to arouse but a limited and rather drab enthusiasm. Uncertainty develops more easily in such conditions than where active aggressiveness is the order of the day.

The government hit on a daring and ingenious plan. The trade-union leaders had mobilized the proletariat for their own purposes, starting with the railwaymen, who, even after the other unions had followed suit, remained the nerve and centre of the movement. This mobilization had been a very real, a terribly effective thing. All it lacked was the legal sanction and the official use of the word "mobilization" with its prestige and the almost mystical connotation of significance which it carries with it. The government remembered that by law the railwaymen could be duly mobilized in time of war. Surely, by stretching a point, the law could be so interpreted as to make mobilization enforceable also in time of peace if the interests of public security demanded it? There were two risks involved. Such an interpretation of the law might be held to be casuistical, and it was possible that the parliamentary parties of the Left, always more sensitive to forms than to realities, might raise the cry of *"Coup d'état,"* of "Dictatorship." But this risk was not very

FLOOD WARNING

serious, far less so than the second. After all, anything is justified by success: an action only becomes criminal when it fails. No, the only thing really to be feared was failure. Would the railwaymen, mobilized by their leaders against the established order, consent to be mobilized by the forces of law for the very purpose of saving that order? Would the second act of mobilization be able to counter the first and neutralize its effects? If the railwaymen found themselves holding mobilization instructions in one hand and their union cards in the other, how would they act? Which of the two pieces of paper would have the greater force, which of the two ideas thus conjured up in the mind would be most difficult to exorcize? Which of two courses would seem the most impossible, to refuse obedience to an order suddenly reinforced by military authority, or to be false to class loyalty in the very heat of the struggle? The attitude of the railwaymen, supported as they were by the body of other trades, would decide the issue. The stake could not be exaggerated. The whole fate of Society, now and for the future, was involved. But the future was concerned in more ways than one. For some years now revolutionary unionism had taken on a definitely anti-militarist tinge. Dissatisfied with empty formulas, with mere academic resolutions against the policy of an armed peace and against war, the movement had set itself to combat these two calamities by means of organized action on the part of the proletariat. Several workers' congresses had discussed in detail the possibility of dislocating mobilization on the eve of the outbreak of hostilities. Mere individual refusal to report for duty would not be enough; any such course of action must be supported by the general strike and by the destruction of a certain amount of material. No country can make war if the railways have ceased to work, if the reservists fail to turn out, if factories close down and bridges are blown up. No matter how bellicose a government might be, it could never, under such conditions, realize its criminal intentions. With a weapon so blunted it could make theatrical gestures in the void for ever.

The press, in order to keep public opinion informed and forearmed, had given a good deal of space to these discussions and to the resolutions which had been their outcome. A great many people in official circles as well as members of the upper and middle classes, not excluding several of a lower social grade (and such are by no means the least patriotic section of the community), had regarded the danger as a very real one. Whenever foreign relations tended to become strained, whenever the French Foreign Office showed an unwillingness to be conciliatory and raised its voice, the same question made itself heard on many lips: "It's all very well, but could we even mobilize? You saw how all those workmen voted the other day?"

To force an issue which might end in the railwaymen refusing to obey a mobilization order would be an extremely dangerous experiment. Uncertainty, still clinging to a hope, might be turned into certainty without any hope at all. The result would be that the trade-union movement would have proved to its own satisfaction that it was stronger than the existing State machinery and could go exactly as far as it liked, and when it liked, on the road that led to revolution. But worse than that, such a result might also furnish incontrovertible proof of national impotence. The foreigner, the inevitable foe of the future, would realize that France was incapable of resistance. No longer would it be possible to beat the big diplomatic drum.

In view of these various considerations the government passed an hour of the greatest possible anxiety. Would the railwaymen answer yes or no?

Only a very few said no.

On the 18th the trains were once more running. The distribution of flour, milk, and meat was resumed. Lights once more went on when the switches were pressed.

The storm had lasted for eight days.

If Paris, and a few other great cities, had been conscious of a slight earthquake, the real countryside had not had time to notice anything. Even when things had been at their worst, Mionnet, sauntering along the streets of M— had been sufficiently undisturbed to notice the direction of the wind and to watch the play of the October sunlight on the walls.

But those eight days were to produce results which would be long in dying. The forces that they had liberated made themselves felt in many obscure and unexpected ways. Not a village, however remote, not a man, but in some way or other was conscious of their effect.

Chapter

MAILLECOTTIN AND HIS LATHE

The appearance of things was once more almost normal both in the streets of official Paris which lie around the Palais-Bourbon and in the industrial quarters of the northern fringe. Life was again much as it had been.

At seven o'clock in the morning official Paris is still silent and deserted. Streets and offices alike are empty. Even the sleepers within its gates are, except in rare instances, of a different kind from those who later, when the sun is higher, will come thither to talk and plan and play their parts. Until that happens, the character of the district remains thin, lifeless, and vague, bodied forth only in the slumber of occasional dowagers or in the waking discomfort of a few low-spirited caretakers. The vitality of the neighbourhood lies at a lower level.

But northwards the muddy alleys are already astir and life has begun to hum behind the great lit windows.

This was the hour at which Edmond Maillecottin, pushing his bicycle before him with his left hand behind the saddle, was accustomed to enter the side gate of Bertrand's factory which was known as the Four-Ways. The main entrance was used only by the carts and trucks which needed more space, and was not permanently opened until later in the morning.

Maillecottin registered his arrival on the new machine which the boss had recently installed for an experimental period, after having tried several other systems. (M. Bertrand had a mania for improvements—or for what he took to be improvements. In the equipment of his factory, too, he loved change merely for the sake of change. It was his particular form of restlessness.) This new gadget of his was, in theory at least, simplicity itself. On Saturday morning, at pay-time, each man was handed a small yellow card marked out into six squares. Each morning of the following week, the workmen, as they arrived, had the appropriate square stamped by the machine, which was, in fact, an automatic register operated by clockwork. It stamped, in thick, smudgy ink, the hour and minute of arrival, followed by the date. The doorkeeper on duty took no part in the process except to rectify mechanical breakdowns and to keep a sharp eye on fraudulent practices. (Occasionally a man would get a card stamped belonging to a pal who had given it to him overnight, with the intention of indulging in an extra hour or so in bed.) At pay-time the cards were handed in. No discussion about deductions or fines was possible, and the cards, it appeared, were filed in the office for future reference.

Edmond, who still lived with his parents, left the rue Compans at twenty-five minutes past six, half past at latest. To reach the factory he had to cover just over four miles, and his average rate of progress was about eight miles an hour. Considering the bad state of the roads, the frequent repairs in progress, and the additional obstacles represented by rain and mud, this was not too bad. Luckily he could get a good start down the straight, steep slope of the rue de Crimée, which, at so early an hour, he could safely take at full speed, doing an easy fifteen or eighteen, so that in five minutes he could be at the canal. At that time of the morning the drawbridge was almost always closed, but it was always a bit of a gamble whether it would be or not. When, by ill luck, he found the chains taut and the spans in the air, he had either to turn sharp right and make a long détour along a bumpy quay as far as the Pont des Abattoirs or to the left by the Pont de la Moselle. This latter was no more than a sort of hump-backed stairway, and he had to make the ascent and descent on foot, running like mad, with his bicycle on his shoulders, and a muddy pedal sticking into his ribs or his rump. Obviously, if there had been any way of guessing on which days the bridge would be

open, he would have made straight for the Pont des Abattoirs in the
first instance, despite the fact that it was a longer way round, but
there was no way of guessing, and it would have been ridiculous to
lose five minutes every morning, and make a fool of himself into
the bargain, just to avoid a difficulty which only occasionally presented itself. Life is like that. It would be foolish to deprive oneself
of pleasures and conveniences because of the possible risk attending
their enjoyment. If one argued on those lines one would end by
never taking a train for fear of accidents, and never riding a bicycle
because one might get pitched on one's head. There are a lot of
young fellows who will never go to bed with a woman for fear of
what they may catch. Caution carried as far as that becomes morbid.
The particular risk presented by the bridge was that, however fast
he might pedal, he might fail to make up for lost time. On several
occasions the bridge had cost Edmond a fifty-centime fine; once he
had lost as much as a franc. Well, that wouldn't break him.

For four months now Edmond had had a job as lathe-tender.
Bertrand's new factory had been going for only a short time, and as
summer approached, a lot of new hands were taken on to deal with
the mass of orders.

At first he did piece work, but, owing to lack of training, found,
when he began, that it was difficult to make more than seventy or
eighty centimes an hour, very much less, that is, than he had been
earning previously. He tried to increase his speed, but, since there
was a very strict system of checking in force, the only result was
that he found himself kept short of jobs and often made less even
than he had anticipated. Little by little, however, he mastered the
work, teaching himself the various processes in use at the factory,
till he was earning as much as a franc, then one franc ten centimes,
and finally one franc twenty. Then a week came during which he
managed to maintain an average of one franc thirty-two centimes
over the whole sixty hours, so that on that particular Saturday he
picked up, much to his pride, eighty francs less a few sous. His fellow-

workmen made a joke of it, but their laughter was mingled with respect, and he had to stand a couple of rounds of drinks. His mother, Mme Maillecottin, lost no time in letting the street know that her eldest son was earning "more than thirteen francs a day" at his new job—that's to say, more than many a tradesman.

A few days later he was informed by the management that from then on he would be paid at the rate of a franc an hour. His first reaction was anger and bitter rebellion, until some of his older pals explained that it was a rule of the works that all men who had been there more than a certain time should be put on a regular footing, and that, in fact, he would benefit from working at a fixed rate. Thinking the matter out for himself, he came to the conclusion that to make one franc thirty-two at piece work he would have had to keep himself slaving at high pressure, and that at the cost of twelve centimes an hour he would be able to buy the right of working in comparative comfort, without having to worry every time he broke a tool or got on a job that wouldn't go right. He accepted the change, therefore, with resignation, though he liked to use it as an illustration of the way in which the proletariat was exploited by the employers.

It amused him, while working at his lathe, to distract his mind by figuring out how much he would be making if he were still being paid at piece rates. The total usually came to about one franc ten or one franc fifteen, never to more than one franc twenty. Under the new dispensation his employer, as well as he, lost something.

Edmond worked in a small, narrow room on the first floor of Building B. His lathe was mounted against an outside wall, beneath a window. It stood in an angle made by the wall with one of the supporting pillars on its right. The corner thus made was rather pleasant. It gave him a feeling of homeliness and privacy. The plaster surface of the pillar, reflecting as it did a good deal of daylight, made him think of some familiar piece of wall in a room of his own on which it might give him pleasure to fix his eyes. He had hung on it a calendar adorned with the portrait of a woman, and drove in a nail to hold his watch. He used it also for pinning up the blue-prints supplied by the drawing-office in connection with the work he might be on at the moment.

The personal and unusual note thus given to this particular corner attracted the attention of his employer on one of his daily rounds. He seemed to be on the point of saying something. He was proud of his new factory and liked the wall surfaces to be clean and unencumbered. He wanted to see the conditions of modern industry freed from the dirt and disorder which had been handed down as an undesirable legacy from the days of the blacksmiths, metalworkers, and locksmiths of an earlier dispensation. But he disliked making too many small complaints and knew that Maillecottin was an excellent lathe hand. He went on his way, therefore, frowning slightly and quite failing to notice the faint traces of a cobweb—a small one, it is true, but nevertheless a cobweb—hanging from the top corner of the window just above Maillecottin's head. There was a window-cleaner on the staff who was under orders to make the rounds of every window once a week. But from time to time one of them got overlooked, and sometimes during the summer a spider, encouraged by the fine weather, would succeed in spinning its web in the interval between these periodic visits.

Edmond was fond of his corner, so fond that he endowed it with certain qualities which existed only in his imagination. He was convinced, for instance, that there were fewer draughts there than in the rest of the building. Not that he was particularly sensitive to cold, but he hated draughts. They had been a constant source of nightmare to him in most of the places he had worked in up till then. People have a way of saying that one can get used to anything, but it is not true. One may resign oneself to the fact that certain disadvantages, certain discomforts, are inseparable from the conditions of one's work, and train oneself to take as little notice of them as possible, but, for all that, one's body is engaged in a constant struggle with them or, at best, accepts them in a mood of sullen non-resistance and shivering resignation. The sense of unease, however insignificant, is no less irritating for being recurrent and merely has the effect of drawing renewed attention to one's lack of well-being and of underlining the unpleasantness of one's surroundings. A man who has already smoked eight cigarettes doesn't for that reason find less comfortable warmth in every puff of the ninth, less pleasant a sharpness, less encouragement or consolation. The material conditions in which a workman spends his day are rich in a whole sequence of tiny discomforts which are in no way related to the actual job or essential to its successful handling. They follow him from place to place or lie in wait for him in odd corners. The workman is one who labours ten hours at a stretch in places which another man, hat on head and hands in pockets, would shiveringly put up with for no more than five minutes, places with an uncomfortable resemblance to gateways, sheds, and street-car shelters or even cellars and tunnels, places from which every quality of a warm interior is absent and which are far worse than the simple out of doors, places which the ordinary man goes through as quickly as may be if he is to avoid the sensation of being "gone through" himself. It is true of course that work warms one, but there are degrees in such warmth. A lathe hand moves about less violently than a smith. When he is busy finishing off a crank-shaft, intent on the tiniest adjustment of his cutting edge, his work warms him no more than that of the designer bending over his drawing-board. It is generally agreed that clerks in an office can't write or calculate if they are cold or bothered by draughts, and for that reason care is taken to make them feel snug. Why, in their case, is a badly fitting door or broken window recognized as an intolerable discomfort? Is it because they are past masters in the art of lodging complaints or because their work is considered to be more valuable than that of others? Not at all; it is simply a matter of tradition. Office workers have inherited from their predecessors certain conveniences which date from a period when locksmiths and farriers, bending over their forges, would have been the first to laugh had anyone asked them whether they minded a touch of cold air.

Edmond sometimes found himself envying the clerks. When all was said and done, many of them had had no better schooling than himself. In the days when he attended night classes he could easily have taken the extra little French, history, geography, and even English necessary to qualify him. But he derived comfort from the thought that quill-drivers of twenty-five or twenty-six, for all their diplomas, didn't make eighty francs a month or even seventy-two. As for three hundred a month, why, many a clerk wasn't earning that when he came to retire.

Modern factories, especially motor-car factories, are a great advance on the old in this matter of comfort. It is only necessary to compare them with the little old-fashioned workshops to see that. Edmond remembered the time he was working at Levallois with a man who did odds and ends of repairs. What a hovel that had been! The broken panes of the skylight had been plugged with sacking, and the rain used to come through drop by drop like water in a coffee-filter. Greasy puddles used to stand for as much as three days together in the hollows of the earth floor. Everything he touched was covered with black slime, and tools just vanished anyhow. The air he breathed was a hotchpotch of every smell known to the district—escaping gas, hot metal, scorched leather, burning oil—all of them with a disgusting stagnant quality, as though they had been hanging about for days and decomposing in the general dampness that hung about the place.

With Renault or Bertrand things were obviously very different. But no matter how much an employer might modernize his factory, it was up to the actual workers to keep conditions comfortable. There would always be fellows who left doors open or who broke the skylight cords the first time they pulled them. Little did they care if the skylight stayed open for the rest of the week and an icy draught descended on the shoulders of their pals.

It was partly because of a draught that Edmond had left Renault. It was not the only reason, but it was one. Edmond had worked there with a door at his back which could quite easily have been

shut, but which never was, with the result that he was always standing in the path of a bitter blast. Time and again he interrupted what
he was at to shut it himself, but he couldn't always be leaving his
work. Besides, it was annoying running about like a servant at other
men's heels. He complained to the foreman, but all the foreman did
was to ask him how long he'd finished his military service and
whether they'd coddled him in barracks. Edmond felt vaguely,
but without quite knowing why, that there was something vile
about such an answer, that it was with such arguments that the
people were kept enslaved every time they made an effort to attain
to a level of human dignity. He gave up his job the following
Saturday.

That, of course, had been in January, and so far he had only been
at Bertrand's during the summer months. But even the heat had
been bearable because the factory faced north-east. The disadvantage
of that would probably make itself felt as soon as the winter came.
He gathered that after the 15th of November the heating would be
turned on. At any rate he had noticed a large flanged pipe emerging
from the floor in one corner and making the round of the room
about nine feet from the ground. Unfortunately, it came nowhere
near the place where he worked.

Maillecottin watched the big metal shavings unrolling beneath
the cutting edge. He took an unceasing delight in this evidence of
the power of hard steel over soft. But there was always about this
pleasure of his a touch of anxious uncertainty, wherein, perhaps, lay
its ability to charm. The light of early morning, still weak and uncertain, illuminated the rounded surfaces of the various objects, but
left their under sides in shadow, so that experience alone enabled
him to guess what was happening in these darker regions. Like a
thin coating of grease, shadow lay in every hollow and recess, as in
the throat and intimate secrets of a woman's form. The metal,
heated by friction to a faint brown colour, gave off a smell of burning. The window was high enough to prevent his eyes from wan-

dering to the view. To see anything of the outside world he would have had to stand on tiptoe, and then all that would have met his gaze would have been the roofs of the next-door buildings, a few tree-tops with the leaves still on them, some chimneys, and a misty distance veiling the far-off country.

Two days earlier at noon Edmond had begun working on crank-shafts for the 11–12 horse-power four-cylinder engine which had been Bertrand's particular contribution to the Motor Show. Unless something unexpected happened, they would be occupying his attention for many days to come. But he might get sudden instructions to meet an urgent order for a dozen or so pistons, in which case the crank-shafts would have to wait.

They came up to Edmond hot from the foundry, and it was his business to finish them strictly to specification, leaving a margin on the moving parts for final adjustment. It was an interesting job, demanding a skilled workman and a lathe set to a fine millimetre. Edmond was very careful about the preliminary preparation of his machine, trying various settings over a period of weeks, and testing it before beginning each new batch. It was a horizontal lathe of first-rate construction, and he expressed his grateful recognition of the fact by the loving intentness with which he carried out his minute adjustments. It was clearly understood that no one else had the right to touch it. If he caught one of his fellow-workmen using it, even for a few minutes only, he reddened with anger, and on such occasions the feeling of the room was with him. He had made with his own hands the various tools for use in connexion with the lathe, and if they were set at a faulty angle, if they lost their edge or were badly fixed, he had only himself to blame. He had no hesitation in scrapping them if they turned out badly, and making others.

The Four-Ways factory was designed to specialize in motor-car engines. Bertrand's ideal was that it should turn out engines for all the various cars which he produced. His intention was that they should be delivered to his Puteaux works ready mounted, tested, and run in, so that they could be assembled straight away with their chassis. Each part was to come from its own particular department and, so far as was possible, from the hands of its own particular workman. Specialization and progressive division of labour were the keynotes of his gospel. Long ago he had convinced himself of the benefits of such a method, and his belief owed as much to imagination and enthusiasm as to reason. When he was a child nothing had excited him more than to be told that so small and apparently simple a thing as a needle involved sixteen (some said thirty-two) different processes. He liked to imagine a line of sixteen women, each with her tools or her machine (the details of which he did not trouble to determine), and the little needle passing from one to the other on its way to completion, a whole series of little needles close-packed as raindrops. When he took up the construction of motor-cars and had mastered the elementary problems and difficulties of their manufacture, he began to ask himself why the principle of the division of labour should be less efficacious in their case than in that of needles. Each time that he planned some new subdivision in his factory, it was safe to guess that the picture of a little jumping needle had helped to determine, however slightly, the trend of his thoughts.

It was difficult, however, at once to adjust practice to theory. The first necessity was to keep pace with demand. The immediate end to be aimed at was not the accumulation of separate parts, but the delivery, with as little delay as possible, of finished cars or of chassis ready for the body-maker. If there were too many big-ends and not enough piston-rings, the man who made the big-ends would have to knock off and take a hand at piston-rings. Things were tiresome enough at the moment, with Four-Ways turning out more engines than the works at Puteaux could fit with gear-boxes. The main problem was to establish a condition of harmony between the two plants without altogether abandoning a system based upon division of labour. It might be easy enough in theory, but how was a solution to be found in practice? Would it be better to slow down production at Four-Ways, or build up a reserve stock of engines which there was no certainty of being able to use before they became out of date? What Bertrand would have liked, had he dared, would have been to get the engine-shops to turn out a certain number of flawed parts. But a man of business must be careful not to court failure too often, otherwise he is apt to doubt his own infallibility and to lose confidence in his star. Bertrand thought he saw another way out of the difficulty. He would try to solve the problem of over-production by marketing his engines separately. For instance, he might be able to persuade small manufacturers that the 11–12 horse-power which he had exhibited at the show was the ideal power-unit for their various undertakings. To achieve this two things would be necessary: a certain amount of special advertising, and the provision of a number of engines mounted on cast-iron beds, with gasolene- and water-tanks of the right type for the sort of employment he envisaged. This, of course, would involve the creation of a new department, a small but adequate staff, and the satisfactory solution of a number of problems of manufacture and mounting, which, in their turn, would bring their own difficulties of specialization and timing. He was in the habit, now and again, of reading articles in the papers complaining of the lack of enterprise shown by French industrialists. Nothing would have given him greater pleasure than to see the fools who wrote such things up against the kind of difficulties he had to deal with.

As a result of all this, Edmond Maillecottin soon found himself in possession of a good deal of inside information on the subject of mass production. But he had no very clear idea of the revolution in working-conditions which was proceeding under his eyes. The problem was not one that touched him nearly. Occasionally at meetings he would hear some speaker with long hair and a flowing tie holding forth against the system. The workman of today, he was told, was nothing but a slave of the machine, a being of flesh and blood caught and ground in the cogs of a soulless factory, condemned to a brutalizing routine of heart-breaking sameness. This wholesale condemnation of existing society was sometimes supplemented by word-pictures of a vague, anarchic future in which the craftsman of past ages would once more come into his own, master of his time, enthusiastic for his task, working happily in a sort of family group, in full enjoyment of all the freedom, leisure, and comfort which, meanwhile, would have been made possible by the liquidation of the privileged classes. Edmond joined in his neighbours' applause, but he was equally ready to approve orators of quite a different type, with short hair, celluloid collars, and ready-made ties, who accused the capitalist system of tradition and impotence, demonstrated with detailed illustration the disorganization of contemporary industry, and offered a picture of the Socialist city of the future, a sort of glorified northern suburb covered with a network of model factories, all shining with white enamel and filled with endless machines of all shapes and sizes running in oil.

Back again with his lathe in his little sheltered corner, it never occurred to him to apply these contradictory views to his own particular case. He was aware of no monotony in his work. Had he thought of comparing his present situation in Bertrand's new factory with the conditions he had known, for example, in the little workshop at Levallois where he had had to obey, at a moment's notice, orders of every sort and kind, the last thing in the world he would have complained of would have been the exchange of variety for sameness. The difference would have appeared to him as one between confusion and order, between a nerve-racking, jostling chaos where he was always behindhand, where no sooner had he started one job than he was called off in a hurry to another, and a state of regulated discipline whose very continuity was restful, where the need for constant attention was a sure prophylactic against boredom.

When he had been working for several days on an order for crankshafts and found himself suddenly told to leave them and turn to axles or bearings, so far from being pleased at the change, he was conscious only of annoyance. He suspected the management of not knowing its own mind, the engineer-in-charge of turning everything upside down because he was muddle-headed. At such times he felt in sympathy with the short-haired orator, though not to the extent of declaring his belief in the principles of mass production, and still less of realizing the future developments of the system. Nor did it occur to him to reflect that he might be living in a very odd time of the world's history, in which mechanical progress, still in its early stages, had brought into the life of the factory worker a mixture of sameness and variety, of discipline and initiative, all in a state of such unstable equilibrium that no conclusions could possibly hold good for more than a few years.

As a matter of fact, although he was apt to swear when some tiresome demand came his way for pistons or bearings, he probably got a good deal of benefit from the change, although at the time it only irritated him. As likely as not he would have found less pleasure in getting back to his crank-shafts if his mind hadn't been refreshed by a temporary diversion to some different kind of job. Besides, even had he done nothing since coming to the factory but turn crank-shafts for the 11–12 horse-power 1911 model, his work would still have been both personal and varied. In the first place there would have been the setting of his lathe, which from the first he had always seen to himself, and the making of his tools. This gave him a chance of imposing his personality on his machine. No two workmen ever set a lathe in exactly the same way, ever make their tools alike or use them in identical fashion. But, above all, the turning of a four-cylinder crank-shaft involves a great many stages and a considerable variety of processes. To make sure that the alignment is correct calls out, so to speak, the best in a man and demands a trained eye, a sure judgment, and a great deal of patience. The concentration that goes to it is not so very different from that exercised by a graduate in mathematics in surveying a road or by a scientist carrying out some laboratory experiment. To ensure the uniform roundness and smoothness of a steel rod demands no less accurate a series of calculations, though the machinist has this in common with the craftsman: that each is in direct contact with the material on which he works. The degree of concentration called for in the workman is part and parcel of the task beneath his hand, not a matter of external discipline nor yet of rational analysis. The sense of his machine is almost like an extension of the faculty of touch. A man working with his hands needs no other guidance than the trained sensitiveness of his fingers. An unevenness in surface, a roughness, a ridge, is to him something intolerable in itself, something that he wants to get rid of with as natural a reaction as he would want to scratch himself if he felt a tickling. The really imperative thing is to know where to stop, to realize that beneath the carefully adjusted edge of his tool the surface of his material will be shorn away, removed entirely, and replaced by another, just as when an onion is peeled one skin is shed only to reveal a new skin beneath it, and to know when to call a halt to the stripping process. Often, when it is a question of turning out some new part or varying an old one, a man in Edmond's position, studying his blue-print for the first time, scratching his head the while and sniffing, has the sense of being not so much a part of the machinery but the creator, the designer. There are decisions to make, details to foresee. "I will do it like this," he says to himself, "or, rather, like that." He measures distances, calculates angles, considering with a ruminating eye the turn of a screw, the setting of a scale. In imagination he reckons the effect of various methods, coughing, perhaps, or whistling gently to himself. His lathe becomes for him at such moments a whole little factory on its own, attendant on his orders. He is the boss.

What will become of all this interesting variety at the next stage of mechanical development? Edmond had heard of a new type of machine-tool already in use in America and elsewhere which performed automatically all those operations at present achieved only as the result of thought on the part of a skilled hand. They could turn out more finished parts to the minute than the older type, without varying a hair's breadth in their action. Much of what he had been told was vague, some of it fantastic. But, for all that, he realized clearly enough that a parallel lathe of the type he was used to was unlikely to be the last word in human ingenuity. It didn't need much effort to imagine a still more complicated piece of mechanism, or, rather, several pieces of synchronized mechanism, easy to control and needing only to be set at the beginning of each new job, capable of producing, say, a certain type of crank-shaft with next to no intervention on the part of a human agent. The workman would merely have to feed the raw material into the machine, receive the finished product, and pass it on to another machine for the next process. There'd be nothing much to worry him. But, on the other hand, would he get much amusement out of such a state of affairs? Probably not. Still, one could never tell; it was all a matter of the period one lived in. Maillecottin would chat now and again to an old locksmith in the rue de Belleville who liked to hear about his work, at first when he was with Renault and later when he had gone to Bertrand. "Well," said the old man, "that kind of thing would bore me stiff! I don't see myself working all day at turning out a hundred or two replicas of the same key. It would send me to sleep." Edmond tried to explain that it wasn't quite so simple as all that, and that a day spent in turning a series of piston-rings was quite enough to keep one awake. But the old man couldn't understand.

Nevertheless, his point of view did derive from an aspect of the business one couldn't avoid. Had Edmond never got free of the sort of life of odd jobs he had known at Levallois, he might have shared the locksmith's prejudices. People who have never worked in a modern factory seem to think that the place just goes on running itself, whereas the only thing that does go on, that never varies, is the actual product of the machines. Perhaps if one began to think about it all, about the ten, the hundred, the thousand identical objects being turned out, one might get a bit depressed. But there's no reason why one should think about them. Once the thing is made, it ceases to be interesting; the interest lies in bringing each separate item to the same point of finish, and to do this in circumstances which are never precisely the same, however often the routine is repeated, since, no matter how similar the conditions of work may be, there is always something arbitrary and unexpected about the details of their recurrence. Not that the fellow on the next bench will notice any difference—unless he happens to be on the same sort of job. Most of the time he will get the impression that everything is going on perfectly smoothly. But that's far from being the case in reality. One's never quite free from anxiety, never without a feeling of constriction in the bowels. One's got to be continually on the watch lest the slightest wandering of attention may result in momentary loss of control and a consequent ruining of the work in hand. If too many minutes pass without some minor crisis, one begins to get worried; it's not natural for things to go so well, unless it happens to be one of those days when one feels in particularly good form, unusually on the spot, the sort of day when everything goes right at the first touch, almost at the first glance. Normally one has to be constantly alert, listening, watching, testing. It's more a relief than not to find details going a bit wrong: if they didn't, one would begin to suspect more serious trouble. As a rule one doesn't have to wait long for the expected snag. One's ear catches some little sound that oughtn't to be there, or something happens to make one think that the lathe is out of adjustment. One's probably suspected something of the sort for days and simply not interrupted the work in the desperate hope that it may, after all, be nothing but an "idea" of one's own. Or it may happen that the metal begins to strip badly, a sure sign that the cutting edge is blunt or broken. One probably thought it would carry on until the evening, but here it is already at its last gasp. Again, it sometimes happens that the metal itself shows a flaw. It's extraordinary what differences there may be, from day to day, in apparently identical deliveries from identical foundries. Presumably the inspectors noticed nothing wrong, but that doesn't absolve the machine hand from vigilance or from suffering the consequences if he passes bad material.

If three pieces running break in one's hands through faulty heating, one may be angry or worried when it comes to the fourth, but one certainly isn't bored. The work may wear one out or even disgust one, but tedium is a less common experience. When does a man get bored? When nothing happens. So long as there are risks, there can't be boredom. Manual labour is a kind of game of chance, a matter of holding good or bad cards. It's true, of course, that as material and machinery improve, the margin of accident grows less. On the other hand, small accidents, tiny accidents, assume an importance they never had before. One notices them more; one becomes more sensitive to details than the old-fashioned workman was. A slight difference in temper, the error of half a millimetre in a measurement, a slight tendency to bias in a sphere, such things used to mean nothing. Nowadays they constitute a major crisis. The margin of error may get smaller still, it will still be there, and the workman of the future, becoming progressively more and more sensitive to shades of difference, will still have plenty to occupy his mind.

Besides, the personal factor has always got to be reckoned with: a man's reactions can never be plotted accurately in advance. There are days when everything seems to be going on oiled wheels. The machine just goes on making its regular movement, never varying by a hair's breadth, and out come the finished products, as like as two peas. No thought needed; one just goes on doing the same thing, again and again, so mechanically that one would have to stop and think before one could do otherwise. Surely *that's* boring? On the contrary, the perfection of the work produces a feeling of elation. Gradually one falls into a day-dream. Ideas come and go unsummoned; a train of thought begins and ends—nowhere. You remember how, when you were a kid and your parents were living in the rue du Télégraphe, you and a friend used to run about ringing door-bells. A moment later you're thinking of something your girl said last night when you were walking on the ramparts. Unless you happen to be particularly worried you don't even pursue an idea to the end. No matter how little your work may occupy your mind, it manages to keep it continually on the move, holding unpleasant thoughts at bay, preventing them from settling. They don't weigh on you as they would if you were sitting thinking in your own room. They're not really thoughts at all, just fleeting, shadowy impressions, the sort that come to you when you're fishing, with your eyes idly fixed on your float. It's no great matter to watch a float, but it's often just the very occupation you need. A man's an odd creature.

An apprentice, coming up to Maillecottin with some vaseline he'd asked for the evening before, whispered that the boss had just arrived, that he was with the fitters at that very moment.

He would come up to Maillecottin's room in a moment or two. He loved making the round of the shops on some pretext or other, sometimes with no pretext at all, and Four-Ways was his favourite port of call. He was always trying to think out some improvement. Sometimes he would bring a visitor with him.

He wasn't bad as bosses went. He always spoke politely to his men, showing them much more consideration than the foreman ever did. He never put on airs. He was interested in the work, and knew about it, too. Although his father had been a boss (he was a body-builder), he himself had begun at the bottom. He loved telling how he and a friend had between them turned out their very first car—which might or might not be true. He loved to impress a newcomer by handling the tools himself or feeding a piece of metal into the machine. But he usually chose an easy job and always stopped before it could go wrong. The men weren't taken in, but it pleased them, none the less, that a multimillionaire wasn't afraid to dirty his hands by using the same tools as they did. He was fond of asking questions about the work in hand to show how intelligent he was—and he listened to the answers, nodding his head and saying: "Ah. . . . Ah," sticking out his tongue and standing with his belly well to the fore and his hands behind his back. He followed the explanations which were given him, bending a little forward to look at whatever object might be under discussion. Sometimes the engineer who accompanied him would interrupt the workman and try to take up the explanation himself. But the boss would always stop him; "Let him alone," he would say, "let him alone."

He gave the impression of being nervous. If he was angry he never let himself go. If anything annoyed him he frowned and hurried off, leaving an underling to do the necessary telling-off. He was terrified of working-class hostility. During the worst days of October he looked ill with anxiety. On the evening of the 15th, after he had paid off the hands, he shut down the shops on the ground that certain raw materials had failed to arrive, and he didn't open them again until the 19th. He wasn't directly affected by the strike. The metal-workers connected with the automobile trade had formulated no specific demand, Bertrand's least of all. They would be the last to come out, and if they did come out it would be only in support of their mates in other trades. Bertrand must have known that perfectly well, but he had shut down his factory for the same reason that a shopkeeper shuts his shop when there is danger of rioting.

If Bertrand visited the lathe shop the odds were that he would stop and have a word with Maillecottin. He had had a letter-box put up in the corridor leading to the cashier's office. Any workman wishing to suggest some improvement, some little gadget, however small, which might be useful in the shops, was supposed to write it down with his name, seal it up in an envelope, and put it in this box. If the idea was regarded as worth while, its author eventually got a bonus. He had to wait some time, because M. Bertrand had to read personally all such suggestions and decide on the amount of the award. Quite often a man might get his bonus and yet never see his idea put into practice. It might be that the boss was holding it up for future application or just liked to encourage his men's initiative.

Edmond had already got an extra twenty francs in this way during August, without seeing anything come of his suggestion. The week before, he had put another envelope in the box, and was hoping for another bonus. But this time he was even more anxious to see his improvement, which had to do with a modification in length and adjustment of the carrier, put into operation. (M. Bertrand did not himself manufacture the lathes which were used in his factory, but there was no reason why changes should not be introduced and embodied in all models supplied thereafter.) It was quite likely that Bertrand would congratulate Maillecottin, or question him about the proposed improvement and ask to be given a demonstration of its possibilities.

Edmond wouldn't let himself wish too violently for such an event. Even when there is no actual state of war existing between a workman and his boss, the relationship between them should be as impersonal and indirect as possible. Even to accept the boss's invitation to the extent of putting forward some suggestion for technical improvements in the shops is held, in itself, to show a suspicious degree of keenness. A really militant party man would avoid doing anything of the sort and would condemn such enthusiasm in another. The moment when your comrades on the railway and in the powerhouses are thinking of sabotage as a duty, and running considerable risks to put it into practice, is not the time to choose for elaborating methods of improving and cheapening production, all for the sake of twenty francs and a smile from the boss. It smells too strongly of servility, almost of treason to your class. At the very least it is evidence of too weak a feeling of solidarity with those who have just put up an epic fight in the interests of the proletariat.

While Edmond's thoughts were thus engaged, the voice of M. Bertrand was heard speaking rather harshly and hurriedly. He had just entered the room in conversation with his companion.

This latter was a man of middle age, rather taller than the boss, very well dressed, with a close-cut beard emphasizing the line of his jaw. The point of junction of beard and hair was thick and luxuriant, giving the impression that the hair had encroached on the whiskers and was arranged in curls above the cheeks. His voice was "distinguished" and rather distant. M. Bertrand, walking beside him, was busy expatiating on the glories of his factory.

"Fifty-four feet from wall to wall," he was saying, "and concrete ceilings everywhere. Here we have just a simple partition running the whole length of the room. . . . You see how the main driving-shaft's arranged? Rather clever, eh?" and so on, and so on.

The stranger seemed to think it hardly worth while to show much enthusiasm. Both men passed behind Edmond without stopping. Obviously the boss was too much excited to bother about envelopes and boxes.

As they were about to leave the room he drew back to let the other pass:

"After you, my dear Count."

My dear Count, indeed! Wasn't it, perhaps, a little tactless to go talking about dear counts in a workroom of the northern suburb just a fortnight after the social revolution had sounded its first ominous notes?

Chapter

A POT OF RED PAINT

M. de Champcenais's promise to visit the Four-Ways factory was of long standing. He could have done so on more than one occasion, having just established a huge oil depot on some waste land to the north of the river, close to the parish of Saint-Denis, but he had been till now too lazy to give Bertrand a ring.

Today, however, he looked in on the chance of finding him.

"Is Monsieur Bertrand in the office?"

"He's just arrived, sir."

After he'd been round and had complimented his host, quite sincerely, on the new factory, M. de Champcenais offered to drive Bertrand to his own establishment.

They talked about the general situation and the recent occurrences.

"It affected us more than it did you," M. de Champcenais said. "Deliveries practically ceased, even those that we get by water transport; but if that had been all, it wouldn't have been so bad. It was getting the stuff away that was the real trouble, and the fact that consumption was more or less at a standstill. Most of the retail trade just ceased to exist. But our costs remained the same as ever. We've suffered losses that we shall never make up. People aren't going to burn more oil now just because they burned none at all during the strike. In your business it's different. The man who was going to buy a car on the 15th may have cancelled his order, but he probably renewed it on the 25th. In the long run it won't have made the slightest difference to you."

Bertrand protested. October had fallen a long way below expectation. The good effect of the Motor Show had been entirely wiped out. Since the end of the strike his figures had been recovering very slowly.

"Once the forward movement slows down, it never recovers. People who had been saving up for a car have had time to think twice and have found other ways of spending their money."

Generally speaking, they agreed that social upheavals on such a scale, quite apart from any immediate consequences they might have, produced in the buying public a state of mind which was very bad for business.

"There's no confidence. People say: 'It's quieted down for the moment, but at the first opportunity it'll begin all over again.' Did you read the account of the debate in the Chamber the day before yesterday? Briand was howled down, why? merely for saying what no sane man would question, that if he'd seen no way of preserving public order and saving Society except by stretching the law, he'd have stretched the law. Do you think if there was a fire in my factory that I should bother my head about violating some labour regulation in putting it out? It's appalling to think there can be two ways of thinking about things like that."

They enumerated the various stages of the strike movement over the past few years. The thing had become a permanent disease, the symptoms of which grew more severe with each new crisis. Business was living in a constant state of alarm; one really wondered at people's courage in starting anything new.

"It's no joke being an employer of labour!" Bertrand said. "Take my own men, for example. I pay them more than any other manufacturer in Paris. I've built them a model factory—well, you've seen it for yourself, and I'm always improving it. They've no feeling against me personally; in fact I'm probably one of the most popular employers going, but, for all that, I'm always conscious of an atmosphere of hostility. Even if I did more for them than I do already, even if I used up all my profits in raising wages and bettering conditions, they wouldn't feel a scrap of gratitude. Just as soon as a more or less general strike was called, they'd leave me in the ditch as they'd leave anybody else. When they start shouting in their meetings about 'exploiters of labour,' they shove me in among the rest without thinking twice about it."

At this moment the two men, their feet white with cement dust, found themselves before a huge cylindrical container made of steel, mounted on a foundation of stone, looking rather like a gas-tank. Three painters, slung at different heights, were daubing it with red lead. M. de Champcenais listened to Bertrand with a slight smile on his lips.

"It isn't," he said in measured tones, "a matter of wages or of claims. They're after our scalps. They'll never be happy until the whole existing order has come toppling down. We'd better face the truth. I've been saying this for years to all those friends of mine, Christian Democrats and all the rest of 'em, who chatter about social reforms. 'Go ahead,' I tell 'em, 'so far as I'm concerned. Do anything you like in the name of charity; after all, the claims of humanity can't be ignored, but don't think you're going to *satisfy* 'em. . . .' The leaders are after one thing, and one thing only: revolution. Strikes, demands for this and that, are just so much prize-money to keep their men in heart, local manœuvres. And every now and then, as happened this month, they stage something on a grand scale. . . . Besides, they hope that that kind of thing will demoralize the enemy. They're the winners, whatever happens. If the strike fails they use the failure to intensify the anger and bitterness of their followers; if they get what they ask for they begin shouting that we're frightened. 'Look,' they say, 'we've got so much; now for some more!'"

"All the same," said Bertrand, "they've had a bad set-back." He spoke like a man trying to fight down his depressing thoughts.

"Perhaps . . . perhaps. . . ."

Champcenais pointed to the container, half of which shone in its glorious coat of new paint, red as poppies, almost redder than blood.

"We're giving ourselves trouble for nothing. . . . As like as not we're building what others will use. . . ."

Bertrand jumped.

"Oh, I say, aren't you being a bit gloomy? I've never known you like this before."

The oil-magnate smiled once more and shook his head. A moment or two later, with the same air as before, of quiet thought, he said:

"Obviously war's a bad thing, a terrible thing, and one must be careful not to exaggerate, but I sometimes wonder whether there's any way out of our difficulties except by war."

Bertrand appeared to be amazed.

"We're on the downward slope," went on M. de Champcenais. "There's no real authority left. A man like Briand has got to twist and turn like an acrobat to maintain even a semblance of government. Where do you see the slightest chance of spontaneous improvement? Where's it to come from?"

"You think that a war would—?"

"I don't know; I merely wonder. Sometimes you can only keep a man from dying by using the surgeon's knife."

"But a war would be frightful. . . . Besides, who can tell how a war would turn out?"

"I'm not afraid of defeat. . . . No. . . . A defeat like that of '70 seems to me an impossibility. . . . We hold too many trumps. And in any case, just think what an amazing renewal of vitality came to us as a result of '70, with what strength the foundations of national order were rebuilt. The rot only set in after twenty years of peace. Socialism, anti-militarism, the persecution of the Church, the power of the trade unions—and they're all part of the same thing—date from when? From the Dreyfus business. . . . It seems to me that we shall only avoid a foreign war at the price of war at home and revolution. Take your choice, but I'd like to point out that civil war is a dirtier business than war on the frontiers."

Bertrand rather timidly remarked that in view of the working-class attitude, of the doctrines on which they were being fed, of the views that were being promulgated in the schools all over the country, it didn't seem a very good moment to plunge the country into war.

"I agree with you. No matter how much our interest, social and national, might demand it, no matter how excellent the occasion, we certainly could not be the aggressors. But with neighbours like the Germans—"

He left the sentence unfinished, and smiled, closing his eyes.

"You mean that they'll attack us?"

"Whatever they do will be done so awkwardly that they'll put themselves in the wrong."

Bertrand felt uncomfortable. He was unfamiliar with the details of foreign policy. He lacked that worldly subtlety which seems to be the necessary preliminary to diplomatic subtlety, that instinct which, in the absence of special knowledge, makes it possible for a certain kind of person to venture into these high regions of policy without appearing to be too ill at ease. On the other hand he had a vivid imagination which forbade him to think of war without at the same time thinking of corpses and burning villages and the bent figures of weeping women. He was not particularly proud of this weakness of his and would never have dared to make use of it in argument for fear of seeming "common." But, for all that, as he listened to the oil-magnate he felt a stirring of conscience.

Perched high up on his rope ladder, one of the workmen who were engaged in giving the container its fine coat of sticky red began to whistle softly, absent-mindedly, and as though the tune were some popular ditty of the day running in his head the verse and refrain of the *Internationale*.

Chapter

5

BRIAND'S MEDITATION ON THE SUBJECT OF PERSONAL POWER

Far away, in the heart of official Paris, Briand was pacing his study. His shoulders were rather exaggeratedly hunched, and with his left hand, which he kept half-clenched behind his back, he rumpled the bottom of his jacket. The right he used to lift a cigarette now and again to his lips, or to hold it suspended in mid-air as though some thought had interrupted the movement, while he flicked a tiny scrap of ash to the floor.

He approached his desk and stood there for a moment, looking absent-mindedly at the papers with which it was covered. Then he sat down.

A few white strands showed in the black hair which he wore parted rather far over on the right side and bunched in a thick tangle over his forehead. Two bushy whiskers grew low on his cheeks. His soft and rather prominent brown eyes were bright and handsome, with a quality in their glance which reminded strangers of a street urchin. His moustache was thick and drooping, his lips full, and every feature large, heavy, and strongly marked. His ears were prominent. Countryman though he was, he had about him something of the good-looking artisan, the look of a man at once cynical and sensual, sceptical and yet sure of himself.

He read, not for the first time, the account of the sitting of the 29th, in the official Gazette. His manner was absorbed, yet detached, showing no outward sign of concentration. He gave the appearance of being relaxed, and looked like a man who has no illusions about the absolute value of anything or of the conclusions he may draw from the facts presented to him. He studied the figures of the various votes with the air of a disinterested observer reading a barometer.

The Chamber had condemned, by 522 votes, the recent acts of sabotage and disloyalty, the Socialists abstaining; had supported the conduct of the government by 415 to 116; had passed a vote of confidence in himself by 329 to 183; and by 388 to 94 recorded its general adherence to the main lines of government policy.

He recalled the details of the sitting, and a faintly bitter smile twisted his lips as he did so. Never before had he had to deal with such a pack of wild men. "A good deal of their hostility was trumped up, of course," he thought; "still, there were moments when I had my work cut out to hold them." The real trouble had come as a result of that unfortunate sentence of his which was duly recorded in the Gazette, though in rather more academic phraseology than he had actually used: "The government has acted throughout with due observance of the law. But if the law had not provided the adequate means for maintaining authority, for controlling the railways, for ensuring the safety of the country, if it had been necessary to break the law, then the law would have been broken." At those words, the whole Socialist group and a whole crowd of Radicals had jumped up, shouting and yelling, shaking their fists, standing on their chairs, leaving their seats and crowding down in front of the tribune. There would have been considerably less uproar if some fellow had got up and said: "I've just murdered my father and mother and outraged my little sister; I'm extremely sorry, but I must have been temporarily insane." Cruppi had screamed; Jaurès, red in the face, had wielded his Olympian thunders; Jules Guesde, with the air of a prosecutor under the Terror, had announced that he would move for an impeachment.

"It must have been rather like that in the old days of the Convention, but things would have turned out rather worse for me then."

Looking at it all coolly this morning, Briand was amazed to think how he could have come to utter the famous sentence. What devil had got into him? As a rule he kept a careful hand on devils. All that was needed was that he should defend what he had actually done, not what he might have done. He could quite easily have stressed the government's moderation and skill, pointing out that the necessary steps had been taken with the least possible fuss. "Even if the safety of the country had involved the suspension of the Constitution, you would have had to absolve me from blame. But the Constitution was not suspended, so what have you got to complain about?" He had yielded to the temptation of making a case. A lawyer, speaking to an assembly more than half of which is made up of lawyers, may be excused, surely, for taking so fine an opportunity for making a case. He had not forgotten his Cicero: "I swear to you that I have saved the Republic." It was not surprising that a muck-raker like Jules Guesde should jeer at Cicero, but Cruppi—Jaurès . . .

It was the way he had said it. Briand did not disguise from himself the fact that he had behaved with less than his usual adroitness. He could have suggested the same idea, introduced it persuasively, without forcing the note of retrospective defiance. He might, for instance, have said: "Another man in my position might have broken the law and used force pure and simple." Why was it necessary to add: "and I was ready to do that had it been necessary"?

He had been moved by the need to relieve himself of what was pressing on his mind, by the desire to tell the truth to people who had lost the power of seeing things as they are. When a man has been fighting for a week to save the country from anarchy and sees himself called to account by a pack of scowling political hacks who would have turned tail the moment things started to get serious, and a few doctrinaires who had never known responsibility and would have been swept aside by any actuality, it is natural for him to delight in telling them the pure, ungarbled truth, truth which they are incapable of seeing for themselves or lifting a finger to resist. It is his way of taking revenge. It's fun to watch them spluttering under the attack like dogs wet by a hose. For all their pretended indignation, for all the noise they had made, they knew in their hearts that the man was right, and secretly offered up a prayer of gratitude to Heaven for sending them a protector in the hour of danger.

Worn out and saddened, Briand brooded upon his triumph, weighing it, examining it, reliving it in imagination, drawing out his memory of the glorious moment.

"They accused me of being a dictator, of planning a *coup d'état,* of trying to revive the Second of December. . . . Suppose the mobilization order had failed or new complications had developed, what should I have done? What *could* I have done?"

He fell into a day-dream, but it was a dream that he mistrusted. He could remember vividly the evening on which he had decided to mobilize the railwaymen. At the moment of making up his mind he had been conscious of a tiny sensation of shock, similar to the jolt one feels in a motor-car when one changes gear. He was leaving behind him the known, familiar world where things went by rule and precedent, to enter another, where all that mattered would be quick decision and success. Everything would be untried; anything might be possible. Nothing would be sure. No one could tell what the consequences of his action might be.

He remembered too the period of waiting which had followed. He had had no idea what might happen, no idea what to do should things not work out according to plan. He had refused to contemplate the possibility. He had smoked ten more cigarettes than usual that day. At lunch-time he had drunk a whole bottle of white Burgundy. When he was told that the men were going back, when he saw from the first figures that came in that the number of recalcitrants would be negligible, he was conscious of a feeling of childlike self-satisfaction quite unlike anything he had ever before experienced. For a whole hour he was within measurable distance of megalomania, or, rather, his scorn of humanity had never been so uncompromising—or so dangerous. He was in the mood to be tempted, to regret lost opportunities. He almost found himself thinking that it was a pity to have overcome resistance so easily. "It might have been amusing to push things still further."

Further? Just how far could a man in his position, a man of his period, go? The question was exciting, but it was difficult to answer.

For fifty years society had been subjected to a series of modifications which had affected it in a thousand different ways. No one knew exactly to what extent it was undermined, nor what the total result of such changes might turn out to be if anyone took it into his head to test them. The working class was better organized now than it had ever been, better disciplined, better equipped. It knew, as never before, what it had to do to paralyse a government. Parliament lived on the reputation of its past successes; its ways were the ways of tradition. It never occurred to it, apparently, that the executive could do without it or take a single step without its due approval. The first sign of an attempt on anyone's part to seize absolute power would be blasted before it could develop. The press might say what it liked about the necessity for a strong hand, but it kept a jealous eye on the least move of those in authority. A minister had only to lift a finger for some paper to start a cry of "Down with the tyrants!" Every change taking place in Europe was towards fuller democracy and against the domination of individuals. And yet there were moments when one couldn't help suspecting that it was all a game, that it didn't, all this business of "tendency," respond to any living reality. So long as the game goes on, everyone is keen to apply the rules. The least little deviation from them produces as much excitement as though the world were being shaken to its foundations. But what would happen supposing one of the players were suddenly to jump up, bring his hand down with a bang on the table, and cry: "Stop—the game's done—*this* game at least; from now on *I'm* going to say what the rules shall be"?

"Suppose the mobilization of the railwaymen had failed or had not been enough. . . . Suppose I'd had to go further. . . ."

True, it was only when it *had* succeeded that he'd been conscious of the itch to go further. The moment had brought a sudden release from tension, a collapse of resistance, intoxicating him, turning his thoughts in a new direction—"You exaggerated the difficulties. . . . When all's said and done, I'm still *master*. It's never events that stand in one's way, but only the doubt of one's own power to control them.

Paralysis of the *will* to govern, that's what I was suffering from—a sort of nervous disease."

Would it be fun really to govern? Of course it would—the sort of fun that no amount of governing in accordance with parliamentary rules could ever give.

What's the fun in being a minister, in being a Prime Minister, even? It means no more than to exercise a little power without seeming to exercise any, to make people do something of what you want— a third, perhaps, or a quarter—while all the time letting them believe that it's what *they* want, what *they're* making *you* do. A matter of walking up and down corridors, of taking influential deputies by the arm, of whispering seeming confidences first in one man's ear, then in another's, of not committing yourself, yet never being caught in an inconsistency; of breaking up hostile combinations and setting opponents by the ears; of flattering a commission by a show of good humour, of working on the Chamber with eloquence, of giving interviews to party chiefs and newspaper editors, of offering cigarettes to some hanger-on of the Cabinet in return for what he is only too glad, too deeply flattered, to tell. You keep your own mind receptive to certain ideas, letting them settle, germinate, and bide their time, while others you set yourself to sow elsewhere. Everything's got to be done by dint of endless and indecisive talking, hints, suggestions. To be officially the man in power is to be no more than the man who'll eventually get turned out, the man whose influence, if it came to taking out a balance-sheet, would be slightly on the credit side. In fact, you never give an order to anyone, not even to the doorkeeper, old though he is and subservient. You merely "suggest" that he bring you some paper or show in the next visitor. The documents you sign have been drawn up by clerks. If they embody any intention, it's theirs and not yours, dictated by some head of department whom you may have met once. Probably it's not even that, but the fruit of the old and dusty collective wisdom which haunts your footsteps however much you may try to ignore it, under the title of Permanent Civil Service, a name as high-sounding as your own, the

Minister's. If you last more than six months without being swallowed whole by Parliament and the Civil Service, you are regarded generally not only as the man in power, but as an individual of exceptional strength and adroitness.

And now, instead of all that, events had combined to show that there was quite another way of governing, a use of power that tasted sharp and strong, filling the mouth with its savour, apt to go to the head of a man unless he keep a strong hold of himself. It had suddenly been borne in upon him that he could give *real* orders, that he could say to someone: "Do this at once and report to me again in half an hour," with the certainty that the subordinate in question would salute, turn on his heels—and be back in thirty minutes. He had realized for the first time that people were looking at him as they never used to look, were ready to *obey* him. Their every movement told him that they were at his service; a sense of military discipline was in the air. He supposed that something about him had changed too, that his very look, his very attitude, was different. How odd it felt to know that his orders would be carried out! It was as though he had been placed in sudden and intimate contact with the State, with Society, so that he could act directly upon them, controlling their movements without conscious effort as he controlled the muscles of his own body.

How far could he go in this new direction if he let himself try? In the first place, how long would it continue to be "fun"? Wouldn't the novelty soon wear off? He wasn't one of those madmen who could find an endless source of delicious intoxication merely in ordering about a few million human beings. He might be self-satisfied, but he wasn't a megalomaniac. There is endless pleasure to be found in the use of persuasion, finesse, counterplotting; it is a game that calls for a clear brain. But to command and be obeyed without question soon palls. Even theologians are agreed that God would die of boredom if it weren't for the fact that He's got to be continually conquering anew that biggest of all constituencies—Mankind.

Of course, with absolute power he could do a lot of good and put through a number of reforms. No longer would it be necessary to intrigue for fifteen months merely to get a clause or two of some law through the Chamber, mutilated, at the best, with amendments. All he'd have to do would be to sit in his office, work the thing out in his mind, discuss it perhaps with two or three intelligent specialists, and then order its adoption. But in that case wouldn't he soon get to the end of his powers of invention? No program, no *practical* program, not even the program outlined in his Saint Chamond speech, can go on for ever. It can only be made to last by dint of piecemeal realization and by calling a halt between the various stages of its application. Like a love-affair, it can only be dragged out, can only continue to be made interesting, by reason of the obstacles to be overcome. Briand didn't flatter himself that his mind contained more than three or four leading ideas. He couldn't shovel them out indefinitely like some of his facile friends.

Give rein as he might to every fantasy of his imagination, throw to the winds every check suggested by prudence and by his own intimate knowledge of himself, he still couldn't see himself really going far along the slippery path of personal power or following for long the terrible footpath that skirts the dizzy heights of absolutism. A man who detaches himself from his fellows, unless, like kings, he is born to that kind of authority, finds himself ever more and more alone, treads a narrow way, exposed to every wind that blows, above abysses that grow more and more frightening the farther he advances. Quite apart from the danger of such a course, how melancholy it must be! A man would have to be a bit mad to start deliberately on a career like that, and Briand certainly didn't think of himself as mad. He might have no illusions about friendship, but he couldn't imagine for himself a career in which he would have to do without friends.

No, no, he could never suspend the liberties of the citizen or adopt an arbitrary attitude to the law, for more than twenty-four hours; could never overawe resistance with policemen and soldiers or deport to penal settlements those who happened to disagree with him . . .

even in return for the applause of a lot of idle fools or the blessings of a crowd of Right-wing reactionaries. "Everyone knows one can't always be as extreme as one was at twenty. Do those fools really think that I should enjoy ruling if I knew that the republicans were against me?" Why, even to know that the Freemasons were against him would spoil his pleasure.

"If at some moment of crisis Lafferre or Bourgeois or an honest old fellow like Rothweil were to say to me: 'We realize that society can only be saved at the cost of a little rough handling. Carry on as long as you have to; the Masons are behind you'—ah, that would be quite a different situation. . . ."

Something of the sort, he reflected, must always be true. He found it difficult to imagine that any man, however swollen by ambition, could find in himself the hardihood needed to outrage the law of a whole people, unless he had some secret assurance, some understanding that he had been given a blank cheque by the men whom he regarded as his associates. "That must have been true even of Louis-Napoleon. . . . Nobody will ever persuade me that he would have attempted the *coup d'état* of the second of December unless the Carbonari or some other powerful body of opinion had first assured him that he could safely go ahead. . . ."

The subservient door-keeper entered at this moment and said, rather deprecatingly:

"Monsieur Gureau would like to see you, sir."

But Briand wanted to be alone with his thoughts for a while longer.

"Ask him to wait five minutes," he said quietly.

Chapter

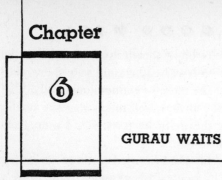

GURAU WAITS

Gurau had brought his own troubles with him.

He sat on the edge of his chair, leaning forward, his head between his hands. He looked at the anteroom carpet, at the bottom of the rather dirty panelling, and then let his eyes wander over the marble mantelpiece until they came to rest on the clock. He was surprised at being sent for like this. "What does he want?" he asked himself. "Is he going to demand an explanation of the way I voted the other day?"

For some months now he had been going through a bad time. He had thought that he had got over Germaine's treachery almost as soon as it had occurred, but it had left a wound which went deeper and deeper as the weeks wore on. In his secret heart the poison had never ceased to work. "She discovered suddenly that I was getting old, or perhaps it was that she began to doubt my future." The more he told himself that she was a sensible woman, a woman who wouldn't be likely to act on a sudden impulse, the more humiliated he felt. He had soon found out that she was Henry Mareil's mistress, and an obvious process of reasoning had convinced him that the shadow he had seen on her window-blind must have been thrown by the dramatist. No doubt he could easily have put himself right on this point and have learned of the part played in that incident by Sammécaud, but only by dint of setting himself to investigate, and that he had no desire to do. The last thing he wanted was to find reasons of any kind to break with Sammécaud.

At first he had found some comfort in the thought that Germaine had left him for a man of the theatre rather than for one of his political colleagues. "She was attracted by her own world—quite naturally." A little later, as the result of something he had heard, he added to himself: "Besides, he's a Jew, I gather, and so is she, on her father's side, at least. . . ." But the more he thought about it all, the more bitter did he become. "She always used to say that she wasn't attracted either by men of the theatre or by Jews. . . . I must have been a terrible disappointment to her."

He began to think more highly than he used to do of literature, to wonder seriously whether he mightn't have made a career as a novelist or a dramatist instead of turning, as he had done, to politics. Surely it wouldn't have been beyond him? He could see himself at his desk, setting down the story of his unhappy love-affairs. A few fine phrases began to take shape in his brain.

Then, the more easily to forget, he had sought a new romance. But he was shy with women and difficult to please. A woman might satisfy him physically for the space of two or three meetings, but if he found her common or stupid, he couldn't go on with her. He even ceased to feel any desire for her. His experience with Germaine had made him more exacting than ever. He began to think he would never again be loved by any woman whom he himself could love. Such a prospect had never before occurred to him, and he found it appalling.

Politics had brought him other humiliations. The difficulty with which he had got himself re-elected at Tours, together with various other circumstances, even though some of them had been anticipated, touched his pride on the quick. His resignation from the government had, or so he thought, caused no sensation. Briand's team had shown no sign of being the weaker for his absence, and the union leaders, preoccupied as they were with all the preparations for a general strike, had made none of those advances, those appeals, to the great man of the *Sanction* which, even if he had turned a deaf ear, would have given him a certain sense of importance. "I don't count any more," he thought. "Nobody wants me. If I vanished completely tomorrow, my place would be filled almost at once."

When, however, the strike situation had begun to look really serious, he had not been above experiencing a certain amount of un-acknowledged relief. "What luck that I wasn't in the Ministry! Either I should have had to leave Briand in the lurch and been called a coward and a traitor, or I should have had to stick by him at the risk of seeming a despicable turncoat. They would have hated me even worse than they hate him. I should have committed political suicide, and the irony of the situation would have been that I should have sacrificed myself for him!" As things had turned out, it wasn't altogether unpleasant to be able to watch Briand's embarrassment from a safe seat on the bank. Gurau had no personal dislike of the man, and was, in fact, rather less jealous of him than he was of many other politicians, but he would have been more than human had he not felt a certain amount of secret pleasure in seeing his cleverest and, till then, his most successful rival up against an obstacle of unprece-dented difficulty, and more than likely to founder.

Unfortunately, Briand had not foundered. He had emerged from the ordeal shaken but triumphant. Gurau realized that this success of his competitor would be, for many a long day, gall and wormwood in his mouth.

But the great crisis of October had saddened him in other and less ignoble ways. For him, and not for him alone, the events of that month had been a painful test of cherished schemes and sincere beliefs. Few could have found the results really encouraging, but with him disenchantment had gone deeper than with most.

For months now he had been living in hopes of a revolution in-spired and directed by the trade-union movement (always, however, with the mental reservation that the attempt must not be made too soon, and with a feeling that the chief value of the idea lay in the fact that it provided an almost mythical source of enthusiasm and hope). But he realized now, not only that such a revolution was further from being realized than even he had thought, but also that the leaders, by dint of preaching it to their followers, had sown the seeds of impatience and allowed the expectation of immediate suc-cess to grow too quickly. The result of all this had been merely to set in motion a premature and ill-prepared offensive which had done no more than put the enemy on his guard and stiffen his defence, and, by the fact of its failure, to give new heart to the forces of reaction. It would be difficult in future to talk of the general strike in the almost mystical terms which had been customary hitherto. The giant had been drawn into the open; his strength had been measured. The bourgeoisie might be no less frightened than before, but at least it knew now what it was frightened of, and was more likely to organize measures of defence than to be stampeded into panic.

While Briand was navigating the worst political storm that had been known for years, Gurau found himself aware, as he had to a degree which he had not experienced since the debate of March 1909, of the thrill of admiration induced by the spectacle of "superb leadership." In all the heat of battle, and despite his natural prejudices as a rival, he had retained sufficient honesty to approve of the way in which Briand was handling a rapidly developing situation. "He's doing his job well," he had told himself, "splendidly. . . . His coolness is superb. . . . He certainly is a man." He had yielded to the temptation of putting himself in his enemy's shoes, had imagined himself engaged in a similar struggle, much in the same way as a man will ape the movements of a runner or an acrobat whose efforts he is watching.

If the defeat of trade-unionism was in a sense his own defeat, he couldn't resist feeling the discomfiture of certain of its leaders as the realization of a personal vengeance. "They wanted to do without the politicians, without me, though I've devoted my life to their cause and only gave up office in my anxiety to stick by them. . . . Well, they've learned their lesson."

Now that the storm had died down, Gurau found himself, in the privacy of his thoughts as well as in his relations with his colleagues, holding aloof from the struggle. He was like a man who had been through a violent spiritual crisis and did not want to be reminded of the experience. He asked himself no questions, and seemed intent only on finding a refuge from the importunities of the moment.

When the new session opened he resumed, as was natural, his place on the Foreign Affairs Committee, the constitution of which had been much improved by a recently adopted method of co-option. The change made it possible for him to take an increasingly active part in its deliberations. He was regular in his attendance and constantly on his feet for the purpose of asking questions. Early he had accepted the post of vice-president, but at the beginning of the autumn session the president fell ill and looked like being unable to attend to his duties for several weeks, so that, in fact, his office devolved upon Gurau.

Occasionally a colleague, meeting him in one of the corridors, would ask him something about Interior affairs, and at such times he was careful to assume a look of knowing detachment quite different from his normal, everyday expression—the sort of mysterious, far-away look the effect of which is to keep ordinary mortals at a distance.

"My dear fellow," he would say, "I'm not at all sure, despite appearances, that the really important things, the really serious things, are to be looked for in the field of domestic politics. . . . After all, the world doesn't revolve round the Trade-Union Congress. Organized labour may be able to stop Paris from getting its breakfast for a few days, but the life of Europe goes on much the same as usual. Europe's a bigger affair than the northern suburbs, and the next political storm will affect more than a single quarter of a single city. Even the leaders, full of their own affairs as they are, can realize that."

Many of his articles at this time gave evidence that his mind was once more preoccupied with the problems which he had, so to speak, made his own, but it was noticeable that a new tone had crept into them. He wrote less as a doctrinaire and more as a man who knew what was going on behind the scenes. His arguments were richer than before in implications, and he set himself to weigh with a greater sense of responsibility the pros and cons of the situation. The problems involved, he pointed out, were extremely complicated.

Nevertheless, in spite of his various activities, Gurau was not, at this time, in a very happy state of mind. Even when things were going well with him he was conscious of an unpleasant taste in his mouth, and felt vaguely, although he did not put the thought into words, that he wanted to wreak a personal spite on everybody with whom he had dealings. He was inspired by a general feeling of malice and sought blindly for some object on which to vent it. At times he achieved a temporary and uneasy sense of relief, but nothing completely satisfied him.

There were moments when he felt that this spiritual restlessness had become intensified to a point at which it was barely distinguishable from physical discomfort. Unable to trace the bitterness of his spirit to any definite disappointment, to any particular occurrence of his days, he began to believe that some physical cause was at the root of the trouble. Never before had body and soul seemed to him more inextricably confused. It was as though the physical sensations of his body and the disgruntled thoughts of his mind were both, in their way, but symptoms of the same general condition of his whole being. His nerves were abnormally active, with the result that whole tracts of his body, usually dormant, seemed sensitized into wakefulness.

There were moments, for instance, when he seemed actually to *taste* in his arteries the bitter sediment of the blood-stream, a sensation so much out of the ordinary, so hateful, that he didn't know how long he could stand it. The experience was so definite that he found it impossible to attribute it solely to his imagination. It was as though the walls of his arteries had taken on the characteristic of a mucous membrane and could distinguish the flavour of the flowing blood, registering the fact that it was bitter, distasteful, repellent.

He was, as it were, immersed in a tangible bitterness, penetrated by it, caught in its ebb and flow, as though bitterness were the normal medium of communication between his individual being and the outer world.

FLOOD WARNING

The thing became an obsession with him. Even though he was aware of no actual sensation of tickling, he caught his fingers going through the absurd gestures of scratching in an effort to reach the nodal point of this bitter irritation and tear it out of his system. "One of these days," he said to himself, "I'll speak to some doctor friend about it," only to add a moment later: "No, I can't do that; he'd merely laugh at me."

Chapter

GURAU AND BRIAND

"You chose just the right moment to get out. I'm not blaming you—but it's true all the same. You felt the ship beginning to break up. Ever since you went I've had nothing but trouble at every turn."

Gurau's face twitched slightly. His reply was suave: "All the same, the elections went well for you."

"You think so? Perhaps they did—but look what happened afterwards—just one damned thing after another.—I'm not sure you weren't my mascot."

Briand said this in a deep voice, but with a mocking intonation, stroking his heavy moustache as he spoke. He took up the Gazette and appeared to be running his eye over its columns.

"And how did *you* vote the day before yesterday? . . . Not very well, I think . . . but not very badly either. I can realize the position you were in, but that doesn't prevent my having my feelings."

He leaned his head against the back of his arm-chair, half closing his eyes. But the glance which he shot at his visitor from beneath his lowered lids was bright and penetrating.

"I was not in very good form on Saturday, eh?"

Gurau voiced a sincere protest:

"Not in good form?—Oh, I wouldn't say that—indeed I wouldn't —on the contrary. After all, what else could you have said?"

"I don't mean altogether—but I did have one bad moment. . . . You've no idea how tired I was—my nerves were in shreds. I made a perfect fool of myself—that silly outburst of mine about illegality— no, don't pretend I didn't. There are some things one doesn't say, that one *needn't* say. . . ."

Gurau compressed his lips.

"Do you really think you could have helped yourself? The question had to be faced."

"Does a police superintendent ever find it necessary to tell the court that he deliberately put a lot of rioters to the third degree? . . . Oh well, let's change the subject."

Briand got up and started pacing up and down the room as though he had been alone. Suddenly he stopped close to Gurau, but without turning towards him or looking at him, and spoke in a low voice.

"Look here, old man, I'm going to ask you—forgive me, perhaps I oughtn't to be so familiar—"

He laughed, glancing at Gurau.

Gurau smiled, and made a little gesture of deprecation.

Briand began again, speaking this time in a more formal tone.

"I should like you to regard what I am going to tell you as strictly confidential You promise not to repeat it? . . . Good. I've mentioned nothing of this to any other living soul. The truth is I want to get out—I'm not joking."

"What! Resign—after such a success as you've had?"

"I'm nothing but a target for my own people. . . . My Cabinet's divided on every fundamental question—I'm sick to death of them, Barthou, Millerand, Viviani, the whole lot of 'em; they're nothing but a pack of weathercocks. I'm fed up, they can go to hell for all I care! You talk about my success—don't run away with a false impression: it looked all right on the surface, but there's no strength in it. I've given up too much for the sake of reconciliation. My enemies are perfectly right. It's no good trying to run the lamb and the lion in double harness. France as a whole is moving towards the Left—you know you think so yourself, don't you?—and that's where my real sympathies are too. The conservatives mistrust me."

Gurau listened very carefully, on his guard against a trap. He was afraid of taking a false step. "Is he sincere?" he thought. "Or is he just feeling his way with me, making a fool of me?"

Briand went on:

"I don't mind betting that within forty-eight hours I shall have resigned—" He paused, then added on a note of banter: "With the whole of my Cabinet, naturally."

Gurau kept himself from giving any indication of his thoughts.

"You'll put the President of the Republic in an awkward position," he said quietly; "I don't see what line you expect him to take. . . ."

Briand merely shrugged his shoulders without speaking.

". . . Unless you become your own successor."

Briand shot a mocking glance at his interlocutor.

"Odder things than that have happened," he said.

Gurau smiled with the air of a man who had seen all along how things were shaping. Both men remained silent. Briand rolled a cigarette. After a moment or two he continued on a quieter note:

"You're the first person, as I said before, I've breathed a word of this to. Suppose I did consent to form a new government—could I count on your support?"

Gurau was conscious, deep within himself, of an uprush of happiness. It was as though he had served a sentence and been released suddenly from prison. Once again he was a man who "counted," a man who could believe in his own destiny. The colour of his luck had changed as quickly as the lamps of a railway signal, but in doing so it had presented him with a problem. The essential thing now was not to snatch at a flying chance but to realize that the chance was there. Now that it was within his grasp he could indulge in the luxury of waiting, of taking his time to decide, even of refusing.

He showed his uncertainty by a little grimace.

"You mean," he asked slowly, "for some new political combination? I should have to think about it—I couldn't say anything definite without knowing more details—your suggested program, for instance, the general tendency of your new government, the kind of colleagues I should have.—The prospect's not a very exciting one, and not very certain.—It rather depends, too, on the sort of post you offered me. . . ."

Briand said nothing. He seemed not to have heard, but continued to move casually about the room, intent on his cigarette.

Gurau found himself obliged to make the point more definitely.

"What post had you in mind?"

"That's a detail I haven't as yet considered. The important thing is that I should be sure of your collaboration. The question of posts, as you know, depends on a whole lot of things—it may have to be decided at the last moment. When one sets about forming a government one finds oneself up against a lot of tiresome fellows who hold pistols to one's head. That's why I want to talk the whole thing over first with a few men of intelligence whose views are not limited by selfish interests. I've not really gone into the question of what I should be able to offer you, though I think I was assuming that you'd be willing to go back to the Ministry of Labour."

The tone of Gurau's reply was curt.

"Labour?" he said; "that's hardly my idea."

"Really? I must say, I thought— You rather surprise me. I know the post's a fairly recent one, but it's important, for all that. In view of the general situation I'm not sure it's not the most important. As Minister of Labour you'd be constantly in the public eye. Besides, I was assuming that you'd want to carry through the program which you initiated when you were last in office. Still, if you feel like that I suppose you have your reasons. It can't surely be that you're afraid of difficulties; you're not that type. What's the trouble?— I imagine you weren't thinking, for instance, of the Privy Seal?—that's the kind of sinecure one keeps up one's sleeve for some old fool of a Senator who's got to be fitted in somewhere.— The Interior is out of the question. If I don't stick there myself, I shall have to offer it to a radical.— The Treasury? You've not got the specialist knowledge. — What's at the back of your mind? War? Navy?— Come, out with it. . . ."

Gurau spoke deliberately, but not without a touch of nervousness:

"I should find the Foreign Office very interesting."

Briand stopped short, half turned, and fixed his eyes on his visitor. He assumed an air of good-tempered amazement, as though he had just made an extraordinary discovery.

"Really, now! Well, that *is* odd—such an idea never entered my head. . . . Perhaps I ought to have guessed—after all, your articles— and then of course you're secretary of the Foreign Affairs Committee, aren't you, or vice-president, rather?"

"Acting president since Forillon's illness."

"Yes, of course—what an infernal nuisance it is—you see, I can't get rid of Pichon. He's one of the few men I simply must stick to. He's done very well, he's got any number of friends in both Chambers, and he's worth twenty votes or more in any division. I can depend on him; he's loyal, unlike Barthou or Millerand—and there's nowhere else I can put him. You see what I'm up against?"

He sat down with the air of a man at the end of his tether, and seemed plunged in gloomy thought. But his eye, which now and again he fixed on Gurau, gave evidence of mental agility still unimpaired. When next he spoke, it was on a note of sincere concern, of friendly warning.

"Besides, don't you see, Pichon's well in with the permanent staff —let's say, rather, that he's not unpopular. He's managed to get himself accepted. They're an odd lot. If you were suddenly unloaded on them, they'd make life impossible for you. A minister, *qua* minister, means nothing to them: in their eyes he's either a puppet or a damned nuisance. They're as thick as thieves, and if once they make up their minds to hamper their chief there's no end to the ways they can find of doing it. It's much the same at the War Office and the Navy, with this difference: that most soldiers, especially those in administrative jobs, are fools. A civilian minister can usually get the better of them. But the Foreign Office lot are as cunning and mischievous as a box of monkeys. They've no reverence for anybody. No matter how distinguished a man may be, to them he's merely an intruder. If that's so, think what the position of a newcomer would be!—someone just popping in from nowhere to upset their applecart! . . . They'd damn well see to it that he was tripped up at once, just to let him understand how things were, and then, if he still insisted on having a mind of his own, if he still refused to be just a rubber stamp and nothing more—especially if he belonged to the Left, to the extreme Left, if he were not merely a damned republican but a dirty little Socialist . . . well, I leave you to imagine the kind of time he'd have. . . . I can assure you, it would break your heart."

Gurau smiled with the air of a man who is hearing nothing new and has no intention of allowing himself to be browbeaten.

"Somebody's got to begin there some time," he said. "After all, there have been ministers who've managed to get themselves accepted, and even to assert themselves, haven't there?"

Briand, as was usual with him, having injected into the mind of his questioner a good dose of salutary ideas, set himself to soothe his ruffled nerves.

"Of course you shall be Foreign Minister some day, my dear fellow, if you've set your heart on it, and you'll be a brilliant success and carry the whole office with you. All I meant was that it can't be done overnight. . . . You've got to serve an apprenticeship. . . . They're extremely sensitive to prestige, to the glamour of success. Once you've held office two or three times, important and responsible office like Labour, or the Colonies, to say nothing of the Interior, and shown yourself thoroughly capable as a leader, they'll be ready to take you to their bosoms and feel flattered to get you. . . ."

"It seems rather extraordinary to me that a thing like that has got to depend upon the goodwill of a lot of officials who are only there to be ordered about. . . ."

"Of course it's extraordinary, but life is like that. . . . It's scarcely for you, surely, for a champion of Unionism, a defender of the petty official against the central power, to be indignant about a thing like that. If you had your way that's how the whole country would be run, eh?"

Briand disguised the biting quality of his malice with a guffaw of laughter.

"I'll give you a bit of advice. If that's really the post you want, and if it's your ambition to make an extended career at the Foreign Office, the way to do it is to be Prime Minister first. Take my word for it."

Gurau stole a sidelong glance at Briand. What had he got at the back of his mind, he wondered. Was he sincere? Was there some hidden meaning in his words, or were they meant as a bait to tempt him? A little of both, perhaps.

He eased the strain by changing the subject.

"Leaving Pichon out of it for the moment, whom had you in mind for the other ministries?"

Briand's expression cleared. The heavy lines of his face softened. Suddenly he was all frankness. He stretched out his hands, palms upward, and looking Gurau straight in the eyes, began to speak with the air of a man who has nothing to conceal.

"In addition to Pichon I should like to keep Lapeyrère, Dupuy, and perhaps one or two more. . . . I'm thinking of offering an important post to Lafferre, simply, I don't mind admitting, because he's a Masonic Grand Master. In that way I shall avoid the charge of playing into the hands of the Church. Speaking in general terms, I shall look to the Left for my chief support. . . . It is essential that I have a cabinet as solidly Left as possible, based on the Radical Party and the Masons, with somebody of the extreme Left to guard my flank—you for choice. Does that surprise you?"

Gurau was once more smiling and plunged in thought.

"What sort of majority are you hoping for?" he asked.

"Small but certain." He tapped the Gazette with the palm of his right hand. "I don't want any more elastic majorities like Saturday's." With his two hands he made the movement of a man stretching and then relaxing a rubber band. "Where I went wrong was in ignoring the verdict of the elections. They gave me a clean republican majority of 300 to 320, not counting Labour. If I can be sure of that I shall be content."

He got up and held out his arms.

"And now all you've got to do is to repeat what I've just told you in confidence, or even a part of it, to bring the whole edifice crash-ing to the ground."

Gurau started.

"My dear Prime Minister, I hope—"

"That I will do you the honour of—putting you to the test!"

Briand shook his hand and went with him to the door. "Don't give me your answer today," he said; "—if it's to be no. Think over what I've said. I know I've given you cause for complaint—nothing serious, I hope—still, cause enough. As for your future career, even if your heart is set on the Foreign Office, a few more months—and that's all I can guarantee—at the Ministry of Labour will help you on your way."

"One last question."

"Well?"

"What will your attitude be to the Trade Union Council?"

Briand made a movement of his head from side to side, passing his hand over first one cheek, then the other.

"There's the rub." He was silent for a moment, then: "That's precisely one of the questions I want to go into with you."

"*With* me?" Gurau stressed the word. "Not over my head, and not in such a way that I shall be left holding the bag?"

"No, no, that I promise you!" He laughed. "I'm capable of im-provement, you know."

"You don't mean to dissolve it, then?"

"What, the Council? Certainly not. That's what they'd like to make me do, but I'm not going to. It's a matter of principle with me. No one's going to make me trample on the ideas of my hot youth to that extent. It's for that, among other reasons, that I want to redistribute the weight of my Cabinet. I want to get some point of contact with your people."

"And you're not thinking—how shall I put it?—of trying to stran-gle it with kindness?"

Briand made an eloquent gesture. "No, I swear. . . ." Then, with a smile, he added:

"When one rides a horse on the curb one may make it foam at the mouth, but one doesn't strangle it. . . . Do you agree?"

Gurau replied with a non-committal smile.

"What one does," Briand said, "one does for its good."

Chapter

BIRTH OF A LITTLE GIRL

"Yes, yes, everything's going fine. You were perfectly right to send for me, but you can take my word for it that everything's as it should be."

The grey-haired doctor adjusted his spectacles and took from a leather case an overall of fine white linen which he proceeded to unfold. He kept glancing towards the corridor and muttering to himself as he worked:

"Basins—towels. . . ."

He was as excited as though this had been his first lying-in, and made no effort to ignore the fact. He realized his state of mind without trying to excuse it. "I must provide an outlet for my nervous tension," he thought. "My hand will be all the steadier."

There was a noise of passing traffic from the rue de Saint-Pétersbourg. A sound of rasping gears came from a taxi breasting the slope. The flat was filled with the smell of drugs, to which already was beginning to be added the acrid stench of gaping flesh and of the tormented intimacies of the body. The general effect of the place, however, was very different from that of a hospital. The curtains, the coverings, the sense of long-established and familiar furniture, produced an atmosphere of cheerful middle-class security. Pain held no hint of permanence in such a spot, but seemed merely a passing visitor.

Women came and went. There was the young sister-in-law, burning to make herself useful, on whom the groans of the patient, the faint smell, reminiscent of a butcher's shop (as strange in such surroundings as would have been the evidences of a crime), the idea of birth, the idea of a child about to emerge from the flesh of another human being, had an effect akin to intoxication, at once kindly, cruel, and sensual. There was the servant, anxious to show up well at such a time of crisis, but afraid of letting her employers impose upon the natural kindliness of her nature. And last of all there was the district nurse, a secularized Sister, with a life-time of experience behind her, slow-moving and acid. Every movement she made seemed a silent protest against the lack of conveniences, against the confusion and insufficiency of the conditions in which she was called upon to work.

The doctor turned to the sister-in-law.

"Is Monsieur Maieul there?"

"We've sent for him, but, you see, he went off as usual to his office this morning. No one thought it would be so sudden."

"I told him how it would be! . . . But I'd just as soon not have him hanging about. . . . Hand me that other basin."

The groans were louder now, but spasmodic.

"We're not just going to stand by and see you suffer—we're going to help—just a leetle pressure—it may hurt a tiny bit more, but it'll be over sooner. Come now, my dear—it's all going exactly as it should—nothing to worry about. Don't lose heart—stick it out."

She heard him as though he were at the same time close to her and a vast distance away. He seemed separated from her by some impalpable obstacle made up of sharp spasms alternating with moments of lethargy. It was as though a wall of pain stood between them. At moments she could hear him, and then she could hear nothing. His words irritated her. "I'd like to see him going through it," she thought. "Easy enough to tell me to be brave. Just another fool man." But if he stopped speaking she would feel utterly abandoned. If he stayed silent for too long, she felt for him with a tight, moist hand, as though she were seeking something in the dark.

She was appalled by the violence of her pains and by the way they spread through her whole body. Their onset seemed to tear at the very profundities of her being as though it sought at the roots of life the element that would give it strength and power and weight. Each spasm was like a breaker on some storm-bound coast, dragging from the bed of the ocean sand, shells, and seaweed, scattering them in a high burst of spray, or like a tree felled by a hurricane and tearing up a great circle of roots in its fall.

At each recurrence she was amazed that so much suffering was possible, that the body could endure such things. If she had not been through it all before with her first child (it had been worse then, because unfamiliar), if she had not known by experience that it was possible to endure such agony and live, she would have been convinced that a few more thundering waves, a few more crashing trees, would kill her.

At intervals the pain left her, and at such moments, with a rapidity that surprised her, confidence, a too easy confidence, returned. The very effrontery with which, in these moments of respite, her whole body profited by the temporary reprieve was proof enough that deep down in her the springs of life were strong and unimpaired. As the torment ebbed from one part of her after another, it was replaced by a delicious sensation of well-being, quite unlike anything that comes to a body racked by continuous fever. "I was foolish to be so frightened," she told herself; "perhaps it wasn't so bad as I thought it was." In these intervals of pain she had time to think: "How happy I shall be when it's all over and they show me the child! If it's a boy I shall call him Robert; if it's a girl, Françoise." But even while the words formed themselves in her mind, the terrible spasms began again. What could she do to make herself bear them? How could she force her mind to fight the enemy, how make it repeat again and again like an incantation: "It's not so bad after all—I won't let it get worse—it shan't go any further"; how force herself to think of something else? What else was there to think of? To what could she fasten her mind that wasn't dominated by the pain or part of it?

Thoughts came to her of their own accord. All they wanted was to be called into being by the agony of her body, to be filled by it, to annotate it. They came too freely, they were too clear, too logical. At such moments she would have given much for the chaos and delusion of fever, for the delirium that protects the mind from thought, veiling it in a dreamlike mistiness.

She was driven to ask herself: "If I had to begin all over again, should I do it? . . . Is it worth all this horror? If I get over this I swear I'll never have another child. . . . What an awful thing it would be to die in childbed, not even knowing what one had left behind! . . . What a long time he's taking to come back from the office! . . . If only he's not here when it happens, if only they don't let him into the room! . . . If I die, will he marry again?"

She heard voices as a drowning man might hear, through the smothering, choking water.

"Strain, child, strain; now's the moment. If you do as I tell you, you'll save yourself an hour . . . it'll all be over in a minute."

Strain? As though this agony wasn't enough! He was telling her to drive herself deeper still into her hell of torment. Didn't he realize that she was at the end of her strength—that her whole flesh revolted from the meaning of this moment, from the end that she seemed to have set herself? She felt as though her body were being turned inside out, as though she were about to expel, not some alien matter, but the very core of her being. In moments of extreme pain, of extreme danger, the natural instinct is to hold it back, to keep it from emerging, and now they were asking her to let it come, to force it out. But suddenly she was aware of something she had not experienced before. Perhaps this bearded man was right after all. The pain, if anything, was worse than ever, but something was different, and it was making everything else different. It wasn't so much the pain that was different as what lay ahead, the reason for all this suffering, the thing she had forced herself to expect. It came to her in a flash that the word "delivery" meant something, was going to mean something. Despite the laceration of every nerve and every sinew, she suddenly felt in herself the necessary strength to do what this bearded man asked of her, to achieve this delivery which now, at last, held meaning for her body.

It was at the same moment that a sort of large, human worm, shrivelled and tight-coiled, felt itself threatened by the slow onset of a disaster the like of which had never before entered its experience, and against which it was completely powerless. For long months now it had been enjoying an existence which became daily richer and rounder, living happily in the moment without a thought of the end towards which it was moving. In ease it had endured, irked by no harsh shock of change, contented, regularly fed, deliciously warmed, exerting no effort of its own. It had hung there in the warmth of the body like one of those "bottle imps" that stay at one level, neither rising nor falling. Nourishment was there for the taking; mouth, as it were, clinging to life-giving mouth. It no more experienced any active desire for the food that filled it than the throat of a drinking man desires the liquid which flows around the tongue. Supplied with rather more than it needed, it took all that it could, absorbing it into the as yet invertebrate sack of its being, building itself on superfluity. Growth became for it a sort of intoxication. Boredom is impossible for an organism made drunk by the principle of its own growth. Fear it knew not; unthreatened, it had no need to face an enemy. Close wrapped in sticky depths, it knew no other universe. Its world was one and indivisible, a world of darkness faintly lit by a reddish glow of which it was conscious through no medium of sight, sensing it rather as a warm mass impinging on the sensitive stuff of its own jelly-like substance. Into the eternal darkness of its world this red light was infused, saturating it, taking from it the power to terrify, for darkness unrelieved has power to frighten even the child unborn.

In this night without dawn it lay curled and unafraid like a chrysalis in its cocoon, rejoicing in the mere fact of living as it would never do in the complexities of mature existence. Of such happiness we may get some faint idea when, after a comfortably digested meal, we sink gradually into a deep sleep, content if only it would never end. At such moments we recapture the sweet security of that moist and secret life. We bathe in it, floating upon its sluggish current, wrapped round by it as by an element. We are aware of ourselves then as nothing but a complex of sweet sensations, as a sum of tiny changes active within quiescent being, irked by nothing more violent than the happy dance of motes in the fixed eddy of existence; and we ask no more of life. But into the sleep of the grown man dreams always come, fragments from his waking cares, like crumbs shaken from a table-cloth, to break the still surface of this happy, landless world. Somewhere within us, like a night-watchman in his shelter, the sullen consciousness of man is vigilant, following the hands upon the clock-face, seeing the grey dawn beyond the blind, waiting to call us back to day and life.

And now its world had crashed upon this great coiled worm. Where hitherto had been nothing but rich and kind security, a raging enemy showed sudden fangs. It suffered to its full capacity for suffering, but blindly, knowing nothing of the future. Wave after wave crashed down upon it; it was caught in the movement of blind forces as in the shattering seizure of an earthquake. It lacked the instinct to know that an end would come, that all was working to an issue. What was to come had for it less power of comfort than for a plant that blindly struggles towards the light or seeks some patch of soft and moistened earth. It was being choked, uprooted, stripped. The sweet, warm world which it had known, the wet, protecting world, where change had been a gentle ebb and flow, was being ripped from it shred by shred. Knowing nothing, willing nothing, it had been caught up in a nightmare of destruction, driven onwards to a world of strangeness, where solitude would be its lot, where men would live alone and comfortless, fighting for food, where perforce it must set itself, by superhuman efforts, to come to terms with an environment which was suddenly remote.

This world it was, with its strange new laws, that broke with the

first sharp light upon the tiny close-stuck eyes (no warm red darkness now for the startled body), with the first rush of air into the
expanding lungs. Nothing now but a few viscous threads, a few
gurgling sounds, to tell of the lost darkness of the womb.

"It's a girl," said the doctor.

The young sister-in-law ran to tell the husband, who, just arrived,
had been left standing in the passage.

"It's a girl."

Chapter

9

A MIDDAY STEW IN THE
ROUTE DE LA RÉVOLTE

As soon as he got to the street-crossing at Four-Ways, Edmond saw his girl waiting for him at their usual corner.

He dismounted from his bicycle and gave her a kiss, taking care to avoid dirtying her dress with the wheel or the pedal.

"Hullo, Georgette darling,—going to lunch with me?"

"Not today. Lucien wasn't very well this morning. I very nearly didn't go to work at Pleyel's. You understand, don't you? I hate leaving him all day with the woman next door without popping in to see how he's getting on. Have you time to walk a few yards with me?"

"Of course."

They walked on side by side. Georgette was a nice-looking woman of thirty or thirty-five, as tall as Edmond, rather fair and full-figured. She was of a type that might tend to fat, but her natural plumpness had fallen away, and the childlike contours of her face showed traces of extreme fatigue and bitterness.

"You know, I had such an odd visitor yesterday evening," she said; "you'll never guess. Isabelle."

"My sister?"

"Yes."

"Does she know where you live, then?"

"She must. I rather think that about a year ago, the evening we all dined together on the river, you both of you saw me home."

"What did she want?"

"She didn't tell me. . . . She's got something to say to you. She'll be waiting for you this evening at a quarter past six at a little eating-house she says you know at the top of the faubourg Saint-Martin, on the right as one comes down the hill."

"I know it all right: but why did she have to send the message by you?"

"She didn't know you were working at Bertrand's. She went to Renault's, but they told her you'd left. That's the only reason. She didn't want your parents to know she had been looking for you."

"Another of her little games. I'm sure I don't want to see her. I've always been sorry she had dinner with us that evening."

"But why? She was charming."

"That may be. But when she left home I swore I'd never see her again. A fine fool I shall look! You've no idea what she wants?"

"No."

"How did she look?"

"Terribly worried, but, apart from that, as well turned out as ever; smart, in fact. She had on a brand-new fur."

"You ought to have said that you didn't know where I was, that we'd given up seeing each other."

The look which Georgette turned on Edmond was shocked, almost anxious.

"Oh, but I shouldn't have liked to say that—unless you'd definitely told me to."

"Never mind. She's going to wait for me, you said?"

"Yes."

"All right. I shall have to think about it. I'm not at all sure I shall go."

In the little restaurant in the route de la Révolte where he took his meals, Edmond kept on thinking about the coming meeting with Isabelle. The idea worried and irritated him, not very profoundly, perhaps, but enough to prevent him from dismissing it from his mind.

About twenty men were there already. Two or three were eating in silence, the rest were chatting casually, laughing, exchanging odds and ends of gossip as they might have done ten years earlier, as they would probably be doing ten years hence. But at the back, two tables set end to end were occupied by the "big noises."

There were about twelve of these, all sitting close together, some of them leaning forwards for intimacy, in a cloud of tobacco smoke and a hum of talk kept low and confidential, above which, now and again, some voice, louder than the rest, made itself heard. But an onlooker trying to hear the subject of their talk would have found it difficult to catch enough to give him a clue. Occasionally a single phrase would be spoken loudly, but it would contain some allusion utterly incomprehensible to an outsider. Perhaps this trick of saying very audibly what the uninitiated had little chance of understanding was the "big noises'" way of marking the degree of their mutual admiration and of stressing their importance as a sort of aristocratic inner circle.

Edmond would have been quite unable to introduce these men to one another. Three or four of them only he knew by name: Loiseau, Tricoton, Franchomme, Schalter. . . . He gathered that these were important names; the least of them meant something to thousands of workers. If at some meeting he happened to mention one of them casually to his next-door neighbour, he noticed that it was received with a look of respect and a knowing comment, such, for instance, as: "Oho! Franchomme—he's the fellow who runs all the Nord-la-Chapelle district!" Decidedly Franchomme was somebody. Tricoton, too, was generally supposed to be a regular oracle for the electricians working around the Place Clichy. But to the general public these names meant nothing at all. None of them, with the possible exception of Loiseau, could be said to belong to that galaxy of stars of the trade-union movement held up to infamy by the bourgeois press, men who, like Merrheim, Pouget, Broutchoux, took no little pleasure in seeing themselves daily referred to as enemies of the human race.

Quite often one of these "stars" would casually drop in and take a seat at the "big noises'" table. Only three days before, Coupon, of the Engineers' Union, and Guérard, the railwaymen's leader, had come in for coffee. Edmond, as a metal-worker, knew a good deal about Coupon and regarded him as a "sound man."

During October the little restaurant in the route de la Révolte had been the scene of a great many councils of war. The "big noises" took to coming at irregular times. At any hour of the day one might find one or another of them snatching a hurried meal, just back from inspecting the line, having eaten nothing, or next to nothing, since morning. That fact alone was proof enough that things were serious. Men in their position think twice about abandoning their comforts and their regular meals.

This little eating-house, scarcely noticed by the casual passer-by, had become one of the advanced posts of the revolutionary general staff. It was conveniently situated. Men could meet there in the general routine of their days and without making any special arrangements to do so. There was no reason to think that the police had their eye on it. Its regular clientèle was composed of men who were known to work in the various factories of the neighbourhood. Strange faces were rare and were confined to occasional carmen who might drop in for a quick drink (since the beginning of the strike these visitors had almost ceased). The proprietor was the last man in the world to be suspected of being an informer.

Those who, like Edmond, were still at work reflected as they watched the "big noises": "Those are the men who have declared war on the government, who in a week's time, with their friends, will be giving orders to everybody."

But now the "big noises" had resumed the even tenor of their days. The place had lost the atmosphere of excitement which had marked it when it was staff headquarters. Nevertheless, the events of October had left their traces. Franchomme and a man called Havy had lost their positions. Franchomme continued to come as before, but Havy was no longer seen. Tricoton and Loiseau had been put under arrest for twenty-four hours and then released. It was said by some that they had given promises of good conduct.

There was an air of forced cheerfulness about these important clients. They still, on arrival, saluted the lesser fry with an air of optimism and a cordial assumption of protective leadership. The talk at the two end tables carefully avoided any appearance of commentary upon defeat. But nobody was deceived. The big men were given credit for trying not to weaken the morale of their followers, but, for all that, it had been weakened. Even Edmond, who was young and, like all those of his generation, could look forward to revenge in the future, reflected as he mashed the potatoes in his stew with a fork: "The middle classes are strong, governments are strong. How long will it be before we can recover from this failure? What resources haven't they still got, perhaps, in reserve for making us go slow?"

Since, too, he was looking forward to a meeting with his sister that evening which would probably result in some unsuspected embarrassment, Edmond was not feeling on very good terms with life.

Chapter

S O S FOR ROMUALD

The café had a very narrow frontage and consisted of a series of compartments which got darker and darker as they receded from the street. Isabelle was sitting near the front, to the right of the door, with her back to a glass partition. Light fell upon her from the ceiling and from the wall mirrors, and her face was further illuminated by the confused glare from the bar which reached her through the glass of the partition.

Seen thus, she looked pretty, thoughtful, and young. She had the melancholy eyes of a lost child. The paint on her cheeks and on her lips was toned down by the half-light of her surroundings.

Edmond recognized the fur mentioned by Georgette. Even he, with his imperfect knowledge of the world, could realize without much difficulty that she was well dressed. "She's more elegant than Georgette," he thought; "prettier even, and more alluring. She's not too much like a tart—just looks like any rich young woman. Pity she lives like that. Pity I've got to worry about it just because I'm her brother."

He held out his hand.

"Aren't you going to kiss me?" she asked.

Their faces met above the table. He gave her rather an embarrassed kiss on her right cheek, close to the corner of her lips, conscious, as he did so, of the softness of her flesh and of the smell of scent and powder.

Then he leaned back, frowned, and said sharply, without looking at her:

"Why did you want to see me this evening?"

"Is it so odd that I should want to see you after such an age? What a question! Anyone would think we were a pair of savages!"

Her smile, as she looked at him, was gentle, but touched with anxiety.

"I'm not blaming you for being hard on me—though you, of all people, might have been less of a fool about it all than the old 'uns. . . . Girls have had boy friends before me!"

He continued to look at her out of the corner of his eye.

"How dare you talk about your 'boy friend'!"

"Why shouldn't I? He's never had a chance. He's not really bad. His education sickened him for work. There are some things he won't do. There are some things that even you wouldn't do, aren't there? Besides, he's not strong."

"Not strong, eh? Still avoiding military service, I suppose, your great slum bruiser?"

Isabelle answered him with an air of pride:

"He served for six months, but then he got himself a discharge. He didn't like the Army—they made him do such stupid things. He's the same as you, he's got anti-militarist ideas."

Edmond frowned, then continued with the same mocking tone as before:

"Served, did he? Where? In the penal battalion?"

"See here, he's never done time!"

"And what were you doing while he was in the Army? I suppose you—carried on, eh?—and sent him a little money order on Saturdays?"

She hung her head and seemed to be struggling with her tears.

"You're always so hard," she said; "you can't imagine yourself in other people's shoes. Haven't you ever been unhappy?"

She was crying unashamedly now.

"And I thought—"

"What did you think?"

"That in your heart of hearts you still loved me. You made me so happy last year when you asked me to dine with her and you on the river. She was so sweet to me yesterday, your friend Georgette. She talked to me so nicely; she understands. . . . She's been lucky enough to find a solid chap like you, but she's had her bad times, left alone like that with two children. She can feel for a girl. She knows you'll marry her some time or other, and good luck to her, I say; I'm not one to be jealous. But it's not every man who'd saddle himself with a woman ten years older than himself, with two of somebody else's children into the bargain. . . . And I thought I could ask you to help me."

She shook her head with a look of resignation which seemed sincere enough and was not without its appeal.

"I needn't have bothered," she added.

"How grown-up she's become!" he thought as he listened to her. "There's not much about life she doesn't know." He felt slightly abashed, but kept his air of arrogant aloofness.

"Out with it."

"I only wanted to help Romuald out of a bit of trouble—but as soon as I mention his name—and he thinks such a lot of you. He's often said that one of the things that most disgusts him with the capitalist system is that it makes a man like you sweat your life out to put money in the employers' pockets. . . ."

"Very kind of your pimp friend, I'm sure. You'd better tell him to let the capitalist system alone. Every time I hear you say 'Romuald' I want to laugh. Guyard Romuald! I bet he wasn't christened that. It's some name he took for business purposes. Before he began living off women he probably wobbled his bum about round the Place Blanche! Well, what does this Romuald of yours want?"

Isabelle leaned towards Edmond and looked him straight in the eyes, shaking her head a little and biting her lips with an air of half-hearted appeal. Finally she forced herself to speak in a low voice.

"I want you to say that you spent the evening of the 19th of September with me—and of course with him too."

"Oh, really, he wants that, does he? To whom have I got to say all this, and why?"

"Don't cry before you're hurt. Just listen to me, and don't go imagining things. . . ."

Edmond gave a mocking laugh.

"I suppose your nice little friend did a job that evening and wants an alibi? Thank you, I'm deeply honoured. I always said my brother-in-law had a future and that I should be proud of him some day. A nice state of affairs! And to think of *you* asking *me* that!"

"Listen to me and don't make such a noise!— He didn't do anything, but there's some fellows he knows—more or less—fellows he's met, they're not really pals of his—but they got nabbed. It seems they broke into a jeweller's that night in the rue de Quatre-Septembre, three of them, and the cops got them. They've not said anything about Romuald, because there's nothing they could say; that's not the sort of thing he'd ever get mixed up in. But you know how it is, there's a lot of cops who don't like him, and they've sworn to get him. And now they're trying to implicate him, just out of pure spite. It's awful for him. He can swear as much as he likes that he wasn't there, but if the cops are against him—"

"If he wasn't there, all he's got to do is to say where he was and bring a few witnesses to prove it."

"Exactly! That's what he thought at once. Where was he? At La Veilleuse; you know it, the café?—with me and a pal. But no one'll believe me, naturally, nor his pal either."

"His pal, why not?"

"Because the cops have got it in for him too. Well then, there's the waiter who served us, and the owner of the place. To keep on the right side of Romuald they'll probably be willing to say that they're not sure—that they don't remember. And that's quite natural. After all, you can't expect them to remember, when it's a case of somebody they see so often, whether he was there on the 19th rather than the 18th or the 20th. But they want to keep in well with the police too, naturally, so we can't count on them. But if a respectable chap like you comes along and says: 'Oh, yes, I remember . . .' the judge won't bother any more about it. There's no evidence against

Romuald, and there's no particular reason why the judge should *want* to convict him."

"What you want is that I should give evidence that I was with you at La Veilleuse, is that it? Aren't you being a little too clever, my dear? Perjury, that's what it would be, and that means five years or perhaps more. Do you really think I'm going to take a risk like that for your pimp? Quite apart from the fact that it wouldn't do any good. It's pretty obvious that the waiter at La Veilleuse would say at once: 'No, that one wasn't there; certainly not. I should have noticed him.'"

"No, listen, you're so impatient. All you've got to say is that you came to fetch us, Romuald and me, not in the café itself, but just outside on the sidewalk, about ten o'clock; that all three of us walked up the rue de Belleville and along a few other streets; that we wandered about on the hill talking, and that about eleven o'clock we went into a bar in the rue Pelleport for a drink. . . ."

"And suppose they inquire in the rue Pelleport?"

"All the better if they do—we've arranged everything with the bar—it's kept by a friend of Romuald's, and he's promised to say that he remembers perfectly well; better still, that it was just as he was going to close down—he's only got an eleven o'clock licence —and he remembers that he was on the point of refusing for fear of breaking the law, and that we promised to be quick over the drinks and made fun of him for being in such a stew. You see, everyone would have thought that his place was empty; no one can contradict him."

Although Edmond was still playing for time, the excitement of the adventure had got hold of him.

"In that case," he said, "it'll be easier still. There's no need for me to come into the picture at all: the bar-tender's evidence will be enough."

But she continued, gently insistent, like somebody only too well versed in such matters trying to convince a rather stupid novice.

"You don't understand. That wouldn't be at all the same thing.

If the bar-tender was the only witness, they'd be suspicious of him.
. . . Besides, we shall have to explain how we came to think of going from La Veilleuse for a walk up the hill, and how it was that it
took us an hour. It wouldn't sound natural. But with you there, it
all hangs together. . . . You wanted to have a chat with your sister.
We walked home with you, slowly. . . . You're perfectly safe."

Edmond seemed to be plunged in thought. At last he came out
with a blunt refusal:

"No, my dear, I won't do it."

She started to cry again, trying hard to prevent the tears from
making her look plain.

"You can't say that Edmond!"

"Oh yes, I can."

Staring before her, she repeated the phrase, her voice gloomy but
determined, as though she found herself face to face with a tragic
certainty:

"You can't say that."

"And why not?"

Isabelle's voice became suddenly husky; a sob broke from her.

"Because he's already given your name to the judge . . . that's
why!"

"He's done that!"

"He had to. . . . He simply didn't know which way to turn. . . .
They'll probably come and see you, or they'll serve you with a
summons. You can't say he told a lie"—she spoke more and more
hurriedly—"that would make it worse for him. They'd argue that
if he'd tried to fake the evidence it must be because he's guilty. And
he's not guilty. You know perfectly well that he's never had a conviction. He listens to me. I'm perfectly sure that I can make him
go straight. But if he gets himself landed in the jug, it'll be all up
with him!"

She added, putting as much pathos into her words as she could
(and what she imagined to be eloquence, like a lawyer making his
final address to the jury):

"And with me too, *I* shall go to prison, Edmond, I, Isabelle Maille-cottin, and it'll be all your fault!"

She looked at him, silently now, with moist eyes, using all she knew of woman's wiles to plead with him. Unconsciously, she allowed to creep into her gaze that quality of invitation which she had grown used to employing in her dealings with men.

Edmond thought: "That's probably just how you look when you're trying to pick up a fellow in some café—dirty little whore!" Although she had used the name Maillecottin, he scarcely regarded her as a member of his family. A public woman—more or less public—is no longer the daughter or the sister of anyone in particular. She was no longer Isabelle Maillecottin, his sister; she was just anybody's woman. "A pretty little kid, not worn out yet, and ready to satisfy the first man who asks her." He still remembered their common past, but any feeling he might have had of the sanctity of the family tie had almost entirely vanished. It was just as though he had met accidentally some little playmate of the old gutter days, with whom, long ago, he had had a casual intimacy, the scent of whose hair and body was familiar to him, some little girl he had alternately teased and championed, who had since given rein to natural vicious proclivities which he had been fool enough not to recognize earlier and take advantage of before others had had her. Out of sheer bravado, from some desire to deepen his disgust, he said to himself: "I wouldn't mind going to bed with her myself." But he left it vague in his mind whether Isabelle's favours would be payment for the help she asked of him, or whether after insolently taking his share of a bit of public property, he would just leave her with a casual "So long—get out of your mess yourself." The thought was momentary, but it went to his head like wine. There was lust in it, and a touch of intellectual audacity, as well as a sense of deliberate contamination and the satisfaction of a desire for vengeance.

She had lowered her eyes and spoke now in a quieter voice:

"If you'd rather not make up your mind at once, don't give me your answer tonight. You'll be served with a summons and you must do as your conscience tells you. You know the story—we came out of La Veilleuse about ten o'clock and walked up the hill, the three of us. . . . The bar is 21 or 23 rue Pelleport. It'd be just as well if you went and had a look for yourself. You might even go in and have a word with the boss. If he's alone you need only say: 'I'm Isabelle's brother,' and he'll understand. When you answer the judge's questions, don't go into too many details; that's the way one gets tripped up. You can always say: 'It's some time ago and I've forgotten.' The important thing is to stick to the same story and not contradict yourself. If someone else contradicts you, tell him he's wrong."

While she was quietly coaching him in his lesson with her air of the elder sister, he suddenly saw again in his mind's eye the room in the rue Compans, the carefully arranged alcove, the two large curtains of patterned cretonne hanging from their rod, the little bracket lamp which he had himself fixed neatly to the wall (nothing had been changed since Isabelle left). He felt a sudden constriction of the heart. He wanted to cry out: "My poor little sister, let me take you home. Leave that rotter to go to prison. You'll be well rid of him!"

But the words remained unspoken. In spite of himself, even while he thought: "I may have advanced ideas, but I'm honest. . . . That's not my idea of fighting Society . . . I've nothing to do with him, there never could be anything in common between a pimp burglar and a qualified metal-worker with his union ticket, whom his boss treats with respect"—he was memorizing what Isabelle had told him: "Ten o'clock" . . . "21 rue Pelleport" . . . "Stick to the same story."

He looked at his watch and got up. He seemed to be debating something in his mind. Finally, in a gentle voice, he said:

"You poor kid—I'm just going to say this. In giving my name to the judge your Romuald behaved like the dirty skunk he is. I shall not take him for my model. If the judge sends for me I shall not say, as I perfectly well might: 'This swine's been lying to you.' No,

I shall say: 'He's made a mistake. I did go once to see my sister at La Veilleuse, because I had something to say to her, but it wasn't that evening; it was another evening. And he's made another mistake when he says that I was with him in a bar in the rue Pelleport, because, Your Honour, I don't make a habit of going about with pimps.' "

Chapter

11

MIONNET IN DANGER

Mme de Quingey accompanied Mionnet as far as the first-floor landing.

"You're coming the day after tomorrow, aren't you?" she said; "or, rather, tomorrow, I mean—it's Tuesday already. You have no idea what a rush I live in! . . . Do try, won't you? I think there'll be one or two people here you'll like. I believe you haven't yet been introduced to Monsieur de Montsauche, have you? He's on the Council, you know. I'm sure you'll find him interesting. I know, of course, that he has the reputation of being a free-thinker, but a good deal of it's put on. . . . Then there'll be a professor, Monsieur Dumas, who'd very much like a chat with you. I don't know whether he was at college with you."

"Dumas, you say? Quite likely. How old is he?"

"Oh, about thirty-five or forty."

"I don't remember his name at the moment."

She said no more for a while, and when, after a pause, she spoke again, it was in a tone that had become very confidential:

"There's something, my dear Abbé, that I don't know whether I ought to tell you or not. But I feel so friendly towards you that I should hate to think of the brilliant career to which you have every right to look forward being injured by a lot of country gossip. Anyway, I think you ought to be warned. . . . You may think it was stupid of me to say anything about it, that I ought to have ignored the whole thing, but then, you don't know country society as I do, having lived in it since I was a child. Believe me, placed as you are you can't afford to ignore anything. . . ."

Mionnet took advantage of this long preamble to imagine several possible dangers, one in particular, and to prepare his features accordingly. At the same time he was aware of a little familiar twinge of pain at the side of his head.

"Thank Heaven it's nothing as definite as a rumour yet," she said. "I don't believe that so far there's been any what you might call gossip. But a little bird *has* been whispering in my ear, and it's not at all unlikely, if you aren't careful, that he may start whispering in others'. . . . I know you must think me very immodest to talk to you like this, but I think you should know that I *have* heard it said—in a tone of carefully assumed concern: 'Obviously this young man's got a fine future; it would be a thousand pities if he spoilt it for the sake of a *casual* adventure.'"

Mionnet took his time. He frowned, smiled faintly and wrinkled his forehead with the air of a man who has just verified a suspicion and wants to be sure of not taking a false step. His whole attitude was expressive rather of polite consideration for his companion than of serious alarm for himself.

"You know what I'm referring to?" she asked.

"I thought when you began that I could hazard a guess. . . . But thinking it over, I'm not so sure . . ."

"May I ask you just one question? Whose idea was it that you should stay at Madame Roubier's pension?"

He showed no agitation; the frown vanished from his face.

"I was taken straight there when I arrived; I was given no choice in the matter."

"Whose business was it to find rooms for you?"

"Canon Delhostal's, so far as I know."

"Ah! . . . You had no idea then of the existence of her two daughters?"

"I only learned of it much later; the two young women were away from home when I first came to M—."

"Do you know that they are regarded as—how shall I put it?—as notorious beauties, in the town?"

He assumed an air of charitable astonishment.

"Notorious—because of the way they behave, do you mean?"

"No . . . there's nothing definite against them, but there's been a good deal of talk. . . . You didn't think it advisable to move, when they came back?"

Mionnet permitted himself an amused, an almost innocent smile.

"I confess that at the moment the idea never occurred to me . . . and even if it had, I should have regarded such headlong flight in face of the enemy as rather comic. . . ."

Mme de Quingey smiled too, as much as to say that she was inclined to agree with him.

He went on:

"Later, I admit, I did half think of it. I made a vague general resolve to find other accommodation, and I was only waiting for some reasonable excuse for going. I didn't want to hurt Madame Roubier's feelings after all she'd done for me."

"Well, don't wait too long," Mme de Quingey said earnestly. "But I mustn't keep you standing here on the landing. If you can spare a few minutes for a chat we'd be more comfortable somewhere else."

She opened the door of a small drawing-room furnished with a few shabby old chairs, a chest supported on four legs, and a mahogany roll-top desk.

She seemed to be very much agitated. The look which she directed at Mionnet was eloquent of a warmth of interest which might have seemed hardly discreet, and of reproachful criticism.

"Please sit down, my dear Abbé. You realize of course that it's very embarrassing for me to have to say all this. . . . You don't think, perhaps, that these young women have been talking, that their heads have been a little bit turned?"

"How can I possibly know? And what is there for them to talk about? Mademoiselle Émilienne may have said that she takes an occasional look round my rooms when I'm out to see that the maid's not scamped her work—which is perfectly true."

"What terms are you on with Canon Delhostal?"

"Heavens above!—on perfectly normal terms. . . . Charity is not

perhaps his strong suit, but one must take people as one finds them.
. . . Once or twice I've had to make an effort to dismiss from my
mind some of the things he's told me about his colleagues."

Neither of them said any more for a while.

"If I understand you aright," Mionnet said at length, "this agreeable piece of news was passed on to you by—by the gentleman we've
just been discussing?"

She gave him the impression that she was suffering acutely.

"I'm distressed beyond words. . . . You'll think of me as the kind
of woman I most hate, always spreading gossip and making bad
blood. But I thought that if I didn't warn you I shouldn't be acting
like a true friend."

He made no direct answer to this, but assumed the air of a man
whose mind is occupied with purely impersonal matters, and remarked perfectly calmly:

"It really is very unfortunate."

"In what way?"

He hesitated, looked at Mme de Quingey, and lowered his voice.

"I happen to be going into the whole question of Canon Delhostal at this very moment. I've dealt with the others and now I'm
just coming to him. I implore you to keep this to yourself, dear lady;
what I'm saying is in the strictest confidence. . . . But since these
inquiries of mine are bound to have certain consequences (they had
pretty serious ones no longer ago than yesterday for someone), you
see in what a very difficult position this talk of ours has put me. I
don't want to seem, even to myself, to be actuated by personal motives. But what you have told me opens my eyes to certain aspects
of his character which I can scarcely ignore. . . ."

He had risen, and added, as he pressed her hand:

"You can have no idea how sincerely I wish that I'd never heard
anything at all about it."

As he went down the great staircase he felt quite exhausted.

WHO CAN HAVE GIVEN US AWAY?

As soon as he got home, he crossed the square and entered the main wing of the Pension Roubier. In his usual good-tempered manner he asked that Mlle Émilienne should come and see him as soon as she could conveniently manage it. "It's about my washing," he said. It happened to be the day when the laundress called.

"You'd like to see Émilienne before lunch, sir?"

"If it wouldn't be too much of a nuisance."

On his way back from Mme de Quingey's, full though his mind was of many matters, he had tried to recapture his normal serenity of temper, or at least to appear to others as though he were care-free. Experience had taught him that a frank and pleasant demeanour, provided it is constant, is an even greater asset in the country than in Paris. Nothing would make so bad an impression as alternate moods of expansiveness and reserve. People would mistrust the first and imagine mysteries in the second. Unrelieved seriousness would be better than that, but gloom was not a good card to play. Consistent cheerfulness is armour of proof: not only does it protect its wearer against ill-natured gossip, but even if he does get found out, it disarms a good deal of criticism. The little weaknesses of such a man are looked on as perfectly consistent with his being a good honest fellow. Knowledge that they exist is comforting to the old Adam in most of us. "There's enough sorrow and trouble in the world," we think; "no good making life more unbearable than it is already." Such is the tolerant wisdom which provincial morality, usually so unbending, derives from the sight of a cheerful sinner.

In ten minutes or so, Émilienne appeared. Mionnet made her

come right into the room, carefully shut both doors, and then, in the hushed tones which he used in the confessional, told her what he had just learned. He spoke without bitterness, but he was careful to do nothing to remind her of their former intimacy. He avoided the use of the word "casual," which he had found both offensive and untrue when Mme de Quingey had used it.

Émilienne seemed to be both sincerely distressed and honestly dumbfounded.

"I don't understand it," she said.

He repeated that it was absolutely essential that he should know the truth.

"Whatever you may have done, I shan't blame you," he said, "but if I'm to defend myself I must know what weapons the ill-disposed can use against me. You see that, don't you?"

"I've never breathed a word to anybody."

"Not even to your sister?"

"No."

"You're sure? You're such friends, you two, that you might easily have confided in her without any intention of being indiscreet."

Émilienne protested that in the first place she had told Clotilde nothing: "She has her secrets and I have mine"; and that Clotilde would rather have been "cut into little pieces" than betray her sister. Any leakage of that sort was, therefore, doubly impossible.

"I've never been seen either going into your room or coming out of it," she insisted. "I'm absolutely certain of that. And even if I had, it would prove nothing, because everyone knows that I make it my business to look after the rooms in the annexe."

They tried between them to discover who could have struck the blow.

Émilienne had no doubts.

"It's the Canon," she said. "He's never seen anything and he's got no proof. But as we both of us sleep in the annexe, he's assumed that we have been taking advantage of the fact, and he's just made a lucky shot."

Mionnet pointed out that where he had been foolish from the point of view of possible gossip was not so much in staying on at the pension after she and her sister had returned as in remaining in the annexe.

". . . Particularly as most of the time I've been the only guest there, and everybody knows it."

"But that's not true. On the contrary, there've been other people here almost all the time . . . an old lady on the ground floor . . . a travelling salesman who was here a whole week . . . an officer in the reserves who came for his annual training. You never noticed them because they were all quiet folk whom I'd carefully chosen for that very reason. Besides, I always arranged things so that the room opposite should be empty."

"What is there on the other side of this wall? Two little rooms like mine?"

"No, only one room. The house isn't symmetrical. The space between the passage and the side-street gets narrower."

"Was anybody in it?"

"A railway inspector had it for a week, but he was never there. He was always travelling up the line. I think he only took it to have an address. . . . Oh yes, on the Sunday he had a young woman with him. They stayed shut in there all the afternoon. You were out."

Mionnet asked her whether she didn't think that one of these people might have found something out and talked about it.

"The old lady is deaf, and the others were only birds of passage. They wouldn't take any notice of us. Besides, what could they have found out? We were always so quiet."

There was a note of provocation in her voice as though she wished to evoke pleasant memories. But he gave no sign of having caught her meaning. She went on:

"Immediately below is the deaf old lady. On this side there's a thick wall—you can tell how thick it is by hitting it with your fist. . . . Madame de Quingey herself mentioned Delhostal. I'm perfectly certain it's he who's invented the whole thing. I say 'invented' because actually he can't 'know' anything for certain."

Mionnet considered the problem in silence. "Oh well," he said at last, "I must try to get the whole thing straight in my mind. Naturally, you won't breathe a word about it to anyone."

He went with her as far as the landing, bowing her out as though she had come to see him about some work of charity.

As soon as he was alone he looked at his watch. Ten minutes past twelve. He decided not to have his lunch at the pension. He didn't want to meet Delhostal too soon. He went to the station buffet and had a bite costing one franc fifty.

Chapter

13

I WON'T BE BEATEN!

If he had been severe in his attitude to the young woman, he was no less so to himself. He spent the period of his meal, as well as the early afternoon, in reflecting upon some extremely unpleasant home truths.

If he had allowed his thoughts to follow their natural bent, he would have been inclined to ask himself some such questions as the following: "Who has given me away, and why? What stupidity was I guilty of? What extra precautions ought I to have taken? Am I merely being driven back on that silly old superstition that everything gets found out sooner or later—especially 'in a country town'?" But he stopped himself sharply from thinking along these lines. "That's not the point," he told himself; "it's not the details of my foolishness that I've got to concern myself with, but the underlying principle—the rule of chastity by which I'm bound as a priest. I've broken it, not so much as the result of deliberate intention as from weakness, from giving in to opportunity. If it's led to unfortunate consequences, so much the better for me."

He would punish himself in the first place by giving up Émilienne and leaving the pension. To change his lodgings was easy enough, but to do so would automatically involve breaking with the girl, and that would need careful handling. As a further penance he determined to allow himself no "fleshly indulgence" of any sort so long as his mission lasted. But suppose it went on for another year, for two years?—Yes, even in that case.—But suppose, in the mean time, he made a little trip to Paris?—Yes, even so—in theory, at least, though that point might call for a little more thought than he had given it so far. If such a degree of self-discipline seemed rather absurd, that couldn't be helped. There can be no discipline without blind obedience, and no blind obedience without a certain amount of absurdity.

At this point the spirit of contradiction began to whisper a few observations in his ear: "Suppose circumstances arose in which higher considerations demanded a sacrifice of your chastity?"— Well, in the first place, such things don't often happen. Sacrifices aren't, as a rule, so pleasant. And, secondly, it would be time enough to decide when the occasion arose. His general rule must be "No exceptions of any kind."

He felt renewed respect and admiration for the Church. "The more one sees of life," he thought, "the more one realizes how wise her basic principles are. The event always proves her to have been more right than one had expected."

The spirit of contradiction renewed its comments. "It's easy for her to be right. If she had not attached such importance to the chastity of the priest, the world wouldn't have done so either, and a trivial slip or so wouldn't have caused you any more inconvenience than a layman. In creating the ban she has created the scandal." But the argument wouldn't hold water. Even stripped of all spiritual significance, the chastity of the churchman was still an extremely powerful weapon. It strengthened him in his every relationship with Society, in his every function, his every duty, especially today when Society, having ceased to believe in the magic of the priestly office, needs more than ever to believe in the virtue of the individual priest. "Besides," he reflected, "there's something exciting about it. If a doctor told me I mustn't smoke, wouldn't there be a sort of pleasure in abstaining from tobacco?"

Reasoning in this way, he managed to make himself take a sort of sporting view of his late misadventure. He even forced his mind to think callously of the whole affair. Each time that the warm reality of Émilienne's face and figure came unbidden to his thoughts, each time that he felt the insidious beginnings of melancholy (tiny clouds blowing athwart his mind: "You'll always be lonely now—have you really thought just *how* lonely—what loneliness means? . . ."), he deliberately countered the reflection by saying to himself: "Luckily you were never in love with her."

But finding his reverie becoming dangerous, he broke it off short by telling himself that this was no time for theorizing.

"Enough self-examination for one afternoon."

He turned his thoughts to his trunk, in the lower compartment of which the two leather-bound books lay so carefully concealed.

"Time enough for that, too," he told himself. Before anything else he must extricate himself from a very awkward situation. "This is one of those days on which one can lose or gain whole years in as many minutes. Casual adventures, indeed!" Even if he recovered the lost ground, he would never forgive himself for having supplied material for one of Delhostal's confidential notes.

"This is the kind of thing that explains many ruined careers. Later on, it wouldn't matter so much. It would just be regarded as the occasional weakness of a grand old man; but at my age I should look like a man whom his vices had forced to his knees."

He thought of all the ruined lives he might have known, and saw in imagination all the roads that led—fanwise—into the future, indefinite perhaps, but each lit with the bright sun of hope; saw the ardent beginnings of many pilgrims, and how, too soon, those same pilgrims were "beaten to their knees"—a whole vista of men beaten to their knees. At what point, he wondered, did the realization come that one was of those who fall to their knees?

The idea depressed him. To cheer himself up he thought arrogantly: "Well, hang it all, even that's better than being a modernist or a member of the Sillon!"

Chapter

FRONTAL ATTACK ON THE CANON

Seated that evening at table opposite the Canon, he began by saying nothing.

Delhostal, too, seemed preoccupied. As he ate his soup he looked thoughtful, even bitter. He fixed his eyes on Mionnet. To keep himself in countenance he spoke of the new number of the *Weekly,* grumbling at the printer, who was old, obstinate, and a fool.

". . . One would think," he said with a sidelong glance, "that all the plagues of Egypt had fallen on this wretched diocese."

As Mionnet gave no sign, he asked him a question:

"Have you heard that Manguy's leaving us?"

". . . I'd heard that he *might* be going, that the possibility had arisen. . . . But no more than that."

"Indeed! I thought you were more in the know. . . . I gather that it's been suggested he might do well to make a retreat in some monastery, and that he's going to be sent somewhere in the Yonne."

Mionnet said nothing more for some minutes. Clotilde brought the second course and then the cheese. Émilienne had not put in an appearance. Clotilde's behaviour was perfectly normal.

As a rule, when the dessert had been put on the table, things quieted down. There was no more handing of dishes, and an air of privacy settled on the room. The ticking of the round-faced clock was once more audible. The eyes of the diners were free to notice that there was a stag's head high up on the wall, and that the antlers threw hard, sharp shadows as high as the ceiling.

"Do you know what I heard today?" Mionnet asked. "I may as well say at once that I don't believe it, but one can't help taking notice of the intention. It seems there are people here who fancy they can make bad blood between us—between you and me. Whether it's you or me they're trying to damage I don't know. . . . But I can't imagine that they take much interest in *me*."

Delhostal had suddenly stopped eating. He laid his knife and fork on the cloth, and set his two hands flat on the table before him. He had gone rather pale.

". . . In short," Mionnet went on, "somebody's taken the trouble to represent you as saying something about me which I'm pretty sure you never did say. But as the thing in question involved a particularly base and hateful imputation, they no doubt imagined that I should react violently to it without giving it much thought and without trying to find out whether the charge had ever actually been made. . . . Thank Heaven, I kept my head."

Delhostal was now very red.

"What on earth," he stammered, "can you have been told?"

"Oh"—Mionnet's tone was playful—"only that you'd accused me of intimacy with the charming Émilienne. The story, no doubt, would have a good deal of added point in view of the fact that I had been sent to restore discipline and morality in the diocese. . . ."

Delhostal, still very red, looked all around to see that nobody was near.

"What an idea! . . . Who can have told you that? . . . Why, the thing's absurd!"

"For you and me, yes. For the man in the street, perhaps not quite so absurd. I can think of nothing less likely to be true."

He smiled, fixing his gaze on the Canon's worried face.

"Unless it had been that I was having an intrigue with Madame de Quingey. But she's in a position to deny such a thing, and any such story would merely have had the effect of putting her on my side. No, no, the actual story's more plausible than that."

Delhostal returned to the charge:

"You won't say who it was who told you this outrageous thing?"

"I can't do that," Mionnet said quietly. "If I did, I should only be capping one stupidity with another. . . . The person who told me had been told by someone else, but she didn't seem anxious to say by whom. What do you say to our doing a bit of detective work, independently of each other? You know the place better than I do, and the channels through which gossip is circulated. You'll probably be able to trace the story to its source. . . . If there *is* a conspiracy, you can help me to expose it."

He finished on a note of ambiguous affability:

"You'll be doing us both a service."

Chapter

A GOOD LETTER

Mionnet reached home much agitated as a result of the expenditure of nervous energy which had been demanded of him since morning. On the whole, however, he was satisfied with himself. Not that he actively welcomed a situation which had tried so searchingly his powers of self-defence, but his reflections on the occurrence were not far removed from complacency. "Sooner or later," he told himself, "something of the sort was bound to happen, and it's probably just as well that it should happen while things are as they are."

On his table he found a letter; the envelope was without a stamp, and was addressed as follows:

The Abbé Mionnet
(local)

He recognized Émilienne's handwriting. Though he had never previously received a letter from her, he had seen frequent notes of hers.

The letter was as follows:

"I have been thinking a lot since our conversation this morning; and I have been crying a lot, too. I'm not such a fool as not to realize what's bound to happen now. What bad luck we've had! We weren't doing anyone any harm, and I think I had arranged things so as not to be too much of a nuisance to you. I want you to think well of me and have only pleasant memories. But I'm not going to worry you with my troubles. You always used to think of me as gay, but now there's a big, big pain in my heart. Of course I know that we should have had to part sooner or later. You might have been suddenly recalled; but that would have been different. At any rate, it mightn't have happened for a month or two, and one makes the most of happiness while one's got it. That's what I used to tell myself—and now it's all over. I'm not crying and smudging the ink like this on purpose, truly I'm not.

"It hurts me too to think that people can be so cruel. I am tortured by the thought that you may have been told lies about me which you didn't like to repeat, but which will prevent you're thinking of me as I want you to think of me. I am miserable, among other reasons, because it never occurred to me to make you my confessor. If I had done that, you would at least have known all about my life. I don't want to pretend I'm better than I am, but I don't believe you would have thought me very bad, because a man who spends his days hearing confessions can't have as many illusions as other people even about fashionable women who set themselves up as so respectable and allow themselves to judge others contrary to our Lord's commandment.

"I must stop now so as not to bore you and so as not to spoil my paper any more. I take this opportunity of saying good-bye. I know that we shall probably see each other again before you go away, but if we do, it will only be to discuss matters of business, and perhaps you'd rather that we met as strangers. I shan't have the right to say good-bye as I want to say it. Let me, then, send you one last, long kiss—as I used to kiss you when you seemed to like your little Émilienne.

"You see, I needn't even sign my name. The letter's come to an end of itself."

This was just the kind of letter to reassure a man compelled by circumstances to break off a love-affair. It removed all fear of complications in a quarter where he might, quite naturally, have anticipated them, and by giving a fillip to his self-complacency it left him free to indulge in a little gentle melancholy.

He gave himself the pleasure of re-reading it. It was written with a simple and charming sincerity wholly consistent with the ideas he had formed of Émilienne's character. Certain phrases made him pause. Reading them, he was conscious of a feeling of unhappiness which, beginning as a gentle sense of loss, went, by degrees, deeper and deeper, until it affected the very profundities of his being, disturbing those hidden sources of the will which dictated habitually the main lines of his conduct.

"What a charming, impulsive girl she is!" he thought. "Less educated, perhaps, than some, but endowed with natural delicacy of feeling. She was exactly the kind of secret little friend I needed. I have a very soft spot for her, and I shall miss her terribly."

He wondered whether a life in which love could be, at the best, but furtive and uncertain was not a mistake. He thought of all the famous examples of attachments between women and priests. "But that was in the old days," he reflected. "We live in sterner times. As a result of the Separation between Church and State, and in view of the present attitude of the Holy See, it looks as though asceticism were to be the order of the day. If an intrigue can last only so long as nobody knows about it, it's condemned to failure before it begins. Sooner or later precautions are bound to fail." In reasoning thus, he deliberately left out of account those who had abandoned all hope of preferment. Resigned to a life of obscurity, such men could afford an occasional small scandal and take no harm from it.

Then it occurred to him that a married layman, in the ordinary course of events, was in much the same position as himself. "Any sentimental relationship except one—his marriage—can endure only on condition that it remains a secret, and a suspicious wife is in a better position than anybody else to discover such secrets." Mionnet decided, with a feeling of cheerfulness, that, so far as love went, his own situation was much the same as that of any "decent and respectable layman" from the moment that he has entered the married state. "The Church is *my* wife, and she's no more intolerant than another man's. As usual, one's driven back on the fundamental verities of existence."

He found this train of thought stimulating. Being young, he did not easily despair.

When he had undressed, and before putting on his night-shirt—which was a perfectly plain one—he looked at himself for a moment in the wardrobe mirror. He found the image there reflected mildly reassuring. "Not a bad figure of a man: tall, fairly strong. My chest might be a bit broader, and my legs are rather poor. . . . But nobody could say that I'd chosen the priesthood in despair of finding anything else." He considered this an important point. Nothing seemed to him more contemptible than to choose a profession merely on the ground that "there was no alternative."

"Stripped like this," he asked himself flippantly, "do I look in any way different from a layman?" Nothing that he could see would have marked him as a cleric except perhaps some hardly definable hint in the cut of his hair and the smoothness of his face. But suddenly he felt a pricking on the top of his head where the tonsure lay. It was like the magic circle drawn by some wizard on a blasted heath. Will-o'-the-wisps, surely, should dance above it!

He couldn't make up his mind whether he found the pricking sensation agreeable (as denoting a way of life that was exotic, difficult, and as dangerous as an acrobat's) or painful (a reminder of servitude, the seal of a compact perhaps too lightly entered into).

Once in bed, he quickly went to sleep though the thoughts that occupied his mind in no way drove him to find refuge in unconsciousness. They were comfortable bed-companions, and set off bravely with him to the land of dreams.

Chapter

FORWARD DEFENCES

He awoke without bitterness, but with no sense of elation. In the cold light of day he found himself face to face with certain facts. With most of them he was already familiar, but they took on for him now a new clarity.

"I may not be seriously compromised, but I'm certainly in danger. I'm just at the point in my career where the kind of thing they accuse me of might prove fatal. Delhostal's more powerful than one might think from merely considering the position he holds and the amount of dislike he arouses. He can certainly damage me. He's got a stranglehold on a lot of people because of what he knows about them or the cases he's made out against them. The Montagnini letters were a serious matter for men of the last generation. He's timid, but he's no longer very vulnerable, because he's got no future and not much of a present. Is there anything really about the little convent to make him uncomfortable? I'm not at all sure, and even supposing my suspicions are justified, it wouldn't be easy to make use of them. If there is a secret there, I should make myself pretty generally unpopular by revealing it. No chance of catching him in anything like my Émilienne episode, and still less of involving him in the tramway scandal. No, the only thing that would help me would be for him to think himself more vulnerable or more thoroughly hated than he is. As a matter of fact, he doesn't particularly dislike me. . . . But I mustn't think I can drop my guard."

Two things, he decided, he must do at once.

In the first place he must correct any bad impression that Delhostal might have carried away from their last evening's conversation. He must make it clear that he entertained no feeling of hostility to the Canon, and that he would avenge himself on him only if forced to do so, and even then very unwillingly. There was no reason to suppose that he was the object of the other's malice, especially since he had in no way deserved to incur it. Far from that, ever since his mission had begun he had listened to Delhostal's advice with respect and accepted his suggestions with every appearance of humility, as witness his choice of the Vicar-General as scapegoat. Manguy's disgrace had established a bond between Delhostal and Mionnet too strong to be dissolved by any indiscreet words, however deplorable in themselves, that the editor of the *Weekly* might have let drop. It was up to the Canon to repair his imprudence by the same means he had used to give it currency.

In the second place he must get Monsignor Sérasquier on his side and let him see that if he was being attacked it was only because he had undertaken to defend the Bishop against the conspiracy that was seeking his destruction, and that in abandoning him the Bishop would be playing into the hands of his own enemies. In any case, he must forewarn his superior against Delhostal's tittle-tattle.

As soon as he had said his Mass, Mionnet went to the palace. He had plenty of excuses now for his visits. For some time past he had been engaged upon the reorganization and extension of the social work of the diocese. Desdombs, who was in nominal charge of these activities, had been only too willing to hand them over to a man who seemed willing to do the work and let him have the credit. Thus it came about that Mionnet found himself busy re-establishing or inaugurating a whole series of undertakings: a study-circle for young people, a savings-fund and fraternal society for the railway workers, an employment agency, a land-bank (limited at first to a few parishes), and a system of garden allotments in the suburbs. He was at work on a pension scheme and was working out plans for several Christian trade unions. These enterprises, each one of which was at a different stage of development, necessitated almost daily conferences and brought him into contact with all sorts and conditions of people—with tradesmen, clerks, working men, country magnates, with men and women, youth and age, good church people and bad—the whole making up a conglomeration of more or less passive humanity which offered a seed-ground in which his personal popularity took root and blossomed. He was well aware that this growing popularity of his was a powerful weapon, and no less well aware that he must use it to bring pressure to bear on the ecclesiastical authorities only in the most trivial matters. The Church has no aversion to the art of the demagogue, provided she can keep it entirely in her own hands. But a priest who attempts to employ it for purposes of personal agitation is soon made to feel that he has backed the wrong horse.

Mionnet found no difficulty in getting an audience with the Bishop, and proceeded to give him an eloquent version of the facts, the accuracy of which it would have been exceedingly difficult for anyone to disprove.

He admitted that he had been wrong to ignore the existence of Mme Roubier's daughters, but pointed out that in taking rooms at the pension, he had let himself be guided by Delhostal. Had there been any danger, or even any impropriety, in his doing so, surely the Canon would have warned him instead of thrusting him into the lion's jaws. He refused to suspect his colleague of such a subtle piece of treachery as would be involved in his deliberately exposing him to danger. But, to make a long story short, certain absurd and hateful scandals were being circulated by people whose motives in doing so ought to be exposed. As soon as he had got wind of it he had decided to come at once to His Eminence.

Monsignor Sérasquier seemed to be deeply interested in the story, and slightly amused. He looked at the young priest, whose emotion seemed evidence of his innocence, with the air of an older man who is not easily to be taken in. Then he became thoughtful.

Finally, he asked a question:

"Who told you all this?"

Mionnet hesitated, managed to achieve a blush, and stammered:

"Monsignor, I had to promise not to tell. But I can have no secrets from you. I only beg of Your Eminence not to mention what I am going to say to a soul."

"You need have no fear."

"Well, then, I got it from Madame de Quingey."

"Ah! Ah!"

The Bishop began to pace up and down his study with a sort of brisk cheerfulness. His mouth was twisted into a smile which was eloquent of spite and contempt.

At the end of a few minutes he stopped, took a cigarette, and offered one to Mionnet. Then, in an almost familiar tone, "It's all very odd," he said. "Perhaps she's concerned for your virtue. . . . Did she say where she got her information?"

"I had an impression that it was Canon Delhostal, but I'm not sure. Perhaps I misunderstood her. Besides, even if it was, it may well be that he was not the source of the rumour, but only repeated some piece of nasty gossip that he had heard. I can't believe that the thing came from him in the first place."

Monsignor Sérasquier shrugged his shoulders, made a non-committal sound with his finely chiselled lips, and spoke again:

"You know, Delhostal—" He broke off; then, "There's something else I'd like to say," he went on. "I don't want to impugn your excellent principles, but aren't you rather making a mountain out of a mole-hill?"

Mionnet shook his head.

"It's not so much the seriousness of the charge that worries me, Monsignor, as the intention which prompted it. . . . I know that my presence here embarrasses certain people. . . . I may have disappointed certain hopes. I have refused to let myself become the tool of certain grudges."

The Bishop made a sharp movement.

"I know what you mean," he said. "You were sent here to get my scalp. . . . Yes, you were, it's no good denying it, but your conduct has been above reproach, entirely above reproach. You have behaved like a gentleman and not like a toady. Like a man of conscience. Rest assured that I have noticed it, and that I am sincerely grateful. I shall remember what you have done to the end of my life."

The Bishop's voice had risen. He was moved by the sound of his own words; he was almost trembling. He stopped and looked at Mionnet as though he were about to take him in his arms and weep on his shoulder as he might have done on his own son's. It was difficult not to attribute so sudden, so extreme, an access of emotion to the effects of his illness.

Mionnet forced himself to show the necessary degree of responsiveness and to assume an air of modesty. He was, as a matter of fact, sincerely touched.

The Bishop went on:

"You can rely on me. If anybody comes to me with a lot of stories about beds and women, I shall know how to receive them. They'd better not try to annoy you. . . . I may be an old lion, but I've still got my claws."

On his way home Mionnet took the street in which the de Quingey house was situated, with the half-formed intention of calling. He would make a lot of excuses and ask whether he could see Mme de Quingey for a couple of minutes. One or other of the charitable works in which they were both interested would furnish an admirable pretext. This vague intention of his was due less to calculated thought than to a rather feverish hope of getting some fresh news about the subject that filled his mind to the exclusion of all other interests. Even to watch her face while he talked would assuage his curiosity.

Suddenly, when he was about fifty yards from the door, he saw the editor of the *Weekly* leave the house and walk quickly away in the direction opposite to his own, his eyes fixed on the ground. He followed, and caught up with him at the end of the street. At the very first words they exchanged, Mionnet realized that he now had to do with a man who had become soft and unresisting. Clearly,

Mme de Quingey had taken a hand in the game. Perhaps she had actually sent for the Canon.

They returned to the pension together by a roundabout route. Mionnet, in fulfilment of his intention, set himself to lull the other's suspicions, without finding it necessary to pick his words too carefully. Delhostal seemed only too ready to take a hint. The Abbé announced that he was going to leave the pension in order to disarm all possible suspicion.

"It's quite unnecessary," said Delhostal; "I'm sure you can afford to laugh at the whole business. . . . But perhaps, after all, its wiser. . . . I shall be the one to suffer. Yes, I shall miss you a good deal."

EDMOND MAILLECOTTIN'S WORLD

Edmond had received his summons to court. Yesterday evening, up to the moment of holding it in his hand, he had still not made up his mind what line he should take. In a case such as this he could certainly excuse himself from attending. No one could compel a decent workman to lose half a day just because a rotter had tried to prevail on him to bear false witness.

Once he had read the paper, however, the problem solved itself. Official documents, whether they take the form of a mobilization order or a summons to the law courts, have an immediate power of persuasion. Even a man with revolutionary convictions can find no way of resisting the hypnotic power that they exercise. A proletarian who would gladly heave a brick at a police squad pales before a piece of paper.

This morning Edmond, after a careful toilet, took his way down the rue de Belleville. He had been told to be present at eleven o'clock and had left the house at ten. There was plenty of time. He could think things over. What was he going to say to the magistrate? He couldn't be sure until the moment came.

His mind would make itself up as he walked, without his even realizing that it was made up. He would avoid a pedlar's cart, follow the curb of the sidewalk, take a look at the window of a newsdealer's, and all this while his decision would have advanced an inch or two one way or the other. He was not skilled in introspection and knew nothing of the art of observing his own mental processes, still less of controlling them, of putting a good face on them, of making them seem important or reassuring according to circumstances. But that didn't alter the fact that they had their own way of working and of extending their operations by a series of little shocks and associations, until, although he might not realize it, they had covered the whole field of existence.

Once in the presence of the judge, he would find himself dogged by his own particular world as closely as the hero in a Japanese tragedy is dogged by his shadow, and it would tell him what to answer.

The actual world as he saw it was a place of confusion. He knew perfectly well that in coming to this conclusion he was not deceived by his own private sensations. It wasn't a question of finding in the events of the moment a purely personal difficulty which he could recognize despite the fact that he lacked both leisure and education. He had a strong impression that the confusion was real and objective. The scene wasn't muddled because he looked at it in a muddled sort of way; it was actually in a state of chaos. Edmond could perfectly well distinguish between the complicated and the confused. He had been on familiar terms with too many bits of machinery to make that mistake. Some machines are terribly complicated, but their parts are beautifully ordered in relation to one another. It is the perfection of the order *within* them that makes them complicated. The contemporary world might, indeed, be complicated beyond the power of a simple mechanic like himself to grasp, without being chaotic. But as things were, he was convinced that even had he been better educated, better equipped to understand the detail of its construction, he would have been more than ever convinced of its lack of order.

One only had to look round one to see how ill fitted the various parts of this world were to run smoothly together, how badly they had been assembled, what friction resulted from the attempt to combine them. Had that, perhaps, always been true? Edmond's knowledge of history was not enough to let him examine the point, but he would have been much surprised to find that the answer was in the affirmative. (Nor would his instinct have been wrong. Of his many predecessors who in past centuries had trodden these selfsame slopes, none had ever felt quite so acutely that the times were out of joint.)

Nothing seemed to be in its right place or capable of long remaining in whatever place it happened to occupy. Ideas, like everything else, seemed to be in a state of flux. Of one or two things he was quite certain. He could, for instance, have given a fair account of the principles of Socialism and have described the general lines on which the revolution would develop—not, perhaps, as clearly as one of the speakers he was accustomed to listen to at meetings, but well enough, for all that. He couldn't but notice, however, that the ideas which he was really proud to claim as his own all referred to the future. Side by side with them went other ideas of which he was not so proud, but which he was bound to entertain so long as things in general were as they were. One must manage to live while awaiting the arrival of an indefinite future, and in order to live one must treat as serious even those ideas in which one has no belief, whether they refer to trivial matters or to great. For instance, here at his hand was a push-cart positively piled with nuts. Edmond was very fond of nuts. He would have liked, as he passed, to plunge his hand into the lovely loose, rattling mass and continue his way with his pockets full so as to have something to crack with his teeth as he walked. In a society ideally organized a workman would be able to take a handful of nuts like that whenever he wanted to, without anybody making a fuss about it. But as things were at the moment, the pedlar would merely treat him as a thief. Even in his own eyes he would be a thief. Or, again, take the jeweller's shop on the other side of the street. In theory Edmond wouldn't admit that there was anything sacred about all the brooches and rings, the gold and diamonds and pearls, exposed before the eyes of the poor wretches who passed the window. (As like as not, the proprietor was a swindler, and his customers, without exception, were the kind of people who exploited the poor or lived in idleness on unearned increment.) Nevertheless, he couldn't imagine himself smashing the glass, not even . . .

The odd thing was that although he had certain convictions, although he was willing to suffer a good deal of discomfort for the sake of his theories, he couldn't help recognizing that deep down he was troubled by doubts. He would rather have had his face bashed in than admit to an opponent that Socialism was—as the bourgeois newspapers phrased it—a "utopia" (if they were polite they called it a "beautiful utopia"; if they were not, "a bloodstained and unholy utopia"); and would have felt even more of a traitor if he had admitted that it wasn't, but there were days when he heard within himself the whispering of a little disillusioned voice, the voice, as it were, of some mocking and weary companion sipping his drink at a café, telling him that things would always be the same, that there would always be villains and always be fools. Still, holding the views he held, he must believe in the intrinsic goodness of human nature. He held that the average workman was a good fellow. If a boss was a rotter it was in his capacity as boss and not as a fellow human being. If there were hooligans who committed burglaries and highway assaults, if there were women who went on the streets and fellows who drank themselves blind, the real reason was that society was badly organized. He held it as an article of faith that the destruction of a state of affairs which automatically produced injustice, violence, poverty, vice, and war would be the inevitable prologue to a period of justice, morality and peace. To believe otherwise would be to believe that men were nothing but a lot of mischievous monkeys who did evil for the fun of it, abstained only through fear, and would always, no matter what the state of society, concern themselves with the satisfaction of their bestial instincts. Fraternity, real fraternity—not the kind inscribed by a lot of lying bourgeois on their public monuments—was the fundamental fact in his political beliefs. And yet he was no fool. He had a secret mistrust of his fellow men—and women. He knew that if his sister played the whore it was partly, no doubt, the fault of the capitalist system (that is to say, if one took the long view), but partly also because she was temperamentally a bitch. After all, she'd always had good examples before her eyes at home, she'd never known the pinch of extreme poverty, she'd never been kept on too tight a string or left to do as she liked. Ever since childhood she had been spoiled by her mother and her brother; she had grown up like a little bourgeois miss. And if her Romuald had become a pimp and, probably, a thief, instead of learning his job as a dentist, which would have been both honourable and lucrative, it was because he was born lazy—a failing which could hardly be attributed to the capitalist system.

When one has been born a working-man, lived among working people, and knocked about a bit, one has seen one's fellow men at very close quarters, one has rubbed shoulders with them in situations in which they have had neither the wish nor the opportunity to pretend to be other than they are. The smell of them sticks in one's nose like the smell of horses or cows or goats, and the smell isn't always very pleasant. Men in other classes, the bourgeois, the aristocrats, probably have ways and means of appearing better than they are, at least to one another. They can smother their natural smell with scent, they are skilled in hypocrisy. Provided one's got decent instincts oneself and is a bit of a fool, one hasn't much difficulty about seeing men as plaster saints and women as angels. But working people, in their dealings with each other, are not so continually concerned with *appearances*. There are times, of course, when they become self-conscious or, rather, when they speak as they've been taught that a refined person speaks, but the rest of the time they say right out just what they think and feel. For instance, only the other day at the factory, when they'd all been discussing some notorious swindler who'd just been arrested, one of Edmond's pals had said: "I'd do the same if I knew how, even if it did mean six months in jail." Or take the case of the grey-haired warehouseman who'd been living with his daughter since the death of his wife. Some of the boys had been pulling his leg, yesterday evening, about her charms, and he'd answered quite seriously: "I'd be only too glad to go to bed with her if she'd let me!"

Most of Edmond's contemporaries, even among the educated classes, were suffering from this same confusion of ideas, from this realization that the world was in a chaotic state. But many of them —the best-educated in particular—seemed to think that the confusion was due to the fact that they had lost their way, that the whole modern spirit had lost its way. They were filled with remorse and regret for the past, regarding themselves as guilty of disloyalty to a principle of order which, through lack of instinct or of energy, they had failed to recognize, or the tradition of which had been lost. They did not, however, despair of discovering it in a flash of sudden illumination. It was probably, they thought, hidden among the many solutions devised by humanity through the ages, but more or less lost to view for the moment. The sole problem would be to identify it and then leave it to operate. They believed in dramatic revelations. Of such men are converts made. If they do not themselves experience the delights of conversion, they never cease to envy the thrill and the comfort of those who are made the objects of so overwhelming an assault of truth. For them the adventure of conversion is the type of all that is happiest in the operations of the intellect. Their attitude is based upon the assumption that somewhere or other the true secret of social order lies ready to their hands, only awaiting discovery. Like the suitors in *The Merchant of Venice,* they stand uncertainly before the caskets. Their perplexity is the perplexity of the gaming-table. "Shall I back the right number?" they ask themselves. Their minds work in terms of chances. They have not moved a step forward since Pascal.

Edmond Maillecottin had got beyond that stage. Of the historical development of the problems to be solved he knew nothing, but in his sense of there being some such development and of its general trend he was well in advance of many men with a far better education than his. In lots of ways, in the ways that really mattered, they stood, these men of education, much closer to the period of Louis XIV than he did. In his effective grasp of reality he was further than they from Louis XIV. In the first place, he realized that he had ceased to attach any significance to certain problems, without quite knowing how the change in his point of view had taken place. He felt in regard to them the same sort of natural freedom that Americans feel towards the age-long enmities of the older continent. The fact that particular questions have a way of losing all reality is, of course, a commonplace among most people of education. The Molinist and Jansenist controversies, for instance, no longer interest them. Even a Dominican monk would nowadays consider as out-moded and childish many a theological subtlety which once might have sent men to the stake. (The Darwinian theory, however, seemed to him to be in quite a different category.) But, for all that, members of the educated classes are constantly being led, by the very traditions of their upbringing, to treat as urgent problems which are in fact dead and to restore them, by so doing, to a state of ficti-tious liveliness. Their education and their position in society both stand between them and the realities of the modern world. Not that they don't notice the objects of the contemporary scene. On the con-trary, they make full use of them, master them, and occasionally invent some mechanical novelty; but they never touch them, as it were, with their naked hands, never deal with them, as do humble workmen, through the long hours of the day. Even when they are in closest contact with *things,* there is always, to protect them, an intervening pad, made up of abstractions and traditional good man-ners, which softens the harsh reality of the moment.

Thus it came about that among Edmond's contemporaries was a large number of educated men who, if they no longer occupied their minds with the problems which had engaged the attention of Louis XIV, had much the same outlook as he had had. Edmond, the working man, was far more modern in his attitude. Had he been able to analyse his thoughts and give them words, he would have said that the world was in a state of confusion, not through any fault of ours so much as of its own. He would have added that the prin-ciple of order is not something existing outside ourselves, something ready to hand, a gift of fortune which we should be wicked to refuse, but rather that it is something which we ourselves have got to apply, slowly and with rigour. It is not a question of *recognizing* order, but of *creating* it.

Aside from his Socialist theories, Edmond found himself forced to admit that he believed whole-heartedly not only that classes existed, but that they differed radically from one another. On one side there was the money-owning class, on the other the workers; bourgeoisie and proletariat. Fundamentally the difference was a moral or spiritual one. He did not feel, as a working man of an earlier period would have felt, that the two classes were racially distinct, though he would certainly, in imagination, have relegated the "aristocrats," the "nobles," to a special and exclusive compartment of humanity known to him only by hearsay. This privileged world was chiefly symbolized by the beautiful and unapproachable women whom he saw getting out of their carriages in the fashionable streets, wrapped in priceless furs. To realize their difference from himself he had only to think: "Can you, Edmond Maillecottin, see yourself kissing them or going to bed with them?" Such an idea, if for a moment it became anything more than a short and exciting fantasy, showed itself as so absurd that its very formulation was eloquent, as nothing else could have been, of the difference which separated the two worlds. But as a rule Edmond didn't waste much thought on these people.

Other social differences appeared to him as less mysterious. He was perfectly well aware that some grubby fellow-workman of former days had become a contractor, that some bar-tender round the corner, as a result of dabbling in stocks, had bought a big café somewhere on the Boulevards and would end by retiring to a little property in the country. One could be an employer without necessarily being an employer on a grand scale. The man who hawked coal at the corner was already a member, although a humble one, of the money-owning class. Many even of the biggest industrialists, such as Renault or Bertrand, had started so low and risen so quickly that nobody could forget, not even they themselves, the humble nature of their origins.

Experience had taught him to divide existing society into three main groups. First of all there were those who had been born lucky, who had started life with money in their pockets. Next came the shrewd fellows who had learned how to make money out of their pals. Luck had come their way too, not perhaps at their birth, but again and again later in life. Finally, there were the exploited, who were where they were as much because they were honest as because they were unlucky.

He didn't blind himself to the fact that account had to be taken, too, of the unemployables, the fools, and the idlers, to say nothing of the born criminals; that one had to admit the existence of a sort of bottom drawer kept for the broken pieces, for all the rubbish, of humanity. But this was a point to which he didn't attach too great an importance. In his more confident moods he told himself (rather too complacently) that in a better-organized society there would be fewer examples of human wreckage, and that means would be found of making some use of them.

The main point to be considered was the existence of these three great divisions; the immediate task was to find some way of preventing the oppression of the third by the first two. It was at this point that Edmond found himself thrown back upon his Socialistic beliefs. Those born lucky presented the easiest problem. The injustice which they represented could be swept away by a stroke of the pen, merely by confiscating all large inherited fortunes. But so long as the machinery of society remained unchanged, the particular form of inequality thus removed would simply reappear in another form, to the advantage of those shrewd men of business who made up the second of his main classes. The men who talked about "sharing the wealth" at street-corners and in the bars of the poorer quarters were fools and ignoramuses. The young men of Edmond's generation realized that what must be done was not to make the winner disgorge, but to alter the rules of the game.

His belief in the society of the future was deeper than he realized. To set oneself deliberately to imagine the details of a state of affairs as yet unrealized, to think of it as something actual, as something already there, demands a degree of ingenuousness rarely to be found in a Parisian. (It is more modest to confine oneself to generalizations—and one runs less risk of being laughed at.) Edmond's visions of the future were extremely vague. People would be better housed and better clothed. Many of the necessities of life would be provided by the public services. The working day would be shorter, and working conditions as comfortable as they could be made. There would be a great deal of leisure, to be used as one pleased. There would be a certain amount of organized sport, theatrical performances, and open-air games. There would be libraries well stocked with books both light and serious, for use in cold weather. The whole week would be rather like Sunday; not Sunday as it was now, with nothing to do and rotten with boredom, but full of life and occupation. Would money have been suppressed, as was proposed by some, and replaced by a system of "tokens"? That remained to be seen. Money itself is a kind of token, the only difference being that it can be exchanged against unspecified commodities. There must be some way of preventing the accumulation of money by individuals. One wouldn't have to be a magician to devise means for that when everyone was living on a wage and not, as now, by the exploitation of others. Not even a miser could amass a fortune if all he had to do it with was what he saved from his wages. Fortunes are only made when a man can use his savings to buy a business or start an industry; that is to say, when he can begin to exploit his neighbours. The real problem, therefore, would be not the suppression of money, but the prevention of the exploitation of one man by another.

In the world of the future, general happiness would be the rule. The longing for it was what made a man enthusiastic for the cause and filled him with sacred fury in the day of battle.

How glorious it would be to feel that he was no longer kept down by the existence of a privileged few who were getting from life all the pleasures that he had never known; getting them, too, without the shadow of a claim that he would have recognized as good or even as adequate! How glorious to feel, as he worked, that part of his labour was no longer going to provide some unknown gentleman with luxurious food, cars, women, and a magnificent villa!

Even should life turn out to be harder, it wouldn't matter so long as it was hard for all, so long as he knew that somebody else wasn't benefiting by his poverty. The awful thing wasn't the having more or less of certain advantages; no, the awful thing was that injustice, inferiority, inequality, should exist. Once they had been destroyed, everything else would be bearable; but so long as they lasted, nothing else mattered. (The only pleasant memory that Edmond had taken away from his military service was that of seeing a mother's darling going through the mill like everybody else and being treated like dirt.)

It was for these reasons that he believed in revolution and had no sympathy with mere reformers. Many employers were reformers. Bertrand seemed to think that he was doing all that could be done for his work-people if he gave them a decent wage and provided them with a large and airy factory. There were others who organized nurseries and orphanages. No doubt they were sincere in what they did; it was just that they didn't understand the problem. They were like the owners of horses who said: "My box stalls are all tiles and varnished wood. My animals have the best hay and the best oats. They're kept as clean as new pins. What have they got to grumble at?"

It's no argument to say that inequality is the natural lot of humanity—as though one didn't know that!—that those with more to give to society should get more out of it, or to contend that without that spur all effort would cease. Who has greater gifts or can be of greater value to his fellows than a great scholar?—and yet isn't it a commonplace of schoolmasters that many scholars are poor, and many writers too, many whose statues, when they are dead, are set up in the public squares? No one bothered to ask whether poverty

prevented *them* from working. And let no one try to persuade us
that if Dufayel was allowed to make a thousand times more than
Pasteur, it was because he was a thousand times more useful to society,
or that if he hadn't been so encouraged he would have given up his
work in disgust. Suppose he had, would society have been the loser?

Equality is a pleasure. Justice is a pleasure—the most widely enjoyed and continuous of all pleasures, as necessary as breathing. To
live and work without justice is like living and working without air.
Other pleasures are secondary, to be thought of only when justice is
secured. The future will prove that.

Edmond's appetites were not insatiable. He was not the kind of
madman whom pleasure excites instead of satisfying, for whom food,
money, love were less the means of fulfilling desire than incitements
to a sort of inborn megalomania. If suddenly something extraordinary
were to happen and the restraints of law were suspended; if, for example, he found himself with one of those beautiful and untouchable
women at his mercy, or swept by a mob into some luxury shop, the
windows with their trays of diamonds crashing beneath his fist, he
would, undoubtedly, like anybody else, feel a mad joy in outraging
the woman, forcing her to his will, or shaking down necklaces and
bracelets like so many cherries; but his madness would be less the
madness of desire than an expression of fury and the will to
vengeance.

And yet in his scale of human values pleasure took a high, perhaps
the highest, place. He had an instinctive dislike for all teaching that
set a premium on abstinence or sacrifice. Even the noblest cause
would seem a sham to him if there was no place in it, ultimately, for
the various pleasures of life. He regarded those who pretended to
scorn pleasure, or who subordinated it to other ends, either as hypo-
crites or as faddists. He felt a particular kind of pity for the pious
folk who deprived themselves of happiness in this life, or who put
up with a miserable existence, in the hope of a heavenly reward. One
didn't often come across them now except in the depths of the country. Even those of his mates who were members of Catholic unions

and played the scab when it came to a strike, didn't, he noticed, in their fond anticipation of heaven, scorn such worldly advantages as better wages or other similar benefits. What was true was that the fables of another life in which they believed did help them to endure more easily the injustices of this one, and that was what the exploiting classes relied on even while they laughed good-humouredly at the propaganda of the Church. He was amazed, too, and tickled, by quite another class of simple souls, the elderly spinsters who, because no one would marry them, abandoned all idea of love. There were even certain young men who were terrified by what they had been told of sin into remaining virgin for an incredible length of time.

For Edmond attached very great importance indeed to the pleasures of sex. Without his realizing it, he assumed that any betterment in human conditions, any system of happiness, would involve as its central fact, duly hedged about with safeguards, a more refined and more equitable enjoyment of sex. Nothing seemed to him more unjust than that all the beautiful and well-cared-for women were reserved, without exception, for the rich. Not content with the women of their own class, they stole the prettiest of the class below, making them adopt the bodily refinements necessary to fit them for the practices of love. (Although Romuald disgusted him, he sometimes wondered whether it wasn't preferable that Isabelle should live with a little pimp who at least belonged completely to the "people" than that she should be carried off by some rich man's son to be his mistress in the world of fashion.) He didn't blame the privileged for thinking so much about women and love. He envied them. He, too, delighted in well-turned-out women whose underclothes were like a bouquet of flowers. (He was bound, on principle, to condemn prostitution, and nothing humiliated him more than to have a sister on the streets, but, thanks to the smart professionals, a man who had long been eaten up with desire for fine women and elegant underclothes could get a certain amount of satisfaction at the cost of a day's wages and a little goodwill. So long as social injustice was tolerated, prostitution would have to remain.) He, too, would like to have his pick of women. But he realized that if society was to remain an ordered whole, there would have to be some check on caprice, and family life would have to be protected. He had no objection to family life provided it centred on a satisfactory enjoyment of sex. One of the rare visions he allowed himself of an ideal state was that of a young family group, well cared-for and well clothed, with plenty of time for love-making and a greater insistence on elegance than passion. He liked, for instance, to imagine a fine sunny afternoon with no work to do; a couple of hours of dallying in bed, followed by dinner at a restaurant. Then a show, of the kind that would work one up a bit, and finally home, with some more love-making before one went to sleep.

Not that he'd carry it to the point of weakening his system or of making a beast of himself. Sensuality ought to have a place in any rational scheme of life, but even when one's young, it mustn't be allowed to interfere with health, though the choice between the two might be difficult. Edmond was very much concerned about health. He professed a great distrust of doctors in general, because he knew that a lot of them were quacks, and that the rest, however good their intentions, thought of nothing but cutting off their patients from all the pleasures of life. But he believed in the future of medicine. He was frightened of violent drugs, but he had a liking for trivial remedies. He would have liked to fill his pockets with pills and lozenges, if only they didn't cost so much: to take occasional tablets, to treat himself to a drop of cordial in the morning or before meals. On the occasions when he took an appetizer, he always chose one that claimed to have some medicinal property.

His ideals, as may be gathered from these facts, were purely of this world. His imagination was almost completely untouched by those dreams by which humanity, through the ages, has symbolized its belief in an origin and a destination outside itself. At one time he had attended confirmation classes for the space of a whole year, but had not gone so far as to take his first communion. In fact, he had treated the affair much as he would have done a course of lessons in

German or Russian. Religious ideas had no more effect on him than water has on a duck's back. He did not believe in any divine sanction for the moral code, holding that anything that makes for pleasure is, in principle, a proper basis of conduct. The only general rule which he admitted was that life should be enabled to proceed smoothly, and in this connexion he agreed that certain modes of behaviour were unwise. For instance, it was inadvisable to allow marriages between brothers and sisters, because their children would be deaf-mutes or half-wits, and for that reason popular prejudice was against cohabitation between people so closely related. There was no point, he believed, in outraging public opinion unless one had to. Stealing wasn't playing the game; therefore one didn't steal. It was all a matter of common sense. Nevertheless, he did not entirely exclude the irrational from his own life. He hated the idea of bloodshed. No argument was necessary to prevent him from committing murder. The sense of proximity to a murderer, the very sight of one, would have made him go white with the sense of aversion. In general it would be true to say that his natural inclination was to help rather than to hurt his fellow men. The feeling of confidence in himself, and the knowledge that he inspired confidence in others, gave him pleasure. If Bertrand had told him to take a hundred thousand francs to the bank, not only would he have been assailed by no temptation, he would have had to resist a sense of pride and a feeling of gratitude towards his employer. He would have explained the matter to himself by resorting to irony: "He knows," he would tell himself, "that you're not such a fool as to slip into Belgium with his cash."

In order to formulate for himself any definite moral scruple, beyond discussion and untouched by irony, to feel the particular emotion associated with definite "well-doing," the warm satisfaction resulting from the performance of something that stirred his being to its depths, to experience the reality in his own self of the kind of moral conscience referred to in school manuals, he would have found it necessary to think in terms of his class, his group, or his factory.

To have continued to work after his union had told him to strike would have seemed to him the height of cowardice. To have allowed himself, as some scabs did, to be used as a strike-breaker, would have been, in his eyes, an almost criminal act, deserving of the most extreme form of punishment. He regarded a workman who betrayed his fellows as an outlaw. If such a man ended by being kicked to death, he only got what he deserved.

Similarly, although he was soft by nature and careful of his own skin, he could quite easily imagine himself risking his life to save a pal from a burning factory. An ordinary house on fire would have made him hesitate much longer.

For some time now he had been turning one particular problem over and over in his mind. "If there was a war, what should I do?" Formerly his answer would not have been in doubt: "The unions will proclaim a general strike and refuse to fight. I shall obey the orders of the working class as it's my duty to do." But things were different now. He had to reckon with all that had happened in October, the railway strike, the mobilization order. The working classes had hesitated to shoulder the final responsibility. Edmond was profoundly worried. He knew that he could never stand out alone. As one of a crowd, strong in the solidarity of his comrades, he could defy all the police forces of the world; as an individual he was nothing but a miserable defaulter whom the first constable could arrest. What then?

Probably, just because his leaders had failed, he would have to let himself and his friends be driven forward like a lot of cattle to slaughter the proletarians on the other side. Such a state of affairs would be utterly ridiculous, without any redeeming feature. He would be wholly without illusions. If such a black day should come, and it might come soon, he knew that he would be carried away by no intoxication. For him such words as "country," "nation," were dead sounds. He loved Paris, and his own district of Paris in particular. He believed that the climate of France was pleasanter, the monuments of France finer, than those of any other country. He was convinced that the average Frenchman was more intelligent and more civilized than any foreigner. The mere fact of speaking French seemed to give him an obvious advantage over other people. But he could see no rational connexion between such peaceable feelings and the embattled struggle of nations in the field. A man from Belleville naturally looks down on a man from Vaugirard, but that is no reason why he should want to fly at the throats of a lot of decent fellows who happened to be less gifted and less fortunate than himself. The country, the nation, military retreats, Fourteenth of July parades, bugles, the *Marseillaise,* were all very fine, but he wasn't quite a fool! He knew perfectly well that the leaders of the capitalist middle class wanted to get him drunk with such things. So long as he and his friends had got their heads filled with Germans, they would leave the privileged classes alone. As soon as the privileged classes took it into their minds to side-track revolution by means of a war, it would be to their interest to get as many poor devils as possible killed in the name of the country and the nation.

And how about God? Well, God was in the same boat. The fact that the "haves" thought so highly of God made Him suspect. One couldn't help thinking that they reckoned on Him much as they reckoned on the country and the nation.

If he were pressed, he would be inclined to distinguish between God as the chief stockholder in religion, the great ally of capitalism, the boss of bosses, and God pure and simple.

Edmond felt nothing that could be called hatred for religion or for the Church. The anti-clericalism of the last generation had worn pretty thin by the time he had grown up. Priests as a whole, of course, were usually on the wrong side, but there were decent enough fellows among them, and certainly no one could accuse them of living in affluence. Religion might be a good thing for children and women. Probably Isabelle wouldn't have gone wrong if she'd been to church oftener. Apart from the mischievous doctrine of resignation which it preached to the people, the Church's principles were not bad. When it came to considering the *truth* of what she taught, the mysteries, the future life, and all the rest of it, Edmond didn't think it worth while even to discuss the question. He remembered seeing a red poster one day announcing that some speaker or other would refute the Catholic view of Jesus Christ, and thinking that the gentleman in question must have a lot of time to waste. No one religion was truer than any other. The only thing that mattered was that it shouldn't be allowed to worry people. It was hardly worth while, in that case, to go about "refuting."

One could believe in God without going into details. Edmond was no atheist. But if he didn't set himself to deny the existence of God, he didn't feel any very great urge to admit it. He was less struck by the "harmonies of nature" than working men of an earlier generation had been. In those days people hadn't known much about mechanics. They were easily amazed, easily reduced to silence, by the "perfection of the universe as a machine," easily led to believe that so wonderful a clock must presuppose a clock-maker worthy of it. It didn't need much thought to tell Edmond that the universe was anything but a good piece of mechanism. Apart from the movements of the sun and moon, nothing operated as it should. Wind and rain occurred just anyhow; seasons were spoiled; whole classes of animals were ill designed and good for nothing but to prey on one another. Even the human body, regarded as a machine, was nothing very wonderful. It was complicated, certainly, but only in the sense that it was a muddle. Most of the time it was out of order. Any piece of modern machinery one liked to name, no matter what its function, was a more beautiful piece of work, more highly finished, and capable of running better.

No, from that point of view nature was evidence of slovenly tinkering. But was that what the argument sought to prove?— Better not talk too much about machines.

What Edmond really thought was that a man, like himself, who knew a thing or two about machinery would regard nature less as something that had been "designed" than as something that had "grown."

But must one presuppose some "force"? It was easy to confuse Edmond by talking of "force" or "forces," even of unknown or psychic forces. He didn't definitely deny the possibility of such things. He had seen displays of hypnotism in cafés. He knew perfectly well that a lot of its practitioners were frauds, and his view of spiritualists was that they were "cracked." All the same, he was of the opinion that there's a good deal that has not been fully explained, that the power of the human mind is extraordinary, that mankind has been surrounded, since the beginning of time, by radiations, emanations, influences, which can perhaps be explained by some analogy with the will and the brain.

He had no belief in the immortality of the soul. He could contemplate utter extinction at death without much feeling of bitterness. His attitude towards his own salvation was on a level with the general modesty and humility with which he regarded himself as an individual. A human being was too trivial a thing to worry about. Seeing that he is born at one definite moment in time, it is surely unreasonable to expect him to continue for ever? What does he take himself for? The finest engines in the world go to the scrap-heap after a few years. Does one demand immortality for a dog, for a snail? Suppose survival possible, what for the most part is it that would, in fact, be perpetuated? Some senile and toothless crone, some old bore in the rue Compans, some mindless dotard of the Buttes-Chaumont who spends his days chewing tobacco and spitting? To think of that going on to all eternity—a museum of mummies! Besides, they'd only be taking up room. And how bored they'd get, a lot of old fogies telling the same stories for thousands and thousands of years!

Still, what is man here for? For what purpose has he been sent into the world? Ask the dog, ask the snail.

Did he, then, feel no need of something beyond himself, of something to inspire his thoughts?— "Feel what I may," he thought, "it won't alter facts. But, actually, there is something that inspires me and points beyond myself: the idea of progress in this world, the idea that some day the reign of justice will begin, the idea that mankind in the future will be as far in advance of me as I am in advance of my ancestors the cave-men."

Meanwhile it was no good taking things too seriously (prone though he was to self-torment). One must shift for oneself as circumstances arose; avoid being put upon, sacrifice as little as possible for a Society that wasn't worth the cost, keep from playing into the hands of those who sought to maintain things as they were.

Certainly, a pimp was no great matter, but in asking your help to get him out of a scrape he was showing that he trusted you, he was appealing to the principle of good-fellowship. It was almost as though he had hammered on your door with the police hot at his heels. Were you going to refuse to let him in out of consideration for the cops? After all, the magistrate needn't have called on you; you owed him no duty.

There must be some non-committal answer he could give which would enable his "brother-in-law" to establish an alibi.

Chapter 18

MADAME DE QUINGEY'S EVENING PARTY

Mionnet had spent the first part of the evening in conversation with various ladies, but later he was monopolized by M. de Montsauche and M. Dumas, with whom he had had a long talk in the well-warmed little boudoir which served on occasion as a smoking-room.

Conversation at first confined itself to matters of literature and ancient history, in which fields M. de Montsauche was almost a professional. For twenty-five years he had devoted his ample leisure to research, and particularly to the philology of Hellenistic Greek. In addition to various magazine articles, he had published a book on *The Language of Strabo* and a volume of more general scope on *Literary Greek from the Antonines to the End of the Western Empire.* He had been responsible for critical editions of the *Meditations* of Marcus Aurelius, and Lucian's *Life of Peregrinus.* But he considered as his chief claim to fame the fact that Teubner had commissioned him to establish the text of Philo. In doing so, the famous publisher had shown a degree of confidence in his scholarship which marked him as exceptional. M. de Montsauche fully realized that this recognition had set him apart, in the eyes of scholars, from the herd of amiable amateurs. He had been elected corresponding member of the Academy of Inscriptions and belonged to several foreign learned societies of distinction.

He had amassed an important collection of texts and specialist works, but he was obliged to travel a good deal in the interests of research. Each year he spent half of his holidays in the public libraries of Paris, London, Oxford, Germany, or Italy. He liked to refer to himself as a "humanist." When colleagues from abroad showed surprise on learning that he was a magistrate and asked him why he had not devoted himself to an academic career, he was in the habit of saying: "As things are, I have much more leisure. My legal work takes up far less time than lecturing, teaching, and examining."

He professed great admiration for the literature and the philosophy of the Hellenistic period, and supported his contention with detailed arguments drawn from his researches. Treating this theme as a point of departure, he set himself to develop certain general ideas which were not very original, but in which he sincerely believed— ideas of the sort that were current among men of specialized culture during the second half of the nineteenth century, such, for instance, as a refusal to subscribe to the conventional view of decadence, and a defence of paganism, especially of paganism at its last gasp. He voiced a kindly hostility to Christianity, maintaining that it was an Oriental superstition, spread by slaves, who had very naturally made it their own, which had ended by overrunning the West and destroying its civilization for many centuries, not without producing now and again, it must be admitted, a few masterpieces which were not wholly without charm. In Paris these ideas would have seemed rather outmoded; uttered in a drawing-room in M— before an audience of admiring ladies who thought it rather daring to read Anatole France, they still produced an enormous effect.

After a few introductory references to the primitive Church and the precise degree of antiquity to be ascribed to the rule of celibacy, M. de Montsauche attacked Mionnet on the general question of professional chastity. The Abbé wondered, for a moment, whether there was not, perhaps, some subtle intention behind this choice of subject, especially as several ladies were seated not far from them, having, apparently, come deliberately within range in order to catch a few crumbs from the two men's learned intercourse, and being, in fact, near enough to overhear all that they said. The question seemed, however, to have arisen quite naturally, and if M. de Montsauche's face expressed malice, it arose, clearly, less from premeditation than from the amusement of taking this chance of touching on a delicate matter, and, no doubt, because it gave the speaker an opportunity of mounting a favourite hobby-horse.

Mionnet tried to give the impression that he was in no way embarrassed by the point at issue, but, at the same time, that it did not greatly interest him. What he said was more or less as follows:

"It's a thing that outsiders are always worrying about, and it's very kind of them, I'm sure, to give so much attention to our concerns. We priests, believe me, give it much less thought. It's the kind of thing that laymen, especially, love discussing. It reminds me," he added shrewdly, with a glance at his female audience, "of something I once heard a lady say in the elevator of one of the big Paris shops, with reference to the operator. 'How,' she asked, 'can he go on doing this all day? Even going up once makes me feel sick.'"

But M. de Montsauche was not to be beaten so easily. Human nature, he maintained, makes certain demands. That the problem was a real one and was not merely invented by the simplicity of the lay mind was proved by the fact that many great churchmen in the past had tried to solve it either by dint of heroic adherence to the law of abstinence or—otherwise. There seemed, moreover, to be evidence that the heroic method had never been quite so universal as was sometimes supposed, since the attested continence of this or that bishop or ecclesiastic had always been cited as a proof of unusual holiness. Nobody writing the biography of the elevator-boy, with the possible exception of the lady in question, would have stressed as a merit his immunity from sickness.

Mionnet replied quietly that he held no brief for the past and admitted that those who wrote the lives of the great churchmen had foolishly underlined, for the benefit of lay readers, a virtue which had probably been extremely common in all ages, except perhaps at certain periods of almost universal corruption. So far as the present was concerned, it was only necessary to think seriously for a moment about the way in which a priest spent his day to be cured of any tendency to be surprised at his continence. He then proceeded to outline the routine of a parish priest, being careful to draw freely on his own memories in order to avoid making his example too abstract. He ran through the list of offices and prayers, detailed the various works of charity, reminded his listeners of all the people who had to be seen, advised, and visited. What time was there, he asked, in such a life for loose thoughts, the self-indulgence of day-dreams, and all that such things brought in their train? M. de Montsauche, he concluded, seemed to think that sexual virtue demanded abnormal self-control, whereas, in fact, the circumstances of such a life were its best guarantee, so that, in most cases, it was not even necessary to invoke the assistance of supernatural grace.

"I don't think," he said, "that I am violating the secrecy of the confessional when I say that there are many not particularly devout laymen who live a life of almost complete celibacy. Such men are prevented by business, anxiety, and overwork from giving any thought to sensuality, and if they do occasionally surrender to its claims, it is often because of some curious prejudice, a sort of feeling that they owe a duty to their humanity. Speaking generally," he added, "I should say that suggestion plays a very large part in these matters, suggestion and the imitation of one's fellows, or of the claims put forward by one's fellows. Evil books have also a great deal to answer for."

He paused before remarking in a low voice, as though closing the discussion once and for all:

"And the priest, you must remember, says his daily Mass."

The ladies were delighted. As for Dumas, the professor, he had listened to both sides of the discussion, taking little part in it himself beyond contributing a few brief and benevolent remarks which had little to do with the subject. For the rest of the time he had been troubled by yawns caused by an imperfect digestive system.

Chapter

19

PART OF A LETTER FROM MADAME G— TO MADAME DE V—

. . . .

Yesterday evening at Mme de Quingey's I met that Abbé Mionnet whom I've mentioned already (he's the man, you remember, who was sent to put the diocese in order, and I don't mind telling you I think he's got his work cut out; there's a story going about that the Bishop's let himself be bamboozled by the Freemasons, and that they got him mixed up in the tram scandal so as to have a hold over him, which would explain some of the very extraordinary things he's been doing this last year or two.) Well, this Abbé is very attractive, younger than I thought, a fine figure of a man, and looks as though he's got a will of his own, simple though he seems; he gives up a great deal of time to games and social work; it's my belief, as I said before, that he abandoned his career, which everyone says was bound to be brilliant, and went into the Church as the result of some disappointment in love; you know he graduated first in his class at the Polytechnic.

It was splendid yesterday the way he absolutely floored that beastly old M. de Montsauche, you know whom I mean?—who as usual was making jokes in the worst possible taste about the clergy, particularly about their morals—you can guess the sort of thing; it was lovely to hear this Abbé M. answering him; I shouldn't say he's virtuous from any lack of opportunity.

There is a rumour going about that he's Mme de Q.'s pet; it doesn't surprise me about her, because she must be finding her *widowhood* a bit long, but it's difficult to believe about him—he could do so much better for himself—but I'm inclined to think that the memory of the love-affair for which he has given up everything is enough to keep him from temptations of that sort; what's your view? It'll be something for you to talk over with your Vichy friends—eh? M. de Montsauche is always doing that sort of thing; he's got a concealed shelf in his library entirely filled with dirty books; he insisted on showing them one day to me and another woman; I don't mind telling you they were perfectly *filthy*.

Have I told you that Mme La Pairolière, whose niece you once met at my house . . . etc. . . . .

Chapter

20

ON THE BRIDGE OF CAULAINCOURT:
MATHILDE'S UNCERTAINTIES

A hundred yards before him Laulerque could see the beginning of the bridge of Caulaincourt where it rose above the crowds and the lights of the late afternoon. It was wet underfoot. For the moment the rain had ceased, though round every lamp there was a halo of fine drops like insects attracted by the glow. The clip-clop of horses sounded in the distance, the familiar harsh rattle of rubberless wheels, and the newer, denser roar of cars and motor-buses. The human voice seemed banished from the medley of noise. Only to hear the damp patter made by the passing feet on the two pavements, inaudible save close at hand, was to be made aware of the strange truth that the human voice was noticeable by its absence.

Suddenly, while he walked, and without any premonitory warning either from the world without or from his mind within, Laulerque became conscious that the scene had become completely detached from his consciousness—all this fragment of the Paris evening, the whole of the damp, dwindling, vista. On the one side lay the picture of the street, on the other himself, Laulerque. The two seemed separated by more than a mere element of space. Not that he could see less clearly, or that the view was misted over. It wasn't that objects became less distinct or more distant; there they were before him as they had been but a moment back, but he no longer seemed to be in contact with them.

The scene itself took on an odd quality, all the more fascinating for being withdrawn entirely from the orbit of his own personality, for having, as it were, escaped him. It was as though he no longer lived in it. He felt that he must lose nothing of its quality. Every detail seemed curiously moving. He had a sense of perfection in things, seeing them as complete and unchangeable.

Half unwillingly, Laulerque set himself not to explain so much as to realize his experience. It was rather, he felt, as though some prodigy of nature had set him, without warning or portentous preparation, in the presence of some perfectly ordinary scene belonging to another period. No one paid the slightest attention to him or showed any sign of realizing his presence. His being there changed nothing. Not a movement, not a sound, was different from what it would have been had he not been there to see and hear, had he not intruded into this world. No act of the imagination could create, no memory recover, so intense a degree of normal actuality. But everything was in a state of completion; everything had passed, long ago and for ever, into that mode of being where no eye will ever look on it again (yet here he looked and saw). All had become part of that world where there was no room more for condemnation or for struggle, freed from time and change. No need now to worry for their fate. Their future—threats, dangers, anxiety—was the future no longer. The terrible power of the years to come had passed. They had paid the debt; they were at rest.

At rest! Only completed things could be so perfectly at rest. What happiness to live thus, quietly and in every detail, through a day for which all tomorrows were as things past and gone! Happiness secure and guarded such as a man knows when he sleeps with his face turned to the wall.

It occurred suddenly to him that he was perhaps living "ahead," a quarter of a century ahead, about 1935, for instance, and that by some means or other he had been enabled to find himself thus face to face with the scene before him—the wet pavements, the haze of raindrops, the dwindling vista of the bridge of Caulaincourt, the two streams of silent walkers separated the one from the other by carts, a motor-bus, and the clip-clop of horses.

A moment later he saw in imagination the cemetery of Montmartre spread out in the damp evening air beneath the bridge, swelling on either side to a gentle rise, a field of the dead, wrapped all in shadow save where its headstones caught here and there a reflection of pale light, holding in its dark embrace the bridge with its wet footways and its lamps. And he wondered whether perhaps his vision of the scene as something achieved and out of time was in some sort due to his sense of this field of the dead, alive with an obscure movement of its own, linking in unity the hillside and the valley, lit by a pallid and reflected light, bearing upon its night-hung bosom the lit and fragile structure of the bridge as the sea, faintly glimmering in darkness, bears on its waves a fragile ship with all its port-holes lit. But even as the idea came to him he realized that the two sensations had nothing to do with one another.

And on the instant he asked himself a question: "Shall I be alive in 1935?" and felt a creeping of his flesh from head to heels.

Then he thought that in less than a fortnight he would probably be in Amsterdam. At the end of November he had received a letter from Margaret-Désideria which ran as follows:

"I have heard that things are getting serious. There is a sense of bustle everywhere. I should be very much surprised if someone from your end didn't turn up here soon. Try to arrange for it to be you. Burn this letter."

There was a postscript:

"Do you realize what has been happening since L.T.'s death? Our friends are extraordinary people. They never *sleep*." She had underlined the word *"sleep."*

A little later he had managed to arrange a meeting with Mascot, and Mascot had asked him of his own accord:

"How long a vacation do you get at Christmas? . . . Would you dislike the idea of spending a few days in the same part of the world as you were in last time?"

As he crossed the bridge of Caulaincourt, Laulerque indulged in happy thoughts of Margaret-Désideria and the canals of Amsterdam.

All of a sudden he saw, a few paces ahead of him, a young woman in a dark beige cloak whom he thought he recognized. He overtook her.

"Good evening, Mademoiselle Mathilde."

Mathilde Cazalis turned with a nervous little start:

"Oh, it's you! . . . Were you following me?"

"Good heavens, no! I wasn't looking where I was going, and then I glanced up and saw you. . . . What are you doing in this neighbourhood?"

She didn't answer at once, and he added hastily: "Perhaps that's an indiscreet question. . . ."

"Not at all; you see—" She looked him full in the eyes. "I'm worried about something. I don't know what impression I gave you when you spoke to me, but the truth is I'm terribly worried."

"Seriously?"

"Yes."

They had reached the end of the bridge.

"May I walk with you a bit? Which way are you going?"

"I'm on my way to see Sampeyre. I'm going by the rue Caulaincourt and the rue Lamarck."

"It's a long way; won't you be tired?"

"No," she said, and added with a smile: "It does me good to walk; it prevents me from getting fat."

"Is there a meeting at Sampeyre's?"

"Oh, no."

"Perhaps you're going to see him about this something that's worrying you?"

"As a matter of fact, I am."

"Ah, a professional secret? . . . You needn't tell me about it if you'd rather not."

She assured him that so far from minding, she would like to have someone of her own age to advise her; only she didn't trust him.

"Why not? Do you think I can't keep a secret?"

"Possibly. But the real reason is that you're a mocker: you're not serious about things of the heart."

He protested that she misjudged him, adding that she would have been surprised could she have seen into his mind the moment before he met her.

"Oh well, then; you already know part of what I'm going to tell you, or, at least, you've probably guessed. I expect you've been told that Clanricard and I were engaged. That's not exactly true. There's no formal understanding between us, but we've been good friends for a long time—and I think he's in love with me."

"And you're not in love with him? Is that it?—Not a little bit?"

"Perhaps I am, more or less, but that's not the question."

"Not the question? The devil it isn't!"

"I believe he'd ask nothing better than to marry me. I'm quite sure of it, in fact. But you know what he's like—always afraid of forcing himself on people. No sooner had he made his intentions clear and realized that I understood what he meant than he was careful not to mention the matter again or to press me for an answer. He probably thought that I was waiting until we'd both saved enough to set up housekeeping. And then there was the question of my mother. You know, don't you, that I lived with her? Somebody had probably told him that I should have to look after her until my sister Constance got a job. My uncle Alphonse, at Barjac, is paying for her education. I'm very fond of my mother, but I've always thought it bad for a young couple to have the mother or father of either of them living in the same house. As a matter of fact, my sister has just got into the Post-Office Department, and she's been appointed to a very nice country district. I took my mother down to Barjac during the holidays, and they've set up house together."

"Doesn't your sister mean to marry?"

"There'll be plenty of time to think of that later. She's three years younger than I am. Besides, in the country there aren't the same difficulties. People are not huddled together as they are in Paris. Something could be arranged somehow. If the worst came to the worst, my mother could live with my uncle, now that he's got Constance off his hands. My sister and I could make her a small allowance. . . . To cut a long story short, Clanricard had got the idea into his head that once the holidays were over, the chief obstacle to our marriage would be removed and that I should let him know that I was ready—especially as I'm living alone now, which is a bit gloomy."

"I should think so. Well?"

"I hate telling you this. You'll probably think badly of me. Swear that you won't laugh at me behind my back, and that you won't repeat what I'm saying to anyone!"

"My dear girl, of course I'll swear."

"Well, then—you remember the day we met Monsieur Jerphanion for the first time?"

"Perfectly. It was quite close to here. Some thin snow was falling, and he and I started home rather late by one of the bridges. I remember that we looked at the Seine and thought how placid it seemed, little thinking what a hullabaloo it was going to cause later."

"He didn't, you remember, take much notice of me on that occasion. Well, we met once or twice afterwards, but not often. You know all about that. We became good friends, as it might have been you and I or any of our group. And then, gradually, his feelings must have begun to change."

"But yours didn't?"

"Let me tell it my own way!"

As she warmed to her theme, a southern quality crept into her voice, becoming more and more pronounced. She still spoke, however, in the past definite tense, forming her phrases with a dignified precision, until suddenly realizing the unconscious elegance of her speech, she dropped back into the vernacular of Paris. At the same moment her charming brogue vanished.

"I realized before the holidays that he was thinking a good deal about me. Of course there are some men who can't help making love to every woman they meet, but somehow he didn't seem to be that kind. When I was at Barjac in September, I got a letter from him. It was a very nice letter, in which he made it clear that on his way back from the Dordogne with his bicycle, on his way to visit relations in the Haute-Loire, he would very much like to drop in on me. I couldn't not answer without looking a fool, or tell him not to come. He arrived at Barjac one afternoon on his bicycle, very red in the face and very dusty. It was a frightfully hot day. He said he was tired and wouldn't go on till the next day, and he took a room at the hotel, though naturally we asked him to stay to dinner with us. Both my uncle and my mother took a great liking to him. They thought him very simple and very high-spirited. I think they were rather flattered by his attention. He ate a lot and had a good deal to drink. After dinner he said he'd like to go for a little walk—the evening was pleasantly cool after the heat of the day. He asked my uncle and me to go with him. My uncle refused, whereupon Monsieur Jerphanion very politely asked my mother whether I might be allowed to accompany him. My mother, who was quite used to my going out when and with whom I pleased, was charmed by his good manners. So we went. It was quite dark by then; there may have been a bit of a moon, I'm not sure. I think that the wine he had drunk had made him poetic, sentimental, and very sure of himself. Our local wine is exceptionally good. He said some charming things to me, and he kissed me."

"You didn't struggle very hard?"

"It wasn't very serious. I should have quite understood if next day, when he had thought things over a bit, he had behaved as though nothing had happened. But not a bit of it. When we said good-bye, he went out of his way to repeat to me, very earnestly, all the things he had said the evening before."

"And after that did you exchange letters?"

"Yes."

"Sentimental letters?"

"His were, certainly."

"Did you see him again when you got back to Paris?"

"Yes."

"And Clanricard, too?"

She made no answer, and he went on:

"But you didn't tell him of—his misfortune?"

"Please don't be funny about it. I feel terribly guilty. I'm very fond of him; he's so straight, so honourable, and I know how much he likes Jerphanion, which will make it so much worse for him."

"And Jerphanion isn't quite so honourable?"

"Indeed he is! Don't try to be sarcastic. It's a horrible position for him, too. But Clanricard's shyness makes everything so much more difficult. He's always been so careful not to plague me, not to pre-sume on our friendship. With anyone else I might have found an opportunity of showing that my feelings had changed, but not with him."

"Still, he must have kissed you sometimes?"

". . . Yes."

"And you let him go on?"

"You don't understand. . . . It's not as simple as you seem to think."

"My dear girl, you're not going to make me believe that a woman in your situation hasn't all sorts of ways of showing a man that it's hopeless, that everything's over, even when everything hasn't gone very far—particularly when everything hasn't gone very far. What little beasts women can be! . . . But there's one point I'm not clear about. Instead of going straight to poor old Clanricard and having things out with him, you're going to Sampeyre. . . . Explain, please."

"I want to ask his advice."

"About what? About which of the two you ought to be in love with? Honestly, now, what is it you want to ask him?"

"Don't pretend you don't understand."

"I want to know. Are you going to ask him whether the time has come to tell Clanricard the truth? I should have thought you could decide that without bothering Sampeyre."

"He can tell me how best to set about it."

"You're remarkably modest for a woman! . . . What you mean is that he may offer to do the job himself. . . . He's quite good-natured enough!"

Mathilde began to laugh despite herself. After a moment she went on:

"There's something else. I've got myself to consider. Sampeyre is fond of me, and knows me well. I'd far rather listen to him than I would to my father if he were alive. . . ."

Laulerque remained for a few moments plunged in thought; then, in a different tone, he said:

"That's very charming of you, and Sampeyre will be touched. But you know perfectly well what he'll say. He'll be deeply concerned for Clanricard, but he's too intelligent and too human to do other than say that you must decide for yourself. 'If you're in love with Jerphanion,' he'll tell you, 'and if he's in love with you, as he seems to be, there's no reason why you two shouldn't settle down together, no reason in the world. It'll be a very happy, an admirable arrangement.' "

Mathilde remained silent.

Laulerque pressed his point:

"What else do you expect him to say?"

"I know; but I repeat, it's not all so simple as that."

"Either I don't understand what you're trying to say, or I'm a fool."

She made a little sound of irritation.

"You're making me say more than I meant to. . . . You see, if it was only a question of deciding whether in three months, or, at most, six months, a year perhaps, I should be calling myself Madame Clanricard or Madame Jerphanion—"

At these words Laulerque's expression underwent a quick change. He looked at the young woman, shook his head, and muttered: "Well?" once or twice.

She hurried on:

"I'm not quite a fool, you know. I know, naturally, that students at the Training College are allowed to marry while they're still taking their course, but I know, too, that he doesn't think it very practical to do so. It's all right for men whose parents have got money and can help them, but—"

"I see. If I understand you aright, what our friend Jerphanion would propose would not be marriage?"

She hastened to interrupt him:

"Don't put a wrong construction on what I've told you, or I won't tell you any more. . . . In the first place, you mustn't think ill of him."

He replied with a laugh:

"Ill of him for that? Quite the contrary, I assure you. I feel considerable admiration for him. There are plenty of charming young women like you who track us down and snare us into marriage and lead us a hell of a dance. . . . Oh yes, we have plenty of time to regret it when it's too late. . . . But now and then, I'm glad to say, a chap comes along who's too wily to be caught. Surely you don't think I should blame him for that? I should have done exactly as he's doing, if I'd dared—and without looking further than you! Perhaps I *have* flirted a bit with you from time to time, but I've never followed up my chances, never pushed things to an issue, because I always said to myself: 'She's not that sort; if she wants me, or anyone else, for that matter, it'll be for keeps.' And I didn't feel ready for keeps. But I see now what a fool I've been!"

She laughed, but she was in a towering temper.

"You're being offensive, Laulerque—as though, no matter how much you'd made love to me— I'll never tell you anything again. . . . If *you* ever had that sort of relationship with a woman it would be from pure caddishness, so as to be able to get out of it when you'd had enough."

"With him, I suppose, it's so that he can introduce you to the pleasures of disinterested love. Well, I admit he's perfectly right. But you're wrong in thinking that I couldn't show a sweet young thing just as many pleasures of disinterested love as he can. Shall I tell you what I think? In a well-organized society men would be forbidden to marry before they were thirty-five, and women before they were thirty. Up to that time they would make love gracefully, irresponsibly, and without bothering about tiresome scruples. There you have my considered opinion."

Her face had an angry expression. "It's always a mistake to talk to you of things one really cares about. You're just a clown."

"All right, all right, I'll stop talking."

She lowered her voice and went on in a more friendly tone:

"But it would have been nice if you'd tried to put yourself in my shoes."

He was touched.

"I beg your pardon, Mathilde, I do, honestly. I realize that you're worried, and I'll try to listen sensibly."

"Yes, I am worried. I don't want to argue like a little middle-class miss, but if what I think of doing is going to land me in misery and disillusion, perhaps I'm a fool to despise an unexciting and prosaic happiness. That's what I want to discuss with Sampeyre."

Laulerque had become very serious.

"You couldn't discuss it with a better person. But before he can give you any advice, he may feel it necessary to ask you questions such as I have no right to ask. You must realize that. In the first place he'll have to be quite clear about Jerphanion's intentions. You say, don't you, that Jerphanion knows more or less how things are with you and Clanricard? I can't believe that, knowing you've only got to lift a finger to marry a young man of whom he's so fond and of whom he thinks so highly, he'll take the responsibility in cold blood of dissuading you from a marriage which offers every chance of happiness, just for the sake of an adventure which may lead nowhere. He's not that kind of man."

"I know—although I remember him saying an awful thing to me once—something rather like what you were saying just now, only worse. It was all in fun, of course, and he only said it for effect, as you did. He said: 'If we'd met one another after you were Clanricard's wife, you'd probably have been perfectly willing to deceive him with me. You'd probably have felt considerably fewer scruples, so far as he was concerned, than you would now, though at the moment he has no rights and after marriage he will have a great many. Certainly you would have very few scruples on your own account.' And he added: 'Why is it that women only give themselves freely to the men they love after they have given themselves, not so very freely, to the men they care nothing about?' "

Laulerque smiled.

"I should never," he said, "have credited Jerphanion with so much cynicism. Still, he didn't conclude his argument, I imagine, by saying: 'Give yourself to me, and let's be happy while happiness lasts; you can always later marry Clanricard, who will have the tact to wait for you'? I'm sure he didn't, nor yet: 'Since the idea commends itself to you, marry him first and deceive him afterwards'—not to mention the simultaneous solution, which, in the words of Legraverend, provides the synthesis."

He pondered, now and again breaking his silence with little bursts of laughter:

"How odd it all is!"

"I mustn't be unjust," she went on. "He's planning to do great things, and he knows more or less how he's going to do them. He's afraid of loading himself too early with responsibilities, of being shackled. He wants to remain free. Love, as he says, doesn't interfere with anything, but marriage and a home to keep up are quite another question. You may make as many high-sounding oaths as you like before it happens, but sooner or later the necessities that married life gives rise to are bound to get you down. For instance, one of the things he's said to me is: 'I want to be able to leave the University suddenly if I think it necessary to do so, to rough it. So long as you're nothing but my mistress, I shan't be making you suffer by taking such a course, or not much, because you've got your own career. If, however, you are my wife, the whole thing becomes impossible. I could never let you keep me. And then, of course, there's the possibility of children. The presiding deity of the domestic hearth has a way of landing one sooner than one expects. Besides, once we are married, even if we don't have children, we shall have to keep up appearances, however modest. There's always something that has to be sacrificed to marriage, and sometimes it turns out to be the most essential thing in life.' He says that among the many young married couples of his acquaintance he knows several who have already come to grief. I've got an idea that his point of view in these matters has been to some extent influenced by his friend Jallez, about whom he's told me a good deal; not that he goes as far as Jallez, who is opposed to marriage on principle. But he does say that it's foolish to rush into it, especially when the woman has a chance of being independent, and that before saddling ourselves with those small duties which inferior folk seem to find necessary for the support of their self-respect, people like us (he says 'us' out of politeness; he's really thinking of himself) ought to tackle the big things of life first."

"What does he mean by the big things?"

"Well, for instance, getting one's ideal clear, and so arranging one's life that one can work for it."

Laulerque's reactions to her words were visible in a series of tiny expressions that played across his face, changing, vanishing, melting into one another. He smiled, then frowned, next raised his eyebrows, bit the corner of his lip. He opened his mouth as though in readiness for a loud guffaw, but closed it again without emitting a sound. Strangest thing of all, he listened to her for moments together without attempting to interrupt.

"My dear Mathilde," he said at length with a certain sententiousness of manner, which, however, was replaced, as he proceeded, by a lighter tone, "now indeed I have imagined myself in your shoes, and that fact doesn't make it any easier for me to advise you—far from it. Not, I must say, that you have asked me to."

"But please, please, I want you to."

"I am far from thinking our young Jerphanion a bad lot. What he said may not have been best calculated to please you, but it is brim full of common sense."

"You men always back each other up!"

"On the contrary, we are terribly jealous of one another. I should ask nothing better than to make you hate him so that I might take his place in your affections. But the young devil is right. . . . Even his cynical comment on women's aptitudes before and after marriage, though it may not be very flattering to your sex, is true enough. You're nothing but a lot of rakes at heart! But our young friend knows how to protect himself—indeed he does, and I regard him as an honour to his fellow men. Listen, Mathilde, my dear; I am a man who goes for all or nothing, and in your place I shouldn't hesitate for a second. . . . The solution offered by Clanricard would seem to me far too tame, far too settled. I should make straight for the worse alternative, with all its risks." In a lower tone he added: "If I wasn't afraid of shocking you, I should feel inclined to support my argument with a bit of cynicism, somewhat in his style, but—" He raised his voice again. "No, don't ask me what it would be. To sum up, you're not me, and you ought to have regard to a minimum, at least, of prudence. Go to Sampeyre and ask his advice. But you must tell him everything, even—"

He stopped and shot a glance at her from the corner of his eye.

"Even?"

"Even if you have to tell him things which you have thought it wiser not to tell me. . . ."

"What are you hinting?"

"Nothing, nothing at all. But in a problem such as yours no detail should be neglected. May I make this suggestion? With Clanricard I can do nothing—and, anyhow, Sampeyre can deal with him a great deal better than I could. But I am pretty intimate with Jerphanion—intimate enough to talk frankly to him. As I said before, there's no harm in him. He may be thoughtless and a bit conceited, but that's all. I promise you to make him think seriously about the whole thing—that would be all to the good, wouldn't it?—and to come to some conclusion myself."

"You must promise not to tell him what I've said."

"Do you think I'm quite a fool—or a bad friend? Now here we are at the corner of the rue du Mont-Cenis. I'm going down the hill this way. I'm due to meet somebody at the rue Flocon; nothing of very great importance, but I'm late already. Don't tell Sampeyre that you've met me, or only after he's given you his advice. Good evening, Mathilde, and good luck."

A moment later he ran after her again.

"One other thing: Sampeyre had better do nothing with Clanricard until I've made Jerphanion declare himself. . . . I tell you what, as soon as I've seen him, I'll write to you. That'll be best."

Chapter

21

LAULERQUE'S LETTER TO MATHILDE

My dear Mademoiselle Mathilde:

I've just got your note, and I've no excuse to make. I *did* see J. last Sunday, and I ought to have written to you at once. But I expected to be seeing you soon, probably next Tuesday at Sampeyre's, and thought it would be easier to explain things to you in conversation. At least, that's what I told myself, but the truth is I was lazy. And now Sampeyre's got the flu.— And talking of Sampeyre, I was much interested by one of the arguments you told me he used. It had never occurred to me, so you see how wise you were to go to him. To return: I had a long talk with J. J.—two and a half hours by the clock, which is not to be sneezed at. He was a bit upset at first at the idea of my interference, and was inclined to think that your asking me for advice, etc., was painful evidence that you didn't trust him. Doubtless you will be able to soothe the wound. I've done all the necessary talking.

My general impression is good. J. J. was prepared to be perfectly serious without any suggestion on my part. He spoke with feeling of Clanr., and of you, too—but I don't think I need tell you that!

His state of mind is a very complex one, and he finds it difficult to make his intentions clear (this was one of the reasons I would rather have spoken to you at leisure than cram everything into a letter), not because he's keeping anything back or shirking the issue, but because he is honestly confused. He said a lot of things to me about planning his life and avoiding the danger of slipping into mediocrity, which he seemed to feel sincerely, and which I couldn't contradict, because I believe them to be right. He wants to do the decent thing by you, but he is anxious to avoid starting his life with a colossal mistake. I have an idea, too, that he doesn't want his friend Jallez to think him a fool.

I was particularly struck by what he said about Cl. It was something like this:

"If I'd thought she was really in love with him, I would have avoided doing anything that might have injured their relationship; I should have been a cad to have acted otherwise. But she showed so little enthusiasm that I thought I might reasonably conclude that she hadn't made up her mind."

My own opinion is that if you show you trust him, he will feel bound by your trust, and may find, rather sooner than he thinks, that what at the moment rather frightens him is, after all, a possible solution.

I know that to show a man that she "trusts" him may mean a good deal to a woman. That's why I only give you my opinion instead of offering you my advice.

Ever your friend,
A. LAULERQUE

Chapter

AN IMPORTANT EMISSARY

With great caution Mascot half opened the door; he recognized Laulerque.

"Oh, it's you; good." He lowered his voice. "There's someone here."

"A member?"

Mascot gave an affirmative nod.

While Laulerque took off his hat and overcoat in the tiny hall, Mascot continued in hushed tones:

"I shan't introduce you. He's all right; you can be quite easy in your mind."

After a moment's hesitation he added:

"Somebody important."

The "somebody important" was seated in an arm-chair in the elegant little drawing-room which always seemed to be so thickly padded. He rose quickly and held out his hand to Laulerque, bowing from the neck and clicking his heels. Not a word was said. He was slightly shorter than Laulerque, rather bald, of a full complexion, dressed in black, and inclining to corpulence. He might have been forty. He had fine brown eyes, a large face, and a flattish nose, the tip of which was adorned with a few curly hairs. His reddish-brown hair was not trimmed into the nape of his neck, but lay across it in a discreet wave which gave to his face—indeed, to his whole person, despite the extreme correctness of his clothes—a faint look of the "central-European artist" type. His light-brown moustache was sparse and so closely clipped as to be scarcely noticeable.

On the whole he made a pleasant impression on Laulerque, but it was clear that his physical appearance would make it difficult for him to pass unremarked in a crowd. It was not easy to imagine him foiling the police of Europe.

"We were just discussing the general situation when you arrived," said Mascot. "This gentleman was saying that a serious view of it is taken where he comes from. Here, and elsewhere too, the prevalent feeling is that things will slow down. But any such delay will be deceptive and purely temporary."

The stranger turned his brown eyes towards the speaker and nodded his head once or twice in sign of agreement.

"It looks," Mascot continued, "as though next year will be decisive. . . ." He smiled, and added: "Definitely decisive, I mean; every year, for some time past, has been more or less so. What it comes to, in fact, is that in the best-informed quarters it is thought that war will break out next summer."

Although Laulerque considered himself steeled against any news, however bad, he was conscious of a shock.

"The summer of 1911?" he said, as though he mistrusted his ears. "Yes."

The stranger backed up Mascot's "Yes" with a movement of the head.

"You mean," said Laulerque, "that this time it won't simply be another of those scares we have grown used to almost every year?" "No."

"But I thought that this coming together of Russia and Germany as a result of the Potsdam meeting was a good sign."

"It seems not; or, at least, it seems that it is no longer so."

This time the stranger underlined Mascot's reply with a little horizontal nod and a backward and forward movement of his raised forefinger. It was as though he and his host had divided between them the resources of language, the latter confining himself to words, the former to gestures. Perhaps the unknown visitor spoke no French, though he seemed to understand it perfectly well.

"Who will declare war? What will the pretext be?"

"Oh, there's never any lack of pretexts. The general attitude of a country is much more important than the question of pretexts."

Laulerque thought: "That man sitting there is apparently an important member of the organization. Now is the moment for me to find out really what it is they're up to and what they think they can do—and to make it clear to them that delivering secret letters in Holland isn't my idea of participating in a great heroic movement."

He said:

"In that case what's going to be done? Obviously the time has come to do something. We've known it was coming for years, and so far no one has done anything. At least, that's how it seems to me."

Mascot and the stranger looked at each other and smiled. On the stranger's face was a look of amused indulgence. Obviously he regarded the young Frenchman's question as evidence of a democratic enthusiasm which found it hard to submit to the society's methods and discipline. He opened his mouth. He had a high, almost treble voice. The only sign of a foreign accent was in his phrasing, in the rather marked hissing sound which he gave to his "f's" and "v's," and in the harshness of his "r's."

"But something has been done. Something is always being done."

"Yes," agreed Mascot, "the work is going on every day, but its effects are necessarily limited; its results are hard to appreciate, because its tendency is purely negative, aiming, as it does, at preventing and delaying. How do you know that we weren't partly responsible for the attempted understanding which you yourself mentioned just now?"

"Nevertheless," said Laulerque, "you admit that we are on the brink of disaster. In what way has anything been changed? How can you speak of 'results'?"

"The disaster might have occurred already," said Mascot.

Laulerque made a little movement of the lips, but said nothing. He was thinking: "That's what's called retiring in order to advance. . . . If they're going to take credit for all the things that *might* have happened! . . . It's what I'd call playing the fisherman."

The stranger was watching him intently. He started to speak again. Very quietly, and in a series of rapid references, he pointed out that the secret of all real energy lay in the conservation of power, in the willingness to work within limits when no more was needed to attain the immediate end in view, to reserve action on a large scale (and occasions for action were not endless) for extreme cases, instead of dissipating it. He went on to ask about French opinion in the matter of Morocco and the general attitude towards Briand. Had his behaviour in the recent crisis made him unpopular? Did the composition of his new Cabinet correspond to some fundamental change of policy? What, he inquired, would be the attitude of the working classes in the event of a genuine mobilization?

"They'd all obey," was Laulerque's instinctive reply. He had no sooner spoken than he realized that the sharpness of his answer had been due in part to a feeling of patriotism. He was aware of the man as a foreigner, and he didn't want a foreigner, no matter what his secret thoughts might be, to jump to the conclusion that France could be discounted. (Loÿs Estrachard had once been the victim of just such an automatic reaction.) At the same time he admitted that he himself was prepared to execute blindly any orders that this man might give him. "Not a very logical attitude," he concluded to himself.

Mascot interrupted with an observation to the effect that in France, as elsewhere, the military machine was still powerful. There might be a little friction, a little unevenness, but at the end of a few days, in the actual presence of an enemy, the wheels would begin to turn. Which was all the more reason for relying on secret and preventive action.

"You agree, don't you?" he said, turning towards Laulerque. "It was hearing you give expression to similar views that first convinced me that you were one of us at heart."

The conversation continued in a desultory fashion for a moment or two. Then the stranger rose and took his leave. Mascot went with him, closing the door behind him. Laulerque remained alone in the elegant little room. It was as quiet there as though he had been inside a box. A sort of secret influence seemed to emanate from the papers and the books.

He was alone for several minutes. Laulerque concluded that Mascot and his visitor were talking in the hall before parting—perhaps about him. But no sound of voices reached him.

When Mascot returned he was smiling.

"Well, what did you think of him?" he asked. "Pleasant chap, isn't he? He's the most extraordinarily generous-minded man; and what a fine face he has!"

He went on, pausing now and again:

"He liked you very much. . . . I wanted you to know each other, though normally our rules forbid that sort of thing. . . . Still, circumstances alter cases. Imagine: he has just thought of you for something in which he needs a man particularly reliable. . . . I had mentioned another little trip to Holland to you. . . . Now someone else will be sent. Does that annoy you? Have you taken a liking to Holland?"

"Oh, not especially. . . . But this time it suited me."

"You will surely not regret it. . . . Well, he asks you to go with him . . . elsewhere. At the same time. You're going on a trip together, in the South, somewhere near the coast, I believe. I can't imagine a pleasanter winter holiday. . . . I don't know exactly what it's all about." Mascot began to smile again. "You're more in his confidence, you see, than I am. . . . All he wanted to know from me was whether you could guide him from your station of destination to some place in the neighbourhood. I said that with a map and a few directions, of course you could. . . . Then he asked me whether you knew anything about houses."

"About houses?"

"Yes, country houses . . . whether, if the occasion arose, you could help him look over one, give him advice about the various details . . . be able to judge its convenience or the reverse, perhaps

—I don't know exactly what it is he wants, he didn't tell me. It may be that he's just planning to go and stay somewhere and doesn't want to attract attention on this exploratory visit. . . . But all that's pure hypothesis on my part. . . ."

"I've no special knowledge of country houses, especially in the South, but I imagine there's nothing particularly mysterious about them."

"Nor do I. . . . I think he's chiefly anxious to avoid direct contact with people where it's a matter of asking for information or finding his way. He's probably a bit shy because of his accent and his slightly foreign appearance. . . . I've no doubt he's exaggerating. In any case, you'll be very useful to him."

Chapter

THE HOUSE BY THE SEA

As soon as they arrived at Toulon, whither they had taken the morning express after sleeping at Marseilles, Laulerque and M. Karl ("Call me Monsieur Karl," the stranger had said when they started on their journey) made inquiries at the Southern Station about trains to La Croix and the length of the trip. It was Laulerque who did the asking.

Both were dressed as tourists. They carried steel-tipped walking-sticks and had rucksacks on their shoulders.

When their questions had been answered, M. Karl's first reaction was laughter.

"How on earth can it take all that time? Are the mountains along the coast so very high and difficult to cross? I imagined we should be there by noon without any difficulty."

He apologized for not having anticipated the delay:

"We ought to have consulted a time-table in Paris and made our plans accordingly."

He had, in fact, thought it sufficient to say to Laulerque, before they set out: "It's somewhere near Toulon," and it was only that morning, after they had left Marseilles, that he had talked about the Southern Railway and mentioned the name of La Croix, adding as he did so: "I don't think it's more than an hour's walk from the station."

Laulerque drew his attention to the fact that it would be quite dark by the time they got out of the train, and that they couldn't start tramping over the countryside that night. They would have to sleep in some wretched ale-house in La Croix and spend a boring evening in the village, a course which would have the added inconvenience of drawing attention to themselves and leaving tracks.

They went into the station buffet to discuss procedure. M. Karl said that if Laulerque thought it better that they should spend a few hours at Toulon, or even sleep there, he, personally, would not be sorry. He very much wanted to get acquainted with the town and to have time to wander about it at leisure. He regretted that he had seen next to nothing of Marseilles.

Laulerque pointed out that, provided they got up early, they could, according to the time-table, still be at La Croix by midday, even if they spent the night at Toulon. They would then be in a position to start their explorations with plenty of time.

"We shall still have most of the day before us, and we can finish everything we have to do by evening, unless we have the devil's own luck. Then we can try to catch a late train and sleep at Saint-Raphaël."

He suggested that they had better guard against accidents by taking something to eat with them in their rucksacks.

With their minds at ease on this point, they set out to explore the town, taking what they guessed to be the road to the sea.

The sun was shining brightly, though the air was cold. It would have been difficult to imagine light with more of the quality of hardness. This light was something new in the experience both of Laulerque and of M. Karl, and they observed with interest the way in which it struck on earth and buildings, the shadows that it made, the limpid clearness of the sky. They looked at each other and laughed with satisfaction, as much as to say: "It's really too much of a good thing! So lovely as to be almost comic!" The passers-by smiled at their clothes, while they, in their turn, found endless amusement in the gait and appearance of everyone they met, pedestrians, shopkeepers, pedlars, loungers, and street urchins.

They submitted willingly to the sense of intoxication which overcomes all Northern people, all who live in harder climates, at their first contact with this Mediterranean land. Life, which till then has been but glimpsed, mere raw material of sad or mad conjecture, is exhibited at last in its true colours, stripped of cowl and habit, naked to the eyes. It is not so terrible, after all, nor so serious. It is seen to be softly dimpled, and every dimple is, as it were, a smile of welcome to the newcomer, a proffer of friendship.

The two men had already achieved a certain degree of intimacy, and this, born of their journey together, was increased by the morning brightness of Toulon, by the prospect of a whole day of aimless idling in which they would be exposed to the delicious surprises of each succeeding moment.

They came out upon a quay bordered by cafés, a promenade for saunterers, prolonged on the sea side by a surface of glittering water, which was covered with multi-coloured boats. Farther out, dark against the light, lay a few blue-grey warships and the harbour-mouth, closed by the sun's disk.

They sat down on a terrace and laid their rucksacks on a chair. Stretched comfortably at ease, they drank some Corsican wine, the existence of which they had learned but a moment or two before from a poster on a billboard. Laulerque accepted the other's offer of a cigar. "This tobacco," he thought, "and this wine will probably disagree with me. But health, after all, is an abstract idea. Long term debts don't matter much. Where shall I be in a year? Where will any of us be? What will have become of these ships?"

They kept up a desultory conversation. Now and again some thought bearing upon their deep preoccupations showed its head between the trivialities of their chat. For the moment Laulerque's curiosity about his companion and about the reasons that had sent them both upon this journey was not active.

Not that it was any nearer being satisfied. The two men had talked a great deal the previous night during the twelve hours of their journey, seated facing each other in their second-class carriage or standing in the corridor, and again this morning as they travelled from Marseilles to Toulon. But if M. Karl's habits of thought, the way in which his mind jumped nimbly among ideas, the tendency which he showed to wander constantly into the regions of the obscure and the transcendental, his liking for oblique approaches and oddnesses of speech, made his conversation extremely exciting and not seldom tantalizing, the same qualities certainly had a way of making it impossible to draw any very positive conclusions from his talk.

Laulerque had thus been reduced to certain hypotheses, most of which reposed on the slenderest of foundations. In the first place M. Karl—or the man who chose to be so called—seemed, like the name with which he had saddled himself, to be of Germanic origin, or, at least, of Germanic culture—Austrian perhaps, or of Austrian citizenship. The way in which he talked of the Germans, especially of the Prussians, was marked by a freedom and a detachment which he could hardly have shown had he been one of them, no matter of how liberal a turn of mind. He was well acquainted with all central Europe, but gave the impression of being in particular attached to, and connected with, Vienna. As a young man he had spent a year in Lausanne, where he had gained his really remarkable knowledge of French. He had travelled much, in the Balkans, Russia, and the northern countries. It was clear that he held an important position in the Organization, of which it was quite possible that he was one of the leaders. He had had, and still maintained, close and repeated contacts with the great ones of the earth, though he did not boast of the fact, nor refer to it in terms of self-satisfaction. A certain note of ironic comment in his conversation, however, made it clear that it was so. Not that he seemed to be on a social equality with such people; rather were there moments in which he showed himself possessed of the sharpness of the gutter. He loved art, its practitioners and its achievements, but not as a man of the world, not, that is, with any hint of condescension. It was clear that he numbered artists among his friends; it was not impossible that he had spent some period of his life among them and had, in some way, shared their preoccupations.

He seemed to have known Mascot for some considerable time and to hold him in high esteem. But it was obvious that he had not come to France with the deliberate intention of meeting Laulerque and making use of him as a guide. Mascot had probably mentioned Laulerque's name in the course of some previous conversation and arranged the recent meeting that M. Karl might form his own opinion on the trustworthiness of a man who had been suggested as suitable for the business.

What was the precise significance of this little trip to the South-east? M. Karl gave the impression of being anxious for it to succeed, but, at the same time, rather sceptical of its having any real value. He was the kind of man who does a job with enthusiasm, but doesn't mind it being known that he is only doing it to oblige a friend. What connexion there could be between this journey and the objects of the Organization, Laulerque could not clearly see.

Up to now, moreover, M. Karl had spoken very little about politics or contemporary problems. At most he had given vent to a few sallies which, at the moment of their utterance, Laulerque had found a bit odd. He had said, for instance: "The equilibrium of Christendom has been impaired ever since the Middle Ages"; and again: "God is withdrawn from the modern world. Our great problem is to bring Him back; if necessary, in disguise"; and yet again: "What we need is a body of, say, thirty theologians sitting in permanent council, with full power to decide what truths are to be promulgated, what truths had better be kept secret, and an adequate backing of temporal force to give effect to their decrees." But the more he thought about such dicta, the more convinced did he feel that the ideas behind them were remarkably like his own, though they might have been reached from a different starting-point; furthermore, that they bore a startling resemblance to the views of Auguste Comte and Renan, and to the aristocratic attitude as it is found in Nietzsche and even in a man like Sorel. In the privacy of his own thoughts he had observed that for many men of intelligence the real conflict of the times sprang from the inability of the mass of mankind to make use of the liberty with which it had been presented, or, rather. to control certain aspects of it, such as economic independence, the useful employment of scientific discovery, and the fact of national self-determination, and to protect itself from the storms of unprecedented violence which the imperfect adjustment of these various modes of liberty would inevitably let loose upon the world. He remembered, even, how, between Avignon and Tarascon, he had drawn up for his own satisfaction a formal statement of the situation as he saw it, attempting to give it the clearness of a chemical formula for, say, the manufacture of high explosive. It was not, perhaps, perfect, but in the absence of anything better, it would serve: "*Freedom* of applied science to produce means of destruction of ever-increasing efficacy; *freedom* of capitalists to develop a system of trusts of greater and greater complexity; *freedom* of every country, no matter how small, to preach a doctrine of national aggrandizement and thus give to capital the means of rousing international enmity whenever it should seem advantageous to do so."

In the intervals of thought he had said to M. Karl:

"The main difficulty for your thirty theologians would be to control the necessary temporal power."

"There is one way, and there has never been any other," M. Karl had replied, looking at him with large, shining eyes.

"And what is that?"

"Terror."

Laulerque had suddenly felt upon his cheek a sensation like the warm touch of a kiss, a sensation that comes when one finds some dear and secret thought of one's own presented in an unfamiliar form.

M. Karl, it is true, had added, passing his hand over the bald portion of his head:

"The theologians of old could inspire terror by preaching eternal torments, a weapon which had the double advantage of costing them nothing and being reserved for their own private use. We, on the other hand, can rely only upon death—which is expensive and can be employed by anyone."

"But that," Laulerque had answered, "is no reason for not using it."

They spent their day in Toulon, as they had hoped to do, in the manner of innocent tourists. They lounged in restaurants and cafés; they watched shoe-shine boys at work, bird-fanciers making sales, and tailors sewing gay rosettes on sailors' caps. They wandered through every sort of street, even through those of the red-light district, which they found by accident, and the illumination of which after nightfall delighted them. They nearly went so far as to buy picture-postcards, and made up for their self-control in not doing so by laying in provisions for their next-day's journey—sausages, four rolls, cheese in a box, six eggs wrapped up in newspaper, and a litre of wine, which they put into an aluminum flask. M. Karl wanted to get a taper as well, in case they might find that they had to explore some caves, but the one offered them by the shopman was so small that they bought two. They also furnished themselves with two military and one Ordnance Survey maps of the district for which they were bound.

The only conversation of any importance which they had took place after dinner while they were taking their coffee on the same terrace of the Quai de Cronstadt where they had sat that morning.

M. Karl was turned sideways to Laulerque. The firm line of his jaw, his mobile lips, his rather wide nose, and his high forehead were clearly visible against the brightly lit darkness of the night.

The substance of his talk was to the effect that all organizations which were free and open suffered from the same disadvantage, which was that every member was at liberty to talk as much as he pleased, with the result that discussion tended to become endless and action always postponed. "The danger, on the other hand, of all societies that are secret and highly disciplined," he went on, "is that since nobody is allowed to say anything, it is quite possible for some members to think one thing in complete ignorance that others are thinking something else. Then, when the day for action comes, a considerable number find that they have been instrumental in pre-paring a dénouement which they don't want."

Laulerque remembered the course that his thoughts had taken

at Amsterdam on the occasion of his first conversation with Margaret-Désideria. It occurred to him that he might have been with her now in some snug tea-room instead of drinking coffee with this man on the quay-side at Toulon.

"What it comes to," he answered, "is that one lot achieve nothing because they talk too much, while the others get something they don't want because they don't talk enough."

They smiled at each other, and the mysterious M. Karl went on:

"The problem, of course, is to avoid being side-tracked without having any sure knowledge of when or where the side-tracking begins."

He thought for a moment, then: "There's another problem, too," he said: "to ensure that all decisions are made by those best fitted to make them. It's impossible that the same man should be best in all circumstances."

"What a weapon you're putting in the hands of the democrats!"

"Not at all. Democrats never spot the right man. The solution offered by democracies is collective deliberation; people think that collective deliberation can do anything. Our forefathers knew better."

A little later he said: "We're living at a time when anything may happen. A great many people protest that they are anxious to preserve peace, or, at least, that they've no reason for breaking it. The trouble is that they've no reason to keep it. . . . Peace is not for them an object of devotion. They are moved by many passions which are stronger than their love of peace."

After a few minutes he returned to the same thought in another form:

"What's so awful," he said, "is that peace is not regarded as an objective."

"It might be argued that neither is war."

"That's not true. There are some people who deliberately want war; others who want something that can only be got as a result of war, that is attached so closely to the idea of war that the two are almost identical, so that for them, too, war becomes almost an end in itself, being the first step necessary for the attainment of their wishes. No one regards peace as an end in itself."

"Still—"

"Do you yourself, honestly? Is peace for you the end of all ends?"

Laulerque turned the question over in his mind, wrinkling and unwrinkling his forehead in the intensity of his thought. At length, "No," he said, "I don't; you're quite right."

"I'm not asking what you *do* regard as the end to be achieved. The point is that you are working for peace only because you realize that if peace is destroyed in the near future, your end, whatever it may be, will be indefinitely postponed. We, too realize that, but to do so involves a form of wisdom that is not at all common, and those who have it are apt to lose it; that's true even of our members."

He added, almost as an afterthought:

"Many of them are already pursuing quite other ends without realizing it."

He finished the argument with a laugh:

"Man is very ingenious in the details of life, but in the matter of controlling his destiny he has always been, and still is, a fool."

A little later, when they got up to go back to their hotel, M. Karl returned once more to the subject.

"As soon as a war breaks out, the man who really wanted it and worked for it can say: 'Good! It's here, it's come. My responsibility's over.' In a sense his mind is at rest. But the mind of a man who wants peace and works for it, of a man whose object is the prevention of war, is never at rest. He can never say to himself: 'It's come.' What he does say to himself is: 'We've stopped war for the time being, but tomorrow it's all got to be done again, and tomorrow's morrow.' Finally he gets to the point of thinking: 'I can't go on stopping it for ever'; and as soon as he thinks that, peace is in a bad way."

The next morning Laulerque was so nervous lest the night waiter should forget to wake him in time that he awoke of his own accord much too early. For a whole hour he lay in bed thinking, and snapping on the light every five minutes to look at his watch.

His mind was still full of M. Karl's last words.

"Why did he say all that? Was he deliberately trying to influence me, or was it simply that he wanted to pour himself out to someone and felt that he could trust me? I'm inclined to think that that was the reason, but if it was, it certainly doesn't increase my confidence in him. The high priest—the sect must have a high priest—seems to me to have lost his faith; not, perhaps, faith in the cause, but faith in success—and that's not a comfortable thought. He referred to disagreements, to side-tracking, to misunderstandings. He's even wondering—or so I read his words—whether a man like himself isn't really putting a weapon in the enemy's hands. . . . And the worst of it all is that he seems to be a fine type of fellow. I like him very much. We have become good friends. . . . What mare's-nest am I getting involved in? What actually lies behind all this business about a house? I've been inclined in the past to laugh at Jerphanion for being cautious and at Clanricard for seeking the safe, middle-class solution, but if this is what comes of making the heroic gesture! . . . I must take advantage of the friendship that's sprung up between us and of the confidences he's made to me, to talk to him of my own uncertainties, to ask him one or two leading questions. . . . Actually I've got a bit of a hold over him, because he's already begun to put me wise about today's trip, and he'll have to let me in on it still more. Obviously I'd be a fool to go so far that it would be worth his while to get rid of me, but I don't think I need bother about so highly romantic a dénouement as that. From what I've seen so far of this little lot, they're not quite so ruthless as all that, nor so quick on the draw."

It was still dark when the train left the South Station. The two men spent the first half-hour of their journey shivering in the narrow compartment, situated right at the end of a coach, which they had chosen for reasons of privacy. Then the dawn began to break. The sky took on the colour of pearl. M. Karl, his face turned towards the sea, and his eyes widening as the light increased, recited four stanzas of a German poem which Laulerque could not understand. M. Karl's light voice seemed to take naturally to the elegant rhythm.

As the darkness thinned they felt warmer, though the temperature had probably not in fact much altered, and were moved to high spirits.

As soon as it was light enough to see in the car, Laulerque's mysterious companion took from his pocket a note-book, and the maps which he had bought the day before. He read attentively the notes, accompanied by sketches, which covered two pages of the book, and then turned to the maps.

He seemed anxious not to keep Laulerque any longer in ignorance of what he was doing.

"I'm trying to recognize the spot we've got to make for. According to my notes, as soon as we leave the station of La Croix we've got to take a road running a little to the west of Cavalière; that's to say, towards the south. After a while, about twenty minutes, we leave this road for a smaller one leading off to the left, eastwards. . . ."

He fumbled in his pocket.

". . . I've got a compass, but"—his whole body shook with laughter —"I'm not at all sure I know how to use it. . . . So far as I can make out, we ought to see a little village called Dourets after we've gone about two hundred yards along the lane in question; see, here it is, marked on the map. We've got to climb as far as the village and then take a path which leads straight into the forest. There are two other paths, but we leave them on our left and continue towards the east. After a bit we shall reach a clearing in the form of a small gully, with a house in it—and there should be a man there to meet us. We shall give him a letter and he will hand us some keys. He's the caretaker of the house we're going to see, which means no more than that he goes and has a look at it two or three times a year to see that the roof's not been blown away. We've got to arrange things so that he won't come with us, and that may not be easy. The house in question is another quarter of an hour's walk into the forest—no, it's not marked on the military map. The man will tell us how to find it. But I'm afraid that instead of merely telling us the way he'll do all he knows to come with us. The letter explains that it's not at all necessary, but the writer couldn't definitely forbid him. It's you who'll have to argue with him, and you'll need all your cleverness. . . . Do you think that with the help of these maps and what I've explained to you, you can manage to find the way?"

Laulerque, after examining the maps in his turn, said that he didn't think it would be very difficult, but he couldn't, he added, guarantee his ability to keep the man from going with them.

"Politeness, curiosity, and distrust will all be working against us."

"Well, we must wait and see," said M. Karl, and closed the discussion.

He was much interested in the nature of the country and the appearance of the coast, which, as soon as they had passed Lavandou, became very lonely. He asked Laulerque whether he knew anything about local history.

"Hardly anything."

"Nor do I, unfortunately. I'm told it's very curious. What's the name of that little town perched up in the mountains which we saw just now to our left?"

"Bormes."

"Bormes?" repeated Karl with an odd inflexion of his light voice. "Bormes? It's easy, isn't it, to imagine what this bit of coast was like in the old days? One's only got to think this little railway out of existence. Look at these rocks and woods and lonely stretches of water. . . . I read once that the people hereabouts were constantly at war with the African corsairs, and that that's why they planted their villages on inaccessible crags with a good view of the sea. I've read, too, that from time to time the corsairs settled in this neighbourhood and also built villages high up so that they, too, could get a good seaward prospect. The result is that when one comes on one of these villages one's never sure whether it was built by the corsairs or as a refuge from them. . . ."

He added, with a sound like a sigh: "They must have been very happy here, for they were in paradise."

He asked Laulerque whether he had heard that a good deal of coastal smuggling still went on in these parts.

"I don't know; I should think it quite likely."

"There's a good deal on the Spanish frontier, isn't there?"

"In the Pyrenees, yes; but it may be more difficult to land stuff from the sea, and perhaps the trade's less profitable round here."

The other returned to his study of the map.

"Yes," he murmured, "I see, the railway cuts across the neck of the peninsula, and leaves the coast; yes."

As station succeeded station Laulerque kept on asking himself whether the right moment had come. After they had passed Cavalière, he made one or two faces as though to get himself into the right frame of mind and took the plunge.

"I've been thinking a lot, last night and this morning, of various things you've said. . . . For instance, your remark in Paris, a little while back, about the likelihood of war breaking out in 1911. You see, it's a matter of enormous importance for me; I can think of nothing else. I suppose the ordinary type of man one meets in one's daily round is perfectly capable of saying quite casually: 'We're going to have a war,' without feeling particularly upset about it. That such a thing is possible is all part of the general idiocy which seems to prevail in the world. The ordinary type of man, I say, but not you, not us, if you like. But since then you've said one or two other things that have worried me. What I really want to know, without asking you to tell me secrets, which you'd refuse to do anyway, is whether we're going to take some heroic steps, whether, in fact, we're going to risk everything, to prevent such a thing from happening. . . . I should never forgive myself if I found that I'd got mixed up by mistake with an organization which was only playing at being fishermen."

"I don't quite understand."

"It's a little expression of my own. . . . What I mean is a collection of people who let themselves be taken in with empty words, as anybody else might be, with titles of rank and the hocus-pocus of ritual, with all the trivialities, in short, which go to make up the life of ordinary society. . . . This house, for instance, near La Croix, which we're bound for—I know you can't take me wholly into your confidence, but can't you give me some assurance that it will serve some purpose, that in going there with you, *I* shall be serving some purpose, doing something definite, something, however small, that's going to help stop this war that you say is so near?"

There was a note of almost pathetic appeal in his voice.

While he was speaking, M. Karl had shown his embarrassment by the way in which he had pulled at the little tuft of hair at the tip of his nose.

"I'm particularly sorry that you've chosen just this time to put your question," he said. "You see, I feel now that my conscience isn't quite clear in the matter of this house. What is the word I want, 'childlike' or 'childish'?"

" 'Childish.' "

"Yes; well, I feel suddenly very guilty because I may be involving you in something that'll turn out to be quite childish. When the affair was first mooted at headquarters, I was inclined to shrug my shoulders, but since it was decided to go into the matter further, I thought I'd better come and have a look at things with my own eyes. I don't want anything to be decided on false or foolish premises. . . . Not that anything has been finally decided as yet. It'll all very much depend on my report. One's got, hasn't one, to take many things into consideration? . . . I realize that we've got to take account of various possibilities. There are chances which we oughtn't to let slip even though we may not have made up our minds what use to make of them. You know how one feels when one comes across a bargain in some antique-shop; one mayn't need the thing at the moment, but one says to oneself: 'It might come in useful some day.' And even if one has got an idea of what one can do with it, it's quite possible that one may find a better use for it later on."

"Has this house got such remarkable possibilities, then?"

M. Karl waited a long time before answering. With his mouth half open and his head leaning sideways, he looked out at the sea. He seemed to be holding his breath when finally he started to speak.

"It's a fine situation," he said at length; "lonely, and with direct access from the sea."

"Is it right on the sea, or only close to it?"

"Not very close."

Laulerque tried to find some way that should not be too offensive of putting the question which filled his thoughts.

"Somebody, then, where you come from, made the proposal? But why to you and your friends? Did he think you wanted a lonely house by the shore in the south of France?"

On M. Karl's face, that was so like a cross between Beethoven's and a child's, a worried smile appeared.

"The owner lives where I come from. . . . The proposal was made through one of our go-betweens. He knew that we were interested in properties of this kind. . . . We have been wondering for some time whether perhaps we couldn't pick up four or five such houses cheap, conveniently situated at various points on the coast . . . and in different countries."

"But . . . I can't guess what you intend to do with them."

"That will depend on circumstances. Bases of that kind would always be useful. Yes, it would be extremely convenient to us to have a base here and there."

Laulerque thought the use of the word "base" odd; it made him feel uncomfortable. It had a military sound to him, though he had to admit that M. Karl did not seem to be using it in any such sense. He was reminded of Jerphanion and of the suspicions he had voiced as they walked together through the thinly falling snow. It was not difficult to imagine an organization of espionage established by the Triple Alliance at some point on the French coast, remote, yet strategically important, ready to help an enemy fleet in time of war (by such means as signalling, providing facilities for secret landings, amassing dumps of ammunition, laying mines, etc.). He even thought of the possibility of submarines, which a great many prophets still said would play an important part in the next war, despite the more recent vogue of aeroplanes.

He ventured to voice what was in his mind by saying:

"It's lucky for you that you're dealing with a man who has decided to trust you. Otherwise he might be tempted to wonder whether he, too, wasn't being used to further something that he had no intention of furthering. . . . It wouldn't be difficult to get the idea that this house of yours might be going to serve as a 'base' for spying—at the expense of France. . . . Try as I may, I can't see how this 'base' is going to be employed for the prevention of war."

M. Karl seemed at first not to understand what he meant, but a moment later he ejaculated: "Oh!" in a tone of great distress, and turned on Laulerque a reproachful gaze.

"That's not kind of you. Do you think I should have brought you here with me if I'd had any secret of that kind? It doesn't make sense."

Still with the same expression of disappointment on his face, he became absorbed in thought. It was clear that he was carefully weighing and reviewing what he should say. The train stopping just then at a station, he took the opportunity of prolonging the silence.

"I will explain the whole thing to you," he said at last, "even though by so doing I shall be guilty of an infringement of discipline. In that way you will be privy to the matter in hand and responsible for its success."

Laulerque was on the point of remarking that this seemed a very specious argument to him, but the other motioned to him to be silent and went on:

"This house has been used in the past for smuggling. I believe they used to land tobacco there, though they may also have dealt in more valuable commodities—drugs, for instance. The stuff came by sea. The great advantage of the place is that one can enter and leave it from that side without being seen."

"Then, as I said before, it must be right on the shore, or at least quite close to it?"

"No, it's some distance away. . . . The people concerned were a group with plenty of funds at their disposition, and they spent a great deal in equipping it suitably. The workmen were brought from a distance to avoid the danger of local gossip. The house is an old one, built on the ruins of a small château which once belonged to some feudal baron, who was probably himself engaged in clandestine trade or had reason to fear that he might have to stand a siege. The new owners took advantage of the various arrangements he had made. I've heard, too, that the house was once a mill, of the kind common in this part of the world, and that the people I'm telling you about made use of that fact. How much of all that is true I can't say until I have seen the place for myself. There, now," he concluded with an air of generosity, "you know as much as I do."

Laulerque thanked him, but observed that he still didn't understand the underlying motive of the transaction, the value that such a house could have for the Organization.

M. Karl extended his arms in a gesture.

"Neither do I, for the moment, as I told you before. Perhaps we shall find a use for it in the future."

Laulerque kept to his point. When one buys something, he insisted, with an idea that it may some day come in useful, one must have some vague notion of what that use will be. Besides, hadn't M. Karl mentioned some scheme already in hand of which he didn't altogether approve? Hadn't he used the word 'childish'?

M. Karl appeared to be amazed. He smiled as might a man who was amused at the difficulty experienced by two foreigners in understanding one another, or as though he found something comic in the odd interpretation which an excess of French caution had led his companion to put upon his words.

"I shall get nothing more out of him for the moment," Laulerque said to himself.

They found their bearings soon after leaving the station. In forty minutes or so they reached the hamlet of Dourets, which stood in the middle of fields, gardens, and small vineyards. They noticed, however, that they had not taken the road laid down for them in M. Karl's notes, and this fact made them all the more careful to adhere, thenceforward, to the prescribed itinerary.

They had not liked to ask their way at Dourets; in fact, they had skirted the village by a rough, overgrown path, so as to run as little risk as possible of being seen. But the only sign of life in the place had been an old woman bending over her work in one of the gardens. They managed to identify easily enough the road which led "straight into the forest." The two paths which they had to leave to their left gave them rather more trouble, because between what seemed to be the two paths in question, there was a very narrow and faintly marked track. Luckily, these two paths were only mentioned in the notes for the purpose of giving them their bearings. There was no doubt whatever about the main route they had to follow.

Their way led downhill and brought them at last to a narrow gully, the sides of which were thick with trees and underbrush. At the lowest point there was an open clearing in which was a single-storeyed house, built of reddish, rough-hewn stones and roofed with semicircular tiles which were much discoloured and very uneven. It stood in the middle of a few small enclosures divided one from another by low walls. In the doorway a man was standing with a large faded felt hat on his head, smoking a pipe. He had obviously heard them coming.

He was a large man, with small black eyes, with which he stared fixedly at them, and a thin, lined, and rather swarthy face. He had a dirty black moustache and an arrogant, obstinate, and almost stupid expression. He barely acknowledged their salute.

Laulerque, to whom M. Karl had given his final instructions on their way there, advanced towards the man and said that he and his friend wanted to see the "White House." They had a letter authorizing them to do so, from the owner, who, no doubt, had written to say that they were coming. The man vouchsafed them no answer on this point, but took the letter which Laulerque held out to him, and read it, or, rather, stared for a moment or two with a sulky look at the unfolded paper. Failing to make out the text, he carefully examined the signature.

Finally he said: "All right," went into the house, and reappeared with two rather rusty keys, one large and one somewhat smaller, tied together with string. He shut the door, slipped the key into a hole in the wall by the lintel, while he kept fast hold of the other two keys on their piece of string.

"Come on," he said, and started to move forward.

"But why should we bother you?" asked Laulerque. "We can find the way all right, and we'll bring you back the keys. You saw what the owner said in his letter."

The man frowned, fixed his little black eyes on Laulerque, and muttered that it was no bother.

Then, with a determined air, he set off along a rough path which led uphill from the back of the house towards the edge of the forest. Laulerque looked at M. Karl with an expression of polite regret. "I might," he thought to himself, "have tried harder if you'd honoured me with rather more of your confidence."

They reached the top of a little hill. Their guide pointed to a glittering patch of sea visible through a dip in the next ridge at a distance of about three miles.

Shortly afterwards they saw the house. It stood on a hillside, with its back to the slope, facing west. At this hour of the day the sun struck it obliquely.

It was a square building of undressed stone treated with a reddish-yellow colour-wash, portions of which were peeling. It was about sixty feet long and thirty deep.

The roof was of old semicircular tiles. There were three rows of windows in front, all of which were close-shuttered. The lowest row consisted of three only and seemed to belong to a range of rooms lying half below ground. The upper rows had five windows each. The side wall, which just now was in the full glare of the sun, had two windows on the first floor, and a single window and a door at ground level. The door was approached by an embanked driveway overgrown with weeds. Below this the wall was hidden by the slope. There seemed to be very little space between the back of the house and the hill, which was rocky and covered with scrub.

At its far end the house was prolonged by another, much smaller building, one storey high and almost entirely without windows. Beyond it there seemed to be a sort of triangular field or paddock concealed by bushes.

Laulerque and M. Karl, clambering at the heels of their guide, examined the site with curiosity.

Laulerque said in a low voice:

"I'm sorry this fool's come with us if his presence annoys you, but there was no way of getting rid of him."

"I know," replied M. Karl, adding: "When we've been over the house, I shall try to leave him a moment with you, so that I can get another look at one or two things. You must try to help me. But I think we ought to talk to him a bit."

They caught up with their guide, and Laulerque, at his companion's instigation, began to chat with him. He complained of the weather, saying that the night had been very cold. He asked whether it ever snowed in that part of the country, and whether the local wine was good. The man understood only half of what he said. The French in which he made his answers bristled with Provençal dialect, in which Laulerque thought he could trace a certain amount of low-class Italian. M. Karl, however, who knew Italian, found it at first very hard to follow.

As soon as they got inside the house, the man went ahead of them, from room to room, opening the shutters.

The interior was in no way remarkable. It was like any peasant's cottage thereabouts except that it was more roomy. All the rooms had tiled floors. Two of those on the ground floor had open beams, roughly squared. The walls were painted in light colours, mostly blue-green, and varnished. A few of them, especially on the staircase and in the passages, were colour-washed. It was not easy to determine what the various rooms were. On the ground floor there was a large kitchen, recognizable by its big fire-place, its sink, and the built-in cupboards and closets. Presumably, from its size, the room next to it was used for meals. But the other two rooms had no particular character. It was the same with the five rooms on the first floor. They went through them hurriedly. Laulerque, going up to one of the windows, noticed that the view, though restricted, was fine. Except in the kitchen and the dining-room there were no fire-places. On the other hand, every room had at least one built-in wardrobe. Some of these were narrow, ending short of the ceiling and having but a single door; one or two, however, were of imposing size. M. Karl, who, despite the difficulties of language, had managed to get on better terms than Laulerque with their guide, asked whether they could see the inside of one of these cupboards. The man replied, helping out his words with gestures, that the keys had long been lost, and that there was nothing to see inside but a lot of old woodwork. M. Karl, bending down to look through one of the keyholes, said that if the locks were all as complicated as that one, they would cost a lot to mend.

The lowest storey, despite the fact that it was lit by windows, had all the character of a basement. It was divided by two walls into three parts of almost equal size, each corresponding to one of the windows. It was littered with a large number of big earthenware jars, most of which were broken.

The place was filled with the peculiar smell of empty houses, but of empty houses of the South—dry, aromatic, and more like a wooden drawer than a cellar. The basement had, in addition, a particular atmosphere of its own, stale and rather sour, reminding the two visitors, faint though it was, of some of the business streets in Toulon.

M. Karl asked about the little building next door. The guide explained with a wealth of gesture, but neither of them could at first make out what he meant. At last Laulerque said:

"I believe he's talking about a mill. . . . He mentioned oil, too. . . . He did, really. You know there are mills in this part of the world which they use for crushing the olives and extracting the oil. Yes, that's it; the building next door must be an old oil-mill. . . . That accounts for the jars in the basement and for this peculiar smell. It's odd that the main house should be so large."

M. Karl showed great interest in the oil-mill, and they paid it a visit. The interior was very dark. There seemed to be a coating of old dirt over everything. The guide began explaining again. M. Karl lit one of his tapers. The guide, by this time very voluble, tried with more enthusiasm than success to demonstrate the working of the stones. While he pointed out a structural feature, about the nature of which the two men were not quite clear, he kept on saying something which sounded like "hell" or even "road to hell," laughing consumedly the while. They joined in his laughter to keep him in countenance, but remained puzzled. M. Karl, taper in hand, made the round of the building, examining the walls, the corners, and the floor. He noticed a small locked door and shook it. The guide assured him that it communicated with the basement which they had already examined. Seeing, however, that M. Karl was still not convinced, he told him to stay where he was while he went round to the other side where the key was hanging, and opened the door. A minute or so later they heard the key fumbling and scraping in the lock, and then the door opened into the front compartment of the adjoining basement. In their hurry they had passed that particular corner without noticing the presence of the door.

In the short time that the guide was gone, Laulerque had asked M. Karl:

"When do you want me to divert his attention?"

"I've been thinking. He seems in a much better temper now. Why shouldn't we go back with him to his house, eat our food there, and ask him to join us? It'll be the right time for a meal. I'll give him a tip. Then, after lunch, I'll make some excuse to get back here. I'm pretty sure he'll stay with you."

Just before they reached the cottage, M. Karl, who had been chatting vivaciously with their guide, stopped him with a tap on the shoulder and gave him a gold ten-franc piece, accompanied with many expressions of gratitude. The man seemed amazed by the size of the gift. He kept on saying: "Thank you, sir," with such earnestness that Laulerque turned to look at him.

A little farther on, M. Karl and Laulerque looked at their watches and remarked loudly that it was almost noon. The man, gazing up at the sky, said it must be about a quarter to twelve. They asked whether they might eat their food on a corner of his table and whether he would do them the honour of joining them. He consented with alacrity, adding that he could offer them some wine, and that his daughter, who had just come in, could make an excellent bacon omelet with the eggs they had brought with them, and a few more of his own added, if necessary.

The meal proceeded according to plan. It was very lively and there appeared to be no lack of food. The daughter was probably not yet thirty, but her face was already withered, and several of her teeth were missing. She was most of the time on her feet, handing the dishes, making the omelet, circulating the wine, and keeping the fire going. She merely tasted each course. The meal was followed by coffee and home-made brandy. The man obviously wanted to treat his guests well.

He ate and drank freely—more freely, it was clear, than it was his habit to do. The wine was by no means bad, and though he showed signs of getting intoxicated, he never lost control of his faculties, but grew mellower the more he drank, and increasingly inclined to take a kind and rosy view of life.

M. Karl took a scrap of paper from his pocket and, while he drank his brandy and chatted, occupied himself with sketching what seemed to be intended for a plan of the White House.

"What a nuisance!" he cried suddenly. "I've forgotten some of the details. . . ."

Laulerque and the caretaker offered to help him, but he managed, by dint of contradicting them and raising fresh queries ("Are you sure the wardrobe stands against this wall?" "Has it got a single or a double door?"), to make confusion worse confounded. The caretaker, who found it difficult to follow the plan, but insisted on making his contribution to the discussion, did all that was necessary to make the puzzle insoluble.

M. Karl finally said, with a glance at Laulerque: "I'd very much like to run back for a moment before we leave; do you mind?"

"Go if you like, but I'm too tired, and too comfortable here. If this gentleman's agreeable, we'll finish our wine quietly while you're away."

Their host, who was by this time in a state of pleasant stupor, showed no sign of wishing to make the journey to the White House a second time, nor of leaving the thin young stranger alone with his daughter and his belongings, and he made no difficulty about handing over the keys on their piece of string to the larger of his two visitors.

Chapter

ON THE PATH. EVENING

"Well, you took your time over it! You must have found a lot to interest you."

"How long was I away?"

"About two hours and a half."

"You're joking!"

"I certainly am not. It was barely one o'clock when you started, and it's now a quarter to four."

"But you must make allowance for the time it took to get there and back."

"Even so, you must have been two hours there. I began to get bored with our friend. . . . His powers of conversation are quickly exhausted."

Laulerque glanced up through the branches at the sky.

"It'll soon be dark. Down here the days are rather longer in winter than farther north, but we've got to set against that the fact that we're well to the east of Paris. . . . Provided we can get back to Dourets before nightfall, I don't mind. . . . If we don't, I can't guarantee that I'll find the path."

Laulerque's tone was peevish. He quickened his pace in order to make his friend hurry, perhaps even with the intention of getting him a bit out of breath. M. Karl caught up with him and gave him a friendly tap on the shoulder.

"Don't be hard on me!" he exclaimed. "I'm in a particularly good humour and full of the most marvellous plans."

"That's good."

"Don't look so gloomy. You ought to have taken a final glass of brandy, as I did, before we came away. You're not a bit drunk, you know, and one can't embark on epic adventures without being a little drunk. You've not even asked me what I found when I went back to the house."

"It's not my place to ask. If you'd wanted to take me into your confidence, you'd have asked me to go with you."

"You're really very unreasonable! You know perfectly well that one of us had to stay behind to keep that fellow quiet. . . . Listen; that house is a perfect marvel!"

He gave vent to a high-pitched laugh in which pleasure seemed mingled with triumph. But Laulerque kept up his pretence of indifference.

"Is it really!"

"There's nothing like it anywhere. . . . When you were a child, did you like adventure stories, all about plots and prisoners and escapes at dead of night?"

"I suppose so."

"And when you were—what's the word?—sprouted, full-grown, weren't you rather disappointed to find that there was nothing of that kind in ordinary daily life?"

"Oh, more or less."

"I realize now that a whole lot of the things I've done in my life, which seemed important at the time, I only did in the hope of recapturing the thrills of my childhood."

The words had a sudden effect on Laulerque. His ill humour began to diminish.

"Imagine the pleasure," went on Karl in the same tone of happy exaltation, "of suddenly finding in one's life something that is absolutely true, true beyond all possibility of doubt, and at the same time just like the kind of thing one dreamed about when one was seven! I'm sorry I used the word 'childish' this morning in a contemptuous sense. It's I who am going to be childish now!"

He forced the note of rather crude simplicity in his good humour.

"My dear fellow, I'm going to ask you a favour, the first I've ever asked, eh? I'm sure you haven't the heart to refuse. Buy this house for me!"

He burst into as full-throated a laugh as he was physically capable of (a sort of a stomach laugh) and, stumbling on the stony path, clung to Laulerque's arm for support.

"I want this house. If you haven't got the money, I'll lend it to you. A little thing like that between friends is a mere nothing. Do please buy me that house!"

He went on laughing like someone who's just told a rather coarse story and can't get over the fun of it. "Is he drunk?" Laulerque wondered, "or is he only pretending to be?" In either case it might be interesting to humour him. "If he thinks this an easy way of letting me see what he expects of me, it's a chance for me to find out what he's after without involving myself in difficulties."

He replied in the tone of a man who's seen the point of the joke:

"Is that all you want? Why, of course I'll buy it for you" (M. Karl began to control his laughter), "but on one condition only."

"And what's that?"

"That you tell me what you want it for."

"If I tell you, you really will buy it?"

"If I approve your motive . . . yes."

M. Karl began once more to laugh heartily.

"And if you don't you won't, eh? . . . Well, I want it to hide somebody important in . . . a royal somebody. . . . Isn't that as good as the Man in the Iron Mask? Anything else?"

"That sounds all right to me—and you can't hide him anywhere else?"

"Show me another house hidden away in a forest, far from any town or village, and—this is the point—less than a mile from the sea. . . . Just think of it! . . . And with a direct underground passage to the shore. . . . Ah!"

Still laughing, he pointed to the little hamlet of Dourets standing on its height midway between the already shadowed earth and the clear green of the evening sky.

"Well, we've got there before night, haven't we?"

Once more they were seated in the little train. Outside, it was pitch dark. The cold, enveloping them from all sides, struck especially at their feet and the lower part of their legs. The oil-lamp shed a primitive glow which turned the carriage into the semblance of some nomad's tent or wood-cutter's cabin. They were, indeed, surrounded by wood, but it was moving wood. Their cabin was very noisy and jolted a lot. Their tent was not so much a tent as a gypsy caravan harnessed to little Hungarian horses and bumping its way over the ruts of the road. With their heads leaned together they talked in rather low tones.

"Ah, now you're beginning to believe me! But back there on the path, what were your first reactions? You weren't sure, eh? You thought I was laughing at you. I'll tell you something worth knowing. In any given period men will believe only what is consistent with the usages of that period. As soon as they are confronted with anything out of the ordinary, they're afraid of being laughed at. If you told a Paris police inspector what I told you while we were walking along that road, he'd think you were suffering from softening of the brain. Good! I don't mind telling you I was a bit doubtful myself when I first heard of this plan. In all matters of action, it's a good rule to use only those means the mere mention of which would provoke laughter and scepticism. You realize that? For instance, if you want to kill a queen, the best thing you can do is to give her an asp hidden in a bunch of roses. If you want to poison a minister, offer him chopped hair in a cup of coffee, because the police mind goes no further than automatic revolvers and high-explosive bombs."

He lowered his voice still further.

"You remember those big wardrobes? I managed to find the right one at last, the one my key fitted. . . . It was in that room on the first floor where you noticed the fine view. You recollect, you spoke about it? It was a huge cupboard reaching to the ceiling, with double doors. Inside it there's a staircase."

"Is there room for a staircase between the doors and the wall?"

"It begins only below floor level. You've got to lift up one of the planks to find it. I'd give a lot to know whether in the smuggling days they really had—how do you call sudden visits of the police?"

"Searches."

"Yes, searches . . . and whether the police often passed that wardrobe."

"There was a pretty good chance that they'd open it, and all the other cupboards too, if they suspected smuggling."

"What would they have found if they had? A few brooms and some old clothes hanging up. There's a shelf about the height of one's head, with a row of pegs beneath it, such as you get in a hotel wardrobe. . . . The staircase is in good repair, and so are the first two cellars. . . . You've got a clear idea of the general plan? It's only at the far end of the second cellar, where the ground begins to slope upwards, that the masonry's crumbled a bit. Just where the water begins the wall's badly smashed, almost as though it had been blown up. The passage begins all right, but it's fallen in just at the entrance to the big room I told you of; so much so that the way's entirely blocked."

"But you told me you'd seen the big room, so you must have managed to get by."

"Not at all; I did a bit of stretching. It's not difficult to make a long neck and a long arm. If you'd been with me I could have ventured my whole body, but I was afraid of getting in and not being able to get out again."

"Was your taper bright enough to show you the whole room?"

"There was a bit of light from the roof; they must have made use of a natural grotto and worked it up into a room."

"Then you've no idea whether this grand subterranean passage of yours ever gets to the sea; it's just as likely to end in the grotto you're talking about."

"Oh dear, no! I distinctly saw the entrance of another passage opposite and rather to the right, like this" (he inclined his hand in the direction he had named) . . . "in such a way as to form an angle with the one I was in. Why shouldn't I believe the rest of the story, since I had been able to verify so much of it with my own eyes? . . . If you had been with me, we'd have gone forward into the big chamber and tried the other passage. It wouldn't have needed much work. But repairing the water system will be a bigger matter altogether."

"You didn't try to make it work, then?"

"I did make an effort to turn the—what shall I call it?—the metal bar, but it was all rusted up, and I was afraid that if I got it open, I might not be able to close it again."

"Where does the water come from?"

"We didn't explore behind the oil-mill, you remember. . . . Well, there's a reservoir in among the bushes, an old—I never can remember these words—an old lock."

"With water in it?"

"Certainly."

"At this time of the year, perhaps; but what about the summer? It looks to me as though this bit of country is pretty dry."

"The floor of the second cave is quite wet: you can see the water dripping from the mouth of the inlet pipe—a big pipe, as big as this." (M. Karl curved his two hands to indicate a circumference about equal to that of a baby's head.) ". . . I don't think the end can be—how shall I put it?"

"Stopped?"

"Stopped?—I didn't know one used the word like that; I thought one spoke only of stopping a thirst. . . . Of course we shall have to examine it all very carefully. That's where the difficulty will come in—we shall have to bring workmen from a distance and keep them from talking."

Laulerque began to smile.

"You really think that'll be necessary?"

"Perhaps not necessary, but advisable. There's a proverb, isn't there, about a wife being too handsome?"

M. Karl sat plunged in thought. At last he started talking again:
"If we do decide to put this plan in action, we shan't be able to
use this train, nor yet the ordinary country roads where there's
always a chance of meeting somebody every other step. But how
about disembarking by night on a little patch of beach, no bigger
than this car—or so I'm told—and surrounded by sheer cliffs on all
sides?"

His eyes were shining like those of a mystic who has just had a
vision.

Chapter

25

LAULERQUE DRAWS HIS CONCLUSIONS

While he was undressing in his little bedroom in the Saint-Raphaël hotel, next door to M. Karl's (whom he could hear through the wall, moving the slop-pail and rinsing his mouth), Laulerque came to the conclusion that certain facts might be considered as definitely established, though there were still one or two contradictions and obscurities which he was not yet in a position to resolve.

It seemed clear that the Organization, convinced that war had now become an immediate danger, had decided to abandon the temporizing and indirect methods of influencing events to which in the past it had confined itself, and put into operation against the individuals who appeared to control the European situation a definite campaign of intimidation and terrorism, preceded by certain warnings which would leave little doubt of its intention. But feeling within the Organization was not unanimous. In fact, such was the divergence of opinion among its members that it looked as though some of them were actually working against the plan that had been decided upon. Nor was that the only difficulty, since even those who represented the majority view seemed only half-heartedly to believe in the success of their scheme and to be embarking upon it mainly to avoid the charge of having done nothing to forestall the coming catastrophe. The result of all this was a marked hesitation as to the actual means to be employed. It appeared, too, that at the last moment difficulties had arisen in connexion with individuals. Certain of the chief men and leading spirits seemed to be holding aloof by reason of class or family ties and, by so doing, to be imperilling the action of the rest.

In short, the assumption was that general agreement had been reached on a policy of attacks, few in number, to be launched at brief intervals and in a prearranged order (unless circumstances compelled a modification of the original plan), but only if the situation should become desperate. If the early stages of the campaign resulted in a slackening of tension and a removal of the danger of war, it would not be proceeded with. A plea for commutation of sentence had already been put forward on behalf of one of the "guilty" (some reigning sovereign, apparently), and family influence was active in an attempt to substitute for his eventual assassination the kidnapping of someone closely connected with him of whom he was known to be particularly fond. In this way it was hoped to bring to bear on the sovereign in question—somebody whose influence must be especially dangerous—a form of effective blackmail which easy access to the prisoner would enable the Organization to modify according to the necessities of the situation.

Meanwhile the chance had arisen of buying cheaply this house near the south coast of France, replete with its quite unusual conveniences, and this accident had been not a little responsible in giving shape to the scheme in hand. The man who went by the name of M. Karl had at first opposed the plan on the ground that it was too fantastic, but had later agreed to examine its possibilities on the ground, though still thinking that it might have to be abandoned. What he had seen, however, had amazed him all the more for having previously seemed impossible, and he had come away converted. Going from one extreme to the other, he had now taken the whole project under his wing and was anticipating considerable pleasure in carrying it out.

Laulerque had been recommended to him by Mascot, and he had at first regarded him as no more than a travelling companion, the less to be suspected since the business in hand would probably come to nothing. Now, however, he wished to use him as a colleague, partly because he had taken a liking to him, partly because, the affair having become serious, the best way of ensuring the discretion of an eyewitness was by turning him into an accomplice. With this object Karl was now doing all he could to arrange for the purchase of the house in Laulerque's name. So far Laulerque had made no definite promise. He had only made it clear that if he was not the man to shirk an adventure of this kind with which, in principle, he was in thorough sympathy—always assuming that it was really going to serve the cause and was not merely a childish prank or a screen for other activities—he would prefer to take a more prominent part. If risks had got to be taken, he would rather they assumed a more heroic guise.

Thus reviewing the situation in which he had become involved, Laulerque was led on to make certain more general reflections. Some of them he found full of meat, and these he would have liked to talk over with somebody like Jerphanion.

What perhaps most amused him, what certainly he had least expected, was the atmosphere, impossible to guess before the event, but now glimpsed from afar, which surrounded these highly placed conspirators, who seemed well on the way to realize the tradition of romantic politics.

"Romantic" was certainly the word to apply to their general attitude. Laulerque, indeed, found it rather too romantic. Although he believed firmly in individual action and the power of strong men to influence history, in what might be called the philosophy of unfettered genius, he liked, all the same, to regard himself as a realist, as clear-sighted, and as proof equally against the intoxication of fantasy and against the opium vended by doctrinaires. His view of himself was that he was always ready to adapt himself cynically to the demands of each recurring situation. The essential motives of these people, their attitude to human affairs, and the objects which they had in view presupposed a fund of enthusiasm, even of simplicity, in contrast with which his own position seemed to be one of cold and prosaic common sense.

But romantic though they were, he noticed that their conduct in detail was hedged about with precautions and modified by a thoroughly middle-class insistence on prudence. This world of conspirators, in which the assassination of a crowned head or a prime minister was regarded as an everyday affair, and in which each participant, waiting to be allotted his part in the tragedy, should, by rights, have been living in a state of ecstatic expectation, was also a world in which personal convenience still counted for much, and where such matters as social precedence, family connexions, and the obligations of friendship had not been superseded. Patronage and influence were as much a reality there as in a minister's antechamber. This or that attempt was postponed in consequence of official representations much as elsewhere action might be stopped by some awkward question in parliament. Peter or Paul must on no account be annoyed. The launching of a thunderbolt depended on a telephone message or on some last-minute alteration of plan. Jealousies he knew there were, and he could guess that there would also be plots within plots, disloyalties and betrayals, grave or trivial as the case might be, but all disguised beneath a convention, a fiction, of solidarity.

"It comes to this," he thought; "that a fat old deputy or a sleepy party secretary would be much less out of his element than one might suppose in this back-stage world of heroes. He would soon be perfectly at home with all this old junk of parliamentary and administrative procedure, with a few remnants of court life under the old régime thrown in.

"And yet," he went on to himself, "it's probably as good an example as one could find of this kind of thing, more closely in touch with reality than most of such movements, more active, and less stupid." What did he want in its stead—terrorism organized in the gutter? Anarchy in the interests of the down-and-outs? After all, he could take it or leave it, but if he left it, what was the alternative? Isolated action? But how could he act in isolation, and what purpose would be served if he could? Better face the fact squarely and without too many illusions; better put his reserves of enthusiasm at the disposal of this wild scheme. Half fantastic it might be, but it was at least half serious too. Even allowing for the fact that it was not too well run and that nobody knew how it would turn out, it was the only way in which his sympathies could find an outlet.

How it would turn out—that was the real question. Laulerque was only too ready to waive his various objections, and many more besides, provided he could feel certain that behind the confused façade of this enterprise there was a real will at work able to influence events, a directive mind capable, so to speak, of achieving its object. But this now was what he was least certain of. "As likely as not," he thought, "nothing whatever will come of all these grand plots." What had started as an intention to assassinate a crowned head had already dwindled into a conspiracy to kidnap a prince of the blood. Who knew but what the kidnapping mightn't become, in its turn, nothing more than the spiriting away of a butler?

Still, in his heart of hearts he was glad that chance had led him to become involved in the movement. His skin was moist, his head hot, his breathing laboured. He knew that as a result of drinking rather too much wine and allowing himself to get overtired, he would probably have a slight attack of fever before morning, but there was happiness in the thought that here before him lay an opportunity for violent—even if slightly ridiculous—action, into which, as into some cool and limpid pool, he could plunge with the assurance of finding there refreshment and forgetfulness.

When all was said, one could never know how things would turn out. It was a mistake to be too fastidious in life, just as it was a mistake to have too much good taste in art. It was more than likely that many of the greatest events of the past, which, since they had actually taken place, couldn't but be regarded as natural and possible, would in their early stages have seemed to the over-subtle both unlikely and ridiculous. Once you put history under the microscope, you find it full of absurdities.

"A choice between absurdities—that's the only real choice I've got.

What, after all, could be more absurd, and more annoying, than that I should fall on some battlefield next summer, just because a few speculators happen to be quarrelling about the exploitation of phosphates in Morocco? Quite apart from anything else, it's not an alternative that I should find particularly amusing."

Chapter

26

A LESSON IN BIOLOGY, AND THE SUFFERINGS OF CLANRICARD

The first class that Laulerque took on the day of his return concluded with a lesson on mammals. The stove was drawing badly and smelt of hot metal. The cold, invading the room through every crack and cranny, numbed the faculties. The boys were inattentive; Laulerque no less so. There was uncertainty in the air as to the value to be attributed to the classification of mammals. Teacher and pupils strove, each in his own way, valiantly to resist the insidious scepticism. The boys thought: "They wouldn't teach us all this unless there was some point in it." Laulerque reflected: "Science is independent of the disasters of history. Looked at from one point of view, it ought to take no account of what happens to mankind. In teaching these children, at this precise moment of this new year, 1911, the difference between whales and fish, I am introducing them to the noblest of all the many aspects of science." But he could not banish from his mind the memory of a harbour twinkling in the sun, of a road running upward among trees, of a large white house with closed shutters, or the still odder vision of an emperor's nephew lying trussed upon a lonely shore or being shoved into the entrance of a subterranean passage as one might pop a loaf into an oven.

"The whale gives milk just like a goat or a cow, and suckles its young. . . . Léotard, if you don't stop laughing like an idiot, you'll stay after school. . . ."

He thought, too, of the letter from Clanricard, barely read as yet, which lay in his pocket. The concierge had given it to him as he came out. He had glanced at the signature and at the last few lines, just to see whether it needed an immediate answer, and had then put it, envelope and all, into his pocket. One can look at a newspaper as one hurries to work, but a long letter from a friend must be digested at leisure as one walks slowly home when the preoccupations of the day are over.

As soon as he was in the street and had got rid of his boys, he took the letter once more from its envelope. It was dated two days earlier. "It's been long enough coming," he thought.

My dear Laulerque:

Let me first pay my due to custom by sending you my warmest and most affectionate wishes for the new year. May it be a happy one for you and for the causes which lie nearest to both our hearts.

Having said so much, I must apologize for troubling you with a letter. I might have waited until we next met to talk to you of my concerns, but there are some things which I can more easily express on paper. Besides, it seems to me no bad thing to take advantage of my holidays to try and get some order into my thoughts.

You've probably guessed already what I'm going to write about. I know that you have recently seen Mathilde Cazalis, and that you are in the confidence of J. Jerphanion. Please don't think that I am blaming you, or even that I am suspicious of the part you have played in this business. I am quite sure that you have done what seemed to you wisest under the circumstances.

But since my point of view is the one that you've had least opportunity of getting to know, I must say a word or two about it.

First of all, I want you to realize that I am deeply in love with Mathilde, that I thought she had at least accepted the idea of my devotion, and that the whole of my life has been planned upon that assumption. I want to say this before I go on to anything else, because, though it may be clear to the persons chiefly concerned, an outsider, however intimate, is probably not in a position to know the exact truth of the matter; also because it is unlikely that I should have had the courage to tell you all this when we met. What it comes to is this: that if Mathilde is now going to give up all the plans we had made, my life is going to be utterly and completely smashed. Look as far as I may into the future, I can see no smallest hope of comfort.

Another rather difficult admission is that up to now I have been on terms of the greatest friendship with J. J. and have never doubted his integrity. I am not quite so blinded by selfish feeling as to say that in stealing Mathilde he has shown himself contemptible; I don't suppose that he ever really thought what a serious matter it was for me, but I should be more than human if I pretended not to have been deceived. My friendship for him has been badly shaken. I will go further and admit that my whole attitude to friendship in general has received a severe shock. My belief in the value of intimacy between men has been outraged. After all, if one's closest friend, the man who has been almost a brother to one, can do something—whether deliberately or not—which inflicts on one the greatest possible wrong and causes one the greatest possible pain, isn't all intimacy a mere illusion, and isn't one driven to despair of all human relationships?

Looking at the matter from a different point of view—and now I really am trying to take an impersonal attitude—I don't believe that J. J. is the sort of man who plays fast and loose with women, and I should like to think that he knows what he is doing. But when I asked Sampeyre: "Is he going to make her happy? Is he going to marry her?" I couldn't help noticing our old master's embarrassment, and that made me think. Is J. J. being as scrupulous in all this as I am? You know that I've none of the traditional prejudices about marriage. The mere fact of official sanction means nothing to me, nor the placating of public opinion, but I do think that marriage gives to a woman a sort of moral guarantee which she can find in nothing else.

And then there's the question of Mathilde's real feelings. Is she sure herself? Isn't she perhaps just being carried off her feet? Up to now she's been used to going about with a rather retiring person

like myself, and it wouldn't be very surprising if I had been eclipsed
in her mind by the brilliant newcomer; all the more so since in my
intimacy with her, as in my intimacy with him, I had done nothing
to avoid being eclipsed. But if that is so, is it any proof that what
she feels for him is profound and lasting—that it springs from a
harmony of personalities without which love is nothing but a flash
in the pan? What about it? I may be a fool, but I can't help feeling
that poor Clanricard was more likely to be the right person for
Mathilde than this rival for whom she has suddenly, at rather short
notice and without much consideration, decided that she is the
destined mate.

The result of all this is that my purely personal pain can comfort
itself with no thought of compensation. I've not even got the re-
source of being able to say that my own unhappiness may pave the
way to somebody else's happiness.

I wouldn't have ventured to tell you all this if it weren't for the
fact that circumstances had already involved you in my personal
affairs. I beg of you to think it all over from the point of view of my
friend and to tell me what you think when next we meet.

I know that we shall have a great many more interesting things
to talk about. Despite the secrecy in which you have enveloped your
recent proceedings, I can't help thinking that you have found your
way, and the means of making yourself useful. If you can devote
yourself whole-heartedly to the course you have chosen, I envy you.
Speaking personally, the future attracts me less than it frightens me.
I have just been casting up the balance-sheet of 1910 in my own
mind. The past year has held little for us but discouragement and
continued anxiety. If this age of ours, this civilization of ours, is
heading for disaster, it is not so much because of our blindness as
because we are apathetic and deserve no better. I won't go so far as
to say that our contemporaries, faced by ever increasing difficulties,
are ready to welcome disaster as an escape from responsibility, but
certainly that attitude does partly account for our present situation.
In this grey dawn of 1911 I blame myself for having believed too

blindly in my fellow men. It's no good their blaming circumstances; circumstances are made in their image.

After this paragraph the letter continued as follows, with a slight difference in the colour of the ink and in the writing, which showed that it had been temporarily laid aside:

All the same, I don't want to give way to a sort of consistent pessimism and, after so often blaming others for not seeing the dangers ahead, refuse myself to see any favourable symptoms there may be. For some time past I have had a feeling that things weren't, perhaps, quite so bad as they have been. You may have had the same feeling. Certain articles by Jaurès which I came across seemed to bear me out. He blames our diplomats, it's true, for not keeping a more watchful eye on the Russo-German flirtation, but he seems inclined to think that, in itself, the understanding is no bad thing. He is quite sure that if Russia on one side and France on the other made it clear that they have no intention of declaring war on Germany in the interests of English imperialism, the danger would be diminished. Possibly, in that case, England and Germany, who are in no position to come to grips, would discover that it was simpler and less expensive to settle their rivalry by peaceful means. It might then be possible to put an end to this armaments race which is ruining and unsettling the peoples of Europe. In any case it would be something if the Russo-German frontier ceased to be one of the tender and inflammable "areas" of the Continent.

One curious and to a certain extent reassuring fact is that an article which I happened to come across the other day in the *Temps* (you know it's not a paper I make a habit of reading) put much the same point of view. When Jaurès and the *Temps* agree, even when it's only on a point like that, the omens are good, don't you think?

And what about President Taft's speech? I liked the sound of it. Perhaps this proposal for general arbitration which he is offering to the world means that the young America may help the old Europe to throw off her nightmare.

Who knows? It may be that after having lived all these years in an agony of panic, after walking down a tunnel which seemed to be getting narrower and narrower, we are closer to the tunnel's mouth than we thought we were. If only we can get there, it will mean the end of this absurd and abominable period of armed peace and partial mobilization in which we're all suffocating. The peoples of the world could then devote their money, their energy, their scientific and industrial genius, not to preparing means of mutual destruction, but to bringing about peacefully that betterment of human conditions, that realization of justice, that achievement of universal dignity, which we call Revolution. If Peace can only be assured, Revolution will sooner or later set the crown upon its head. Peace *is* Revolution. That's what we've got to go on telling ourselves to keep our faith alive (in despite of those who preach disaster), and that's why we've all got to work for Peace as hard as we know how.

My personal troubles, you see, however serious they are, haven't made me blind past praying for.

Perhaps I shall see you on Wednesday.

Always yours,

Ed. Cl.

Chapter

27

GURAU CLEARLY PERCEIVES
THE DANGER

Ever since the formation of the new Briand Cabinet, in which, on the terms proposed, he had refused to participate, Gurau had been engaged in stressing with ever increasing emphasis his own political position.

Briand himself he regarded with growing irritation, though he still admired him and even felt for him something of their old friendship. What really annoyed him was the careless ease with which the man had assumed the position of leader, retained it just so long as it was necessary to do so, and then, without any fuss or bother, reverted to the casual good nature of parliamentary government, accomplishing the necessary changes in his Ministry with the slickness of an accomplished conductor. At the same time he felt that the comfort he had once derived from the thought that he had not been in power during the crisis of October was becoming less and less operative. He no longer felt moved to say to himself: "I got out of it just in time; I saw which way the wind was blowing"; nor, to others: "You see now where he's landed us."

What remained constant, alas, was a sense of complete disenchantment. Almost every day, at the most unlikely moments, but usually as he lay, unable to sleep, "in the first stirrings of the dawn," he asked himself whether perhaps he hadn't taken the wrong road. "Have I," he wondered, "allowed myself to become the victim of a tendency which men of sounder sense have resisted? Is a Syndicalist revolution really possible? Won't it always be neutralized by the natural conservatism inherent in the body politic? Briand had a perfect right to say to those who accused him of having turned the events of October to his own advantage that he was nothing but the instrument of circumstances, and may not the same argument be applied to the wider question? Is it even desirable, since it would bring inevitably in its train an orgy of destruction, complete disorganization of the social machine, an uprush of the stinking dregs of the State, and that anarchic agitation which springs from the dread of the ineffective for all authority, even that of their own leaders?"

More and more he found himself making use of Foreign Affairs as a refuge and an excuse. No less a person than Jaurès, to whom he had confided his intellectual doubts, encouraged this interest of his. "Get away for a bit," he had said, "from all purely social problems, if you feel that for the moment you can't see your way clear before you, and get nothing from them but anxiety. While you're in that state of mind you can do no good. Foreign affairs interest you? Well, then, concentrate your attention on them. There's work of first-rate importance to be done there. The danger is appalling, and it grows daily worse. There's scarcely a man capable of, I won't say, fighting it, but even of seeing it. I do what I can, but I'm not enough, and there are so many varied calls on my energy. You could play a part on the committee which none of the rest of us has either the time or the strength to fill. I'll do everything I can to help you."

As a result of all this, Gurau was fired to a very unusual degree with enthusiasm for the Foreign Affairs Committee, and this enthusiasm carried with it a renewed belief in the parliamentary machine. "One's apt to forget," he reflected, "when one criticizes it, that behind the façade of the two chambers stands the structure of the committees, and that this is more than ever true nowadays when the committees are a direct expression of the parties." Indeed, his whole conception of the régime underwent a change. "The Republic is a more complicated affair than the foolish are inclined to realize. It contains at least two governments. Of these one, consisting of perhaps a dozen ministers, harassed, bewildered, and at the mercy of a stormy and sometimes melodramatic Chamber, seems to have all the power; but actually it is a body of uncertain tenure, controlled by a clique of chatterboxes, a window-display set up to attract and occupy the political passions of the crowd. The real administration of the country is carried on behind the scenes by twelve or fifteen permanent departments answerable to an equal number of committees of public safety which criticize, instruct, suggest, and reprimand. That is the government that matters, working without show and unshaken by passing crises. It draws its authority from two main sources, the State offices with their age-long traditions, and the parties with their various creeds, rather than from the confused and childish verdicts of the constituencies. Government of this kind, organized on a basis of disciplined and clearly defined interests and groups, competent, powerful, and supreme, is not, in fact, so very different from the theory of the organic State which we know as Syndicalism."

He was present at every session of the committee, and tried to be in his place as soon as business began. Up to the middle of December he had led most of the debates. As soon as the President, always in a state of exhaustion, resumed his seat, it was Gurau who gave life to the discussions. It was he who asked questions of the Minister or prevented him from eluding those asked by his colleagues. To the officials of the Foreign Office he listened with attention, and when he questioned them, did so with caution, being careful not to antagonize them or to betray their inadequacy. He followed closely the reading of all minutes and constantly suggested alterations in their wording, which were invariably adopted, since, as a result of his constant attendance at every sitting, he was often the only man present who had heard certain debates through to the end. He was in frequent consultation with the secretary.

His colleagues, for the most part, had no illusions about the purity of his motives, but attributed his enthusiasm to private ambitions. "He wants to put a spoke in Pichon's wheel," they said. "He's getting back at Briand because he refused him a place in his Cabinet. . . . He's trying to make himself indispensable to the next combination. . . ." But despite these hole-and-corner criticisms, his influence grew. In parliamentary circles such ends can be pursued quite openly. Indeed, a man's ambition seems to derive strength from being known, as though it succeeded in dazzling his enemies and rivals by the mere fact of its public manifestation. And this, it is true, is probably the result of another and counterbalancing belief in such circles: namely, that all are inspired by at least a minimum of concern for the common weal, so that good taste dictates the assumption that such a minimum forms part of the mental equipment of every politician who seeks a career or adopts an individual point of view.

Gurau, therefore, would have gained nothing by protesting his disinterestedness.

Besides, it would have been difficult for him to deny that his attitude on the committee, to the Minister and to the Government represented by Pichon, lacked sympathy. Even when he kept himself in hand, he could not altogether disguise the malice that inspired him. He contradicted Pichon on every possible occasion and went out of his way to pick quarrels with him on points that were often trivial in themselves. He forced him into making awkward admissions, and now and again attacked him openly. "What is the moving spirit of your policy? What are you trying to achieve? Peace? I doubt it. Either you are deceiving yourselves or you are deceiving us." At such moments a wave of excitement would agitate his listeners, and the extreme Left would make a great show of applauding. When asking questions, Gurau had a way of quoting Jaurès, not as though he were citing a friend or supporter, but with a sort of academic solemnity which added weight to his words: "Our distinguished colleague said the other day . . ." "It is a pity, sir, that you seem to have ignored what a great man like Monsieur Jaurès has not failed to perceive. . . ." The Socialists, far from laughing at the pomposity of such phrases, saw in them a tribute to their leader and were grateful to Gurau for having uttered them.

In this guerrilla warfare, Pichon, as a Minister, had resources at his command which Gurau knew that he himself lacked. A member, for instance, would criticize some recent action of the Foreign Office, and Gurau, taking advantage of the opportunity, would press the attack, insisting upon an official answer. Pichon, taken unawares, would make some half-hearted reply, Gurau would underline its unsatisfactory nature, and the committee would adjourn deeply impressed by the exchange and full of encouragement for their champion. But at the next sitting the Minister would arrive armed with a dossier of terrifying proportions hurriedly got together by his permanent staff. Referring with a practised hand to some duly dated and classified documents, Pichon would then make it abundantly clear that his questioner had spoken without knowledge, that in fact the question was covered by a certain correspondence which had taken place in 1907, which correspondence referred to an exchange of views dating back to April 1904, ignorance of which must inevitably result in a complete misunderstanding—such as the honourable gentleman had shown—of a whole series of conversations initiated, interrupted, and finally resumed, between the years 1902 and 1903. The questioner would stammer: "Of course I knew all about that"; but nobody would believe him, and the incident would then be closed.

One of Gurau's chief efforts, therefore, consisted in getting together a mass of information for his own use, not on general matters of policy—which would have involved an appalling amount of labour and would never have been as good as the superior documentation at his adversary's disposal—but on certain specific points about which he had reason to believe that the department was imperfectly informed or which it wished to keep secret. A particular and more or less authenticated fact, chosen from among those of which the public knows next to nothing, is surrounded by a sort of mystic aura and produces an effect comparable to that obtained by the sure handling of chiaroscuro in painting. It focuses the attention on a single point and seems to shed a flood of light on the obscure recesses of a problem. It leaves the impression that the speaker knows a great deal more than he says. Finally, it flatters the laziness of his listeners who would be bored by a long argument, but are thrilled by a succession of dramatic points.

Gurau was more particularly drawn to this method since he had lost the habit of careful research in libraries and record offices, could no longer pursue an extended course of reading, and disliked working in solitude. When he was alone he was fond of indulging in day-dreams and letting his thoughts wander, but could not apply his mind methodically to a problem. As a result of spending his life in public places—such as the Chamber or the editorial offices of newspapers—where every thought is worked out before witnesses and takes place in an atmosphere of vicarious excitement, he had, like Bérénine, got into a state of mind in which long seclusion with a pen or a book led to boredom or sleepiness. Conversation was his chosen method of getting information, and he could only work out his own ideas by dint of talking. A time would come very soon, he knew, when he would have to dictate his articles. In the absence of other companions he could always rely on Léon Manifassier, whom he had taken away from the Department of Commerce and made his right-hand man at the Ministry of Labour. Manifassier was now his private secretary and sub-editor of the *Sanction,* receiving in his double capacity the sum of three hundred francs a month. His salary was charged against the paper, an indirect advantage by which Gurau, despite his scruples, had allowed himself to profit.

Manifassier had introduced him to a certain Alfred Maykosen, upon whom he now depended as the source of his most valuable supply of official information. Maykosen gave himself out to be from the Baltic Provinces, of noble parentage, Russian by birth and American by naturalization. As a young man he had served on the staffs of several important Swedish newspapers, and had been the *Times* correspondent first in the Balkans and later in Russia. While thus employed he had made contact with several American journals, one of which had employed him as a reporter during the Russo-Japanese war (was he still a Russian subject at that time?), in which capacity he had achieved a certain notoriety. More recently he had led an independent and rather mysterious existence as a free-lance journalist and globe-trotter. He undertook, at his own expense, special missions, the results of which he held himself free to dispose of to the highest bidder in the newspaper world, and had interviewed many of the leading personages of Europe, from whom, if he could be believed, he had obtained the most astonishing revelations. Part of these he published, part, by agreement with his informants, he kept to himself. It was generally supposed that his popularity with the great was due to the extraordinary tact with which he managed to edit their confidences for public consumption, and to the remarkable services he had thus been able to render in the handling of delicate international situations. Nor did his usefulness end there. It was almost certain that he had been employed directly in several private missions, and it was safe to assume that he had sometimes acted as go-between and investigator in matters too fragile to be entrusted to the ordinary channels of diplomacy. It might well be that he played the part, as many such men have done in former times, of observer and agent in the services of reigning princes who mistrusted the honesty or efficiency of their official representatives, and there was reason to think that the secrets of which he had been made the recipient in the course of his many wanderings, carefully concealed though they might have been from the world in general, had not always lain completely buried in the recesses of his memory. It should be added that ever since his childhood he had had a fluent knowledge of German, Russian, Swedish, English, and French; that he knew English well enough to write it excellently; and that, in the course of his various journeys, he had picked up a sufficient smattering of Italian, Spanish, and the Slav dialects of southern Europe to enable him to go anywhere without difficulty. During the war of 1905 he had even mastered a certain amount of Japanese.

He had expressed a desire to make Gurau's acquaintance. "Most French politicians are mere puppets; it is a matter of indifference to me whether I get to know them or not. It is not part of my duty as *Times* correspondent to dress up and go about to tea-parties in order to listen to a lot of trivial talk. I go only where it amuses me to go. I am interested in Monsieur Gurau."

They had met on four separate occasions, the last two of which had been of considerable duration. To Gurau it was a completely new experience. He had never travelled, and his knowledge of foreign affairs was confined to the generalizations of political doctrine, to parliamentary reports, and the speeches of politicians. Never, until now, had he heard anyone speak of William II, Edward VII, some Austrian archduke, Nicholas of Montenegro, or Merry del Val as familiar figures, the very sound of whose voices could be reproduced, whose every mannerism and trick could be imitated, whose absurd adventures and dishonest subterfuges could be retailed, as though they were people of no more importance than casual parliamentary acquaintances. At first he had been dazzled, feeling himself to be nothing but a Paris provincial in comparison with this man of the European world. But he was no fool and had soon got over the sense of inferiority. He had set himself to discount what was merely amusing in the other's conversation, the better to absorb what was of real importance. A very few questions had convinced him that Maykosen was no mere bluffer. It was clear that he had first-hand knowledge of a great many problems and had made himself master of their most significant and secret ramifications. Clear, too, that the natural bent of his mind was just, that he was fundamentally truthful, and that if, on occasion, he took refuge in lies, it was only for some carefully thought-out reason.

Their third conversation had, as a result of this new-found confidence, been entirely confined to a discussion of the most obscure developments in the recent politics of Europe. They had talked of the negotiations between Russia and Germany which had been the outstanding fact of the latter half of 1910 and which were still disturbing public opinion in France, of the meeting between the two Emperors at Potsdam, of the personal points of view of these two rulers, and of the real attitude of their governments and chancelleries. In addition to his other sources of information Maykosen had recently had a long talk with William II, so that he was in a position to give Gurau information of an extremely definite kind which he couldn't have invented and which at that time probably nobody else in France possessed. Gurau tested its probable accuracy in various ways and satisfied himself that it was undoubtedly true. He had indirectly questioned Jaurès on the point, knowing him to be one of the best-informed of French politicians despite the fact that the bourgeois newspapers like to describe him as an unpractical dreamer.

"There's something funny going on," Jaurès had answered. "I'm going to raise the question in the Chamber myself during the next few days when the foreign estimates come up for discussion. I shall take advantage of the occasion to show how dangerous this policy of alliances is, in what a condition of crass ignorance it leaves the country, and how it may very well lead to our suddenly finding ourselves face to face with an infuriated Germany, with nothing to rely on but the broken reed of a Russian treaty. I admit, of course, that a slackening of tension between Russia and Germany would, in itself, be a good thing for all of us, provided it conceals no secret agreement. If we can be sure of that we should do well to profit by the lesson. England is obviously doing her best to drive the Triple Entente into hostility with Germany. It's the old story of getting somebody to pull the chestnuts out of the fire. Russia has made it clear that she doesn't want to risk a war simply to protect English interests in the Persian Gulf and elsewhere. But it's no good simply relying on Russia's attitude . . . Russia alone can't guarantee peace. . . . I say again what I've said a hundred times already, that I'm profoundly convinced of the impossibility of any security for France, and consequently for the rest of Europe, unless we come to a frank and friendly understanding with Germany, and that such an understanding will never be brought about unless we take the first step. It's up to us to make it perfectly clear that, while we maintain our right to compensation pacifically determined, we have entirely given up any idea of retaking Alsace-Lorraine by force. The whole trouble, my dear chap, is that we can't rid ourselves of that wretched catchword, and that Germany's always waiting to hear it. So long as that state of affairs goes on, the Germans can't help regarding us as enemies who are preparing revenge and waiting for our chance. . . . I shall show, too, that if the scheme of our alliances and the policy of German encirclement to which we have committed ourselves are not a means of preparing revenge, but, as its authors maintain, actually a policy of peace, it is, none the less, pure idiocy, since it is bound to lead straight to war. . . . That's what I shall try to make clear, and I shall do it, as far as it can be done, without getting our conservative friends on their hind legs, because that would jeopardize the whole situation. . . . We must wait and see. . . . About what's been going on behind the scenes at this Potsdam meeting, I admit that I know almost nothing at all, and doubt very much whether anybody can honestly say that he knows any more than I do. . . . I believe that Nicholas II means well. . . . But he's entirely at the mercy of influences. . . . The Russian court's nothing but a robbers' cave."

Gurau also put his questions to the young Tardieu, whom he way-laid in one of the passages of the Chamber and whom he knew to be one of the shining lights of diplomatic journalism and a man of courageous and realistic views. Tardieu said to him: "Russia thinks that she's got to bring pressure to bear if she's to get any of our money —and she wants it pretty badly. She's hoping that as a result of this little turn of hers with Germany we may become rather less difficult to manage. Is there really anything more behind it, anything more frightening, than that? I hardly think so, though I know nothing for certain."

Gurau made his boldest move before the committee itself, where he added to his reputation by his successful handling of two or three debates. By making use of certain pieces of information provided by

Maykosen, he completely silenced the Minister, who could only stammer: "I hardly think that can be the case, sir. . . . What you say amazes me. . . . Won't you tell me where you got your information? . . . What, you can't? . . . Ah, that's a pity. I will go further into the question."

At the next session the Minister could produce only a few empty phrases. "We have every reason to doubt the accuracy of this information. . . . The affair seems to have been grossly exaggerated. . . . In any case, the committee can count upon our keeping our eyes open."

It was clear that the department was not in a position to give the lie to what had been said.

But these talks with Maykosen had had a far deeper and more important effect upon Gurau. They had left him with a conviction, almost an obsession, that a real understanding between France and Germany was a matter of the utmost urgency.

Until this moment he had regarded it as no more than one idea among many, saner, perhaps, and more plausible than most, well worth supporting in conjunction with Jaurès, but, for all that, at best but a "point of view," something, that is, about which it would be natural to hesitate, to argue, to think at leisure, a debating-point to be valued less for its own sake than as a weapon of attack. One might, he felt, have argued its opposite with a perfectly clear conscience if considerations of domestic policy had made it advisable to do so. His attitude, in short, had been a purely forensic one, and in some such state of mind he had written his tendentious articles of September and October.

Prolonged contact with Maykosen, however, had resulted in a radical change of outlook. His ideas had suddenly assumed that clearly defined solidity which in the affairs of daily life leads to immediacy of action. The owner of a factory on a river-bank, warned by telephone that the water-level upstream was three yards above normal, would never dream of treating the news as a thesis admitting of arguments "for and against." Not that Maykosen had made any effort to persuade him. On the contrary, his attitude was one of serene detachment. He took the view that the best thing to do was to abandon Europe to its wretched fate. "Thanks to America," he said, "there will always be a way out for the white races." But from what Maykosen had said, from his evocation of scenes and persons, from the atmosphere, as it were, of second sight which he had contrived to collect about him in the various places of his pilgrimage and now carried wherever he went like a personal aura, Gurau had deduced a number of staggering truths. If things went on as they were going now, Germany and France would find themselves at each other's throats, even though the pretext might be furnished by some third power. There were many causes of conflict in the world, but none so capable of starting a general conflagration. The fire might start anywhere, but it could only become general if France and Germany were involved, and neither in France nor in Germany did the Government —to say nothing of the people—really and deliberately want war.

"Are you quite certain about Germany?" Gurau had asked.

"Absolutely certain. The Chancellor is a 'pacifist.' Why, the Emperor's always making fun of him for it. And the Emperor himself said to me: 'There is a war party here, but it's very small. I am for peace, and so is my Chancellor; that's why I support him, in spite of the fact that he makes me laugh and often annoys me by his way of doing things.'"

According to Maykosen, the two Governments would give a great deal to avoid a quarrel, but each time some definite proposal was made, they each of them cried out: "Utterly impossible! Something else, perhaps, but not that!"

"That's what makes it so serious. Isn't it a fact that it has become extremely difficult to eliminate the causes of conflict without having recourse to war?"

"Not at all difficult. On the contrary, very easy."

Maykosen had a way of bringing together for comparison the various things he had heard, the various confidences of which he had been the recipient, in each of the two camps, the effect of which was to show that the adversaries were, in fact, much nearer to complete agreement than either of them imagined.

"Quite easy," he repeated, adding carelessly: "What a pity it is that no one can do such an easy job!"

Another of Maykosen's ideas had had a profound effect upon Gurau. Not content with prophesying, as others did, that the next war would quickly become general even if it were not so at the outset, this adventurer from the Baltic Provinces refused to subscribe to the theory, at that time almost universally advanced, that it would be "terrible but short."

"Terrible, yes," he said calmly; "more terrible than you've any idea; but not short. Certainly not shorter than the Russo-Japanese war. Possibly longer. What reasons have you for thinking it will be short? Not that the actual length matters, because even if it's no longer than the Russo-Japanese war, Europe will be left in ruins."

Maykosen based this double thesis less upon argument than upon his own first-hand impressions. His experiences during the Russo-Japanese campaign had given him a notion of modern warfare that was very different from that conventionally held by Western peoples, even, perhaps especially, by soldiers. He gave Gurau a description of some of the engagements at which he had been present, and told him of some of the things he had seen on the battlefields when he had walked or ridden across them on his little Manchurian pony after the armies had withdrawn. Two or three times Gurau cried out: "Oh, but that's horrible!"

Maykosen laughed and proceeded to make it clear to his friend that this "horrible" thing was apt to move leisurely and was in less of a hurry than people were inclined to think. It established itself, he said, slowly and deliberately, rending a country from top to bottom, digging claws into its very entrails, radically modifying every aspect of the national life. Once it had settled on the body of a people, it couldn't be just flipped off with a gesture. "If the Russians," he remarked, "had been a bit tougher and rather better led, if their artillery had been more efficient, every one of the battles I witnessed would have gone on much longer. So would the war, if only they'd had better railways and their finances had been more honestly administered."

He added: "I saw Russia just after the war. The country was already in a state of collapse, and the rot, I assure you, had gone pretty deep. You have no idea of the extent to which your country would be destroyed as the result of a war."

Whereupon Gurau had sworn in an access of deep and sincere emotion: "I will get the portfolio of Foreign Affairs at the earliest possible moment, if only to stop that from happening."

One of the immediate effects of this new determination was to make him forget his physical ailments. For some time now his body had been giving him cause for anxiety. It was no longer a question of vague sensations in unaccustomed places or of insistent messages emanating from those deep-seated organs which normally draw no attention to themselves.

The trouble had begun two days before the end of the year. He remembered the occasion perfectly. He had just done one of those things of which a man may feel justifiably proud, one of those rare, intuitive actions which stand out in the memory as signifying an unusual, a profound victory of humanity over dignity, of the heart over the self-will; something to be all the prouder of since no one is likely to congratulate him upon it, still less to understand its motives.

Passing a shop-window filled with New Year presents, he had suddenly said to himself: "How pleased poor Brigitte would be! She has so little to look forward to . . ." adding, with a pleasurable twinge of self-mortification: "And how disgusted *the countesses* would be if they knew!" (He had got into the way of thinking in this term of his hostesses of the Boulevard Saint-Michel and their set, among whom he was entertained and made much of.) He had gone into the shop and chosen, then and there, a large and expensive box of preserved fruits, which he had ordered to be sent to Mlle Brigitte Lechapelu, Les Œufs-Durs, near Cerelles, Indre-et-Loire. And between the lid and the ornamental paper which covered the fruit he had slipped a card on which he had inscribed in handwriting so carefully legible that it resembled the efforts of his schooldays:

Happy New Year
MAXIME.

Then he had left the shop with a slight sense of constriction about his heart, caused not indeed by love, but rather by kindliness and a consciousness of humility.

That same afternoon he had been worried more than once by an itching in his left forearm. To begin with he had scratched it rather absent-mindedly, at first through his sleeve, but later rolling up the cuff to get at the skin. Finally he had become obsessed by the irritation. Perhaps, he thought, it was a flea-bite, or even a bug-bite, because there was a soreness at the heart of the tickling which didn't feel like a flea-bite. Two or three times he had shut himself in his room, taken off his coat, and rolled up his shirt-sleeve. But the only thing he could see was a vague redness on the inside of his forearm, with, here and there, a few rather redder scratches which were the marks of his finger-nails.

Later in the day his work, the people around him, and the conversations in which he had been involved had occupied his attention to the exclusion of everything else. But no sooner was he alone than the tickling began again. At first it had been very slight, just enough to recall itself to his consciousness. When he got home he bathed his forearm in cold water and applied some vaseline. He went to bed. But the warmth seemed to excite the irritation to renewed activity as though it had been some half-torpid animal which he had taken to bed with him. He began to scratch again, despite the vaseline. At first he scratched with care, and the vaseline got into his nails. Scratching, he found, gave him peculiar satisfaction of a kind and degree

which he had never before experienced. As he fretted with his nails
at the itching, subtle, intense, irritation, it turned into a definite pain,
hot and constant, rather like that produced by a razor passing over a
rough surface. After a minute or two this hot little pain was replaced
by a deceptive sense of relief, which in its turn gave way to a maddening sensation of pricking. He was driven again and again to use
his nails, just as, when snow is falling fast, one keeps being forced to
use the scraper to keep a road clear from the repeated obliteration of
the flakes. And he was less inclined to refrain since, in the privacy of
his bed, he found a curiously voluptuous pleasure in this alternation
of intolerable tickling and smarting relief. The nerves of his arm
showed themselves quite unexpectedly to be as sensitive as those
commonly associated with the sexual act and capable of passing
through a whole series of reactions, ranging from taut intensity to
quiescence, the like of which he had never before experienced. Now
and again the scratching became accelerated, and at such moments
the area of irritation became extended. It began at his wrist and went
right up his forearm, finding in the moist and fleshy part inside the
elbow a cosy spot in which to establish itself with particular ferocity.
For a long time he lay awake, and finally fell asleep on his right side.
From time to time, unconscious though he was, he continued to
scratch his arm.

When, three days later, he decided to see a doctor, he had a well-
developed attack of eczema.

Since then he had taken a certain number of remedies both external
and internal, had kept, though not very strictly, to a diet, and had
begun to train himself in a discipline of heroic resistance to his bouts
of tickling. He found that the diversion provided by his work was a
great help, but that when he was alone a degree of will-power was
called for which kept him continually marvelling.

The vague physical discomforts which had troubled him three
months earlier, however, had now disappeared. Contrary to what
might have been expected, he felt better. Or, rather, he would have

said he felt better had not common sense assured him that he must be worse, since he now had a definite ailment which caused him a good deal of discomfort, not, perhaps, very serious, but intense enough in its way.

AN ALLIANCE IN THE GREAT WORLD

The Count said to Marie de Champcenais:

"The Zülpichers are in Paris. I simply must show them some attention. How about asking them in quite quietly tomorrow to spend Twelfth Night with us?"

"Tomorrow? But that leaves me no time to ask anybody else. I shall be rushed off my feet as it is, just seeing about dinner and ordering things."

"I know I can get Bertrand, and I'll send an invitation to Allory by messenger. They're always available at short notice. Then there's Duroure and his wife. . . . Leave it all to me. If I can't get them, I'll ring up one or two fellows I know at the club. We don't want to have too many—just enough to make it possible for me to have a quiet quarter of an hour with Zülpicher after dinner."

Marie waited, rather nervously, for him to mention Sammécaud. But it didn't seem to occur to him to do so. She said:

"I don't like arranging things at the last minute like this, especially for people as rich as the Zülpichers."

"Make it look like a family party. I'm told they're really very simple—or he is at least. He'll like it all the more for not being too grand. I'll tell them not to dress. There's no need for me to make a show with a man like that. He's fifteen or twenty times as rich as I am, and he knows that I know it. He'll take our simplicity as a mark of respect; he'll realize that we're not stupid enough to try to impress him."

"But is Bertrand smart enough? He's so crude."

"He knows how to behave. People like the Zülpichers haven't the same idea of society as we have. I don't mean they're as slack in their ways as most Belgians; far from it. She, in particular, is very elegant and distinguished. But there are countries where the serious side of things takes precedence of the merely worldly. There's no need for Bertrand to have the manners of a great gentleman for them to appreciate him at his true value. They know what he sprang from, what he's done, and what he's worth. Besides, Zülpicher wants to make his acquaintance."

She still looked worried, almost sulky. After a moment's hesitation and with a flushed face, she said:

"If I'd known, I'd have stayed a day or two longer in the country."

"Why?"

"Then you could have invited them to dine at some restaurant. You could have had your talk much more easily there. I shan't really be any use to you, and I needn't have left poor Marc so soon. . . ." She seemed to be choking back her tears. "I can't help thinking of the way he said: 'Why didn't you let me come to Paris for my holidays?'"

M. de Champcenais smiled, but said nothing.

After dinner, assisted by his wife's manœuvres, M. de Champcenais managed to get Zülpicher to himself in the study.

In the drawing-room George Allory was talking to the Countess of what was for him the chief news of the winter—his candidature for the vacancy at the Académie Française made by the death of the Comte de Vogüé. The election would take place at the beginning of February.

"I only decided at the last moment. My friends in the Academy insisted that I should. My chief opponent will be Henri de Régnier, the ex-symbolist. Of course he's Hérédia's son-in-law, and he's got a 'de' in front of his name, but, as Albert de Mun said to me the other day, his novels are an outrage against modesty, and his poems an outrage against French prosody. I, unfortunately, don't know enough about pulling strings."

Mme Duroure was explaining in great detail to Mme Zülpicher that her father was no less a person than the Comte de Rumigny; that she vas the eldest of four daughters, and that in his disappointment at having no son, and contrary to French usage, he had always regarded her as the heir to the title. He had, she said, insisted on her being called "Vicomtesse" when she was little, and had made her promise that when she was married she would use the title on every possible occasion. But it wasn't easy. The simplest solution would have been to style herself Vicomtesse Duroure de Rumigny, but that would have involved technical details, and her husband objected. She understood, however, that in central Europe, and especially in French refugee families, it was the custom for young girls to use titles, which was almost proof that similar usage had once obtained in France. Mme Zülpicher seemed not to grasp the full importance of the problem.

Bertrand was chatting with Lieutenant-Colonel Duroure in the pink boudoir. He held certain theories which he liked the chance of discussing with soldiers of experience. He claimed not only that motor traction would eventually be used in all armies for purposes of transport on lines of communication, but that the infinite resources which it provided would quite possibly be adapted to the needs of artillery and to the transportation of front-line troops. He was amazed that the General Staff had not yet taken the matter seriously. Duroure, like all Frenchmen, was quick-witted and could take in at once the various aspects of a problem. Before Bertrand had finished speaking, twenty objections had already occurred to him. But he thought it unnecessary and impolite to refute at length a layman's vagaries, and carried his forbearance to the length of trying to imagine tens of thousands of soldiers being taken into battle in an endless line of bumping motor-cars, like a holiday crowd going out to Longchamp. The picture thus conjured up was a fantastic one, not altogether unsuited to the setting provided by the pink boudoir. But Duroure would have preferred to hear absurdities of this sort from the lips of a pretty woman. "No one," he thought, "minds a pretty woman with a serious turn of mind talking pleasant nonsense."

Meanwhile Zülpicher and de Champcenais were taking up the

thread of a conversation which they had started six weeks before at Antwerp.

M. de Champcenais had gone to that city to negotiate the lease, with the option of purchase, of a site on the quay which he thought might be useful to him in handling his various imports. But before he could carry through the business it would be necessary to persuade the Luxemburg Steel Company to renounce its own claims in the matter. The company's representative informed him that M. Zülpicher, the head of the firm, was passing through Antwerp, and offered to bring the two men together. "It can all be so much more easily arranged between the two of you," he said. The next day the Count was invited by M. and Mme Zülpicher to luncheon in a small but expensive restaurant in the business quarter of the city. The matter of the waiver was soon settled, and the rest of the meal passed in pleasant conversation (both the host and his wife speaking fluent French). Champcenais already knew vaguely that Zülpicher was an important industrialist. In the course of their talk he obtained a very much more detailed view of the situation. Zülpicher was officially a citizen of Luxemburg, where he owned a château, several blast-furnaces, and a group of factories. He also owned—or controlled—two other groups of factories, one in Germany, near Essen, the other in Belgium, in the valley of the Meuse, a few miles downstream from Namur. It was pretty certain that he had other interests elsewhere. The production of his various plants was of an extremely varied nature, ranging from iron, castings, crude steel, timber, sheet metal, and armour-plate to instruments of precision such as stamping-machines, torpedoes, and machine-guns. Champcenais thought it just as well to assert his own importance when faced by so eminent a prince of industry. He spoke of his own enterprises, his factories, his new depot at Saint-Ouen, but without insisting overmuch, realizing that he could not dazzle Zülpicher merely by detailing his business concerns. He therefore set himself to stress the nature of his personal connexions both in society and out of it. But M. Zülpicher appeared to be very little impressed by his catalogue of counts, countesses, and marquises, though his wife smiled amiably enough. The names of certain men eminent in business and politics produced a much more noticeable effect. The mention of Bertrand, Gurau, and the *Sanction* seemed to interest M. Zülpicher.

A little later—perhaps to impress Mme Zülpicher, to whose charms he was far from being indifferent—Champcenais admitted that, though he applied himself conscientiously enough to his business as an oil-magnate, he needed other outlets for his energy. Oil, at least as the industry was at present run in France, was too simple a matter to occupy him fully. There was no future in it; it lacked problems to be solved; could offer him no adventures. He explained that he had dabbled in other enterprises, and mentioned Celle-les-Eaux. He adopted the tone of a gentleman of breeding who admitted the necessity of making money, since modern life demanded money, but who was bored if he made it too easily. Then the two men began to discuss the general European situation. The Count brought the conversation back to a more personal level. Like many people in France, he said, he was afraid of domestic upheavals and felt that a war was imminent, without being sure which would come first. In either case the oil industry would suffer. Didn't his host agree that, like the motor business, to which it was so closely related, it depended on peace and prosperity? He would have liked to insure against the future, but didn't know quite how to do it.

To all this M. Zülpicher listened attentively.

Now, in the study in the avenue Mozart, it was M. Zülpicher who led the conversation.

He was a man of about forty, rather large of build, dried up, and with an austere face. He had a clipped moustache and wore gold-rimmed eye-glasses; was very neatly dressed, with a white edging to his waistcoat, and showed no signs of putting on weight. His voice, which had the timbre of wood-wind, was sharply defined, pleasant, but slightly daunting. He spoke French perfectly, but like a foreign language. He was a good listener, never interrupted, and clearly resented interruption in others when he was speaking.

"I've thought a good deal," he said, "about what you told me in Antwerp. You are an energetic man and still young. If your business doesn't occupy you fully, you ought to seek some additional outlet. I should like to talk to you a little about certain plans of my own."

He then roughly outlined what was in his mind, making it clear that if the oil-magnate was interested in what he was saying, the matter could be developed at greater length on some future occasion. The Count, might, for instance, pay them a visit at the château.

He had long wanted to establish business connexions in France, but hitherto he had been prevented from doing so by, among other things, the relations existing between him and Schneider of the Creusot works. He disliked the man thoroughly, and nothing would induce him to come to any arrangement with him. But he fully realized that if he had to rely on himself alone, to say nothing of being faced with the hostility of the Creusot concern, he would find it extremely difficult to obtain the necessary backing from the banks, from the press, and from the politicians. If Champcenais would come in with him, that particular problem would be solved, while the Count would find a first-rate field of activity for himself and at the same time could guarantee himself against any future eventuality. All he need do was to raise a certain amount of capital and provide a sufficient number of directors to ensure the business having a thoroughly French complexion.

"How much would it need?" Champcenais asked.

"There's no need to be too definite on that point. The actual amount of capital is of no very great importance, though I don't think it ought to be too big, and only part of it would have to be paid up. After all, I should always be behind you. Do you think you could raise ten million or so?"

"Easily."

Champcenais had taken care to answer without any hesitation, so as to give the impression that if ten million was nothing to him, he realized, too, that it meant little to his interlocutor. Zülpicher concluded that the purely financial side of the affair was the least important. What he was really keenest about was to give the proposed concern the best possible form, to ensure for it a favourable reception from the public, and a general atmosphere of goodwill in which it could develop satisfactorily.

Champcenais interrupted him for a moment to give expression to a doubt that was lurking in his mind. He knew, he said, nothing whatever about heavy industry.

"That doesn't matter a bit. I'll provide all the technical staff necessary, heads of department and lower grades as well. A man like you, who's handled big business and shown what he can do, will have no difficulty in mastering the details."

The oil-magnate felt that since their first meeting Zülpicher had been making inquiries about him and had come to satisfactory conclusions. He was as deeply flattered as though he had been a young man.

The question of what the factory was to turn out could be settled later, according to circumstances. Zülpicher thought there was a good deal to be done in the way of machine-guns. He based his views on information that had reached him from beyond the Rhine. By dint of using a little tact, by mentioning certain French schemes, real or imaginary, by associating his interests with those of a great German armament firm, he had discovered that the German Government was paying a great deal of attention to the question of machine-guns. His own establishment at Essen and this other firm had, between them, received orders to the value of forty million marks in the last three years. This meant that France was in a condition of serious military inferiority and would have to work hard to recover her lost ground. It was a fine opportunity to establish a French branch. It was the reason, too, why a distinguished man like de Champcenais might easily find himself in a position of importance, a position which could never be adequately filled by a mere technical director. One could always make machine-guns; the difficulty was finding buyers and making sure that what buyers there were came to the right place. To concentrate demand might involve a complete political program. France unaided would never wake up to its need of machine-guns. Public opinion must first be informed and then roused. The enemy's preparedness, which they two were in a position to know something about, must be declared to the world, the marshalling of forces in a probable European conflict fairly faced. This state of affairs could only be assured if co-operation was forthcoming from every department of national life—the press, Parliament, the civil service, the Army. The same general argument would hold true of armour-plate: indeed, the manufacture of machine-guns and of armour-plating could proceed simultaneously.

Even discounting the hostility of Schneider, there was no reason why the proposed company should not have a brilliant future and succeed in establishing itself beyond all fear of competition. The composition of the board must be very carefully considered. In addition to the usual names of men well known in business and in the great world, Zülpicher wanted to see on it, if possible, a former Minister of War and a retired general of repute. Nobody could look after this side of the affair better than de Champcenais. To look no further than his immediate circle, why shouldn't Bertrand be persuaded to take a hand?

The oil-magnate replied that doubtless Bertrand could be persuaded to accept a seat on the board provided that he were asked to take up no more than a bare minimum of stock. It was no good, however, counting on him for any considerable amount of capital, since his own business absorbed most of his available funds.

"That doesn't matter; it's his name we want. If, at the last moment," added Zülpicher, "we find that we haven't enough French stockholders, I could always arrange some sort of an exchange with Monsieur Bertrand. I would provide all the money necessary in return for a block of stock in his business."

M. de Champcenais made a face. So far as he knew, he said, it was not a corporation, and he doubted whether Bertrand would agree to his cherished independence being threatened, to however small a degree.

"How about Colonel Duroure?" Zülpicher went on. Mightn't he be, here at hand, the very retired general of repute for whom they were looking? And Gurau, whom de Champcenais could so easily approach, hadn't he once been Minister of War?

"No, he was Labour."

What of the *Sanction*? Was it a really influential paper? It was very little known abroad.

At this moment the Count saw Bertrand approaching. He made a sign to Zülpicher, who immediately became silent. In any case, their private conversation had gone on quite long enough for good manners.

Chapter

29

AGNES WRITES TO MARC

Dearest little Brother:

It is eleven o'clock. My child is asleep. My husband has gone to bed. Large though this house is, I am sure that if I listened, I should hear in the general stillness a sound of light breathing. To tell the truth, love of her little brother is all that keeps his little sister up. She, too, would like to go to bed. From head to foot she is overwhelmed by the labours of the day as by some weight of water that turns her strength to weakness. If her bed were here beside her, I think she would just fall into it.

As tired as all that? you will say. Yes, as tired as all that. I was up at seven. This morning I helped the maid to do the dining-room, and that meant moving the furniture, at the cost of much expenditure of energy, two broken nails, and a pinch on my little finger. In the afternoon I went over all the child's clothes, sewing on buttons, mending torn linings, taking out spots, etc. . . . All that was in addition to the ordinary business of getting him off to school, hearing him recite his home-work, arranging for meals, and all that. . . . I even washed some of my own underclothes which I didn't want to leave to Frosine's heavy-handed methods. I tell you all this, my dear, as though you hadn't a family of your own to keep you tied to the prosaic details of life. Still, you must admit that you let it worry you as little as possible. You've probably never really considered all that your poor Thérèse has to do with her days. Men have a way of thinking that the normal work of a household gets itself done automatically, as the sun rises and sets, and that they are the only people who know what it means to be rushed. Every now and then they pay a perfunctory compliment to the domestic virtues—"the humble life of hard and easy toil"—and then think no more about it. Don't imagine that I can't sympathize with the irritation which a busy man must feel, even though he keeps it hidden, when he's got a lazy wife, especially if she hasn't, or has no longer, the excuse of keeping her beauty fresh and is stupid enough to whine about her imaginary grievances when he comes in tired from a day's work and hoping to find smiles and relaxation and a little kindly sympathy.

You remember that nice plump Ravenaz? I introduced him to you when he was a third-year student and I was working for my degree. You liked him, and he speaks most warmly of you whenever I meet him. Since he has the reputation of being a good doctor, and hasn't put up his fees, he's got an enormous practice, mostly out of town, and is terribly overworked. Incidentally, he used to reproach me for not having kept on with my studies, but he says now: "The work's too hard for a woman, except perhaps in a big city, where she can specialize and choose her own patients."

Well, to come back to what I was saying, his wife is a typical little middle-class doll of the worst kind. She's got no children, but she insists on a maid and a cook, on the strength, I suppose, of having brought him fifty thousand francs on her marriage and having expectations to the tune of a hundred or a hundred and fifty thousand more (a regular Rockefeller heiress, eh?). If she does manage to produce a baby, of course she'll want a nurse as well. She spends the whole morning titivating herself, pays one or two calls in the afternoon, and then, when he comes home in the evening, she sulks and complains that she's got a selfish, hard-hearted husband, who prefers sitting down in an arm-chair, looking at the paper, and having a moment's breathing-space, to petting his little "wifekins," anxiously feeling her pulse, rushing off to fetch her bag from the drawing-room, the handkerchief she left beside her bed, or the lipstick that's rolled under the chest of drawers. If I was him I'd throw her out of the window. It wouldn't hurt her much, because they always live in a ground-floor flat. She has the cheek to complain of him to her friends, and there are enough kindly fools about to establish the theory that she's not very happy.

But I'm not writing to my dear little brother just to tell him about the Ravenazes. I'd much rather talk about myself. Yes, about myself, if I knew how. Do you know I've never before felt so like confiding in you and telling you all about my thoughts, because—this will surprise you—I realize that I haven't ever done so? We've gossiped enough, Heaven knows, ever since I was a little girl, when you used to listen so patiently to my chatter, though, at the age you were then, you must have thought it intolerably childish! But since then we've been apart for longer and longer periods. Whenever we could we've taken up the old intimacy and rattled away in the old style; we've been good correspondents. But there are things we've never mentioned. We've been shy with each other, reticent, or perhaps just lazy when confronted with all the things we should have to talk about if we were to get back to the old footing. Whatever the reason, part of my life is hidden from you, part of yours from me. Besides, in the intervals between our rare meetings, life has been changing all the time for both of us. Our circumstances have altered so radically that, if one comes to think of it, we should have to spend hours and hours in mutual explanation if we wanted the old contact to remain unbroken. When one's way of life has altered most, one writes about it least. I remember, for example, that when I wondered whether I was going to accept Charles, I used to write you endless letters, and even after we were engaged I still wrote, though less frequently. But once I got married, I more or less stopped sending you news of my changed condition, though that was just when you would have found my news most interesting, since I should have been able to tell you, not, as I used to do, of my dreams for the future, of my vague fears and hopes, but of the actual experiences of every day. Of course, when we've met, there have been hints and allusions, but nothing more intimate than what might have been spoken between strangers. It's not likely, is it, that in those few casual phrases much of importance can have been said about matters so profound, so complex, so delicate, when one thinks how difficult it is to explain even the simplest thing to another person?

The same thing has been true of you, only more so, since you are so much older than I. Either because I'm too much in awe of you to ask about certain sides of your life or because you instinctively refrain from mentioning them to one who is still, in your eyes, a rather simple younger sister, a tradition of silence on these matters has grown up between us.

Do you know what it is that has set me thinking like this? The long letter you wrote me in July. You haven't forgotten it? You'd never spoken to me like that before. I would have answered it at once if I hadn't suddenly felt that any little confidences I could make were utterly trivial compared with yours. I simply didn't dare to write then, and your letters since have been so short and hurried that I've never again had the same excuse. But at last I've plucked up courage, and this is the result. But courage isn't enough. The trouble is I don't know where to begin. It's silly to unburden oneself, just for the fun of it, when there's no particular reason to do so. Time and time again, when I felt stifled, I said to myself: "If only I dared write to Marc . . . if only he was here, if only he didn't make me feel so nervous. . . ." It would have been such an enormous relief. I didn't want to spoil that feeling of relief by anticipation. I wanted to wait until I really did feel stifled. And that reminds me to say how terribly disappointed I was that you didn't come here in the holidays. Do you remember that passage in your letter where you said: "What endless talks we would have! It would be the old days come again, but with strange, poignant overtones made of our experiences . . ."? I've read it and re-read it twenty times; I've cried over it. Your cruelty in refusing me such a pleasure made me realize how heavenly it would have been. Oh, I know my husband would have been here, and your brother. (I hesitated to write "our," and it never occurred to me to write "my"—which shows that I'm not very anxious to claim the relationship.) But all that could have been arranged.

By the bye, now that we're talking of "your" brother, I must tell you something I said about you the other day. You'll probably think I acted foolishly. Tell me if you do. He condescended to ask us to one of his grand dinner-parties. I won't bother you with a list of all the people who were there; they belonged, as you can guess, to the cream of provincial society. Among others, there was a certain Maître Sableau, one of our leading lawyers, and his wife Madame Sableau. For some reason he asked after you. Dear brother Paul became rather embarrassed and vague. "He's got some small post in Paris," he said. I'm not quite sure whether he actually said "small," but the tone of his voice and the way he looked implied it. It was obvious that he wanted to avoid going into details as he would have done if he'd had a brother who was an office boy or a street-car conductor. I plunged in with: "He's managing secretary of the United Bank of Europe." "Oh, but," said Sableau, "that's a very important position!" Paul tried to argue. "Not managing secretary," he said with a patronizing smile. I shut him up at once. "I know better than you what he's doing," I said. "We write to each other every week." Paul gave a slight shrug and said no more. But Maître Sableau kept on repeating: "Think of that, now—managing secretary! It's a very important bank." I added: "They don't pay him as much as they ought, because he's not the sort of man who can look after his own interests. . . . His family's terribly expensive, and living in Paris is very dear," etc. I hinted also that you had achieved a very enviable position in the literary world and would go far. I was properly worked up. But thinking it all over, I rather wonder whether, in my anxiety to squash our dear Paul and dazzle my lawyer, I didn't perhaps make a mistake about the name of your job. . . . But Sableau won't bother about checking my words, and I don't care if he does.

But enough of trivialities. I want to tell you something that's been bothering me. I keep on saying to myself: "You made a vow once that you'd do something worth while with your life, or, if you didn't actually make a vow, you *ought* to do something with your life to be worthy of Marc. . . . But *are* you doing anything? Far from it;

you're well on the way to becoming a humdrum, respectable little middle-class wife. You're fond of your child, you're going to—(I'll talk about that later), you don't dislike your husband, and you're strictly faithful to him. You keep your house decent. Well, hundreds of thousands of women can say as much. You've nothing to be particularly conceited about."

I know the nice little poem that gives the other side; I quoted it just now when I was criticizing you: the quiet sanctity of the daily task, "the humble life," etc. But if I feel annoyed to think that my mild household merits are not appreciated by those who benefit from them, I can't take any very great credit for them. Doing "something worth while" doesn't mean that.

But what does it mean? I find the question difficult to answer. All I can say is that I can't imagine anything being "worth while" in the life of anyone, man or woman, unless it implies some kind of *spiritual* value. So what it all comes to is that I find that I have spent too little time in, have too seldom visited, the world of the spirit, if, indeed, I have ever been there at all. Don't ask what I mean by the world of the spirit. I have a feeling about the words, but I can't explain them. It seems to me that to think of oneself and one's actions in a certain way, to pass judgment on oneself and on them, getting them, as it were, in perspective, looking *down* on them, means, to that extent, getting into the world of the spirit. So many people round me seem to live without ever asking themselves any question more profound than: "What's the best thing to do in order to get this thing, to gain this advantage?"

You asked me once why I went to church. What you really meant was: "So far as I know, you don't believe in the Christian faith, so why do you behave as though you did?" It's perfectly true that I haven't much real belief, though I may be a little less uncompromising in my scepticism than I was ten years ago. In my opinion, if sincerely devout people deceive themselves, it's only by giving too clearly defined a form to the general mystery of existence. People, on the other hand, who in the name of science deny that there is any mystery deceive themselves just as much, and are arid into the bargain. When I say a prayer to the God of the Catholics, I don't feel myself any more guilty of dishonesty than you would do in invoking the Muses when you write a poem. I admit, too, that I am influenced to a certain extent by the common usages of my neighbours. In a country town like this, the fact that a woman in my position goes to church doesn't mean much, and certainly doesn't involve her in any very great obligation. *Not* to do so, not to have one's children baptized, not to be buried in consecrated ground, means a lot. It is an exaggerated gesture which expresses more than one intends and can only be justified if one is, at the very least, the wife of an atheist, a militant anti-clerical, or a well-known Freemason. But with me there's a more personal reason, which is really the thing I want to talk to you about.

When I'm in church on Sunday, unless household worries make me absent-minded, a moment always comes when I find myself wondering why I'm there, and considering the question of my faith or absence of faith. The question, and the answer, don't always take the same form. It all depends on my mood at the moment, on what I've been reading the day before, on some annoyance, big or little, of which I may be conscious, even on what I saw when I looked at myself in the glass that morning (a wrinkle more or less, the certainty that one's looking pretty or the reverse, the sense that one's still young or that one's already old, etc.). Whatever the actual circumstances of the moment, I find myself thinking, pondering. No doubt much of what I think is superficial and foolish; nevertheless, I do go over a lot of things in my mind which I might never bother about at all for weeks and months together if it wasn't for this fact of being in church. You will say that reading would have the same effect. That's true, but it wouldn't be quite the same thing. In the first place, I'm not in the habit of reading very serious books, and secondly, just sitting at home with a book on my knees doesn't influence me in the same way as do the vestments, the chants, the whole ritual of the service. All of which brings me back to what I was saying about living in the world of the spirit.

Have I ever mentioned to you my two Didier-Vignac friends? They're cousins who married brothers. They come of a very con- servative, Protestant family and are both very charming, besides being exceptionally loyal and steadfast in their friendships. They are modest in just the ways I like. (One of these days I must talk to you about the shamelessness of good women.) Whenever we meet we have a lot to say to each other and are on the most intimate possible terms. I sometimes envy them for being Protestants. Their religion seems to bother them so little, and though they regard themselves definitely as devout, they never seem forced to ask themselves all those questions which break the charm of religion, such as: "Do you believe this, or don't you? Can you really bring yourself to accept such and such an impossibility?" Of course, their faith has a more or less official dogma, deviation from which brings disapproval from some of their pastors and from rigid Huguenots. But there always seems to be some pastor, some theologian, more daring than the rest, who can be quoted in such cases as a champion. Some Protestants, it seems, go pretty far. From what I gather, provided they treat the Scriptures with proper respect, they are free to interpret them more or less as they like, or are sincerely and conscientiously led to do, and no blame attaches to them for it. These ladies tell me that there are Protestants, particularly abroad, even active clergymen, who have ac- tually called in question the divinity of Christ, not to mention His existence, and whose conception of God is so general that only a thoroughgoing materialist would be bothered by it. I once went to church with them, and I have been at one of their funerals. I have nothing to say against their services, which are perfectly decent, nor against the sermons I heard. As a matter of fact, I think their pastors speak to their flock in a more human and more direct way than our priests do, and are less apt to make use of ready-made discourses. What they say has an immediate application to the needs of their listeners and obviously interests them. Going back to one of our own churches, one realizes that the priest is really doing no more than indulge in a rhetorical exercise on allegorical subjects, and since he's more often than not a bad speaker, one usually has to listen to some nice little man stammering a lot of eloquent phrases about the virtues of the Virgin or the infinite goodness of God. If he said it all in Latin or Hebrew, his congregation would be no worse and no better off. If what he talked about was the incarnations of Buddha, it would be all the same so far as his parishioners were concerned. But this is the point: when I go to a Protestant service I never feel that I'm really in church. There's nothing to put me into a religious state of mind. That may, of course, be due to the way I've been brought up. . . . Still, I sometimes say to myself: "When all's said and done, I live far less constantly in a spiritual world than these Didier-Vignac women. I seem to exist at a lower level; I'm more middle-class, more prosaic. I'm less worth while."

Do you think that religion's got something to do with this feeling of mine? You would be doing me a real kindness if you'd say what you really think about all this. Actually, I know absolutely nothing of your views on this subject. If anyone asked me, for instance, whether you believe in God, I just shouldn't be able to answer. Do try and explain a little of what you believe; it would be such a help.

In return—you see, I'm paying you in advance—I'll tell you a secret. I'm expecting a baby—probably in May. I haven't said anything to you about it till now because the doctor wasn't sure. It probably started last August. It was quite intentional on my part. I was feeling so terribly lonely just about then. But now, when I think of all the new anxieties I've got to face, I'm rather less enthusiastic. But I've got you as an example. You've had several children, so I imagine you think it's a good thing?

I'd almost forgotten a message Charles asked me to send. You know we've got a tiny, really a tiny, bit of invested capital, and this is a time above all others when we ought to be careful. Most of it's in Government securities, but we hold a few industrial stocks. A friend of Charles's has told him that the three per cent will continue to go down. In any case they bring in very little. He advises him also to sell his industrials. He says that French business is badly threatened by labour unrest, and that there's going to be more trouble, and that it may be worse than before. People say that things in Champagne are going very badly, and that the peasants are going to follow the example of the city workers. He says we ought to buy Russian and Turkish securities. According to him, Russia is once more very sound and very prosperous, with a strong Government which can keep the revolutionaries in their place, and that Turkey, now that affairs in the Balkans are straightening themselves out, appears to be doing well. The same amount of capital would bring us in a bigger income, which is a consideration not to be sneezed at now that there's going to be an addition to the family, and the capital itself would appreciate.

Another of his friends, M. Coulomb, who knows a lot of people in Paris and whose son is a captain on the General Staff, says that we shall have a war sooner than we think, and he agrees that we ought to sell our Government stock. But he thinks we'd be much wiser to send our money abroad and buy *Rios* or some American shares.

Forgive me for bothering you like this, dear brother, but you're in a better position than anyone else to tell us what to do. I send you my thanks in anticipation. I'm particularly anxious to know whether you think that war is possible, perhaps even imminent. Send me an answer as soon as you can. Charles will do nothing till he hears from you. And till I hear from you, I shan't really be happy, for all the other reasons.

Kiss Thérèse and the children for all of us. I send you a special kiss of my own.

AGNES

Chapter

MARC STRIGELIUS'S REPLY

Rarely, sweet sister, has my mind been more divided. I know that you are hoping for a quick answer, yet your dear, your marvellous letter is something that I like to carry with me wherever I go, to ponder, to turn to again and again, to answer perhaps in a week, perhaps in a fortnight, when all the thoughts it sets stirring in my mind shall have had time to do their work upon my spirit. It isn't that I lack leisure either now, this evening, or tomorrow, little though I have of it, but that I am anxious not to shuffle off your questions. I want to give them the serious consideration that I give to my own problems. When I seek an answer to *them,* I hold a fortnight to be short shrift indeed.

What am I to do, then? I can see but one solution: that you regard what I am now writing, not as a reply, but rather as only an acknowledgment of your letter. I will slip into it the few bits of information—or absence of information—on mundane matters of which you say you stand in need, but my real answer will follow later.

But I must just say how deeply your letter touched and interested me. Let me rather use the present tense, since the effect is still operative in me, and say how deeply it touches and interests me, opening long vistas to my view, holding out to me for the future the prospect of strange delights born of a warm affection, filling me with regret that we did not earlier adopt this tone of intimacy. Once more I must resist the temptation to reply to you on the spur of the moment. I am thrilled by all you say about the spiritual world, about the religious feeling and religious observances, about how dogmas and places and ceremonies help or obstruct the life of the soul, and excited by your stark call to action, by the way you summon me to leave the cloudy land of poetry, where so much is approximate only and irrational, where so many thoughts lie as yet undeveloped, as in a chrysalis, to stand before the bar of your judgment and declare on oath, with a plain yes or a plain no, that I believe this or don't believe that. Your questions force me to a very necessary review of my ideas, to a general cleaning up of my mind. I, too, must "do the dining-room . . . moving the furniture, at the cost of much expenditure of energy. . . ." I'm not, you see, going to beg the question in a spate of words. If I wanted to do that, I could do it here and now.

I am interested, too, by your valuable dicta on the condition of women, home life, and the married state.

But what intrigues me most, I think, is this odd, this suggestive idea you have about "worth-whileness," because it brings us face to face with the whole question of individual destiny. A fool might think it simple, but in fact it is compact of so many ideas that merely to touch it superficially sets the mind rocking on a sea of surmise.

But let us confine ourselves for the moment to matters of more immediate concern.

First of all, let me congratulate you on your impending or probable motherhood. I say "congratulate" because the word is customary in such circumstances and because I think that, on the whole, I want to congratulate you. The deeper question of propagation in general I find difficult and hedged about with qualifications. It is important that the human species should be continued. It is important that its higher manifestations, or that certain local variations of them, should be maintained in due proportion to the general human swarm. It is arguable that by multiplying individuals we increase the chances, as a result of the law of averages, of producing a few outstanding men and women. But wholesale reproduction of the species has its dangers. We could well afford to see the world inhabited by a quarter or a tenth of its present population if that meant a higher general level of education, culture, health, and material comfort as opposed to actual conditions as we see them today, in which a few men worthy of the name out-top an ignorant and degraded multitude. I should consider the world quite full enough if it contained a hundred million wise men and beautiful women. Nor must we forget that wars are, without doubt, due to a prolific and unplanned growth in population, and that of all methods of selection for survival, none is more senseless than war.

When it comes to considering the value of children as a means to personal happiness, I confess myself vague. I am ready to believe that physically women are adequately equipped to undergo the disturbances of motherhood. To a certain extent their health is dependent upon it, but to what extent? And doesn't it very soon wear them out? It's probably a question of type—of what type should or should not be preserved. One or two children would probably do Mme Ravenaz no harm, and I hardly think that two children will exhaust my darling sister or leave her without the time necessary to pursue her ideal of the "worth-while."

But you mustn't quote me as an argument either way. My four children prove nothing. Their existence gives me considerable pleasure (though I don't know what their view of the matter may be), and I certainly shouldn't think of calculating what they have cost me in comfort and tranquillity. I should say that they are the equivalent of a certain number of books, but I can hardly complain of that, provided the equivalent is a good one. But I disclaim all responsibility in the business. It would be absurd for me to claim any merit for a state of affairs in which my will has played no part. Absent-mindedness or lack of precaution has alone been the cause of their birth. Some people can't write without getting their fingers dirty, but they don't regard the fact as particularly meritorious.

And now about this advice you want me to give. But before I go further, let me tell you that I am not managing secretary of the U. B. E. Would I were! It would indeed be a job worth having. I am private secretary to the managing director (one word misplaced makes all the difference). That's that. But when it comes to giving financial tips I'm terrified out of my life. When the course of events bears me out I get no thanks, and when my advice turns out to be bad the people who asked me behave as though I had stolen their money. The fact is I don't believe in financial tips. The current price of any given stock, except in rare instances, seem to me to be determined by the state of equilibrium between the equal chances of appreciation and depreciation—that is to say, by the point at which it doesn't very much matter whether you buy or sell. A little reflection will prove that I am right. The larger the number of stockholders, the more accurately can this point be gauged. The genius who determines it is the Man in the Street, whose "sense" for such things is made up of varying facets like the eye of an insect. You can't keep any secrets, not even State secrets, from the Man in the Street. He weighs every risk.

And talking of State secrets, I'll tell you one. It really is a secret. I won't mention names, because they wouldn't mean anything to you. But anyone in the know could guess them. Besides, if it got about that I'd been talking, no matter with what precautionary warnings, I should lose my position and be generally disgraced into the bargain. So I needn't urge my dear sister to say nothing. But I do ask this, that if she isn't sure that her drawer is *absolutely* sacrosanct, she will tear my letter into tiny bits and burn them.

Well, then, the other day we were visited by an extremely important gentleman representing a very powerful Empire. Let us call him M. Choubersky. M. Choubersky, all smiles, and speaking in a charming singsong voice, told us (you realize, of course, whom I mean by "us") that his August Master was far from satisfied with certain persons whom he had hitherto employed, and had done us the honour of thinking that we might replace them. And what was it all about? No less than undertaking to distribute yearly a considerable number of millions among certain big newspapers and certain influential people, who, in return, would undertake to forward the interests of this powerful Empire, allied to us, it is true, and to support the views of its August Master (or the views that a few clever folk on the spot, perhaps M. Choubersky himself, can induce their August Master to adopt as his own; M. Choubersky refrained from giving details). It seems that up to now these millions have not been distributed to the best advantage and have failed to produce the expected results. There is reason to think that they have been dissipated *en route* like water in badly maintained canals, or else that they have been used to irrigate a sterile patch of ground. M. Choubersky, who doubtless gets a very good rake-off from these millions, appears to resent the fact that the other go-betweens have an appetite equal to his own. He is the kind of man who swears by honesty—in other people. We went into the whole question very carefully and sat with our heads bowed over a list of items drawn up in two parallel columns. On the left were the names of certain newspapers, not all of them equally long established, but the least important of which ranked as sane and important organs of French opinion. On the right were entered various sums of money. They, too, varied in size, but the smallest was far from negligible. And so, too, with the names of influential individuals. We discussed, calculated, balanced this against that, weighing merit with the careful accuracy of a jeweller at his scales. Now and then someone would exclaim: "The *Evening Star's* not worth that! . . . The *Yell's* robbing you; its circulation's dwindled to nothing! . . . M. Duchamp-Desnavets is entirely discredited; absurd to give him as much as a thousand francs a year . . ." and the air would be filled with similar protests, expressive of our sincere convictions. M. Choubersky nodded his handsome and disillusioned head. We recommended an increase in a very few of the amounts to be expended. We announced that we would be willing to take a smaller commission as middlemen. But since one of the chief objects of the campaign which we were to organize would be the floating of a loan for the powerful Empire on the French stock exchange, he undertook in return to see that we got the lion's share of the holdings. Which means, dear sister, that the lucky Frenchmen who happen to be our clients will have an unrivalled opportunity of lending their money to the aforementioned and powerful Empire.

But at this point, beloved, I want to draw your attention to a remarkable complication. Two days previously we had been visited by another gentleman, equally important, but in quite a different way, a certain Monsieur Z. This Monsieur Z. is also a great man, but in less public fields. He is one of the steel-kings of Europe. He was accompanied by a Frenchman, Monsieur de C., himself the head of a prosperous concern. Monsieur Z., who is a foreigner, wants to establish in France a factory, or, rather, a group of factories, for the production of weapons of war. Monsieur de C. will be associated with him in this enterprise. These gentlemen did not come with the object of raising money, because they've got more than enough of it already. But for many reasons, the details of which I will spare you, they want the support of a leading bank such as ours. At first we hesitated to promise what they asked for fear of antagonizing Monsieur S., who is the biggest armament-manufacturer in France. He is not one of our clients, but no one would deliberately get into his black books. Now it happens that in order to get from the French Government the orders necessary to make their factories a success, Messieurs Z. and de C. find themselves, like M. Choubersky, compelled to bring pressure to bear on public and parliamentary opinion, and this they wish to do through the normal channels of the press and of men influential in the life of the nation. It seemed, however, not to have occurred to them to make us the distributing agents of their generosity, any more than it had to use us for the purpose of raising capital for their undertakings (with the honourable profits which would have accrued to us in the process). The business was not, therefore, one which was likely to excite us, since it appeared that we should play but a small and unimportant part in it.

But no sooner had M. Choubersky left us (may I repeat that I use "us" in the same sense as that implied by a salesman in one of the big stores) than a great light dawned on us, comparable to the synthesis which led Newton to his great discovery. We argued as follows:

"How are M. Choubersky and his August Master to ensure an uprush of enthusiasm in the French consciousness for their powerful Empire strong enough to float a new loan and subscribe it whole-heartedly without prejudice to other marks of friendship which may be desirable at some future time? Primarily, of course, by painting an attractive picture of the resources, greatness, and impending prosperity of the said Empire, but chiefly by persuading the Man in the Street that the safety of France depends upon that Empire's friendliness and support, and upon French willingness to make it greater and more powerful still. How is such persuasion to be applied? By forcefully demonstrating the dangers that threaten France; by showing that Germany is piling up enormous armaments with the object of attacking us; by proving that our only hope of resisting such an attack lies in the readiness of the powerful Empire to take the enemy in the rear; by hinting that Germany is at this very moment engaged in making overtures to the Empire in the hope of an alliance, and that it is therefore to our interest to attach it to us by behaving well, and doubly so to lend it as much money as possible, thereby winning its gratitude and enabling it, by means of the money thus lent, to manufacture or buy a great quantity of weapons, to build a large number of strategic railways, and so ensure the discomfiture of the common foe."

Now ask yourself this question: how are Messieurs Z. and de C. to get orders for their armaments? Surely, by impressing upon French opinion the danger that threatens us from abroad, by painting a gloomy picture of German preparedness and our own relative weakness, etc.

The two objects, therefore, are not so different as might at first sight appear. Isn't it only common sense to assume that success will be more likely to ensue if they are taken together than if they are separated?

The result of all this is that we are planning a most ingenious combination. We shall ask M. Choubersky to see to it that the potential loan is used to buy a large quantity of armaments from the—also potential—factories of Messieurs Z. and de C. It may appear simpler, if the two parties agree, to establish within the Em-

pire itself a branch of the business in question, so that our ally may
have ready to hand the weapons which our friendship will have
persuaded them to be necessary. A dream of beauty is it not? We
think it likely that, in return, Messieurs Z. and de C. will arrange for
us to play a considerable part in their schemes, and may give us
the pleasure of showing our zeal in their cause by finding capital
of which they do not stand in need, so far at least as the new branch
is concerned, since that branch will have come into being solely as
a result of our efforts. (Please note the far-seeing nature of our
plans: the honest profits to which we are accustomed will be turned
over several times on the same capital, once when it is transferred
from the pockets of our French clients to the treasury of the powerful Empire, once when it leaves that treasury to pay for the orders
filled by the associated factories, and yet again—but this time in
small amounts—when it reaches, in the form of dividends, the stockholders whom we shall have found. And don't forget that by the
time we find them we shall already have had our pickings.)

In view of all this, even if Messieurs Z. and de C. don't entrust
us with the administration of their propaganda funds, we shall take
it extremely ill of them not to give us the right of control and advice.
We shall make it clear to them that our common object is to rouse
a fervour of patriotism, and that such fervour is more likely to move
harmoniously if the orchestra is conducted by a single man. They
will also have to consider the material disadvantages which would
result from competition. Where there are two purchasers, the seller
is apt to develop a sensitive conscience and yield to the highest
bidder. By becoming the only purchaser we get complete control of
the situation. Vice and virtue will pass entirely into our hands. We
shall, in fact, establish a trust.

Naturally we, the U. B. E., must have the entire handling of the
combination, manœuvring the turn-tables and switching the trains
as we think fit. We shall so arrange matters that every set of rails
will pass through our organization, or come to grief if they don't.
That is the A B C of our calling.

Have you followed the reasoning, sister dear? It's a bit daunting perhaps, but you need only, my pet, apply that gift of patience which was yours in the old days of your medical training when you had to master the secrets of some cyclical process in chemistry. The cyclical processes of money are no less subtle and deserve just as much attention. If we fail to give it, then we are merely as sheep led to the shearing—or to something worse, though I'm afraid that the mere fact of seeing where we are going doesn't mean that we are any the less sheep, and subject to a sheep's fate. But even if no good comes of it, there's a certain pleasure, don't you think, in seeing what lies before us? And it may have the effect of putting us, however little, on our guard.

You will say that I have not answered your request for advice, nor told you what I think is going to happen. Are you quite sure I haven't? Read over again what I have written (and burn it, I repeat, when you have done so).

That's all very well, but what are you to say to our good Charles? Tell him not to fuss. But if he wants to fuss—and fussing does help to calm one when one is worried—he might do worse than buy a few American shares; not too many, but a few. There are times when it gives me great happiness to think that I have no savings, because if I had, I, too, should have to ask myself similar questions, and it would annoy me to have to answer them so unsatisfactorily.

Give my love to everyone, including the newly-born to be, if you have some secret way of getting messages to him. I shall now try to think of all the serious matters you have mentioned, but don't let that prevent your writing again in the mean time.

My fondest love to you.

MARC

A SIMPLE POWER OF ATTORNEY

"I asked you to call at the shop this morning because I shan't be at home this evening, and I must get this off today, since it's Thursday. . . . We'll go together to a notary I know. He'll put it all in correct form for us. I hope there won't be any complications. . . . Read it, please. . . . You'll find that it's the normal form of words in such cases. . . ."

There was a knock on the door of the office. A head appeared.

"Don't disturb me," said Mascot. "I'm busy. If it's anything important, Monsieur Auburtin will attend to it."

He returned to the matter in hand.

"You must have given many powers of attorney in your time. . . . The thing's the merest formality."

Laulerque was holding a sheet of stamped paper. For the third time he read through the few lines of text which it contained. As a result of concentrating too much on what lay before him, he found it difficult to take in fully the gist of the sentence. Besides, he was easily intimidated by matters of this kind.

"What am I binding myself to?" he asked.

Mascot adopted a tone of good-natured patience.

"Practically to nothing at all. The purchase money, including all legal costs, will be deposited with our lawyer as soon as you have signed, and thereafter no one will have any financial claim on you. Taxes will amount to perhaps fifty francs a year—a mere nothing—and we will see to all that."

"Who is this Monsieur Risso to whom I'm giving power of attorney?"

"One of our agents. His part in the business is limited to this single point. You will hear no more of him."

Laulerque remained a prey to uncertainty. "I see, I see," he said, and continued to look at the stamped paper with a musing eye.

"Please realize that you will be responsible for nothing that may happen in the house. All you've got to do is to write a short note to someone whose name I will give you, agreeing to lease him the property in question, just as it is, in return for an annual rent of three hundred francs, payable each quarter in advance. There will be no need of a formal agreement. You will keep a copy of this note, and he will write back to you accepting the offer. Let us assume for the sake of argument that someone starts asking you questions. You need merely say: 'I was told about the house, and it seemed to me to be a bargain. I went to look at it on the chance during my Christmas holidays. I liked it and I bought it. But since I couldn't make use of it at once, and haven't got money to throw away, I arranged to let it to a temporary tenant.'"

"But if that's all, I don't see why I've got to be brought into the business at all. Why doesn't this future tenant buy the place outright? If he doesn't want his name to appear, he's only got to sign a power of attorney in favour of this Risso fellow."

"Excuse me: before a man can sign a deed of purchase, he's got to give certain references as to his civil status, and they've got to be genuine. . . . You'll say that such things can be forged. . . . Well, they can of course, but that's a dangerous game. Somebody might come along and start asking questions. 'Who is this chap?' And then, if they find that the references have been forged or can't be verified, their suspicions are immediately aroused. . . . Whereas by doing as I suggest, we run no risks. 'Monsieur Laulerque is a Paris schoolmaster'—it's all as clear as daylight. But what about the tenant, you will ask. Well, when you lease a house you're not obliged to take precautions. Somebody gives you his name, some means of identifying him, possibly by letter. . . . You're not bound to verify his statements. You're not a lawyer. That sort of thing's done every day. The worst that can be said is that you've been careless of your own interests, and, after all, that's your business. In any case it'll be assumed that he's paid his rent in advance. Obviously he couldn't make off with the house."

He stopped talking. Laulerque, his eyes on the ground, said in a different tone of voice:

"Won't you give me till tomorrow to think it over?"

Mascot looked distressed. His voice was still mild, but he didn't yield an inch.

"Unfortunately I can't. I must send it by registered mail today, before the office closes."

Laulerque raised his head and looked hard at Mascot.

"Is it as urgent as all that?"

"It is extremely urgent."

"Ah! . . ."

Laulerque hesitated a moment; then:

"In order to do—what's been arranged?"

Mascot raised his eyebrows and wrinkled his forehead.

"That I don't know. Honestly I don't. . . . I don't even know exactly what you mean to imply. I wasn't present during your conversations with Monsieur Karl. . . . When he got back here he told me practically nothing. You're undoubtedly much better informed than I am."

Laulerque smiled. Then he sat down with the paper before him, took the fountain-pen which Mascot held out to him, made a few faces, and signed.

Chapter

32

SOMETHING SAID BY GURAU TO
BRIAND COINCIDES UNFORTUNATELY
WITH THE RECEIPT
OF A THREATENING LETTER

Briand was very much surprised to be rung up at half past eight in the morning by Gurau.

"I want to see you as soon as possible. . . . Yes, this morning. I tried to get you the other evening after the session, but you were with a whole lot of people. I've got something new to tell you."

"All right, come along at once. I shall be dressed by the time you get here."

"Well, what is it? Has something happened? . . . You see, I've not even taken time to tie my tie properly. . . . Take this chair, you'll be more comfortable. . . . Cigarettes?"

"No, thank you, I'm trying not to smoke in the morning."

While he was moving his chair before sitting down, Briand noticed that Gurau looked serious, even strained.

"Nothing important, is it?"

"No; or, rather, yes, it is important, but it's not unexpected. I didn't want to ask a question in the Chamber. In the first place, I knew that Jaurès was going to make his big statement—we'd talked it over together, and, secondly, it was no time to parade a personal success. . . ."

Briand appeared to be surprised by the almost solemn way in which Gurau was speaking. He stroked his moustache and cleared his throat.

"I don't understand. . . . Thing's aren't going too badly. . . . Pichon's speech on Thursday was very well received abroad."

"Indeed?" Gurau said with veiled irony. "So much the better."

"You can rest assured on that point. Even in Berlin. Pichon has

shown me the press clippings. The general view is that he spoke
with great moderation, that his tone was reassuring."

"Optimist!"

"And why not? Some of his phrases were extremely happy;
'European patriotism,' for example." Briand winked. "Not bad, eh?"

"He said that?"

"Certainly he did."

"I didn't hear it."

"That only goes to show that when Pichon is speaking you don't
listen. . . . I'll show it to you in the Gazette. . . . He said something
too about the Russian alliance, though I don't remember exactly
what . . . the gist of it was that the object of the alliance was to
guarantee a general peace. . . . But he put it rather well."

"Since we're on the subject, hadn't you better quote also what
Jaurès said towards the end of *his* speech? I'm no better at giving
actual words than you are, but it was something like this: 'According to you, Monsieur Pichon, we've got so many allies that we've
no choice but to double the size of our army without more ado in
order to deserve them.'"

"You're sure he said 'without more ado'?"

"No, not absolutely sure."

Both men laughed.

"Hang it all," Briand went on, "it wasn't Jaurès's business to give
us bouquets. He's as fond of phrase-making as the next man, and
he has a weakness for noble sentiments. But they don't always come
off. You remember his remark about tow-headed Austria and the
waltz? It seemed to me a bit crude, all that about the dancing
bear. . . . But you must admit that on the whole he treated us
kindly. . . ."

"Oh, so long as the Government was pleased . . ."

Briand threw back his head and shook his thick mane, opening
his eyes wide. He seemed to have lost the desire to laugh.

"Oh yes, he was kind enough. . . . He didn't even bring up the
Potsdam business against us. He said that, in the circumstances, it

looked as though Russia, instead of driving us into war, would drive us into holding our hands. . . . You're joking. . . . He quoted young Tardieu in his support. Don't you find the picture of Jaurès hand in hand with Tardieu rather touching? He has realized that the Russian alliance is so far of value that it will make us strong enough to avoid being drawn into a struggle between England and Germany. . . ."

Briand slowly raised his right hand, forefinger extended, and moved it to and fro. Then, suddenly, looking Gurau straight in the eyes, he said sententiously, almost rhetorically:

"That's the really serious thing, Gurau; that's where the danger lies. You're too much inclined to think of things in terms of Franco-German relations. You've got your eye glued to the wrong end of the telescope. Pichon's told me that you're always harping on that line in the committee. My dear fellow, the real danger's going to come from the struggle which is preparing between English and German imperialism. The risk for us is finding ourselves suddenly in the position of hostages. It's we who shall suffer if they come to blows. Take the Bagdad railway, for example. Whom does it annoy if not the English? It doesn't matter a damn to us. Russia? It's enough for Russia to seem to say: 'After all, your railway doesn't bother us much,' for Germany to discover that she's got no real cause of quarrel with Russia, and for the Tsar and the Kaiser to start flirting with one another. The point is that if war breaks out between England and Germany over the Bagdad railway, or for any other reason, it won't be fought at Bagdad. No, it'll be fought here in France, on our frontiers, in Lorraine or in the north."

Gurau was annoyed. He felt that Briand was lecturing him. He answered sharply. Despite himself a note of passion crept into his voice. And because Briand had once more relapsed into his attitude of the calm and watchful elder statesman, always ready with an answer, he felt himself to be ineffectual, and the sensation irritated him.

"That's all very fine," he said; "but to my mind Jaurès kept the whole thing too academic. He'd been chewing for months on this big idea of his, and he wanted to get it across. He knew that if he let tempers get high, questions would be asked, secondary issues would emerge, and his whole plan get side-tracked. That's not my method, as you very well know. If I think something's true, I go a lot further than Jaurès. . . . Be that as it may, it didn't prevent his getting under your skins before he sat down." (Briand made a show of expressing surprise.) "Did he or did he not say that no peace was possible in Europe until there had been a reconciliation, a sincere and loyal reconciliation, between France and Germany? . . . It's not a question of England. . . . Did he or did he not say further that no such reconciliation could ever be brought about until France had made a clear and definite statement that she had abandoned once and for all any intention of recovering Alsace-Lorraine by force of arms? By legal means, possibly, at some future time, but not by force."

"Legal means, indeed!"

"Yes, legal means; he knows perfectly well what it is he wants to do. . . . In the course of his speech he made use of certain quotations from that book of Norman Angell's."

"What the devil's that?"

"*The Great Illusion,* by Norman Angell . . . I've not read it myself, but I'm told it's an amazing work. The author proves mathematically that any future war must be idiocy, that a war fought under modern conditions will inevitably ruin everybody, including the victor. . . . Well, without any fuss or bother Jaurès just gave your war party that nice little fact to play with. . . ."

"Don't talk like that, Gurau!"

"I shall talk like that."

"Whom do you mean when you say war party?"

"Not you, Briand—certainly not you—but other people. . . . Not you personally, but those, all the same, who work at your orders and under your protection."

"Not Pichon? Your hatred for that poor man blinds you to everything else."

"Poor indeed—the epithet is an admirable one! I have no personal feeling against him. I think he's a public danger, but that's quite a different matter. He's not even dangerous by intention. . . ."

"You may as well say at once that you think he's a fool."

"Not quite that either. . . . No, he's dangerous because he doesn't really exist, because he's without any sense of reality, because he's a mere puppet. You've often talked to me about the Foreign Office crowd. Well, they've made Pichon in their own image. This time *I'm* telling *you*. And knowing this, you, Briand, as head of the Government, do nothing to stop their game. Either as Foreign Minister simply and solely or in conjunction with the War Office, he's playing a game which will have far-reaching consequences. Another point: Jaurès said: 'You're playing a dirty game in Morocco.' Those are his exact words. They may have been softened down in the official report, but I don't care a damn about official reports. Oh yes, you're playing a dirty game in Morocco. General Moinier's raid was bad enough, but there's been worse than that. There are things that can't be said in the Chamber; not even before the committee. . . . Shall I give you the details of just one little incident among many? I've got all the facts here. . . . The worst feature of the whole business—or perhaps the funniest—is that I'm ready to bet you know nothing whatever about it. They're too cunning to let it get to your ears. . . . Well, listen, then; you can have all the necessary facts if you want them—name, places, dates. A certain officer, I believe of the Intelligence Department, who has a perfect knowledge of Arabic and long experience of local customs, arranged to work his way into the confidence of one of the tribes. He succeeded in his efforts and finally roused them against the French and against the Christians generally. So well did he do his work that one fine day the poor devils actually attacked a small French column. . . . That's what he meant them to do and what those who employed him meant them to do. . . . We lost about ten men killed, a few wounded, and some prisoners, who were promptly beheaded. . . . A pity, but we had the pretext we wanted. . . . A little while later a full-dress expedition was dispatched. . . . The way was clear for pacification by high explosives."

Briand forced himself to maintain his attitude of patronizing amusement.

"And you really believe all that?" he asked.

"I'm quite sure of it."

Briand spread out his arms and hunched his shoulders.

"I've no doubt that the same sort of thing goes on elsewhere. . . . What about the English? I can assure you that plenty of people will regard this officer of yours as a hero cast in the antique mould."

"But what about you, Briand? Doesn't it make you sick with indignation? Do you really think it's worth while men like us getting power if it's only to countenance that sort of thing?"

"Of course, of course. . . . But you'll never prevent a certain amount of dirty work going on. Suppose you were Minister of the Interior and you wanted to stop tobacco-smuggling, do you think the police would always tell you about the methods they were going to employ? . . . A cook doesn't ask her mistress's leave every time she spits in the sauce. What do you want me to do? Get out of Morocco and make way for the Germans? No doubt you think they would behave better than we do?"

"Look here, Briand, I'm not a child. I know enough about politics to realize that one's got to wink at a little nastiness sometimes, to avoid something worse. But little nastinesses in Morocco may lead to war in Europe. Every time one happens it means another scuttleful of coals on the fire. You know that perfectly well, Briand. Jaurès reminded you of it, too mildly for my taste, and I've dotted his 'i's' and crossed his 't's.' . . . But there's something else I want to say to you."

"Go ahead."

"I saw Jaurès yesterday evening. You know the wording of the resolution he's going to submit today?"

Briand affected an air of careless indifference. "The actual wording, no," he said; "I did hear something about it—something to the effect that it was fairly mild. Do you know its precise form?"

Gurau fumbled in his pocket.

"Yes . . . there may be a few last-minute alterations, but the essentials will remain as they are. It is based on President Taft's statement. Here we are. I took this down from Jaurès's own dictation:

"'The Chamber invites the Government to associate itself with the noble gesture made by the great American Republic with the object of settling by methods of arbitration all conflicts of an international character, and to submit to all the governments represented at the Hague Conference a series of treaties based upon that principle.'"

Gurau waited. Briand seemed to be plunged in thought. After a moment's pause he said:

"I should say he'd get about a hundred and ten or a hundred and twenty votes—not a very serious matter."

Gurau smiled bitterly.

"And that's all it means to you, Briand!"

"You're not seriously suggesting that the Government should act upon this resolution?"

Looking Briand straight in the face, and in a loud voice, Gurau said: "Yes."

"My dear fellow, you're mad! You're not even sincere. You know perfectly well that we couldn't commit ourselves to such a course. I needn't explain that to you."

"All the same, it's got to be done."

Briand stared at his visitor with curiosity. A mischievous look came into his eyes, as though he were suddenly the prey of some fantastic idea.

Gurau pressed his point.

"It must be done. It's a question of the national honour, or, if you prefer, of the national ideal. . . . It's also a question of national safety."

Briand stroked his chin, and a smile showed for a moment on his lips. Then, opening one of the drawers of his table, he took from it a paper which he held out to Gurau.

"This little billet-doux comes from you, then?" he said, deciding to turn the smile into a laugh.

Gurau took the document. It was a single sheet of thin, greyish paper, of the kind used in business houses. It was covered with close typewriting which showed several faults of alignment and a good many deleted letters.

15 January 1911

Monsieur the Prime Minister
Dear Sir:

You are advised, if only in your own interests, to adopt without a moment's delay the suggestions herein contained, despite the fact that they reach you in rather an unusual fashion.

We feel no particular hatred for you; in fact we are willing to believe that in general you mean well. But you are doubtless aware that hell is paved with good intentions.

Your position lays upon you a particularly onerous responsibility. Whether you wish it or no, you are one of the men on whom at the present moment the question of peace or war in Europe depends. It so happens that we have strong views about peace, and we have determined to use every means to ensure, with God's help, that the cause of peace shall prevail.

You have a remarkable opportunity of showing that your enthusiasm for peace is sincere. Tomorrow will be presented to the Chamber a resolution demanding the adherence of France to the proposal put forward by President Taft and the immediate opening of arbitration negotiations with all other countries. You will be well advised to support the resolution in the Chamber and to ensure its passage by treating it as a vote of confidence.

You will also be well advised to get from your Foreign Minister tomorrow a document which has already been submitted to you, bearing the register number A. M. 173, and to countermand without a moment's delay the instructions contained in it, if necessary by telegraph. We believe that the contents of this document will outrage your conscience as violently as it has ours, and that you were hurried into approving it in despite of your better feelings.

If you fail to follow this advice an attempt will be made on your life in the course of the next few days. No precautions, whether of an ordinary or an extraordinary nature, will be of the slightest avail.

If, on the other hand, you act in the way we hope, and in the only way consistent with your publicly announced convictions, you can rest assured of our enthusiastic support. Nothing but good can result both for you and for your country.

Gurau's face, as he read this letter, had gone scarlet. He did not think that Briand seriously suspected him, but the coincidence was too remarkable to be anything but embarrassing.

"How was this sent to you?" he asked.

"It was delivered to me yesterday evening while I was dining with —with somebody." ("His mistress," thought Gurau.) "As it was Sunday, it was unlikely that anyone but me would open it. . . . My secretary might have thrown it into the waste-paper-basket without showing it to me."

"You take it seriously?"

"Oh—no—I'm not sure. . . . What do you think?"

Gurau made a non-committal movement with his shoulders. He read the letter through once more.

"It's odd," he said, "that the authors of the letter" (Gurau used the plural intentionally) "seem to know all about Jaurès's resolution. . . . Not that there's anything very secret about it. . . . Still, outside a certain number of persons. . . . And then all this about the document A. M. a hundred and—I've forgotten the exact figure—has that got a basis of fact?"

"Of extremely accurate fact."

"Ah! Is it a confidential document?"

"Very confidential. . . . You know what happens in such cases —it's probably been through the hands of half a dozen or so officials and of about the same number of soldiers, if not more; nevertheless," he concluded with a laugh, "it's what we call a secret document."

The usher entered with a card.

"All right, in a minute or two," Briand said.

Gurau felt once more completely at his ease. He could say now with a perfectly clear conscience, and in a tone of friendly concern: "You've mentioned it to the police?"

"Oh, I gave them a ring last night, just for the principle of the thing. . . . If anything did happen they'd haul me over the coals for not warning them. . . . They sent me Coutelard; you know whom I mean?"

"What did he say?"

"Nothing. The man's a fool. . . . I didn't think it even worth while to give him the letter. . . . You don't really think I'm going to make myself ill for a little thing like that. . . . It happens every day at the Élysée . . . I've had a good many of them myself. There are so many fanatics and visionaries about. . . . Not that there's anything particularly mad about this letter, except the phrase 'with God's help.'. . ."

Briand burst out laughing.

"Unless, of course," he added in qualification, "it was written by a foreigner. God's still very popular abroad. And there are one or two points about the style. It's quite possible that it was first drafted in a foreign language and then translated by someone with a good knowledge of French."

He got up, holding out the card which had just been given to him. "You must excuse me. I must see this chap."

On his way out Gurau thought it well to stress his anxiety: "Do take care, all the same."

"But how, my dear fellow? I'm not going to the Chamber surrounded by cavalry! If I did, the chances are that everyone would say I was out to make myself dictator."

THE ATTEMPT

On the 17th Laulerque had just started back from his school and had reached the square which marked the first point at which the returning crowd of children began to break up into divergent streams—it must have been about five minutes past four—when he heard the cries of newsboys calling a special edition. He thought he could distinguish the words "attempt," "Briand," "Minister." Already fearing the worst, he hurried across the road to waylay one of the venders and bought a paper.

A staring headline occupied the whole width of the front page:

ATTEMPTED ASSASSINATION OF M. BRIAND IN THE CHAMBER

The actual news was confined to a few lines printed in heavy type and occupying the full width of the two middle columns:

"Precisely at 2.55 p.m. today, the 17th of January, during the sitting of the Chamber, a man seated in the public gallery fired two shots from a revolver at the Prime Minister, M. Briand. The Prime Minister was untouched. M. Mirman, however, Director of Public Health, who happened to be sitting near him, was seriously wounded. The man in question was at once disarmed and placed under arrest. The sitting was adjourned.

"Further details will be found in later editions."

Laulerque was seized with a fit of trembling, which was succeeded by a sudden desire for violent action. He didn't know whether to run at full speed to the shelter of his home, whether to take refuge in aimless flight through the streets, or whether to seek some means of relief no less efficacious if slightly more rational.

His first thought had been of Mascot, and he tried now to fix his mind upon him calmly and clearly. A motor-bus belonging to the G route, drew up at the square. Laulerque got into it.

But the motor-bus seemed to him to move very slowly, far more slowly than his own thoughts.

When they got to the Place Clichy he could contain himself no longer. Seeing a taxi, he hailed it, got out of the bus before it reached the stop, and told the taxi-driver to go to the D— bookshop.

"You want to see Monsieur Mascot? I'm afraid he's busy at the moment, but I'll tell him you're here. Monsieur Laulerque, I believe?"

The clerk disappeared.

"He's remembered my name," thought Laulerque, and realized the imprudence of his visit. "Today of all days I oughtn't to have come here. The clerk will make a note of my call. Besides, there may be someone in the office who will hear him mention my name. That makes two witnesses. That's just the way people put two and two together. On the other hand, I couldn't have waited until this evening."

Mascot, usually so calm, betrayed a certain amount of annoyance in his manner of greeting Laulerque.

"I'm sorry," said the latter, "but I bought a paper a few minutes ago, just as I started to go home, and I must admit—"

He left the sentence unfinished. Mascot, rather white about the nostrils, was engaged in straightening a pile of books which stood on the left-hand corner of his table. As Laulerque remained silent, he asked him point-blank:

"Was there anything special in the paper?"

"Haven't you seen it?"

"No."

"But the newsboys must have come this way."

"I can't hear them from my office. . . . None of my people have said anything to me. . . . Besides, this is a very quiet street. Tell me, what was in the paper?"

Laulerque smiled with the air of a man who appreciates a piece of play-acting, but is not taken in by it. But Mascot gave no sign. Finally the younger man said:

"Do you really want me to tell you?"

"I do."

"Well, then, read for yourself."

He held out the paper.

Mascot read through the paragraph twice, apparently digesting its contents. His eyes never left the few lines printed in heavy type. With his right hand he stroked the lower part of his face.

Laulerque suddenly remembered something that "M. Karl" had said: "Kill a queen with an asp hidden in a bouquet of roses, poison a Minister by putting chopped hair in his coffee."—"Instead of which," he thought, "they use a revolver like anybody else—and miss."

Mascot put down the paper, closed his eyes as though he felt tired, rubbed them, screened them with his hand, and, without changing his position, said very quietly:

"Well, at least you can see now that we *are* trying to do something."

At this answer Laulerque felt his tension relax. He gave a sigh, and lowering his voice, "Then it was—we?" he asked.

Mascot opened his eyes and looked at him. His voice, when he spoke, was curt, but controlled.

"Let me say first that you had no business to come here at a time like this, no matter what you were thinking. It was a ridiculous thing to do."

"I know, I know," said Laulerque miserably.

"I thought you were made of sterner stuff. Secondly, this business has nothing to do with me."

Laulerque did not quite know how to take this last remark and he showed his uncertainty in his face.

Mascot added on an incisive note:

"I knew nothing whatever about all this until you told me."

"Ought I— do you want me to pretend I believe that, or really to believe it?"

"You should believe me."

Laulerque showed his amazement.

"I don't say," Mascot went on, "that I hadn't some inkling of what was afoot, but I had absolutely nothing to do with putting it into effect." He stressed the word "absolutely."

Laulerque's heart was beating violently. After hesitating a moment he asked:

"You see that the man has been arrested?"

"Yes, I noticed that."

"Isn't it rather—unfortunate?"

Mascot pondered this for a moment; then, very calmly, he said: "No."

"Is there no danger of—his talking?"

"No."

"You know—who it is?"

"I have a shrewd idea." He broke off, then, with a faint smile, added: "If my information is correct, the individual in question has no idea who employed him."

"Is that possible?"

"More than possible; it's our rule."

As though he had caught a look of incredulity in Laulerque's eyes, he went on (speaking all the while in the lowest of murmurs):

"His identity will probably be given in the later editions. You will be able to verify what I'm going to tell you. I rather think that his name begins with a G, that he was once employed in the civil service, that he is related to someone fairly prominent in the political world."

As he finished, he broke into a smile.

"Do you mean to say," Laulerque asked, "that a man like that could be used without suspecting anything?"

"Yes, given certain peculiarities of character."

"And there's really no danger of their putting two and two together . . . of their getting on the track of his associates?"

Mascot made as though to brush the question aside with a
gesture.

"Actually, I think not," he said. "Of course, there's always a risk
. . . otherwise— But I want to say again that no responsibility attached to me personally for the success of the attempt."

Laulerque was made aware by the heavy beating of his heart and
by a contraction of his throat that he had not yet asked the most
important question of all. He took his courage in both hands, and
broke out with:

"May I say something else?"

"Certainly . . . but I can't spare much time. . . . I'm sorry. . . ."

"Was the house—you know what I mean—*that* house—meant to
play any part—?"

"In what's happened? None at all."

Mascot got up from his chair and held out his hand to Laulerque.
In a tone of kindly tolerance not unmixed with contempt, he said:

"There is no need at all for you to worry about anything you may
have done yourself in the matter."

Laulerque got up in his turn.

"One last question, please"—his voice was almost beseeching.

"Why Briand? Why him rather than another? . . . Is he really
the chief danger?"

"By what right do you say him *rather* than another? . . . Please
wait a moment."

He was standing by his table. Turning to it, he took up a pencil.

"I'm going to give you an order for three books—any books. Don't
forget to make the clerk give you them. And don't look so dazed."

Chapter

34

CONVERSATION OF BRIAND WITH GOULVIC, THE FRIEND OF HIS YOUTH. ALLORY IN THE DUMPS

"It was too good of you, my dear old friend, to put yourself out like this; it really wasn't worth your while. But it's always a pleasure for me to see you."

"I had been to Versailles. I only saw the news just now, when I got out of the train. It knocked me all of a heap. . . . And how are you? I must say you don't look much the worse."

"What did you expect?"

"But what did you feel like when it happened? It must have upset you?"

"No, I really didn't notice it happening. . . . You see, there was all the usual noise going on. Of course I heard a bang, bang, and for a moment I thought someone might have shot himself at one of the desks. Then I saw Mirman collapse just beside me. . . . That and one or two other things pretty soon showed me what had happened."

"But when you realized it all, surely it was something of a shock?"

"Yes, but not overwhelming. It all seems a great deal worse in retrospect."

Briand looked at his friend and began to smile. Suddenly his face took on an expression of humility; not so much humility of Briand the politician as of Briand the human being. "What insignificant creatures we are!" it seemed to say. "How silly all this pretence of cleverness is!" For a moment, face to face with this childhood friend, he was just a little boy again.

"Who was the fellow who fired the shot?" Goulvic asked.

"Somebody called Gizolme—I think I remember hearing that he

was about forty and came from Saint-Flour. That struck me at the time. Saint-Flour's hardly a breeding-ground for political assassins, eh? If it had been some dirty old Breton like you from Guérande, it would have been easier to understand! But the oddest part of the whole business was what happened when his name became known in ministerial circles—such a ringing of telephones! You see the permanent secretary of Lafferre's department is called Gizolme! What a nice little bit of scandal that made—permanent secretary of the Ministry of Labour, and Grand Master of the Grand Orient, attempts to assassinate the Prime Minister! What possibilities *that* opened up! As a matter of fact, it seems that my Gizolme really is a brother of Lafferre's—so that even if it doesn't make as good a story as it might have, still, it's something. My man's a retired clerk who's had bad luck. The other brother, the one who's not the assassin, says that they're not on speaking terms. . . ."

"But why did he do it?"

"I've no idea. . . . The police theory is that he's mad—persecution mania. It seems that he made an attempt on someone else. When he was questioned he made some perfectly incoherent statement."

"And what's your own opinion?"

"Mine? I think he's probably mad—either mad or pretending to be mad—but that he's been used by certain people who are perfectly sane. . . . That kind of little game can go on for a long time."

Briand hesitated a moment. Then, opening one of his drawers, he took from under a pile of papers the threatening letter and held it out to Goulvic.

"Take a look at that. I got it yesterday evening. Read it, but don't breathe a word of it to any living soul."

Goulvic read the letter very carefully. Then:

"You say you got this yesterday evening?"

"Yes. Sunday, at dinner-time."

"And you did nothing?"

"I warned the police."

"And then—?"

"Nothing was done. . . . No, I'm wrong, I believe they put one or two extra detectives on duty last night round the ministries."

"And now? Hasn't this business set them wondering? This letter isn't the work of a madman. . . . It looks to me as though it doesn't come from an individual at all . . . as though there's some sort of organization behind it."

"I think I agree with you."

"I'm not sure—but it reminds me of some of the papers that used to pass through my hands when I was working for some months at counter-espionage in the rue Royale. . . . You'd better get them to make a careful inquiry. . . . After all, old man, it's your life that's at stake. . . . Besides, if our suspicions are correct, it means that some organization's at work which may spell danger for the whole country and which ought at all costs to be unmasked."

"My dear friend, do you really think I can do what I want? The police theory is, first, that the whole thing's a mare's-nest. If I make too much of it, if I seem to take it seriously, they'll think I've got a screw loose, that fear has turned my brain. . . . And, secondly, they take the view that even if the man wasn't mad, we've got to pretend he was. That's the way these things are managed in England. From time to time there's an attempt against the sovereign or against some minister. It's always hushed up. The official account is always that such things are the work of a lunatic, because only a lunatic could dream of assassinating such excellent sovereigns or such honest ministers. What happens to the guilty party nobody knows, but public opinion is reassured, and the risk of contagion is removed."

"That may be so, but don't tell me that the English police, even though they might put this Gizolme fellow away without fuss, wouldn't first of all find out, either from him or from other sources, who had written this letter and who was behind the business."

Briand shrugged his shoulders, smiling at some idea that had occurred to him.

"My answer to that is that we're not in England. Besides, they may be right. If one began forming theories, one really might go mad. What do you think of this?"

And in a low voice, and with the same mocking expression, which had never left his face, he told his friend of the visit he had received from Gurau the day before.

Goulvic listened wide-eyed.

"So you see," Briand said in conclusion.

"What am I to see?"

"That the police are right in holding Gizolme to be mad."

"I don't understand."

"You don't understand because you're a hard-bitten old soldier."

As George Allory left Jules Lemaître—the twenty-third visit he had made in the course of canvassing votes for his election to the Academy—he heard the newsboys shouting the news of the attempt against Briand, "with all the latest details"; but he paid very little attention to it.

In the first place, he had no opinion of politicians, despising, as he did, the mediocrity of their ambitions and the spirit of intrigue which animated them. But another reason for his lack of interest was that he was a prey, just then, to particularly violent emotion. Lemaître had just said to him:

"Let me give you a word of advice. I've spoken to Faguet and he agrees with me." (Faguet was Allory's chief supporter in this matter of the Academy.) "Give up the idea of standing for the vacancy left by Vogüé, and become a candidate for Barboux's. The election will be held only eight days later, and your only serious competitor will be Roujon, who hardly counts. I can't guarantee that you'll get in, but you'll have pleased Hérédia's friends by making way for Henri de Régnier, and they'll remember it in your favour the next time you stand."

Seeing that Allory looked disappointed and said nothing, Lemaître had added:

"You can take it from me it's no misfortune; very much the reverse. Here you are with a chance to do a service to people whom, in all probability, you would never otherwise have been able to influence. Don't forget, too, that a question of decency is involved. Both you and Régnier are published by the *Débats,* and violent rivalry of this kind between two of its authors is alien to the traditions of the house. You will tell me, no doubt, that you have been associated with the firm for a very much longer time than Régnier, and that he was only added to their list for political reasons. . . . That may be true, but it doesn't affect the point at issue."

George Allory had reached the street in a state not so much of indignation as of collapse. Not that he had expected to be elected at his first attempt (Victor Hugo had stood three times), but the casual way in which he had been treated filled him with anxiety for the future. "They let me hang on until the last possible moment so as to increase the number of votes for Régnier and frighten off other competitors. Now they're getting rid of me. . . . What line will Madame de Ruje take? Probably she, too, will leave me in the lurch. If I'd stood out for the Vogüé vacancy I should have been sure of nine votes, perhaps eleven; if I transfer to Barboux's I can reckon on only six. It's all very well for Lemaître to talk, the fact that Roujon's a nonentity is what makes him dangerous. Besides, he's a clever old fox. He's not very likely to have made the attempt without first being pretty sure of his success. I shouldn't be surprised if they'd asked his leave before urging me to oppose him. . . . The worst of it all is that everyone will think I've withdrawn in order to avoid a defeat, so that my failure will look more significant than it would otherwise have done, and I shall never recover the ground I have lost. It's all up with my hopes of the Academy."

A REPROACH, A DISCUSSION, AND
A SCHEME

About eleven o'clock on Friday evening, in the third-floor study (known also as the Palace of the Cubes [1]) which they had occupied since November, Jallez remarked to Jerphanion that it was now almost a month since their last considerable expedition through Paris.

He made the point calmly, but rather bitterly. "I suppose the fact is that the proximity of the exam is weighing on us as much as it does on the others."

Jerphanion felt that this remark was aimed particularly at him, but at first he made no attempt to counter it. Instead, he made use of the weather as an excuse.

"Don't forget," he said, "that each time we had the chance, it was a wretched day."

Jallez was in a disillusioned mood. He pointed out that for those who really seek adventures in Paris, there are no "wretched days." One can go on walking a long time through thin rain, and if it rains hard, it never keeps on long. There are always clear intervals, and nothing is lovelier than a clear interval, with sunlight breaking through on the walls of buildings and reflected on the wet pavements. One gets muddy, of course, and one's shoes get wet through, but at five o'clock, in the back room of some café, one puts one's feet up on the cross-bar of the table and shivers happily till all sense of wet fatigue is warmed out of one. If one always insists on fine weather, then, when fine weather comes, one ought to give up everything else and take advantage of it. If one doesn't, one's caught

---

[1] "Cubes" is the slang name given to third-year students at the École Normale Supérieure.—Translator's note.

in a vicious circle. Things that one pretends have got to be done go on increasing in number. Why are so many of the middle-aged men one meets such miserable specimens? Because all their hours, all their quarter-hours, are mortgaged in advance to something that's "got to be done." They've got to take little Adolphe to the dentist; they've got to attend the monthly meeting of the Old Fogies' Friendly Society. Such degradation comes slowly. Once, perhaps, they were young fellows who set out in search of adventure. Then a year came when they went out less, another year when they waited for a fine day, and then, when one came along, it unfortunately coincided with something that couldn't be put off, as, for example, analysing a chapter of Fénelon's *Letter to the French Academy,* if they happened to be sitting for a literary degree, or working up some point about marriage settlements if they were reading for law.

Jerphanion still made no attempt to defend himself. He was not feeling particularly aggressive, and he had a bad conscience.

Finally, however, Jallez went too far.

"You're just a good little schoolboy," he said.

Up to this moment Jerphanion had been sitting with his pen in his hand. Now he laid it down and turned to Jallez, who pulled himself up sharp, thinking: "Now I've hurt his feelings. What a brute I am! I'm behaving abominably."

But Jerphanion gave no sign of anger.

"You're rather unfair," he said quietly. "In the first place, you're not really so indifferent about your degree as you pretend to be."

"I'm not the slightest bit indifferent. If I get a degree I shall regard it as a miraculous event of very great advantage in my future life. But I refuse to let myself get into the habit of sacrificing things that are sacred to things that are merely advantageous, no matter how admirable they may be. Why do I want a degree? Because a degree will assure me a livelihood, guarantee me against poverty, which I dread, and provide me with a certain amount of leisure, which I hope to use in a proper way—that is, by devoting it to what I consider to be really worth while in life. But if in preparing for my degree I sacrifice everything else, everything in the present, the things that can't be replaced, that will never come again, on the pretext of increasing my chances of success, I run the risk of making a fool of myself, of dropping into a dreary routine. I shall get into the habit of always sacrificing the things that can't be replaced, the things that 'will never come again.' There will always be something calling for attention, something that's got to be done or prepared, something rational, useful, urgent. And the demands of such things will grow more and more insistent, because, my dear chap, we shall be growing older, and as we lose our youth, we lose the power which youth gives of resisting the claims of the rational and the prudent. Once I've got my degree, I shall argue to myself that I've got to be noticed, that I've got to be well thought of, in order to get a Paris appointment as soon as possible, or that I ought to give more lessons because they bring in money. Therefore I shall spend my time correcting a lot of papers and giving a lot of lessons, with the result that I shall have no leisure. The sum total of which will mean that I shall have got a degree and lost everything for the sake of which I wanted to get it. . . . *Propter vitam,* etc. . . ."

"That's all very well, old man. We agree about principles, but circumstances force us to differ about their application. You want a degree, but you sacrifice less to get it. Let's say that you work less, partly, perhaps, because you're cleverer than I am. . . . Oh yes, you are. . . . Partly because you rely more on your wits, on your power of improvisation, on your natural, town-bred sharpness. But the chief reason is that if your success would be gratifying, your failure would not be a tragedy, whereas mine would."

Jallez started a friendly argument. Jerphanion went on quite calmly:

"No, our cases are not the same. If you flunk, I know that you'll manage to get along, though I may not know exactly how. Either you'll take another year, which won't break your parents, or some job will come along, of which you've no idea at the moment, but which will suit you much better than a post in some country school."

(Jallez ventured a mild protest. His friend's prognostications were not displeasing to him, for they went far to allay a fear of the future which, unaided, he found it difficult to resist. "This," he reflected, "is what others think of you and your destiny, what this man, seeing you from outside, and therefore better able to judge, foresees as your future.")

"I, on the other hand," Jerphanion went on, "am poor. . . . Oh yes, I know . . . I don't want to be indiscreet, but in matters like this small differences count for a lot. My parents are very, very humble. . . . I say again, if I fail it will be a tragedy. I can't afford to wait and I can't accept an allowance from them. My only chance would be to take a job in some obscure university and start all over again studying for a degree in conditions which would be horrible, discouraging, and calculated to destroy any keenness I may have. I should submit to them if I had to, but I don't know what their effect on me would be. I am prepared to sacrifice anything to avoid such a catastrophe. If I succeed, I don't think I shall really feel that I've made a fool of myself."

They proceeded to consider and discuss the idea of poverty. They faced fairly the question that only the children of the rich are spared, but that becomes an obsession, more or less intense, in the minds of all others, even though they may not always admit it, setting its mark on them, explaining most of their actions even when they are old, even when the danger seems to have passed—the question: "What must we have to keep us safe from fear?"

They agreed that the answer need not always be the same even for any one man. What would be enough if it involved no service in return, and left him free to live his life and dream his dreams, would be too little if it tied him to a trade. Freedom keeps at bay the sense of poverty just as salt prevents water from freezing.

"If somebody told me," Jallez said, "that for the rest of my life I could count on having two hundred francs a month, I should never be afraid of the future."

They agreed too, contrary to general opinion, that with very small

means—and freedom—a man would feel himself less wretched in
Paris than buried away in the country, provided always that he knew
how to make use of Paris. He must know the cabmen's eating-
houses, where a good meal can be had for just over a franc, and the
cafés on the Boulevards where one can get a bottle of beer on the
pavement for thirty centimes; he must be a good walker and have
by heart the plan of the city, with its bus and subway lines; he must
bear in mind the various public entertainments, and get into the
habit of treating them as his own with as much freedom as though
they were his private flat, thinking of them as "my" National Library, "my" Louvre Museum, "my" Tuileries Gardens, "my" view
up the Champs-Élysées, and so get into a state of mind from which
all sense of poverty was banished.

But as soon as they got to grips with the problem, the two friends
found that they differed on certain points of detail. In the first place
it was obvious that Jerphanion took much less seriously than did
Jallez this theory of the "bare bones" of life, or rather of life reduced
to a wise minimum; that he treated it as a game, and didn't really
think of it in terms of his own existence. Jallez was disappointed.
He told himself that Jerphanion was deficient in a sense of poetry.
But there was another surprise in store for him. Having argued
how little was necessary to keep a man from destitution, they went
on to discuss what was the "most desirable" income for a man of
their age and their period—that is to say, what amount of money
could ensure him the satisfaction of his needs and legitimate tastes
without involving him in social injustice. (For some time now they
had both of them shown an increasing sensitiveness on this point.
They had decided—and here Jerphanion had made certain concessions to Jallez—that though it was possible for a "wise man" to
doubt the efficacy of all theories of social reconstruction and suspend
judgment on the question of society as it was at present constituted,
he ought, meanwhile, to keep himself, as far as possible, from participating in any form of social iniquity. The best way of keeping
himself unsullied in this respect—always allowing for the fact that

one doesn't really know the value of what one gives to others—would be to avoid bearing too heavily on their shoulders, to make sparing use of goods and services held in common, even to refuse some of them in token of virtue.) Jallez maintained that four or five thousand francs was a reasonable figure, Jerphanion held out for seven, and absolutely refused to go below six.

"Aren't you forgetting," said Jallez, "that when you've got this precious degree for which you're willing to sacrifice everything, you won't even get, at first, as much as four thousand clear? What are you going to do, then? Are you reckoning on outside work? On giving lessons? Your feet are on a slippery slope, old man, a damned slippery slope!"

Jerphanion, when called upon to explain himself in greater detail, took refuge in vague generalities. There were a whole lot of things, he said, which they mightn't feel the need of now, but would do later, many expenses which would be forced upon them as they grew older. Nor was this his only line of argument. One mustn't, for instance, be priggish.

"It's odd," thought Jallez; "there's something behind all this. He's not telling me his real reasons."

By this time it was after midnight, and Jerphanion, as though wishing to give some pledge to his friend, declared suddenly that he would arrange to be free the next afternoon as soon as lunch was finished. They could therefore plan one of their long expeditions through Paris, even if the weather was "wretched."

They agreed to abandon for once their usual habit of casual wandering and to plan their outing in advance. With this end in view they set themselves to work out the details of a fantastic itinerary.

"What I suggest," said Jallez, "is this. Try to be free in the morning. I'll wait for you at the corner of the rue Lhomond at nine o'clock sharp." Since the beginning of the term Jallez no longer slept at the College, though continuing to take his meals there. At the moment he had a room in the rue Lhomond. By this arrangement he received the partial board of a day student. "Let's go straight to the Panthéon and climb up to the dome. We've never been there together. Then, on the principle of water finding its own level, we'll go down, across Paris, and up to the summit of the Sacré-Cœur, which also we've never visited. We'll lunch in Montmartre. We'll get back here before night. You'll still have nearly three hours for work before dinner."

But the "wily mountaineer" withstood the suggestion. "I said: afternoon. That's final. Besides, your program, which I like, can very well be carried out between one o'clock and nightfall."

Chapter

HISTORY (PERHAPS RATHER TOO MUCH OF IT)

The weather on Saturday afternoon was pleasant— brief showers followed by blue skies and gleams of sun; sudden eddying gusts of wind succeeded by gentle breezes, damp and slow, that blew as from some inland water.

They did not stay long on the dome of the Panthéon. For one thing, they were afraid of wasting time; for another, the wind brought suddenly across the city roofs a driving rain that stung their faces. Besides, they felt themselves to be too near their usual haunts.

Nevertheless, true to their role of sightseers, they looked about them with exploring eyes. The rain hung like a curtain, insistent though not concealing. Seen from here, Paris, they found, spread all its history before them to a far greater extent than they had anticipated.

"Rather as it looked that day from the College roof," said Jerphanion, "only there's more of it. One can see farther, and one's less dependent on the foreground."

The number of monuments seemed beyond all measure. Mellowed by time they looked, made rich by the memory of old solemnities. Swift to the watching mind there came the thought of endless institutions, and ceremonies more than it could count. The garden fronts of houses, courtyards, rows of windows, showed as sudden patches, light or dark, revealing here an ornament, there some noble contour, withdrawn, it seemed, into a world that was not that of every day. Even the distant quarters of the city and the suburbs looked as though they had long formed part of some pageant of pomp and circumstance, set with their duties and their toil upon the lighted stage of history. The Seine seemed farther off than might have been expected, and had the air of flowing between banks heavy with curious secrets.

When they came out of the Panthéon, the rain had stopped.

"Just our luck" said Jallez, "to be down here in the street as soon as the distance clears."

On their way down the Montagne Saint-Geneviève they passed through the rue Descartes. Jallez thought of Verlaine, of Verlaine's death, but said nothing. A little later they drew near the river, reaching it at the bridge of Notre-Dame. To their left Jallez saw the shop of Messein the bookseller, successor to Vanier, and once more his mind was full of Verlaine. But this time the subject of his brooding gave rise to another association for which he had no difficulty in finding words.

"You saw that Henri de Régnier was elected to the Academy the other day? I couldn't help feeling rather pleased about it."

For a moment or two he seemed lost in reverie; then:

"It's such an age since they last chose a real poet. Most of the time they just sit on anything that's really great. . . . Do you remember that summer evening—some time ago now—when we discussed the persecution of the true Church? The Academy played a prominent part in that game. As a matter of fact, it's been becoming iess and less significant ever since the middle of the nineteenth century. Before that, it is true, it made a good many mistakes, was often dim, and absorbed a fair number of nonentities, but sooner or later almost all the really important men did find their way into its fold, and since they weren't inevitably wirepullers or social climbers, one's forced to the conclusion that wirepulling and social climbing were only necessary for the second-raters. The great Romantic period was the last to be adequately represented. From that moment it's really extraordinary how the Academy deteriorated. Take the greatest of the poets, the men whose names have already become classic, and note how an evil chance seems to have kept every one of them from being elected: Baudelaire, Banville, Verlaine, Mallarmé, Moréas, even

Samain! With the novelists the rot had begun to set in earlier still: Stendhal, Balzac, Flaubert, Barbey d'Aurevilly, Maupassant, Zola, Daudet, Huysmans—all the really *great* writers in their various fields. . . . Then there's the theatre . . . a few of the dramatists did get in . . . but Becque didn't, and you'll see Courteline won't. . . . One could write a pretty sound history of French literature since the Romantic period simply by taking care to mention the name of no single Academician. And yet not all the great men I've mentioned were vagabonds and drunkards. Even if they had been, why should it have mattered? A good few of the Academicians of 1760 boozed and womanized. . . . It wasn't Richelieu who founded the thing, but Montyon. . . . So when one sees that a man like Régnier's been elected, although one can't help feeling that there must have been a good deal of scheming to get him there, and that he must have had the deuce of a job to get himself forgiven for the literary company he kept, and for the sin of having talent, one can't help being a bit pleased about it, and thinking that perhaps there is a principle of justice at the heart of things, and that spirit can move mountains. The thought of the dead comes back to one—of Verlaine, Mallarmé, Moréas, and all the rest who were persecuted for the faith. . . ."

Suddenly his tone changed:

"Not," he said, "that it matters a damn, any of it."

"You honestly believe that?" Jerphanion asked.

"With my hand on my heart."

"Why, then, do quite decent and disinterested folk get into such a state about the Academy? Why, you do it yourself. . . . You certainly weren't talking just now as though it didn't matter a damn."

"Ah, but that's for the sake of the past. The Academy's the oldest of our great institutions; it was brilliant once, and it's difficult to resign oneself without a struggle to the thought of what it's become. Suppose the Observatory of Paris, still with its great name, still housed in its old buildings, dwindled some day into the sort of place where a lot of old men showed the moon through a telescope to country bumpkins and soldiers on a spree, at a penny a peep—shouldn't we at moments feel affronted at the change? Still, so far as the Academy's concerned, I do think one's a fool perhaps to let oneself get angry. In fact, I'm not at all sure that people like Régnier oughtn't to refuse election unless it were accompanied by a definite undertaking that the whole place was to be reformed from top to bottom. Actually, they know perfectly well that there's no chance of such a thing. They realize that they've got in on false pretences, either by accident or for reasons that have nothing to do with their merits, and that in so far as the Academy knows who they are, it has admitted them against its better judgment just to score off the folk who are always casting 'modern' literature and 'new' poetry in its teeth. 'How can you say,' it cries, 'that I'm not up to date, not contemporary, that I'm superannuated, when I've just elected young Henri de Régnier, who's a decadent poet and a writer of vers libre? What more do you want?' It needn't bother its head for another ten or fifteen years over any writer, poet or whatever, of really first-class importance. All it's got to do is to exclaim: 'But surely you've forgotten, it's only yesterday that I let one of them in. . . .' And Régnier will shout as loud as any of them. It's only human nature. It must be rather pleasant to say to oneself: 'The Academy as it is at present dislikes either originality or talent. Such dislike can be overcome only in the case of an exceptional individual with a great movement of public admiration behind him, and it's unreasonable to look for such a phenomenon every day.' Why, look how they elected Roujon only a week after Régnier. Roujon, I ask you!—a man, I'm told, who's the author of a pretty little novel which he wrote in the intervals of being a civil servant. And then think of Zola, of Flaubert. . . . What a world!"

"You must remember that Roujon had nobody against him except that wretched Allory."

"It was all in the family. Allory'll get in all right, don't worry your head about that. They'll pile up their Roujons and their Allorys just as makeweights for Régnier. On second thoughts, I was a fool to be so pleased about Régnier; as a matter of fact, his election merely perpetuates the present ridiculous state of affairs. Look at the Academy of Fine Arts: *their* goose has been properly cooked. It's a matter of general knowledge that since the beginning of the impressionist movement not a single painter or sculptor of the first rank has ever got in. Everything that's been done of any importance has been done outside it or definitely in opposition to it. There's something fantastic in even imagining that Rodin could be honoured by being made a member. . . . If all the great writers and great poets had declared publicly: 'You wouldn't have our great predecessors, so you can do without us,' the Academy's goose would have been cooked in just the same way."

"Well, that's not happened. . . . What strikes *you* most about it all, I think, is the abstract injustice of the affair, the *intellectual* scandal; but I'm chiefly concerned about another aspect of the situation. What occupies *my* mind is the thought of the people hidden away in the country, the sort of people I spring from, the petty, semi-educated bourgeois, the local intellectuals, thousands and thousands of little schoolmasters and others, who have never been warned and go on thinking of the Academy in terms of its past, thinking of it as a collection of all that is brightest and best in the national genius. . . . They've been misled. And since the Academy makes pronouncements, enunciates judgments, gives decisions, and even takes sides in public controversies, this fact that they've been misled can easily have serious consequences. What it comes to is this: that they've been led to suppose that the Academy is capable of taking the lead and showing the way . . . all because in the eighteenth century, for example, everything that was daring in the thought of the period was embodied in its members, whereas in fact it merely makes use today of the reputation accruing to it from the past in order to prevent things getting done, to slow down the wheels of progress, and to support a policy of frightened conservatism fit only for a lot of old women. All it can say is: 'Not that way!' and 'Go back!' Look at it for a moment from another point of view.

Assume some historian of the cold, objective, sociological type to be examining the fabric of French society. Well, starting without any preconceived ideas and driven merely by the logic of facts, he finds himself forced to regard the Academy since its foundation as a sort of barometer of public opinion, or, to be more precise, as a barometer of public opinion in matters of intellectual achievement. He is struck, as you have been, as anybody must be, by the way the mercury in this barometer has dropped during the last fifty years, right down to the bottom, and he can't resist the conclusion that this drop corresponds to something in the public conscience. Even allowing, therefore, that in itself the present state of the Academy is of no very great importance, it immediately becomes important as a symptom. For it shows that our society is old and sick, that, as the result of some deep-seated weakness, it rejects all that is best in itself, acquiesces in the second-rate, and manufactures a group of leaders who are warped and imperfect. A doctor by looking at your finger-nails can tell that you need drastic treatment. It may be that only by looking at the Academy a historian can see that France needs a Revolution."

Jallez did not need much pressing to agree. The best way of rousing his revolutionary enthusiasm, as Jerphanion had long ago discovered, was by working on the indignation which he felt at sight of any example of intellectual chaos. He was careful, however, to add a comment:

"I admit that every kind of injustice is rife, that indiscipline in things of the mind marks our national culture. I see no inherent improbability in tracing a connexion between the expansion of a grubby middle-class capitalism which has gradually muddied the whole of the nineteenth century, and the degradation of the Academy —to go no further than the Academy in our search for symptoms. But I am inclined to wonder whether the people who would actually make the Revolution, preoccupied, as they would be, by purely political and economic considerations, would do much to help the cultural situation. I can't make up my mind about it. The low level of public taste is the result, not of the supremacy of money, but of the rule of the majority. Merely to ensure the economic freedom of the majority isn't enough to ensure a spiritual renaissance. *My Baby* appeals to a very much greater number of people than Mélisande's theme in *Pelléas*. I have a horrible feeling that for most people the ideal future State would be a place where they could hum *My Baby* while fishing on the river-bank. The suppression of capitalism won't make working men take any less pleasure in singing *My Baby*. We can hope to disgust them with it only by dint of long and patient labour. It's not enough that they should like something else better; they must be made to realize that until they do like something else better, conditions for them won't really have altered at all. I should like to feel sure that the revolutionary leaders and their followers had got hold of this truth. The Revolution will be a *spiritual* blessing only if it replaces an aristocracy of money by an aristocracy of intellect capable of giving to the masses leading ideas, taste, and a sense of values. . . ."

About one thing they were in complete agreement—namely, that the commonplace generalization about "old institutions" being a danger to the life of any society was based upon a profound truth. (It is true to say that profound and unalterable truths may lie, as it were, imprisoned and latent within a formula whose triteness repels the curious mind.) The social animal may be immortal, but its organs grow old and will, unless they are removed, result in death for the whole. But there are ways in which the fortunate animal can rid itself of outworn organs and replace them by new ones. This labour of renewal is very exhausting and takes on all the features of an acute sickness. When that happens it is called Revolution. Needless to add that it is no good waiting to achieve this renewal until the animal is dead.

Chapter 37

HOW TO MAKE AN "ACADEMY"

Jallez and Jerphanion proceeded to imagine that a Revolutionary Government had laid upon them the duty of creating for France an entirely new Academy. Such a thing could be done only by decree. There would have to be no explanations, merely a giving of orders, a statement that such and such "is our pleasure." Individuals concerned would not be consulted, nor would they be asked to mend their ways. Public opinion would not be considered. In times of upheaval there can be no advantage in letting public opinion express itself directly, since the very fact of upheaval assumes that public opinion is in an unhealthy state.

Reformist zeal led them to the preliminary decision that no members of the present Academy should be admitted to its successor.

"By accepting election they have shown a willingness to acquiesce in present conditions which must make them highly suspect."

The case of Anatole France, however, made them pause. Hadn't he redeemed the initial error by refusing to take part in any of its sittings? The mathematician Henri Poincaré was excused on the ground that he had acted from lack of judgment (which, alas, was only to be expected of a man of science, if those at the College were to be taken as typical). Exceptions, as they proceeded, became more and more numerous. Jerphanion insisted on rescuing Barrés and Loti, and Jallez said that in that case he must ask clemency for Bourget and Rostand. To this first list of acquittals were added, for various reasons, and after much belittling and vexatious criticism, Marcel Prévost, Maurice Donnay, Brieux, and later still, Faguet, Lemaître, Richepin—as being King of "Cubes" —and, of course, Régnier. This gave an irreducible total of thirteen.

Twenty-seven places remained to be filled. To avoid serious mistakes, they decided to do as they had done in the case of their game of "preferences" and adjourn to a bar where they could put down their decisions on paper. The first one they came to was in the rue de Richelieu, opposite the National Library. The double coincidence seemed to augur well.

Certain new rules were adopted: admission of foreigners, provided they had contributed to the glory of the French language, and the admission of women. After considerable argument they agreed to abide by the traditional usage of the Academy and, while seeking recruits primarily from among writers, to admit a few eminent practitioners from other walks of life.

They proceeded next to nominate those about whom there could be no argument, preferred as they were by the insistent—if sometimes rather mysterious—voice of fame. This first choice gave: Verhaeren, Claudel, Maeterlinck, Jammes, Jules Renard, Paul Fort, Courteline; and these were joined almost at once, by reason of achievement in their specialized, though not strictly literary, fields, by Jaurès, Bergson, Debussy, Rodin, Jean Perrin, and André Antoine. A second group followed hard on the heels of these, consisting of Gide, Paul Adam, d'Annunzio (in recognition of his *Saint-Sébastien*), the Comtesse de Noailles, Claude Monet, the elder Rosny, in spite of his catch-penny novels, Maurras, in spite of his fanaticism, Porto-Riche, in spite of his "smartness," Romain Rolland, in spite of what Gourmont called his muddy style, Gourmont himself, in spite of his limited outlook, and Elémir Bourges, as a "precautionary measure." This last consideration was put forward by Jallez, who admitted that to him Bourges seemed as an author empty, silly, and almost unreadable.

After counting up these names they found that only three vacancies remained. For these there were about a dozen candidates, many of them with strong claims. Jerphanion pressed strongly for Ferdinand Brunot, maintaining that it would be scandalous if an institution which set itself up to lay down rules for the language did not include the only man who really knew its history. He was inclined to regard favourably the election of Émile Fabre, whose *Ventres dorés* he had much admired, and of Dürkheim, who, he said, deserved a place next to Bergson. Jallez agreed about Brunot, but put forward Tristan Bernard as an alternative to Fabre and argued that if they'd got to have a philosopher, Lévy-Bruhl was better than Dürkheim. He said, too, that they ought to give wider representation to criticism and the art of the essay. Suarès, Thibaudet, Péguy, Alain? The last two were still very young, the first was becoming long-winded, the third was obscure. Jallez felt kindly towards *Images de Grèce* and *Images de la Grandeur*. He remembered certain phrases of Alain's, close-packed as crystals.

But the sky was clearing, the sun was good, the wind keen. The finest Academy in the world would grow old like its predecessors, and, like them, would have to be killed. There was something better to do than shut up forty good brains in a museum before they were dead.

The last vacancies remained unfilled.

Chapter

A PUZZLING ATTITUDE

They had climbed the Butte by its steepest face.

This was all part of the game. Having chosen to imitate the action of water finding its own level in their journey from the Panthéon to the Sacré-Cœur, it had seemed more honest and conclusive to take the most direct route. (It was hard, of course, to justify the interlude in the bar, but then, surely, every game admits of certain breaches, certain suspensions, of the rules? Even Louis Bastide had sometimes carried his hoop across a square.)

Jallez said:

"I adore this district."

He pointed to the rue des Martyres, rising before them like a true triumphal way, and to where, on the right, the little streets wound on from far beginnings, luring the feet to unseen goals, beckoning to adventure.

"Because of Hélène Sigeau?" Jerphanion asked.

"Perhaps."

Jerphanion next attacked Jallez on a point which the latter, ever since they had crossed the Boulevards, had seemed anxious to avoid (and not for the first time).

"There's one thing about you I don't understand and you've never explained. I understand it less and less because, since I knew you first, it has become more and more marked and because it seems now to respond less than it ever did to circumstances. . . . Yes . . . you've changed. . . ."

Jallez almost blushed; he seemed to be annoyed and worried.

"Changed? In what way?"

"Do you remember showing me one evening an article on the Latouche-Tréville explosion? We went on to talk a good deal about Baudelaire."

"I remember. It was, as a matter of fact, an article by one of these Academicians we've been discussing."

"Quite right. By that rotter Henri Lavedan, wasn't it?"

"Yes."

"To cut a long story short, you gave evidence of an indignation which delighted me. So far, so good. . . . Now try to remember what happened a little later. . . . I had come back from walking in the slums; my mind was all at sixes and sevens. You listened quite calmly to all I had to tell you of what I'd seen, of what you must have known about already from other sources. You didn't contradict me, but you were completely detached. . . . You'd begun to change then."

"I don't quite understand what you mean."

"How can I explain? . . . What I mean is this. You're not the kind of man who's insensitive to impressions . . . the kind of man who can go through a period of upheaval without thinking of anything but his office job or wondering how he can add to his collection of medals. . . ."

"Not such a bad kind of man to be!"

"Don't pretend. . . . That's not your type at all. . . . I've got an idea that you're fully alive to everything of importance that happens. In some ways you're extremely sensitive to injustice, to lack of order. You'd hate to take deliberate advantage of injustice. You're by nature a revolutionary. You don't acquiesce easily. You don't bow down to the idols of the market-place. You've not got that fear of the unknown which explains, I think, the faint-hearted attitude of so many. Only just now you were saying good things about revolution, but somehow—it's so difficult to explain—without conviction. . . . It amused you to reconstitute the Academy, but if I'd suggested reconstituting Society, you'd have let me play the game alone. . . . The deeper you go, the more completely do

FLOOD WARNING

I feel that you are detached from actuality. The worse conditions
become and the nearer we approach to a crisis, the less do you seem
to bother. If you were like that fellow who's just gone by with
his portfolio under his arm, probably some insurance agent or
something of that sort, I'd say that you felt it as all too remote,
too complicated, too tiring. He probably doesn't mind chatting
about the world now and then with a colleague who flatters himself that he's 'got ideas,' but if he thought about it too often, he'd
feel he'd got a screw loose or was becoming 'odd.' Up to now in
every society there's had to be a certain number of men like that
to make it possible for the chaps on top to carry on. . . . What
bothers me is that almost all the men of the seventeenth century
were of that kind, even men like Racine and Boileau. . . . They
said to themselves: 'These problems are no concern of ours. Let us
trust to the wisdom of our great Prince and of God, whose instrument he is.' I hope, for their sakes, that there was a bit of the
hypocrite about them, and that in the privacy of their own room
they sometimes murmured: 'When shall we get rid of this old
tyrant who's ruining and killing us with his magnificence?' It was
a fine time for the ruling classes. '89 messed it up a bit, but without finishing it. There are still millions of more or less willing
slaves who say: '*I* don't know anything about politics.' Will there
ever come a time when there are no slaves, when Democracy will
be a reality? But that's another question. Let's go back to you. . . .
I imagine that in the main you and I have the same presentiments
about the future. Are you so superficial that you won't bother your
head about it? . . . No, you're far from being superficial. . . .
So modest that you feel you're not competent to deal with it, and
that in any case there's nothing you can do? . . . No, I don't think
you're modest. I don't mean that in a bad sense, but you certainly
are not inhibited by modesty—thank Heaven! Nor are you the
kind of man who won't think about a thing because there's nothing practical he can do . . . which, anyhow, is a silly thing to
say, because even if he can't directly influence circumstances, a

man's always got to take up some personal attitude to them and has got to think that attitude out for himself."

Jallez smiled. "What exactly are you thinking of?" he asked.

"You know what's happening, you know what's occupying the mind of every man who thinks at all—are we going to avoid a war? As the months go on, fears recede or come nearer. One may say: 'I'm not going to think about it, I'm not going to let it poison my life or my youth . . .' but one can't alter the facts of the situation. . . . The war is the closest object on the horizon. Either it will happen or it won't—we shall soon know—but whether it happens or doesn't happen, there's still the other great event."

"Namely?"

"You know perfectly well what I'm referring to—the change *within* the structure of Society. Kindly note the care with which I avoid grandiloquent phrases. . . . Do you realize, my dear fellow, that unless we die in the mean time, we are bound to see all that happening? And happening how?—as a process of orderly planning or emerging from chaos? I admit that to answer that question is beyond me. I try to think about it, but after a minute or two my mind becomes confused. If we fail to keep the peace in Europe and war breaks out, will it, in the long run, hamper or assist the Revolution? I can't say, I can't guess. . . . Anything seems to me to be possible. . . . But that particular mystery is not what's bothering me just now; it's *you* who are bothering me. Do you really wash your hands of war? Do you really wash your hands of Revolution?"

For a few moments Jallez said nothing. When he did speak, it was in a voice that betrayed sincere embarrassment:

"The indiscretion of your questions is devastating. . . . I don't want to have secrets from you, but there are things that I avoid, where possible, putting into words, even in the privacy of my mind, lest by formulating them too haphazardly I may detract from their importance and generally cheapen them. It's perfectly true, of course, that thoughts which have never been expressed cannot, in any real sense, be said to exist at all, and that one is rightly suspicious of a too facile retreat, no matter how private and personal it may be, into the sham transcendental and the sham profound. But it's also true that a form of expression into which one may have been tempted some day when one happened to be in an eloquent mood has a way of perpetuating itself even in despite of one's later and better judgment. It ceases to be a question of facts on one side and you on the other, and becomes an arrangement of facts, yourself, and, between the two, like some third person who can't be got rid of, that unhappy definition of a passing moment. Sometimes the results are very serious, because one finds it impossible to recover the sense of the facts as one once perceived them, and discovers that one can possess them only in the verbal form into which they have been forced. . . . Let me try to explain what I mean more clearly.

"I am here, in this street, in direct contact with everything that surrounds me. A thousand details take form and vanish. My consciousness includes equally this crack between two paving-stones and the casual meeting of those two women. I am aware of the movement that each makes to avoid the other, of their effort to recover the direction in which they were walking before they met. I am aware of the thousands of simultaneous things going on around me which no eye can catch, secret things, things that have more affinity to music than to anything else. . . . In short, of the continuity of life, of its sound, and of the underlying quality of that sound which it is impossible for our sense of hearing to register. I can only describe it by the word 'endurance.' An endurance comparable to that of great forests, of grassy plains that harbour myriads of insects. They have a way, all these things, of submitting their lives to the season, of patiently awaiting the changes of the year. They are affected and modified only by changes recurring over long periods, by time cycles. Do you understand what I mean? An order of nature, a profound organization of existence, which makes of this spot of Paris a part of nature, with all that nature has to give to man of peace and mystery and contact which no words can explain. Then I think of one of those theorists you and I know so well. I see him sitting at his table covered with books, working away at his notes. He cares for nothing beyond knowing whether some particular theory of value, or of the division of labour, or of profit, is consistent or inconsistent with some other competing theory. He is intent only on determining by statistics whether or no capitalism is evolving along some preconceived line of development. . . . And I get the idea—the illusion, if you prefer the word—that a man like that is working away, not perhaps·with his head in the clouds, I won't go so far as to say that, because I admit that such problems are real and important, but on the surface of things only, that he is concerned with forms that are relatively superficial and quickly outmoded, and that the things which interest me, which move and affect me nearly, are at a deeper level. I say 'relatively superficial.' I admit that the forms in question do ultimately have an effect on the facts of life, but the facts are stubborn; they resist such treatment and pursue their destined way. What I mean is that there is a way of approaching sociological problems which seems to me to be purely superficial. I would even say that what is usually described by that word is, in itself, superficial. I would go further still and maintain that history itself suffers from the same fault, strictly in confidence, of course, because such a statement might seem to be merely foolish and perverse. . . . Let me illustrate my meaning in this way: Let us assume that while we're here in the rue des Martyres, while we're in the very act of crossing the avenue Trudaine, a revolution breaks out at the City Hall or at the Élysée. The whole régime changes completely. Well what of it? Everything here goes on just as before, and this particular section of the city calmly accomplishes its fundamental destiny."

"But you must admit that sometimes the events of history do influence essentials, do, as it were, plough up the field."

"Oh, obviously. . . . But please remember that I'm not trying to prove a theory. You wanted to know the reason for my attitude, and I'm trying—I warned you that I was a bad hand at explanations. . . . I'll tell you another of my convictions. Suppose I was walking at this very moment along a street in some other capital—London perhaps, or Berlin. I'm quite sure that I should feel perfectly at home there and in familiar contact with everything that surrounded me, that I should be aware of a whole heap of things which would have the power to delight and inspire me, to work on me with a sort of secret intimacy. In such a case the *real* would be the street in which I happened to be, and *myself*. If during that time the chancelleries of Europe happened to be exchanging acrid notes, it would be the chancelleries that would be living in the phenomenal world of chance and change. . . . Once more let me insist that I'm not trying to convince you. You have asked me a question, and I want to make you realize that, by dint of constant thought and a special kind of training, one can, without being either mad, trivial, or egotistical, arrive at a state of mind in which one perceives and experiences the facts of life in a certain way. Secure in this state of mind, one sees from afar, and with a detachment which is perfectly sincere, that other state of mind which occupies itself with all those occurrences which we've got into the habit of calling political, sociological, historical, and national. Such a condition brings great tranquillity. . . . I know better how to attain it than I did once, you will say. Perhaps. That's what you mean when you say I have changed. And now let me say that I'm glad to have had the opportunity of talking about it just here."

"But doesn't all that mean merely that you're drugging yourself or intoxicating yourself with the trivial facts of daily existence in order to avoid thinking of the things that really matter?"

Jallez looked faintly disappointed.

"Certainly not. . . . If that's the effect my words have had, I must have explained myself very badly. . . . Let me give you an analogy. We will assume that you are a young, deeply religious, perhaps even a slightly mystical priest. You pass in your walk the various people we see here around us—this street pedlar, that woman with the tormented eyes, the child playing alone over there. What matters to you, what you automatically ask yourself, is something like this: 'Is God helping that woman in her pain? Is she near to, or far from, God? Is her agony helping her to find salvation? Or are her feet set on the path to damnation?' You note the expression on the pedlar's face, at once foolish, calculating, and jovial, and you wonder whether he is ever troubled by even a suspicion of religious doubt. . . . You fall to questioning whether the child is being brought up by unbelieving parents, whether the idea of God has ever occurred to it except as forming part of an oath. . . . You find yourself considering what must be the condition of a human soul in utter loneliness. Now suppose somebody tells you that you are bothering yourself about trifles, that what really matters is the condition of the police administration which issues a licence to the pedlar, or the amount of his daily earnings, or what school the child attends, or whether his father is or is not a trade-unionist . . . you won't consider such comments particularly apposite. You may be ready to admit that it's not everybody who can take the spiritual point of view, but if that happens to be your point of view, you're not going to abandon it merely because somebody says that the spiritual is of secondary importance. . . . What I've been trying to describe to you is a sort of spiritual plane within the life of the community, and the tranquillity which it gives."

He added in a lower tone:

"You mentioned the name of Hélène Sigeau. Many of our joint experiences took place in this neighbourhood. I think I've told you of the sort of peace of mind she exemplified for me . . . of the attitude of surrender which I learned from her. . . . Yes, learned, for when it comes to that, I think that nobody ever taught me so much as did Hélène Sigeau. . . . I don't know whether I managed to convey all that when I talked about her before. . . . I don't want to lose that sense as of private music which surrounded us

as we walked the streets so long ago. Indeed, I want to impreg-
nate with the virtue and the saving grace which it gave all the
circumstances of my life as I have lived it since I knew her; I want
to make permanently my own that power of floating in the current of things which came to me then, not of my own choice, but
from my association with her."

Jerphanion walked on a moment or two deep in thought. He
made one or two casual remarks, then:

"I think," he said, "that I do understand now a little of what
you mean. I don't think I could ever practise that particular form
of quietism, but I admit that it's possible. It must, at times, taste
curiously sweet. . . . It is, if you like to put it so, the detachment
of the philosopher, the outcome not of a withdrawal from human
affairs, but rather, paradoxical though such a statement may seem,
of a close and intimate contact—at least that's how you think of
it—with the immediate place and the immediate moment. It's a
kind of nirvana attained not by the practice of solitude, but by
its careful elimination. Am I right? . . . But even if I could reach
such a state, I don't believe I should find much comfort in it.
It seems to me that this attitude of yours is only possible for you
because so far you have not been exposed to any very severe
shocks. But whatever your point of view may be, there's one
question which you've no right to ignore. What shocks are in store
for us? Even if you care nothing about politics or history or the
nation, even if you hold all those things to be nothing but a
scratching of the surface, you must ask yourself to what extent,
in the next few years, that surface-scratching will affect the roots
of things, what profound changes it will bring, in what way we
shall have to face it. Look at the matter from the point of view of
pure individualism (and, speaking generally, there's a good deal
in common between individualism and mysticism). A man might
well say: 'I've been born into this epoch without my choice. What
interests me is *myself*, my way of dealing with the general situation,
the general direction that I can manage to give to my life. . . . But

the epoch doesn't seem to be one of those in which a man can live to himself alone. What is in store for me?' You can't help asking yourself that question, as I do, as we all do: 'What is in store for us?' Reduce the problem to its simplest form, you can't help saying to yourself: 'If there's a war, or a revolution, or both, what will be the effect *on me?*'"

Jallez smiled.

"Possibly," he said.

He looked at Jerphanion and added:

"We might be excused for answering: 'Wait and see'—because we are young, because events are infinite in their possible combination, because, too, whatever admirable resolutions we may make now, we shall sooner or later turn them upside down ourselves without waiting for the processes of history to do it for us. Do you remember one day when we were discussing the problem of women that you said very wisely: 'It's difficult to dogmatize, to say what exactly one would do. . . . It all depends so much on whom one may meet . . . on the person . . .'"

Chapter

SOME NOT VERY CREDITABLE CONFESSIONS

Five minutes later, when they had reached the big flight of steps in the rue Foyatier, just in front of the school where Jaurès had lectured, Jerphanion had become involved in certain very intimate confidences.

"I'm damnably worried. Am I in love with her? you'll ask. Oh yes, I'm in love with her all right, but neither you nor I are the sort of men who use the word 'love' as a sort of magic formula with a definite and unalterable meaning. A man can love a woman without losing his head about her. He may even lose his head about her and yet be so divided in his mind as to call himself a fool for doing so. One thing's quite certain: I'm more in love with her than I have been with any woman up to now."

"Including the tailor's wife?"

"Yes, including the tailor's wife. . . . But that proves less than you might think. What irritates me most is the feeling that I've let myself become the victim of circumstances. One never sees things straight until they've happened. We laugh at the cautious fellows who do nothing on instinct, who plan out every action beforehand. We say they've got no sense of poetry. I know all about that. But it annoys me to have to take stock of a situation now which I ought to have foreseen clearly six months ago."

"Forgive my insistence—but what exactly is the situation?"

"Simply this: that one can't fall in love with a girl like Mathilde and let her respond, no matter how honourable one's intentions, as they say, without a lot of other questions automatically arising. In this case there's the additional complication that Clanricard was in love with her and was perfectly prepared to marry her. In fact, I think he was anxious to do so. You realize, of course, that the idea of a love-affair, even of a serious love-affair, didn't frighten me in itself. In a way I was just waiting for one to come along. But I thought of it as something purely lyrical and romantic. I no more thought of it in terms of marriage than—oh—in terms of taking my degree."

"One question, just one—the only one I shall ask. Do you want to get out of it?"

They climbed the staircase, one on each side of the double iron balustrade that divided it. Now and again they touched it with their hands, but the metal was cold and hostile, and worn so smooth that it felt greasy. The west wind, blowing on to the side of the slope through one of the narrow side-streets, played above the unfinished gardens and went on its way to the eastern hills, which shone far off like the promised land. It brought with it a sense of gaiety, a sort of irresponsibility bred of the sea. Jallez, without noticing what he was doing, started to hum the sailor's song from *Tristan*. A feeling of Brittany was in the air, of separations as inevitable as the returning tides, of passions destined for impermanence as clearly as though they bore some white mark on their foreheads, of deep things treated lightly. It was a wind heavy perhaps with the tears of women left, but comforting for men with its promise of release and healing counsel.

Jerphanion had not yet answered his friend's question.

"Let me ask you something else first," said Jallez; "it will give you time to think out your answer. To what extent do you regard yourself as bound?"

"To an extent which I alone can judge. That's the trouble. It's one of those cases in which the situation rather than any definite person tells you that you're free to behave like a cad."

"Oho!"

"What?"

"I mean that Situations—to use your own word—are usually only as frank as that with people like ourselves. With real cads they're apt to be less expansive. I strongly urge you not to let the situation get you down."

"It's all very well to talk like that. In similar circumstances you—"

He left the sentence unfinished. They climbed a few more steps. Jerphanion changed his tone:

"I don't want to give you a false idea. If the whole thing came to an end, of its own accord, tomorrow; or if Mathilde broke it off . . . I should be very sorry; I should probably be terribly cut up. You see, what makes me pause is not what you might like to call my natural perversity, but a sort of general prejudice in favour of freedom which I've always had up to now—and still have. But I don't want this prejudice to stand in the way of my doing what, perhaps, in the depths of my being I really want to do. . . . Look here, there's something I hardly like to ask you. You met Mathilde once, for a very short time, I know, but—"

"For five minutes."

"Oh no, it must have been at least half an hour. Still, even that's short enough. I'd set my heart on that meeting, but I managed it badly. Tell me, what was your impression of her?"

"I told you at the time."

"I know, but tell me again, or tell me your later and more considered opinion."

"I remember that I thought her pretty . . . and, yes, unspoilt, sincere, light-hearted . . . very simple. . . . I should say she's a thoroughly good girl. Is that enough? I can hardly say more without looking a presumptuous fool."

Jerphanion's voice as he asked his next question was anxious and subdued:

"Not perhaps a tiny bit vulgar?"

"Certainly not. She's of a Southern type, and that's not, perhaps, quite so refined as some. But she has a charming voice. I share your liking for that particular quality of tone she has, and for just that amount of brogue."

"I mean more from the point of view of education, of intellectual training."

"How can I possibly say?"

"But you must have got some sort of an impression."

"I should say she's intelligent and quick-witted. It would surprise me to hear that she let herself be seriously worried by ideas, even by yours. But that's probably all to the good. I imagine that you don't want a blue-stocking or a woman like Louise Michel?"

"I see; you're not very enthusiastic about her; is that it?"

Jallez waited a few moments before replying.

"I thought I'd said nothing but good of her. . . . But if what you want is for me to take you by the shoulders and *push* you into this marriage—and that's what it comes to, isn't it?—I think I should refuse."

A prolonged gust of wind helped them up the last few steps. Rather sadly, rather solemnly, Jallez said:

"I see now, you old ruffian, why you wanted seven to eight thousand francs a year!"

THE NORTHERN SUBURBS ONCE MORE

When they reached the dome after a long, dark climb, Jerphanion, fascinated by the brilliance of the sky seen through the vista of slender columns, set himself at once to breathe in the vast seas of air which spread around them, while Jallez, leaning on the inner balustrade, lost himself in contemplation of the depths of the church.

"Come here a moment," he said; "doesn't it look odd?"

At the bottom of a great gulf of darkness, far below them, and widening as the gaze descended, lights were moving in a circle, one behind another. They were large, heavy, and slightly diffused. They moved slowly in a broken figure of eight. The two watchers were suspended, as it were, over the very centre of the abyss, which seemed to broaden more and more and to plunge far below the level of the earth. It was hard not to imagine it as a sort of nether firmament, a section torn from the sky and dropped into these depths. The lights were not like stars, at least not like any stars known to us. Their size, their movement, the way they crept along in single file, their round and misty radiance, brought to mind the phosphorescence of worms or caterpillars, the *ghosts* of stars. Yes, phosphorescent ghosts was what they looked like, ghosts of animals or ghosts of the universe. Seen from this distance, it was impossible to guess how large they really were.

"It must be some procession in the church," said Jerphanion; "it looks extraordinary, seen from here."

They exchanged a glance of mutual and smiling understanding, eloquent of a dozen unspoken thoughts. Then they turned away from the darkness at their feet and went to look on Paris.

They surrendered themselves at first to the sensations of the place, to its strangeness, its mere height. It formed a balcony open on every side to the vast spaces of the sky. Beneath, the enormous dome swept downwards, white in colour, set with scale-shaped tiles, a great, dazzling curve that was touched with grey towards the east, a balloon with its car not slung, but set atop, like a howdah on an elephant's back. A wild and gusty wind tore at its sturdy immobility. It was the horizon that seemed to move and shake in the onset of the gale.

No vestige here of the "historic city." Rather, what lay before them looked like some huge surface quickened by a power that for long ages had worked upon the matter of the globe, moulding it to a form, driving it to an expression of violence, such as humanity had never known till now. Among many extraordinary things, not the least extraordinary was that a man could comprehend it thus within the limits of his vision (as amazing as his power to see at a glance the whole sweep of the night sky, perhaps more so).

They looked towards the west, which was very beautiful in the stormy glow of the setting sun (the city on that side seemed responsive to every change of light); towards the south, where the texture of the town merged into an indefinite distance of grassy slopes and patches of forest; towards the east, where a seeming cliff of white and gleaming brilliance led the eye onwards to grey distances, exciting and unplumbed, a land of mystery where a man might wander for ever, seeking and finding without end. But it was the north, there behind the tower, that held their eyes the longest, because they had so seldom had occasion to see it at all, and because from this high vantage-point they saw it as they could never have seen it from elsewhere.

They were close to the northern suburbs, which began almost at their feet and could be easily distinguished, separated from the lower districts of Montmartre by the line of the old fortifications. They showed a huddle of stark, uncompromising buildings, some very long, others reared upwards on their ends. Here and there squat

blocks of factories, separated by naked squares of earth, were set
in irregular files, one behind the other. Smoke-stacks by the dozen,
of varying heights, stood in compact groups, like lances of some army
of old days, like the masts of ships in a harbour, like batteries of guns
aimed upwards at the sky. Some of them were smoking. Now and
again above the plain, white puffs in twos and threes, drifting in
different directions, showed where trains were moving. The whistling of locomotives came up to them, detached from their points of
origin, and sounding like the voice of all this vastness.

There was nothing specially threatening about the view, only the
sense of something different, something not yet achieved; an air
of uncertainty about the place and the plan; territory occupied in
haste by forces impatient for the next advance. Seeing it thus, an
observer found himself thinking suddenly of camps, seeing in
imagination beneath the rising smoke the flames of bivouac fires.

Jerphanion let his mind play vaguely round the picture of some
great critical period of history; of Rome, heavy with age and riches,
a great fruit ripe to rottenness; and there, beyond the northern slopes,
of some encampment of barbarian hosts. For a long time now, for
years, their tents had been pitched. They were growing restive, were
making raids for plunder. But so far the City had not been entered.
What were they waiting for? What was it that still held them back?
Could it be that, having come so far, they didn't really want to enter? Or were they afraid? Possibly. They wouldn't want to confess
the feeling of respect that moved them at sight of this great and
famous Rome, of all this complex life of which they could make no
use. They were waiting until they had grown accustomed to it all.
But to what? Not, surely, to the complexity which for so long had
been before their eyes, but rather to the fact of its nearness, and also,
perhaps, to the fact of waiting.

"What are you thinking of?" Jallez asked.

On the point of telling his thought, Jerphanion found it naïve,
crude, and stupid. The analogy with which he had dallied seemed
to him now one of those swollen and rhetorical ideas with which

dull minds are fond of playing—fit only for a moment's unspoken reverie.

All that he said in answer was:

"I was thinking that of all this spreading view, this northern suburb is, perhaps, what moves me most—just the sight of it, without any thought of all the life that it conceals."

"Why do you think it affects you like that?"

"I don't know. . . . It has a quality of drama all its own. . . . I can't find words for what I mean. . . . It speaks to me of our present, and of that future which will be so difficult. . . . But it doesn't depress me. . . ."

SUMMARY

Early morning in the northern suburbs. Broad streets and narrow lanes. The suburb's growth; its vitality and its importance in the life of Paris. Industrial development and the growth of the trade unions. Two powers face to face—the General Strike of October 1910. The mobilization of the railwaymen.

Edmond Maillecottin goes to work. The money he makes; his position in the Bertrand factory; his experience as a worker. Bertrand's industrial psychology. Specialization and mass production. —Bertrand and Champcenais, who has come to see him, discuss the political and social situation.

Briand's day-dream. His unfortunate phrase in the Chamber; the ballots. The nature of Government; personal power.—Gurau, waiting in the anteroom, chews the cud of bitterness and disappointment. He turns his attention to Foreign Affairs. His vague sense of physical discomfort.—He refuses the Cabinet post offered him by Briand.

Accouchement of Mme Maieul. Her sufferings and her thoughts. The little Françoise leaves the dark comfort of the womb.—Maillecottin meets his girl, Georgette. He takes his midday meal in the Route de la Révolte. "The big noises." Edmond keeps an appointment with Isabelle, who asks him to help her save Romuald Guyard.

Mionnet learns that his love-affair is suspected, and takes council with Émilienne. A serious meditation. Mionnet makes a show of force against Delhostal and takes steps to win the Bishop's support. Émilienne agrees to break with him.

Edmond obeys the magistrate's summons. His thoughts on the way to court. The world as he sees it.

Conversation between Mionnet and M. de Montsauche at Mme de Quingey's. The general opinion of Mionnet as given in a letter written by Mme G—.

Laulerque approaches the Caulaincourt bridge and has a strange experience. He meets Mathilde Cazalis and hears from her the story of Jerphanion.—A few days later he writes to her.—Mascot introduces Laulerque to M. Karl. The latter's trip to the South with Laulerque. Their day at Toulon, and their journey in the local train. The sea-coast; the White House and its caretaker. M. Karl half confides in Laulerque, who begins to wonder about the real objects of the Organization and about the adventure in which he has got himself involved.—On his return to Paris he receives a letter from Clanricard in which the latter speaks of his trouble.

Gurau's enthusiasm for Foreign Affairs; his activity on the committee, and his attitude to Pichon. His sources of information. Maykosen; his past, his contacts, the importance of personality. Gurau is haunted by the danger of war and by the Franco-German problem. His bodily ills.

Champcenais gives a dinner to Zülpicher, with whom he has recently entered into relations. The powerful steel-magnate proposes a partnership.—Agnes pours out her most private thoughts in a letter to her brother, Marc Strigelius. Marc's reply. He relates certain transactions of Zülpicher and Champcenais with the United Bank of Europe.

Laulerque gives a power of attorney for the purchase of the White House.—Gurau speaks to Briand of a resolution to be put in the Chamber by Jaurès. Briand shows him a threatening letter which he has received.—Laulerque, walking home, reads in the paper of an attempt on Briand's life and hurries to Mascot.—Goulvic pays a visit to Briand, the friend of his youth. Allory is dispirited as the result of his twenty-third attempt to canvass support for his candidature in the Academy.

Seated in their study, Jerphanion defends himself against Jallez's criticisms. Sacrifices involved in studying for a degree. A discussion of poverty.—The two friends start on a long walk. From the top of the Panthéon they see Paris as an expression of its historic past. Decadence of the French Academy. They play at reforming it. Jerphanion accuses Jallez of aloofness. Jallez tries to explain his state of mind. Jerphanion's confidences on the subject of Mathilde. The dome of the Sacré-Cœur. The northern suburbs.

BOOK TEN:

THE POWERS THAT BE

Chapter

STEPHEN BARTLETT'S TRAVEL DIARY

I'm not sure that I wasn't a fool to choose this subject for my new series of articles; or perhaps I'd have done better to find some *petit trou*[1] on the south coast and write them *de chic,* seated at a café table. The more I document myself on the spot, the more confused do I become.

I must confess, too, that I'm beginning, for the first time, to have doubts about my master Torchecoul. I'd been cynically counting on him to help me out, fully expecting him to provide me in the course of an hour's talk with a complete theory of *Les Pouvoirs* in France as new and as lucid as his theory of "Stratification." Can it be that he regards the question as too far removed from the sphere of Economics to think about? But the Shaksperian problem is still further removed. Perhaps he's tired. Other things make me think that that may be the explanation. When I pressed him on the point, he got out of it by means of one of his typically insolent comments on my countrymen. What he actually said was: "That's an odd thing for you to be bothering about—a bit too abstract, surely. Do you really think that English readers would make head or tail of it?"

I had to make some excuse to get back here. I've got to the stage of not being able to do without this uncomfortable country. I never stop laughing to myself about the things I see here, but I miss them as soon as I go away.

But did I really choose a subject so *calamiteux*? No; once more I've let myself be manœuvred into my present position by the man whom the presiding evil genius of England—which once inspired the Boston Tea-Party—has set at the head of one of our leading

[1] The words in italics are in French in Bartlett's manuscript.

newspapers. My single consolation is that I've learned enough by this time to see through his satanic plans even when I let myself be used to further them. Having employed me to rouse the hatred of the mob against the fine old English landed interest, having tried to reduce our wretched peers to a condition of starvation, his idea now is to strip them of the poor remnants of political power that still remain to them. I think I can detect Mr. Lloyd George's Welsh grin at the bottom of the plot. He's sworn to destroy the Upper House, or to reform it utterly, and first of all he wants to discredit it, to show it up as an anachronism as absurd as the procession of tenants at the young squire's coming of age. He doesn't want to destroy the Commons—after all, he must leave something—but he does want, by the same stroke, to alter the basis of representation so as to benefit the radicals. I've been sent here for the avowed purpose of observing the working of the French parliamentary machine, and the unavowed one of singing its praises. The idea is that my readers should be forced to exclaim: "How well these things are managed in France! What initiative the Chamber shows! How intelligent the Senate is, how modern, how sensible! Why can't we get rid of our wretched antediluvian Lords? The Commons, too, need a good deal of making over before they'll be as good as the Continental model."

(What part is the Right Honourable Mr. Asquith playing in all this? I used to think that he was merely a puppet in the hands of our Welsh wizard, but now that I've seen him in action I'm not so sure of his innocence.) So far as I'm concerned, I shall carry out my task of hired bravo in complete innocence of heart, for I know almost nothing about the English parliamentary system, and have thought about it still less. I've never, till now, had to concern myself professionally with it, and I naturally didn't go into the subject for pleasure when I was working in London. Only once did I listen to a Commons debate, and I'm hanged if I can remember what it was all about.

I've no idea what use the Upper House is, but if it disappears or loses its distinctive character as a result of this plot in which I've become involved, I shall be sorry. England, in my opinion, ought to be a country where completely useless institutions are preserved with the utmost care. It's the only thing that prevents us from becoming Americans.

I'm quite convinced that many of our individual peers arc fools, and that, regarded as a body, they are quite incapable of doing a serious job of work. But if we destroy them, we shall destroy a number of essential virtues which, God knows why, have chosen to fix themselves in this odd corner of the national life, much as musk has got itself secreted in the pouch of the musk-rat. That's my private opinion, but I shall be careful not to put it into words. I'm being paid to make the English ashamed of their Parliament.

That'll be easy enough, I think, so long as I haven't got to explain the subtle workings of the political machine. Yesterday I sat through a long session of the French Chamber. My brain's still in a whirl, but that doesn't mean that I wasn't delighted. What a varied and interesting sight it was! When I try and remember that Commons debate at which I was once present, I seem to conjure up the vision of a dignified and boring ceremony, in the course of which a lot of very formal gentlemen delivered set speeches interlarded with spinsterish jokes, in low voices and without paying the slightest attention to their audience, while the occupants of the neighbouring benches, who were the only people who could hear them, expressed their feelings in polite laughter. The whole thing was rather like the conferring of honorary degrees at Oxford. Here, on the other hand, what animation, what vitality, not only in the Chamber itself, but outside it too! The speakers behave as though they are rousing an enormous mob to frenzy. None of them are alike. The deputies never keep still for a moment. Sometimes whole groups, sitting together, jump up shaking their fists in the same direction and uttering cries of fury, while with their disengaged hands they bang the lids of their desks, which, being hollow, make a grand row. In the *couloirs* they get together and argue in crowds, seizing and shaking

one another by the lapels of their coats. Then, suddenly, these con-
claves are interrupted, and their component members dash back into
the Chamber by the first open door just as if they were going to
rescue their wives and children from a fire. The ushers keep an
anxious eye on the fray, ready at any moment to dash between the
more violent of the gentlemen, whom it seems to be their special
duty to watch. Even the public galleries catch the general infection.
I'm not surprised that somebody last month fired a revolver from
one of them. It must be very tempting if one happens to have a
revolver, and can follow what's going on.

I was prepared for the general slovenliness of the members, but
it quickened my former impressions. The number of beards is enormous. (I've had to revise some of my earlier views about the popularity of beards in France. I asked one of my colleagues about them,
and he assures me that they are extremely common among the provincial middle classes, and almost universally worn by those who
pursue the more serious callings, or like to be thought to, such as
medicine or the law; hence their prevalence in Parliament.) I'm
rather afraid that I shall have to reconsider my conclusions about
dress as well. Isn't it perhaps insular prejudice that makes me think
that most Frenchmen are badly dressed? When, in the Chamber, I
see endless pairs of trousers completely innocent of any suspicion of
a vertical crease, but proudly displaying every kind of horizontal one
on knees and thighs; when I see braided coats worn with common
shirts of lemon yellow, or bright blue soft collars on fawn-coloured
dickies with violet stripes, or a hundred other curious combinations,
I begin to ask myself whether it wouldn't be fairer to speak, as we
used to do, of a national costume. In former centuries the French
dressed differently to the English. The fact was generally admitted
and was regarded as perfectly natural. It may be that French costume
is just as national today as it ever was, and that we are wrong to
criticize it. Dominated by an ideal other than ours, it aims, perhaps,
at a sort of refinement beneath its apparent carelessness. I'm ready
to believe that the real French dandy finds a certain thrill in com-

bining a full-dress coat with a tramwayman's shirt, and carefully instructs his servants on no account to eradicate, by mistake, the resemblance between his trousers and a broken column, attained with such difficulty.

To return to Parliamentary matters, I am struck by the charm of this life. How dearly I should love to be a French deputy! I should feel every day that I was taking part simultaneously in an election meeting, a Hyde Park rally, a trial of the Inquisition, one of Shakspere's historical tragedies, a boxing match, a students' rag, a Salvation Army service, a session of the Revolutionary Tribunal, in everything, in short, ever invented by man to canalize his emotions. And the various parts and annexes of the Chamber itself seem to me to offer all the amenities of a club with none of its dreariness.

I must admit that the session in question was rather out of the ordinary. I was present at the fall of the Ministry, or, rather, I gather that I was, because I shouldn't have known it. Left to myself, I find it difficult to follow debates. I can understand anything that is said directly to me, but for some curious reason I still only partially comprehend words which are not deliberately intended for me, whether in a crowded room, in the theatre, or elsewhere. Luckily, a French colleague who was sitting next me whispered in my ear the general trend of what was going on. He told me that a certain M. Malvy was trying to pick a quarrel with the Government on the ground of their alleged criminal weakness in dealing with the clergy. At the end of it all, the Government, according to him, succeeded in getting a majority of 26. I rejoiced in the Government's success. I was a bit surprised, therefore, to find, this morning, that M. Briand had resigned with the whole of his Cabinet.

This is one of the mysteries which I find it difficult to fathom, and about which, if I'm not careful, I shall write a lot of nonsense, and discredit myself as an observer of the political scene. This whole question of ministerial instability in France is a thorny one. Governments here rarely last longer than six months. The one that's just fallen came into office last November. Part of my job will be to stress the advantages of this system.

Ernest Torchecoul, whom I met for a moment this morning when I was taking my *apéritif,* deigned to let drop one or two passing remarks on the subject. I didn't catch their full significance at the moment, but I shall think them out later. "In England," he said, "governments last longer, but the ministers change their minds frequently during their term of office, as it is inevitable they should when circumstances change. In France, when circumstances change, the government changes, since no single government is held to have the right of altering its point of view. This has been carried to such an extreme that when a prime minister wants to alter his policy, he must first bring about his own downfall. In other words, he himself becomes the instrument in a change of government." (This, presumably, accounts for the fact that although M. Briand got a majority of 26, he turned himself out of office.)

I have thought this all over since, and I have come to the conclusion that in fact Walpole, Pitt, or Disraeli couldn't have stayed in power as long as they did without constantly changing their points of view, and even their policies. I can't think of any actual instance, being completely ignorant of English history, but I can look it all up in some school-book when I get down to writing my articles.

Another thing that Ernest Torchecoul said was: "France is a mixture of Democracy and Bureaucracy. She is like one of the deciduous trees, like the sturdiest of them, the oak. Bureaucracy is the trunk, Democracy the leaves."

Having delivered himself of this remark, Torchecoul left me as though he wanted to avoid a longer discussion. I believe I know the reason of his present melancholy. When he had gone I said to the *garçon:* "Don't you find that M. Torchecoul has been less forthcoming than usual these last few weeks?" He answered: "He's worried about his health. He's had himself examined at the hospital, and one of his friends who's a doctor has told him that he's got the beginnings of diabetes." The *garçon* said also: "That's why M. Torchecoul confines himself, as he did today, to white wine with a lot of water, instead of taking his old *apéritifs bien tassés."*

As a matter of fact, I was just going to ask Ernest Torchecoul's views on an ingenious idea which came to me this morning while I was shaving. I must write it down so as not to forget it.

It is to the interest of all us foreigners that this state of ministerial instability in France shall continue unabated, and that the French people shall continue to devote much time and passion to questions of politics. Otherwise France might become much more of a threat than she is to the peace of Europe. Ever since I have come to know this people really well, I have grown convinced of the fact that they can endure boredom much less easily than their neighbours. Not that many individual Frenchmen don't resign themselves to lives of extreme boredom. On some of my weekly walks on the outskirts of Paris I have often noticed men still hale and hearty who seem to have nothing to do but sit idly in front of their cottage doors or spend their time fishing. Impossible to imagine anything more utterly expressive of boredom. (Worse even than the old gentlemen at home playing croquet in the vicarage garden.) But collectively the French are impatient of boredom. I imagine that those who put up with the drabbest of existences at home still count on a number of public excitements for distraction and a means of keeping themselves from being completely divorced from life. If the day ever comes when the French no longer have their attention occupied with the fall of ministries and the quarrels of politicians, they will begin to turn their minds to military adventure, to war and to all that war brings in its train. They would quickly become as tiresome to their neighbours as they were in the time of Louis XIV or of Napoleon. (My fear is that neither ministerial crises, colonial wars, nor Seine floods will be enough for them. I remember how somebody said to me last year about the time the river was giving so much trouble: "France is bored.")

The fact that my master Torchecoul is in the early stages of diabetes has deprived me of that admiration which I had hoped to rouse in him by the expression of my views. To the same cause is due the weakness he showed the other evening at the *Closerie* when dealing with Maykosen, who had been talking the whole time.

I hate this fellow Maykosen. It would be hard to find anyone more fatuous than this naturalized American from the Baltic Provinces. He dominates every conversation, and seems to be *à tu et à toi* with every crowned head in Europe and with all the millionaires of America. To hear him talk, one would believe that neither William II nor the Pope could come to any decision without first consulting their dear friend Maykosen. Although he's been only three months in Paris, he's managed to get into touch with more important people than I've scraped acquaintance with in two years. He works his way into every circle. What's such a grandee doing at the *Closerie?* M. Sulzbach pretends he's a spy, but there can't be much occupation for a spy at the *Closerie des Lilas.*

He really is odious. He is much richer, much better dressed, and has seen much more than Ernest Torchecoul, but compared with my master in Political Economy, with his natural generosity of mind, his warmth, and his wit, he's about as appetizing as a brick would be, served up in the same dish as a pudding. He almost makes me hate all Northerners (although I'm partly one myself). As a matter of fact, I don't believe he's a Scandinavian at all; he's more like a cross between a Prussian baron and a Lapp.

But, for all that, I admire him, after Torchecoul, more than any man I know—professionally, that is. He has carried to the supreme point of perfection this career of journalism in which I'm still only a beginner. He wanders about the world with the nonchalance of a Lord Byron and then, in the various palaces he visits, writes articles which newspapers tumble over one another to get at the most enormous prices. He bargains with editors like a prima donna. When he's in Paris he stays at the Hôtel Continental (when I think of my *garni!*), eats his daily beefsteak in the most expensive restaurants, and must get through, I imagine—quite apart from any secret expenses—not less than four pounds a day.

He adopts towards things in general an utterly cold-blooded attitude. He affects to consider all the major problems as essentially simple, maintaining that they have become complicated only because of the idiocy of the ruling classes, or because theorists have tied them up in a tangle of words.

He says, for example, that the whole problem of society can be reduced to the single question of how to provide every family with a bathroom. The possession of a bathroom brings with it inevitably certain other additional advantages such as clean clothes, good manners, a decent standard of education, and electric light. According to him, America is already well set on the right path, and, incidentally, he gives William II a patronizing pat on the back, since that monarch seems, in his friendly talks with Maykosen, to have displayed the proper attitude towards this particular problem.

He argues that countries like our own could solve the difficulty here and now were it not for the fact that as soon as one of them has reached the promised land, or just before it reaches it, it finds itself compelled to fight the others or go under as a victim of competition. As soon as the standard of living rises, production in every field becomes more expensive, with the result that the price of goods gets so high that they can no longer be sold unless they are imposed on foreign markets by force of arms.

From this he deduces that the first thing to do before the social question can be dealt with is to suppress all competition on any considerable scale between nations. For instance, before the conditions of the working classes in England, France, and Germany can be bettered, some sort of European unity must be achieved which will ensure that the standard of living, and consequently the cost of production, will rise at a uniform rate in the various countries concerned.

But he thinks that it is too late to do anything now, and has no confidence in the future of Europe. He sees her as fated, in the near future, to become the victim, not of natural circumstances, but of her own amazing lack of political instinct, and of the blindness which alone would be sufficient evidence of her stupidity, even if she had not already given a hundred different proofs of it.

The chief of these is that she has never fully realized the marvellous position which she has made for herself in the course of centuries, and which, despite the beginnings of decline, she still retains. She does not see that she has succeeded in setting the whole world to work for her profit. This she has done either by exploiting it directly in the form of colonies, or by the establishment of lucrative enterprises, all the hard work of which she gets done by native labour, or, finally, by remaining content to lend it capital to enable it to work at its own risk while paying heavy interest to its creditors. Europe (he says) is like an aristocratic family, living in its château on the proceeds of its own lands, and surrounded at a comfortable distance by farms and tenant holdings which pay rent in various forms, and by villages inhabited by work-people who spend their lives finding in the sweat of their brows the back interest on their loans.

Failing to understand the situation, she does nothing to perpetuate it. On the contrary, it looks as though she were doing everything in her power to destroy it. She has been at pains to provide the exploited peoples who had been reduced to the position of servants and debtors with every conceivable kind of military and industrial equipment, and has taught them how to use the very weapons which will inevitably be used against her—against her in particular! As though she hadn't found it difficult enough to conquer them in the first place! As though their new-found strength wouldn't be used, at the very first opportunity, to shake off the fetters with which Europe keeps them shackled! The Russo-Japanese war should be sufficient warning of what will happen.

But, alas! nobody seems to have read the obvious lesson. Nor is this the full count of Europe's idiocy. Not content with fomenting discontent among the subject races, she thinks of nothing but tearing herself to pieces with her own hands. Instead of using her wisdom, her genius, and her resources to protect her threatened hegemony, she is setting feverishly to work to prepare a terrible war within her own frontiers.

Maykosen sees in this a return of what he calls the *maladie grecque,* that curious madness of the ancient Greek peoples, who were so marvellously endowed and created to rule the world, but were so politically inept that they could only tear out their own entrails.

"The only man in Europe," he said, looking round at the Frenchmen seated at his table, to see how they would take his words, "the only man in Europe who begins to understand the situation is the Emperor William. He has been forced to give most of his attention to the hostility of the Triple Entente, but if he could have his way he would soon make short shrift of the difficulties inside Europe and would devote all his energy and all the power of his Empire to safeguarding, in partnership with England, France, and Russia, the position of Europe and of the white races throughout the world."

"On condition," put in Ernest Torchecoul, "that he was allowed to assume the leadership of the aforesaid Europe."

"Someone's got to be leader!" Maykosen answered with a shrug. "Europe can't lead itself."

This statement was not popular with the assembled company, and Ernest Torchecoul and I exchanged a meaning smile.

Thereupon Maykosen quoted the case of Napoleon, of whom he condescends to entertain a high opinion, maintaining that he would in time have made the term "Europe" a reality had he not been prevented from doing so by "the blind jealousy and criminal obstinacy of England."

I noticed with sorrow that my friend Ernest Torchecoul agreed unreservedly with this thesis and showed his willingness to forget his previous divergence from Maykosen's point of view, for the pleasure of condemning English policy.

I tried to forget this painful impression by asking Maykosen what he really thought of William II, and what good or ill results he imagined this monarch's attitude would have for Europe.

He replied:

"He is half a great man and half a fool. He dreams of becoming, by peaceful means and at the head of his people, the shepherd of a united Europe. The happiest moment of his life occurred during the Boxer rising, when Field-Marshal Waldersee commanded all the allied troops of Europe in his name. He believes that it might have been possible to revive the ideal of the great emperors of the Middle Ages, when the sovereigns of Europe were content to accept the unity imposed by a feudal hierarchy without any loss to their own prestige, and when the peoples of the West were ready to march shoulder to shoulder to the Crusades. As things are, he is disillusioned and beset with doubts. He asks himself whether he may not be forced to lead his Germans to war against other nations of the Continent. He does not understand democracy and therefore mistrusts it. He is surprised that his fellow sovereigns, many of whom are his blood-relatives, do not treat him with greater confidence. He sets too much value on personal friendship. He alternates between bouts of enthusiasm and of bitterness, and listens too easily to advice. He is quite capable of seeing the faults of those who surround him, but his regard for their feelings goes often to fantastic lengths, with the result that he often prefers lying to them and acting behind their backs to taking the straight course of opposition. He has lying in the blood, and he is vain. In his heart of hearts he is terrified of the future."

Chapter

HUMILIATION OF GURAU

A little before seven o'clock in the evening, an express messenger brought Gurau a summons from Monis, who had just been entrusted by the President of the Republic with the task of forming a new Ministry.

It was worded in the most polite terms: "If it is inconvenient for you to call on me, I will run over and see you. But I'm up to the eyes, and you would be doing me a great kindness by coming here."

"I thought of you at once," Monis said, in his warm, soft, Bordeaux brogue, "and so did my friends. Your name calls forth nothing but the sincerest expressions of friendliness. You know, of course, that I am forming a Government of a definitely Left complexion. Caillaux has promised to take the Treasury. May I include you among my ministers?"

"I have no objections to the policy which you represent, but before answering, I must know what position you can offer me."

"Naturally, naturally, but you're of greater importance than your possible office . . . as a man, I mean . . . as the embodiment of all that you represent. . . . I will try to keep Labour for you."

Gurau smiled, but he was clearly annoyed.

"I refused Labour when Briand offered it to me in November. It's not likely that I should accept it now."

"Oh, I didn't know. . . . Forgive me. . . . You've upset all my ideas. . . . But we'll fix things up, never fear. I suppose it's no good my suggesting Agriculture?"

Gurau continued to smile without troubling to answer.

"I don't quite know what to do. . . . What exactly were you thinking of?"

"Foreign Affairs."

The words were uttered as though they had been an ultimatum.
Monis's expression was one of sincere hopelessness.

"Foreign Affairs! . . . But they're promised to Cruppi! . . .
Cruppi is one of the main pillars of my Cabinet! . . . The most I
could do would be to cancel the arrangements I had made for the
Colonies. . . . You can't pretend that the Colonies are child's-play?"

Gurau was on the point of remarking rather bitterly that if Monis
really valued his collaboration he might have spoken to him before
making all these promises, and that he, Gurau, might have been as
good a "pillar" as anybody else. Instead, he rose from his chair,
saying, as he did so, in a tone of carelessness that masked a mind
made up:

"I'm only interested in Foreign Affairs at the moment."

Monis kept him from going.

"I beg you, my dear fellow, not to say no straight off. I attach the
greatest possible weight to your collaboration. Give me a little time
to turn round. . . . I've accepted this job, as you must realize, only
from a sense of duty. The important thing is for some of us to get
together and work for the Republic."

Gurau returned home a prey to unpleasant thoughts. "I'm the
kind of man they consider—but only as a second string. I have no
group or party behind me. As Jaurès once told me, I stand alone."

He tried to reassure himself:

"The fools don't realize that a man with the whole mass of the
Syndicalist movement at his back isn't in quite the same boat as the
leader or assistant leader of some vague group composed of twenty
or so deputies."

But he compelled himself to pass a more modest verdict on the
facts:

"You're forgetting that, in fact, the whole mass isn't at your back at all, that they don't care two figs for you, that, according to your enemies, it's *you* who are running after *them*."

He took a sudden decision:

"Hell, I won't think any more about it!"

The only result of which was that he thought of nothing else for the rest of the evening.

The next morning he received from the company with which he was insured against fire a letter which mystified and annoyed him.

It stated that since he had failed to pay his last premium despite several bills, and had left unanswered the original communication which had been sent to him by registered mail, the company found itself with no alternative but to cancel the policy and to make application for the amount already owed and for the fine which he had incurred as a result of breach of contract.

Nobody had mentioned these repeated applications to him, nor had he received any letter from the company, registered or otherwise. He went down to the concierge and questioned her. She had no recollection of the postman having delivered a registered letter, but thought she remembered a collector calling one day when Gurau was out, though she was not sure even of that. In any case, he had been only once.

"The asses have made a mistake," he decided, "and to add insult to injury, they make me suffer for their blunder."

He thought at first that he would send back a sharp answer. But that would mean all the bother of writing it, and he would have to wait several days for an answer. He wanted there and then to get rid of the irritation which the incident had caused him.

He looked at the clock. "I could be there by subway in twenty minutes. I'll give them a piece of my mind, and settle the whole business at once."

He was surprised at his own anger and sense of impatience. It would have been more sensible, he knew, and more in keeping with the dignity of his position, to write or telephone, and he didn't doubt for a moment but that the company would end by apologizing. But somewhere inside him there was a worrying absence of certainty. Some inner voice whispered: "You must get this thing off your chest at once; otherwise you'll think about nothing else all day. You'll imagine them ignoring your claim, replying that they're sorry, or not even condescending to reply at all. You'll be haunted by the fear that fire might break out while the policy was in abeyance, or that some further complication might ensue. However trivial the original annoyance, official obstinacy or mere ill luck will swell it to ridiculous proportions. You're essentially a man who's dogged by ill luck. Besides, although you're nominally a lawyer and (perhaps also nominally) the son of a Town Clerk, you're terrified by formalities and unnerved by the sight of a piece of stamped paper."

A sudden tickling in the hollow behind his knee bore out his theory of ill luck. "And now I've got chronic eczema," he thought. The idea that he belonged to a definite physiological class, condemned without hope, affected him painfully. "No sooner is my arm almost well than I feel the irritation trying to establish itself somewhere else. It's more difficult for it to get a hold this time, because I've learned not to scratch—or only very little (sometimes at night when I'm just dropping off to sleep). I've found out that it's better to bite my lips hard rather than give in to the delicious torment of scratching as I used to do. But the damned thing's on the watch the whole time, ready to take advantage of the first sign of weakness."

Absent-mindedly he entered the subway and found himself standing in a first-class carriage, reading a leading article in the *Sanction,* written the evening before, in which he had dealt with the ineptitude of the late Government in its handling of the labour situation.

The conductor was standing before him. Gurau felt for his ticket, but failed to find it in its usual place (his lower right-hand waistcoat-pocket) or anywhere else. He thought he remembered that it had been the last of a book of tickets, and that when he had shown it at the entrance gate the stub had been still attached to it. He visualized the scene perfectly and could feel again the thick stub, with its uneven edge, in which the ticket was set like a thin blade.

"I've gone and hidden it in some corner or other," he said to himself, "or perhaps I threw it away by mistake, just because of that stub."

The conductor was waiting, his hand, with the punch held ready, in front of his body. He had assumed an air of patient expectation in which already there was a hint of mockery. He was a man of rather more than thirty, clean, thinnish, dark-skinned, and fine-featured, but with that turn of the lip and gleam of the eye which betray nervous ill-temper and lurking malice, evidences of a vengeful temperament which loves to humiliate and punish its victims. He was the type of man who, in the Army, would have been a strict and bullying sergeant-major.

Gurau hated him at sight with a deep and instinctive hatred. Nevertheless he continued to search his pockets. His immediate neighbours began to take a vague interest in the proceedings. All the time he was searching, Gurau was thinking: "It's disgraceful that I, that a man in my position, should have to go through this fantastic business under the eye of a miserable little official, and all for a lost ticket! It'd be much simpler just to pay for another one."

But he didn't dare. He was by no means certain that he could control himself sufficiently to say with the necessary carelessness: "I don't know what I've done with it. Give me another." He had waited a shade too long. "I've made too much fuss; I've shown too much concern. If I did that now, I should look as though I were admitting the fault and throwing myself on his mercy."

The other turned on his heel, saying:

"I'll come back—perhaps you'll have found it by that time."

There was a note of polite mockery in his voice, and his glance round the carriage seemed to say: "I know all about this sort of chap!" He had spoken, too, with a sham refinement which made his common accent more odious even than it had been before.

Between the next two stations he went on his way round the car, carrying out his duties, but watching Gurau carefully out of the corner of his eye. He behaved to the other travellers with exaggerated politeness and good temper, and his "Thank *you*," "Thank *you*," was distinctly audible. Gurau gave up the search and adopted an aloof and obstinate air.

The conductor came back and halted before him, his punch well in evidence, and a nasty look in his muddy brown eyes. Had Gurau been free—really free, free of all social inhibitions, free of witnesses, free of his own respectable prejudices and fixed ideas of conduct—he would have driven his fist into the face confronting his own. Only one blow would have been necessary, for it would have been irresistible. He would have put into it all the pent-up violence which lies dormant in even the weakest man, would have hit hard enough to smash the fellow's jaw, to floor him, to break him in two.

As it was, he merely said:

"I can't find it; I've lost it."

He left unspoken the other words which were burning his lips: "And don't think for a moment that you can frighten a deputy, a former Minister, with all this nonsense! Now you're going to see what's what!" He left them unspoken because they were his trump card. To have played it would have meant risking his whole social position on a single throw. The occasion was too trivial, the stake too high. He would have had to be absolutely sure of its effect. What added humiliation if the other had merely replied: "The hell you are!" How intolerable would have been the onlookers' laughter!

The conductor remarked:

"You haven't even got a second-class?"

"It's not a question of second-class," Gurau answered, letting his annoyance get the better of him. "I had a first-class ticket from a book of first-class tickets. I must have absent-mindedly thrown it away. There's no need to make such a fuss about it."

He held out a franc, but the conductor didn't take it.

"Can you show me your book of first-class tickets?"

For a moment Gurau was at a loss.

"No . . . I'm afraid I can't. . . . I remember that it was the only ticket left. I can't show you the book. I must have thrown the whole thing away. Are we really to waste two hours discussing a ticket worth twenty-five centimes?"

The thin brown face with its ill-tempered eyes assumed an expression of triumph. The voice, however, was still calm:

"Where are you getting out?"

"Quatre-Septembre."

"Right."

When they reached Quatre-Septembre, he came back to Gurau, opened the door, got out with him, signed to his colleague in the last car to hold up the train until he returned, and led the way, with a "Follow me, if you please, sir," to the station master's office. A great many of Gurau's fellow-travellers were witnesses of the scene, and he felt that he must look like a pickpocket taken red-handed, or, more probably, some nasty old man with a quirk, caught in the act of committing an indecent assault.

The conductor handed him over to the station master. "This gentleman was found without a ticket in a first-class car."

That was all he said, but the tone of his voice, the way in which ne uttered the words "without a ticket"—and the fact that what he was doing was obviously out of the ordinary—supplied all necessary comment. He left them.

The train got under way, and through the window of the office Gurau could see the row of moving heads as the occupants turned to stare at him.

"I entirely fail to understand the reason for such behaviour," he said; "the whole thing's absurd. It's not a crime to lose one's ticket. I offered to pay, but the man refused to accept any money. Why? Why has he made me come here and waste valuable time? It's inexcusable—an outrage."

He spoke sharply, but avoided giving the impression that he had any grievance against the station master. On the contrary, he seemed to be enlisting his sympathy in a matter of subordinate zeal which called for official reprimand from a sensible superior.

"That may be, sir, but I'm afraid I shall have to ask you for your name and address," said the station master in a bored voice.

Gurau went pale.

"Oh, all right."

To himself he said: "Monsieur Maxime Gurau, Deputy for Indre-et-Loire, formerly Minister of Labour." He heard the words as distinctly as though they had been actually spoken, and measured their probable effect. Would it be sufficiently stunning? Would the pause following their utterance repay with interest the quarter of an hour's humiliation to which he had just been subjected? "Formerly—" What a pity that he had to admit to that modification! The word "formerly" was like a worm gnawing at the "Minister" which it accompanied, emptying it of significance. He couldn't even restore the balance by adding: "editor of the *Sanction*." In the first place, he wasn't editor, and in the second, to a station master on the subway, aware of the importance of the *Petit Parisien* or the *Journal,* the *Sanction* would mean nothing at all.

One was a fool, he thought, not to amass all the titles possible, not to inflate one's value in society, one's position as a social being, by every means in one's power. After all, nobody would refuse the editorship of a paper on the ground that in fact he controlled its policy and didn't need the label. That sort of thing was nothing but one of those refinements of simplicity which were bound to be regretted sooner or later. It was a fool's trick to refuse the offer of a place in the Government just because one couldn't get the department one wanted. A wise man accepted office whenever it was offered him (short of betraying his principles). It was merely childish to refuse to admit that a hierarchy exists as much today as ever in the past. The important thing was to make sure of occupying in it a position equal to one's merits. That was the least one owed oneself, and if it was a spectacular position which could be relied upon to dazzle fools, so much the better. (That of course had been the value of uniforms, decorations, and differences of dress in the societies of former days. It was merely stupid to try to look like "just anybody" when one knew that one wasn't just anybody; an illusion bred of democracy. Soldiers knew a trick worth two of that. Would that wretched conductor with the nasty eyes have made him get out of the train if he'd been a general in full dress? Hence the value of decorations. It was merely ridiculous that Parliament had adopted the self-denying ordinance which forbade its members to accept decorations. A former Minister should be at least a Commander of the Legion of Honour.) What possible purpose was served by this modern, this pitiful depreciation of rank? Only this, that one's inferiors trod on one's toes and took delight in humiliating one. All very well to talk of comrades of the proletariat . . . but a man could be a proletarian and yet a dirty skunk with the soul of a slave-driver. Men like that could understand no argument but force. The only pleasurable relation one could have with them—and it *would* be pleasurable!—would be kicking their bottoms in public.

Meanwhile the station master, without hurrying himself, had taken down a ledger from the shelf, opened it, and wiped his pen on his sleeve.

At the very moment that Gurau, striving to make his tone as politely ironical, as calmly superior, as possible, was about to let drop his crushing phrase (after all it *was* crushing): "Monsieur Maxime Gurau, Deputy," etc., and the station master's pen, after circling like a bird, was preparing to alight on the open page, there flashed before the deputy's mental eye a scene from the distant past. He saw in imagination a second-class compartment somewhere between Orléans and Blois, the ticket-collector (a great strapping fellow with a fierce moustache) studying with terrifying precision the return ticket which had just been held out to him. . . . In a sudden fit of panic Gurau thought: "One never knows! The very fact that I'm well known may end in that old business being raked up as a result of today's incident—it would be just like my infernal luck! What a hideously significant connexion! What a gift for the yellow press, the comic cartoonists, the ballad-makers of Montmartre! . . .

They could plague me with it for the rest of my life. . . ."

But if this sudden vision had the effect of modifying his original intentions, he was sufficiently master of himself to proceed as he had planned, and it was with a very pretty air of irony and frigid politeness that he said:

"I think I ought to warn you, station master, that I'm not just anybody, as you will see for yourself in a moment. You're perfectly within your rights, of course, in proceeding with what I consider to be a highly insulting formality, but I consider myself as being also within *my* rights if I decide to pursue the matter further—I tell you that perfectly frankly. And now, you will kindly give me the name, or, if you don't know his name, the number, of the man who started this ridiculous scene. . . ."

The station master took his pen from the paper, raised his head, and looked at Gurau. He seemed uncertain what to do.

After a moment's thought he said in a conciliating tone:

"We've got to obey orders, sir—but of course there are ways of doing these things. . . . Those chaps aren't always very good judges of persons. . . . I don't have to say that I'm sure you acted in good faith, sir. . . . It's a pity he didn't just let you pay for another ticket. . . ."

"Which I was perfectly ready to do, and still am." The station master's eye seemed to be searching the shelf for something that wasn't there. He raised his arm.

"Oh, well, if that's the case, sir . . . you're quite free to go. . . . I can assure you that nobody will ask any questions."

Gurau, his temper suddenly appeased, was rehearsing to himself the precise shade of condescension which he intended giving to his parting phrase—"that's all right then, my good fellow"—but the station master suddenly determined their relative positions in a manner quite other than that intended by Gurau, by adding shortly:

"And see that it doesn't happen again."

Gurau made a face, confined himself to a formal "Good day," and left the office.

Chapter

3

HOW MINISTERS ARE MADE

"Ah good! . . . You've come to give me your answer? . . . Well, I only hope it's the one I want. . . . You're rather late with it—not that I'm blaming you. . . . But, you see, we're in a terrible hurry—the President's getting impatient." (Monis shifted some papers on his table.) ". . . Well, now—I've promised Paul-Boncour that he shall have Labour. . . . It's tiresome, but there it is. . . . Wait a moment, let me look through my list again. . . . Perrier, Cruppi . . . Berteaux at the War Office . . , Delcassé . . . Caillaux. . . . Oh dear, what a nuisance it all is! . . . No good suggesting the Colonies now, Messimy must have them. I might at a pinch—at a pinch, mind you—manage Public Works. . . . I've almost promised it, but the man in question hasn't yet given me his formal acceptance, and, in any case, he's not really a first-rater. . . . He'll probably be annoyed, but I can't help that."

While Monis was busy with his polite odds and ends of talk, Gurau was hurriedly giving substance to the words *"Public Works."* He saw in imagination the Government building on the boulevard Saint-Germain, its façade, the fine sweep of the stone staircase, the great courtyard. He repeated the title to himself, weighing its social as well as its parliamentary significance—"Minister of Public Works." He saw in dwindling perspective bridges and highways, road-menders and engineers, a whole army of workers; harbours, mine-shafts; finally, as a subordinate activity, the Post Office services (even that!)—the whole length and breadth of France covered by the innumerable servants of the Post Office . . . and, in less detail (though not the less distinctly), the railways, the whole machinery of transport, the subway. He saw it all in his mind's eye, even to the station master at Quatre-Septembre in his little glass box, with a gentleman, an unknown traveller, standing before him in the yellowish gloom. Suddenly this unknown, like a mediæval emperor raising his vizor, exclaims aloud: "I am the Minister of Public Works"—the words crashing downwards with the force of a thunderbolt (in that sulphurous subterranean darkness "Foreign Affairs" would have sounded comparatively aloof, dull, harmless). Could one conceive anything more weighty, more crushing? "I am the President of the Republic"? But presidents of the Republic don't travel by subway:—the official in question would merely say to himself: "Don't seem right to me; must be a bit soft on top"—or he might take him for a madman who *thought* he was President of the Republic. Whereas the Minister of Public Works in that world of ill-lit shadows would be, if an extremely distinguished, at least a by no means impossible apparition. Far from impossible indeed, nothing more natural, nothing less suspicious—a Minister come to see for himself, even in those humble depths—Napoleon and the sentry over again. How could the incident fail to redound to his credit? Every situation could be made to bear witness to his power, to assuage his vanity. "I understand that the checking of tickets is done very thoroughly; so far so good. But also that it is carried out with deplorable absence of tact. I will not have the public bullied!" A prince ever thoughtful for his subjects ("If only the King could know how we are treated!")—mysterious expeditions of Grand Viziers in the *Arabian Nights* ("He wanted to know what extortions were practised on the poor")—and, not least, the pleasure of revenge. How sweet to find that miserable, weedy, sallow little worm, to catch him, to be able to say: "Now I'll break you!" . . . Not necessarily to do it, but just to be able to know that he could do it—it, and a thousand other things. . . . What subtle beauty lies in impersonal vengeance! How sweet a savour in vengeance long drawn out!

One hour later the official composition of Monis's Government was communicated to the newspapers. It showed Cruppi as Foreign Minister, Berteaux at the War Office, Delcassé at the Navy, Caillaux at the Treasury, and Gurau as Minister of Public Works, etc. . . . The Interior being reserved for Monis himself.

Chapter 4

GURAU DINES OUT.
MADAME GODORP. THE CREOLE

Two women in evening dress were moving about a table laid for about twelve persons. The elder held in her hand a packet of gilt-edged, oblong cards, on which names were written diagonally. Both appeared to be preoccupied.

"So you've finally decided to have Monsieur Luymarié on your left?" asked the younger of the two.

"Why not?"

"You're not afraid of offending Monsieur de Pelledoux?"

"Certainly not; he regards himself almost as one of the family. Besides, I'm putting Madame de Pelledoux next to your father. . . ."

"You said just now that he was to have Madame Veneuil-Rennetin on his left, and the Baroness Wulf on his right."

"So I did. The Veneuil-Rennetins are older than the Pelledoux, more or less. . . ."

"I love that expression of yours—'more or less.'"

"Please keep your witticisms till later. I want to get my table balanced. It seems to me natural that since I've put a politician in the place of honour, I should put a politician in the second place as well."

"On the contrary, it seems to me absurd that you should sandwich yourself between a Municipal Councillor and a Minister—and not very flattering to Monsieur Gurau."

"How would you arrange it, then? Monsieur Gurau can talk to his right-hand neighbour all the time if he likes."

"I know you're going to say that I'm always criticizing you, Mother, but really it'll look very odd."

"Why odd? Just because Madame Godorp'll be sitting next to Monsieur Gurau? Nobody'll notice it."

"Won't they! Everybody knows what you're planning."

"If they do it's because you've told them. *I've* not breathed a word to a soul."

"Oh, you brazen-faced woman! It's not a question of breathing words. You've already brought them together at least two or three times. A blind man could see what you're after."

"What if I have? They're free agents, aren't they? Why should anyone mind?"

"I should hate you to get the reputation of being a match-maker. It's a thing I dislike excessively."

The Vicomtesse de Crauze, who was just about to put the Baron de Pelledoux's card in a glass, paused, looked at her daughter, and, still holding the card in her fingers, said, with a suspicion of anxiety in her voice:

"Simone, this habit of yours of teasing me has become a regular game. . . . I never know whether you're serious or not. . . . I certainly don't want to turn into a match-making old lady."

"Of course not—because you're not an old lady."

"Thank you. . . . Have you really heard people say that I'm trying to get them married? Are people laughing at me? Tell me the truth, please, the real truth."

"If I'm to tell you the real truth, Mother dear, no. I think they may have suspicions, but that's all."

"What do you think yourself? Does it seem to you such a silly, such a ridiculous idea? Have you talked to your husband about it?"

"Oh, Jacques's got other things to worry about. . . . I confess I've laughed at you a bit—both of us have . . . but that's only because we always do. Still, as I said before, match-makers get on my nerves."

Mme de Crauze sat down with every symptom of an uneasy conscience. She was still holding the Baron de Pelledoux's card in her fingers.

"I can't help it," she said, "and I expect I'm a fool. I've got a soft spot for Monsieur Gurau. In some ways he's so vulnerable. At bot-

tom he's such a kind man. I've seen him look so gentle, and sometimes as though he'd been wounded. He's never had much luck—in
certain respects. He wants to help people, and he's very lonely. I
can't help feeling that his lack of means and his desire to remain
poor are rather touching. He's so utterly unlike the general run of
greedy, gambling politicians who come to Paris from their constituencies with only one idea: to make as much money as they can in
ten years, no matter how they do it, and to find jobs for all the
brothers-in-law and cousins whom they've left behind them in the
country. Your father told me that Monsieur Gurau used to be at the
bar and could still practise if he wanted to. Only think how most
lawyer-politicians have managed to feather their own nests. . . ."

"Then all I can say, Mother, is that you're a sadist, a satanist!
Here you are, the friend of the kind of politician who's almost ceased
to exist, who wants nothing so much as to remain poor, and your
one desire is to get him married to a woman who has, or lets it be
thought that she has, three hundred thousand francs a year! Do you
want to corrupt him?"

"Lets it be thought indeed! . . . She certainly doesn't do anything
of the sort. Gisèle is far too well-bred for that, and too discreet. Other
people may talk about her fortune, she certainly doesn't. . . . But
what you've been saying worries me, Simone. I must think about it,
but meanwhile let me get Monsieur Veneuil-Rennetin settled. He'd
better go here, don't you think? I must put Monsieur de Pelledoux
on Gisèle's right. Unfortunately he's an awful talker, and he'll try
to monopolize her all evening. She and Monsieur Gurau won't get
a chance. Look, I'm going to put you on Monsieur de Pelledoux's
other side. You must try and draw him off."

"Oh, Mother, you do make me smile!"

Mme Lambron de Crauze sat down once more, and her face took
on its former expression of anxious thought.

"You've really upset me, Simone. Heaven knows I've no wish to
make Monsieur Gurau do anything he doesn't think he ought to do,
or to act against his better judgment. . . . I should hate to do a thing

like that. But he deserves a more comfortable life, if only because he'd never do anything low to get one. He deserves to be independent. Madame Godorp would never be a bad influence on him. She'd teach him how to wear his clothes and how to entertain. She'd give him a certain amount of luxury, and help him to look the great gentleman he is, whereas, as things are, a lot of people, quite naturally, think that he looks like an old bookworm, rather bohemian, and not over-careful of his appearance. Even his ideas would benefit. He's so very theoretical, so—so naïve. . . ."

"Does she want him, or is all this only a private little scheme of your own?"

"Do you take your mother for a perfect old fool, Simone? . . . She likes him very much. . . . If I wasn't afraid of exaggerating, I should say she was in love with him . . . she certainly has a very strong feeling for him."

"And he?"

The Vicomtesse made a non-committal gesture.

"Haven't you sounded him at all? That's rather odd, isn't it?"

"I've made one or two vague references to the subject, but I don't think he took it in very good part."

"He knows how rich she is?"

"I've managed to let him know it—indirectly."

"Do you think it had any effect on him?"

"I'm sure it did. For instance, when he was here the other day, I mentioned Gisèle's apartment on the avenue du Bois, and he interrupted me. 'It's not hers, is it?' he asked. 'I thought it belonged to one of her relations.'"

"Where had he got that idea?"

"From me. I'd spoken about it once before. . . . I did not add that, in fact, Gisèle is paying a pretty heavy rent. The Comtesse de Moëvre isn't very anxious to have the fact known, and it's nobody's business but theirs. But that's not the question. I only wanted to prove to you that he's no more disinterested than anyone else, when he wants to be."

"You think, then, that he'll end by letting himself be tempted?"

"I'm not sure. It's his happy-go-lucky ways, I think, that chiefly hold him back, the habit he's got into of being unattached. I was very much amused one day by hearing him talk of all the trouble these big dinner-parties must give him. I'm quite sure he'd shudder at the idea of being the kind of man who's expected to give 'big dinner-parties.' . . . Oh, of course, he'll soon get used to it. After all, money makes everything so much easier."

Gurau was not drunk, but he had taken enough wine to make him feel that the mere fact of being alive was a rich and exciting experience. It was as though he were floating on the strong current of his destiny, as though wave after wave took possession of him and swept him onward, each higher than the last, a flowing tide of power. Even the pauses between the succeeding rollers were but breathing-spaces in the triumphant sweep, moments of relaxation in which he could gather strength for the next forward drive.

He was in one of those moods which owe nothing to the illusions of intoxication, in which the effect of alcohol is merely to produce a sort of internal tension sufficient to arm the spirit against circumstance, to strengthen pride and self-confidence to the pitch of being proof against the reaction of success, capable of resisting those onsets of weakness which go by the name of surprise and uncertainty.

Such a feeling was the very reverse of the spirit's low ebb in the creeping light of dawn. Not that he felt either sleepy or confused. His mind was perfectly clear. But everything in the universe was so perfectly relegated to its just and proper place that the sense of obstacles, of remorse, of danger, of anguish, seemed to find voice and cry: "Oh yes, we're here right enough; we're not pretending that we're not; but, for all that, see how splendid life can be!"—much as His Majesty's opposition, by the very fact of its existence, is guarantee that there are no hidden rancours and secret plots within the realm.

Why take things so tragically? The insurance company had only to look into what had happened to admit—as, in fact, it had already done—its error and make the inevitable apology. The adventure in the subway certainly wouldn't go any further. If the station master proved obstinate, the board of directors would have to rectify the mistake.

He was still young—even by the test of his birth-certificate. But if he wanted further proof, it was here, in the person of this woman at his right hand who was planning to marry him, in that of the hostess on his left, who thought it perfectly right and proper that her friend should be in love with him, and was urging on the plot as the most natural thing in the world. Seen in its daily progress, the greatest of careers must sometimes seem to lag. "Twice a junior Minister at my age!" A little later, when he could see things in their right perspective, he would approve this measured progress, seeing its successive achievements as rightly spaced. Too rapid an advancement almost always brings disappointment. The sturdier the tree, the slower its growth.

Mme de Crauze was asking him a question:

"Why did you choose the Department of Public Works? I was surprised. . . . You find the work interesting?"

"Very interesting, dear lady. You see, it gives me an opportunity of studying at close range certain problems of growing importance in the modern world, such as the function of the State in industry, the question whether it shall itself become producer or merely intervene to control and regulate. . . . I regard my department as a sort of experimental laboratory."

He had said the first thing that came into his head, but on second thoughts it seemed extraordinarily good. His prestige certainly wouldn't suffer from it.

M. Veneuil-Rennetin, who had been listening and seeming half to understand, launched into a violent polemic against State control. Gurau smiled, remarking politely that the right way of reaching conclusions about the evils of State control—if they really were evils—was by experimenting. He added that State control was only one of the formulas to be considered. Quite possibly it would be found to be already outgrown; many reformers already condemned it on grounds quite other than those advanced by M. Veneuil-Rennetin. He let it be understood that he himself was a revolutionary of the most up-to-date kind. (A revolutionary is rather out of place in aristocratic company, but if he is "up-to-date," he is in a position to neutralize the incongruity by a certain reputation for "smartness.")

The Baronne de Pelledoux, who looked like a great lady of the eighteenth century and traded on the resemblance, deplored the inclusion of Caillaux in the Ministry. He was much more dangerous, she thought, than the Socialists because he was far abler and far cleverer. She knew all about him because she had met him.

"He's madly ambitious. He'd shrink from nothing; he'd turn France upside-down if by so doing he could get into the limelight."

Mme Godorp, he thought, had fine eyes; rather large, perhaps, and slightly prominent. Their particular shade of blue might not be very unusual, but they were full of good humour, of a love of life, of a certain healthy sensuality. There was a remarkable similarity between Mme Godorp's eyes, the way in which she pouted her lips forward when she spoke, and the way in which her breasts swelled and pressed together beneath her dress. She was obviously one of those women for whom sexuality presented no separate problem, but was merely an extension of her delight in eating, in walking, in enjoying a bath. It involved her in no complications, no sense of sin. Gurau wondered whether he were deceived by a momentary impression or by some subtle and preconceived idea in finding in her a certain family resemblance to Germaine. Was it just that they were both fair, both had blue eyes and rounded curves? But it wasn't the same fairness or the same blue. Their colouring was different. Mme Godorp was altogether on a larger scale than Germaine, and the expression of her face was quite different. There was something watchful, something determined, about Germaine, a dominating, almost a hard quality. Probably it came from having to work, but fundamentally it was the expression of a nature that knew how to control itself and others, without prejudice to an enjoyment of sentimental surrender.

The mistress of the house had turned her attention to M. Luymarié. What a pity that he wasn't a count or a marquis! A title would have given him just the finishing touch. There is in Paris a type of aristocratic municipal councillor unlike anything to be found in the Chamber. Obviously it is easier for a man of fashion to win over the electors of a smart district than to sway a whole constituency, and it involves him in fewer humiliating condescensions. Mme Lambron de Crauze was anxious to know how long the boulevard Saint-Michel was going to be poisoned by smoke from the Sceaux railway.

"Just walking casually along the boulevard you don't notice those things that look like newspaper kiosks, but as a matter of fact they're chimneys. If you look carefully at them you'll see that there's always a certain amount of black smoke coming out of them. We're being asphyxiated by slow degrees."

The Vicomtesse was full of sympathy for the wretched people who lived on the street.

"When my father built the house, he put the part we were to live in at the far end of the courtyard in order to escape the noise of the boulevard and to get a feeling of privacy and homeliness. . . . There was also the question, of course, of a good return for his money. . . . He certainly never dreamed for a moment of this ordeal of smoke. . . . On the whole, though, he chose well. I don't mean that we aren't affected—all our visitors notice it, though they're too polite to say anything. It's amazing how quickly everything gets dirty! . . . There's a sort of deposit of greasy soot on all the covers and curtains. . . . But apart from that, it's a pleasant district—so near the Luxembourg. I wake up to the sound of the bells of Saint-Jacques. . . ."

The Baroness Wulf, who was terribly pock-marked, seemed absorbed in watching Gurau and Mme Godorp. She probably knew what was afoot. "Let her listen to her heart's content," he thought. "She won't hear much. I'm not even flirting with the woman!"

345

The general resemblance of Germaine and Mme Godorp was hard to specify. Something about their effect in a room. They both had that same apparent confidence in life. "Germaine caused me a great deal of pain, but only because she was unfaithful, and only when I knew she was. In herself, her personality, her state of being, she never made me suffer."

He was conscious of a sudden twinge, of a passing sense of distress, as temporary as a moment's feeling of sickness on a long, calm sea-crossing. For the first time he completely understood the state of mind of those husbands who are wrongly accused of shutting their eyes because they go on living with women who deceive them, but with whom they are still in love. "They don't want to be cuckolds, but they know from experience that the presence of a certain woman makes them happy, and they are aware, or feel instinctively, that such happiness is no common thing. The mere proximity of another might be more painful to them than the known infidelity of their wives.

"It may be that I need the kind of woman who's at peace with herself, who doesn't suffer from a tormented conscience, but radiates a sense of balance. Or perhaps it is that that kind of woman needs me, that I attract her."

He noticed that he had carefully avoided thinking of Mme Godorp's fortune. Nevertheless he couldn't help, now and then, considering it despite himself. "She's very rich, according to Madame de Crauze, who knows her well and understands that sort of thing. A big income, I believe, rather than a big capital; probably the result of her divorce. But how solid is it?"

He felt that he must now and again take part in the general conversation flowing round the table, at the end of which he was sitting. Young Masson, Simone's husband, was giving voice to exceedingly liberal views, in compliment to himself. He was laughing at the conservatives and maintaining that there was less fundamental difference between the Action Française, to which several of his friends belonged, and the Trade-Union Congress than between those two parties and the republican views of the moderates and radicals. He didn't belong to the Action Française himself, but pretended to believe in the probability of a revolution as a result of which the leaders of labour would be willing to accept the arbitration of a king. He assured Gurau that he was, of all politicians, the one regarded with least dislike by the Royalists and the Camelots du Roi.

"You may be sure that if they win they won't make a general clean sweep of the fellows who've been running the Republic. They know perfectly well that they'll need men of experience and proved worth."

Gurau smiled. Mme Godorp, noticing his expression out of the corner of her eye, smiled too.

M. de Pelledoux, who had a great admiration for Maurice Barrès and was not quite sure of Gurau's political views, declared, with no intention of hurting anybody's feelings, that Syndicalism was "all humbug," that the social revolution was a lot of demagogues' nonsense, that all the alleged differences of opinion in the country would vanish as soon as there was threat of a foreign danger, and the only problem for France was how to keep her Army in a state of readiness.

"These people," thought Gurau, "make me smile. They're all so sure of themselves that they'll voice opinions of the most uncompromising description in the presence of a man whose position in the Government does, at least, ensure his possession of a certain amount of information which they cannot possibly have. But they none of them know what they really ought to think. The interests of their class dictate their views and motivate their actions without giving them any clear indication of the road to take. They're much less happy than their fathers, the 'Haves' of the nineteenth century, who believed in a definite creed and were not bothered by qualms of conscience. For them, any questioning of the rights of property led straight to the June Revolution or the violence of the Commune.

They're less happy even than their great-grandfathers, their ancestors, who were the privileged class of the days before '89 and played so elegantly with fire.

"They're worried. They don't ask for a faith. They would be quite happy with a few simple remedies, or, better still, they'd be perfectly ready to sign a bargain with the Devil, provided the Devil was a decent fellow who wouldn't ask too high a rate of interest. 'How much will you see that we're left in peace for? It's not sacrificing things that worries us, but the feeling that what we've sacrificed is never enough, that there'll be a second demand in next to no time. Have you no remedy to suggest? Let it be drastic if it must be, provided only that we can rely on it. What do you say? Monarchy, with just the tiniest touch of red in it? A king sufficiently a "people's man" to be able to ride the people on the curb? H'm! Well, that's something for the young folk to get excited about, but we feel, somehow, that it'll never happen. A good war with a quick victory, to restore discipline, to treat the world to a little wholesome blood-letting and canalize our political unrest into honest hatred of the foreigner? That would certainly be drastic—but one's never quite sure with a war. . . . If the worst came to the worst, a revolution made by the lovers of order—Thermidor and Brumaire carefully tacked on to the Fourteenth of July? No, no, that would be the most dangerous solution of the lot.'

"Here they are, swarming round me, coaxing me, just as though they think I may have a remedy ready-made in my pocket. How odd it all is! I attract people like this just as I attract women of a certain temperament. My first dinner with Sammécaud was proof of it, and everything he's done for me since. Is it that they suspect me of being a possible renegade, a man who can be easily corrupted? Most unlikely, because I'm obviously the kind of man whom nobody can pin down—no party, no group, no clique. It's probably just that I attract them. Perhaps they feel instinctively, all these 'realists,' these people who disbelieve in ideals, that I'm a man of strength and integrity, the very reverse of a mere talker. It's just another case of personality."

He spoke to Mme Godorp of her travels, of the European countries she knew and of which he, unfortunately, was ignorant. He hinted darkly that he would get more than most men out of seeing the foreigner at close quarters and making himself familiar with the life of other lands.

"Have you been to Germany?"

"Oh yes, often; I even lived there for a time."

As he listened to her his mind was busy. What she was saying about Germany was not very important, but she had fine eyes and lovely breasts, a body well graced by nature. "Magnificently calm and dowered for love" she was, with every quality calculated to give poise and certainty to a man like himself who had a weakness for Baudelaire.

Mme de Crauze took advantage of a moment during which her friend Gisèle was being monopolized by M. de Pelledoux, to lean towards Gurau and whisper with protective enthusiasm:

"Don't you find her charming?"

He indicated politely that he did.

"Ought I," he thought, "to undeceive them, to show them that I'm perfectly aware of their little game?"

Why should he? It was all very pleasant. Gurau adored (perhaps even more so than Mareil) feeling that he was an object of desire, liked knowing, even, that a trick was being played on him, so long as he was sure that he was aware of what was going on and could retain perfect liberty of action. What more delightful, more flattering way than this of being courted? Here was a beautiful and wealthy woman obviously in love with him, though he hadn't a penny to call his own (only yesterday, just because he had been let down by a little bitch, by a kept woman—may as well face it— an actress who was everyone's property and only just not a whore— why mince matters?—he had been wondering whether life held any future for him, whether he wasn't too old to think about love); and all these smart folk, so far from laughing at him, were delighted with the whole affair and doing all they could to throw this deliciously fair and plump little morsel at his head! Her eyes might be a bit prominent, but how delectably they would close beneath his lips! How intoxicating to crush those breasts against his body!

She was rich. While he listened absent-mindedly to the Vicomte de Crauze telling M. Luymarié about a new shooting-ground that he and some friends had taken near Compiègne and explaining that they still had room for a few more guns if he liked to take a share, Gurau was imagining what it would be like to be married to a rich wife. (No one could read his thoughts, so why should he be ashamed of them?) There would be the apartment on the avenue du Bois, or another like it, and it would be his: he would be completely at home there. Tall windows and high ceilings. A huge bedroom hung with silk—or perhaps two bedrooms, the larger and more luxurious for his wife. There would be a valet to bring the master's trousers freshly pressed, the master's waistcoat, the master's tie,—not forgetting the master's coffee. All the tiresome little details of existence which wasted time and frayed his temper when he had to do them for himself, relegated for ever to a world of servants, a world which need never be thought about, with which he need never again have any dealings. He'd soon forget how to go about getting new laces for his shoes. The car would be waiting for him—his wife, busy at her dressing-table, wouldn't want it until later. . . .

Gurau's meditations were suddenly interrupted by a new thought. Why, after all, shouldn't he lead that kind of life now? After all, he was a Cabinet Minister—even if his appointment was only a few days old. He had been one before for almost a year. A minister's salary was large—as large as a handsome income. He could perfectly well afford to take a handsome apartment, buy good furniture, and engage a valet. He had a car—well, not exactly one of his own, but a car at his disposition, and of course that *did* make a difference. For instance, he hadn't dared take it this evening.— Why hadn't he?—

Oh, simply because he was shy, because he didn't want to bother the chauffeur, who regarded himself more or less as a public servant, because he didn't want to have him hanging about for hours in front of the house, gossiping with the other chauffeurs and finding out things about his hosts. Well, but leaving the car out of the question, what about all the other things?— The first time he hadn't known how long he would remain a minister, nor did he now, for that matter. Why should he risk upsetting all his habits, changing his whole way of life? Besides, it would be silly, contrary to all his principles. He could have gone to live at the Ministry—he had slept there once or twice, but it had been vast and melancholy, impersonal, empty, rather like sleeping in an ill-kept museum, with a lavatory which was used during the day for washing old ink-pots. No, it was much better that he should keep the rooms he had had as a student, much healthier for his self-respect.— But what about the money? What had he done with that? It was really rather ridiculous—paid off one or two small debts which amounted to next to nothing, lent a couple of thousand francs to his brother-in-law, sent a few presents to his old parents—all that hadn't made much of a hole in it. Then he'd increased that bitch Germaine's allowance, bought her one or two fairly expensive little things, allowed himself a bit more for pocket-money, treated himself to a good restaurant now and then, made a few small advances to sponging friends, subscribed to this and that. Of course there had been his election expenses. Far from helping him, Lesouchier had said: "I set your foot on the ladder, my boy, and now you've got money and everything else you want. Things are going badly with me. Let me have ten thousand francs on account of what you owe me. . . ." He had given him five thousand. He must have about three thousand in the bank.

It looked as though some men never got poverty out of their system. Now and again money came their way, but they never managed to assimilate it. They never really throve on it, but remained "undernourished." They never seemed to be able to spend. Money did them no good. They went on living a wretched hand-to-mouth existence which many a poorer man wouldn't put up with for a moment. Obviously to make money for a few months wasn't at all the same thing as having a private fortune or being married to a woman with one. Being a deputy, or a minister off and on, was all right as a foundation, a good solid, concrete foundation, and once that was secure, one could build on it by marrying a rich woman. In that case one could regard a salary as so much pocket-money (enough to spare one the humiliation of asking one's wife every morning for a couple of louis). As pocket-money it was fine—even allowing for subscriptions and a few loans here and there. . . . How independent it made a man in his relations with his colleagues ("I'm not the kind of fellow to go round hunting after jobs; I don't need to"); or with local committees ("I don't need so-and-so's support. Spent a thousand francs, has he? All right, give them back to him.")!

It might be rather painful to be really tempted, but it was pleasant enough to *play* with the idea of temptation, to let himself get a little giddy at the idea. That's the way to keep the mind fresh. But how far could he let things go without finding them a nuisance? It was all a matter of tactful handling. Affairs might turn out rather differently from what he had expected. Instead of Gurau married to the rich Mme Godorp, for instance, the situation might resolve itself in terms of the lovely Mme Godorp becoming Gurau's mistress, which wouldn't involve the same difficulties. "The fun of the whole thing is that at the moment I'm more or less completely master of the game. There's really no reason why things shouldn't turn out exactly as I want them to." It wasn't every day that a man was so wholly in a position to control his fate. The important point was to see that his feelings were under sufficient control to make the most of the opportunity. Used rightly, it could make up to him for many humiliations.

He felt a pricking behind his knee. This time it did not pass. It was continuous and threatening. He had probably drunk too much wine. It had heated his blood. His "eczema diet"—even allowing for the modified form in which he followed it—had got him out of the habit of such rich feeding. If only he dared, he could rub the hollow of his knee against the edge of his chair, the knee and the chair being in convenient proximity; but a better way of quieting the irritation would be to fling himself into the conversation which had just broken out on his left about the recent events in Champagne—concentrate, contradict, work himself up, forget all about his skin and these acidities that were trying to work themselves out.

A footman was bringing round liqueurs. Should he risk a brandy? Yes, and damn the consequences!

Ah, sweet society of men and women, of all defences the most sure, the only true escape. Who would have the heart to go on living for ever alone, for ever beset by his secret troubles? Short of complete and irremediable renunciation there can be no happy loneliness. Blessed be these jewelled women, blessed these men with their dress clothes and receding hair! Mighty is their magic, for they weave spells among which a man may lose himself, set him about with circles of power which hold from him all but pleasing thoughts. Before such talismans even the ailments of the body draw back and dare not threaten. Later, in the solitude of sleeplessness, they will creep back, seeking their revenge, and bitter will be the struggle, unaided then by the comforting support of friends.

Could it really be almost midnight?

In the hall, Mme de Crauze said to him, lowering her voice: "Have you got your car?"

"No, not this evening."

"Then I'll ask Madame Godorp to drop you—if you wouldn't be bored?"

"Why, of course not, but—"

He indicated with a glance the other guests, who all seemed on the point of departure.

"Go first, since you're ready. . . . Wait a few moments in the passage by the front gate. . . . I tell you what I'll do, I'll get my daughter and her husband to go in the car with you. It will make it less embarrassing for you. . . . You can drop them first at the Île Saint-Louis, where they live. . . . Go along now. . . . I'll tell Gisèle and the other two to follow you."

Gurau laughed as he crossed the courtyard.

"No procuress like a woman of fashion!"

While he waited under the arch, he allowed himself, as a special favour, the delicious indulgence of a little scratching. The fine cloth of his trousers helped him to obtain exactly the right degree of relief.

When they had left M. and Mme Jacques Masson at their home in the Île Saint-Louis, a slight awkwardness made itself felt between Mme Godorp and Gurau.

"You are going straight home?" she asked.

He hesitated.

"No. . . . I want to look in at the office of my paper."

She smiled.

"As late as this? . . . Do you do that every night?"

"When I'm not a minister, yes. . . . When I am a minister, I allow myself a little latitude. But tonight I really must look in there."

It gave him a certain pleasure to suggest this oscillation between periods of office as the normal rhythm of his existence. . . .

They set off towards the *Sanction* building.

"If I wasn't afraid of asking too great a favour, I'd—"

"You'd what?"

"I'd ask whether we might go by—by the Left Bank as far, perhaps, as the Pont-Neuf. It's only a very little out of our way."

She seemed to be interested.

"You want to stop—somewhere?"

Her voice trembled slightly as she spoke the words.

"Oh no. . . ." He smiled. "But I should like to take that particular route with you. Am I asking too much?"

After they had passed the Place Saint-Michel, seated as he was on her left, he had only to lean forward a little to get a good view of the house-fronts on the Quai des Grands-Augustins.

He directed his gaze frankly towards the upper storeys of the houses, without attempting to hide what he was doing from Mme Godorp's watchful eyes.

"Would you mind asking the chauffeur to drive a little slower?" he said.

Opposite one of the houses he leaned still farther forward and seemed to be examining the upper windows with care.

Then he turned towards Mme Godorp and smiled at her with an expression of obvious distress. Her left hand, holding a glove, lay beside her on the seat. Gurau took it, as though to do so had been the most natural thing in the world. The sadness in his eyes seemed to excuse the gesture.

"Dear lady, one of these days I hope I shall be able to tell you why I wanted to come this particular way on this particular evening. . . . I should like to tell you my secrets. . . . It's not a thing I do with many people."

He could scarcely know that it was almost in exactly the same way that on another evening, at almost the same moment, and in a car not so very different from this one, Sammécaud had taken Germaine's hand in his.

As the car moved off he raised his hat once more to Mme Godorp, who waved her hand and smiled. He walked slowly towards the *Sanction* building, as though with the intention of entering it, but stood for a moment in thought upon the threshold. Then he turned suddenly and set off at a quick pace along several streets, hesitating a moment now and again before crossing some of the intersecting streets.

He proceeded in this way for about twelve minutes, until he reached a narrow-fronted house of three storeys, of which the highest formed a mansard roof. Its appearance seemed to be familiar to him. It was white and had the respectable look of a private house dating from the Second Empire, or of a family hotel. It showed no sign, however, save the single word "Modes" inscribed above one of the two windows of the ground floor, which stood a little above the level of the pavement. There was no light in any of the windows, and some of them had the shutters closed. There was a lamp in the fanlight above the front door.

Gurau pressed the bell, and footsteps sounded within. A maid in a white apron and frilled cap opened the door, gave a quick glance at the gentleman in evening dress before her, admitted him and closed it behind him. A short passage led to a few steps, at the top of which there was a narrow landing. The colour of the walls was oak and cream. The air of the place was that of a middle-class apartment-house.

As he mounted the steps Gurau kept saying to himself: "Why on earth have I come here?"

A young woman of about thirty-five, rather plump, neatly and quietly dressed, who might have been the hostess of a decent commercial hotel somewhere in the provinces, cried out, the moment she saw him:

"What, you! How nice to see you, and what a surprise!"

She smiled broadly at him, holding her closed right hand pressed against the open palm of her left and rocking gently backwards and forwards on her feet, as though to express a mood of nervous cheerfulness. She spoke in a fresh and slightly common voice, which she lowered when she again addressed him:

"You've not been here for a long time, though I must say when you were here last you made the most of it!"

She nodded her head and bit her lips. She looked admiringly at Gurau and added in a tone that was almost a whisper:

"I congratulate you. We're all delighted at your appointment."

She seemed intent on some thought.

"I hardly like to offer you a drink. Our last lot of wine was poor —much too sweet, and I remember you don't like that. I imagine, too, that you're in rather a hurry?"

She took his hat and his overcoat.

"Anyhow, sit down a moment."

She lavished attentions on him, though she did not lose her pre-occupied air.

"Listen. I don't know whether you'll like the idea, but the fact is that I've got a little creole here tonight—it's the first time she's been here—and she really is charming, in every way. She's dancing at the Olympia, a thoroughly decent girl; it's the merest chance that we've got her. Not a Negress you know, only just a little dark, and with a perfectly lovely body. I think she's come on a sudden impulse; I don't believe she'll take up the life regularly. I should be so pleased to think it was you who were benefiting from our luck—if it's the kind of thing you like, of course."

The young creole came into the room where Gurau was waiting. She was wearing a loose wrap adorned with red flowers, and seemed not so much nervous as bored and rather aloof. She pouted her lips as she looked at Gurau, but he thought the gesture perfunctory.

"Good evening," she said.

She took off her wrap, beneath which she was naked, but instead of throwing it casually aside, folded it carefully and laid it across a chair which she pushed up to the corner of the fire-place. This gave Gurau plenty of opportunity to observe her body from several angles.

It was a light tobacco colour and of very even tone. The skin was remarkably fine in texture, but of a mat surface, with the soft, dull finish which is seen in certain expensive materials.

She was, on the whole, well enough made, though on the stocky or sturdy side. Her waist was rather thick, her hips prominent, the curve of her legs strongly marked and muscular, while her breasts, though firm, were narrow and prominent. Their tips, which were extremely pointed and of the colour of tea-roses, stood out with re-markable distinctness. Her face was not striking, being round and rather large, with a small, snub nose which was in no way flat, a mouth rather too large, with fullish lips, and eyes of no particular distinction. But for the colour of her skin she might have been a Breton peasant. Her hair, loosely coiled in the nape of her neck, was not very thick.

Gurau looked at her with detachment. "I don't really want her," he told himself (was he quite sure of that?), and added: "nor anybody else, for that matter . . . not tonight. . . . Why have I come here?" But he put the question without any feeling of distress, rather as though he were considering the actions of a stranger, fastidiously aloof. "There is certainly a very odd side to me; my motives are sometimes very difficult to define."

"Aren't you going to undress?" she asked him.

"Yes, yes," he replied, in a tone of polite absent-mindedness such as he might have used to say "Why, certainly," to some hostess who had asked him whether he would like coffee in the garden.

She came across to help him. At first he waved her aside, but found it pleasant after a moment or two to let her have her way. There was no hint of provocation about her. Her manner of quiet helpfulness might have been that of a well-trained maid helping her mistress off with her clothes. But, for all that, her every movement contrived to be a caress, subtly and momentarily exciting.

He tried to determine of what it was this woman smelt who was moving about so close to him. Something, he decided, not at all obvious, half aromatic, half highly spiced, but, whatever its exact nature, scarcely perceptible and not at all heady. It reminded him of the smell one gets in well-kept museums full of carefully dusted and polished furniture; a little, too, like the interior of a fashionable church.

The young mistress of the house was lying in wait for him.

"Well," she asked anxiously, "what was she like?"

"Admirable, really admirable."

"Perfectly clean, I'm sure, and well-behaved, eh? . . . But does she know how to make herself agreeable?"

"I have no complaints at all. She was extremely forthcoming. . . ."

He hesitated a moment, started to laugh, and began to speak, without coarseness, in the tone a man might use to explain to someone of experience the details of some rather interesting piece of technique: "She did a great deal more than I expected in several ways, but in one particularly. I don't mind telling you that on that special ground she would be very hard to beat. A great many people, you'll find, will be extremely appreciative of her."

"Good," said the young, quietly dressed manageress, without the vestige of a smile; "so much the better . . . but—"

"But, all the same, she's quite extraordinarily cold. . . . It's really very odd. . . . There are a great many women like her, of course, who feel nothing at all . . . that's quite easy to understand, and I dislike it intensely when they make pretence of something that isn't there. But at least they respond—which is quite a different thing. . . . But she doesn't, not in the least. What makes it all the stranger is that in the preliminary stages she showed herself very active and very—expert."

Gurau had sat down in the neat little drawing-room facing his hostess. "A curious sort of conversation," he thought. "Here am I, quietly seated in this room, talking like this. . . . Oh, well!"

The young manageress listened with respectful attention and showed by occasional nods that she understood what he was telling her and that she was giving his remarks her serious consideration.

"Yes," she said at last, almost solemnly, "most of those women are made that way; it's very odd. Once or twice I've told them about it, but it does no good. Do you think it's a matter of race? . . ."

"What women do you mean? Negresses, Arabs, or just creoles like this one? There's a good deal of difference, you know."

"Oh, I realize that. . . . Genuine Negresses throw themselves into it heart and soul, I believe. . . . But on two occasions I've had Arab women, and they were exactly as you describe your creole. . . . It's probably due to the training they've received from their men at home and which they pass on. . . . But you must admit it's odd. Have you ever seen them dancing—doing the belly-dance, for instance? I'm told it's just the same in the colonies or the Antilles. They go through the most extraordinary contortions, and their love-dances are the most passionate affairs. They give the impression that they're in the very ecstasy of desire; so much so, I gather, that it becomes rather embarrassing. . . . Why is it, then, that at the very moment they seem to have been working up to, when you'd say they most wanted it, they're less satisfactory than a great many Frenchwomen? . . . The only explanation is that the native men like to be worked up, but that once they've reached that point, they prefer to have the initiative left to them. There's a great deal to be said on the subject, of course, that can't very easily be put into words. As my husband says, you don't hear that sort of thing discussed, people don't make a study of it, because it's not thought decent to talk about except jokingly. All the same, it's just as curious and interesting as a lot of stuff one sees in the newspapers."

Chapter

5

MARGARET IN PARIS.
THE PLOT THICKENS

Laulerque thought he recognized the handwriting on the letter which the concierge gave him. But the stamp was French, and the postmark showed that it had been posted in Paris.

He opened the envelope and looked first at the signature: "Margaret-Désideria"; then he read the text, which occupied only a few lines.

Friday

Dear Armand:

I am in Paris. You mustn't be angry with me. I want to see you as soon as possible. Write to me at the address below. It will be quite safe. I'm free any day after half past nine in the evening. [She had originally put "ten o'clock" and then scratched it out.]

Yours always,
MARGARET-DÉSIDERIA

My address is: Mademoiselle Margaret Kreuz, c/o Madame Bouillon, 6 rue Octave-Feuillet, La Muette, Paris.

It was already six o'clock. Laulerque thought that an express letter would get to the girl in time. He went to the nearest post office and wrote as follows:

Dear Margaret-Désideria:

I have just got your note, which fills me with amazement. It's a delightful surprise, but it *is* a surprise. What has happened? I'm just as anxious to see you as you are to see me, and I will be at the

café at the corner of the Place Victor-Hugo (I've forgotten its name)
any time after a quarter to ten this evening. The café I mean is also
a tobacco-shop, and is quite near where you're staying. You won't
have any difficulty in finding it. Don't mind about being late.

Yours affectionately,

ARMAND

Laulerque had not seen Margaret-Désideria since their first meeting in Amsterdam. But they had written to each other regularly.
About once in every fortnight he received a letter of twelve or so
close-written pages which showed, from the various dates which it
contained, that it had been composed at various times. His answers
were rather shorter. The tone of this correspondence had become
very tender, even high-flown; so much so that if some of the letters
had fallen into the hands of a third person, they would have given
the impression of a passionate love-affair. Starting on a note of detached emotionalism, their exchange had rapidly become more and
more personal. The two young people had not only exchanged
photographs, but had reached a point where they confided to each
other the nature of their tastes, the details of their past lives, and the
various adventures and experiences which had come their way in
the world of the intellect as well as in that of every day. Thus they
now had at their disposition a whole fund of mutually comprehensible allusions and were able to treat each other, not without
feeling pleased amusement at their skill, as friends of long standing.

None of Margaret's letters had contained any hint of an intention
to come to Paris. She had expressed great disappointment when their
plan to meet in Holland at Christmas had had to be postponed. More
recently she had complained, with ever increasing bitterness, of the
boredom of having to go on living with her diamond-merchants, of
the gloom of the Dutch climate in winter, of her loneliness. But
there was nothing new in all that.

What had been remarkable in her later letters had been certain
rather obscurely phrased outbursts—occasioned probably by inci-

dents of which she said nothing—about the general beastliness of the human race, the readiness of people to take refuge in lying when by so doing they could cloak their vices or their dishonesty, and the unhappiness that comes from discovering such humiliating truths.

"What is she doing in Paris? Has she come here with her Dutch family? How long will she stay? Am I the cause, or partly the cause? Ought I to be pleased? . . . When I suddenly see her again in the atmosphere of Paris, without the canals and the moonlight, without the excitement of a mysterious journey, and after all these letters in which we've been working each other up, what shall I feel about her?"

From six until ten he pondered these problems with scarcely a pause, and was still turning them over in his mind, especially the last of them, when he chose a quiet corner in the café on the Place Victor-Hugo.

He saw her come in with a shy and awkward air. She turned to nod her thanks to a strange man—some passer-by, obviously, of whom she had asked the way. She moved forward, looking anxiously round her as though unaccustomed to her surroundings. The dark-green coat which she was wearing appeared to be made of some heavy material and looked slightly odd to Parisian eyes, but her hat, of black felt, very deep in the crown and fitted with a peak, was not unlike the hats which Laulerque had seen that winter surmounting the faces of various pretty women, Mathilde's among others. It was in no way odd or funny and suited the young girl to perfection. Its only fault was that it neither deliberately harmonized with nor formed a contrast to the green of her coat, which, however, set off her figure so admirably—giving an impression of height and strength—that its actual colour was soon forgotten. Her body thus displayed presented, from shoulders to hips, from throat to waist and legs, a firmness of silhouette and a grace of carriage which, though they had little in common with the daintiness of female Paris, completely reconciled the observer to its absence.

Laulerque had about as much time as it takes to empty a dice-box to ask himself a variety of questions. These were, in their nature, of prime importance, and concentrated in one brief moment the matter of a hundred idle reveries, striking to the very heart of his intention and forcing him to take a definite attitude from which there could be no subsequent turning back. Many moods, many actions, many decisions, might later flow from this instant's verdict, taking the line of least resistance, and dependent upon the consequent force of inertia.

"Is she pretty enough? Well enough made to neutralize the plainness of her features and compensate for her foreign air of oddity? Will she be willing to abandon fantasy for action? Does she want a real love-affair, with all that the words imply? Does she want it as much as Mathilde, for example, whom I never had and never tried to have, but whom I might still be able to have if I really wanted to, had sufficient cheek, and really took advantage of the fact that her present situation is rather like that of the 'Donkey and the Two Thieves'? Or does she want more? . . . What it all really comes to is this—will Margaret (who has just caught sight of me, who is smiling, who, in another second, will be wringing my hand) be my mistress in a week's time?"

He wouldn't allow himself to answer the question at once, but sought to delay the decision and made use, for the purpose, of a plausible enough argument: "Wait until you know why she has come. Don't go off the deep end. . . . Wait at least until you know whether she will be here a week from now." But he felt himself inclining to a sort of easy, intoxicating affirmative which seemed to open somewhere on his left in a golden mist, much as Margaret-Désideria's rather brownish lips were opening in front of his eyes, to display her white teeth in a nervous smile.

She spoke at first with the anguished expression, the pouts, the bursts of uncertain laughter, of a child who is trying to forestall a reprimand and to soften, before it can fall, the expected severity of a rebuke.

She had left her Dutch diamond-merchants; yes, for good, and with no regrets. She had left Holland too, but whether for good she couldn't yet say. One never knew for certain about a thing like that. She had been in Paris for three days as governess to two children of apparently very rich parents.

How had all these changes come about? Well, one day she had read an advertisement in the *Figaro,* which her diamond-merchants took in regularly:

Wanted. A governess with knowledge of German; preferably Austrian by birth. Must be young and well educated. Two children. Send photograph and references to Bouillon, 6 rue Octave-Feuillet, Paris.

She had written, stressing the fact that she was an Austrian. She said that she wanted to leave Holland because of the climate and because she wanted to get to know France, of which she was very fond. She had added that she had a good knowledge of French.

At first they had tried to get her to come in return for her board alone (a condition which they had carefully kept out of their advertisement), but after considerable correspondence she had agreed to accept a very low salary—sixty francs a month.

"But how are you going to manage on that?" Laulerque asked.

"I'm hoping they'll give me a rise, or that, now I'm here, I shall be able to find another situation."

"At least they sent you your fare?"

"Yes, third class. I've also written to my parents. They're very pleased to think that I'm coming to France. I let them assume that I should have to pay my own fare, and that I should have other expenses. They sent me rather more than five hundred francs. . . ." She laughed rather shamefacedly. "You see, I wanted to come. I should have managed to come in any case." She laughed again. "If the worst had come to the worst, I'd have stolen one of my employer's diamonds."

"But why were you so keen to come?"

"Don't you know?" Her eyes grew misty and she seemed to swallow. Laulerque took the hand she stretched towards him and pressed it quickly. While appearing to accept the tender implication of her words, he continued to encourage her confidences and soon came to the conclusion that the desire to be near him had not been her only reason for leaving Amsterdam in a hurry. He gathered that the diamond-merchant whose children had been in her charge had more than once taken liberties with her, but this part of the story was not very clear, and he hardly liked to ask for details. In the first place, he found it difficult to question her about the lengths to which these liberties had gone, and, secondly, a point came in the narrative at which the merchant's wife began to participate in the action. A cynic might have wondered whether, in fact, Margaret hadn't waited until the situation became intolerable before letting the lady get wind of it. Probably the truth lay half-way between the two versions. It seemed likely that the young woman had submitted, reluctantly, but without taking the matter too seriously, to a few harmless and rather vulgar familiarities, and that the Dutch wife had found something out and kicked up a row. Even if the husband had been entirely to blame, she must have felt that his house was scarcely the place for her.

Nevertheless, Laulerque felt annoyed. There was something not quite frank about what the girl had told him. He decided that he would try to find out more later on. For the moment he wanted to talk about something else. What part had the Organization played in all this? Had she asked permission to leave Amsterdam and come to Paris?

Margaret swayed the whole upper part of her body once or twice from left to right, with an expression of distaste.

Then, without looking at him, she whispered:

"You know that there's been a— Oh, what's the word for *Spaltung*?"

"*Spaltung*?"

"Yes, division, breach. . . . *Trennung,* if you prefer."

She made a movement with her hand as though she were cutting something in two and separating the halves.

"A schism?" Laulerque imitated her gesture.

"Yes, that's it." She repeated it: "Schism, schism," as though to get used to it. She seemed to find amusement in the exercise.

"Really? . . . Who told you so?"

She smiled mysteriously, lowering her eyes and resting her cheek on her hand.

"I know it."

"But a schism—what kind of a schism? . . . What does it consist in?"

There was a note of irony in her voice as she said:

"Have you forgotten that we're forbidden to talk?"

She stopped, then continued:

"Naturally, I don't know everything . . . but I do know . . . from people in my own country . . . people related to me."

She went on, becoming more and more excited as she proceeded:

"The chief has been coming in for criticism—the big chief. . . . Haven't you any idea who he is? . . . You haven't? . . . Well, I shan't tell you. . . . You see, I'm not absolutely certain, but it's someone high up, someone very high up. . . ." (She raised her hand above her head, following it with her eyes.) "He's been blamed for doing nothing himself and for preventing other people from doing anything. He's *too* high up, you see, he's got too many friends. They say he's deliberately adopting an attitude of philosophic detachment so as not to have to decide, and that if that goes on, nothing will ever be accomplished."

"If what goes on?"

She continued as though she had not heard:

"It is said that he started the Organization—he and others, because he didn't do it alone—just to save the Empire."

She stopped short as though suddenly frightened of saying too much.

Laulerque experienced what he took to be a sudden flash of intuition.

"Look here, Margaret—it's just occurred to me—I'm probably all wrong—but this high-up person—it isn't by any chance the Tsar?"

Even while the words were on his lips, he felt that he wanted to give vent to a bitter laugh, so absurd was the degree of disillusion which they implied.

"What an extraordinary idea!" she said, completely disconcerted for the moment.

"You're right, I was a fool. . . . It was only because of this rumour that he's been working for peace. · · · But I see what a stupid idea it was. . . . Go on."

"I was thinking of the Austrian Empire. But don't start imagining. . . . You'd better not try to guess, you never will. . . . You've never even heard his name. All I meant to say was that nothing good can happen so long as the Austrian Empire exists. It's easy enough to see why. The fact that it oppresses the people that compose it stands in the way of everything. There can be no peace in Europe while all those peoples are enslaved: the Southern Slavs, the Czechs, the Slovaks, the Roumanians, and all the rest of them—all under the heel of the same Empire, which is nothing but the very incarnation of Antichrist. It's all very well talking about preventing war, but when preventing war means that all these people are prevented from revolting, that the folk in Vienna and Budapest are just to be allowed to go on living in comfort and ruling like Turkish sultans in the old days, surrounded by their viziers, it's . . ."

The young woman had worked herself up into an extraordinary state of excitement, but since she was trying, at the same time, to keep a hold on herself, she could find words, in the excess of her feelings, for nothing but a confused jumble of ideas.

From the first, Laulerque had listened with amazement, which rapidly turned to discomfort. He was far from understanding all she said. He suspected that the girl's mind was filled with a medley of facts of very unequal value and very indifferently mastered; that she ranked matters of purely local interest with events of international significance; that she gave as much weight to gossip and the inventions of disgruntled individuals as to well-supported evidence.

He was aware of two separate sets of impressions, both of which saddened him. In the first place he felt that something was taking Margaret from him, that they were drifting away from each other with swiftly gathering speed. . . . She was headed for some unknown hurly-burly of ideas, passions, and people which, even at this distance, reeked of the Near East, something which the Western mind could only guess at with feelings of disgust, terror, or mockery. . . . "And this," he thought, "is the Margaret of those Dutch canals, of that Amsterdam, so dear to memory, so full of kindly shadows, yet so free from troubling mysteries, taking its place so easily in the long pageant of our European tradition . . . the Margaret who once seemed to me the typical young woman of today, modern and liberal-minded as the best of us . . . capable of taking my most allusive meaning . . . worthy to be a member of Sampeyre's circle. . . . Yet now I feel her haunted by alien and unfriendly ghosts, so that I am driven to wonder what this cause of ours really meant to her, what she hoped to find when she decided to devote herself to its furtherance."

But this was not all. His doubts spread beyond the figure of Margaret and began to play about the Organization itself. "What's behind it all? Is it simply, too simply, a disguised agency of espionage, as Jerphanion suggested? No, it almost certainly isn't that. But still less, I'm afraid, is it what I hoped to find it, what others like me, the members, for instance, of our 'little set,' might hope to find it, according to their varying temperaments, a secret society on modern lines, positive and realist, ready to make use of every manifestation of direct action which has been tested by experience and tempered by use, from the up-to-date versions of the anarchist bomb to the disciplined technique of organized labour, strikes, sabotage, and the paralysis of the essential public services . . . all directed to the attainment, not of vague, misty, and doubtful ends, but to the achievement of a limited and definite objective, about which all good men, no matter where they might be, could be in agreement—the prevention of the war that is daily drawing nearer, just because such a war would be absurd and could benefit nobody (as Norman Angell says in his book. Ah, there's a man who ought to be one of our leaders, though he's probably not even a member of the society). Yes, that, stripped to its bare bones, is really our object—to prevent a European war because that, we think, is the task lying most urgently to our hands, because, apart from all the hateful bloodshed of such a war, its occurrence or non-occurrence is bound to influence the whole of that future in which we all, whatever our reasons, so passionately believe. . . . And because we have only limited resources, we seek to prevent it, not by the isolated manifestations of individuals, but by applying the maximum of pressure to a few vital points at carefully chosen moments. Well, I see now that that's just what it isn't. . . . Mascot may believe it is, but it isn't. . . . And if that's so, what is it?"

He couldn't say definitely what was in his mind. He had merely one of those vague intuitions which need no detailed proof to be utterly and completely convincing. He remembered the confidences which M. Karl had made to him, or, rather, their general impression. They did not contradict Margaret's veiled references. Seeking an appropriate background for this feeling of his, Laulerque found himself vaguely recollecting certain facts of history—the Emperor Alexander I, Mme de Krudener, the Holy Alliance. . . . "That's not exactly it, times have changed, but it's of the same general kind."

Nevertheless, he wanted to get greater clarity into his thoughts. Certain points he found particularly irritating because they involved his personal destiny.

"Listen, Margaret, my dear," he said, trying to speak and look as naturally as possible, "I don't want to bore you about all this or spend too much time on it. I'm in a hurry to discuss our own future, yours and mine. . . . We've written lovely things to each other, and it's such a delight for me to have you here by my side! . . . But I want to get this tiresome business off my chest. You see, you've given new life to my doubts. . . . I don't want to make you say more than you wish to, but you can't, really you can't, leave me a prey to all these worrying ideas which you've put into my mind. . . . Not that they weren't there a little already. . . . I'd like your opinion on one or two points. . . . We don't have to dot the *i*'s and cross the *t*'s. . . ." He lowered his voice. "You yourself said in one of your letters that things were going to happen—do you remember? It was some time early in the winter, just after Tolstoy's death? . . . You didn't seem at that time to be so completely disillusioned as you are now. . . . No, no, let me finish. . . . And since then . . . you know what I mean . . . they have tried to do something . . . here at least. . . . You knew about that?"

"Briand?" she said in a very low voice.

"Yes. . . . So you knew. Good! . . . There's a question I've asked myself frequently since: was there anything similar elsewhere? I've heard nothing. Do you know of anything?"

"Yes," she said, with a touch of scorn in her voice, "in Russia . . . and in Austria."

"Really?"

"In Germany, too; there was an attempt on the 5th of February, on the occasion of Paul Singer's funeral, in Berlin. There were more than a hundred thousand people at the funeral."

"Paul Singer?"

"One of the leaders of the Social-Democratic Party."

Laulerque made a face. "Oh, the Social-Democrats!"

"It was the occasion that counted. An attempt was to be made against one of the Emperor's friends who has been giving him bad advice. The idea, you see, was that the Emperor would think: 'Here's one of my most familiar companions killed . . . and down there all

that crowd of revolutionaries . . . all on the same day!' But somebody sold the plot to the police."

"And in Russia?"

"The same thing happened."

"What do you mean, the same thing?"

"What I say. There was an attempt, but it was against the wrong
person—and he wasn't killed. It is said that the Okhrana—that's
what the police are called in Russia—arranged the whole thing and
changed the victim. . . . The Organization has an agent in the
Okhrana. But it may be that he sold us to them. You see what I mean?
It's so difficult to be sure. Others say that it was the Maximalists who
made the change, because the assassin was one of their own men, and
their objects are not the same as ours. All they care about is revolution
in Russia."

"Who are these people you call the Maximalists?"

"The newest type of revolutionary—the most extreme." The light
of admiration was in her eyes. "They're extraordinary people," she
said, "their energy is terrifying. We need some of them in our
country!"

"In our country? You mean—?"

"In Austria-Hungary—that's what I mean."

He felt discouraged and tired. He wanted to get away by himself
and think. He hoped that all these amazing and mutually irrelevant
ideas which he had picked up would fall of themselves into some kind
of order, would at least formulate themselves into one or two questions which he could ask later.

One of the other occupants of the café seemed to be paying them
rather suspicious attention, and he made this man's presence the
excuse for proposing a short walk.

Once outside, he took the young woman's arm as he had done that
evening in Amsterdam. It was cold and the pavements were wet. It
must have been raining while they were in the café.

They reached the avenue du Bois and walked up it on the left-hand side towards the Porte-Dauphine. This part of the town was completely deserted.

He asked no better than to let his mind dwell on thoughts of love. He gave himself a little private lecture. "At your age, with this charming, this alluring girl on your arm, you've got something better to do than to try to straighten out this tangled skein of bogus plots. So has she. In any case, there's a time for everything. Your immediate object is not to put the brake on the next war, but to go to bed with this young woman. She's certainly worth going to bed with. Take a leaf out of Jerphanion's book. Bad though the times may be, and however noble his soul, he's managed to whisk away Mathilde from under the nose of Clanricard, the idealist, and to— I wonder, as a matter of fact, whether they have been to bed yet. Problem number one. Problem number two, which should I like best, to go to bed with Margaret or to go to bed with Mathilde? Unfortunately, there's not much doubt about the answer. But going to bed isn't the be-all and the end-all. There's a quality about Margaret, an exciting strangeness, a hint of character, that there isn't about Mathilde. . . . Still, there are points about a little French girl from the South."

After a quarter of an hour spent in dallying beneath the leafless but already budding trees of the avenue, and two kisses of a rather mild kind, Laulerque was inclined to think that going to bed with Margaret was not one of the world's insoluble problems. It looked, in fact, as though it would be rather too easy for his taste. The story of the diamond-merchant began to worry him again. He would have liked to know rather more about her reasons for leaving Amsterdam. He approached the question in a roundabout way:

"I'm thinking about something I asked you before, darling. How did you manage about the Organization when you left Holland? You must have been under somebody's orders there?"

"Certainly I was."

"Well, how did you work it, then?"

She burst out with it then, as though she had been only waiting for this opportunity to unbosom herself. The chief agent for Holland, whom unfortunately she knew only too well, was a horrible creature; not a Dutchman at all, but a German-speaking Swiss, who was more or less obliged to live away from his own country because of certain scandalous episodes.

"He's a pervert," she said. "He was caught one day with the son of a Federal Councillor."

But his unnatural tendencies went, it seemed, with a weakness for women as well. He was fond of staging intimate orgies at which both sexes were represented. The precautions which he used to cloak his political activities provided him with convenient shelter for his debauches. He tried, too, to take double advantage of his authority. It seemed to be his opinion that the young women members of the Organization, those at least with whom he had most to do, ought to refuse him nothing.

"He summoned me one day to one of his parties. I didn't go and he was furious. Oh, he probably didn't want me for himself, but he may have promised me to somebody else."

He had the impudence, it seemed, to formulate a theory in defence of his vices. He maintained, for instance, that the members of a secret society ought to have sexual as well as disciplinary relations with their chief, and, in certain cases, with one another. In this way their solidarity would take on a sort of sacred and mystic significance.

"But that doesn't hold water!" Laulerque exclaimed. "I was told quite definitely that one of the chief rules of the Organization was that its members shouldn't know who one another were."

"That may be . . . but some of them can't help knowing each other. Besides, every chief agent is a law to himself. . . . I'm pretty sure, too, that this particular one is in with the police. When I refused to go to his party, he threatened me—not very definitely, but I saw pretty clearly what he meant."

"Threatened to denounce you to the police?"

"I imagine so. . . . He was my real reason for coming away in such a hurry. . . . It wasn't very likely that I should ask his leave. He thinks I'm still there."

"But he'll very soon see that you're not!"

"Yes, but not at once."

"Did he summon you often to his house?"

"Yes, at first I used to go and see him every Friday. But he'll think I'm staying away because of his threats. If he makes any inquiries, my employers will tell him that I've been called home, and that I'm spending a few days at Agram."

"Are you sure they'll tell him that?"

"Yes, they think themselves that I've gone home. What reason can they have for saying that I shall come back soon? And he's not quite comfortable in his own mind. If he's not in with the police, he'll probably be afraid that I may denounce him, just to get my revenge. If he is in with them, he may think that I've found it out, and that I'm going to give him away to the Organization."

"You said just now that he'd threatened you. What did he say?"

"He said: 'I'll teach you to make a fool of me!'"

"No more? And you interpreted that as meaning that he was in with the police?"

She shrugged her shoulders.

"He might have friends in the police and manage, through them, to get me deported or imprisoned as a revolutionary or an anarchist or something. You see, the police wouldn't know that he was one of the heads of the Organization. A man in that position, however honest, however loyal to the cause, finds it almost necessary to have friends in the police, so that he can know in time if it comes to helping one of his friends or averting official suspicion, and it's not easy to be sure whether he's betraying us or not."

"Yes, I understand all that, but if he denounces you he must know that there's a risk of your talking, of your telling other people who he is?"

"It all depends on how much he can get the police to believe. . . .

He may just have wanted to frighten me into going to his beastly parties."

Laulerque looked uncomfortably at the girl. "How odd she is!" he thought. "Is the whole thing an invention? Or is she just exaggerating? . . . There was nothing of all this in her letters, unless, indeed, I failed to catch the allusions. . . . Was she already hiding all these mysteries from me that time we went walking by the canals?"

He gave rein to his reflections:

"Perhaps it's not so extraordinary after all. Isn't it just among rather abnormal people that they would be most likely to find the kind of recruits they wanted, especially women, individuals more ready than others to adopt a rebellious and desperate attitude towards the social order? She may have been led by a naturally vicious imagination to make it all up, or this man may really be what she says he is—neither alternative is beyond the bounds of possibility. . . . But then where do I come in? . . . Compared with that kind of chap I'm normal enough, but I suppose I should seem a bit cracked to others, if they knew what I was doing."

His recent problems returned with added strength to plague him afresh, and this time there was no reason why he should side-track them.

"There's another thing, Margaret. You spoke a little while back of a schism. I didn't understand exactly what you meant. What kind of a schism?"

The explanation upon which she now embarked was extremely confused, either because she wished deliberately to keep her story vague or because she was bewildered by all the details she had picked up.

So far as he could make out, the members of the society in central and eastern Europe, including its chiefs and originators, were obsessed, more or less consciously, by the idea of some sort of nationalist agitation, under the pretext that the main obstacle to the establishment of European harmony and a durable peace was the continued existence of that "political monstrosity" the Austro-Hungarian Empire. With this attitude Margaret was now in sympathy. The first thing to do, according to her, was to smash the monster. A break within the Organization was inevitable, not primarily because it contained followers of two mutually incompatible doctrines—"Peace at all costs" on one side, "Destruction of Austria-Hungary" on the other—but because a large number of those who had originally organized the society and now gave it the protection of their patronage had a lively interest in the existence of the Empire and believed, perhaps honestly enough, that its fall would be the prelude to general disaster.

"But," he insisted, "you spoke just now of an attempt . . . of a stroke, which had been recently engineered in Austria. . . . We dropped the subject at the time and forgot to take it up again. What was this stroke? If there really are two tendencies which diverge just on this question of Austria, which of the two arranged it and hoped to benefit from it?"

The girl replied that, so far as she could make out, this particular business had been a triumph of treachery on the part of their leaders. They had made a great show of proving their *bona fides* to the terrorists. At first it had been planned to make an attempt against the Emperor Francis Joseph, not necessarily to kill him, but anyhow to frighten him. Later, this was changed to an attack on one of his close relatives, someone he was particularly fond of, the object, as before, being to terrify the old monarch. Finally kidnapping had taken the place of assassination. But under colour of carrying out an act of terrorism, the big men of the movement, and its real head in particular, had been scheming simply and solely in their own selfish interests. The man they were arranging to kidnap was someone who stood in the way of their personal ambitions.

"Did the kidnapping actually take place?"

"Yes."

"Where did they take him?"

"Somewhere abroad."

"Do you know where?"

"No."

"But if they haven't killed him, he must be just as much in their way as he was before. I don't understand. If, for instance, they wanted to make away with an heir to the throne, they'd have to kill him."

The girl seemed to be nonplussed by his questions. "It wasn't that exactly," she said, with considerable show of embarrassment.

Laulerque was deeply worried. He couldn't help putting two and two together, but he wouldn't let himself draw conclusions too quickly.

He pressed the point:

"Have you no idea what country they took him to?"

"Absolutely none."

"What is his name? You must have heard it from somebody."

"No, I don't know."

She added, as though excusing her ignorance:

"I only heard of the matter from one of my cousins." Her voice trembled slightly as she said the words "one of my cousins." "He wrote about it in a letter. But since he was afraid that his correspondence might be opened by the police, he used a roundabout way of telling me and worded it as though it had to do with some family occurrence. Consequently I didn't grasp all the details."

"Are your cousins members of the Organization, then? . . . If I remember rightly what you told me that evening in Amsterdam—"

"They weren't members then. But they may change their minds now. . . ."

She was obviously speaking against her will. "That's enough for this evening," he thought.

For some time they had been near the entrance of the Bois. They walked to and fro beneath the trees; now and again they crossed the avenue.

Laulerque felt rather like a man who wakes, with a headache, in some disreputable place where he had been keeping it up late with a few casual acquaintances, and sees a lot of strange faces among the debris of last night's orgy. He remembers that when the fun was at its height he lent his note-case to one of the strangers. "What have I let myself in for?" he wonders. "Where is this adventure going to land me?"

He would have thought about it a good deal more but for a certain sense of self-respect.

Chapter

⑥

IN WHICH TWO FRENCHMEN CONTEMPLATE THE MYSTERIES OF CENTRAL EUROPE

Laulerque had just said to Mascot, in the intimacy of the latter's quiet and cushioned room:

"That, making allowances for details of places and persons which I have suppressed, is the sum of what I have been able to learn. I didn't ask for these confidences, and I'm perfectly ready to believe that they contain a great deal that has been exaggerated and possibly even invented. But some of the points which emerged tally too well with what I have been able to gather from other sources to be ignored. I can't help feeling worried."

"Does the person who told you all this belong to the Organization?"

"That's a difficult question for me to answer, seeing that I don't know the person's real name."

"It was foolish of me to ask. . . . Such close knowledge of detail presupposes an intimate connexion. Besides, no one but a member would have thought of going to you."

"Surely that doesn't follow?" Laulerque replied, looking rather mysterious. "After all, life's full of queer coincidences."

Mascot was deep in thought.

"If someone belonging to the Organization is passing through Paris, it's devilish odd that I shouldn't have been told of it."

"I repeat," said Laulerque in an anxious voice, "that anything I've said has been said as man to man and not as a subordinate talking to his superior officer. I've treated you as I might any friend at whose reasons for being in this society I might make a shrewd guess and who might be puzzled by the same questions as are puzzling me . . . as a Frenchman, in short. . . . Nothing I have said ought to go outside these four walls, or be used in any way."

Mascot looked down at a brochure which he had picked up automatically and the pages of which he was now turning.

"That of course is understood," he said. "What I have heard, I have heard simply and solely as a man."

He stopped. Then, in a franker, more direct tone than was usual with him, he added:

"I've as much reason as you have to be worried; perhaps more, since my responsibilities are greater. I became a member from much the same motives as you did and am similarly induced to remain one." He waved his hand towards the closely packed bookshelves as though calling the volumes to bear witness to his words. "What other motives could I have? You certainly won't find me staging orgies with young women. . . . But while I listened to you I was trying to get at the exact degree of truth contained in your story. . . . How reliable is your informant? You've given me no evidence on that point, so that I lack an important part of my documentation. . . . Still, I'm ready to believe in the general accuracy of what's been told you. The gossip you've heard about this unknown gentleman's morals may very well be true (though we ought to know his nationality; the same degree of depravity may carry very different implications in Russia, for instance, and in England), as may some of the other and more important details. . . . All this business about understandings with the police is particularly irritating. . . . But we must be careful not to judge like outsiders. . . . A secret society is bound to take the question of the police into consideration. It may have to protect itself from them or make use of them. The police are an essential factor in the problem, and that being so, there must be means of approach, points of contact, between the two bodies, and these may become very complex and exceedingly difficult to explain to those who are outside the Organization. Suppose, for example, that I had a man working for me at police headquarters and that somebody from outside discovered the fact, you must admit it would be difficult for him to decide whether I was betraying the Organization to the authorities or spying on the authorities for the benefit of the Organization. His conclusions would depend upon his general attitude. On the other hand, if I really was a bad lot it would be perfectly easy for me to take advantage of this very complicated state of affairs to mask a genuine piece of double-dealing. That's why I consider the question of a man's character of such prime importance, especially in enlisting recruits. If I was in a position to do what I liked with this 'leader' you've been telling me of without informing me of his nationality, and had satisfactory proof of his private carryings-on, I shouldn't bother to find out the exact nature of his relations with the police, I should—*execute* him."

He looked Laulerque straight in the eyes long enough to let him determine whether the word should be taken figuratively or not.

"But making allowance for all that," he went on, "I've often wondered whether a society such as ours isn't somewhat disappointing to those who've come to it with the grandiose ideas and fine preconceptions of the idealist. But I don't see how it can be helped; we've got to work with men as we find them, and we're not in the position to insist, as the Jesuits do, on a fifteen- or twenty-year noviciate. We must have the wisdom to realize that the greatest enterprises of history, the noblest undertakings, the schemes which in the long run have most benefited the human race, have always shown, at close range, just this unedifying mixture of meanness, selfishness, and general nastiness. Pure idealism has, on the whole, counted for very little with the individuals concerned. Nevertheless that's how humanity moves forward. I sometimes feel very grateful for my medical training. It has taught me that for a whole, made up of a large number of atoms, to show a bias, to manifest a tendency, an inclination to move in one definite direction, a particular urge,—I use the words in their most general sense, spatial or whatever—it is by no means necessary that the graph of each atom taken separately should be definite and undeviating. Regarded in isolation, each may seem to move as erratically as it did before it was combined with others. It needs only that each, perhaps even only some, however random their apparent activity, should submit to a slight pressure in the desired direction. The problem is merely statistical. The force of an ideal is perceptible only in the long run, only when the general situation can be viewed in just perspective. . . . If, of course, we could organize in Europe generally a group of, say, two or three thousand men, not more, who were intelligent and of absolute integrity, yet ready to take every risk and submit to every sacrifice, prepared to obey without question, that would indeed be marvellous! . . . Given such material, we could do anything we wanted. The thing's self-evident. . . . The introduction of such a factor into the course of events would act like an explosive. The whole course of history would be altered; it would become, literally, 'incalculable.' "

"That is what we must do."

"Certainly we must; it is what we have all dreamed of doing. People who found a movement such as this must be inspired by an ideal if they are to achieve even the minimum of success. But we know, you and I, that the dream is too golden. Things don't happen like that. What you find you've got, when it comes to the point, is a few decent fellows without the guts to do anything, and a few men of action whose credentials won't bear looking into. The Foreign Legion isn't recruited from Sunday-schools."

He had rolled the pamphlet into a cylinder, with which he struck the table at intervals.

"I've seen something of other societies. . . . For instance, I've had a good deal to do with Russian revolutionaries. I can assure you there's no lack there of bad eggs and police spies, to say nothing of hangers-on, and vague nondescripts without a will of their own, who are probably the most dangerous of the lot. Still, by and large, something does get done. One man may be a blackguard, another a dreamer or a feckless idealist, but in the long run you do find virtue, you do find courage, and it's the Group that produces it, the Corporate Body, the Organization. Naturally, the Body mustn't let itself be poisoned by its putrid elements. I'm all for as frequent purges as possible; make no mistake about that!"

He seemed once more to be plunged in thought; then:

"But there's another question, and it's the more annoying of the two."

"What?"

"This tale of a schism, or what your informant calls a schism, of some internal divergence of views which has suddenly developed or increased. The fact that I've felt it coming for some time doesn't make it the less worrying. And I've been so sure of its imminence that I don't even need to verify your statement."

"Monsieur Karl warned you of something of the sort?"

"He and others."

During this discussion, which had become frank and confidential —rather too much so, perhaps, for his liking—Mascot had managed to maintain his attitude of a superior officer. He clearly disliked this weakening of discipline which he'd been led to tolerate, and Laulerque tried to minimize its effect by saying as little as possible and by listening with an exaggerated deference.

Nevertheless, this sharing of disenchantment was not without its pleasurable moments for both of them.

"An organization like ours," Mascot went on, "is alive, and when a thing's alive it must, of necessity, change. I don't think I'm betraying any secret—I rather think you know all about it already—when I say that it started in rather a haphazard way. . . . As a matter of fact, it started as the result of a schism. . . . No doubt you're thinking: 'Well, I hope it won't end in the same way.' . . . It's certainly a curious coincidence; but that's another story. In the early days the whole affair was rather nebulous and sentimental, a matter of utopian dreams indulged in by people with too much refinement and too much leisure. . . . We can be thankful that there was an early change of direction, a reorientation, a closer coming to grips with reality. A few genuine men of action got mixed up in it. They may have been a bit mad, a bit dubious, perhaps, but at least they were men who knew what they wanted, for the time being at least, and who realized that you can't make omelets without breaking eggs. It may well be that the form they gave to the society couldn't last either. They brought with them certain interests, certain passions, certain potentialities of fanaticism, with which to feed the common idealism of the society. It was strong meat, and there was considerable danger that it might prove indigestible. Just think for a moment. Only extremely civilized and intelligent men could realize steadily that this abstract, indefinite, apparently negative thing called Peace, the prevention of war, is, in itself, an end so overwhelmingly important that it contains all other ends within itself, as the big end of a telescope contains all objects in the visible field, and justifies the endless expenditure of enthusiasm and heroism. The generality of people go on for a while in a sort of state of auto-suggestion, saying that it is, but gradually they begin to find this business of Peace rather dull and rather vague. This is particularly so if they're young; and the younger they are, the more they're inclined to think of Peace as nothing but a good subject for prize essays and official orations, a nice soporific ideal for old gentlemen. What they want is a more full-blooded ideal. Young people want to fight. Not that we can't give them plenty of opportunities. 'Want to fight, do you?' we can say. 'Well, fire away, then; there's no lack of enemies. And if you're anxious to take individual risks, we've got the very thing for you.' That's all very satisfactory so far as it goes, but it only goes as far as finding employment for those who just want to *do* something. Give them something to feed their aggressive instincts on, and they don't ask anything more. But the trouble is that with us these fellows who just want to do something, who crave only action, are the exception. The kind of men who join us are usually 'men of imagination'—you know what I mean, men who will work themselves up for an ideal, who don't mind taking risks so long as they can have the ideal clearly before them the while. And that's where our weakness comes in. The official ideal of the society is too quiet, not sufficiently intoxicating, not *childish* enough.

"What we need is some genius who could invent a really good vision for our people, who could do for them what, in another field of action, when great assemblies of men have got to be worked on, is done by those who compose songs like the *Marseillaise* and the *Internationale*—who could formulate our object so that it would be emotionally potent, so that it would be like, for instance, what the dream of the fall of the Empire, and the liberation of their countries, is to these Croats and Czechs of whom we've got so many. . . . They've always got before their minds' eyes the vision of Prague or Zagreb dressed out with flags to welcome the liberators, of people kissing one another and crying in the streets, while in their ears for ever sound the old national songs sung by assembled thousands. . . . There's nothing they wouldn't do just to live through such an experience or to make it possible for others to live through it.

"And that's not our only weakness. What our ideal lacks is the sense of something extra that doesn't exist already, of something new that's got to be fought for and won, a prize, a reward. Our more aggressive members say to themselves: 'After all, what's it all about? —just to keep peace, just to keep things as they are. We're being asked to endure all this discomfort, why? Simply to maintain a state of affairs that's good, or relatively good, but which nobody could get excited about, because everyone knows it.' . . . Only people who've reached a certain age realize the importance of maintaining the known good, avoiding the known evil. . . . It doesn't matter how absurd other ideals may be, or how reactionary. Provided they can offer that little more, that something new or rehashed, that something that may exist but doesn't exist yet and can put the spur to enthusiasm, they're sure of finding supporters. The young Frenchman who has fallen a victim to Barrès sees this 'little extra' in the form of Alsace-Lorraine—a definite something on the map, a piece of frontier line thrusting out eastwards to join the Rhine, a scrap of territory stuck onto the right-hand limits of his country. The young adherent of Maurras sees a whole mass of wonderful things superimposed on the dull life of the Republic which he knows so well: royal processions, princesses of the blood blowing kisses, provinces renewed with song and dance, sunning themselves in the mere glance of the king. . . . I am talking now only of Frenchmen. If they can find such intoxication in the imagined glory of the future, think what it must be for the people of central Europe!

"Do you know what I sometimes say to myself?" He lowered his voice and leaned towards Laulerque with exaggerated caution. "I say that a movement like this ought to have started with us, here in France, because we are the only people—or the best among us are the only people—capable, not of enthusiasm for abstractions, because it's not a question of abstractions, not in the bad sense at least, but of feeling genuine emotion for secondary causes. Do you understand what I mean? For instance, we know that in preventing war we are not only preventing its inevitable train of ruin, we are making possible a whole sequence of new and additional things, things that at present don't exist at all, things newer, more important, having a greater real effect on the future of humanity than the restoration of a province, the return of a king, the purely political liberation of a small people. All this we know, and we are capable, in addition, of seeing with the eyes of enthusiasm all these secondary effects, much as a mathematician is capable of seeing in imagination, and delighting in, all the developments that he knows are potential in what, to ordinary minds, look like a series of dead and dismal signs." He smiled, but a moment later relapsed into his former reserve. "Most of us here in France would never have been mad enough, of course, to set such a movement going. There are times when a few madmen are indispensable. Once the thing's started, they can be got rid of. There ought to be a much sharper line of demarcation than there is between the élite who provide the motive power, the initiated, the intellectual General Staff, and the main 'mass of manœuvre.' What we ought to have done was to arrange for the common troops, the mere men of action, to be provided with more spectacular ideals, more showy objects of worship; we ought to have worked on their fads and their local patriotisms more systematically, more cynically than we have. Only in that way can one keep control and avoid being made a fool of. Once we let them get the upper hand, once we let them contaminate us, the whole future of the cause will be undermined and distorted. One of these fine days, for all we know, we shall wake up to find ourselves in God knows what sort of a pickle—as like as not furthering the private ambitions of a lot of central-European terrorists."

"But surely a thing like that couldn't happen? There couldn't be such a reversal of ideals! When, at Christmas, Monsieur Karl referred to some such tendency, I found it difficult to believe him—and talking of Karl, he may not be a Frenchman, but I've got a pretty shrewd idea that he sees where the danger lies and is in no danger of confusing the ends to be pursued! . . . "

"I'm afraid he's as bad as the rest of them. . . . You see, the trouble with these fellows is not that they're not clear-sighted, but that they're clear-sighted only in spasms. They're as energetic when they're wrong as when they're right. All one can do is to take advantage of their moments of sanity and to see at once when they're going off the rails. . . . But it's not easy. . . . You say that a thing like that couldn't happen, but it could. It only needs a little sophistry. . . . Assume for a moment that you were a subject of the Austrian Empire, that you were a member of one of the oppressed nationalities, you'd find it easy enough to get into the state of mind in which you'd believe that the best way of preventing war was to smash Austria, that the same stroke which would liberate these oppressed peoples would have the effect of replacing a dangerous Empire which was intriguing with another Empire equally dangerous, on the diplomatic map of Europe, by a group of young democracies with something else than war to fill their minds. . . . It's only a step from believing that the best way of assuring peace in Europe is to provoke a war. It would, of course, be a holy, an essentially pacific war. As I see things, this shifting of the basis of our society, this divergence of aims, started with the rank and file, particularly among those energetic recruits whose enlistment, as I said before, was at first such an advantage. . . . (This is one of the cases in which we've suffered from our cunning method of getting new blood, from the freedom allowed to our members to remain members of any other organization with which they happened to be connected before joining us. The point of this rule, of course, was that we hoped to exercise an influence on, more or less to control, these other organizations through them. That, I need hardly say, would have been possible only if we'd been actuated by that cold and cynical attitude to which I referred awhile back, and which, as things are, doesn't exist. What, in fact, has happened is that instead of influencing these organizations, we've allowed their ideas and propaganda to seep into our own ranks. . . .)

"To cut a long story short, this divergence of the rank and file has provoked a counter-movement in the general staff. That staff contains individuals who have suddenly discovered that the destruction of the Dual Monarchy is not at all to their advantage. . . . I don't say that these individuals are not inspired by the most generous intentions, but one can hardly ask them to execute their own death-sentences, especially if they believe—and I must say I agree with them —that European stability is not going to be furthered by working for an upheaval in Austria. . . . Consequently they have reacted— at least, so I understand—though it may well be that this reaction has gone rather too far if it takes the form of saying that the best way of maintaining peace in Europe is by saving the Austrian Empire! . . ."

"Certainly rather too far from what interests us!" cried Laulerque in a tone of indignation. "We didn't get mixed up in this business just for that!"

"Certainly we didn't. But this reaction will last only as long as the movement which has provoked it. As soon as the others leave the society, and I'm pretty sure they will leave it, the Organization, cleansed of their nationalist poison, will stop the manufacture of violent antidotes. We shall then be in a position to get back to our proper work."

"You think, then, that if the schism develops, it is still our duty to remain members of the society?"

Mascot appeared to ponder this question conscientiously before replying.

"Taking everything into consideration, and in the absence of a tolerable alternative, I do."

"You're not afraid that the common action will show a progressive tendency to degenerate . . . that our efforts will be sacrificed for ideals, or, what would be still worse, for interests, which are entirely contrary to our intentions?"

"Honestly, I don't think that will happen. We can only wait and see. I'm just as anxious as you are, and you can rest assured that I will be the first to warn you if I find myself wrong."

Laulerque thought silently for a moment or two before saying rather timidly:

"There's another question I'd like to ask, a very particular question which is worrying me a good deal. What's happening down there?"

"Where do you mean?"

"In 'my' house on the coast."

"I've absolutely no idea. . . . Nothing at all, I should say."

"But you're not sure?"

"Nobody's said anything."

"That's tiresome."

"Have you any reason to believe that something's happening?"

"Heavens above, I should think I have!"

"Somebody's spoken to you?"

"I've merely put two and two together."

"I can't see that there's any reason for you to be worried."

"I do!"

"Well, then—I'm not sure—I find it very difficult to advise you . . . it's not really my business. . . . But when all's said and done, there's nothing to prevent you from going down and having a look at it, is there—quite secretly of course? You get a fairly decent holiday at Easter, eh? I'm merely giving you my personal opinion, as man to man. I should have thought the idea might have occurred to you without any prompting."

Chapter

7

JERPHANION IS SEIZED WITH REMORSE

Jallez had gone out (on some mysterious errand of his own). The morning sun filled the study. Jerphanion was engaged in arranging a lot of odd pamphlets which were cluttering up a corner of his locker. It was the sort of job he liked doing, although the clouds of accumulated dust irritated his nose.

Suddenly he noticed a red-coloured leaflet which he had no difficulty in recognizing: *La Flamme,* containing Clanricard's article: "We Are So Much Alone."

He hadn't realized that he had kept it. He had forgotten to give it to Jallez.

He re-read the article and found, as he did so, that he knew a great many passages by heart. Despite this fact, as he read them over, they seemed to come alive again in the most amazing way. Never before had he felt so deeply moved by their deliberate rhythm.

The further he read—he read slowly, letting each period gradually establish its meaning as though he were seeing it for the first time, and half murmuring the words to himself—the more conscious did he become that his heart was beating and that drops of perspiration were standing on his forehead. At the end of one particular paragraph he was so affected that he had to stop to prevent himself from bursting into tears. Then he went on again, saying to himself as he read:

"Is this the man I've injured—the man who could write this, the man I first got to know because he had written this—the man who waited for me one evening in a bar on the boulevard Sébastopol—the man who welcomed me with so kind a smile? Little did he know that the stranger he was greeting would take from him all that he held most precious in life. . . . We are so much alone. . . . At the sound of that calm, deliberate cry I had turned my head, seeking in its author an unknown brother lost in the great desert of the world and calling for help in a faint and muffled voice. The sense of comradeship had started me off—and see where it landed me! It's not merely that I stole something he had made his own and long possessed . . . what I stole was something which was not yet his own, his comfort to be, his hope for the future. We are so much alone! He had found a way out of his loneliness, and I, who had answered his call, I set him to flounder in a worse loneliness than any he had known before. I was no better than some night-prowler who, hearing the cry of a lost and frightened wayfarer, takes the opportunity to rob him of all he has. I'm a monster. In the eyes of others, in my own, I stand excused on the grounds of rude health and country upbringing. Rather should I have been condemned for clumsy selfishness as a greedy boor, a cad. Jallez, I'm sure, though he said nothing, must have despised and condemned me. He's as self-centred as anyone, but that's the kind of thing he'd never have done. He's all sensibility and consideration. . . . He had good reason to laugh, that day when we climbed to the Sacré-Cœur, and I accused him of standing aloof from the problems of society, seeming to charge him with egotism while I paraded my nobility of soul, my heart torn with thinking on the sorrows of humanity! . . . That must have been why he found pleasure in giving me cynical advice about Mathilde. He did it, surely, to bring me back to a sense of my own behaviour. What he really meant was: 'You stole her from Clanricard, who treated you like a brother, and now you want to get rid of her. If you must act like a cad, do at least be consistent!' "

He had laid the pamphlet aside. Now he took it up again. A feeling of compassion and remorse took the place of self-condemnation. He wanted to humiliate himself, to repair the damage he had done. "Forgive me, my brother, who trusted in me, forgive me, poor, dear Clanricard, whose happiness, no, worse, whose hope, I have destroyed, whose *loneliness I have intensified*! Tell me what I must do to heal your wounds. . . ." He read over the sentence in which Clanricard described the children in his class-room. The sour, exhausted smell of the place was in his nostrils; he could picture in imagination the pale faces and the eyes too large and round. He saw at the desk the figure of a young man seated with his cheek resting on his hand, a thin young man with a weak moustache, a young man who longed to give more and more love to these children, to dedicate himself more completely to their service, yet doubted all the while his power to achieve anything, unsure even of the end to be attained, and through it all aware of his own appalling loneliness.

His chin began to tremble. He tried to hold back his tears, but they stung the corners of his eyes like needles. He thought: "How foul human nature must be if I, who am so far from wishing to harm anybody, can do a thing like that!"

Jerphanion saw on the opposite pavement a chattering procession of little boys all dressed in black, and, walking along the curb, a young man slightly bent, who kept his hands before him as though to guide and control the sea of childish heads.

He followed at a little distance as far as the square, where he thought the convoy would begin to break up into divergent streams.

As he looked at Clanricard he kept repeating to himself: "How much better he is than I! How good he is at his job, how conscientious, how patient! And it's not because he can't do other things more worth while. He it is who wrote what I was re-reading this morning. Nothing escapes him; he realizes the drabness of this little crowd he tends so carefully, the half-pathetic, half-comic role he fills as shepherd of the flock, the melancholy of the street, the gloomy vista of his life, the wrong I have done him."

After one last glance to make sure that none of his charges had run underneath a cart, Clanricard turned on his heels. He looked tired and seemed uncertain which direction to take.

Then he saw Jerphanion, and for the fraction of the second in which he recognized him, his eyes lit up with a smile that was almost as friendly and as trusting as that with which he had greeted him when last they met. Jerphanion's heart melted within him. A moment later Clanricard's expression darkened, but even so, it seemed to express more pain and astonishment than rancour.

"I've been thinking about you ever since this morning; I've made myself ill thinking of you. I can't bear the idea of the part I have played in all this. I feel most horribly guilty. This very morning I was re-reading those fine passages in *La Flamme* that first brought us together. . . . How bitter your thoughts of me must be! You were never for one single moment in the wrong. You behaved throughout like a perfect comrade—I can hardly now say friend."

Clanricard walked with his head bent, listening attentively. He seemed moved by the other's words, but he said nothing.

Jerphanion went on:

"I'm not going to excuse myself or plead the force of circumstances —no, that would be too easy. But I want you to know this, that what I did was not done lightly. I can't forgive myself for the pain I have made you suffer. I should not be proud of having made anyone suffer like that—don't think of me as worse than I am—but you, of all people!"

Clanricard at last found words:

"I'm pleased you've spoken. It's not for me to judge you. I know that you didn't mean any harm, that you were just thoughtless. . . . I suppose it had to happen." He added without the slightest hint of harshness: "Please don't let us discuss it any more."

They walked in silence along the rue Ordener towards the Batignolles. Neither was quite sure whether they were deliberately keeping together or whether their ways happened to coincide.

"Look here," Jerphanion said with an effort, "I don't just want to say I'm sorry and get out of it that way. . . . That would be merely to add insult to injury. . . . I've been asking myself all sorts of questions. . . . What I'm going to say isn't just words. If you can still be happy with her, I'll get out. Nothing has happened between us that you need think of as past repair, nothing that need be an obstacle between you. Our relation has been nothing but the kind of thing that crops up every day between young men and young women. You'll forget it in next to no time. If you really feel that you must make a life together, this little incident needn't stop you. As far as I'm concerned, the pain I shall feel will be evidence of my forgiveness."

Clanricard looked long at Jerphanion. His eyes expressed doubt and torment. When he spoke at last, his voice trembled.

"Have you said anything of this to Mathilde?"

"No."

After a moment's reflection Jerphanion added:

"Don't you think it would have been rather lacking in delicacy to do so, perhaps even rather cruel?"

"Perhaps. . . . But do you think she'd agree . . . I mean, don't you think she'd be sorry?"

"Quite honestly, I don't know."

"Can't you even guess?"

"I think she may be rather annoyed—with me. But that really proves nothing."

"Does she love you?"

Jerphanion said nothing.

"But of course she does," Clanricard said softly, with rather touching sincerity. "And you, do you love her?"

"Yes . . . but that ought not to affect the question. I could have loved her without saying a word about it and still remained your loyal friend. The mere fact of loving would have given me no rights in the matter."

Clanricard reflected again before he spoke. Then:

"She must decide," he said; "but she must know that she's free to decide—that you leave her free." He sighed. "I know it's not easy for you. And even so the test's not a fair one. I don't want her to come back to me just to spite you."

Jerphanion listened, but his face told nothing of what he felt. Clanricard went on:

"What you've said has knocked me all of a heap. . . . My brain's not working properly yet. I must think it all over. . . . So must you. You mustn't rush into this—as you rushed into the other. But whatever happens, your words have brought me great happiness. . . . When one has admired someone, felt affection for someone, it's awful to think that one has been deceived."

Chapter

8

A MINISTER AT WORK.
A CIVIL SERVANT'S CONSCIENCE.
NGOKO-SANGHA

For the last hour Gurau, assisted by Léon Manifassier, whom he had taken with him to his new
office as private secretary, had been going through the conduct sheets
of a certain number of minor postal officials. Against these men, who
were charged with insubordination and with acts of revolutionary,
antimilitarist, or what the reports termed "anarchistic" propaganda,
some local postmasters wanted action to be taken in the form of
either reprimand, dismissal, or forfeiture of seniority.

This was one of the most frequent and least agreeable of the
duties attached to his new post. In his greed for power, he had
foolishly assumed responsibility for the Post Office, which normally
would have devolved upon an under-secretary acting under his instructions. He was well aware that the service had become a wasps'
nest of intrigue. Simyan's misfortunes were evidence enough of
that, but he took the attitude that his predecessor had not known
how to handle matters, how to deal with the rank and file. "The
union men," he thought, "won't play tricks on me." Besides, having
said yes to Monis in a fit of personal grievance, he deliberately made
light of such minor troubles as his duties might involve.

Nor had he had much to complain of. Directly after taking office,
in the optimistic mood bred of a return to power, he had told Manifassier to summon to an official conference three of the chief subdirectors of the service. He had not been wrong in thinking that he
knew the right line to take. When the men left him, they agreed
that he was on their side, that he would do everything he could,
and that they must not put difficulties in his way. To a certain extent
they had been as good as their word. More than once, at union

meetings, they had said (without compromising him too deeply by actual quotation) that they had got to be sensible, that they must have patience, and had stressed the necessity of distinguishing between the real enemies of the working class who were intent only on breaking its power, and those of its friends who "couldn't always do what they wanted and ought not to be discouraged." Once or twice, even, in the early days of the Ministry, several postmen in uniform had raised cries of "Good old Gurau" in the Chamber—an unprecedented display of support for an active Minister. But, despite this, the extremists of the movement could not be altogether controlled, nor the impetuosity of the hotheads, which had lately been increasing, wholly checked.

Among these subdirectors, those who wanted to avoid scandals or who sympathized with the rank and file were delighted to think that Gurau's presence at the head of affairs would result in a slowing up of disciplinary action, and they were all for minimizing small irregularities. Others there were, however, who were only too glad to show this subversive Minister, this leader who had been foisted on the service by the *Sanction,* this parliamentary champion of trade-unionism, how his theories would work out in practice. They picked, as test cases, a few incidents in which a technical misdemeanour could be made to bear the weight of some outrageous act of propaganda which in fact had no connexion whatever with official conduct. The linking-up was worked with considerable skill and in a variety of ways. Sometimes it was made to appear that the accused man, though clever enough to keep within the law, had inspired others to acts of illegality which sometimes even took the form of sabotage within the service. Was it fair, the accusers asked, to acquit a ringleader, just because the evidence against him did not touch him in an official capacity, and punish his tools?

It was just these attempts to establish connexions between official and non-official acts that Gurau, aided by Manifassier's marshalling of the material, had set himself to expose. It was not always easy, because he hesitated, in exploding these trumped-up cases, to use the tricks that the accusers had stooped to in order to present them. Where he could not ignore actual propaganda, he tried to distinguish between the mere preaching of a theory, which, he held, should be respected however extreme the ideas involved might be, and the actual instigation to subversive action or to conduct calculated to lead to such action. He was careful, in each proved case, to dissociate propaganda carried on outside, as, for example, in meetings, from propaganda spread by conversation during a man's official duties. His blue-pencil marks in the margin of a report meant, as a rule, that the fault referred to had been committed during working hours.

Manifassier was a great help to him. He was ingenious in the matter of solving difficulties, had had long experience of the ways of civil servants, and, above all, was sincere in his wish to steer honestly among the shoals of political jobbery.

The door-keeper bowed and held out a visiting-card.

FRANÇOIS COURSON
Under-Secretary of the Political Department
of the Foreign Office

Beneath this, and running over to the back of the card, was written in ink:

"would appreciate a few words with the Minister in person, on a matter of great urgency."

"Didn't he ask for an interview in the ordinary way?"

"No, sir. I pointed that out to him, but he said that the matter was extremely important and that no doubt you would see him."

"Ah! . . ." Gurau turned to Manifassier and held out the card for him to see. "Do you know him?"

"No."

"Under-Secretary of the Political Department—he seems to be somebody of importance, eh?"

"I should say so."

Gurau carefully scrutinized the card.

"He probably wants to ask me some favour—to urge the claim of a cousin or brother-in-law who's due for promotion. . . . It's a frightful bore. We were just getting on so well with these reports. I thought we should be through with them this morning. . . . Couldn't we let Martinet see him, or Descheneaux?"

Manifassier pursed his lips.

"It all depends on what he's come for. . . . He might be offended. He obviously knows the ropes, and if he wants to see you personally, he's probably got good reason to."

"You're right . . ." and turning to the door-keeper, Gurau said: "Show him up at once. . . . Stay where you are, Manifassier; this business can't be as private as all that; and, in any case, your being here will prevent him from staying too long."

M. Courson came in. He was a large man of about fifty, with a high colour and a large head. Despite his corpulence, he gave an impression of elegance. He wore a short black coat and a wing-collar. His attitude of respect to the Minister showed a natural shyness combined with considerable familiarity with the routine of such interviews.

Gurau tried to avoid bores, but having resigned himself to the necessity of receiving one, he made it a rule to be as pleasant as possible. It was with a great show of amiability, therefore, that he said:

"I was anxious to spare you a long wait, my dear sir"—he indicated the files before him—"but we were in the middle of an extremely urgent piece of business. I mention that to show why I can, unfortunately, spare you only a very few moments."

"The matter I have to speak about, sir, is of the greatest possible importance. . . ." With a glance toward Manifassier, he added:

"and of a very private nature."

He spoke deliberately and with an air of caution. He had a way of catching his breath between phrases which gave the impression that he was constantly saying: "Excuse me," "If I may say so," "I beg your pardon."

Gurau introduced Manifassier.

"Monsieur Manifassier, my private secretary, the oldest and most intimate of my colleagues. You need feel no awkwardness in his presence. In any case, unless the matter of your visit was purely private, I should have to tell him the gist of our conversation, in view of possible consequences. We shall save time by having him here."

"In that case—I agree. . . . I must say at once, sir, that in coming to you like this I am guilty of an irregularity and of a breach of official confidence. But I feel that the public, the national, interest is at stake."

Gurau and Manifassier became very attentive and exchanged a momentary glance.

"You don't mind if Monsieur Manifassier takes a few notes?" Gurau asked.

"He needn't bother, sir. . . . You'll see why in a moment. I've come to you like this because in the course of my duties at the Foreign Office I have had occasion to appreciate your activities both in the press and on the Foreign Affairs Committee. I know that certain questions are familiar to you, and that you attach to them the importance they deserve. Many of the replies that were given to you on the committee were prepared by me"—he accompanied the words with a well-bred smile—"replies which, alas, did not always reflect my personal views. . . . But let me say this: if my visit is irregular it has not been made without much thought." He paused. "I didn't sleep at all last night."

Gurau was deeply interested, even excited. All thought of his postmen had vanished. He said: "I am all ears," in a tone of encouragement.

"Doubtless, sir, you have followed the Ngoko-Sangha affair—not, perhaps, in such detail as I have, since it formed part of my routine duties, but sufficiently to make it unnecessary for me to remind you of its nature. Further, although you were not a member of the Budget Commission, you know something of the debates which took place this winter on the subject, and of the Violette report. I won't stress the point. The situation at the moment is as follows: Two years ago we arranged with Germany for joint action by the French Ngoko-Sangha Company and the German Cameroons Company. Both Governments, remember, were directly concerned in the negotiations, which, therefore, took on the character of a regular diplomatic instrument. You will ask, doubtless, how much it really meant. Well, of course a lot of nonsense was talked on the Budget Commission, but, in fact, it meant what most diplomatic instruments do mean, which is just as much as they can be made to mean. It did, at least, have the merit of putting an end to a lot of tiresome local friction, Franco-German as well as Franco-English, and of terminating a period during which infiltration had been going on at our expense, and a good deal of underhand competition had been rife. But that wasn't the real point. The real point was that this proposed joint action was the first attempt at peaceful collaboration between France and Germany, the first attempt to combine the interests of the two nations on a point of definite and concrete importance, instead of setting them against each other over a wide field and in an atmosphere of increasing tension.

"But there is something else which I am inclined to think was of even greater significance, and that is the effect of this agreement on German mentality. Rightly or wrongly Germany attached the greatest possible importance to it. In her eyes it was a test case, providing an answer, based on actual experience, to the question: 'Is co-operation with France feasible? Is it possible, all appearances to the contrary, to look forward to a future in which France and Germany may be able to work together in a field where they have been forced into proximity, instead of endlessly trying to trip each other up.' In other words: 'Is it still possible to play a friendly game with France, or must we clear our minds of all illusion and realize once and for all that she is the enemy, always will be the enemy, and cares really about nothing but recourse to arms at a moment chosen by herself? And if that is so, ought we not to take all necessary steps without wasting any more time?' It's a perfectly simple situation. For the last two years Germany has been waiting, with what impatience you may imagine, and with ever increasing amazement. She has been waiting for us to implement this agreement, or at least to ratify it. And we just don't take any steps. Germany can't understand what we mean, or, rather, she's beginning to think that she understands only too well. Every added month of delay is an encouragement to the German war party. People are beginning to laugh in Germany at those who say: 'We can have an understanding with France; war is not the only solution,' and to treat them as poor innocent dupes. If, finally, we don't ratify at all, Germany will be terribly disillusioned, and her disillusionment will take disquieting forms.

"Please don't think, sir, that I imagine everything to have been above-board in this Ngoko-Sangha business. It is quite possible, even probable, that there has been a lot of underhand wirepulling and bribery. The 'agreement' may have been used to mask and support methods of colonization which the members of the extreme Left rightly condemn as immoral. All that, alas, is true, but we've got to take the world as it is. Once we begin to apply standards of strict honesty, the whole colonial system goes by the board. What we've got to realize is that the opponents of the agreement, those who've attacked it most violently during the winter on the Budget Commission and elsewhere, have exploited the situation for purely internal reasons. They've found in it a marvellous weapon against the Government. Today, when a good many of these gentlemen are within shorter distance of power than they were and can see certain aspects of the question rather more clearly, they would probably like to modify their attitude. But they don't dare. . . . Meanwhile the question of ratification is still dragging on . . . has been postponed

indefinitely. . . . And I've recently been given reason to suppose
that there's serious intention of dropping it altogether."

An almost pathetic note had crept into M. Courson's voice, despite
his efforts to keep it carefully under control.

"Excuse me, sir, if I speak with greater passion than perhaps I
should do . . . if I seem to forget our relative positions . . . but—
but what we're about to do may have the most disastrous consequences."

Drops of perspiration were standing out on his forehead. He
hastily wiped them away with his handkerchief. When he spoke
again, it was in a tone of polite urgency.

"We *must* ratify, sir; and without a moment's delay."

Gurau, who had been listening with anxious attention, made a
movement which was as much as to say: "*I* can do nothing."

"I understand your position, sir. Unfortunately, you are not
Foreign Minister . . . but you can interfere. . . . You can bring
influence to bear on Monsieur Cruppi. . . . Perhaps you might also
say a word to Monsieur Caillaux. . . . I know, of course, that he's
been deeply committed to the party of opposition, but he's not the
kind of man to refuse to listen to reason. You're in the fortunate
position of not having taken sides. . . ."

Gurau frowned in an effort to concentrate his memory.

In the course of the guerrilla warfare which he had waged on the
Foreign Affairs Committee against Pichon, had he never made
incidental use of the Ngoko-Sangha business? He rather thought
he had. And hadn't he repeated the charge in his articles?

M. François Courson, guessing what was worrying him, came to
his rescue.

"Once or twice, sir, on the committee, you did, I think, support
one of your colleagues in some question he put to the then Minister
(I can look up the dates), and made it clear that you were in opposition to Monsieur Pichon on this as on other points. But you said
nothing that could possibly tie your hands—I am sure of that—or
prevent you from declaring that if two years ago you thought it best

to reject the intended agreement or to substitute another for it, today, when the word of France has been given, ratification is imperative."

Gurau turned to his colleague.

"How about the *Sanction*?" he asked in a low voice.

Manifassier had been deep in thought. He answered, in the same tone (but their visitor was close enough to hear):

"No—I think not—a few casual passages of criticism, perhaps. . . . But you never treated the question at length. . . . Your impression, if you remember, was that this campaign wasn't making things any easier for a Franco-German agreement. . . . I believe you actually said something of the sort one day to Monsieur Jaurès."

"Perhaps," Gurau said with an air of relief; "it's quite possible I did."

M. Courson went on with that hint of vehemence which seemed natural to him:

"I implore you, sir. A tragic blunder's got to be prevented, and you're the only person at the present moment who's in a position to do anything, the only person who has the necessary moral authority. You could begin, I am sure, by speaking a word to Monsieur Cruppi, as colleague to colleague. . . ."

He fumbled in his pocket.

". . . I've brought a memorandum with me—quite short, no more than two typewritten pages, but it contains all the essential points, and I can vouch for the accuracy of every detail. . . . If you need my help in any other way, I am entirely at your disposition. . . ."

He had addressed these last few words as much to Manifassier as to Gurau, and it was to the former that he held out the document.

". . . If Monsieur Cruppi proves obstinate, you mustn't hesitate to raise the question at a Cabinet meeting, if necessary at a Ministerial meeting; but you must see to it that Monsieur Caillaux is at least neutral in the matter. No one can possibly be surprised at the initiative coming from you, seeing who you are. . . . You are particularly fitted to take an interest in matters of foreign policy."

Gurau almost blushed with pleasure.

"... You have a definite policy ... or at least a general attitude
... a consistent attitude towards the future destiny of France and
of Europe. I realize that Monsieur Cruppi may be annoyed at your
interfering in the business of his department, but the position is
unusual and the question far-reaching. ... France has got to choose
between two policies, while the choice is still open to her ... between two courses immediately ahead. ... It is essential that we
know what is really intended."

He paused. Then, in a curious tone, at once confidential and intense:

"If they want war," he said, "they've only to go on as they're going
at present. ... They'll have it soon enough."

He hesitated a moment, scrutinizing the two men there before
him in the huge, solemn room, seeming to probe their intentions, to
be weighing them in the balance.

"Speaking for myself, I have a prejudice against war. ... I am
not one of the people who believe that it is the solution of all difficulties. ... I am a sincere Catholic—I don't mind admitting that
to you, sir, who are no fanatic in religious matters—a 'Christian'
Catholic, if I may be allowed the qualification. ... I hate and detest those bloodthirsty Catholics like Joseph de Maistre, who are, in
fact, no better than pagans. I believe neither in the executioner nor
in the sword. ... I am also a loyal republican. I do not regard the
separation of Church and State as a disaster; and now that it is an
accomplished fact—with faults on both sides—I do my best, in my
modest sphere, to find a reasonable *modus vivendi* for France and
the Church. ... I am happy to be able to say that I gave a little
advice in that matter to Monsieur Briand himself, and that he did
me the honour of listening to me. I am honoured by Monsieur
Briand's friendship."

Gurau interrupted:

"In that case, why didn't you go to him?"

"I did, on at least one occasion during the winter. I didn't make
quite so—so solemn a statement to him as I have done to you, but

I took advantage of an interview I had with Monsieur Briand on another question, to mention the subject to him and to urge the necessity of ratification. . . . I found that he saw things in the same light as I did. . . . At that time there was every reason to think that Monsieur Pichon, who had sponsored the agreement in the first place, would feel himself committed as author to bring it to a successful conclusion. No one expected the Ministry to fall so soon. . . . As things are today, Monsieur Briand can do nothing. . . ."

He altered his tone:

"Don't think, sir, that I haven't explored every possible avenue before taking the final step of coming to you, or that I haven't tried every routine method open to me. I have exhausted all possibilities. Monsieur Cruppi is at this moment in possession of a completely documented statement which I gave him a day or two ago, with a résumé of the situation, almost identical with the memorandum which I brought here for you. Not only did I explain the situation orally to him when I handed it over; I was careful to embody in my text, for purposes of record, my view of the extreme urgency of the matter . . . of the perils which our present attitude involved. . . . Needless to say, I was careful not to overstep the reserve and objectivity which belong to an administrative report of that kind, nor to make myself guilty of a breach of the respect due from a simple Foreign Office official to his Minister . . . but I went as far as I could. . . . I defy Monsieur Cruppi to say that 'his administration' is not in favour of ratification, because in this case I am 'his administration'—I and, if you like, our Ambassador at Berlin. For Monsieur Cambon stresses exactly my point of view, and in almost precisely similar terms. I have seen all his dispatches. . . ."

"But how in the world, then, do you expect Monsieur Cruppi to listen to me if he won't listen to you or to Monsieur Cambon?"

M. Courson shook his head violently.

"He may listen to you . . . he *will* listen to you, if you speak strongly enough. . . . The difficulty for Monsieur Cruppi is solely one of internal politics. . . . He is afraid of the Left, of the extreme

Left. . . . If he knows you are on his side, he will feel armed against the critics of the Left. . . . Besides, let me add, with all due respect, that one of the chief arguments of those who oppose ratification is that the agreement is a stalking-horse for dishonest financial interests, an affair of bribery and bought consciences. Your intervention will deprive them of that weapon. I needn't tell you what a weight your name carries in matters of that kind. It will be evident to all the world that one can support ratification, not from motives of self-interest, but because one believes it to be best for France . . . and for the future of peace."

Once again Gurau almost blushed.

On leaving them, M. Courson excused himself again for the irregularity of his visit and expressed the hope that it would be treated as strictly confidential.

"If it were known, my career as a civil servant would be at an end. . . . I don't think there's any need to bring me into it."

"But aren't you afraid that Monsieur Cruppi may put two and two together himself . . . if he finds me too much up in his business?"

"No, sir. It's generally known that you interest yourself closely in a great many things . . . and that you have ways and means of keeping yourself informed. . . . The important thing is that you shouldn't mention my name. . . . Apart from that, people can think what they like so far as I care. . . . After all, Monsieur Cruppi won't go on for ever."

"Well, I'll think it over. Whatever comes of it, I am very grateful for the mark of confidence you have shown me in coming here."

"Think quickly, sir . . . and act quickly! Monsieur Cruppi is on the point of making a decision which, once made, can't be rescinded. If he determines to abandon the agreement, as everything, alas, seems to point to his doing, we shall soon see a recurrence of Franco-German incidents, whether in Morocco or elsewhere. The peace party in Berlin will no longer be able to make itself heard, the General

Staff will push on with its preparations, incident will follow incident, and war will be inevitable—war, sir, and in the very near future."

"What's your opinion, Manifassier?"

"It's all very exciting."

"I agree. . . . But don't you think he's let himself get a bit hypnotized by this agreement business? He's like everybody who's got a bee in his bonnet. Ratification's not going to solve everything, nor is everything going to come toppling down just because we fail to ratify."

"He didn't say it would! All he claims is that the question has become of prime importance in German eyes . . . of symbolical importance, which is very possible. I don't think you ought to neglect his warning. . . . After all, he occupies a high post in the civil service, and he's risked taking a step which is unheard-of for a man in his position. He could only have done so under pressure of deep conviction. If you do nothing about it, you are taking a grave moral responsibility."

"But who's talking of doing nothing, my dear chap? I'm only anxious not to make a blunder."

"The first thing to do is to get information."

"But how—how?"

"To begin with, by making a few discreet inquiries at the Foreign Office, to find out whether Monsieur Courson has the reputation of being a crank or a fanatic."

"Can you do that?"

"Yes, I've one or two friends there. Then I rather think it would be as well to get some independent views on the Ngoko question. I still see something of my old colleagues at the Board of Trade—I might get an inside tip from them. There's another friend of mine at the Colonial Office, a very intelligent fellow. . . . But of course all this won't amount to much more than the official attitude; it'll be prejudiced. . . . I should like a word with young Bailly of the *Humanité*."

"What for?"

"He's a man of distinction, a university graduate . . . and he's the best fellow I know for gossip, well up in every story that's going round, a regular old woman. If there really is something fishy about this Ngoko business, he'll have it. We needn't bother about details, but it might be as well to get a rough idea of what it's all about."

"When can you find time to do all this?"

"This afternoon . . . if you'll lend me the car. I'll catch Bailly in the press gallery . . . the others'll be easy enough; they don't move about much."

"And what about our postmen?"

"They must take care of themselves. This other thing's more important."

Gurau acquiesced with a grimace.

"Right you are, then. I can't help smiling at one thing, though."

"What?"

"The idea that I, of all people, should be engineering this retrospective success for Pichon; that after accusing him so often of being reckless, I should now admit that he was laying the first stone in the structure of Franco-German understanding!"

"Oh, if you're going to let a thing like that influence you—"

"Of course, of course. . . . When can you let me have the results of your inquiries?"

"About six this evening, or say half past."

"That's no good. I'm taking the chair at the committee then."

"So you are. How about later?"

"No good, I'm dining out. Look here, I tell you what, give me a ring while I'm at the committee."

"Wouldn't you rather I came and reported in person tomorrow morning?"

"There's no reason why you shouldn't do both. I should like to hear something tonight. You know what I am when I've got anything on my mind."

"All right, then. But I'd better not speak too plainly, in case somebody's listening in."

"That you, Manifassier?"
"Yes, sir. Can I speak freely?"
"Yes, I'm in the little anteroom. There's no one here."
"Splendid. About the gentleman in question, first of all: good news, very good. Not in any way unbalanced. Rather obstinate and likes to speak his mind, but generally respected. His relations with B., just as he said."
"Ah! . . . Is his position such as to make his opinion valuable?"
"At the Foreign Office? Yes, undoubtedly. . . . About the general situation, nothing very startling to report. One or two names of alleged stockholders. I think some of them will make you smile. In itself the affair is hardly a *casus belli,* but it's quite possible that our neighbour attaches a good deal of importance to it. We're committed up to the hilt."
"Another of Pichon's blunders. . . . And your general opinion?"
"My general opinion is that we've got to act. I've got the impression, unfortunately, that in the Chamber most of the members' minds are made up already. . . . It'll be a difficult course to steer. Even if the pilot's willing to listen, it's not at all certain that he won't find the opposition too strong for him. That's the snag."
"Yes, that's certainly annoying. Come early tomorrow morning. A dirty business. . . . Thanks, all the same."

Chapter

9

TWO DAYS LATER

"Well, sir, did you see Cruppi?"

"I saw Caillaux. You see—"

A slight scowl came into Manifassier's face.

"Don't you think I did right? It was Courson's advice, remember."

"It may have been Courson's advice, but my opinion is that you ought to have sounded Cruppi first and let his attitude determine whether you should talk to Caillaux or not. I've nothing against Caillaux, but you know the line he's taken. You've run the risk of having to use on Caillaux the eloquence which you ought to have reserved for Cruppi."

Gurau appeared to be worried.

"Listen," he said, speaking as though he were interrogating his own thoughts, "I don't suppose that if I had seen Cruppi first— Anyhow, it was Caillaux I saw. . . . He was very pleasant, very frank, as he so often is, very direct. The gist of what he said was: 'Yes, I know. . . . We were probably guilty of a good many stupidities on the Budget Commission, but there you are! Domestic politics are rather like love; at the moment one thinks of nothing else. . . . Let me say, too, in our defence, that the people mixed up in the Ngoko-Sangha business were not a very reassuring lot—well-dressed brigands who would take an ell if we gave them an inch and wouldn't hesitate to shoot us in the back if they got the chance. . . . What's done's done. The last Government fell partly because of the feeling we managed to work up about this very question. . . . It's not our job now to work for ratification. Think for a moment of the figure we should cut. To get a majority—and it's not at all certain he would get one—Cruppi would have to sing the praises of Pichon, Ngoko, and the agreement. We should be a laughing-stock! And suppose he didn't get his majority, which is more than probable—then the Government would fall on the issue of Ngoko-Sangha! Do you really see us all going down, like the crew of the *Vengeur,* holding hands and singing "Ngoko-Sangha or death"?'"

Manifassier listened with the expression he usually wore when he disapproved of anything.

Gurau noticed this.

"There's one thing, my dear chap, that you don't yet understand," he said, "because you've not been long enough at your job, and that is that politics have their own rules, which have got to be reckoned with even if one doesn't bow to them. When Monsieur Courson was here the day before yesterday, you saw with your own eyes how keen I was to hear what he had to say, and I don't think I missed any of his meaning. Today I had to listen to Caillaux and to admit that if Monsieur Courson was right from the point of view of things as he knows them, Caillaux is right from another point of view, about which Courson is completely ignorant. We don't work in a vacuum. I may have eternal justice on my side, but if I'm a Minister, eternal justice will be no good to me until it can be formulated as a resolution which will get me more than three hundred votes."

"I bow to your judgment," said Manifassier with a slight smile. "How did your interview with Caillaux end?"

"Caillaux told me a lot of very interesting things. He's got an extraordinary nose for foreign affairs and he blames himself for not having concentrated on them, but he's been too much absorbed—is still too much absorbed—in financial matters and the enemies they make him. His opinion is that unless we do something drastic to change our course, we're headed straight for war, and he shares my view—yours too—that Franco-German relations are the dominating factor. He is far from being opposed to a policy of collaboration, but he doesn't want to be carried through by a lot of bunglers and incapables. He believes that the Ngoko-Sangha business is on its last legs, and that we've got to let it die. But that doesn't prevent us starting something else of the same kind with Germany, something better planned, more sensible, and with fewer swindlers mixed up with it."

"And you really think that Germany will be so simple as to start all over again?"

"Caillaux thinks so. He seemed to be quite sure, in fact."

"Oh come! . . ."

"I had a feeling that he's already started some sort of negotiations. He didn't say much. I gather, in the first place, that he doesn't think the present Government will last long."

"Oho! . . ."

"But, my dear chap, isn't it self-evident? After Clemenceau and Briand, Monis can't very well be anything but a stopgap. . . . He doesn't think it a good time to start a long-range scheme in the field of foreign affairs, which would be more or less bound up with Cruppi and would inevitably go to the scrap-heap with him. . . . It's quite obvious that he dislikes Cruppi, that he attaches no importance to him, and that if he has to form the next Ministry, it won't be Cruppi he'll think of for the Foreign Office. He considers that the inclusion of Delcassé in the present Government is a blunder, and a useless provocation in German eyes. Nor has he any illusions about Berteaux, whom he regards as a decent, conceited busybody, surrounded by flatterers because of his money, and thinking himself a second Napoleon ever since he went to the War Office. 'A Chauchard with a difference,'[1] as he puts it. Berteaux is for ever inspecting, reviewing, inaugurating. . . . He dreams of flying. . . . Apparently he said the other day, echoing William II, and speaking like an editorial-writer: 'Our future is in the air.' . . . It seems, too, that he's been

---

[1] Chauchard was a rich business man who owned the Grands Magasins du Louvre and amassed a large collection of old masters, which he left to the French nation. He was vain and ignorant, and many of his pictures were fakes foisted on him by unscrupulous dealers. For many years he was the butt of caricaturists and gossip-writers, and passed generally in France as the typical "parvenu."—TRANSLATOR'S NOTE.

doing things behind our backs, and taking very grave responsibilities in Morocco which may lead to a general bust-up, without even referring his decisions to Monis. . . . In short, Caillaux thinks that people like us ought to hold ourselves in reserve and not spoil things by acting too soon."

It was on the tip of Manifassier's tongue to say: "So you're going to play the same game with Caillaux as you did with Briand? When will you grow up and learn to paddle your own canoe?"

But he swallowed the words, not without regret, and refrained from giving expression to his rather bitter thought.

"And what did Cruppi have to say?" he asked, with an assumed air of innocence.

Gurau seemed to be ill at ease.

"Cruppi? Oh yes—well, I confess that I was so much impressed by Caillaux's arguments— You see, I'm more than ever sure that Cruppi would have said no. . . ."

"You mean you didn't see him?"

"No, I didn't see him," Gurau went on with greater firmness; "I don't like beating the air. . . . I've thought the whole thing out. I'm going to change my tactics. It is more than probable that at the next Cabinet council Cruppi will announce his decision not to proceed to ratification. If he says nothing, I shall raise the question myself. In either case I shall ask leave to speak, and I shall make a full statement of my point of view. I shall say that I have no reason to like the agreement of 1909, but that it is a serious matter for a French Government to fail to keep its word, and no less grave a one to let Germany believe that we are lacking in good faith. I shall add that I was prepared to support a policy of ratification, despite a certain feeling of repugnance, but that if the parliamentary situation makes ratification difficult or impossible, then the blunder which has been made must be paid for, and the price must take the form of a radical —and sincere—change in the orientation of our foreign policy. I am not afraid of making it clear to all that I regard the Minister of the moment—even the Ministry of the moment—as unsuited to handle the necessary changes. That's what I shall say, and then I shall sit back and see what happens. Delcassé no doubt will come into the lists. If he does, so much the better. I can deal with him."

While he spoke, he had recovered all his self-confidence, and he finished now on a note of challenge:

"I consider that a braver line to take, a line more worthy of myself, and more useful, too, than to allow myself to be politely shown the door by Cruppi."

"And at the same stroke," observed Manifassier rather dryly, "you put in for the succession."

"And why not?" By this time Gurau was in a high state of excitement. "You don't think, I suppose, that I'm going to give up the former scheme just to make way for somebody else? I'm not that sort of man! I share all Courson's anxieties; I had them before he came along. But Courson's advice is impracticable. It would be extremely dangerous even to try to follow it. Just imagine the situation if Cruppi was persuaded by my arguments, if the rest of the Cabinet sulkily acquiesced, and then, a week later, the ratification was defeated in the Chamber, and the Government fell! (Which is by no means improbable if you take into consideration last winter's campaign.) An adverse vote of that kind would immediately assume the significance of a definite anti-German move—which, in fact, it wouldn't be at all. The President would have to summon one of our great anti-German patriots, one of our disaster-mongers—perhaps Delcassé himself or a cold-blooded adventurer like Poincaré—and then the fat *would* be in the fire!"

Manifassier's face had lost its expression of irony. Gurau's argument had swayed him. He saw that it was true and unanswerable; that to take into consideration the needs of the political situation was not necessarily a proof of cowardice or base calculation.

"Wouldn't it be better," went on Gurau, "instead of trying belatedly to patch up other people's mistakes by underhand methods, to come into the open with a policy of my own? Shan't I be in a better position to make peace secure, to build a durable understanding between France and Germany—because that's what it all comes down to?"

"In that case," said the younger man in a tone that reflected his happiness at being able to feel once more the admiration for his chief and confidence in him which were a prime necessity of his being, "in that case, the sooner this Government of oafs—you and Caillaux excepted—comes toppling down, the better."

Chapter

SEEING WITHOUT BEING SEEN

After leaving Dourets, Laulerque, though he no longer had M. Karl and his notes to help him, found the way without much difficulty. He hesitated, as he had done the first time, when he came to the intersection of the two paths which he had to leave to his left, but a cork-tree, stripped of foliage to the height of its lowest branches, and as brown as the picture of a red Indian, served to remind him of the road.

He had not yet made up his mind what he was going to do. "Ought I to interview the caretaker, who's got nothing to take care of now, unless my 'tenant' is employing him? He might have something to tell me, fool though he is. On the other hand, if I want my visit to remain secret, that's hardly the way to go about it. . . ."

He remembered the effect of M. Karl's piece of gold. "Ten francs is a bit too much for me." He opened his purse, saw a five-franc piece, and transferred it to his waistcoat-pocket to be ready for emergencies.

The sun was warm, but the air was sharper than he had anticipated. "Odd," he thought, "that the temperature's so little different from what it was in December."

The excitement which the beauty of the day roused in him was faintly tinged with fatigue. "Is it," he thought, "the sudden change of climate, or is it my illness? I mustn't forget that the spring's a bad time for me."

He said "my illness" with no feeling of shame, because there was nobody by to hear him. He even felt a sort of affection for the words. "All men's lives are short; mine is of the kind that's rather shorter than the average. All flesh is born to suffer; my suffering is not excessive. It's hardly suffering at all, as a matter of fact; anxiety's more the word. I probably shouldn't bother about it if I didn't happen to know that I was a sick man. . . . One of the disadvantages of being too well must be that one lets the days go by without getting a grip on them. At least I do get a grip on them. I feel each one to the full as it slips by. I'm not absent-minded, and I daren't let myself be bored."

He saw a man bending over a bundle of wood between two trees. It was the caretaker. "I must say something to him now. Whatever I do, he'll recognize me. Does he know I've bought the house? Shall I tell him?"

"Good morning. I hope you're well. You weren't expecting me, were you?"

The man smiled, took off his hat, and said something. He seemed surprised, but not excessively so. He asked whether the fat gentleman had come too.

"Not this time."

"I hope he's well."

"Very well, thank you."

"Has he sent you about the house?"

After a moment's hesitation, Laulerque said: "Yes," in a tone that might have meant much or nothing.

The peasant scratched his head, then shook it, accompanying the movement with a grimace. With his lips he made a clucking noise which seemed meant to express disapproval or scepticism of some situation or of some persons about whom he was thinking.

"Have you still got some of your wine left? I'd like to drink a glass. It's hot work walking."

They descended to the house, which was empty, and sat down in the kitchen. The man put on the table a bottle of wine *rosé,* a hunk of bread, some dried figs, and some black olives. A moment later the girl came in, carrying some half-dried bunches of grass and leaves which she was taking to the rabbit-hutches which stood outside the kitchen door. She greeted Laulerque, showing by her smile that she recognized him, and gave a glance towards the table to see whether they had everything they needed. Then she went about her business without taking any more notice of them.

At first Laulerque was very careful about what he said. He very soon got wind of how the man envisaged the situation. Obviously he thought that the fat gentleman had bought the house after coming to see it at Christmas. A little later he had let it to some people from a distance, and these people had taken possession of it in stages. Two days running the former caretaker had noticed two wagons covered with tarpaulins arriving in the afternoon. They probably contained furniture, and had come from inland, doubtless from a distance. He wasn't sure, however, that he had seen everything. It was possible to reach the White House by a longer but better road which came from Ramatuelle. In any case, he had not seen the people themselves arrive. One day when he was taking a walk, out of sheer curiosity, in the neighbourhood of the White House, he was amazed to find himself stopped, a few hundred yards from the house, by a great lout of a fellow in an extraordinary get-up and armed with a gun. He must have been some kind of gamekeeper, but he was unlike anything usually to be seen thereabouts.

"Had he any right to stop you?"

That was as might be. The former caretaker didn't know for certain where the fat gentleman's land ended. He'd had no reason to bother his head about it up to then. No one within living memory had ever blocked the right of way. The woods were not a preserve.

In this way Laulerque learned that he was the legal possessor of a certain amount of land in addition to the house. But he couldn't get any precise information about either the extent or the shape of his estate. The caretaker could talk of nothing but his meeting with the armed man, and the anger which the incident had roused in him. The man had said nothing, had seemed unable to understand any words addressed to him, but had made it clear by his attitude that he would allow no one to pass. He had taken his gun from his shoulder. The caretaker frowned fiercely and thumped the table with his fist as he described the humiliation to which he had been exposed. He explained that he, too, had a gun and had had half a mind to get it. If he had, things might have happened! But he wasn't certain that the other fellow, however rough a customer he might be, wasn't within his rights. Besides, he didn't want to make trouble for the fat gentleman, who had treated him well and probably didn't know what savages his tenants were. The caretaker expressed a hope that Laulerque, whom he obviously took for the fat gentleman's agent, would tell him how they were behaving.

"But who are these people?"

The peasant kept on repeating, with violent shakings of the head and very fierce looks, that they were "no better than they should be."

"But you must have had opportunities of seeing them since? How many are there? What are they like?"

At first the man pretended not to know. It wasn't that he wished to disoblige his visitor, but having been turned away like a dog, he was unwilling—or so it seemed—to appear sufficiently lacking in pride to bother his head further about such an ill-bred lot.

Laulerque looked at his watch, pretended to be still hungry, and then, putting the five-franc piece on the table, asked very pleasantly whether they couldn't have another of those excellent omelets.

When they had finished their coffee and brandy (the girl had some too, and was invited to clink glasses with the visitor), the old caretaker assumed a very knowing expression, smoothed his stained moustache at great length, winked, and then, having motioned to the girl to leave them, leaned towards Laulerque.

"You just come with me," he said.

Together they left the house. The man gave a few instructions to the girl and appeared to add, in patois and in a nonchalant tone, that the gentleman from Paris wanted to take a little walk.

They went into the woods, heading due east, taking a line at right angles to the road which led to the White House.

The path zigzagged a good deal through the undergrowth. They crossed a clearing, and then re-entered the woods, bearing slightly to the right. The man moved slowly, apparently with the intention of making their walk look like an aimless saunter. From time to time, without turning his head too deliberately, he carefully scanned the thickets through which they were passing.

It seemed to Laulerque that they had described the arc of a circle and were now striking inwards towards the centre. In this way they covered about a mile and a half. Most of the time they were away from any path.

They reached the slopes of a sharp rise covered with trees, which, towards the rocky summit, gave way to shrubs and bushes. The sun shone full on the stony outcrop.

The man motioned to him to stop and seemed to listen for a moment. Then he led Laulerque to the top of the hill, signing to him to follow closely and make as little noise as possible.

They reached a little platform just short of the crest, from which the farther slopes were visible through a curtain of brushwood. To their right was the slope of the hill, which was comparatively bare of trees only in the direction from which they had come.

He made a sign which seemed to mean: "Come nearer; bend down and look."

Suddenly the White House appeared below them. From this point its full length was presented to their view at a slightly oblique angle, the front foreshortened, and the oil-mill, with its pond, in the immediate foreground. It must have been about five hundred yards distant, but seemed less, so clearly were the smallest objects visible. To south and to west the sea shone in the distance, with, midway, a dip in the intervening land.

The two men sat down on the ground and stared. Laulerque soon noticed people moving about near the house. They looked very small, and at first it was difficult to distinguish one from another. But by degrees his eyes took in the differences in their appearance. The peasant, for whom the sight was obviously by no means new, helped his companion to pick them out.

"That's the old man," he said.

"What old man?"

"*The* old man."

A few minutes later:

"And who's that?"

"The same."

"Are you sure?"

"Yes."

The man explained that he was waiting for the "young man" to come on the scene.

"Is there a young man?"

"Yes."

"Ah! . . ."

Laulerque next asked whether, when they were last there, the kind of terrace which he could see in front of the ground floor had been in existence.

"Yes, but they've cut back the shrubs."

"Is that a woman?"

"Yes, the only one."

"What's she doing there?"

The caretaker shrugged his shoulders evasively and made a movement as though he were turning an omelet in a pan or poking a fire.

"She looks fat. Is she old?"

"Not very."

The man put a finger to his lips.

"What's up?" Laulerque asked in a low voice.

The peasant extended his forefinger with extreme caution. Laulerque saw two men walking towards what he called the terrace. One of them was carrying a folding chair, of American pattern, which he proceeded to set up. But it was the other one who, first testing it to see whether it was firm, sat down.

"That's the young one," murmured the ex-caretaker.

Laulerque made a great effort to get an accurate impression of his appearance. He seemed to be thin and rather tall. He was wearing light trousers and a dark coat. On his head he had a sort of yachting-cap of some dark colour, the peak of which, added to the distance, made it difficult to see his features.

Laulerque thought for a moment before deciding what question to ask next.

"How many are there all together?"

The peasant replied that he couldn't say for certain, but he thought there must be four or five of them at least, including the woman, but without counting the two men with guns.

"Are there two men with guns?"

The ex-caretaker shook his head with an air of importance.

"Perhaps more than two."

"But you have seen two? The one who stopped you, and another?"

"Certainly."

"Did the other say anything to you?"

"I saw him, but he didn't see me."

Laulerque looked at his watch. He saw that they had been there nearly two hours, though it seemed no more than ten minutes, so intent had he been on this business of looking, which partook at once of the nature of hunting, warfare, and an experiment with a microscope.

"What am I going to do now? Go down? Suddenly appear down there, announcing myself like the man in *Les Burgraves:* 'Behold in me the Emperor Barbarossa'?"

Was it necessary to go down? What if one of the fellows with a gun stopped Barbarossa from approaching? "I've nothing on me to show that I'm the owner. Besides, if I had, they mightn't take any notice. And I can't complain to the police."

He continued to concentrate his attention on the view of this house set in its little valley; on the behaviour of these people, whom he never saw all together and couldn't count; on all these movements, which could probably be accounted for quite simply, but some of which had taken on for him the dignity of things wrapped in mystery. He felt towards them that mixture of intense interest and detachment, of nearness and of powerlessness to take part in them, which the dead might feel if they could return and watch the living.

Chapter

SPRING AT THE MILL OF SANNOIS

The beauty of this Sunday had been, from the first moment of dawn, scarcely believable. Milkmen, tramps, night-watchmen, raised their heads as though saying in so many words: "What a sky! If you stick in bed you don't see that! It's almost worth while being up so early!" and the paper-sellers remarked to their first customers, as they took down the shutters from their kiosks:

"Hot as anything already, isn't it? Worse than midsummer, and it's not Whitsun yet!"

For some time now the pageant of the year had been a thing of splendour. The bad season, instead of following its usual custom and cheating expectations by promises never quite fulfilled, seemed to have emptied its sack of miseries once for all and gone for good. Contrary to all normal expectation, the days of sunshine had not been traps to lure poor city-dwellers with a hope of brightness, only to plunge them, a moment later, into a week of rain.

For once, the smiling face of spring had not been false. Radiant mornings showed no eagerness to turn to murk, nor did strong sunlight, striking between clouds, snigger maliciously in the face of an adoring world. No, day followed day with added brilliance, setting, as it were, a tradition of fine weather, establishing a claim of beauty.

Young people, sick with the memory of disenchantment, saw the measured tread of spring advance about the banneret of May with a splendour that was worthy of its legend. "Our fathers haven't lied," they thought; "this spring they talk of is real, after all."

Perhaps the flooded months of 1910 had marked, by their very violence, the end of one of nature's freaks. In some such way all periods of disorder find their grave. The gorgeous example of this springtime brought courage to a world of ills and dangers. But Heaven grant that every age of quiet need not be heralded by storm and deluge!

The people of the suburbs were almost surprised to see as yet upon the trees the leaves so scant and thin. They should have got a move on! . . . Six weeks ago the buds were formed and promising—hard buds, soft buds, fresh, pointed, good-looking buds; grey-green and touched with pink, purple-tipped, and silver. Expectant eyes looked to find them now broken to tufts of green, spread in a new maturity. They had no right to stop like this, half-way. The year had been gently nurtured; even the moon had shown a tinge of summer rust.

The hills about the city were set as though for an endless holiday. Sannois and Robinson, Saint-Cloud and Romainville called like a carillon of bells above Paris. The little country restaurants stirred to new life like flies waking from their winter sleep. Cider and wine frothed in their bottled prisons in the cellars of Argenteuil and Mont-Valérien.

For Robinson it was still between seasons: a little too early, a little too late. Its northern slope was still plunged in a moist and chilly dankness, and the great trees, catching the sun as yet but in their upper branches, seemed still in winter's grip, and where it faced the east, the great stretch of cherry-trees and apples, all in bloom, lying like a huge bed spread for beauty, had already begun to shed its glory.

But Sannois, on its green and rounded hill, bare to the sun in the sheltering flank of Cormeilles, took full count of this early splendour of the year.

At seven o'clock, men abed, opening their eyes earlier than was their wont on Sunday mornings and guessing from various signs the glory of the day, turned to their sleeping wives and said: "I say, I've got an idea." Their wives dozed on, but still they said their say:

"Let's get off early, have a good day in the country, and take a bite at the mill of Sannois."

And to himself the man would add: "We might ask the Pellissiers to come with us." For nothing is pleasanter in the spring than a country walk with friends, provided good humour rules the day.

And as he dressed he thought of Sannois, because of the marvellous sun that streamed between the double curtains. He remembered that it was Sunday, and he was seized with a sudden desire to do something fantastic, something heroic, to go farther afield than usual, to find some splendid and unusual spot, somewhere high where Sunday seems to mock the work-day week, where the pleasure of the moment can snap its fingers at the toiling hours and the dead level of every day. Sannois ends, and stops short the northern plain. From its mill the eye, wandering to the distant Eiffel Tower, thrice spans the winding Seine. Sannois dominates and limits the lazy river-lands given over, like a rice-field, to the endless pullulation of humanity. Sannois displays upon its spreading heights a tract of country which the industrial rash has not yet reached, and will not reach for many years, challenging Paris to invade its privacies. Sannois defies the tide of labour to rise and swamp those lands reserved for pleasure. Sannois is a Montmartre which seems to have retreated through the ages, in flight from the spoiling hand of man.

On such a day the sky is clear and blue on every side. Birds sing with that particular note they keep for the suburban fastness, a note that sounds as clearly as though they were hidden deep in woods, but with an added trill of fear and vanity caused by the close proximity of man. The smoke of Argenteuil rises into the air, eddying and thinning. One can almost pick out the contribution of the baker's chimney.

Montmartre, that Sannois of days gone by, lies opposite, down in the plain, humped against the sky, a little to the right of the sun. Despite its distance it fills the scene, and upon its top the Sacré-Cœur stands like an enormous marble statue.

Between the watcher and Montmartre lies an unaccustomed view, which stretches below him like a huge sheet raised at either end. Huge as a city it is, but the eye misses familiar landmarks, towers and domes and spires. Or, rather, it notes a medley of unfamiliar forms, chimneys, gas-tanks, long factory blocks, white, dusty, and round-backed. And between these groups of buildings lies a whole chain of open spaces filled with the ferment, the surge, the bursting sap of spring.

From this point the northern suburbs are seen, as it were from behind. They are difficult to recognize, muffled as they are in stretches of herbage, in copses, in fields. Seen thus, they seem to be no longer striding forwards; they hold no threat. They fill the view, but as a dancing crowd might fill it, waving branches.

How sweet this air can be when the fancy takes it! Whence comes this mild perfection, this softness, this freshness from which all trace of winter has been banished? No sad memories are here, no drizzle of cold rain from reservoirs of dun and mirky days. The clean, new air soars like a lark to heaven, slowly losing itself in the spacious firmament. Such days seem vocal. "See," they say, "what we can do when we try. This is life as it should be." The weather at such times is like a spoiled and pampered woman, fearing to be loved no longer should she be less capricious.

Nowhere else is the bravery of the early year so keen. The smell of the earth, of its greenery, of its growing things, gains from its unexpectedness an added poignancy, an added mystery. As he left his home this morning, the wanderer passed a freight-depot. The yard gates were open wide. A two-horse wagon was crossing the space within, making a fine dust that had a faint taste of plaster. Sparrows were singing in a laurel-bush against a wall. The smell of locomotive smoke was in the air. And over all the fineness of the day spread with a sense of gaiety, giving hope of long, happy hours to come. From end to end of the station reigned a feeling of confidence, the carelessness of May, the sweet atmosphere of young love.

Or, sauntering on his way along the pavement, the pedestrian, moving aside to avoid a roped-in excavation, was conscious of the smell of gas mixed with the smell of watered earth. The sun poured down on the upturned soil. No need to raise his head to feel above it the clear and azure sky.

However marvellous the spring, man does not ask of it that it should hide familiar things. He needs them to bear witness to reality. Without them he would doubt his senses, and his heart would be less full. Even here, among the rustling trees, even here, whence he can no longer see the extent of the northern suburbs and the mass of the distant city, save across orchards and woods, market-gardens, and gleaming river-reaches, he is aware, on this perfect day, of the faint smell of dust that is not of the fields, of hewn stone, of cement poured from sacks, of a hundred indefinable scents which mark the scene with a reminder of the many scattered factories that the Sunday quiet has stilled. It is the smell proper to a fine spring morning between the mill of Sannois and the Sacré-Cœur of Montmartre. But not for that reason have the heady days less power to move the spirit. The smells are the smells of every day, but touched with spring and bright with hope, bringing the colour of young love and the song of birds. The years of childhood have stored up, unconsciously, the sense of all these city things, half-forgotten, vague, unattached, and vagrant, lying at the heart of that will to happiness which now the early year brings to fruition under the impact of little gusts of country air blown across suburban spaces.

People were climbing the hill from every side: from the station of Sannois, from the two stations of Argenteuil, from Herblay, and from Cormeilles. Others, who had come by the Colombes tramway, had had to cross the Seine bridge, and breast the slope, gaining each foot with painful effort. Yet others, from the tramway line of Épinay, had tramped for miles along the road, glorying in their heat, delighted to think that in less than an hour they would have earned the right to sit and drink the whole long afternoon, the men carrying their straw hats in their hands and string bags full of food.

Cyclists were struggling up the rise, making it a point of honour to reach the top without dismounting. Motor-tricycles were spitting and stopping. Here and there a motor-car steamed and clattered: wagonettes and family buses jingled along with the same sound of bells, leaving behind them the same train of yellow horse-dung, as old-time coaches. Waiters were wiping the tables, propping up the legs of rustic benches, and setting beneath the trees collapsible iron chairs, which had become difficult to open because of the rust. Cooks were stoking fires beneath their frying-pans. Restaurant proprietors were chalking up the current price of sausages.

The hill was one huge eating-house. There were inside rooms and rooms half-open to the air; kiosks and sheltered nooks; dining-rooms and dancing-rooms; higgledy-piggledy, cheek by jowl, one on top of another, clinging to the side of the slope. There were terraces, gardens, groves, staircases, rockeries, walks, and sheer drops. And everywhere were people, bottles, food, and the sense of Sunday and of distant views.

Scarcely anybody looked at the view, but people sat glimpsing it from the corner of their eyes, turning their backs on it as though it formed part of the furniture of some casual, family gathering. Every quarter of an hour new groups of friends arrived and took posses-sion of the tables on the hill-top. Round every beaded bottle a little host of glasses clustered like chickens round the mother hen. A feeling of eternity was in the air. In just such a way, from the begin-ning of time, on just such a hill, the folk of Paris had come from the city where history was made, to defy in peace and quiet history's onward march.

Small folk, gay folk, honest folk, and wicked folk.

They came to show that they had the right to live their daily lives despite all the big and empty things that might be happening now or would be happening in the future.

There beneath them the cauldron of history seethed and bubbled, sending up sweet smells, sending up stinks; there in the misty dis-tance to which eyes wandered absent-mindedly between glasses; there in the chasm which spread behind disregarding backs, while the thoughts of all these thousands were intent on nothing but the mill and its bottles.

What was the clink of glasses but a sign that though they had made history or been its victims, that though they would have to turn to and make it once again or once more suffer in its grasp, knowing their destiny and their lot, their will was yet to live in the way that pleased them best?

Through all the ages there has ever been a meal to eat, a drink to take, in all pleasantness, and these things have counted most, have never been entirely interrupted. Theories there may be, street-fighting, risings, but always, through all and beyond all, the little restaurants of the hills with their familiar pleasures. And to these the people have turned (as the conquered and converted have turned time and time again to the shrines and temples they have lost).

There must have been some Sunday on which the people of the Commune came here to take their wine.

Decent folk and wicked folk, but chiefly happy friends, though a few scamps always get into every crowd, a few young fellows who drink elegantly and dance well. "Patrons are requested to refrain from rowdyism"—there it is, written up. But all it means is that you are advised not to come there in a bad temper or to start breaking things. With that one qualification, the place is open to anyone. It takes all sorts to make a world.

Chapter

12

A CELEBRATION

"Sit down, ladies. I think you'll do better on this side. There's a lovely view."

Romuald indicated the bench with a courteous flourish of the hand, but it was with a gesture of liberality that he drew attention to the distance spread before them, from the Sacré-Cœur to the Eiffel Tower. He gave the impression of a man who was offering a present. He turned for a second look, as though to draw personal satisfaction from the scene.

Georgette and Isabelle sat down facing the view. Edmond and Romuald turned their eyes towards the mill.

"A nice little place, I must say," Romuald remarked.

He rapped on the table, which showed evidence of the preceding party in the shape of circles of moisture.

"What'll you have?" he asked his companions.

But Georgette was making eloquent signs at Maillecottin, and now, with a muttered "Edmond!" recalled him to a sense of good manners.

"Oh yes, of course," he said hurriedly, and rapped the table in his turn; "this is on me."

Romuald protested:

"No, no, I insist. Another time, if you like, but this is my treat."

He spoke in a determined tone which gave short shrift to the other's attempt at politeness. He intercepted a passing waiter with the assured air of a man of the world.

"Have you got some fritters? Well then, bring us a litre of white wine, a bottle of lemonade, and two portions of fritters—just for a bite."

"But we're not hungry," said Georgette with a giggle; "we've only just finished eating."

Romuald looked round him at the shady paths and the general scene of gaiety. A little higher up the hill two couples were taking advantage of a clear space to dance. The sound of the orchestra came through the large open windows of the ballroom, playing some kind of cake-walk. Solemn couples could be seen within, and others contorted in the vagaries of impromptu steps. Romuald smiled. The dancers looked to him like scavengers on a spree, bustling, noisy, and rather silly, easily amused and just happy to be alive; in fact, thoroughly common. But he felt in a tolerant mood.

The two girls were on their best behaviour. Isabelle was prodigal of little attentions, while Georgette, addressing her a moment since, had ventured to call her "Madame Guyard." Edmond had frowned, but Isabelle had savoured the compliment with a feeling of gratitude.

Of all four, Edmond was least at his ease. The situation in which he had found himself involved since morning still gave him a sensation of nausea. He fought down his embarrassment until it was hardly noticeable. But it never quite vanished. It had welled up anew when he sat down at this rustic table. When Romuald stretched out his arm to clink glasses or, after watching with scornful good nature the neighbouring groups, the dancers, and the women, turned on Edmond his brown and rather dissipated eyes, his already rather puffy face, Edmond felt as though something at once flabby and dirty were approaching and touching him, felt as he would have done had he been compelled to handle the greasy handkerchief of a man who had a hard cold.

He took out a packet of cigarettes. He couldn't get out of offering Romuald one.

Two days earlier, Georgette, meeting Edmond at the corner of the square, had said:

"Your sister has been to see me."

"What, again?"

"Yes, yesterday evening, just as I was getting my meal. She brought me a lovely bunch of flowers."

"Go on!"

"Carnations and roses—and they're still terribly dear. Don't you think it was awfully nice of her?"

"What did she want of you?"

"The charge against Guyard had just been dismissed, and her first thought was to thank you. Everything's all right now, but Isabelle's still a bit frightened of you. She thought it better to tell me first. And she brought me a bouquet worth six or seven francs, at least. You must admit it was a nice thing to do. And then she said that Romuald wanted both of us to join them next Sunday. His idea is that we should all lunch somewhere in the country, just to celebrate."

Edmond at first had said:

"Leave me alone! I don't want to hear another word of the swine!"

But he realized that Georgette was disappointed. Perhaps he, too, had been attracted by the unusual nature of the invitation. Although he detested Romuald he couldn't help being just a little fascinated by him. Edmond rather liked coming in contact, now and then, with a fellow like that, just to renew his impression of how a pimp lived, spoke, and brazened out his lies.

But his chief reason for accepting was his desire to show that he was not in the least afraid of meeting Romuald. Sensitive though he was to people and to atmosphere, and easily scared, he made a point of never allowing himself to be frightened of any moral aberration. This courage he regarded not so much as a personal as a class quality. The bourgeois, especially the petit bourgeois, is a man who is frightened of everything, a man who lives in constant terror of compromising and dirtying himself. The worker is a man who fears nothing. He ought to be able to expose himself to all contacts without bothering his head about them. He has to mess about with oil and handle bits of greasy machinery. If he's a scavenger he's in constant contact with dirty hand-rails and pumps and filthy water. The worker's a man who doesn't have to wear gloves, who doesn't have to shut his eyes when something nasty comes his way. He may have a sneak-thief as a factory companion, or some depraved creature who boasts that he spends his time waiting for small boys outside public lavatories. It takes more than that to upset him. He refuses to admit that anyone is of sufficient stature to influence him in any way. The worker is strong and inviolable—meaning that he allows of no encroachment on his personality. He will go on acting as he pleases, thinking as he finds it good to think, deviating neither to the left because he's pushed nor to the right because the left shocks him.

Nevertheless, Edmond was beginning to feel that this particular celebration had lasted long enough. The little drink at Argenteuil, the second little drink at Sannois, the lunch, the walk up to the mill. . . . A pimp's company is all right up to a point, but one can have too much of it. They'd played a trick on the magistrate all right, or, rather, they'd let the magistrate tangle himself in the "web of his inquiry," as the papers like to put it, after having carefully cut one of the threads. So far so good. Everything that disturbed the bourgeoisie, that jammed the machinery of the bourgeois State, was a stroke for the Revolution. But that was no reason why any swine should think that getting a swine off was equivalent to taking the Bastille.

When he got Georgette alone he'd have something to say about that "Madame Guyard." No need for the whole family to get on its hind legs just because Isabelle Maillecottin happened to have gone wrong; but to run about calling her "Madame Guyard" as though everything was lovely and they were as proud as Punch of her—well, there was a limit!

It was impossible to talk of going home just yet. One had to show that one knew how to behave even with a pimp, especially when one happened to be the pimp's guest. Meanwhile, cigarette in mouth, and elbows on the table, Edmond sat sideways on his bench and looked at "the view" in a mood of pleasant Sunday relaxation. There was nothing particularly pleasant about his thoughts, but he found it agreeable to see this stretch of country, with one aspect of which he was so familiar; to see, as it were, the wrong way round, against the grain, all this northern suburb which he approached daily from the other end on his bicycle, dropping down on it from the misty heights of the distant horizon; to try to recognize, not without difficulty, not without surprise, the familiar scene behind the smiling country foreground which it presented from this point of vantage.

Over there was a factory, behind the trees, and another; a clump of chimneys. Impossible to say what factories, or whether one had seen those particular chimneys from the other side. Never mind. It was the same old world of factories and chimneys, the world where things happened. Nothing trivial about that, nothing in common with dancing and the excited shrieks of girls in a country restaurant. Life there was serious, weighty, significant. Nothing in common with pimps. Sunday was all right in its way, but it was the week-days that made one feel that one was someone, someone from a different world from that inhabited by this miserable little gutter-rat with his puffy cheeks. The setting of a lathe; the working drawing pinned to the wall; the contour which one knew so well how to get on the part one was working at. The new world, with all the dramas that lay hidden in its womb, to be brought to birth only by the future. Bertrand was an exploiter like all his kind; some day one would have to balance accounts with him. But, for all that, he had in common with his men—in common or in opposition, there's not so much difference, after all—these serious matters of weight and significance. Boss or no boss, he was worlds away from this little beast with the puffy cheeks. One would be only too glad to obey a Bertrand elected by oneself or nominated by the union, a Bertrand who would be there, not to make money by crushing the workers, but just to give orders; a man who would say: "Boys, we're going to turn out next year's best engine." But as things were, the army of labour was discontented and restless because it could not love its leaders.

Life lay there encamped, in that huge plain, behind the nearer green. There, shoulder to shoulder, men were working to build the world that was to be.

Romuald? Bah! A flea; a white louse!

Chapter

13

LETTER FROM ROLAND DE LOMMÉRIE
TO MONSIEUR DE LOMMÉRIE

Sidi-Gueddar, 17 May

Dearest Dad:

I'm sure you won't recognize my writing, because my hand's quite numb, almost dead I might say, with clutching the reins. We're advancing at a terrible pace; we must have done another forty miles today, and it's longer for me, because my men are on flank guard almost the whole time, and I have to keep on galloping round to them to see that everything's all right. But the poor infantry, of course, are the chaps I take my hat off to. They've had a frightful grind of it from the Sliman fort (where my last letter but one was written) to El Kenitra. I don't like to tell you how far it was, because our maps are not very accurate, and I shouldn't like to have you think I was exaggerating, but I can honestly say that the stages were much longer than the average, and the pace was killing. Just think: they talked of getting us to Fez about the 4th or 5th! It would have had a wonderful effect if we could have done it. A whole lot of bother would have been prevented. But we've had bad luck from the word go. I wonder whether you got my letter from El Kenitra. When I sent it we'd been kicking our heels for three days. It's never stopped raining ever since. We were kept from moving for a whole week by mud which extended as far as one could see. At Lalla-Ito we halted again, this time for other reasons. Paris, having suddenly realized that the situation was serious, decided to send us reinforcements at top speed, and we had to give them time to come up with us. I can't say they dawdled.

I'm taking a chance with this letter. The regimental postman assures me it won't get lost, but I have my doubts. Still, I'd rather write than not. It's the last bit of leisure I shall get before we arrive at Fez, which they now say will be about the 21st, and that's where the trouble's due to start, see?—so I should like to think you'd had a line from me.

By the bye, don't let Mother read this part. I think you'd better go on as we agreed you should—just telling her my news, but not showing her the letters. You can make the excuse that they contain *military secrets* which you've promised to mention to nobody. And now, don't *you* start worrying about me. There's very little danger; up to now there's been practically none. It's natural to expect a bit of a skirmish when we get to Fez, but the chances are that it will all go well and be over pretty quickly, since we shall have an enormous superiority of numbers.

You see, since I wrote last, we've become a real army. General Moinier and General Dalbiez caught up with us here, and General Moinier, as we anticipated, is taking over the command. But what wasn't anticipated a fortnight ago was the number of effectives we should have. Brulard's flying column has become a "group." I'm part of it, luckily, because I think Brulard's a fine chap, a really remarkable specimen. But the composition of his force has been modified a little. In the first place, my squadron has been cut in two, and I'm with the half that's staying. They've given us two machine-gun sections, but have taken away one battery of 75's and one of 65's. In exchange, we've had Colonel Simon's six native contingents of Chaouïas attached to us for keeps, with the result that we're a good deal stronger now than Dalbiez's group. Of course he's got the Legionaries and the Zouaves, and if there really is going to be trouble, the Legionaries and the Zouaves will bear the brunt of it. I realize that, so you see, Dad, that my "esprit de corps" doesn't blind me to facts.

Gouraud's column, too, has been ready for the last two days. It will march to our rear, with the train and the *impedimenta,* as we used to say in our Latin exercises (which reminds me that I keep on thinking of the battles they made us analyse in Sallust and Livy;

it's extraordinary how one finds oneself being reminded of them). This column of Gouraud's will be very heavy. It's not only got to feed us; it's taking along food for the troops who've been shut up in Fez all this time, and whose numbers have been swollen by Brémond's column, which set out to relieve them, but got caught in the trap themselves. There's a rumour that Gouraud doesn't much like the job, which he thinks is a second-line affair.

I gather that the situation in front is getting worse and worse. I don't know how much news they let you have in France, but we're afraid we may hear at any moment that the dirty dogs have captured the city and massacred the garrison. The siege has been effective for the last month, and complete since the 8th. The city is absolutely isolated. You can imagine our state of mind. We've had moments of cursing the reinforcements because it meant waiting for them to come up. The last straw is that the rebels have proclaimed a new Sultan, and in a country like this that's no laughing matter. Even if the new Sultan's a fool, his presence will be enough to regularize the revolt in the eyes of his people.

Well, I suppose that, short of some unforeseen snag, we shall be off at dawn tomorrow. It's coolish in the mornings, even cold, after the heavy rains. It only begins to get hot about nine o'clock, and it doesn't get really bad for us Northerners until between ten and eleven.

The advance is easier than we expected. The country on the whole is very bare. Except in a few places, the ground offers no difficulties, and there's a field of vision as far as the eye can reach. This sort of march would have to be much slower and more cautious in a country like France, all cut up by hedges, walls, and woods and dotted with houses.

It's ideal ground for a column to move in, and moving like this, one sees it at its best. You've no idea what a fine and exciting thing it is to see this long, creeping snake of men, over a mile in length, feeling its way with its antennæ stretched out in front and on all sides.

The other day, between El Kenitra and Lalla-Ito, we had an

alarm on a small scale. (It was before the reshuffling, and the two batteries of 75's were still with us.) A party of horsemen, quite small in number, suddenly appeared on the horizon. They had no intention of attacking, but they fired off their guns. Just for the fun of the thing, and to give the troops confidence—perhaps, too, for the sake of practice—Colonel Brulard ordered the 75's into action. It was simply amazing, unbelievable. The artillery horses galloped out about fifty yards to our right flank; the batteries were in position in the twinkling of an eye, and each fired a salvo. One whole section of the horizon was suddenly blotted out by a line of exploding shells. They hadn't had time to aim properly, and only one shell dropped near the horsemen, but three or four exploded and the rest didn't wait for any more. The battery commanders would have gone on, but Colonel Brulard laughingly gave the signal to cease fire. We haven't got so much ammunition that we can afford to throw it away. Besides, the demonstration had had its effect. We were terribly excited, even the native troops, by this example of speed and accuracy.

On the whole I'm very pleased with my men. They don't grumble much. I think this life amuses them, and that the prestige of France stands higher with them than it did. What will they be like when it comes to fighting? My captain says they'll be all right, but I expect he's prejudiced. I've had one of two chats with some of my pals in the native contingents. Two of them are with the Spahis. They say that the Moroccans are magnificent, far better than the Algerians. They may be right. Certainly the native Moroccan troops are a fine-looking lot. It doesn't bother me. I've never felt so happy. I'm longing for tomorrow morning, and I don't think I shall sleep much. I want to see what our army will look like in open country. They say it's the biggest that's been seen hereabouts within living memory. I hope they're not going to detach us from Dalbiez's group. It would be extraordinarily impressive if they made us advance in two parallel columns with a single system of advance and flank guards. But I don't know whether the lie of the land will make it possible.

You say in your last letter: "Naturally, I hope that you will do your duty, but don't take unnecessary risks. Think of your mother and me." You see how carefully I read it, since I can repeat it by heart. You tell me also never to forget, whether I'm giving orders to my men or dealing with the enemy, that they're all human beings and God's children. You say war's a horrible thing and that we shouldn't make it worse than we need; that we ought to make France beloved by showing that she is not cruel. Be easy in your mind, Dad; none of us wants to get killed if we needn't be. As to being cruel, I believe it's about the last thing any of us thinks about. Self-control may be rather harder for our men if they get worked up and if they see their friends falling; but we'll keep an eye on them.

Love to Mother and everybody, and lots of love to yourself.

ROLAND

PS. Just let me say this, Dad. If anything *should* happen to me, I've left a little key with my friend Lieutenant Mallerbe (spelt almost like the poet) of the Spahis, who is staying behind in the camp at Boulhaut. This key opens the cash-box in the hight-hand drawer of my little desk in Paris. In that box there are a lot of letters. Please don't touch anything until Mallerbe can get to you, and then let him take the box and do what I've told him to do. This is important. No need to mention it to Mother yet. Thank you, Dad, and don't worry. All my love.

A TERRIBLE ACCIDENT

"That's fine. . . . Shaved already? Marvellous! What time did you get up?"

"Half past four! For Heaven's sake don't be funny! I can't stand it! They might at least have picked on one of those fine days we've been having lately. . . . What weather, I ask you!"

"It's not so bad as all that. You'll see."

"I'm sick to death of all this talk about aeroplanes; they've become a regular religion with these fools. Don't you think I could have got out of going? Monis and Berteaux'll be enough, surely?"

"Certainly not. Why let flying become a monopoly of the soldiers? The aeroplane's got something better to do than merely to drop bombs."

"Was my car waiting?"

"No. What time did you order it for?"

"A quarter past. It's only just that now. The thing's begun already, you know. . . . Oh well, I don't care! Do you think I'd better take an overcoat? Did you manage to get some sleep?"

"No. It was half past one when I left the *Sanction*. I went and had a wash, and then I wrote two or three letters."

"You're looking as fresh as paint. You're a marvel. Anything in the papers?"

"Dispatches from Morocco. Moinier's column has effected a junction with some caid or other who's brought all his tribes along with him—some name like Ouessan. . . . They're nearly at Fez. I gather that things are beginning to move. Obviously the rebels didn't expect such a demonstration in force."

"The 'rebels'! You make me laugh, young man. . . . The start of the Paris-Madrid flight, the relief of Fez, Berteaux'll jump out of his skin! . . . Come along! Handkerchief, cigarettes. . . . Have you got matches?"

"I've got my lighter."

"Good—so long as the car's there."

Gurau and Manifassier entered by the Porte de Sèvres; but it wasn't easy. The police had not got the crowd under control, and it made approach by car difficult. The sky remained overcast. There was no appearance of gaiety in the scene.

They got out and told the chauffeur to take the car to the official parking-place. An official showed them where the stands were, to the right of the flying-fields, in front of the balloon-hangars.

"Let's take our time. . . . I'm in no hurry to join all those old sheep."

They stayed for a while by the entrance. A few groups of spectators, who, from their dress, seemed to be ticket-holders, were scattered here and there. The crowd was pressing against the barriers and the police cordon. In the background the slope of the fortifications was black with onlookers.

Now and again Gurau recognized someone he knew and raised his hat.

"I say, Manifassier, even some of the ordinary ticket-holders have put on top-hats. What's it going to be like in the grand stand! Perhaps I was wrong to come in a derby. . . . Anyhow, I'm glad I've got an overcoat."

He turned up his collar.

Manifassier smiled at his chief's bad temper.

They saw a machine come towards them, slowly leave the ground, climb with a rather frightening lack of steadiness, turn about a hundred and fifty feet above them, head towards the south, and apparently recover its balance. The starting-point seemed to be at the other end of the ground, towards Issy-les-Moulineaux. Obviously, it was to take advantage of the wind that the machines were starting like this north-eastwards, towards Paris, before turning onto their proper course. The crowd was still out of hand and continued to break through the cordons. Little Lépine was bustling about as usual. Now and again he sent a section of cuirassiers ambling off to clear one of the corners of the ground.

They had reached the left end of the grand stand. A certain number of official seats, especially in the front row, were still unoccupied. Many of the guests were standing. There was a goodish number of top-hats. Gurau's temper did not improve.

Manifassier waved to a man of about his own age on one of the tiers. The latter returned the salute and raised his hat politely to Gurau.

"Who's that?" murmured the Minister.

"One of Caillaux's secretaries. His name's Geoffroy. A nice fellow."

Gurau went up to him.

"Isn't your chief here?"

"No, sir."

He smiled, as much as to say: "He's not as brave as you."

Gurau indicated the empty places.

"Where are all the others?"

"Down there, sir. They've gone to the starting-point, to get a closer view of the machines and to watch them take off. You can see them—there, just behind those cuirassiers who are moving away. . . . You won't be able to see much from where you are. The troops are in the way. . . . I think they're coming back. Look! There's one of the machines just starting."

A monoplane passed in front of the grand stand and rose from the ground, rolling a good deal. The onlookers could hear the engine spitting. The machine seemed to check in its flight. Before reaching the Porte de Sèvres, it swung to the left, as the others had done, but instead of climbing in a south-westerly direction, made a complete half-circle, bumping badly and noisily misfiring. It looked as though it were turning back and meant to land again over by the starting-line.

It passed once more in front of the stand close by where Gurau and Manifassier were waiting. It was only about a hundred feet up and was descending rapidly. It looked as though it would come down straight into the backs of the receding cavalrymen. The spectators were too much appalled to cry out. But the noise of the motor caused some of the soldiers to turn, and they shouted a warning to their comrades. The detachment split, with amazing agility, into two halves, the horses rearing and jostling, and in this way a space was made almost big enough to allow free passage to the aeroplane. But no sooner had this happened than it became apparent to the onlookers that the course of the machine was blocked about thirty paces farther on by a group of gentlemen in top-hats or heavily braided military caps, who were, in fact, the members of the committee on their way back to the grand stand. They could be heard shouting; they could be seen raising their arms and starting to run. A few tripped and fell. The machine had come down on top of them.

For nearly a quarter of an hour Gurau and Manifassier found themselves at the centre of a sort of vortex. A mysterious panic had developed. Hundreds of people were shouting, crying for help, stampeding in every direction. Fashionably dressed women were jumping from the stands with shrill cries, hurling themselves into the thickest part of the crowd, and being flung back and trampled underfoot. Men were waving their sticks and hitting out blindly in all directions. A riderless cavalry horse was galloping across the congested ground to an accompaniment of agonized shrieks.

Gurau and Manifassier had taken up a position with their backs pressed against the stand just below the spot previously occupied by the young secretary, who had disappeared.

Gurau kept on repeating:

"They're all mad! What do they think they're doing?"

It was, in fact, difficult to see any normal connexion of cause and effect between the accident which had occurred—in so far as its precise nature could be ascertained—and the reactions of the crowd. What had happened was shocking enough, to be sure, and seemed to be serious, but it had been confined to one corner of the ground and had occurred in a flash. In any case it was over now and done with, but the crowd was behaving like the audience in a burning theatre, or the staff of a powder-magazine with sheds going up one after another all round them. "But at least," thought Gurau, "people in a theatre or workmen in a powder-factory, however panic-stricken they might be, would respond to some one definite impulse; they'd be trying to get out of the burning building or away into the fields." Here, on the other hand, though there was a general tendency among the onlookers to escape, it showed itself as an effort to run away from *the spot where each happened to be standing at the moment,* quite irrespective of the actual proximity of the danger, which by this time had entirely ceased to threaten. Little groups here and there, rags and tatters of the crowd, seemed to have been caught up at a distance and swept into the whirling orbit of the storm, and these seemed to be not so much avoiding the danger, in which, actually, they had never been involved, as going out of their way to meet it. This general effect was probably the result of an unusual combination of curiosity and terror, both wrought up to a pitch of delirium by the solemnity of the occasion and by the idea, disseminated with the quickness of lightning, that several of the highest functionaries of the State had just been killed. And all this excitement had come on top of a general condition of hysteria due to the fact that many of those present, in their anxiety to get good places, had not had a wink of sleep the previous night.

The experience of this quarter of an hour was for Gurau one of curious intensity. Outwardly he seemed perfectly calm, and the spectacle of all this collective panic served but to increase the lucidity of his mind. Not that he was entirely unaffected by the emotional quality of the scene, but with him it took the form of a power to make judgments and to see ahead with a quickness, a facility of association, a clearness of vision, and a richness of implication far in excess of anything that would normally have been possible for him to achieve.

He was able, as it were in a flash, to compare and test every one of his fundamental ideas on crowds, on public emotion, on the power of human reason, on the origin of historic events, on the instability of civilization, on the persistence, side by side with all the elaborate complexities of the modern world, of a set of primitive instincts ready at any moment to take control and influence events. He was proud of his own behaviour. Once more he realized that he was one of those who seem to be nervous and excitable because little things affect them to an excessive degree, but who at moments of real crisis can achieve complete self-mastery, one of those in whom tense nervous organization acts like the steel network in reinforced concrete. "I lose my head when a ticket-collector makes a scene, but if France went up in smoke tomorrow, I should probably be among the two or three men who could keep their heads, just as I'm keeping it now while I'm standing with my back to the grand stand." He felt himself over mentally, as an athlete feels his muscles and finds them taut and responsive to his will. "I'm ready for anything that comes along."

After having said once or twice: "What are they all doing?" he relapsed into silence. Manifassier, though he remained unaffected by the general panic, was showing a certain feverish nervousness, an impatience to penetrate to the centre of the storm, to what might be called the area of attraction, created by those whose curiosity was stronger than their desire to escape, where, too, the instinct to help had resulted, as it were, in a sort of human solidarity before the assaults of accident.

He said to Gurau in a voice that trembled slightly:

"Don't you think we ought to go and see? . . . There may be a whole lot of victims, and it's quite likely that there's no one to take charge of the rescue work."

"Certainly not, my dear chap. In the first place, we should never get through this mob, and if we did, what could we do? We should only be in the way. The police and the military seem to be keeping the crowd back. It's not my business to do Lépine's job for him. No, for the time being, we'll stay where we are."

Manifassier assumed an obedient expression. Gurau's calmness was having its effect on him. He suddenly realized anew that difference of rank between his employer and himself, which the familiar intercourse of every day tended to obscure. "He's my chief; he's got the qualities of a chief; he is someone." He felt happy and comforted. Gurau, realizing what was going on in his mind, was happy too.

When this strange quarter of an hour was drawing to a close, since the panic seemed to be at an end and the crowd, though still excited, behaving more normally, Gurau said to Manifassier:

"Now you can go. . . . You'll find me here. I'm sticking where I am."

Manifassier returned in the company of Geoffroy. The two young men appeared to be shaken and excited. They both started speaking at the same moment:

"It's been a most awful business. . . . Berteaux was killed on the spot . . . and there's not much hope for Monis. . . . A lot of the others were injured, too. . . . The machine came right down on top of them . . . right on top of the official party. . . . They tried to get away. . . . Berteaux was too near the middle, he hadn't time to do anything. . . . Monis started to run, but he's fat and he fell. The machine ran right over him, and over Deutsch de la Meurthe too. . . . That's what saved them—if they are saved, that is. One of Berteaux's arms was caught by the propeller; you can imagine the amount of blood he must have lost; and his skull was fractured. He was killed at once—can't have suffered much. . . . They're not sure about Monis. It's his head, they say. Pretty bad. . . ."

With hardly a moment's pause they passed to a totally different subject:

"It seems the Government will go."

"Who said so?"

"Some newspaper men who've just been talking to some members who saw the accident . . . one of Geoffroy's colleagues, too . . . and a friend of Pams. . . . Even if Monis survives he'll be out of action for months . . . and somebody'll have to be found to take Berteaux's place. . . . Besides, things weren't going too smoothly in any case. . . ."

"Aren't you going a bit fast?"

"It's not a case of us," Manifassier retorted; "it's what everyone's saying. . . . Why, a fellow from the *Débats* actually told Geoffroy he supposed his chief would be asked to form a Ministry."

Gurau frowned and then smiled. His expression betokened a degree of bitter irony, contempt, and a self-confidence which as good as said: "Well, whatever happens, *I'm* ready."

Then he asked:

"Where have they taken them? I should like to see them. . . ."

"Oh, probably to some hospital or other . . . we don't know which. . . . But now that things have calmed down a bit, we can easily find out."

Chapter

15

GURAU ACHIEVES HIS OBJECT

"Well, Mother, have you seen your friend Gisèle?"

"Indeed I have, we spent more than three hours together. She came for me in her car. Have you seen it? It's a marvel, much more comfortable than ours—a Rochet-Schneider, the great Lyons people, you know. I must talk to your father about it, now that ours is getting so old. Which reminds me, it really is time the dressmakers realized that the woman of today is always in and out of cars. They ought to modify these absurd fashions. Why, getting into Gisèle's car, I ruined the brim of my hat, just because I wasn't used to the way the doors were placed. It was very annoying; not that I care much for that hat, but we had to go to one or two rather smart places. It spoiled the day for me. Gisèle assured me it wouldn't be noticed. . . . Of course when I say 'spoiled' I'm exaggerating a little. I enjoyed myself quite a lot. Gisèle's a charming companion. She wanted first of all to take me to the Durand-Ruel Galleries to look at some Monets. She's mad about Monet. But I can't make up my mind about him. His colour's interesting, or rather his experiments in the rendering of light, but there's no design in his pictures. The various objects seem as though they were all melting and falling to pieces in a fog. It's natural for the English to like that in his London scenes, I can see what he's after in them. But French landscapes, French light—that's quite a different thing. . . . The atmosphere of the Île de France, for example . . . it's not hard, but it's clear-cut. The silhouettes of the houses and buildings, I agree that they ought to be rendered with a sort of softness . . . but the lines, the shapes, are always so definite . . . one's always conscious of precision and solidity. . . ."

"Perhaps he sees things like that. . . ."

"Of course he doesn't! Modern artists don't try to show things as they see them. What they're trying to do is to establish a style—very attractive sometimes, but highly artificial. . . . She wants to convert me to Debussy, too. Oh, I know you agree with her there. There are things of his that I admire very much . . . the things you play, *Cortège,* for instance, and one or two passages in *Pelléas* I like enormously. But I can't think of *Pelléas* in the same terms as I think of the great masterpieces. There's an absence of strength and passion. It's all pretty rather than beautiful. I can't compare it even with *Tristan.* I know you agree with me more or less about *Tristan;* it's the one Wagner opera, fortunately, that you young people *do* admire. But leaving Wagner out of the question, *Carmen* . . ."

"Oh, Mother!"

"I know exactly what you are going to say; we won't discuss it. You'll change your mind about *Carmen* one of these days. It's a very beautiful work. Gisèle realizes that in Germany, where she lived at one time, the critics and lovers of music rank Bizet very high. . . . She reproached me with not having been to hear the *Martyre de Saint-Sébastien.* . . . She says I should have had to admit that it has a certain nobility. . . . Oh, she's not fanatical . . . she argues very sweetly. . . . She just *likes* certain things. . . . I'm not sure that she could ever really convert anybody. She's not good at explaining herself. She likes something, and there's an end of it. Well, after that, we went to the Bois and looked at one or two dresses. Skirts are still being worn narrow. I noticed a new and rather amusing material that one or two young women were wearing. Gisèle says she knows what it's called, but she couldn't remember the name. She promised to write it and to let me know where it can be got. . . . I think you'd look well in it; and since you *are* just getting a new dress . . ."

"Quite right, Mother dear."

"Then we had tea at the Pavillon d'Armenonville. It was *such* a lovely day. What a year we are having! If Monet can go on in weather like this turning out his dishes of mincemeat seen through a fog, he must be as obstinate as a mule. And if he's afraid that nature will disturb his ideas, he'd better shut himself up at home and paint out of his head!"

"But, Mother, didn't you talk of anything but music and pictures? . . . You must, I'm sure, have squeezed a few confidences out of poor Gisèle."

"As though I should! You talk as though I spent my time squeezing confidences out of people!"

"Be honest for once, Mother dear. I don't mind your saying that you enjoyed letting her have your views on Monet and Debussy, but you must admit that your real reason for giving up a whole afternoon to her was your desire to find out how she was getting on with Monsieur Gurau."

"Simone!"

"Now, Mother, don't play the innocent with me!"

"Can I be sure that you won't repeat anything I say to a soul, not even to Jacques?"

"How many times have I got to tell you that Jacques would be bored to death by that kind of gossip? As soon as there's something definite, as soon as the engagement is announced, I'll tell him—and it'll amuse him for perhaps a couple of minutes."

"You see, I should never forgive myself. Gisèle poured out her heart to me as though I had been her elder sister or her mother. . . ."

"I swear to you to be discretion itself. There, now, will that satisfy you?"

"If you really must know, she's suffering terribly, poor dear; she doesn't know where she stands."

"It's really serious then?"

"Very serious indeed. You may find it hard to believe, but she's deeply in love with Monsieur Gurau, passionately attached to him. . . . You are young, Simone, and you tend to treat certain things rather too casually. . . ."

"That's where you're wrong, Mother. . . . I wasn't wondering because I doubt the truth of what you say, but because I'm trying to understand. . . . I want to get a clear idea of each of them."

"A lot of women would find Monsieur Gurau extremely attractive."

"Far be it from me to deny it!"

"Do you mean that ironically?"

"Not at all. I don't think he'd turn my head, but then, when I think of most of the men I know, I'm not sure that to fall for him might not be rather less absurd and meaningless than to make a fool of myself over one of them. . . . Does that satisfy you? . . . I will make a confession to you. It may sound cynical, but at least it should make you easy in your mind about my virtue. The immense majority of men seem to me to be just about worth a woman's marrying, and nothing more; capable of rousing as much love as will fit comfortably into the 'holy state of wedlock.' If Jacques weren't my husband—and you know how devoted I am to him—it would never occur to me for a moment to have him as a lover—him or anybody like him. It's not in that side of life that I find myself tempted to look for adventure, mystery, and excitement. Women who do, it seems to me, must be harlots by nature, always hankering after change in what is, after all, the stupidest and crudest aspect of life. I regard it as inexcusable to deceive an ordinary man with another ordinary man. But with Gisèle the question in that form doesn't arise. . . . She wants to marry him—rather a different situation, to be sure, but one which I fully comprehend. She has money; she has no need of a rich husband—she's just got rid of one! It's something, after all, in spite of what some of our friends say, to be the wife of a Minister; she might find such a position very interesting. There's no reason why she shouldn't be smart as well. . . . What, then, is the trouble?"

"She's as heartbroken as a young girl, because she thinks her feelings are not reciprocated."

"What! . . . Has he made it so obvious that he doesn't want her?"

"He hasn't made it obvious at all; he just avoids the question. His

455

attitude to Gisèle is charming and very attentive. There's no reason to suppose that he's trying to avoid her. . . . A fortnight ago she made me promise, as a great favour, that I would ask him his intentions. . . . I half said I would. But at the last moment my courage failed me—partly because of something you said. I remembered that you had called me a 'matchmaker.' . . . Now listen—but you must promise to keep this part, especially, of what I'm telling you to yourself; it would be so easy for malicious-minded persons to misinterpret Gisèle's behaviour. . . . She invited him to dine alone with her. . . . She made up her mind to stake everything on that one throw. 'For reasons of his own,' she argues, 'he may not want to marry. On the other hand, I don't think he's indifferent to me. There's no mistaking the way he sometimes looks at me. But he is well-bred, not the sort of man who runs after women or treats them lightly. He respects me, and he's heard me spoken of as respectable. . . . Well, so much the worse for me. If he merely wants me to be his mistress, I'd rather be that than nothing, because I'm in love with him.' She has every right to add, as she well may have done: 'After all, I'm not a young girl, and I shan't be the first woman of my age and in my position who's been a man's mistress before becoming his wife. It may be the best and least troublesome way of ultimately achieving marriage.'"

"Go on, Mother—you're killing me with impatience! I suppose she received him in a provocative négligé and heavily scented? And I suppose he resisted? But first tell me: when did all this happen?"

"Yesterday evening."

"And you actually forced yourself this afternoon to discuss Monet and Debussy? Really, you deserve a medal! Oh, do go on."

"I think they were both rather shy. Gisèle believes that she made bold advances and put him completely at his ease; but I suspect that in fact things were rather different from what she imagines them to have been. No doubt that great apartment of hers with its huge dining-room seemed simple enough to her, because she sees it every day, but it must have all looked very formal to him, very respectable, and not at all the natural setting for the sort of pleasing conclusion she had been anticipating. I don't suppose, for instance, that it occurred to her that the mere going and coming of the butler and footman would keep Monsieur Gurau from making advances, and even from holding a conversation on a sentimental level."

"How do you think she ought to have stage-managed it?"

"I don't know. . . . She's got a charming boudoir, and she could have had the table laid there—it would have been easy enough to explain, if she'd had to—and the meal served by her maid. The whole thing ought to have been more on the lines of a frivolous little dinner or supper, which would have done away with the difficulty of having the servants constantly in and out. . . . Besides, she could have made it perfectly clear by the sort of orders she gave in his hearing that the maid would come only when she was rung for. . . . Of course I realize that he would probably have seen through it all, but she could easily have saved the situation by stressing the note of easy friendliness, of casual picnicking, by making it clear, without any hint of suggestiveness, that she had wanted the evening to be informal and charming, the sort of thing that might be arranged between two men. Or she could have kept him in his place, if she'd wanted to, by putting just a touch of formality, of the great lady, into her tone—a 'Really, I don't know where you think you are' note. It would have dissipated the first slightly ambiguous quality of their meeting, and it wouldn't have prevented things taking their natural course later. . . . The effect on the gentleman would only have been to make him keener, and—well, she ought to know her own mind, oughtn't she? . . . She told me she was staking everything on this, and if one gambles like that, I suppose one does it with one's eyes open. . . ."

"Mother dear, you'll make me die of laughing! . . . Your abilities as a stage-manager are really quite frightening!"

"Don't be a fool, Simone. I've been talking to you as I would to a friend, to another woman, and you suddenly make me realize that you're nothing but an irreverent little gutter-snipe! . . . What are you laughing at? What are you trying to insinuate? I've said nothing I wouldn't say in front of your father. . . . Do you imagine that a woman of my age who's read novels and been to plays, who's listened to her friends' confidences and who's thought a good deal about life, can't have views about things of that kind without having experienced them personally? . . . When the Humbert affair was on, I remember that your father said a lot of very wise things about the blunders committed by swindlers . . . but that didn't prove that he'd ever done any swindling himself."

"Please don't be angry, Mother. Surely I can be amused if I like? . . . What a pity it is we haven't still got the château. You could have invited them together. . . . A seaside villa's not so easy."

"Really, Simone, is there no end to your foolishness?"

"Well, what happened? I suppose Monsieur Gurau was terribly well-behaved in the grand dining-room, under the eyes of the footman and the butler. He and Gisèle probably discussed the political situation!"

"You're nearer the mark than you think. She couldn't have chosen a worse day. The Government had just resigned. That was something the poor girl couldn't possibly have foreseen. The accident was a month old, and everyone thought that Monis would pull through, in every sense of the words. . . . Monsieur Gurau was terribly preoccupied. . . . He's very ambitious and full of plans for his future, and he feels that the moment is a critical one for him. Sitting there opposite Gisèle in that huge room, he must have felt rather foolish, and so he naturally took refuge in politics. At the moment, she was delighted just to listen to him and to admire him. She felt touched at such an undoubted proof of his esteem. She may even have said to herself: 'There may be another way—the way of friendship.' She must have been trying, the whole time, not to make a fool of herself by saying the wrong things. It was only the next day—that's to say, this morning—that her thoughts may have been less pleasing. What's your opinion, Simone?"

"About what, exactly?"

"About what's worrying Gisèle. How do you explain Monsieur Gurau's attitude?"

"I'm not so well placed as you to guess. . . . He can't have been so preoccupied as not to see that he was the centre of that particular picture, and I don't suppose he found the knowledge displeasing. His going there proves that. He could easily have excused himself on the ground of political business. But he didn't; he preferred to spend an evening chatting with her. More than that I can't say. There may be some other woman in the case to whom he means to be faithful."

"I don't think there is."

"Have you induced him, too, to confide in you?"

"He had an affair, of course, with Germaine Baader, but that was a long time ago, and it's all over now. If there'd been someone else, he would still be in the early days of his passion. . . . One would have noticed something. One always knows when a man's in love. He, on the contrary, gives me the impression of being quite unattached."

"Have you any theory of your own?"

"No."

"Do what Gisèle wants you to do, then; ask him."

"I can't possibly do that now—after yesterday evening. Really, if I did a thing like that, I shouldn't be a matchmaker, I should be more like a—more like a—"

Manifassier, seated in his office, was busying himself about "current routine matters" with that air of detachment which belongs to periods between governments and is a mark of that philosophic calm which so pleasantly pervades such moments in the world of politics. The principal job left on his hands by Gurau was to prevent the shelving of the departmental Honours List for the 14th of July which they had drawn up together. They must leave to the newcomer, as yet unappointed, a selection of names sufficiently well chosen and strongly backed to ensure it's not being superseded, but they must see, at the same time, that there were enough vacancies remaining for Gurau's successor to have the pleasure of filling at his own discretion. It was up to Manifassier, therefore, to shake the tree of their own planting, in the hope that a sufficient number of the less urgent nominations would automatically fall to the ground. He thought it would do if he could get rid of one commander of the Legion of Honour, three or four officers, and seven or eight simple members.

The commander was giving him the most trouble. Unfortunately, the list as originally drawn up contained only two—one for a highly deserving civil engineer who had almost reached the age of retirement, the other for a journalist in rather bad odour, whose only connexion with the department lay in the fact that he had extracted a considerable number of bribes from the larger industrial concerns. Manifassier hated the man and all that he stood for. He would gladly have run a blue pencil through his name, while regretting that the times had gone by when a simple *lettre de cachet* would have sufficed to send an adventurer of that kind to jail. But the fellow in question was counting on the honour, had moved heaven and earth to get it, and was capable of taking every kind of mean vengeance on Gurau if he found that Gurau had been responsible for his failing to get it—and he would know it, since he had his finger in every pie. The engineer, on the other hand, was a thoroughly decent chap, who had very little influence, hated publicity, and was quite incapable of making difficulties of any kind for a minister.

The young man made no attempt to hide from himself the baseness to which he was about to lend himself. "It's a thoroughly dirty piece of work. Here am I, going to take out the name of this poor old man who's the salt of the earth, just to keep that rotter's in. It would be nothing but cowardice on my part to suggest to the boss that he do the other thing. I know perfectly well that he's not free to act as he wishes. . . . How about leaving both names in and letting the next man get out of the difficulty? But the next man'll say: 'We must have one commander's collar to give ourselves,' and if we replied: 'Well, then, decide for yourself,' in the first place we'd risk upsetting the whole list, and then the new fellow might be so damnably polite as to say: 'Certainly not! I shall do nothing of the sort. I insist on leaving you one.' "

At this moment Gurau arrived with the force of a hurricane.

"I've done it!" he said.

"What?"

"Caillaux's given me the Foreign Office. His Cabinet's complete except for one or two unimportant details. I had a long talk with him. We're in full agreement on all essential points. His policy at home will be to avoid throwing away what's been gained already, and to govern with a strong hand. . . . But he agrees with me—with us—that the job which takes precedence of everything else lies in the sphere of foreign politics—to keep peace in Europe. . . . My dear fellow, at last we're going to be in a position to do something!"

Chapter

JALLEZ IN JUNE 1911

It sometimes happens, when you are taking a long, solitary walk in Paris, that little by little everything begins to go wrong, the taste of the day to turn sour. You are conscious of irritation, you become depressed. The very streets take on an air of perversity; the corners seem oddly placed, the streets, for some curious reason, are hard to cross. Something seen in a shopwindow gives rise to ideas which, by some lightning and fantastic turn of thought, become suddenly humiliating. The fatigue of the body turns to a weariness of the spirit. Instead of being a pleasant and languorous background to day-dreaming, it invades and permeates the mind with a sense of uncomfortable anxiety.

At such times relief is often to be found in some corner bar wide open to the street. The projecting counter conforms in shape to the sharp angle of the containing walls. The handsome metal mouldings shine, like the streets outside, with the reflected light of evening and, like them, seem to show less darkly than the overarching sky. Standing, you drink your coffee and cream, or, seated within on a bench at the far end, before a wooden trestle table, you contemplate with half your mind, set there like a stage scene before the open window, the street which waits for your returning feet.

But other days there are when all goes well, sailing before a soft and favourable breeze. Hour follows hour in orderly progression to some crowning moment. This very moment may be what you have been waiting for. Since you set out you have kept, balanced ever so gingerly within your mind, an illusion of adventure, a conviction that you didn't know where you were going. But the charm is fragile; a mere nothing serves to break it, and with it will go the sense of astonishment that was with you on your way, the lovely counterpoint that played about your wish to walk.

Jallez saw before him a wide boulevard, rising slightly to a hill, and not very long. The two lines of thin trees were barely visible against the house-fronts. The grey-green of their foliage seemed sunk into the walls as though it had been drawn on blotting-paper, so that it was visible only as a confused medley of pattern. The distance showed as a perspective of misty factory walls, of shining roofs, stressed vaguely here and there by vertical lines, and looking like the faint design on postage stamps or the watermark in paper.

He liked the indeterminate sense of place, and carefully avoided indentifying this street, whose name, obedient to his will, lay shrouded in the misty places of his mind. He forgot to which particular district, which particular suburb, these blue-veiled tenements belonged which he could see in the hollow below the descending slope. He wanted to remain sensitive to the individual quality of every object, but without naming it, without having to infringe the integrity of its loneliness. Only in that way could he be conscious of all around him and yet feel free of an unchristened world. From the moment he had entered this boulevard until he had reached the summit of this broad and gentle slope, so like a mountain pass, he had been aware of a feeling which he never ceased to seek. (It was not merely, as it once had been in the rue des Amandiers, a "state of being which already dwelt within." Jallez had gone far since then. It was not even, or not exclusively, a "state of grace" in so far as a state of grace implies self-satisfaction and a feeling of pleasant ease.) This particular and impersonal emotion came to him only occasionally. It brought with it, to be sure, a sense of comfort, a consciousness of steady and directed thought, but its main characteristic was the power it had of transcending the bounds of his personality, of effacing in a swift surge of feeling the limitations of himself. He would have found it difficult to define it accurately, and for the moment he was less concerned to do so than to prevent it from escaping. But he knew enough of it to be sure that it was connected in some way with the movement of the street about him, its animation, and with the relation that subsisted between that animation and his own awareness. He understood and willed, as it were, those movements; he made them his own. He had an impression that of his own volition he could create them if they were not there already and if he could have the same material to work upon. This, he realized, was an illusion, but an illusion that served to make him conscious of his own happiness by freeing him of the limitations of himself.

It was connected with the direction and the speed of all that moved about him, with the spaces that opened between the passing figures—including his own—with the angles at which objects impinged upon his sight, with the way in which everything seemed to "compose" to the satisfaction not so much of his eyes as of some deeper and more intimate part of his nature.

It was connected with the people who thronged this boulevard, those who belonged to it of right and those who merely passed temporarily along it; with the quality of life here and now, with the actual moment of existence to which his own presence had been added; with the particular vitality of the place, with the balance it struck between uninhabited emptiness and intolerable congestion; with the slope of the ground, with the dimensions of the street, with the buildings. It was connected with those recessions of perspective, sensed but unseen, attached to no visible points, but felt like threads about the moving feet; with the proximity of objects behind and beyond the immediate field of vision, with distant things, with the successive planes of the circumambient air, with the density of life around him, with the difference of each separate thing that pressed upon him. It was connected with all that the eyes could see or the ears hear; with the message of those misty buildings glimpsed there in the low scoop of the hill; with the way the breeze brought the sound of traffic, of motor-horns, of the distant hoot of sirens; with its touch upon his cheek, soft and sweet and moist; with the sky's unfathomable depths of greenish blue dotted with anchored clouds, from which

464

reflected light touched every passer-by, every person in every house, with a brooding gentleness.

Jallez walked on. As he began to descend the farther slope he was aware of a vague sense of vision which came to him at rare intervals and which he had often tried in vain to capture in its passage. He attached particular importance to it, because it came to him only at moments when circumstances made him peculiarly sensitive, and also because it released in him a curious feeling of excitement, the quality of which was cold, flat, and sharp, like the sound of a gong set ringing and then suddenly stopped by a muffling hand. What in that moment he saw, without any clearness of definition, was something like a balcony set high up on a house to his left. Beyond it was a distant horizon, which, he felt, must be dense and glowing and veiling many things, but which, from his position below it, he could scarcely see. He could imagine what that horizon must look like seen from a higher level, and the thought made him raise his head hungrily. He was convinced, though he could not explain his conviction, that he had only to get up there to be able at will to move freely along behind that light railing, to rest his arms upon it, or, moving back, to sit at a table, reading, talking, drinking, in some room opening on that balcony which would be close at hand and on a level with himself. If only he could do that, he felt, difficult things would be made easy and his thoughts would flow with a new freedom, a new lucidity. Privileged and enfranchised, he would know secrets to be shared only with a chosen few. . . . But even as he formulated the thought, the vision, shattered by the concentration of his mind, wavered and was gone.

The experience forced him to realize that he had no power to control what gave him most delight. Not that he did not fully admit the beauty of a state of mind controlled and stabilized by conscious will, the state of mind of a man capable, in his dealings with the world, of always taking the initiative and holding his senses taut and disciplined. He saw clearly the value of stoicism in the modern world, but he could not bring himself to accept the deprivations which such an attitude of stoicism would impose—deprivations not so much of pleasure as of adventurous discovery. The mind could not hold itself at a stretch without limiting its sensitiveness, could not foresee and set itself to ends without playing traitor to the unexpected, be its own master without at the same time condemning itself never to be possessed by the casual and the wonderful.

On the other hand, the stoic can be sure of happiness, or at least of definite periods of interior harmony. Jalley knew that well. In his present state of mind he was reduced to waiting on happy accidents, on circumstances he could not control, to seeking. And seek as he might, the search would always be without method, for its rewards, like those of love, were shy of those who trod a trail too carefully blazed.

These walks of his were part of his desire to seek. But he was careful not to pursue them on too strict a plan. He preferred to feel his way like those who venture into the wild places, the forests and the deserts, of the earth, trusting to an instinct ever on the watch, passive, and ready to respond.

For some time now he had felt a liking for broad, short streets, full of movement, like this boulevard, and his rambles were so arranged as always to include something of the sort. Or rather it would be truer to say that when he came on some such street, he felt his expectation pricked, his heart filled with a more particular sense of hope. His "emotion" must be genuine and intact. He never counted upon it. Indeed, he would have felt suspicious had it come too often, for he was on his guard against anything that savoured of mechanical regularity.

On the other hand, he noticed that this "emotion" of his had more than once come to him in old and narrow streets, where passers-by were few and carriages still fewer. He never anticipated anything, but took each experience as it came.

He was convinced that what he sought obeyed no plain and constant law. He had tried his luck in suburban streets hedged in by factory walls, where no one moved except himself. He knew that apparent animation was no necessary condition. But some interior movement there must be. One day when he was wandering aimlessly near Montreuil, he found himself in a narrow lane, running, like others that he knew, between long, blank walls, and, like them, seemingly devoid of life. Nevertheless he had been conscious of a change deep down in his being. The current of life had stopped, but something had taken its place, something quite different from what had gone before, as clear-cut as those subtle changes of climate which make themselves felt when one passes from one slope of a hill to another, or when one turns a corner. He made no effort to analyse the feeling, but experience had taught him when to feel, by instinct, the approach to these particular frontiers of consciousness, and the moment at which he would pass beyond them.

Today he felt himself perfectly in tune with this broad and populous thoroughfare. He liked the sense of noise and people. He had taken, recently, to brooding deliberately upon the ideas that came to him whenever he contemplated scenes of bustle and speed. More and more he was coming to realize that one could only see clearly to the heart of all this movement which so impresses the spectator of modern urban existence, no matter how used one may be to its daily recurrence, if one kept oneself detached from all personal objectives. Not only do personal aims obsess the mind; they lead one by analogy to exaggerate the importance of such aims in the general modern turmoil.

Jallez stopped for a moment to watch the passage of several motorcars. They passed and crossed one another's path with incredible speed and dexterity. He brooded upon this ever increasing itch for speed, upon these shuttles weaving ever more rapidly a pattern of always thickening density. The explanation, he thought, was not nearly so simple as some people imagined it to be, and even while the idea came to him, he smiled to think how typical it was of his temperament to entertain it.

He always leaned towards the "other explanation," especially in problems that concerned the working of the human hive. If Jerphanion had been there, he would have tried to understand, and, being intelligent, his comments would have been far from foolish; but fundamentally he would have failed to grasp the significance of the spectacle.

"And the fault would be mine," Jallez thought. "That winter's day when we climbed the Sacré-Cœur and he asked me questions, I explained myself badly. It was only natural that he should suspect me of taking refuge behind a cloud of words, behind a literary formula. But, as a matter of fact, it was just words that wouldn't come to me. How can one explain an experience which must be felt to be understood? Does it very much matter whether one explains it or not? . . . It would be pleasant to have a companion with whom one could share the experience instead of having to explain and argue about it. I must be content, it seems, with silent sympathies, but I feel sometimes that I should like to have one that would be vocal and expressive. A woman perhaps? . . . Ah!"

He crossed a long bridge spanning some railway tracks. He slowed his pace and looked. A signal dropped; lights changed. He loved such sights. Not that he felt in himself any tendency to worship the new world of machines. He mistrusted particularly, in their growing, threatening power, all manifestations of most recent date, because it was impossible to say what dangers they might bring in their train, what doubtful gifts they offered, but chiefly because they had not yet had time to grow into the structure of man's universe. Railways were by now deeply embedded in the stuff of humanity, in its least material aspects, even as deeply as houses and streets.

He thought again of the differences that separated him from Jerphanion. "He thinks that I play with life . . . it is difficult for him to think otherwise. In his eyes I am a man whose opinions and whose acts are inconsistent, a man of the kind known to school authorities as whimsical. . . . At other times I amaze him by a power of decision in circumstances where he expected to see me, as he has so often seen me, drift with the current or take refuge in non-resistance. . . . He was astounded the other day when I told him that I had applied for a discharge because I realized how impossible it was for me psychologically to do a second year's military service after the Training College course was over. He didn't dare question my decision; he was even rather envious of it. He admitted that he looked forward to his second year with repugnance, but could see no way to avoid it and therefore refused to think about it. Nervousness about the outcome of his examination, he added, made it impossible for him to look so far ahead, and he hoped that if he got his degree, the delightful sense of reaction produced by success would deaden his mind to the boredom of barrack life. 'Besides,' he said, 'it won't be quite the same, as an officer. . . .' But because he didn't want to seem conceited before the event, and didn't want me to understand his words as meaning: 'It would be different for you, since you'd have to go back as a private,' and even more because he disliked the idea that I might think his antimilitarist leanings would be lessened by his getting a commission, he added: 'It's an expensive way of winning experience, but I shall at least have the chance of seeing both sides of the life.' All the same, I believe he was annoyed that I'd said nothing about it before. As though he had kept me posted in the progress of the Mathilde Cazalis affair! Still, in a sense he's right; I am a bit secretive."

He saw a little church on the left and went in, taking a seat in one of the back rows of chairs in the nave. The place was almost empty. Someone was playing the organ. He could hear the rattling of a censer. The perpetual scent of incense grew more pungent, thickened, seemed to form into a cloud.

He felt happy. He enjoyed being in churches. He wondered why he did not make a point of sometimes spending long hours in them; not, for choice, at service time, when they were crowded—he had unpleasant memories of certain psalms screeched by a pack of women —but in the late afternoon, when he could be almost alone.

"In the course of centuries," he reflected, "at the cost of much search and many errors, the Church has succeeded better than any other organization in amassing a remarkable quantity of the true elements of magic. Magic is a reality. Certain lines, certain shapes, certain arrangements of space, the number and the setting of lights, the transformation of silence by music and of the air we breathe by scents, all these things together or arranged in a particular order have the power of sweeping the human spirit to the limits of one of its potential experiences. No one formula is adequate for all men or for all periods, but, by and large, certain combinations are more successful than others. In fact, there is no place in a great modern city better calculated than a Catholic church, fairly old and vaguely reminiscent of the Middle Ages in its general design, but enriched within by the pleasing adornments of many centuries, to set the casual passer-by, entering with his barren load of daily worries, and his vision limited by the constant cares of business, in contact with a level of reality where he is most likely to find some spiritual experience to make him one with the great spaces of the universe, with what, for want of a better name, one may call the divine." All this Jallez realized. The tormenting problems of dogma no longer had power to prevent him from realizing it. He suspected that the man of the modern world meant by "the divine" something else, something more intimate, more tangible, and that for those with such desires there were places better suited than a church. But what those places were he had been trying to discover all his life.

Daylight was beginning to fail. Scattered lights sprang up. The grey house-fronts took on a soft and pallid beauty which made him think of clouds, of the sea, of places touched by cold. Lamps came to life in windows, shone for a moment, and then disappeared.

He walked beside a canal. He was surprised to find himself thus affected by poverty and squalor, by objects that moved him so little to a sense of pity, so deeply to a consciousness of friendliness. "Jerphanion was right," he thought, "that day when he came back from walking in the slums. If anyone had spoken to *me* of pulling down those hovels and replacing them by healthful modern dwellings, I should have felt a pang of regret. It would have seemed to me like some sort of personal deprivation. Heartless æstheticism? Inhuman love of the 'picturesque,' of all that has 'character' and a 'pungent quality,' even though that quality may be the product of a decay from which I don't have to suffer? Easy mistrust of material progress? . . . A little of all that, perhaps, though I am not conscious of it. And yet I am readier than most to accept for my own lot a way of life consonant with what I see around me here. Yes, I can imagine imagine myself living in one of these rooms with a red-tiled floor and a square of curtainless window. (My room in the rue Lhomond is not much better.) I can see myself in one of these ale-houses, eating my meal in the corner, dreaming, all the more vividly because I've lived like that once already. It's not a question of just accepting dirt and squalor. Dirt and squalor are neither of them things that touch the essential me. Poverty's not the word either. No, what I mean is something more like nakedness, simplicity, the rejection of all outward show, life in its basic form. Life, in those conditions, would be like the faces one sees in certain pictures: pale, with the eyes rather too large; pure, pathetic. . . . Oh, it's all so puzzling. I shall probably think quite differently another day."

Then he heard what he always thought of as his "vanished voices." He knew them of old, and recognized them. He could hunt them out in the spaces above the roof-tops, between the clouds and the rising smoke, between the wind that blew along the streets and the wind of the high spaces of heaven, in the wide immensities above the city, there where no one would think of seeking them, where he wandered freely in thought like a fisherman alone in his boat. If he had had to tell someone about them he would have tried to give them form in words. He would have said: "Do you hear the whistle of that train? That siren? The small sound of that bell coming from far, far off? That nameless rumbling, that sound as of some hammering on iron?" But for himself he liked to leave them vague and unidentified, or at least not to use for them the words of every day, which belong only to their "superficial definition." When he wanted to isolate them for his own consciousness, he first set a great silence in his spirit, and then, in that silence, there came a sound which, by means of some inflexion, by the striking of one particular note, by some resemblance vaguer still, imitated one or other of these lost cries.

Sometimes, between the banks of a canal, he would be aware of one of them, drawn thither, as it were, by the quiet waters. It was as though it descended, touched him, and was gone, and he alone, perhaps, would be aware of it before it went for ever. People have other things to think of. Maybe, far away, in some distant part of Paris, beyond the deep valleys of the city, Louis Bastide may have heard it, for he too had ears; or maybe Hélène Sigeau? But whether she still lived he did not know.

Would he, if he could, have Juliette by him now? No, not at this moment, not on a day like today. There would be too many things he could not share with her, too many presences which hers would drive away. Oh yes, he loved her still, could think of her without bitterness. But between them she had stretched the curtain of a lie, which nothing since had altogether drawn or destroyed, which even the fire of passion could not burn, since, like asbestos, it was proof against all flames. Times there had been when it seemed to have vanished, but always, of itself, it formed again, solid before his questing hands.

The thought came to him of a particular day, not long past, of a particular house to which willingly he never would have gone (how often hadn't he gone out of his way to avoid even its neighbourhood!), but whither his footsteps, in despite of better judgment, had taken him. He remembered the strange look on the janitress's face, the janitress's answer, which had set his temples throbbing. The three flights of stairs, the door—all came back to him now. He had knocked.

If all had been as she had said it was, no one should have answered. And, in fact, for a minute or two there had been silence, but finally she had answered. Why, then, had she said that she had left the house for ever? He had not asked her.

So much did he love his "vanished voices" that it was partly to hear them night and morning, as in his days of childhood, that he had taken that room in the rue Lhomond. In the imperfect privacy of his college cubicle it was not "vanished voices" that he heard, but other sounds, close and depressing, importunate as the scampering of mice: a shoe dropped on the floor, a creaking plank, the sound of a cough, ridiculously clear and precise, somebody spitting in the lavatory, the heavy breathing of some sleeping lout; dormitory noises, reminding him always of the forced promiscuity in which he lived with his companions, the clock-like ticking of his servitude (much as it had been at the barracks, to which now he would never return).

His room, high up in the old house, was not as receptive as it might have been to "vanished voices," nor well placed in the city to attract them, but, for all that, now and again one or two of them would find him there. He had grown accustomed to expect their advent, aware, before they came, of their surprise attacks. At times they worked on him with added power; at dead of night, for instance. Uncertain how long he had been asleep, he would suddenly find himself wide awake, though ignorant of what it was had roused him. Surely it could not be that distant sound of hooting so faintly heard that only after some seconds was he aware of it? But he would feel a sudden desire to get up and to "make contact." Make contact with what? In the dawn, just before waking, his sleep would seem a wonderful network of divergent paths along which his jostling dreams were urgent to set forth. At such moments the vanished voices beat on his consciousness from every side. Roused anew to life, standing on the threshold of the virgin day, he felt himself enveloped by their emblems, warmed by their greetings, responsive to their appeals.

Sometimes he dreamed of finding the perfect room. He could imagine exactly what it would be like, but as yet he had not quite decided where in Paris it would be. Sometimes, in some crowded street of the city, he would look up at the top storey of a building, wondering whether it did not house, perhaps, the room he sought.

More and more he was persuaded that the soul is always on tiptoe for "escape." It would not, necessarily, have far to fly, but ever above the serried ranks of fact it lay like a mist, couched like long wisps of lovely cloud over the world of History, timeless, eternal. Beyond the noise, the rumbling bass of cities, it held for ever the secrets of the "other explanation."

Strolling alone, on days when he had been most overwhelmed, like today, he longed to celebrate in himself the complete disappearance of Solitude. It was his gospel. He longed to say to the first passer-by: "I am no longer alone. No one is any longer alone."

He thought about Jerphanion, about Clanricard, about all those who cried aloud the persistence of their loneliness. Ceaselessly they sought a Church which they could never find. Or if, after much questing and repeated hesitations, they found one at long last, they were tormented before they were ever past its portals by the thought that it might not, after all, be theirs. Yet here by the wayside he had found by chance a little church, had entered for a moment and come out, and lo! it was his own for ever.

In Jerphanion's eyes he might seem to be detached from the problems of the day, indifferent to the drama of the world, of History. But, for all that, he knew strange moments when the ghost of the future seemed to press him close, setting him shuddering at the contact; when the spirit of prophecy was quick about his ears, like another vanished voice, unclear as yet, but full of fears and portents.

Chapter

17

GURAU AND MANIFASSIER DRAW UP
A PLAN OF CAMPAIGN

The very day that the new Government was introduced to the President of the Republic, Gurau said
to Manifassier:

"Tonight, my boy, we will have dinner together. I will take you to
the Quatre Sergents de la Rochelle. Don't you know it? It's close to
the Bastille. . . . We've got a lot of work to do. Before confronting
our friends of the Foreign Office, who will be fully armed to receive
us, it is essential that we discuss, consider, and decide what our attitude is to be."

Gurau was a sight for sore eyes, sparkling with vitality, self-
reliance, and lucidity. He had never felt so young. "Mine's a grand
age," he thought; "I'm at the tip-top of my powers—sufficiently experienced not to make a fool of myself, but not too firmly set to dislike the thrill of taking risks. I've got enthusiasm and enough to
spare, and I know men. I've seen enough of life not to let myself be
turned from great ambitions by the craving for pleasure, by passion,
or by the little things that make existence sweet. There's no end to
my possible future."

Manifassier, taking his courage in his hands, gave words to something which had been worrying him for the last two days. It cost him
something to say it, but elementary honesty demanded that it should
be said:

"I'm perfectly well aware, sir, that you mean to keep me with you,
and I'm touched by the intention. You know there's nothing I should
like better than to stay; but my conscience . . ."

"What's all this nonsense?"

"I managed pretty well at the Ministry of Labour and at the Ministry of Public Works, because, after all, they were neither of them so very different from what I'd been used to. I didn't have to be a wizard to fit in there. But at the Foreign Office I shall be completely out of my depth."

"And what about me?"

"It's not the same thing at all, sir. . . . Besides, that's all the more reason why you should have someone at your elbow who's familiar with what's been going on and who knows the ropes and what traps are likely to be set for you. I remember what Briand told you last autumn."

"On the contrary, it's all the more reason why I should have someone I can trust. That's what matters. Two sets of eyes, my dear chap, are better than one. So long as we're together, they won't catch us napping so easily. Naturally, I shall see to it that I have one or two specialists on my staff. . . . Your opinion, my boy, has not been asked; your job's to do as I tell you."

He slapped the other man's shoulder with an affectionate heartiness which sat strangely on him. He even added—Manifassier could hardly believe his ears, and blushed with pleasure:

"I warn you that from now on I shall call you by your Christian name."

They dined in a small room at a table that was rather too large for two places set opposite to each other, though its size was otherwise convenient, since from time to time one or other of them had to make a note, scribble a name, or illustrate on paper the details of some explanation. At one moment the table-cloth at Gurau's right hand found itself doing service as a rough map of Morocco. Their conversation was so lively and so continuous that neither man much noticed what he was eating. But they paused to sing the praises of the Pouilly. They found that good wine was an excellent aid to the discovery and approval of solutions.

Gurau spoke of the two interviews, both of them unfortunately too brief, which he had just had with Caillaux.

"He was much occupied with his program. He showed me one or two passages. It is concerned almost entirely with domestic affairs. He's all for strong government. Only a short while ago—a few days, even—he was obsessed by the foreign situation. But he's a changeable sort of fellow. I got the impression that his hobby-horse of the moment is bold policy in home affairs and finance, realism before all. But he means to keep order and maintain authority, so as to rally to his standard all those who hate anarchy but are not afraid of progress —all those, for instance, who were upset by the troubles in Champagne. I'm beginning to see why he took the Interior for himself instead of sticking to the Treasury. . . . It's a pity, in a way, that his declaration will contain so few references to the foreign danger. Parliament and public opinion ought to be warned of the gravity and urgency of the situation, so as to be ready to accept solutions which may upset a good many preconceived ideas. . . . Well, so much the worse for him. My own hands will be all the freer. He's a restless fellow, and it's just as well that his attention should be diverted from that particular field of activity. He'd always be wanting to interfere, and that would worry me. . . . He pointed out that since the Chamber isn't sitting, I should have time to look round me, which is true enough, and a bit of luck. . . . He made a point of telling me that Berteaux had made some terrible blunders in Morocco, entirely on his own responsibility, without consulting anybody. The poor old chap just forced us into the position of violating the Algeciras Act, with the result that there are going to be a whole lot of new complications with Germany. Caillaux added that he hoped Messimy wouldn't embarrass me in the same way. There's one thing, though, that I didn't dare ask him, and that is what form his negotiations with Germany have taken since the ratification business became a dead letter. It seems that he passed on to Cruppi certain new proposals from Berlin, and that Cruppi just snapped his fingers at them. I hoped he'd talk about them to me of his own accord. . . . It would have helped me a good deal. . . . But no doubt there'll be other opportunities later on. . . . The important point is that he seems willing to give me a free hand. . . . It's a nuisance, of course, generally speaking, that he thought it necessary to include Delcassé in the new Government. But I don't think he'll do much more than treat him as a spare wheel. . . . And now we've got to deal with those fellows at the Foreign Office."

To assert the necessary authority from the start, certain conditions appeared to be absolutely essential. In the first place, Gurau must have the right sort of staff. Two or three colleagues he would have to have of unquestioned competence, and sufficiently in the know to warn their chief against possible intrigues, and two or three others, like Manifassier, representing the new dispensation. The attitude of these men would be something of a mystery to the permanent clerks, and it would be well that their loyalty to the chief should become as soon as possible a matter of "legend." They must gain the respect of the office at the earliest moment, and this should not be difficult, provided they avoided any very blatant mistakes.

Next, it was important that Gurau should make it clear from the first moment that he was not the ordinary type of young minister, equipped with nothing but a few prejudices and complete ignorance, masked by a grand manner which would quickly pass. He must impress on his subordinates that he was, on the contrary, a man with a definite point of view and a knowledge of the questions at issue, letting them see that if he made use of specialists to implement or work out a decision, to provide him with ammunition for a debate, he did not expect them to tell him what he ought to do. He must show that he was their superior in all matters involving general policy, a knowledge of men, and a realization of the interdependence of a large number of various political facts. It wouldn't be a bad thing, either, to let the impression get about that he had "taken a long lease" of the Foreign Office, and this would be the tactful job of the personal staff, and particularly of Manifassier. There was no inherent difficulty in making them believe it. Delcassé had set a precedent, and opinion generally would be only too glad to accept the idea of a few islands of ministerial stability establishing themselves in the general flux.

"I might give colour to the story by going to live in my flat at the office. . . . I should risk nothing; my possessions are few enough to make a move easy."

"Not at all a bad idea, sir."

The apartment in question had the reputation of being luxurious, so that the prospect was far from being an unpleasant one. "A bit of spring cleaning perhaps. . . . It would give me a chance of repaying Madame Godorp's hospitality. She'd be thoroughly impressed."

Manifassier said:

"I suppose you realize, sir, that civil servants are rather like school-boys. There are some masters who always get ragged, and others who make it clear from their first appearance in class that they're not going to stand for ragging. If at the end of the first week everyone, down to the doorkeeper, realizes that 'Monsieur Gurau knows what he wants; he's come here with a long-distance program, which he's going to see through, no matter how long it takes,' the rest of the business will be easy. It takes a good deal of courage, even for heads of departments, to run counter to the wishes of a minister who will hold their fates in his hands over a number of years. They won't do it light-heartedly. The important thing is to get the idea firmly fixed in their minds. You must make them realize that your program is solidly constructed. They must see, even if you don't go into details with them, that it stands four-square, that there's something to it. . . . Flattery apart, sir, you start with certain advantages. They've all read your articles, they all know your reputation on the commit-tee. They're not going to think of you as just a nobody. But there's another point: When we were getting up your briefs this last winter, there was a whole heap of things—we said so at the time—that we hadn't either the leisure or the means to find out. Now we shall have both. But the permanent staff mustn't be allowed to think that they're providing the information."

They agreed that they wouldn't at once be able to dispense with such useful sources of official knowledge. At the same time, from now on, this material must be utilized only with the greatest possible care, and without giving away anything. The essential thing would be to discover how best to avail themselves most fully of the permanent establishment, with its unrivalled resources of records and other things, both material and intellectual, without letting it become an embarrassment.

"You remember Lepage, whom I consulted in that matter of Courson? He's extremely shrewd about nosing things out, and I think he'd be loyal. What do you say to taking him on to your staff? He's got a brother-in-law, whom I know too, called Villechamp, who's secretary to the Embassy in London and was formerly in Berlin. He happens to be in Paris at this moment, on leave. . . . They're the sort of men we want, or others of the same kind. . . . If I was in your position, I'd make as much use as I could of Courson himself."

"Would you? Really?"

"Placed as he is, hard-working and conscientious as he seems to be, he must, I imagine, have more information than most about the things which interest us, and, in particular, about the Franco-German situation. For years now, everything has passed through his hands. He must, almost certainly, have stored up in his mind information that you will find in no official dossier—memories of ambassadors who have poured out their troubles to him and told him more than they ever wrote in their dispatches, of ministers who have made him free of their uncertainties, told him of their visitors, or described the pressure that has been brought to bear on them—a hundred and one things like that which appear in no records—reports of secret agents which have never been reduced to writing, but with which he must be familiar. In short, every time the truth has been modified or altered for public consumption or for inclusion in ministerial archives, the odds are that he's known about it—at least in so far as it affects the particular questions with which we are concerned. He may not tell you all he knows, or not at first, but every opinion he expresses will be coloured by his knowledge. The great point about him is that he *will* express opinions. He's no fool and he's not indifferent to what is going on, not the sort of man who treats diplomacy like a job that's just got to be done and forgotten. I've been thinking a good deal about the way he approached you the other day. It was a happy inspiration, and as rare as it was happy. Naturally, he had to be cautious. He may, of course, turn out to be a busybody; he may say and do more than he's asked. . . . That we can tell only by experience. But the fact that he did approach you puts you in a very strong position. It gives you the right to show that you expect a greater degree of sincerity and courage from him than you would from anybody else. He can't now behave as though he were merely a subordinate anxious not to compromise himself. It makes it impossible, too, for him to assume the superior airs of a patron, because in coming to you he took the initiative and showed by his conduct that he recognized you as his leader, almost as his feudal overlord. In making use of him, to whatever extent, your behaviour will be that, not of a man running after a piece of information which he can't get otherwise, but of one who takes advantage of loyalty freely offered."

Gurau listened attentively, while he drew six-pointed stars on a scrap of paper and shaded them with meticulous care.

"You're probably right," he said. "But if you were I, would you carry your belief in this fellow to the extent of reopening negotiations with him now, at once—I mean before I've really taken over—before the routine of the office brings me naturally in contact with him? . . . You see, that's what I want at the moment—to establish certain sources of information, to throw up defences, to get on those 'man to man' terms with him which we achieved the other day and which we may not achieve again if we wait until later. . . ."

"Why not? When is Cruppi handing over to you the power and introducing you officially to the staff?"

"We've arranged it provisionally for tomorrow afternoon—the morning's impossible."

"Well, then, try to see Courson tomorrow morning. I'll warn him early and arrange to have him at any place you like to name."

"Let's say the *Sanction* office, about ten o'clock; there'll be nobody there then."

"All right."

"One thing in particular's bothering me. I don't know how you feel, but I've got a definite impression that very soon, possibly in the course of a few days, I shall have to make decisions, take an initiative, adopt an attitude, which may have a serious, an irremediable effect on the course of events . . . which may—yes, I'll go even as far as that—which may influence the whole future of France, her relations with Germany, the chances of peace or war in Europe . . . the very fate of the world. Do you agree, or do you think I'm exaggerating? Do you think I'm becoming just a victim of megalomania? Ever since Caillaux offered me the post, the idea's been with me—night and day. Sometimes it excites me, sometimes it terrifies me. . . . But there's one particular aspect of it which I can't get away from, and it drives me nearly distracted. It's this: that I may not have time, before I'm compelled to act, to get the necessary information, to probe the situation to the bottom. I tell myself that I've written articles about it, asked questions in committee, made fighting points, read casually here and here, listened to reports and speeches, heard Jaurès's views as well as Pichon's, young Tardieu's as well as Maykosen's . . . but that what's enough for an article isn't enough to form the basis for conduct which may involve the destinies of France and of Europe. . . . I tell myself that before taking up my pen as Minister, before signing my name to the very first scrap of paper that's put before me, I owe it to my conscience to go over the whole ground again, to remodel my attitude, to get an all-round view of the general situation. . . . I don't mean that I've got to review the position in Turkey or our relations with America—not that such things mightn't be useful too, but I haven't time for them now, and they can wait. No, what seems to me essential is that I should have a clear and sound point of view about the Franco-German question. By 'clear' I don't mean one that has gone into every detail, but one that has been *conditioned* by every detail and by every contributory factor, which leaves nothing out, but sees things straight and in their proper perspective. Rather a silly mania, perhaps, for a new Minister. Do you feel tempted to smile at my simplicity?"

"Far from it, sir!" Manifassier cried with genuine emotion. "Such thoughts do you honour. It's because you're like that that we love you."

"Oh come! . . . But whom can I ask? . . . Who can help me to such a point of view—now, at once? . . . I've got to get my information without wasting a moment, I've got to make myself familiar with it. . . . The amount of detail's appalling. . . . It will be almost impossible to see the wood for the trees . . . I shall probably never again have the time, the freedom from immediate duties, I may never again be in the right mood, even, to see the wood clearly. Do you understand what I mean?"

"Perfectly."

"Do you think that I could ask a man like Courson, or anyone else, for that matter—but who else, especially at such short notice?—to talk in such a way that without losing ourselves in the undergrowth or getting caught up in a medley of facts, but conversing like men who know the general background, we could try to get a bird's-eye view of the Franco-German question and see within what limits action is possible? You see what I'm after? He'd have to do the talking; we should merely listen and ask him questions. We wouldn't bother about details except in so far as they might be necessary to correct a false idea or suggest hitherto unexplored possibilities. . . . All this, you see, presupposes a man with all the facts at his finger-tips, but who isn't a short-sighted pedant with nothing but an encyclopædic memory to recommend him, and an inability to distinguish between a significant point and a mere record in a file. . . . Do you think that Courson's likely to be, even approximately, a man of that kind?"

"We can but try."

"If it got known that we'd had such an interview, mightn't it make trouble?"

"He'd be the only person who could talk about it, and he's not such a fool as to do that. It wouldn't be to his interest. Besides, even if it did get known, it wouldn't be so very terrible."

"It might create rivalries in the office, wrangling between him and the others . . . prejudices, and a general feeling against me."

"We will tell him that you attach the greatest importance to his discretion. . . . It would be unwise, I think, to ask him at the same time for information about the personnel, or the ins and outs of the department, or to consult him about possible colleagues. . . . No, better keep the two things distinct. . . . Don't let him get too big an idea of himself. . . . All that part of the business may seem urgent, but it can wait. You needn't decide on your personal staff for a week or a fortnight. . . . I've other ways of finding out the kind of men you'll want. . . . It's the easier job of the two."

Chapter

18

SCRUPLES

When he heard what was wanted of him, Courson sat for a minute or two in silence.

"I am deeply sensible, sir," he said at length, "of this mark of your esteem, but you are laying on me a very heavy responsibility. I agree with you that there is nothing more urgent in politics today than the Franco-German question. . . . I have been intimate with it for fifteen years. . . . Nothing could be more important than the work in which you ask my collaboration, nor more useful, provided it were well done"—he repeated the words with an air of great solemnity: "provided it were well done! . . . But the difficulties are immense! . . . How much time can you give me?"

"Please understand, Monsieur Courson, that I am not asking you for a report, nor even, at the moment, for a formal outline. We can consider the details later. What I want to do today is just to chat, without files and without supporting evidence . . . to get your first-hand, personal views. You are a man whose life has been spent in this particular world, who has had fifteen years of it, who has digested all the facts, assimilated all the documents. You have only got to interrogate your own experience and to speak out of a full memory. . . ."

M. Courson shifted on his chair, and his voice took on an anxious note.

"I understand exactly what you mean, sir, but to do even that is a serious matter. . . . It's not a question of this or that incident, but of seeing the position, the problem, as a whole, as it has appeared from time to time. As things now are we can't afford to make a mistake. If, as a result of haste, I give you a false impression, I run the risk of being guilty of a crime. I must have time to think. Give me two or three days. I won't go hunting through files, sir, don't be afraid of that. . . . All I want to do is to marshal my ideas, to compare them. I have, in my time, held many different views, and they are not wholly consistent."

"Two or three days are too many—or too few. Your mind will be confused, you will have lost the power to see clearly. At this moment I happen to have the necessary time to spare. If you really must have an interval in which to think things over, see me again this evening, say at six o'clock."

"I'd rather make it tomorrow morning, sir; as early as you like."

"Why? You're not going to spend the whole night in thought, are you?"

"It would be a very good thing if I did. But it's not so much that, sir. I shall be in a better state of mind tomorrow, more fully master of myself."

"All right, then. I shall expect you here at nine. We shall be less liable to disturbance than we should be at the Foreign Office. . . . Oh, and by the way, when Monsieur Cruppi makes his official presentations, I shall pretend never to have met you."

Chapter

19

ANALYSIS OF THE FRANCO-GERMAN SITUATION

M. Courson sat down warily in the chair which was offered him, and glanced round as though to confirm his impressions of the room and of the relative proportion of the objects which it contained. (The previous evening he had been to his regular confessor and had said to him: "I wish to take Communion tomorrow morning. I have business of great importance to transact during the day." He had, in fact, got up very early, having slept hardly at all, had heard Mass at Sainte-Clotilde, and had taken Communion.)

"I'm afraid you are going to be disappointed, sir. I have given a great deal of thought to this matter, but I realize, alas, that I have no revelations to make. Nothing that I can say will be at all new; you know it all already."

He sighed and raised his right hand:

"Ask me what questions you like, sir. I will do my best to answer them."

"We'll come back to questions of detail later, if we have time, or leave them till another day. What I want at the moment is to have the views of a man like you on the general aspect of the question. How do you see the Franco-German situation? How would you put it in a nutshell?"

"That is indeed an embarrassing question! . . . The Franco-German situation as it really is! . . . How can I condense it into a few phrases that will have any value? . . . In principle I entirely agree with you. When it comes to action, nothing is of any value but succinct and definite formulas. . . . I've never before been asked to do such a thing. Some such question might well be put about the Republic of Liberia if the Government happened to be dealing with some dispute in that part of the world; but Germany's quite another matter, though I realize that we ought to be able to summarize the position. . . . The first difficulty is to decide on a point of departure. The war of '70? . . . We're not going to talk about that all over again, but we can't ignore it. We can't really ignore even Napoleon. Without Napoleon, German nationalism wouldn't be the thing it is. Without Napoleon I and Napoleon III, Germany would probably never have been unified, or not in the way that in fact it was. The Bonaparte dynasty, and the aura of romance with which it came to be surrounded, are primarily responsible for the situation as we see it today. We shall pay for the follies and the illusions of that historical event for many years to come. For our present purpose the one important thing to remember about the war of '70 is that it could have been avoided, up to the very last moment. You will say: 'It would have broken out in any case a few years later.' That may be. No diplomat, no government, has a right to argue on those lines. If a doctor cures me of pleurisy, the cure may last for a long time, but if I die from pleurisy the very next year, it's not his fault. So far as he's concerned, I may just as well die of heart-failure when I'm eighty. It's not a problem with which he need worry himself. If, on a definite occasion, war is avoided, it may be avoided absolutely, or at least for so long a time that if war does break out at a future date there is no historical connexion between the two events. . . .

"I have been all through the Fashoda files, and I can assure you, sir, that all the elements that make for war were in that affair—for a terrible war into which the whole world would have been drawn by degrees. Russia would have been involved, not so much out of respect for her alliances, but because she would have taken the opportunity of bringing to a head a quarrel of long standing between Asia and England. Japan would have fallen on Russia a few years earlier than in fact she did . . . and so on. It is more than likely that in the long run William II would have been called in as arbitrator, and that peace would ultimately have been dictated by him. . . . As it is, war between England and France in our lifetimes is of all things the most unlikely. To have avoided war in '70 would have been child's-play. Even the so-called Ems telegram was a trifle. . . . I tried to explain that to one of your predecessors, documents in hand, as a salutary object-lesson, but I could see so clearly from his expression that he thought me a traitor that I didn't press the point. The war of '70 stands four-square as a fact; we lost two provinces and all our self-respect, and we've never since been able to feel really comfortable. That, sir, is where I should plant the first of our signposts, for from that point two roads diverge. If, deep down in the secret places of our hearts, to which some of us believe that only the eye of God can penetrate, we truly think that, no matter what prosperity or what degree of honour we may enjoy in other respects, France cannot consent to live without Alsace-Lorraine, nor fully recover her self-respect unless she avenges the defeat of '70, then it is useless to go on bickering about trifles, to search our consciences or make believe that we are a peace-loving people forced by ill-intentioned neighbours to arm ourselves to the teeth and maintain an unrelaxed watchfulness. William II is not going to give us back Alsace-Lorraine. He has neither the wish nor the power to do so. (I was going to say: has them no longer, but that's another question.) And even if, years hence, as the miraculous result of long friendship, or by dint of bargaining, the question of Alsace-Lorraine came to be amicably settled, it would still be impossible for the German Emperor to turn Sedan into a French victory. If, therefore, France determines to keep that grievance green, there's nothing for it but to prepare for war by every means diplomatically and militarily within our power, and to see that it breaks out at the first favourable opportunity. . . .

"That, then, is one of our possible roads, and if we mean to follow it, we'd better resign ourselves to reading the word 'War' on the signpost, with an arrow pointing straight ahead. Any other course will merely turn the weapon against our own breasts. As things are, instead of going forward frankly and energetically along the road that leads to war, we take first a step towards it, then half a step back. As a result, the country finds itself leaderless and divided. A large number of voters, sincerely persuaded that France seeks peace, believe that they are serving the national interest by returning a pacifist Government to power. What happens then? A few ministers who honestly wish to pursue a policy of peace find themselves working with others who don't. It sometimes happens that in the irony of circumstances both ministers of National Defence are convinced partisans of peace and disarmament, while their colleague at the Foreign Office is thinking only in terms of revenge. The working classes and the school-teachers are, I believe, perfectly honest in their attitude of extreme antimilitarism (some would go further and call it disloyalty), and if the official policy of peace doesn't exactly encourage them, it does at least make it very difficult for any government to take action against them.

"Please understand, sir, that I'm not presuming to pass judgment on anybody. Those who believe that revenge is necessary for the continued existence of France may be right. To be honest with you, I admit that, in my heart of hearts, I doubt it. As a Christian, and as a man of the modern world who has thought much about the new sources of strength which lie open to contemporary societies, I hesitate to believe that the possession of a particular piece of territory by any particular State really dominates the field of politics to the exclusion of all other considerations, or that the honour of a country can be bound up for half a century with the accident of a single campaign. Even if we interpret the word 'honour' in a purely material sense, I should have said that the conquest of our colonial empire would have repaid us three times over for that old story of defeat. . . . That's as may be. As I said before, those who believe in revenge may be right, but they are certainly wrong if they try to conceal that belief or deny it. 'But,' they will argue, 'by concealing it we deceive the enemy and give him a false sense of security.' The answer to that is that we don't do anything of the sort. We merely make him nervous and defiant and put him in a mood which inevitably ends in an outbreak of bad temper and an increase of armaments. We may keep him guessing, but that is more than neutralized by the resultant sense of uncertainty in the minds of our own countrymen. . . . I know that such a policy is often defended on other grounds—on the grounds, namely, that where a country is deficient in courage it must be pitchforked into a period of trial which its honour and its history make necessary, without being told where it is going. . . . I find this the most difficult of all points of view to accept. . . . It is more widely held, sir, than you might think. It is hardly the kind of argument that would be openly paraded before a man like you. . . . It implies, in my view, a degree of mistrust of the people, of the country as a whole, which would be hateful in a despot, but which in the mouths of those who pretend to be the servants of Democracy becomes a hellish lie. . . ."

He wiped his forehead. He had raised his voice, but now, when he spoke again, he tried to smile.

"Forgive me, sir; I realize that I have somewhat departed from that standard of objectivity, of complete absence of passion, which I undertook to observe out of respect for you and in the interests of the question we were to examine. . . ."

Gurau assured him that he sympathized too strongly with his sentiments to be surprised at so natural a display of feeling. After all, objectivity need not mean indifference.

"I thank God, sir, for those words. Put shortly, my case against all these people is that they are either lying to themselves or to others."

"You don't think they may be doing both at once?"

"Quite possibly. . . . In any case, they are defeating their own ends. They'd win much more, even from the enemy, if they shouted from the house-tops: 'We want Alsace-Lorraine, we want revenge on the battlefield, and we'll have both. Nothing else matters."

"You said: 'even from the enemy.' . . . Isn't that a bit paradoxical?"

"The Germans are an odd people, sir. . . . They'd rather like a bit of brutal frankness. They'd think better of us for it."

"Wouldn't it make them more anxious than ever to fall on us and give up the coup?"

"Not necessarily. . . . Don't let us bother any more about that question. . . . The advantage to us would be certain—a consistent policy, a vigorous military program, enthusiastic public opinion, and the maintenance of an aggressive spirit in the race. . . ."

"Yes, but if they don't talk like that, it's because they know that nobody in France would listen to them."

Courson seemed to be impressed.

"Do you really think that, sir?" he asked.

"Well, don't you?"

"I'm not sure. . . . I live so out of the world."

He paused, and then burst out with:

"Do you really think, sir, that the majority of Frenchmen want peace?"

"An enormous majority! I'm quite certain of it. Don't you agree, Manifassier?"

"Absolutely."

"So much the better, sir. . . . You know more about such things than I can do. You live in close contact with public opinion, with the man in the street. . . . So much the better!"

But he appeared to be not wholly convinced.

"Don't people want to make war for Alsace-Lorraine?" he went on.

"No. They cherish a vague, sentimental regret. They'd be delighted if Alsace-Lorraine were handed to them on a platter, but it doesn't go further than that."

"And how about the feeling that France has had to swallow a defeat?"

"Much less than it was. There's been such an enormous increase of confidence in other ways since '70. . . . The working classes quite frankly laugh at the whole business. Their minds are preoccupied with other defeats and other victories. The middle classes, upper

and lower alike, are proud of our colonial successes. The only people
who react to the old ideas are a few half-pay officers and a handful
of intellectuals on the look-out for a sensation . . . like the disciples
of Barrès. . . . There's one other factor of importance, though. A
certain number of rich men who feel or think themselves threatened
by labour agitation tend to regard war as a supreme diversion, as a
means of re-establishing discipline. But they're not bothering their
heads about the lost provinces, and they're not particularly antago-
nistic to Germany; on the contrary, they probably feel a good deal
of sympathy on certain points for the German ruling caste. . . .
Others, and not seldom the same, complain, rightly or wrongly, of
the stagnation of business and imagine that a war would stimulate
the economic life of the country. They cite in proof of this the Russo-
Japanese war, the South African war, and even, with a shameless
display of cynicism, the war of '70. They include, naturally, the contractors who, in the event, would supply the armies, and the big
industrialists for whom a policy of national defence means work."

"Yes, but they no more than the others dare say outright what they
are after, and the whole lot of them can't form more than a small
minority."

"I agree . . . but it's a powerful minority because it has the
money. . . . It more or less controls the stock exchange and the
banks, and a lot of politicians and newspapers are under its
thumb. . . ."

As Gurau spoke these last words he was conscious of an unex-
pressed thought. It was only after he had uttered them that he was
aware of a certain fleeting sense of discomfort and noticed that
Manifassier was giving him a timid wink. But the full flood of his
eloquence carried him on.

"It's comparatively easy for these men to work public opinion up
to a state of patriotic fervour, which can then be exploited by those
who preach a policy of revenge. At moments of diplomatic tension
they can play on the nerves of the country, without openly advocating war, can work the sentiment of patriotic pride and jingo enthu-

siasm for all it's worth, and can accuse of weakness and treachery any minister who tries to avoid disaster. . . . You see, I'm echoing now all you said a moment or two back. . . . All I mean to say is that if we want to get an accurate idea of the situation, since we're talking of imponderables like public opinion and national feeling, we must, on the one hand, distinguish between 'will' and 'power,' and, on the other, avoid a miscalculation of motives. The will to war in France is very small, but the power which it wields is considerable. So far as motives are concerned, those most frequently quoted are, in fact, the least important. Let me put it this way: the regret for the loss of Alsace-Lorraine and the bitterness of defeat do still exist, but transmuted into a sort of vague melancholy in the hearts of a lot of honest folk who, at bottom, want peace more than anything else. But the motives of the few powerful men who want war are of a totally different kind and are not in the least sentimental. What is true, and what complicates the whole situation, is that this small and powerful group, animated by extremely realistic motives, is in a position, given the favourable moment, to exploit this vague sentiment that still lingers among the mass of the nation. The desire to win back Alsace-Lorraine and to wipe out the memory of defeat, taken alone, wouldn't persuade the nation as a whole to raise a finger for war, but it can be used to make them acquiesce in the policy of war as soon as the machinations of these other folk make war inevitable."

M. Courson nodded his head.

"Yes . . . yes. . . . But what really interests me in all this is finding, from what you say, that in pursuing a policy of peace we are not running counter to the essential wishes of the country. After all, France is a Republic, isn't it, sir? Surely I'm not wrong when I say that; it's the nation that is the Nation, and not a king, a clique, or a caste?"

"Precisely." Gurau smiled as he spoke, for he relished the form in which the other's question was put.

"I want to hear that conviction of mine expressed in words . . . I live among people who sometimes seem to me to be not quite sure of its cogency. . . . You'll soon see what I mean, sir. . . . I want, too, to be assured in words that the majority of my countrymen do not want war. I have been working for seven years, if I may so put it, under the shadow of Monsieur Delcassé."

He paused with an air of caution.

"Perhaps he's a friend of yours?"

"Oh, far from it!"

"Good. I've seen Monsieur Delcassé at close quarters, day after day, acting and intriguing. . . . I didn't hold the same post as I do now, but I was well enough placed to notice things. . . . Time and time again during those years I said to myself: 'The French are not generally thought to be fools. . . . It's perfectly obvious that Monsieur Delcassé has broken sharply with the policy which was left him by his predecessor and which did at least assure the maintenance of a durable peace in Europe, and is carefully preparing a war against Germany. . . . My countrymen can't be blind to it. If they let him go on like that, it's because they want him to. . . .' "

Gurau tried to recall his impressions when he first became a deputy. Had he, in those days, seen Delcassé's policy in quite so clear a light?

"God knows I don't want to defend Delcassé," he said, "but do you really think he was pursuing so premeditated and consistent a policy?"

Courson pondered his answer for a few seconds; then, as though he were carefully weighing his words, "Yes, sir," he said.

Gurau made a face.

"You amaze me. . . . It is so difficult for us politicians, whatever the strength of our convictions, to pursue for long a consistent line of policy. We have to make so many concessions to circumstances. . . . Frankly, I find it difficult to believe in these stories, after the event, of premeditated policies. . . ."

"What you say, sir, perfectly well applies to normal politicians. But Monsieur Delcassé was a madman. . . . I say 'was'—he may be one still, but it is less obvious, or perhaps it is that I am losing my power of noticing these things."

Gurau started. This verdict was in strange contrast to the attitude of studied moderation which Courson had obviously been forcing himself to maintain. Whatever the words, however, his visitor's tone remained calm.

"A madman!—isn't that going rather far? . . . A madman!"

"No. . . . There are madmen and madmen. The most dangerous are those who, behind a quiet and reasonable manner, pursue their dominating idea with merciless logic."

(As he heard these words, Gurau remembered something he himself had said to Jaurès about those doctor-mathematicians who treat their patients as though they were so many geometrical theorems and hurry them to the grave as swiftly and certainly as though they had been fired from a gun.)

". . . When you do me the honour, sir, as I trust you will, to let me show you certain old files, I will give you some curious and very detailed evidence of Monsieur Delcassé's madness. But there is one particular point, of great importance and pretty generally known, which will, I think, support my contention. . . . I shall never forget the spring of 1905. All of us at the Foreign Office felt that the country was heading straight for a rupture with Germany, and that the Minister was engineering it. Even the most violent and foolhardy nationalists were staggered. We had friends at the War Office who told us that preparations were not complete and that the General Staff was well aware of the fact. They knew through their intelligence service, as we knew through ours, that Russia's war against Japan, having ended as a military disaster, had just loosed a serious revolutionary movement at home, of which French public opinion was being kept in ignorance, and that Russia couldn't be counted on for action in the West for a long time to come. We had no guarantee of what England's attitude would be (any more than we have today). In short, there we were, without reliable allies, and with an army and a navy both unprepared. . . . Disaster was inevitable."

"In spite of the seventy-fives?"

"In spite of the seventy-fives. . . . Seventy-fives don't make up for everything else, and they can't fire without shells. I repeat, disaster was inevitable. Warnings flowed in on Monsieur Delcassé from all sides. He knew as well as we did what the position was. . . . If he hadn't been turned out on the 6th of June, we should have had war in July. If that wasn't the behaviour of a madman, I don't know what madness is."

"That may be so . . . but a moment ago you were inclined to accuse the whole of France of similar madness, since you assumed that France was behind Delcassé."

"Excuse me, sir; the general run of Frenchmen might well assume that the Government knew what it was doing, had reason for confidence, and wouldn't rush blindly into an adventure of such magnitude. The man in the street couldn't be expected to know that Monsieur Delcassé was mad."

"I agree . . . and what happened raises awkward questions about the delegation of power in a democracy. . . . But you said something just now which struck me with special force. You seemed to be of the opinion that before the advent of Monsieur Delcassé we were heading towards a stabilization of peace in Europe and a definite improvement in Franco-German relations. I wasn't a deputy at the time; my life was far removed from all contact with Government circles, and I was deeply absorbed in the Dreyfus affair. I'm not quite sure what it is you are referring to."

M. Courson lifted his eyebrows, and his voice took on a tone of slight surprise.

"Why, sir—to Hanotaux's policy."

Gurau felt humiliated. He had forgotten that M. Hanotaux had been Delcassé's immediate predecessor, and the words "Hanotaux's policy" carried for him only the vaguest of connotations.

He hid his embarrassment.

"Were you working with Monsieur Hanotaux?"

"I can scarcely say that. . . . I had just been transferred to the

Foreign Office after filling certain posts abroad. . . . I was still quite
young. Nevertheless, I saw a good deal of what was going on, and
in the years that have since elapsed, I have been over all the ground
again on my own account . . . I have gleaned much information
from our agents and from my colleagues in the service. . . . In fact,
I think I can say without boasting that I know that particular period
through and through. . . . And what an intensely interesting period it is! . . . No one, in or out of Parliament, seems to remember
anything about it. . . . Home affairs at that time happened to be
very spectacular, and they have remained so ever since—the Dreyfus
affair, which you mentioned just now, and its consequences, the religious quarrel, the sudden seizure of power by the radical party.
. . . The man who was chiefly concerned—I refer to Monsieur Hanotaux—has been extremely self-effacing of recent years. He might
have made capital, sometimes with dramatic effect, out of the mistakes of his successors, and out of the foresight, of the remarkable
ability, which after events proved him to have shown. He might
have come forward again as a candidate for office. . . . He would,
I think, in the long run, have found a host of supporters. . . . He
might well have been called back to power. . . . But in fact he did
none of these things. Why? . . . Perhaps from the timidity of good
breeding, perhaps because he had turned his energies in other directions, perhaps because he thought that by throwing in his lot with
radical and anti-clerical ministers he would be thought to be disloyal
to his convictions and to his friends of other days. . . . It's all something of a psychological mystery. . . . Do you remember, sir, the
details of the Münster memorandum?"

"Indeed I do not."

Gurau turned a questioning look on Manifassier, who pleaded
guilty to a similar ignorance.

"Monsieur de Münster, with whom I had had personal dealings,
was at that time German Ambassador in Paris. He was a man of
distinction and fine character; one of those German aristocrats the

existence and influence of whom we do not sufficiently realize, men who, when they set themselves to the task, can show a real European outlook. I believe that Monsieur de Münster had a feeling of sincere friendship for France. In his heart of hearts he longed to see an end of the old hatred persisting between his country and ours. I stress the point because the part he played at that time was of the greatest possible importance. The memorandum in question had been drawn up by his Government, but I suspect that he had approved of its being sent and had been responsible for some part, at least, of its wording. It proposed to France, in the politest terms, joint action of a rather complicated kind in the colonial field . . . I won't go into details which would take too long to explain . . . I will expatiate upon them any time you wish, sir, with the evidence before us. . . . All I need say now is that this document, which had come into being after a great many exchanges of views on other subjects, after much negotiation conducted in an atmosphere of subtly growing confidence, which the Emperor knew all about, showed a willingness on the part of Germany to envisage a real mutual understanding and offered the possibility of a long future of peaceful collaboration, in which England, too, would have been included. . . . It deserved to be examined and discussed with care. . . . What would Monsieur Hanotaux's attitude have been? One can't say. Many answers were possible, including a polite but definite refusal, assuming that the responsible minister was one of those who habitually mistrust the Germans or who have sworn never to come to a friendly exchange of views with them. . . . The one inconceivable course to pursue, especially in view of the happy relations which till then had subsisted between Monsieur de Münster and ourselves, was that of giving no answer at all, of refusing to condescend to an answer. To think that France, with all her traditions, should have been guilty of so gratuitous and so vulgar an insult! We had made war in '70 as the result of a refusal on King William's part to discuss matters with Benedetti, a refusal which, in itself, was no worse than what we now proposed to do ourselves."

"You're making me feel extremely uncomfortable. . . . How could such a thing be possible?"

"The note was dispatched, I believe, on the 19th of June. The Government had resigned of its own accord on the 15th, and Monsieur Hanotaux had been involved in its fall. Berlin couldn't know that this document, so carefully prepared, would be handed to a Minister who was no longer in power . . . who had taken his departure, and was not in a position to answer it. . . . The Minister who succeeded him and who wouldn't condescend to reply was Monsieur Delcassé."

Gurau, deeply stirred, sat sunk in thought. He did his best to resist a too hasty judgment. A thought which was only indirectly connected with what had been said found voice for a moment:

"Who was the head of the Government which had just resigned?"

"Méline."

"That's very odd," he said in a low tone. "The old progressives . . . the country party. They were a decent lot, who wanted peace and did their best to make it certain. . . . Very odd . . . Heavens, how sick we were with them for their attitude to the Dreyfus business! It only shows how complicated things are. Why did he resign?"

"Chiefly because the elections had just shown an increase in the radical vote at the expense of the progressives and the moderates in general. You remember, of course, that it was Monsieur Henri Brisson who formed the new Ministry."

Gurau turned towards Manifassier.

"It really is very odd," he said again. "One is tempted to put two and two together . . . or is it simply coincidence? Must one conclude that the radicals, the party of progress, pacifists by definition and by duty, have always adopted or sponsored a policy of aggression?"

Manifassier smiled and shook his head. Courson made a deprecating gesture, as though disclaiming any competence to express a view.

"But why?" Gurau went on, intent on his own problem. "Is it

because they represent a Jacobin and demagogic tradition, part of which is to follow every Platonic flirtation with the idea of universal peace sooner or later by a cry of 'To arms!' which is all the more effective for being strictly circumscribed in its application? Is it because today they draw their strength from the lower-middle-class elements, which are as credulous and as inflammable in matters of patriotism as the Breton peasants in the old days were in matters of religion? . . . I think so. . . . But there are other reasons too, of a more purely political kind, the chief of which is that a radical leader is always terrified lest he be accused of treason by the newspapers of the Right. He would set fire to Europe if by so doing he could set his mind at rest. The radicals have never had the Socialists' magnificent indifference to public opinion. The Dreyfus affair and the Church quarrel were but reasons the more. They had been accused, had they, of disorganizing the Army and demoralizing the country? Well, they'd save their faces by shaking a mailed fist at Germany. To think that it was Brisson, high priest of Freemasonry, who hatched out Delcassé! And that a little later it would have been General André's army and Pelletan's navy that would have been given the job of winning the war with which Delcassé had saddled us! It's enough to make one die of laughing! . . . I'm simplifying the situation a bit, perhaps . . . still . . ."

Suddenly he altered his position and spoke in a different tone:

"But tell me—what's to be done now? Germany's pretty sore with us, I imagine?"

"Quite sore enough."

"You know all about their latest proposals, I imagine? Monsieur Caillaux must have spoken to Monsieur Cruppi about them?"

"Had they to do with the Congo?"

"I gather that they were concerned with the project of a Cameroon-Congo railway."

"And we've said 'Nothing doing' again, I suppose?"

"Apparently."

The three men fell silent.

Gurau swayed backwards and forwards on his chair, his gaze fixed on the table.

"It's the devil of a business," he muttered. "If only Cruppi had done nothing . . . I could at least have tried to set it going again. . . . He never breathed a word to me about it. . . . I can hardly begin my period of office by opening negotiations with Germany. . . . What is your opinion, Monsieur Courson? I'm speaking to you now as a man, not as a civil servant."

"I don't know, sir. Perhaps if the Prime Minister has kept in touch with Berlin, he might let it be known there, through official channels, that there has been a change of atmosphere in Paris . . . that people would be readier now than they were to exchange views. . . ."

There was a hint of annoyance in Gurau's voice as he replied:

"Monsieur Caillaux has said nothing to me about being in touch. If he has, I'm not supposed to know anything about it. Besides, I don't want to encourage him to meddle in foreign affairs. Any go-betweens he may have had were men, undoubtedly, of his own choosing. From now on they will be dispensed with, because from now on there's somebody at the Foreign Office who won't shut his ears to information. . . . I want to have nothing more to do with 'official channels.' I mean to look after everything myself . . . and I'm sure that Monsieur Caillaux will approve of my decision."

"Then all we can do is wait until some opportunity arises."

"I shall arrange to see Herr von Schoen as soon as possible. What sort of man is he? I know very little about him."

"He's not a second Monsieur de Münster; all the same, he's affable, influential, and, I think, anxious to see his period as Ambassador commemorated by some definite success. He's more than once given us very useful advice."

There was another silence.

"Speaking of ambassadors," Gurau said, "I took a hurried look through the files yesterday afternoon as soon as I took over—with the help of my friend here—and I made a special point of having all Monsieur Jules Cambon's recent dispatches brought to me. We went back quite a way, though naturally we hadn't time to go into details. I confess that I don't find this Monsieur Cambon of yours very reassuring or very encouraging. His suggestions are certainly very sensible, and he seems to hold sound views on conciliation—I found that memorandum of his you mentioned about the Ngoko business—but, heavens, what a lot of warnings he's sent, and how pessimistic he is, despite the moderation of his language! There's not much he doesn't know about the Germans, and he sees pretty clearly what they're after. I gather from his letters that the war party is still making headway, and he seems to think that the big colonial merchants in particular, the Hamburg magnates, with a certain Monsieur Simler or Semler at their head, are becoming more and more resigned to the idea that the only way out of their present difficulties lies in making a clean sweep of everything. In their case, in addition to other things, there are economic and financial problems to be considered. They've got to find new markets, and the big industrialists, who are very influential, see eye to eye with them. It may be that the political chiefs haven't definitely made up their minds yet, but they're beginning to waver in a very alarming way. Monsieur Cambon seems to think that their recent willingness to discuss matters with us is only a manœuvre to gain time.

"I read something too—in the report of some other agent, I think it was—Manifassier and I haven't been idle, you see—to the effect that if the Potsdam meeting had had more definite results, if William II had really thought he could detach Russia from us and assure her neutrality, the men at the head of affairs would have pretty soon come to the conclusion that the moment had arrived to settle their account with us before Russia could recover and our alliance with her should be reaffirmed, and before Italy had left Germany completely in the lurch . . . all of which shows, by the way"—he glanced towards Manifassier—"that the question of the Russian alliance can't be treated lightly. That particular situation, however, having failed to materialize, it looks as though their present plan is to build up an overwhelming military superiority, which means being patient for a year or two, and that until they are sure of their advantage they will keep things simmering by arranging a couple of dramatic incidents and meanwhile assume a comparatively conciliatory attitude in order to put off as long as possible the inevitable moment of rupture."

Courson, who for the last few minutes had shown an eagerness to interrupt, now hastened to say, as though he were defending himself against some unspoken charge:

"I don't want you to think, sir, that I've been advocating a pro-German policy, or that I want you to shut your eyes to any aspect of the situation or to any of the dangers which are present in it. In what I said I carefully refrained from stressing the fact that the Germans are extremely difficult to deal with. . . . If you will do me the honour of going through certain papers with me, you will find many proofs of their goodwill, and even of the overtures which they have several times made to us in the course of the last few years, of which the public is in general ignorant. But you will find also not a few indications of their brutality, of their bullying methods, of their lack of courtesy and their calculated insults. Many incidents of this kind are already too well known to need underlining. Their attitude towards us has always resembled the climate of Scotland, an alternation of heat and cold. I don't think it's been altogether due to a deliberate and cunning plan. One's always got to take their national psychology into account. The Germans are far more unstable, impulsive, and wayward than we usually give them credit for being. The general opinion in Europe is that it's France who is capricious, who plays the part of the spoilt beauty, although time and time again France has acted like an obstinate and curmudgeonly old peasant. . . .

"Then one mustn't forget the luck of history. Prussia in 1860 had her Bismarck, Germany today has not—she hasn't even a Delcassé —not that I'm comparing the two men. But I can't repeat too often, sir, how foolish it would be to think that just because Germany happens to be in a smiling mood, we're all well set for a long period

of mutual love and forbearance. . . . It would be equally foolish to
judge her fits of brutality by standards which might apply to a more
adult or a more 'gentlemanly' nation, or to let ourselves be intimidated too quickly into surrender. . . . That would be extremely
dangerous, because it would encourage in her abuse of her strength
a country which is already markedly lacking in self-control. . . .
We must go carefully, and play a cautious game, by which I don't
mean that we should exasperate her or make her regret her generous
impulses. . . . Some of Germany's fits of temper have been deplorable, but it is only fair to judge them in relation to circumstances.
. . . One piece of advice I have at least not been guilty of giving—
in so far as I am competent to give advice on such a subject at all—
and that is that a policy of conciliation and sincerely pacifist intention should involve any weakening of our military strength. . . .
I'm far from thinking that! . . ."

"Remember, Monsieur Courson, I'm not Minister of War. . . ."

"I know that perfectly well, sir . . . but . . . there are times when
War and Foreign Affairs ought to be in the hands of a single man.
In any case, it seems to me the A B C of political wisdom to follow
a line exactly the contrary of the absurdity of which you were so
rightly scornful: namely, the bolstering up of a Delcassé policy on
an army controlled by a General André. . . ."

"A policy of bluster with a lead sword—we're certainly agreed
there. But let me remind you again that, unfortunately, one of the
two terms is not in my power to control."

"It ought not to have been beyond the power of a man like Monsieur Delcassé, committed to a policy of adventure, to control. There
were ways and means by which he could have kept in touch with
his military colleague. 'Make a good program,' it used to be said,
'and I will make you a good budget.' It ought to be possible to say:
'Provide me with a good army, and I will see that you have a good
foreign policy.' . . . But to return to those dispatches of Cambon's
which seem to have made such an impression on you, sir. Monsieur
Jules Cambon is obviously a first-rate man, but in judging his reports

one must take into account an ambassador's state of mind. It is bound to be a mixture of conflicting elements. A minister abroad is naturally inclined to view sympathetically the country whose guest he is. He lives in it, he understands it, many of its inhabitants are his friends. He doesn't want his time there to be marked by a disaster. Think what a bad mark it would be professionally for a diplomatic representative if war broke out between us and a country to which he had been accredited with the general object of maintaining friendly relations. That's one side of the medal, but there is another. An ambassador who has been long in one country develops an extremely sensitive mind. He doesn't want it to be thought that he has become blind to the faults of the country in which he lives. If anything, he bends backwards. At first he is inclined to go through a period of infatuation for his new home, a sort of honeymoon. 'These people,' he tells himself, 'are not a bit as I was led to expect they would be. They've got their ways, and we've got ours; that's all there is to it. They're as nice as nice can be.' Then comes a period of weariness, of saturation. A minister who has been abroad for a long time is usually much more on his guard than a beginner, against the manners, the crudities, the national vices of which he has so often had to take note, much more inclined to be suspicious on principle, to watch for possible traps. Finally this attitude of caution, this over-sensitiveness, falsifies the reality just as violently as does the innocence, the excessive confidence, of the newcomer."

For a moment or two M. Courson hesitated as though he were weighing his next words. Then he smiled.

"With an ambassador like Monsieur Jules Cambon, who is a gentleman as well as a man of first-rate intelligence, there is something else to be taken into account. . . ."

His smile broadened; he glanced at Manifassier.

"Assume for a moment, sir, that you were in office, say, in 1915 or 1917, and that a war was raging between France and Germany. Bearing that assumption in mind, the assumption that war had broken out, re-read Cambon's most recent dispatches. You will find in them full evidence that Monsieur Cambon had foreseen the event, had appreciated the contributory factors, had noted the inevitable development of the situation, and had warned successive governments of the danger ahead. Assume, on the other hand, that at the time we are considering, an agreement shall have been reached between France and Germany roughly parallel to the present Entente Cordiale. You will find in Cambon's dispatches full evidence that he had never shut his eyes to such a possible solution, that he had wished for it, that when a possibility offered he had collaborated in an effort to bring it about, in spite of the fact that he may have despaired at times of the wished-for consummation. Why do you find all this? Because a man like Monsieur Cambon is highly intelligent, keeps his eyes open, and sees two sets of facts, each of which is true, though each may contradict the other . . . signs and hints, some of which point to war, others to an understanding. He will appear in the light of an exact and sensitive instrument adjusted to register all the chances for and against. . . . Such a man naturally looks to the future, naturally anticipates the minister of '15 or '17 who will read through old files, naturally thinks of the verdict of history. . . . He is anxious to establish his reputation for clear-sightedness *however things turn out,* and he knows that only by contradicting himself sufficiently often can he be sure of going down to posterity as a man of almost infallible judgment."

All three smiled. Courson waited politely for the Minister to ask him some more questions. But since nothing was said (the Minister was deep in thought, his eyes fixed in a vague stare), and since Courson's shyness made him talkative and he was devoured by a wish to better his best, to elaborate his case with exciting details, and to appear in a better light than his listeners had anticipated, he continued:

"No doubt you noticed, sir, in one of Monsieur Cambon's latest dispatches, what the Crown Prince said to him at the Grünwald races? Unless my memory's at fault, it was on the 10th or 12th."

"About our troops entering Fez? He congratulated him, didn't he?"

"Yes. . . . 'So you're in Fez. Well done!' But he added: 'Morocco is a very nice cake. Give us a slice and we'll say no more about it. . . .' "

"Well, as a matter of fact, we're just about to evacuate Fez. . . . As to the Germans in Morocco, I foresee endless difficulties."

"Obviously. . . . The advantage of that old 'agreement' was that it removed the question altogether from Morocco. . . . If the Germans get a footing in Morocco, to however small an extent, it will be the thin end of the wedge. England won't stand for it any more than we shall."

"That's true . . . there's always England to be considered! . . . We haven't mentioned England up to now. . . . That wasn't what we were talking about, was it?"

"We'll talk about it whenever you like, sir; we shall have to some time." He checked himself and then added, with a charming hint of jealousy in his voice: "Or let me say you'll have an opportunity of discussing the question with Monsieur Herbette, who is probably better qualified than I am to have views on it. . . . Nothing that we have said is complete, or, strictly speaking, accurate, if England is left out of account. . . ."

"What an awful profession this is! One tries to isolate a single thread, and the whole skein starts unravelling in one's hand!"

"You see, sir, everything that we've said has to be reconsidered as soon as the English factor comes to be introduced. It's like going from two-dimensional to three-dimensional geometry: Monsieur Delcassé's behaviour, the extent of his—mistakes, if I may so call them; their inner springs, the fundamental causes of European unrest . . . the objects of German policy—it occurs to me that we haven't even mentioned the objects of German policy!"

"True—that's very odd!"

"Yes—and yet, on second thoughts, perhaps not so very odd. . . . The objects of German policy are not perhaps what chiefly concerns us as Frenchmen. That's one of the points that make for tragedy in the general situation. It may be that we shall find ourselves making war to prevent Germany from attaining certain ends which it is vital for others to prevent . . . but not for us. . . . One of these days, sir, you must put aside a few hours to discuss this point . . . with me or with Monsieur Herbette. . . . But I should very much like to be present. . . ."

Gurau was silent for a moment or two. Then:

"Yes, we'll talk about all this again, taking all the factors into consideration, as soon as I've had a chance of mastering the records. . . . I'm expecting any day now to have a talk with Monsieur Cambon. He said he'd be here soon, didn't he?"

"Yes, he ought to have arrived by now. . . ."

"Probably he didn't want to be involved in a ministerial crisis," Gurau said with a smile. "I gather, from your picture of him, that he's pretty shrewd. . . . I'll ask him what he thinks of William II. That gentleman interests me."

"We've not taken as much advantage of him as we might have done. . . ."

"You really think so?"

"It's certainly my impression. It's clear that he's always shown a very real desire to please us. . . . He's very responsive to attentions, extremely sensitive to caresses where his vanity is concerned. . . . I've often thought—though I've never dared mention it to anybody, for fear of being laughed at—that it would have been a real masterstroke to have invited him to visit the 1900 Exhibition, and to have given him a really good popular welcome. . . . Naturally, a thing like that would have had to be long and carefully prepared. He would have given a lot for a bodyguard of cuirassiers in the Place de la Concorde, and some cheering crowds . . . more, perhaps, than we think. . . . People are fond of saying that France is like a woman. . . . Well, women have a way of doing things like that, and doing them with an air."

"It's an amusing idea. Do you mean to say you're the only person it's occurred to?"

"Oh, I won't swear that in '98, just before he retired, Monsieur

Hanotaux didn't have an imaginative glimpse of such a scene, didn't envisage it as forming part of one of those grandiose stage-sets which he alone had the gift of planning. But we shall never know."

"Mm . . . and now it's too late."

Chapter

AGADIR

Four days later (the official ministerial manifesto had been issued the day before), Gurau, pale and with hands that trembled slightly, stood facing Herr von Schoen, who, before turning to leave the room, laid a sheet of paper on the Minister's writing-table between the sand-box and a pile of leaflets.

"Here, sir," said Herr von Schoen with an air that was at once polite and shy, evidence that he, too, felt the quality of tenseness in the moment, "here is the little note the contents of which I have just communicated to you."

Gurau ran to the little door and opened it.
"Manifassier!"
"What is it?"
"Something's up."
"What?"
"Read this. The German Government announces that, in order to protect the interests of her nationals which are, at the moment, threatened in the neighbourhood of Agadir, she intends sending a warship there."
"But—but I say, that's serious, isn't it?"
"It most certainly is."

Chapter

21

AT THE CHÂTEAU ZÜLPICHER

"She's queenly, that's what she is, queenly."

He repeated the phrase to himself with increasing pleasure, giving to it an added richness, a new significance. It drew from iteration an almost ritual quality.

Regal she seemed to him in carriage and in pose, though, thank the Lord, there was nothing Junoesque about her, no assumption of dominating airs. She was not in the least like one of those Amazons of five foot six, with a man's profile, capable of commanding a regiment and reviewing it in the field. She was regal because of a sort of inimitable serenity. She gave no impression of trying to be either "noble" or "simple," but her every gesture was proof of her privileged position, of her unquestioned right to rule. In her presence it was difficult to be anything but respectful and worshipping. When she moved, he felt that he must keep his distance, clear a path before her advancing feet, submit at once to her orders, bow as she approached. With a sense of delight he thought of himself as a symbol of the bodyguard that her majesty demanded.

He looked at her where she sat, close to him and a little to one side, in a light arm-chair of white enamelled wood. While she talked she worked at a piece of knitting intended for the poor children's home which she had established on the outskirts of the estate. Although she was intent upon her work and seemed to knit quickly, there was little of the "housewife" about her appearance, or just as much as a queen might show, ought to show, to give to the humblest women of her realm an example of pride in unpretentious labour.

At her back was a hedge of roses, and behind that another hedge of dark and close-packed shrubs. All around stood rose-trees ranged in ranks, and shrubs of various kinds, box and yew carved into shapes, baskets, flower-beds, and sanded paths, all set between an avenue of high trees that led towards the château.

"I'm afraid the sun will drive us in soon," she said. Then:

"It's a pity that there's no nice shady spot down by the water's edge. It would have been easy to make one near where the boats are moored. Of course this is a very unusual summer. One of the chauffeurs who went to Luxemburg yesterday to fetch the big car told me that he'd seen the thermometer there. . . . I don't like to tell you how many degrees, for fear of saying something silly."

"In the afternoon it must have been something like ninety-eight or a hundred in the shade in the city."

"I think he may have said a hundred. Don't you think we shall all die of heat? Or perhaps fires will start in all these forests at once, and then there'll be a conflagration like the one in the *Ring*.

Her very name was queenly—Christine, which her friends shortened to Christa; and her profile, which came to life as she spoke without losing any of its dignity. Queenly too were her voice and her intonation. Never before had he found such pleasure in listening to the French language, although she did not speak it as a Frenchwoman would have done. Never till now had he realized why it was that French had for so long been the language of courts. What other language, he thought with self-satisfaction, could have so freed itself from its earthy origins, from the constriction of mere locality, as to find on foreign lips an added charm and elegance?

To their right the château, seen from one side, closed the view. It was a huge building of uncertain age, probably rather less than a hundred years old, though there may have been an older portion which had been submerged by additions and restorations. Its mountain range of tiles glittered in the sun. There were two large towers and eight smaller ones with pepper-pot roofs. There were battlements and an archers' gallery. The walls were of red brick mixed with small, greyish-pink stones (sandstone, perhaps), which to the eye of a Frenchman evoked no period or style. It stood on a terrace encircled by a moat, or rather by an ornamental canal spanned by foot-bridges. Opposite the main front the terrace was broader than elsewhere and overlooked a gentle slope. At this point the wall of the canal was supported by an embankment of masonry, and midway stood a shallow reservoir through the medium of which the surplus water was fed downwards, between lawns, to a huge, irregularly shaped pond, which, in the wide, romantic landscape, looked like a natural lake. To the right of the château spread the gardens and the flower-beds between two lines of tall trees, and it was here Mme Zülpicher and Champcenais were seated.

Champcenais was thinking of his own home in Sologne. Without being learned in such things, he knew enough to realize that La Noue, with its air of breeding and quality, was finer than the huge Zülpicher château. But he would not let himself take pride in the comparison; far from it. "La Noue's all right," he reflected. "I'm fond of it, and it's big enough for my needs. But here everything is on a different scale. This is a royal residence." He even went so far as to admit that a certain degree of bad taste is the natural concomitant of such royal residences as he had seen in the pages of illustrated papers. It was as though in choosing the material background of their lives the crowned heads of today had been less concerned to win the approval of the cultured than to strike the imagination of the herd, while at the same time satisfying the glorious dreams of the middle class.

Birds were flying across the sky, singing despite the heat. They flitted from edge to edge of the high-piled forest between the arms of which lay the Zülpicher château with its gardens, its lawns, and its lakes. They evoked in his mind a vision of dark woods and endless paths, of dense growths of oak, of beech, fir-trees, and birch, crowded together in a green twilight.

Champcenais looked at Christa Zülpicher knitting her wool. "Does she notice the songs of these flying birds, which are hers as much as are the woods to which they speed?" He would have liked to talk with her of things unconnected with the urgencies and the habits of the great world, of the flight of birds, of their songs, of the half-light of forests, of the faint sounds that drift at night through open windows, of the dreams that come at the moment of waking, of the mixture of intoxicating excitement and sadness that stands on the threshold of a new day, nowhere more so than in the upper rooms of the Zülpicher château—those mornings when the visitor, leaning from his window, sees below him the roses and the box hedges of the garden, the terrace, the lake, the tethered boats, and the sea of forest tree-tops and hears the thin and distant sound of water falling in the reservoir.

But courage failed him for the task, and he gloried in his fear. "That is how love affects me," he thought. Even in those days, long ago, when he had been in love with Marie, he had never been able to satisfy the need he felt for knightly submission and for the delicious mental complications that are its accompaniment. "My nature craves men to rule, but a woman to obey." Marie, even in the flush of her youth, had never been anything but sweet and yielding. Unarmed and vulnerable she had seemed, seeking always the protection of her man, though never showing gratitude for his support, never adoring, never clinging to his strong right arm. Champcenais accepted the duty of defending her, though he never found pleasure in the role of champion to a cringing woman. He was one of those men who are irritated rather than softened by the spectacle of weakness in others, who even while they give, show their scorn of the suppliant. He would far rather have felt himself dominated by a subtle violence, far rather have obeyed the caprices of an imperious mistress, have yielded before a fine and brazen glance. What he would have refused to an appeal to generosity he would have yielded in the ecstasy of slavery, provided he were left the illusion of free choice and were not driven to obedience by physical force.

One of the things that he found most pleasant, almost without knowing that he did so, in the Zülpicher château was a certain harshness in the appearance of the building and the grounds, in the atmosphere of the house, in the relationships between the people who inhabited it. Each time that he heard an order given to a servant he experienced a little shudder of delight. Not that the order was given brutally or shouted, but that it never took the form of an appeal to better nature, never assumed that better nature might have anything to do with its being carried out. The relation here between master and servant was free of all that vague humanity which is nothing but a compromise, of that modern kindliness which is nothing but fear disguised. "In France we have lost the courage to speak like that. How much wiser they are than we!" Christa Zülpicher with her own hands knitted woollen garments for poor children and had built a house for them on her estate. But M. de Champcenais liked to think that she pursued her charitable tasks without diminishing the distance that separated her from her dependents, that she was kind without being foolishly kindly. As a matter of fact, he knew nothing whatever about what she did or how she did it, but by thinking thus, he idealized his model and put the finishing touch of poetry to the object of his worship.

The same sort of assumption lay behind his interpretation of the confidences which she had made to him. She was the second wife of M. Zülpicher, who had had two sons by his first marriage. These two sons, one of whom was eleven, the other fourteen, did not live in the château, did not even spend their holidays there. It might be that they were there for an occasional week during the summer. Champcenais had got the impression that they were being educated at a German school and lived in a professor's family. He gathered, too, that Zülpicher had not yet succeeded in having any children by his second marriage, though he very much wanted to and though Mme Zülpicher had been his wife now for five or six years. That was the sum total of his information, but he wove round it a legend which he purposely left vague and regarded more in the light of a day-dream. He imagined Christa saying once and for all to her husband at the very beginning of their marriage, perhaps even when they were still only engaged, quite calmly, without cajolery or brutality: "I want to have nothing to do with these children of

yours. I don't want even to know them. Do what you like with them.
You're rich enough to give them an excellent education. You can
go and see them from time to time. If you want to bring them to
the château once or twice a year, I can easily arrange to go and stay
with friends while they are here." (The form of this speech was
particularly improbable, since he had always heard Mme Zülpicher
speak to her husband in a very informal and intimate way.)

He persuaded himself also that she was not in love with Zülpicher.
There was nothing to give colour to this theory. Their relationship
seemed to be remarkably harmonious and to be reflected in their
way of life more than would have been the case in France in similar
circumstances. Nor did the Count say to himself that his legendary
Christa was perfectly suited in the man of her choice. In fact, Zülpicher showed to her, in their domestic dealings, all the respect that
she could normally have demanded, and in his behaviour to the
world in general he displayed just the quality of harsh severity
combined with strict politeness which might have been expected to
appeal to a woman of her kind in the man whose name she bore.

But Champcenais was not trained in reading accurately the minds
of those with whom he was brought in contact. It wasn't that he was
incapable of doing so, but the exercise held no interest for him. His
failure to exercise his understanding in this way was due to laziness
and to the fact that other things amused him more. He had an instinct about people, but the necessary gift of criticism, of patient
observation, which was needed to save his generalizations from error,
was quite alien to his tastes. He preferred to think of people in the
way which best chimed with his prejudices and his moods, in the
way that seemed to him "easiest." That being so, his imagination
was free to roam. He liked to give it its head. He was naturally
inclined to day-dreaming, and his dreams usually ended by influencing his ideas. As a rule the "easiest" way of judging people meant,
for him, the right to despise them (whether with or without reason).
He liked, for example, to think of Bertrand as coarse, vulgar, and
rather stupid, despite the evidence of his material success; of Gurau

as a greedy and corrupt politician, cleverer than most in disguising his intentions, and difficult to put in one's pocket; of Sammécaud as a combination of knave, fool, and mischief-maker; of the working class as an inferior race animated by an implacable hatred and capable of understanding nothing but force.

In forming his imaginary picture of Zülpicher he was chiefly influenced by a very real feeling of admiration. In many respects he would have liked nothing better than to resemble him. If there was any point on which he could legitimately despise him it was this one of sexual prowess. Zülpicher was not the kind of man whom any woman could love passionately or in whose arms she could hope to find pleasure. He was probably incapable of giving any zest to his love-making—not exactly impotent in the strict sense of that word, but unable to fertilize a woman, or, if he once had had the power, unable any longer to do so. It was even possible that he was not the father of his two sons—which would explain his willingness to exile them, since their presence would have been a standing witness to his failure. At moments, when he was least in control of his fantasies, his imagination would go further still. He pictured to himself Zülpicher deciding, with the calm detachment of a judge, that his first wife must die, and himself undertaking to execute the sentence in some manner not unworthy of the traditions of a strict family morality, by slow poison or by means of some injection the traces of which no post-mortem would ever reveal. Champcenais stopped short of actually approving this imaginary crime. He would not have done such a thing himself. There were times when he had been obsessed by the thought that Marc was not his son—could not, seeing what he was, be his son—but, for all that, it would never have occurred to him to kill Marie, even if he could have done so without fear of discovery. He would have preferred the sudden miraculous disappearance of the horrible little monster. More recently he had wondered whether his wife's fidelity still mattered very much to him, whether if he had suddenly received indubitable proof of her intrigue with Sammécaud he would have felt uncontrollable anger.

He had, in fact, carefully avoided finding any such proof, contenting himself with despising both of them. But it seemed to him natural that Zülpicher should be violent, and perfectly compatible with his having an untroubled conscience.

In short, he had decided that marital relations had ceased between Zülpicher and his wife, and took advantage of this theory, if not to indulge in definite hopes of success, at least to give free play to his reveries. "I could satisfy her. In her eyes I should stand for something more refined and freer than she has ever known. Paris, France, the aristocracy of France . . . to sin with me would be, for her, to sin without crudity, and since she seems to be a devout Christian, there would be a certain charm in the very fact of sinning. She is a Catholic, her husband a Protestant. To deceive a Protestant in the arms of a Catholic would not seem to her a mortal sin, all the less so since she would regard it as a casual misdemeanour, a mere holiday adventure."

Seated opposite to her, as he was today, devouring her with his eyes, he often tried to imagine their first intimate coming together, their first enjoyment of the carnal act. This free play of the fancy was not, however, so pleasant as it ought to have been. As in certain nightmares, he found himself brought up short by moments of embarrassment, by unexpected obstacles. His invention hesitated in the choice of details or hung wavering between two possible developments of the situation, sometimes deciding, in sheer perversity, for the most painful of the proffered alternatives. He imagined, for instance, Christa suddenly getting angry after contemptuously permitting him a few intimacies, boxing his ears, or even biting his hand, and then spitting out, with an air of inexpressible disgust, the blood which had trickled into her mouth.

At times, too, he was so vividly conscious of the respect with which she inspired him, had so clear a vision of the regal dignity in which his fancy draped her, that he wondered whether he would ever have the courage to possess her; whether, at the critical moment, after the first intoxication of desire and pride, his physical powers would not play traitor when confronted with the actual moment of sacrilege. Though not normally very highly sexed, it was unusual for him to experience this kind of anxiety. But at such moments it attacked him overpoweringly. To resist it he had recourse to various means. He set himself, for instance, to visualize his genital organ with all the pride of a growing schoolboy, telling himself that, even in repose, it was of no ordinary size, and that no woman could see it for the first time without realizing that it gave evidence of masculine power—an argument which he knew, from his own experience to be specious. But this confidence which Christa, like every other woman with whom he had slept, would feel would be bound to set his anxieties to rest. In any case, it would prevent his making a fool of himself. "I've had my failures, like everybody else, but on each occasion the woman has always taken the line that it was her fault, that she didn't know how to please me, that she had let me down." More than one woman had been frankly terrified at sight of him, filled with the disquieting anticipation of discomfort that made them look forward to the experience as though it partook of the nature of a surgical operation, and losing all hope of pleasure in the certainty of pain. The idea that Christa, too, might feel frightened like this, might see him in the light of a messenger of torment, cheered him up even more than his assumption of her flattering confidence.

At other times he allowed the idea itself of sacrilege to act as a stimulant. Christa would not be like any other woman whom one just possesses. She would be a queen surprised and outraged by a subject; a divinity whose sanctuary one profanes.

He enjoyed these fantasies, but he was not really impatient. The only annoyance he felt in the swift passage of the days (he had been there a week and had only another week to go) was that the nearer the moment of his departure came, the less chance was there of his dreams being realized. He decided that the consummation must be postponed until just before he left. "I will get her into my room on some excuse or other. I will make her realize that I want her. I will have seen to it that the door is locked. I'll either have her or make her hit me or bite me. I won't let her go without something happening. If necessary, I'll work on her fear of a scandal."

But at other times still, he revelled in the chastest of chaste dreams, appeasing his hunger on a diet of pure adoration. "She's the kind of woman whose image one carries in one's heart, who moves one to no coarse desires, one of those angelic creatures who, from time to time, come down from heaven to tread the earth. She is a lady whose face for ever lies enshrined in the bosom of the crusading knight. Here is her castle, her frowning, feudal castle, and I am the knight setting forth with her picture as my gage. In my extreme unworthiness I can hope for no more, before I depart, than that I may be allowed to kiss her finger-tips, the nails of her fingers . . . to kiss her feet. . . . My comfort will be the knowledge that no one in the world will ever have loved her as I love her, and the certainty that she knows it. But will she know it?"

He reflected that he had never yet made any declaration to her. Perhaps she thought of all this as some harmless flirtation, as a friendship faintly tinged with sentiment. He thought of Arvers's sonnet. He envied the poets. He told himself that with a little concentration he, too, might be able to write a sonnet. Poetry is more dashing than prose; it expresses things less crudely; it sets the adventures of the heart in a world where there are more chances of an honourable consummation.

He thought of the poem he might compose. As yet he dared not form a single line, nor had he even a confused idea of how the whole rather terrifying business would get itself into shape. He must wait until he was alone and undistracted before he could try to remember the rules of prosody and sketch his theme. But even now his anticipation of the effort he would have to make, of the strange task to which he would have to set his mind, filled his head with an odd buzzing which sounded as a bass to all his thoughts of love and was not without a charm all its own. Separate words came and went: "queen," "pardon," "regal glance," "bite," "strike"—he must have "bite" and "strike" in his poem.

Mme Zülpicher raised her head. Her eyes wandered to the end of the avenue.

"I think," she said, "that my husband is looking for you. He must have finished telephoning."

M. Zülpicher, dressed in a light-grey suit of admirable cloth and perfect cut, was coming quickly along one of the side-paths, between banks of roses.

Chapter

22

A MAN OF DUTY

"I've got a good deal of interesting news. I was speaking to Nieuwenhove. He tells me that the Brussels papers were very gloomy this morning, but that they're nothing to what people are saying. Four or five people in Antwerp, and even in Brussels, rang him up to ask whether he thought war would be declared at the end of this week. He was talking with Paris too, but the connexion was bad. Bamberger is in a hurry to be off to Saint-Denis. His new assembling plant is almost ready, but he complains that he can't get the right men. He wants me to send him two foremen fitters from here or from Oberhausen. But I've no one here who knows the new model, and at Oberhausen they're up to their eyes in work. I suppose you realize that we've been much too slow. I never could understand why it took so long to get that factory into working order, once the building was up. If we'd been able to open in May, we should have had a French plant in full running order by this time. As things are, you'll see, we shall have all sorts of trouble. I managed to get Oberhausen at last; I'd been ringing them since eight o'clock this morning. The sales department was rather nervous about talking to me. They seemed to think we might be overheard. They tell me that it's getting very difficult to send stuff out of the country. They've had no official orders yet, but if I understood their hints right, they're afraid that the railway people may have been told to hold up the cases until the situation admits of definite instructions being given to refuse transport facilities. If that happens, we shan't be able to get stuff into France at all, separate parts or anything else. I felt that would happen, and that's why I was so anxious to get the French branch established."

M. Zülpicher gave signs of a degree of nervousness unusual in him. Now and then, as he passed a rose-bush, he would finger one of the flowers absent-mindedly, or even pluck it, with an appearance of deliberateness, then close his right hand upon it and crush the heart of the bloom with his thumb. Petals fluttered down on the sanded path. Or he would carefully choose a small branch of laurel, cut it, and proceed to strip the leaves one by one. Champcenais, listening to his words, realized that they were intended, in part at least, as a criticism of his own conduct. "What a dominating fellow he is," he thought, "and how violent! It wouldn't take much to crack that veneer of good manners."

He felt that he must justify himself. He pointed out that he had put a great deal of energy into getting the branch started, and that all the financial and legal part of the business had been put through in remarkably quick time. Nor had any time been lost in choosing a site and fixing things up with the architect and the contractors. It wasn't his fault if certain trades in France worked more slowly than others. He had gone so far as to take a whole lot of men from his yards at Saint-Ouen and lend them to the new works at Saint-Denis. Nor was it his fault if French fitters hadn't been sent to learn their job at Oberhausen or somewhere like that. Bertrand, who had all along shown his willingness to oblige, would certainly have let two or three of his best men go. French workmen might lack discipline, but nobody could deny that they were quick. They could have learnt all about assembling machine-guns in a fortnight, and then they could have been sent back to Saint-Denis as instructors.

"Don't let's talk about it any more," said Zülpicher; "it's no good crying over spilt milk. If necessary, I'll go to Oberhausen this afternoon and see whether we can get the stuff through more easily by way of Holland. There's a good service of fast boats from Rotterdam, or, failing that, there's always the railway. It would be worth the trouble."

"How long do you reckon it takes to Oberhausen?"

"Four and a half hours with the big car. I don't have to waste time at the frontier. The German customs men know me. I give them something each time I go. . . . But there's something else I'm bothered about. What's Paris up to? I thought there'd be more doing there by this time. Good heavens! Here's a people who in less than a fortnight may have the enemy on their frontiers, an enemy armed to the teeth, the greatest military machine in the world . . . to say nothing of the German fleet, which will bombard the whole coast-line from Dunkirk to Cherbourg if the English don't chip in . . . and they're ordering next to nothing! . . . Are they doing anything with you in the matter of gasolene and crude oil?"

"There's been a certain amount of buying for the Army. Jessicot, my manager, wrote me that a lot of officers whose names I've forgotten had been to see him. They were making inquiries about stocks and facilities for transport. But there's nothing particularly unusual about that."

"And people say the French are lively! . . . You're nothing but a lot of slackers!" Zülpicher cried irritably. "Surely you're not going to let yourselves be smashed in the second battle of the war, as you were in '70! What are you all thinking about? Do you really believe that a few bayonet charges by Zouaves are going to settle things as they did in Morocco? Do you really want these Prussian swine to be masters of Europe and tell us all what to do?"

He spoke the last words with obvious sincerity.

M. de Champcenais replied that, judging from the newspapers, French opinion was seriously alarmed. He knew that there had recently been a good many troop movements behind the frontier.

"I know it too. Who is this fellow Messimy?"

"I know nothing about him. He's an old regular army officer, I believe."

"Old regular army officers are no good as ministers, especially in your country, even when they've got to make decisions in matters they're supposed to know something about. I've never heard anyone talk more nonsense about modern artillery than that Colonel Duroure whom I met once at your house. And yet, whom can one rely on? Delcassé has the reputation of being an extreme chauvinist. Four months ago I got somebody to submit to him plans of a new type of torpedo which I would have turned out exclusively for the French Navy at a very low price, to keep my factories going. You've got a fine fleet of torpedo-boats, but I happen to know that there's a shortage of torpedoes, since your arsenals turn out nothing but revolutionary propaganda. I also proposed, not quite so cheaply, but still at a very reasonable figure, armour plating made from a new steel of which I alone possess the secret, with a coefficient of resistance to shell-fire twice that of the plating at present in use—1.86, to be precise. For the last four months you would have been in a position to build up a stock of torpedoes and to improve the protection—in vital spots at least—of all your ships in commission, at a remarkably small outlay. I could have given advice, too, about a lot of economical replacements. Well, would you believe it, that great patriot Monsieur Delcassé refused my offers!"

"It was probably a question of the budget. Our statesmen haven't always the necessary credits in hand. They hesitate about asking Parliament for them, for fear of exciting public opinion and giving our friends on the other side of the frontier an excuse. And they've got to take account of Socialist outcries."

"Yes," said M. Zülpicher, frowning; "that Jaurès of yours is a dangerous fellow—more dangerous than the leaders of the Social-Democratic Party in Germany, because he sees further. Speaking generally, your Parliament is a great source of weakness."

"Germany's got its Reichstag!"

"That's not at all the same thing. When it's a question of military credits, I can assure you there are ways and means of going behind the Reichstag. . . . Your system is the worst of all systems. I really believe I'd rather deal with the Russians. When one's in difficulties with a statesman or any other high functionary in Russia, one can always buy him."

Anxious though he was to make his own interests the touchstone of truth, Champcenais could not repress a start of rather horrified amazement as he heard Zülpicher voice this last sentiment without the faintest hint of irony.

The other, however, continued in a dissatisfied tone:

"What's the United Bank of Europe doing for us? They know my instructions."

He broke a twig first into two, then into four pieces, stopped, and frowned at the path.

"The papers are doing no good. They no sooner take up an attitude than they change it the next day. One morning they say it's going to rain, the next they announce that the weather's fair. The public gets restless, and all to no purpose."

They started to walk again. The beautiful Mme Zülpicher was still knitting, though she had changed her position in order to get out of the sun. The sound of voices must have reached her.

"Do you know what I think?" went on Zülpicher; "that you could be of the very greatest assistance. But there's not twenty-four hours to lose."

"I? What can I do?"

"Get the *Sanction* to publish two or three very pessimistic articles."

"But I can't do that."

Zülpicher's reply was sharp:

"Oh yes, you can!"

"I have absolutely no personal influence whatever with the *Sanction*."

"Get Monsieur Sammécaud to arrange things. He can scarcely refuse. You never ask any favour of him."

"Monsieur Gurau would never let such articles get by."

"Monsieur Gurau's got something else to bother about just now. Do you really think he sees every article before it's printed?"

"As soon as he reads the first, he'll stop the others."

"If the first is well enough done, it may have an enormous effect by itself."

Champcenais smiled and slowly shrugged his shoulders. "What sort of effect? . . . You have an exaggerated idea of the *Sanction's* influence. Its circulation doesn't amount to a hundred thousand."

"Everybody in France, and not a few in other countries, know that it's Gurau's paper; in other words"—he mouthed the syllables —"the paper of the French Minister of Foreign Affairs, of the man who, with Herr von Kiderlen-Wächter, knows more than anyone else about the chances of peace or war in Europe. If tomorrow morning the *Sanction* says: 'War is inevitable,' it will be tantamount to an official Foreign Office announcement to the effect that 'We have done everything that could be done, but war is now inevitable.'"

The oil-magnate was conscious of a shock.

"It's a serious matter," he said.

"Of course it's serious; but you're not going to show the white feather, are you?"

"Besides, who's going to write these articles, or this article? It won't do to get just anybody, and those who've got the ability aren't going to turn out stuff like that to order."

Zülpicher screwed up his eyes in a concentrated effort to remember something.

"Wait a moment—what was the name of that fellow—you know—who wrote those articles you showed me the first time you came here? . . . Lafeuille, wasn't it, Pierre Lafeuille?"

"How on earth do you come to remember his name?"

"I remember what I want to remember. . . . Don't you think that's the very man we want?"

Champcenais said nothing. He was nonplussed, and wanted to think.

"Look here," went on Zülpicher; "I'm going to Oberhausen this afternoon. If you're the man I take you for, you'll go to Paris. There's a good train by way of Reims. We'll have a talk in my study before lunch and put down on paper a summary of what you can get done. There's a whole lot of things which need the presence of one or the other of us. We've no business to be sticking here smelling the roses while every hour is precious. You know as well as I do that being on the spot is more important than anything else. We've each of us got a job to do. You can come back in two days' time."

The oil-magnate, having made his decision, replied without enthusiasm:

"All right . . . I'll go if you want me to. . . . But I'd rather not go until tomorrow morning. When do you expect to be back?"

"Lunch-time tomorrow, or perhaps not until evening."

"Well, then—in view of the important news which may come through at any moment, it would be well if we weren't both of us absent longer than is absolutely necessary, and that you should know where I can be reached."

They continued their stroll through the gardens. A little later, in quite a different tone of voice, as though he were merely giving good advice to a friend, Zülpicher said:

"You might as well take the opportunity of getting rid of a good few of your three per cents. I sold my German and Belgian holdings this morning. Half a million's quickly got, and it's just as well to make sure while the going's good."

Chapter

CHAMPCENAIS DISCOVERS POETRY

As soon as M. Zülpicher had gone off in the large car with the black and yellow body, M. de Champcenais shut himself up in his room like a man who means to work undisturbed. He knew that his absent host's private secretary would not bother him there unless he had a really important message to deliver.

The oil-magnate was going to try to write his sonnet. The task was frightening, but it was exciting, too, in a way that he had never known before. It seemed to him suddenly that, of all jobs, this of writing poetry must be the most interesting, yet at the same time the most tormenting to the spirit.

He remembered only confusedly how sonnets ought to run—fourteen lines, divided into two groups of four and two of three. He thought he had heard that there were certain rules about the choice and placing of the rhymes, but couldn't recollect what they were. And he took courage from another memory, clear in his mind, this time, that all the greatest poets had made their sonnets irregular.

There was no vagueness, however, in his recollection of the general rules of prosody. He had learned them at school, and they came clearly now to his mind. He thought about mute *e*'s, about the hiatus and the cæsura, about alternating rhymes and the rules governing singulars and plurals.

What he knew least, he realized, was how professional poets set about the business of writing a sonnet. Oh well, all the more honour to him if he managed it!

He took a piece of paper and on the right hand side, towards the bottom, wrote, one above the other, the two words "bitten" and "smitten," which he wanted to use for his final rhymes. Then, a little higher, also one above the other, the words "greet" and "feet." For a long time he remained lost in thought over these four words spaced on the page before him. Next, he scratched out "bitten" and "smitten" and substituted one for the other. Something told him that it would be better to end with "bitten," which was an unusual word with a cruel and disturbing connotation.

He took another sheet, keeping the former one close beside him, and tried to complete two or three lines to act as a stimulant to his imagination and to fix his leading ideas. Not without several erasures, he hammered out the following:

> Sweetly I swoon beneath your queenly gaze
>
> If I may not be kissed, let me be bitten
>
> You will not salve the wound wherewith I'm smitten
>
> Kneeling before your throne my spirit stays.

Before proceeding further he decided that it might be as well to get some general ideas of what it was his sonnet was going to say. At first he wrote nothing, but let the shape of the poem establish itself gradually in his mind. All the while he kept letting his eyes stray to the four provisional lines which, as it were, kept his thoughts from wandering too far and served as a framework to his inspiration.

Then he seized his pen and set himself to write.

At the end of an hour and a half he had used up four sheets of paper and had completed the first state of the sonnet as follows:

> When in this magic spot I came to stay,
> My heart was burdened with those sordid cares
> Which Satan sows in human breasts like tares;
> But through them all your beauty found a way.

Kneeling before your throne my spirit stays,
Living your slave, or scorned, to sink and die;
In royal haven of your glance I lie,
And sweetly swoon beneath your queenly gaze.

Alas! fell duty calls me to be gone.
Sped by your frown I take my way alone,
Too late for peace, so sorely am I smitten.

Yet with my latest breath would I implore—
Since love you cannot, make me to suffer more;
If I may not be kissed, let me be bitten.

Another hour and a half was necessary, and three more sheets of
paper, before he had completed a version which, though it fell far
short of his intentions, was as good, he felt, as he could manage:

When in this magic spot I came to stay,
My heart was burdened with those sordid cares
Which Satan sows in human breasts like tares,
When to their depths beauty has found no way.

I sweetly swoon beneath your queenly gaze,
Living your slave, or scorned, to sink and die;
In royal haven of your glance I lie;
Kneeling before your throne my spirit stays.

Alas! fell duty calls me to be gone.
Even unchidden, I take my way alone,
You see not e'en the wound wherewith I'm smitten.

Avert your eyes, my Queen! Yet I implore
Since my desire is vain, torment me more.
Go I will not save I am kissed or bitten.

He carefully copied out the poem again, substituting, after much
hesitation, "touch" for "see" in the eleventh line. Then he folded it,
put it into an envelope, and addressed it to *Madame C. Zülpicher*.

Finally, with the aid of a stick of green sealing-wax which he found on his table, the flame of his cigarette-lighter, and his signet-ring, he managed to seal the envelope very suitably with his armorial bearings.

Passing along the corridors and down the great staircase, he reached Mme Zülpicher's room, on the floor beneath his own. He knew she would not be there at this time of day, and meant to slip in, unseen, and leave the envelope prominently displayed on some piece of furniture. As he reached the door, he ran into one of the maids. But he showed no embarrassment and held out the letter to the girl as though his being there had been the most natural thing in the world.

"Please put this on Madame Zülpicher's desk. Tell her that it's the poem she asked me to copy out for her."

He lived through the next hour in a condition of ecstatic delight. He went for a walk in the park. This waiting to see the effect of his poem was enormously stimulating. He thought of it lying there in Mme Zülpicher's room, like a time-bomb. Something, he felt certain, would happen, whether trivial or portentous, when it burst.

But this was not all. He was the prey of a sensation without precedent in his experience. The labour which he had put into his sonnet had left him feeling better and happier than he remembered ever to have felt before. Doubtless this was partly due to the satisfaction of having carried through more or less successfully a difficult piece of work for which he was not by training suited, but there was more in it than that. "Poetry," he said to himself, "is not just triviality. It is very important; it is powerful and it goes deep." He had a feeling that his more dubious emotions had taken on a sort of dignity, had become almost different, now that he had succeeded in enshrining them, however imperfectly, in verse. He felt himself to be "better," not in the prosaic sense of the word which implies that the soul experiences, as it were, an invasion of "goodness" and a routing of all shameful thoughts, but in a sense that provides for a transfiguration of the shameful elements into something else. He had discovered that there is a close aristocracy of feeling to which a man attains by reason of certain states of conscience and as a result of those states having undergone a particular kind of treatment. Until he has undergone the experience, he does not realize that it exists.

Only the fear of making a fool of himself prevented him from adding: "I believe I've got a gift for poetry. If I go on I shall do better."

When he got back to his room, there was still an hour before dinner, and he filled in the time by answering a letter from his wife which had been lying on his table for two days.

My dear Marie:

You mustn't be annoyed at my not having written to you before. Zülpicher and I are up to our necks in business, and there's a great deal to be decided. The situation, as you must realize, if you read the papers, is extremely grave and may get worse at any moment.

I'm glad that the news from La Noue is good, that you're having a pleasant time, and that Marc seems happy there. You say that I oughtn't to judge him by what happened the other day in Paris, and that he has since confessed that I made him terribly nervous. I assure you, my dear Marie, that I took all that fully into account, and thought it only natural that he should feel shy after so long a separation. I am quite sincere when I say that I thought him much improved by his time abroad. He is still awkward, as many boys of his age are, but you were quite right in foreseeing that nothing could better hide his lack of liveliness and brilliance than a smattering of English manners. I find it easy to believe you when you say that several people who have seen him at La Noue are agreeably impressed. I think it better, however, for reasons which you will understand, to keep these social contacts to a minimum.

For other reasons, connected with the general situation, I think it might be wise if you took him back to England rather sooner than you had planned. Anything may happen, and, I'm sorry to say, may happen soon. It is not at all certain that in a fortnight from now the Channel will be practicable for ordinary traffic, and even if it is, the risks may be greater than I should like either you or him to run.

I think, therefore, that you would be well advised to go back with him next week. If the unexpected happens and things straighten out, you can go over and see him again at the end of the holidays. I'm making plans to come back here about then for the shooting. M. Zülpicher is very anxious that I should, and there's still a great deal that we've got to talk over (that is to say, if the situation doesn't develop meanwhile as I very much fear it will; perhaps even if it does).

I'm planning to go to Paris tomorrow on business for twenty-four hours. I certainly shan't have time to dash down to La Noue.

I'm quite sure that you ought to get the roof of the left wing seen to at once. It will be a long job, and we ought to take advantage of this exceptionally dry weather. Yes, let Porcheron do it. He'll be slower and probably more expensive than a contractor from Romorantin, but I don't want to antagonize him.

Don't discuss the price with him. Tell him to send me a detailed estimate, and let him start without waiting to hear from me.

I shall probably be back in Paris for good in a week or ten days. We can decide what to do for the rest of the holidays when we meet. It's no good looking too far ahead just now. If you take Marc back to England next week, it might be as well if you returned by Havre and ran over to Trouville to see that everything's all right at the villa.

Love to you both.

During dinner, which was served in the enormous Gothic hall of the château and at which only three other persons were present—an old aunt of Mme Zülpicher's, a young nephew of her husband's, and the private secretary—M. de Champcenais noticed nothing unusual in Christa's behaviour. She only said one thing which led him to suppose that she had read the sonnet and understood its meaning. They were discussing M. Zülpicher's departure, which had taken place as arranged, when Mme Zülpicher, turning to Champcenais, said:

"My husband told me you would be leaving too, tomorrow morning?"

"Yes, I've got to go to Paris."

"But you'll come back again?"

"I don't know," he replied, trying to look mysterious. "That depends on a great many things."

There had been no trace of a sentimental inflexion in Christa's question, and she seemed scarcely to be listening to his answer.

About ten o'clock the aunt said good-night, and her departure led to a general movement among the other guests. Champcenais managed to intercept Mme Zülpicher, who had gone upstairs with the older woman and was now returning to the drawing-room. The secretary and the young nephew had already sat down again to finish a game of chess.

He spoke in a low voice:

"If you don't mind, I think I'll go up too. . . . I will knock on your door at midnight."

(He knew that it was her habit to go to her room at eleven o'clock, and that the whole household, with the occasional exception of her husband, were fast asleep shortly after that hour.)

She started.

"What did you say?"

He repeated softly:

"Midnight."

Her expression was half fearful, half mocking:

"I forbid you to do any such thing!"

"I shall come. I must say something to you . . . before I leave."

"Say it here."

He shook his head. There was sadness and tenderness in his eyes.

"No."

"I shall not open the door!"

"Yes, you will. . . . You'll have to open it quickly to prevent my presence there and the sound of my knocking attracting attention."

She replied:

"You must be mad. . . ."

But he had already bowed politely, and turned to shake hands with the chess-players. This done, he made for the door, taking care to pass within a few feet of where she stood. The great size of the room made it easy for him to do this. He was aware that she took a step forward as though to intercept him and then hesitated.

He reached the hall and swiftly mounted the stairs.

Chapter

TO BE KISSED OR BITTEN

At midnight precisely he knocked on her door; five urgent little taps—a few seconds' silence—five more, and again five.

He was still in his day clothes (nobody dressed for dinner at the Château Zülpicher).

He waited for about half a minute, then knocked again, this time thrice, more loudly and with a longer interval between the taps.

Through the door he heard a voice which strove to articulate clearly while making as little noise as possible:

"Go away! . . . Go away!"

He bent forward, almost pressing his lips to the panel.

"Let me in."

She repeated:

"Go away! . . . I beg you to go away. . . ." The tone this time was more nervous. The Count, however, far from weakening in his intention, felt encouraged.

He gave three more taps, very slowly, very loudly—so loudly that the whole wall trembled.

The door was opened a very little way, and through the chink he caught a glimpse of half Mme Zülpicher's face and one shoulder.

"I implore you," she said, "to leave me in peace. You are behaving like a madman. If you don't leave off I shall summon help."

He slipped his foot between the door and the jamb. "Summon whom you like, madame; it makes no difference to me. . . . But you would be better advised to let me in for a few minutes. I mean no harm; I merely want to say good-bye. I am leaving tomorrow morning, and you will never see me here again. But I must say good-bye to you."

He spoke in friendly and reassuring tones. She opened the door a little wider. He could hear the sound of her breathing, which was short and sharp. He pushed the door gently. Another moment and he was inside the room. He closed the door behind him. The idea of slipping the bolt flashed through his mind, but he abandoned it.

Mme Zülpicher had recoiled as far as the night-table, on which stood a telephone and a movable slab fitted with a number of bell-pushes. She, too, was still in her dinner dress, which was of pearl-grey silk, rather low in the neck; but she had exchanged her shoes for high-heeled sandals.

She kept her eyes fixed on him. With her right hand she touched the slab with the bell-pushes. Her fingers had only to move a fraction of an inch to press the three buttons.

Smiling, he advanced two or three steps, then fell on one knee.

"I adore you!" he said. "That I should upset you like this is a matter of the deepest distress to me. What I have to say to you could not, really and truly, be said in a drawing-room; not even in a garden. It is not a question of caution, but of decency. I must throw myself at your feet. Not only must I say in words, I must *show*" (he laid great stress on the word "show") "that I regard you as my queen, that I ask for nothing better than to be accepted as your slave. . . . If you read my poor verses, you took them, doubtless, for mere rhetoric . . . commonplaces borrowed at second hand. As verses they probably deserve no better. But, for all that, each word of them is true; each word expresses, no matter how ineptly, what I feel for you. . . ."

He had got to his feet and now, very politely, and carefully avoiding any brusqueness of movement which might frighten her, fell once more to his knees, this time at much closer range. Still speaking in a voice the deep sincerity of which could not be doubted, he took her left hand where it hung by her side, and gently kissed the tips of her fingers.

She withdrew it without any hint of coquetry and, making a great effort to control herself and hide her nervousness, said:

"Now that I've listened to you, please be sensible and go back to your room."

He smiled, but when he spoke, there was an odd note in his voice.

"Everything that my poem said is true. I want only what I said in it—but I do want that."

Once more he seized her hand. She tried to free it, but he held it fast, though he tried to avoid injuring it.

"You're hurting me!"

Instead of answering, he rained kisses on as much of her hand as he could reach without letting it go.

"Please stop!" she said angrily, still twisting her arm in an effort to free herself. "This is all extremely distasteful. Stop. . . . Let me go. . . . Otherwise—"

"Punish me if I am at fault!" He punctuated the words with kisses. "I am your slave. If a slave does wrong he must be punished!"

She had reached a state of fury which was as likely to find vent in tears as in nervous laughter.

"Well, then, if that's what you really want!" she said, and with her unimprisoned right hand she gave him a half-hearted slap high up on the side of the face. She repented of the blow almost as soon as she had given it.

She was once more the well-bred woman of the world.

"Oh, did I hurt you?" she said.

But he had seized his opportunity and now held her right hand as well as her left in his. He covered them both with kisses, showing, however, a sort of ecstatic preference for the right.

"Dear hand!" he stammered, "dear hand, which deigns to punish me!"

As though speaking to her hands, but in clearer tones, in which playfulness strove with sentiment, he added:

"And what now will be the sentence of that delicious mouth should I ask it for a kiss?"

Once again Christa agitated her hands in an effort to tear them from his grasp.

"That's enough!" she said; "you have had your slap. I'm sorry if I hurt you. But that's all you're going to get. Please leave me."

Try though she might to be stern, she was on the verge of laughter. Despite herself, a hint of playfulness had crept into their relationship, of teasing fun, which, however hateful, was not without power to excite her and seemed oddly pleasant. Everything, on a sudden, was different, and what might have been serious took on now the deceptive colour of a childish pastime. To the exigencies of a game Christa yielded an acquiescence which she would have refused had nothing been in question but Champcenais's insistence. In the same tone, coaxing yet provocative, he said again:

"What will that adorable mouth do if I try to snatch a kiss? Perhaps it will give me a tiny, tiny bite?"

It was the sense of play that dictated to his companion in pearl-grey what she should do to carry through her part. She had ceased to be a woman and had become again a nervously excited girl.

The Count had risen to his feet, still keeping close to her, still holding her hands in his. Half-fascinated, or perhaps persuaded that this was all a game, she did not turn her head aside. Quickly advancing his mouth, he touched her lips. For perhaps a second she made no sign; then, with a sudden little movement of her body, part angry, part playful, she drew back her face and, not very violently but, for all that, quite definitely, like someone making a gesture against her will, not quite knowing how to make it and furious at being compelled to, bit him on the cheek.

He released her hands and stepped backwards. There was a look of rapture in his face. He gazed at her with an air of adoring gratitude.

She stared at the cheek which she had just bitten. The mark of her teeth was clearly to be seen and was beginning to turn red. Two minute drops of blood appeared upon the skin, and two thoughts came simultaneously to her mind, each equally sincere: "I hope I've not hurt him too much!" and "I hope it won't be too visible tomorrow morning. What will people think!" But chiefly she was aware that all sense of intoxication had vanished. She wanted one thing only: that he should go away at once.

He sank once more to his knees and kissed her hand, which this time she made no attempt to withdraw. Then, without another word, he left her, opening and shutting the door with extreme caution.

Chapter

WHAT IS HAPPENING?

Seated in his office, Manifassier turned over paper after paper, but could not interest himself in any of them. He kept his eyes now upon the little door through which his chief might enter, now upon the telephone which might summon him into his presence.

For the last half-hour Gurau had been closeted with Herr von Schoen. It was obvious, before it began, that the conversation would be important, perhaps decisive. Its long duration was proof that it was indeed so. How should this long delay be interpreted? Clearly, negotiations had not been broken off, for had they been, the German Ambassador would have left after five minutes. The inference was that the two men had encountered very great difficulties. Probably Gurau was making a desperate effort to make the other see that his demands were impossible, to make him understand that no minister, however anxious for peace he might be, however determined to leave no stone unturned in an effort to avoid war, could impose on his Government, on Parliament, on public opinion, sacrifices which the nation would be at one in considering as insult added to injury.

"If only," Manifassier thought with a qualm, "the chief keeps his temper. He was in a terrible state yesterday evening, when he flung the paper-knife on the floor and said: 'They're simply maddening! There's no end to what they ask. One keeps a tight hold on oneself, one keeps one's temper, one gets ready to say: "All right, then"—and suddenly they trot out some utterly unheard-of and unexpected claim. . . . Cambon tells me to be patient . . . perhaps he knows how! I'm not at all sure that Herbette wasn't right when he advised us to send a warship to Mogador. I don't mind telling you, there are moments when I want to say as Clemenceau did: "You want to go, Mr. Ambassador? Well, then, here's the railway time-table!"'

"Yes," thought Manifassier, "it's a pity I can't be there just to give him a wink now and then."

The telephone rang. Manifassier snatched at the receiver.

"Is that you Manifassier? . . . Courson. . . ."

"Yes, yes."

"Are you busy?"

"Yes and no. . . . I'm waiting."

"Hasn't the Minister finished yet?"

"No."

"You don't know how things are going?"

"No, I've no idea. They've been talking for an hour—fifty-five minutes, to be precise."

"Ah. . . . I want to see you as soon as possible. . . . Can't you run over here for a moment?"

"Absolutely impossible. The chief may be here any moment now, or he may send for me."

"I'd come to you, but if the Minister comes back he'll want to see you alone. . . . He might wonder what I was doing there."

"Oh, do you think so? Have you got something important to say to me?"

"Fairly—very, as a matter of fact. . . . I've got some documents here which I don't want to let out of my sight, not just now anyway. . . . If you came you could see what they amounted to, and you could tell the Minister that you had seen them. . . ."

Manifassier's curiosity was aroused.

"I say," he said, "that sounds serious."

"It is."

"Look here, I'll give you a ring as soon as Monsieur Gurau is free, as soon as he's spoken to me."

"All right . . . but I repeat, I'd rather talk to you first, with the documents in front of us. Then you could give him a preliminary idea of them. I'd prefer that for many reasons—let's say, if you like, that I'm shy or don't want to meddle in things that don't concern me—or anything you please. . . . You'll understand better when you know what I've got to tell you. . . ."

"Listen. . . . There's only one way I can manage it. . . . As soon as he's told me the most urgent part of his news, I'll ask him to let me run over to you for five minutes. . . . Will five minutes be enough?"

"Better say ten."

"All right, then, ten minutes. . . . But I shall have to ask him to be patient while I'm away, and he may want to go to lunch. . . . It's one o'clock now. . . . I gather that you want him to be told as soon as possible?"

"Of course I do."

"Right. I'll do my best. . . . Stay where you are."

Gurau slowly opened the door. He had an anxious expression, and his lips were pursed.

"Well, sir—has he gone?"

"Yes."

"What happened?"

The Minister replied by a little wordless sound.

"No break-down?"

"No settlement, either. . . ."

"Things might be worse, though? . . ."

"I'm not sure. . . . There's something suspicious about the whole thing. . . . I got the impression that he didn't want to speak out, that he was avoiding the issue. . . . It was as though he'd come with the deliberate intention of playing for time. That's what worries me most. If he was just the ordinary sort of diplomat, I should conclude that Berlin didn't want to give him a free hand to decide things. But, von Schoen—a man in his position! . . . I'm inclined to think the worst. Perhaps they want another ten days or a fortnight before launching their attack. It may be that their General Staff's asked them for the delay, or they may be waiting for assurances from England or Russia. . . ."

"But the English—"

"No one's to be trusted! We'll talk about it all quietly over lunch. We must lunch together."

"But—the fact is, Courson rang me up just now. There's something urgent he wants to tell me . . . something he wants to show me in his office, which he's anxious I should communicate to you."

"What's it about?"

"I don't know, but it seems to be serious. Will you give me ten minutes?"

"It's all very odd; still, go if you want to. But don't let him get the idea that he's Minister of Foreign Affairs, and don't stay there an hour."

"Only ten minutes, I promise. . . . By the way, there's something else I'd better mention before I forget it. When I went down to the *Sanction* last night, I took the liberty of suppressing an article of Pierre Lafeuille's which they'd stuck on the front page. It would have been disastrous to let it go in—a summary of the situation in the blackest possible colours, and all the worse for seeming to be considered and official. It couldn't have been more effective if it had been written to prepare the public for war the day after tomorrow."

"Who told Lafeuille to write that?"

"I've no idea. Since we've had to neglect the paper, he's had a more or less free hand."

"We must get to the bottom of this. Perhaps Sammécaud's been trying to rig the market."

"They've had to fill up with any old thing. It'll be rather a scrappy issue. Perrin was furious, but that can't be helped. . . . Well, I'll just run over to Courson."

"All right, I'll go on and wait for you in the rue de Bourgogne, you know where. I'll choose a quiet table on the first floor."

Chapter

THE SECRET IS OUT

It was Gurau's turn to scan with anxiety the face of the young man whom the head waiter brought to his table at the far end of the room near the window.

"You don't look particularly cheerful," Gurau said in a low voice. They gave their orders hurriedly, so as to get rid of the waiter.

"Well, what's it all about?"

Manifassier hesitated a moment as though to collect his thoughts; then:

"Tell me, sir, when was it exactly you took those three days off?"

Blushing slightly, the Minister replied:

"You know as well as I do—the 14th of July. I left on the 13th, and it must have been the night of the 16th that I got back."

(He had accepted Mme Godorp's suggestion of a little trip. She had taken him by car as far as Lucerne, where she was planning to stay for some weeks. He had remained there two days with her and had returned to Paris by a night train. During those two days she had become his mistress. This adventure, snatched from a period dark with anxiety, had remained in Gurau's memory as an oasis in the desert.)

"I forget," said the young man, "whether you handed over your department officially to Monsieur Caillaux during your absence?"

"Yes. . . ."

"Ah! . . . I expect you did . . . but I don't remember having to record the fact."

"Anyhow, it was the merest formality. . . . Why do you ask me? Nothing of any consequence happened during those three days. No decision had to be taken in my absence."

"It's only that I want to get my mind clear about the details. . . ."

"But what details, my dear fellow?"

"Wait a moment, sir; I'm just coming to that."

Manifassier told his chief what he had just learned.

Courson had discovered that for some weeks past the Prime Minister had been conducting direct negotiations with Germany unknown to, and over the head of, his Minister for Foreign Affairs.

Many things had made Courson suspicious—references in official correspondence, and the conversation of his colleagues. But it was only the previous evening that he had managed to get positive evidence.

This evidence had been provided by the text of certain code telegrams sent from Berlin to the Prime Minister. Presumably they had been duly delivered, but Courson had seen the copies.

"I've seen them."

"But how did he get them?"

"He wouldn't tell me. I imagine that Monsieur Caillaux gave instructions to the Code department. He passed on to them the code telegrams which reached him from Berlin, and they returned them to him decoded, taking precautions, of course, to prevent them from getting into our hands. There may have been a perfectly genuine mistake, or somebody may have pretended to misunderstand and to think that the messages were intended for the Office. It's possible, of course, that Courson may have got his duplicates from some of his friends in the Code department by working on their dislike, as loyal civil servants, of obeying orders that ran counter to every official tradition. That, I think, is the most probable explanation, though I don't know. I didn't like to insist, because by doing what he did, Courson had already given good proof of his loyalty and astuteness."

"But what was in the telegrams? This thing's serious."

"As serious as it well could be. But I had time only to glance at them, and since the business is too important to admit of merely approximate impressions, I'd rather you got the details from Courson, point by point. I've told him you'll see him at seven o'clock. You know how methodical he is; well, he's managed to reconstruct all the latter stages of these secret negotiations. He'll give you a report correct to the last comma, and he'll tell you where his information is faulty. All I can say meanwhile is that they concern the Congo, our own and the Belgian, a Congo-Cameroon railway, some railways in southern Morocco . . . and the question of quoting Bagdad Railway stock on the Paris exchange. . . . There's a damned lot of railway business involved. . . . And, oh yes, I was forgetting, something to do with one of the South Sea Islands."

Gurau listened to this catalogue with his eyebrows raised and his mouth half-open, like a man who is still partly stunned.

"I can scarcely believe my ears!" he said at last. His voice, too, was different. He was trying to find some reason for disbelieving a piece of news which constituted so sharp a blow to his pride.

"But look here . . ." he went on in a tone which betrayed his anxiety to find some point of encouragement, "there's one point you've forgotten, old man. You mentioned dispatches in code. . . . Well, did they come from the German Government and not from our Berlin Embassy?"

"Yes. Courson was careful to underline the fact that Monsieur Cambon had been kept as much in the dark as ourselves."

"Then they weren't in our official code?"

"No, they were in a code agreed upon between Monsieur Caillaux and Berlin."

"In that case, Caillaux wouldn't have passed them on to the Code department . . . he would have been particularly careful not to. The story doesn't hold water."

"You're wrong, sir. A decoding job can't be given to just anybody, especially when it's a matter of decoding replies. . . . Assuming that Berlin supplied the key, Monsieur Caillaux would have gone to the department and said: 'Here's a key to be used for both sending and receiving; it's to be used in connexion with certain documents which I shall give you.' The difficulty would have arisen over asking them to do a job of this kind at all, over establishing that particular kind of relation with them. That's why I asked you about your absence. The fact that you were away for three days made the whole thing so much easier. The Prime Minister, being temporarily in charge of your department, would have every right to say: 'Let me see everything that comes in.' Then, when you'd got back, he could add casually: 'There may be one or two things for me still coming along. I'll hand them all over to you—here's the key. Don't let anyone but me see the versions in clear.' At least, that's how I figure the thing out. Besides, official channels accounted only for part of the stuff. A good deal was probably done through go-betweens."

"Do you know who they were?"

"Fondère and Spitzer on our side, Lancken on the German."

"Fondère? . . . Maykosen mentioned him to us, if you remember."

Gurau hardly opened his mouth again during the rest of the meal.

He remained sunk in thought, an expression of extreme bitterness on his face. He seemed to be holding in his anger with deliberate and meticulous self-control. Manifassier, who watched him closely, would have preferred an outburst, however undignified, to this silence, and more than once attempted to provoke one. But the only definite answer he could get was short and far from reassuring.

"When you've got all the evidence you need from Courson," he had asked, "are you going to demand an explanation from Caillaux?"

The eyes which Gurau raised towards the top of the window shone with a curious light between their narrowed lids. For a moment or two he sat in thought; then, scarcely opening his lips:

"No," he said.

Chapter

27

A LETTER FROM JERPHANION TO JALLEZ

My dear Epistemon:

Across three hundred miles I stretch to take you in my arms and press you to my heart. Barely an hour has passed since the postman brought me your telegram. First of all, thank you for sending it. There was a lack of fervour in your promise, and I'd resigned myself to the thought that you wouldn't do anything about it. When I held it in my hands, I hardly dared to open it. I was terrified at the possibility of bad news. I argued that if the news had been bad you would have thought the ordinary post a quick enough messenger. But one never quite knows with you.

So you're through! I set my mountains echoing to the sound of triumphant shouts. Honestly, until this moment I haven't had the heart to rejoice in my own success, and if anything were needed to prove the depth of our friendship, surely it's that. May nothing ever make it less!

That was partly responsible for the lack of enthusiasm which you noticed the other day when we were walking down the boulevard Saint-Michel after the results of the Arts examinations had been announced.

It wasn't the only reason—I don't want to make myself out more unselfish than I am—because I was still dazed by the news that I had got through myself. It's only when it's all over that one realizes what a frightful anxiety it all was even when one didn't allow oneself to think about it, and how little certainty one had. I am quite sure now that in my heart of hearts I thought I had precious little chance of a degree, and still less of a *"cum laude."* I was a great deal more modest than I seemed. I'm still in a condition of amazement; I'm, as it were, feeling myself all over. But these are humble and poignant emotions which you, very naturally, know nothing whatever about.

Since the close of that particular chapter I've been thinking of a whole heap of things, very obvious, most of them, very "undistinguished," but for the moment I'm not in the mood to be ashamed of them. Great men, like our friend Valhubert, would have a pretty bad opinion of me if they knew, but I could chat very happily to you about them on the roads and footpaths of this countryside (you'd like it, I think; it would be lovely if you could come. Is it absolutely impossible?). You could tell me if you shared my feelings. You could contradict me. Even if we reached no definite conclusions, we could taste with philosophic enjoyment the pleasure of that true and familiar sense of a spiritual adjustment, however imperfect, to circumstance (noting as in a mirror the effect on ourselves of the changing background of our life).

In particular, I've been thinking a lot about what we call *security*, or, if you prefer it, the sense of security. You can guess what set my mind on that track. By getting my degree, I told myself, I am quite suddenly guaranteed against all those material worries that haunt the steps of young men without resources, am made sure of a decent livelihood to the end of my days (because I can even rely on a pension!). Of course, if I want to get on quickly, if I'm keen on a job in Paris, if I'm to make my way in the service *(infandum!)*, I shall have to put in a lot of special work. But merely to keep my official academic position all I need do is to take care not to appear too often drunk in class, not to assault little girls in the neighbouring copses, not to stand up each morning at my desk and declare that the President of the Republic is a stinking dung-heap. Even the special work I mentioned just now will be nothing in comparison with the tension, the anxiety, the rush of those months of concentrated cramming for my degree, or with the mental acrobatics and violent concentration of the actual examination. The kind of work I'm thinking of will be relatively tranquil, spread out over a long period of years, and with a whole lifetime in which to deal with it.

THE POWERS THAT BE

All around me here I see the peasant and the dwellers in the village and the neighbouring market town, fine fellows of an antique mould who have not yet lost touch with the essential facts of life. There's nothing they rank higher than security (and the kind to which I am now entitled would seem to them a seventh heaven). They know that somewhere in the world there are brilliant "positions" and the chances of living in luxury, but such things are valuable in their eyes only in so far as they are *certain,* and, in general, they don't much bother their heads about them. They regard them much as you would some newspaper account of a feast given by the Maharajah of Bijapur, and hold them to have as little bearing on the troubling problems of their personal destiny as you would such a distant scene.

It is easy to laugh at this hungering for security. At the moment I find it touching rather than comic, probably because I have found security for myself and can bask in it happily. I accept its protective embraces and feel the delicious thrill that deep down I recognize as its gift to me. In my thoughts I take it fully into account as, it seems to me, one must take into account all that is genuine in life.

But my thoughts on the subject go beyond my own special case. I generalize, I "objectify." All society, I tell myself, rests on this need for security, and yet the history of every society is the long tale of failure to ensure it. If only men would realize that security is the object of all their communal arrangements, that for security alone they unite their efforts, they would establish it and maintain it with less trouble than they have done in the past and with fewer mistakes. They would see more clearly the dangers that beset it and find some better way to overcome them.

Yes, I look around me on these mountain folk from whom my parents and my forbears came. From the days of Louis XIV, from the Middle Ages, and perhaps from further back still, the material conditions of their lives have changed but little. We can say at least that the fundamental facts making for their happiness and their satisfaction are now much as they were then. Being what they are—and I know their natures pretty accurately—they have needed little, I am convinced, in any period to make them happy. (Heretical though the view may be, I am convinced that their lives, so far as houses, furniture, utensils, clothes, cattle, means of heating, and even food are concerned, were no more poorly equipped five hundred years ago than they are today. Remind me to tell you, some time, of a household inventory of the fifteenth century which I tumbled on; it's an amazing document.) I agree that in those days there was no guarantee against feudal exactions or the unreasonable demands of this or that abbey, no safety from the incursions of armed bandits or the attacks of brigands. Life was lived in constant dread of increased taxation or the pressing of men for the king's wars, taxation which might strip the humble people of their all and plunge them in poverty for twenty or thirty years to come, levies which brought in their train separation, heart-break, bereavement, and homesteads laid in ruins. There was no protection, if you will, against a series of bad harvests and epidemics of disease, nor yet (for we must forget nothing) against the danger of abandonment and poverty in old age for that small number which could look for no help from children and relatives. But my point is that the provision of security presented no insoluble problem, was, given the *material resources of the time,* perfectly possible. We've always been wrong about these things, and that's why I'm insisting on them at such length. We seem to believe that quite *irrespective of the way in which society was organized* and of the possible goodwill and wisdom of the ruling classes, these people were inevitably condemned, by reason of the lack of natural resources and the lack of means to make use of them incident to the times, to periods of recurring destitution, to living the lives of starved and hunted animals. No, no, no; it's just not true. I don't say that their resources were inexhaustible, I don't say that disasters, arising from circumstances that they could not control, weren't now and then inevitable. But such things could have been made the exception rather than the rule, could have been so rare as to be forgotten from one generation to another. It would have been perfectly possible so to arrange things that the sense of security would have been a natural and continuing expectation instead of that never ceasing anxiety which our ancestors have left us as a heritage and which still frets at our hearts.

Why, then, did humanity fail in this respect? Because the cause of security was badly served and had too many enemies; because its *leaders,* the men whom the Bible calls the "princes," though they held their power simply and solely by reason of this need for collective security, were continually thwarting it and turning to other ends those very resources which had been confided to them for this end, and this end only. That's what we must never forget. I repeat that at every period of history there have always been sufficient resources to make the mass of mankind happy—as it understood happiness—and to organize security on its behalf (which was all it ever asked). But at every period, too, there has always been a shocking waste of those resources, caused by the need felt by the "princes," not to enjoy a security which was common to all, but to find an outlet for their boredom, to slake their pride, or to crush their rivals. I am absolutely certain that four-fifths of the taxes paid by my ancestors in money, corn, and blood went, not to guarantee their security—which was the real object of the social contract—but to pay for the mad adventures, the fits of megalomania, the orgies of luxury and self-indulgence, of the great ones of the earth and their parasites, from the feudal lord, the abbot, and the bishop up to the high constable and the king himself. It's not simply in order to avenge my ancestors that I'm making such a song and dance about all this (they got some revenge in '89), but to prevent myself from falling into that fallacy to which we're all of us prone, into which I've felt myself slipping time and time again, which consists in saying: "It's no good asking of Society more than Society can perform; in every period the organization of the life of mankind is what that period permits it to be; in times gone by, Society couldn't distribute prosperity and security to all because the resources and the means were lacking. Our first business is to increase the wealth of the world and to perfect the means of distribution. Economic evolution must proceed according to its own laws. Only when we are assured of an abundance, a surplus, of everything, will the problems of Society admit of easy treatment—even the problem of war. People won't want to fight when they're filled to bursting."

That's all a lie, the arch-lie, and it's dangerous too; dangerous because it shifts the problem and gives us a wrong idea of who the enemy really is. When there's a surplus of production it's just possible that a few crumbs may fall to the people, to my poor mountain peasants; but what they chiefly long for, the one thing they had in mind when they entered into the social contract—security—will not be increased by a single inch. It will, in fact, be diminished, for the "princes" will turn a state of surplus to the advantage of their mad adventures, their megalomania, and their self-indulgence, just as in the old days they turned sufficiency or poverty. Abundance will go to their heads; they will be more frantic than ever, more than ever hostile to the general security of mankind. And what nonsense it is to say that plenty will put an end to war! Except in the most remote ages, for which we have no sure evidence (who really knows what started the first of those barbarian migrations which set in motion all the rest?) *a war has never been fought because a nation was hungry,* because it lacked the bare minimum of material resources necessary to enable it to live up to the average standard of its times. "The hunger which brings the wolves from the forest"? Bah! Just a stupid literary cliché of the historians. All wars have been caused by pride, anger, spite, grandeur, imagination, fanaticism, greed (and greed's not the same thing as hunger), so far, at any rate, as the aggressor was concerned and when the business didn't start spontaneously on both sides at once.

Nothing, for instance, gets on my nerves more than hearing people say, as everyone is saying just now, that if the Germans are preparing to attack us it's because their country is too small to let them breathe freely or too poor agriculturally to feed them. Lies and gibberish! You used to talk occasionally, didn't you, with some of our friends who were reading modern languages and had lived for a year or two in Germany? This story of German poverty's a joke! What the people there lack, just as we lack it, is freedom to devote their resources to their own needs and to the organization of security *within* their frontiers, instead of seeing them sacrificed to the pride of their masters and being forced to follow a policy of aggression against their neighbours with the object of building up external security at the expense of the foreigner. I can quite easily believe that their masters tell them that they're on the brink of starvation and that their only hope lies in a good war—but that's simply a matter of suggestion.

You see, of course, what I'm getting at. What's always stood in the way of the kind of security dreamed of by these peasant villagers of mine is not lack of resources at home nor yet the driving force of famine abroad, but the presence here and elsewhere of *violent* and *greedy* individuals, and the weak way in which human society has tolerated them. The first thing to do is to find out how many of them there are, the second to decide how we can get rid of them. You notice that I'm putting the problem in as anti-Nietzschean a way as possible. There was a moment when I was taken in by Nietzsche; at present I detest him. He was an eloquent madman who succeeded in providing the violent and the greedy with a new war-cry. (His effect on me was to make me feel considerably more kindly towards Christ.) To continue: how many of them are there? Not a great many, I think, but we must go into that in more detail. How are they to be got rid of? By police action, using the term in its noblest sense; that is to say, as in '89, by the Revolution. But this time it must be carried through to the end.

Another point: There may be nations in which the violent and the greedy are so numerous that one is almost justified in saying that the nation as a whole is violent and greedy—nations in a state of nervous morbidity, bored by security and not averse to bloodshed, nations that are driven to seek war by some inner necessity and not because they are forced to it by their "princes." I find such a thing difficult to believe, but I admit it as a possibility. Certain travellers' tales of a more or less sociological kind have sometimes made me think so, as you may remember. In the course of a single expedition, under more or less similar conditions and at more or less the same level of culture, sometimes in the same island or the same forest, "peaceful" and "warlike" tribes have been found by explorers, living side by side. Their attitude is reported as being entirely different. Among the first the stranger is received with smiles and an offering of gifts; with songs, dances, and the welcome of noble-looking elders; among the second with a shower of poisoned arrows as soon as he shows his face.

If there really are, making allowances for different conditions, whole nations which may be regarded as "bad," then humanity must be protected against them. They must be detected and reduced to impotence. How are they to be detected? By other nations adopting an attitude so peaceful, so free of all provocation, that the "bad" neighbour, by taking action against them, must inevitably put itself in the wrong. (A method of behaviour which seems to me utterly different from any now in force.) How are they to be reduced to impotence? By the sort of war that our masters wage? I think not. Here, too, it seems to me that Revolution is the only possible method, but Revolution on an international scale so that it becomes real combined police action.

No doubt you will find little to call heroic in this idea of Revolution which started with the intoxicated reflections of a young man who has just got his degree, and proceeded through a set of variations on the theme of peasant security.

You may be right. But each time that I renew my contacts with this countryside and with these peasants of my homeland, who really are *my* people, I get the impression that they are silently laying on me the duty, which has its roots in the distant past, of protesting against heroism. Do you understand what I mean by that?—against an age-long abuse of confidence, a lying and windy way of making men who live together do what they least want to do, what they have expressly charged Society to keep them from having to do. These true and honest men of whose will I am the incarnation have laid upon their "princes" throughout the ages one charge and one charge only: that of organizing security and peace to the best of their ability. They regard heroism much as they regard belief in God, as a matter for the individual conscience, which they've no desire to have foisted on them.

It can hardly be a matter of surprise to you that my mind is working like this just now. I have been suddenly plunged into a state of extreme anxiety. Isn't that true of you too? We get the papers here only very late, so that I sometimes have the agonizing feeling that while I'm strolling among the pines in the glorious sunlight, something catastrophic has already happened in Paris. I get the idea that one of these days, perhaps, at the turn of some path, the distant tocsin of Saint-Julien-Chapteuil will bring me the news that mobilization has been ordered. (That, I gather, is how we shall be told.) Have you had any inside information since we parted?

Did I tell you, that time on the boulevard Saint-Michel that I was dining next day with the Marquis de Saint-Papoul? Alone, at a restaurant? He was just passing through Paris on his way to attend to some business in his constituency (something to do with granting tobacco monopolies, or appointing local officials, etc.). He wanted me to write him a speech (to do with the opening of some school). He'd taken advantage of being in Paris to look in at the Chamber, where he'd met one or two people in Government circles. By the way, it's odd how easily he's slipped into the political world; he seems to find his way about there without any difficulty. He's no fool. Well, he told me what people are saying. All the rumours, of course, are contradictory, as you might suppose, some of them about as gloomy as they could be, others offering a ray of hope. On the one hand, nothing but stories of regiments near the frontier being put on a war footing, reserve officers being called up, munition-factories working night and day, and dramatic interviews between Caillaux, Messimy and General Joffre. On the other, there seems to be a feeling that Caillaux is all for peace, for an arrangement which would lead to some easing of the tension and a durable truce, but that he's up against Gurau's extreme views. The Prime Minister would have

our Ambassador at Berlin on his side, while the Foreign Office naturally relies on the permanent staff and the policy of revenge which
they've inherited from Delcassé. It really looks as though peace and
the fate of France and of Europe are going to be the plaything of
two warring cliques. . . . I'm trying to tell you how I see the situation. One or two points, I must say, amaze me—Gurau's attitude, for
instance. Can it be that the effects of holding office have wrought
such a complete and sudden change in him? I don't think our friend
Saint-Papoul is actually making it up, but I suspect him of rather
over-stressing the romantic antithesis which pleases the Cyrano part
of his Bergerac soul. So far as he himself is concerned, he's on the
side of peace, in the first place because he's a loyal partisan of Government, and Government is Caillaux rather than Gurau, secondly because he's naturally shrewd, and finally because his recent contact
with the inhabitants of the South-west has persuaded him that they
are no more anxious for heroic methods than my mountaineer friends.

You must admit it would be pretty annoying if, just as we had got
our degrees, this wretched dog-fight came along to spoil our satisfaction. You of course— But I'll leave you out of it; let's just talk about
me, the poor wretch who was just now playing happily with his
dreams of security! It seems to me that while we—all the young men
of our age—were entering the world by one door, security was going
out by the other. I have an idea that if it really vanishes now, we
shan't see it again for a very long while. Once peace is disturbed, the
shock is apt to be of long duration.

When damned earthquakes like this come along, everybody's
house is affected. No sort of detached and private life is possible. The
very day of my Saint-Papoulesque luncheon, a few hours before my
train left, I ran into M., who, like me, was just off for home. I got the
idea—after we'd parted—that she had expected my success to show
itself in a sudden optimism about the future, a new-found willingness
to shoulder novel and intimidating burdens. What, in fact, happened, was that, without meaning to, I talked less of my pleasure in
getting a degree than of my fears of mobilization, about which, still

under the influence of my host's eloquence, I was freely vocal. I couldn't very well hide from her, could I, the fact that my immediate future seemed to be one either of active service or of life in a garrison town? She thought, of course, that I was trying to make excuses, and said, rather bitterly: "If that's how you feel now, what would you say if you'd not passed?" Since seeing her, I've had a more than usually sibylline letter from L., that man of mystery. M. must have taken her grievance to him. In it he seems to be gently pulling my leg, and makes certain references which I don't quite understand to "the possible consequences of my attitude."

I'm a good deal bothered about all that business. I've promised to bicycle over and see M. at her home (it's a lovely ride), but the arrangement was that she should drop me a line saying when she'd like me to come. She sent me a card telling me of her arrival, but so far not a word about my visit. She's sulking and pretending that she isn't.

So here, my dear Epistemon, you have somewhat of the deeds and notable reflections of your brother Jean des Entommeures. He longs to see you and would give a good deal to have you here for a few days.

Joking apart, it would be wonderful if you could manage it. Do you realize, my dear fellow, that our ways of life are bound to lie apart? I think constantly about this, and it weighs on my spirits. Oh, I know we shall write, and arrange meetings, but the jolly intimacy of these three last years will be gone, with its freedom, its absurdities, and all the silly little adventures (they were really so vastly important) with which it filled our days. It's an appalling prospect when one really thinks of it. Temperamentally, I'm in love with the future; I'm not one of those who greet life with an eye turned nostalgically backwards, but I have a lively and painful sense of what things have meant to me, when the time comes to leave them behind. I know that we shall not cease to be friends, at least I hope not; but I am going to lose your companionship, and I realize now what a spreading prospect, what a whole world, it has meant to me. I have hopes that the loss of mine will leave in your life, too, a little gap. The day we first really got to know each other, do you remember, you said—so many of your sayings are written in my heart—you said: "A time comes in all men's lives—and we're very near it—when the question of friendship, I think, is settled once and for all, or more or less settled. . . ." That was the day, too, that you said that you realized how short life was, and you spoke of a terrible sense of loneliness. . . . We mustn't, my dear chap, let that "loneliness" come between us, must we?

There's another thing that's drawing to a close: a definite period in our existences (which, as you say, are terribly short). I want both of us to have lovely and exciting stretches in our lives. You will, I know. But let us not say good-bye to these three years which seem so unimportant, but which were so oddly full and rich, without a little tribute of tenderness. Yes, odd they were, unusual, extraordinary, inimitable, and perfect (don't forget how deeply attached you are to the idea of the *perfect life*).

So do come here, old man. Give me that pleasure. We will put upon our three years the seal of a few unique days. Because it will be a unique experience to walk through these larch woods, to climb these cliffs, to tread these fields that hang above a view that stretches for thirty miles or more, to do, in short, what I do every day, but with you at my side, discussing the world and everything in it as we used to do. I will take you to little mountain inns in upland valleys. You will see men in blue smocks drinking in corners; you will eat of sausages hung from the ceiling.

Let's make that a reality, old man. We shall never regret it. Drop me a line or send a telegram. I will meet you at the Puy station. You can stay with me. You needn't bother about anything.

I shall expect you.

Yours always,

JEAN DES ENTOMMEURES

Chapter

JALLEZ'S ANSWER

My dear Old Man:

The end of your letter did the trick. Up to this morning I had made other plans, and now, at the last moment, I must knock them endways. You made use of certain passwords before which even castle gates must open.

I shall take an evening train the day after tomorrow (Wednesday). I've not yet had time to get an up-to-date time-table to make sure of the exact hour, but you see which train I mean. If there seems any chance of your making a mistake, I'll telegraph.

You're right. Nothing else matters. If we can spend three or four days on your mountain-top like some of the days we have spent here, it will be something so precious that I'm convinced we shall remember it to our dying days.

As a matter of fact, when your letter came I was just in the right mood for it. I passed yesterday evening with Tellière and Gentilcœur, and I found the experience so—how shall I put it?—so moving, so shattering, that I hardly got a wink of sleep all night.

Why? I really don't know. The thing's beyond explaining. Those two fellows have always had a curious effect on me, but yesterday it was stronger than anything I'd ever felt before.

You remember what the Place du Tertre and the Place du Calvaire look like? Well, they've taken a shabby ground floor in an old house at the top of the steps, on the left-hand side. It consists of three big rooms communicating with one another, and a kitchen opening straight on a terrace—a terrace paved with cracked flagstones and pebbles black with age, edged with a peeling balustrade, and adorned with a few musty old plaster pots of honeysuckle. They've fitted the

place up with some bits of furniture which look as though they'd
been there from the year one. The terrace is very broad. One can see
the whole immense stretch of Paris, its creeping mists, its darkness,
and its lights. Wherever you are, you can see it, from the depths of
each of the three rooms, from the kitchen sink. When one turns one's
back on the view and looks at a wall or the panels of a door, one sees
on the door a sort of dim radiance which has a thrilling quality,
because it is, as it were, the reflection of all that vast panorama.

But the two men themselves are more thrilling than anything else.
I've never before felt it so impossible to explain what I mean, what I
felt. (That's the reason I didn't sleep.) I was always rather silly when
I spoke about them to you. You think of them as just a couple of
buffoons, two rather vulgar men who live comfortably. If you do, it's
my fault. They're not that at all. The only other person there besides
myself was a charming young woman who is, I think, Tellière's
mistress. The whole thing might have been an ordinary enough,
not very amusing, art-student evening, instead of which it was a
triumph from beginning to end. I sat there as full of amazement as
though I'd been watching some incredibly graceful ballet, or as
though I'd been looking at one of those old masters in which we see
some familiar scene, yet never get bored with the miracle that has set
it there.

They had arranged a dinner, or, rather, a snack, with a few dishes
made out of nothing at all, and a good supply of drinks. When it was
over, they served—I say served deliberately—coffee on the terrace.
There was a subtlety, an intelligence, a lightness, about everything
they did, whether it was setting the cups or placing and spacing the
wicker arm-chairs. I can only explain it all properly by saying what
it was *not*. You know the idiotic and disgusting way some people
have of doing things, so that even when they pour out coffee they
seem to be displaying a sort of idiotic middle-class complacency.
Well, it was just the reverse of that. And yet there was nothing laboured about it, nothing heavily deliberate. One felt that they were
just going on with some lovely picnic which had begun a long time

ago, to which they had admitted one with a friendly smile of welcome, without thinking it necessary to explain the usages and ritual of their lives or the allusions of their talk. What was their talk about? I hardly like to quote any actual sentence in isolation from the whole. All I know is that I laughed almost without stopping, not loudly, but with a sense of comfort and release.

The young woman laughed too, frequently, and rather more loudly than I did. My hosts didn't laugh at all. I don't mean that they gave themselves any solemn airs. They smiled, and now and then they exchanged a candid glance or two.

All this presupposes considerable natural gifts and a background of civilized behaviour so mellow that there was not the slightest trace of effort about it. It was as though they *gave out* something. Every incident, no matter how trivial, seemed drenched, one seemed drenched oneself, in a kind of magnetic influence which emanated from those two men. That's what makes it so difficult to give any specific example of what I mean, to describe it all so that you can understand. You remember one day when I was telling you about them—I think it was on that long walk we took to Saint-Ouen—how I quoted as an example of what I meant those schoolboy "gangs" which manage to maintain a never ceasing atmosphere of happiness. If one tried to describe to a stranger the sort of things those schoolboys did, he would merely say: "I don't see anything very funny about that."

I see that even what I have said in this letter makes it all seem less important than it was. It's as though I'd been talking of two amateur clowns performing charades for the amusement of themselves and their friends. I'd have done better if I'd stressed the *poetic* quality of the evening. The state of mind they get one into resembles more than anything else that sort of transmutation of one's whole being which is produced when one reads genuine poetry (the effect of one's first discovery of Verlaine or Francis Jammes). Everything seems to yield to the rush of the verse, to be bathed in the glory that comes from the book and persists long after the book is closed.

The miracle that Tellière and Gentilcœur achieve is of the same sort. If they were merely "amusing," if they did nothing more than take one out of oneself—like two good clowns—that would still be something; but they do much more, or it would be truer to say that much more "gets done" under the influence of their presence. All the ideas and worries, personal or otherwise, all the judgments of life, all the fretting torments and calculations which one brings with one, undergo an amazing, an alchemical change. It's as though the whole of life had been transposed. These two admirable performers just introduce the necessary number of sharps and flats, and the whole of life is set singing in a totally different key. This was very noticeable yesterday evening. I was terribly worried when I went there, really terribly—something to do with my family, which touched me only through my family, but which was a source of acute torment to me; and you know how unfortunately prone I am to torments of that kind. This particular worry came on top of my general anxiety at the present situation (you'd be quite wrong if you thought that my "detachment" kept me from sharing in national anxieties; my "detachment" is probably nothing but a sort of defence mechanism to save me from too great an absorption in things). Well, I should have been sufficiently grateful if, thanks to them, I'd been able to pass four hours without thinking about my troubles, but what happened was far better than that. *I found I could think about them as much as I liked.* That didn't prevent my feeling a sort of gurgling stream of comfort running through all my being. Even this morning when I got up I felt all the better for it, and I was still under the beneficent influence when I got your letter. The proof of it is that I at once decided to recapture a bit of the perfect life with you on your mountaintops.

I'm not forgetting their terrace, their large old shabby rooms, with the long windows opening on the cracked paving-stones and the dirty gravel, the reflection in the door-panels, and there before one a view over Paris with sublimity enough and to spare, a wonderful midsummer twilight, deepening into a night full of drifting mist, the sounds, the lights, the vibrant bass of that incomparable horizon. But all that is part of their excellence. Where they live and how they live is the result of their conscious choice; it didn't just come of itself.

Till Thursday, then. I've said nothing about your letter and all the staggering things it contains, because we're going to talk our fill about all that—since you're charming enough to want to—on the roads and footpaths of your homeland, treading the larch woods and the high mountain pastures (when it comes to *position,* we shan't do so badly).

To be quite sure, I'll send you a telegram when I've consulted a time-table and fixed up the details of my journey. But don't be frightened that I shall change my mind. My intention is as firm as a rock.

Ever yours fraternally,

PIERRE JALLEZ

Chapter

THE MOUNTAIN INN

"Don't you really think you could manage an omelet? Oh, come on! We've got at least five miles more to do—three, or three and a half, and then two. . . . By the time we're home we shall have been on the go not much short of eight hours. Besides, you don't know what their omelets are like!"

They were seated at a table set close to the wall. Two other tables, one in the middle of the room, the other in one of its corners, were occupied by men in smocks and large circular hats, carrying goads or long whips, the butts of which they rested on the ground. These men were conversing in local dialect, sometimes confidentially, with their heads all leaned together, sometimes in loud bursts accompanied by dramatic-sounding oaths and queer, shrill ejaculations and much noisy slapping of the tables.

"Can you understand?"

"Fairly well, when I catch what they're saying. But every now and then there's a word or a whole phrase which differs entirely from those in use at Saint-Pierre. It's extraordinary how these living dialects, unstandardized by writing or the printed page, differ in vocabulary and shades of meaning from village to village. On the other hand, when, as sometimes happens, one of those wandering harvest hands from Spain comes along, they seem to be able to get along with him perfectly well. In all this old vast stretch of country, deriving linguistically from the Latin heritage, in which scarcely any two hamlets speak alike, there seems to be a generally comprehensible basic tongue."

The woman of the inn had set the stove on the fire-dogs. It was an enormous erection made of that black, dull-surfaced iron which used to be turned out by village smithies in the old days. The metal was almost a finger's width in thickness. A sort of long continuation, like the handle of a fork, as big round as a crowbar, projected to the height of the woman's breast. From the chimney-piece hung a long chain fitted with two pulleys, between which this continuation was adjusted. The smell of wood-smoke mingled with that of the curing meat which hung from the beams.

"What a curious taste this wine has! Where does it come from? Surely there are no local vineyards?"

"It's probably some quite ordinary Southern wine, but it's stored in caves in the hillside, and that gives it this light, fresh, stony flavour."

Jallez was thinking: "Even in this smoky room I can feel how high we are. The air loses none of its purity."

He waggled his left leg and made a face.

"Are you tired?"

"A bit. Just a comfortable sort of laziness. . . . But I rather think I've got a blister on my foot."

Having finished their sausage, they set to work on the omelet. Rather anxiously Jerphanion asked:

"You really do like this country?"

"Tremendously."

"You're not saying that just to please me?"

"I more than like it; I'm obsessed by it. If I don't say much, it's from a feeling of awe. I didn't expect such grandeur, such a feeling of timelessness. It's as though we were on the roof of the world."

"What about it has struck you most up to now?"

"The moorlands—so high, with such a sweep of view, in which everything's so visible. The villages, which seem to have been here for a thousand years, like the one we passed through just now. The wind. One feels that before nightfall it will have reached the Alps, that tomorrow it will be blowing across the Russian steppes, the next day over Asia."

"Then you're not sorry you came?"

"Of course I'm not! I've got a lovely feeling that I don't want to make any effort. I think this wine's gone to my head. All the things we talked about as we trudged over the moors are buzzing in my head like the dreams I shall have tonight in that great bed you've given me. It's enough for me just to think that we're together, that whatever happens, old man, this day will be our very own for ever."

Chapter

SURELY YOU WON'T PUNISH FRANCE?

As soon as Geoffroy came into the room—for some time past he had taken to wearing a single eye-glass like his chief—Courson made as though to go. But Manifassier stopped him.

"Please stay."

Then, addressing Geoffroy:

"You've come on routine business, I imagine?"

"Well—yes—oh, certainly. But business of a rather particular kind."

He showed by a slight movement of the eye that he didn't consider Courson's presence to be very desirable.

But Manifassier pretended to have noticed nothing and addressed the newcomer on a note of rather forced joviality:

"Yes, yes . . . well, take a seat. . . . I think Monsieur Courson may be very useful to us. . . . You know, of course, that Monsieur Gurau has the fullest confidence in him."

"No doubt—but—excuse me for speaking plainly—what I have to say concerns only Monsieur Gurau's personal staff."

"Monsieur Courson is not a member of the personal staff, but you can talk as freely as though he were. When the interest of the service is at stake, we have no secrets from one another."

Geoffroy did not flinch under the allusion, but seemed to resign himself to the inevitable, sat down in front of Manifassier's desk, adjusted his eye-glass, and smoothed his handsome moustache. Courson resumed his chair, pushing it back to a point midway between the desk and the corner of the room.

"It's all rather awkward," said Geoffroy. "You see, I'm charged with a somewhat delicate mission from the Prime Minister. . . . He can't quite make out what's happening. . . . He's been trying to get Monsieur Gurau on the telephone for the last two days without success. . . ."

"Monsieur Gurau has had a good many personal worries. . . . His mother is ill."

"Really? Now, that's very annoying. . . . You know, of course, that there's a Cabinet meeting called for tomorrow?"

"Yes, the news had reached us," said Manifassier on a note of irony.

"There's no fear, I suppose," said Geoffroy with an air of concern, "that Monsieur Gurau's family troubles will prevent him from being present?"

"None at all."

"That's good. . . . The Prime Minister would have liked to have a word with him first. Tomorrow's meeting will be almost entirely concerned with the Berlin negotiations and a discussion of the general lines of the proposed agreement, and the Prime Minister wanted to talk over—procedure with Monsieur Gurau. He is particularly anxious that the Foreign Secretary should give the Cabinet a résumé of everything that's happened since the Agadir incident. . . . He doesn't want to go to the meeting without first discussing with Monsieur Gurau the substance and the wording of the suggested arrangement. Certain points are still rather provisional, and then there's the question of how best to phrase it, of the right line to take in defending it before the Chamber. . . . It's essential that it be unanimously agreed upon."

"Monsieur Gurau has received the little memorandum which the Prime Minister sent him two days ago. I know that he's carefully considered it. It follows, therefore, that he's fully aware of the latest developments."

"Yes, but what is his opinion?"

Manifassier raised his shoulders in a gesture of caution.

"That I can't say."

"Has he said nothing to you? It's most important that we should have some idea."

Manifassier smiled slightly, again shrugged his shoulders, and glanced at Courson, who was looking very innocent in his corner.

Then:

"If Monsieur Gurau has any objections to the text, I imagine that he will make them known."

"Yes, but when? At the Cabinet meeting?"

"Possibly."

Geoffroy started and let his monocle drop.

"You don't really think so! That would be disastrous!"

There was a silence. Then Geoffroy continued on a new, more confidential note:

"I think I ought to tell you that the Prime Minister is deeply concerned at the attitude which Monsieur Gurau seems to have been taking up recently. For instance, at the last meetings of the inner Cabinet, he felt that Monsieur Gurau was extremely, even excessively, non-committal. More than once Monsieur Caillaux asked his advice and invited him to express his point of view on the general question, if he wanted to and if he thought it differed from the official attitude. But Monsieur Gurau always avoided the issue. That he said nothing might, of course, be interpreted to mean that he agreed, but it'll be a shocking thing now if, after letting the Prime Minister commit himself completely and in all good faith, Monsieur Gurau puts himself in opposition."

Manifassier, glancing again at Courson, repressed the reply it was on the tip of his tongue to make. He merely said:

"What makes you afraid that Monsieur Gurau would do a thing like that?"

"Well—you see—I mean—" Geoffroy looked uneasily towards Courson. "I don't know that I ought to say what I was going to say before this gentleman, but I have your authority to speak freely, haven't I? It seems that a rumour has been going about, these last

573

few days, which has come to the Prime Minister's ears. It's said that Monsieur Gurau means to resign. . . ."

Manifassier's gesture of astonishment was apparently quite sincere.

". . . and to resign rather dramatically. The Prime Minister has naturally put two and two together, with the result that he wonders —once more I must apologize for talking like this—whether it may not be Monsieur Gurau's intention to make this rather conspicuous gesture of resignation at tomorrow's meeting. . . . I'm sure you realize the importance of getting this quite clear. If the Foreign Secretary has any serious objections to raise, if he thinks that the Cabinet policy is misguided, let him say so before it is too late. The Prime Minister is perfectly ready to discuss the whole situation with him frankly and at length. He is willing to go over all the clauses of the agreement one by one and to submit them to the strictest examination. There's nothing he wouldn't do to satisfy Monsieur Gurau, but he can't allow Monsieur Gurau to give him a stab in the back by resigning suddenly at a Cabinet meeting without due warning. Nobody in his position could. . . . You must see that it's a question for Monsieur Gurau of loyalty to his colleagues. . . ."

Manifassier made a sharp movement, which he quickly repressed. He allowed himself, however, to appeal to Courson by a jerk of the head which as good as said: "Well, of all the cheek!" Courson smiled, glanced at Geoffroy, and then lowered his gaze to the corner of the table.

"There's one thing I should like to ask," Manifassier said to Geoffroy. "Is your chief's conscience perfectly clear in the matter of his behaviour to mine?"

"I don't understand."

"Dear me, you don't understand. . . ." Manifassier turned over in his mind all the ways of saying what he wanted to say as indirectly, as bitingly, as politely, as he could. He was perfectly well aware that he was probably exceeding Gurau's wishes in thus showing his hand so openly, but the temptation was too strong. He was trembling with indignation and aggressiveness. "Ah," he said again, "so you don't understand." Courson shot him an anxious look which meant: "Look out, control yourself!" but the young man was still seeking some formula that should be at the same time cutting and yet not too outspoken.

Geoffroy interrupted quietly:

"I don't see. . . . I was not present at all their meetings. . . . My impression was that during these past months the Prime Minister had done all he could to keep in touch with Monsieur Gurau, to do nothing without informing him, to make sure of his reactions, even to go out of his way to get them. . . . It's not been his fault if—"

"Since when has the Prime Minister taken all these precautions—which, by the way, are the least he could do?—or appeared to take them? . . . Because—"

"But—I don't know—I—"

"Well, then, I'll tell you. Since the 22nd of August. About what happened between the 1st of July and the 22nd of August, I'll tell you what I think, as man to man and in perfect confidence, and that is that your chief behaved like a cad!"

Courson repeated his wordless signs of distress. Manifassier replied with a gesture the meaning of which was: "Leave me alone, I know what I'm doing."

"I don't know in detail what may have happened at the time you speak of," answered Geoffroy, who seemed like a man on the rack, "but I wonder whether you weren't wrongly informed. . . ." He regained a little of his lost confidence and continued: "Whether the whole thing wasn't a misunderstanding deliberately engineered by those who wanted to drive a wedge between the Prime Minister and Monsieur Gurau. . . ."

Manifassier countered with harsh incisiveness:

"My dear fellow, you really needn't bother. . . . I can assure you —this, too, is between ourselves—that we have ample proof of the direct negotiations that were initiated by Monsieur Caillaux with Berlin. Since you don't want a scandal, don't force us to make one. But when you come here in the name of your chief to read us a lesson in loyalty—well, it's rather too much, that's all."

Geoffroy looked Manifassier up and down for a moment, glanced towards Courson, and sighed. The muscles round his monocle quivered slightly. Finally he rubbed his well-kept hands together.

"My dear sir," he began in a more serious, a more sincere and more human tone than any he had used up till then, "I have no right to doubt your word. . . . Nor have I any right, as you know well, to pass a personal judgment on those facts of the case which are duly established. I am very fond of my chief. I admire him. He has many faults which harm him more than they harm other people. But he's more far-sighted than most, and more than most he knows how to combine personal ambition—legitimate enough, God knows! —with a passion for the public weal. . . . I know him well. . . . I know that he's thoughtless and impulsive, and that even with people he respects—and I can assure you that he has the greatest respect for your chief, that he ranks him very high—he is apt to forget how he ought to behave. I'll go further, and say that he forgets sometimes that other people have any right to consideration. . . . He's perfectly capable, without any ill intention, without even thinking twice about it, of doing things that are bound to hurt people's feelings. He loves all the business of intrigue, the combining of groups and individuals into patterns, and he won't trust anybody but himself at the game. But don't forget this, Manifassier"—there crept into Geoffroy's voice a note of emotional sincerity which came oddly from a man of so smart and trivial an appearance—"because it's the one really important thing. . . . We've just managed to scrape out of having a war . . . or, rather, because it's unwise to count one's chickens before they're hatched, we're almost certainly going to scrape out of it, and we've got off cheaply. You can take my word for it that my chief has had but that one object before his eyes, and that the ingenuity, the power of invention, the adaptability which he has shown in handling the situation is almost beyond belief. I've watched him at work and I know. Short of accepting the challenge and declaring war, nobody, as things were a few weeks ago, could have come better out of the mess. War—well, leaving aside any general views that you and I may have about war, you know what Joffre said when the Prime Minister asked him his opinion point-blank. . . . Look here, Manifassier, what's a little personal huff compared with such an achievement? Oh, don't think I don't realize how angry your chief is. It's not for me to criticize him, but wouldn't he have done better, Caillaux being Caillaux, to have had it all out with him frankly instead of keeping the grievance to himself and brooding over it? There might have been hard words between them, but they'd have understood each other in the end. Monsieur Caillaux is a kindly man at heart. No doubt he would have found excuses for acting as he did, but he'd have done it charmingly. . . ."

Manifassier made a face and shook his head.

"All that would have happened would have been that they would have broken then and there!"

"You really think so? Well, even that would have been better than— But the point is that now, at whatever cost, we must avoid a scene. There must be no rupture. It would mean the end of everything. You know as well as I do what a weak-kneed, hypocritical lot this Government is. Most of them are terrified at the thought of responsibility. For two pins they'd leave the Prime Minister in the lurch, and then good-bye to any hope of a settlement. . . . There can be no two opinions about that; and if that happens, my dear fellow, we shall be mobilizing in four days and at war in six. Look me in the face and deny it if you can!"

Manifassier, deeply moved, could say nothing.

". . . You must know," went on Geoffroy, "that a change of policy on our part at this stage, following on and strengthened by the resignation of the Foreign Secretary, even an attempt to refer the matter again to Berlin, a reopening of all the fundamental questions at the last minute after we'd managed, in spite of every kind of difficulty, to reach a basis of agreement, would be regarded by the Germans as the worst kind of affront. They're sensitive enough already about what they regard as our former rebuffs, and there's only one answer they could make—an ultimatum, the withdrawal of Herr von Schoen, and the closing of the frontiers. . . ."

"I must say," interrupted Manifassier who was not displeased to find a chance of making a minor point, "it's rather comic to hear you, of all people, talking about our former rebuffs to Germany! When I think of what your chief's attitude was in the Ngoko-Sangha affair! Has he told you that Monsieur Gurau approached him last March with a request to support him in a protest to Monsieur Cruppi? Has he happened to mention what his attitude was then? . . ."

"My dear chap . . . I don't mind confessing that he was utterly in the wrong. . . . I know perfectly well that my chief took an erroneous view of that matter, or that, it may be, he thought it ill-timed. . . . I know too that last winter his position was open to criticism, that he allowed himself to be blinded by the immediate requirements of domestic politics . . . that's all part of his impulsive temperament. . . . Would you rather he'd stuck to his mistake and landed us in a war for fear of being inconsistent? . . . I've said once, and I say again, that I'm here with full authority from him to admit his mistake. I can't believe that just in order to punish him you're willing to punish France with a war—and what a war! To do that would be a monstrous crime!"

Manifassier sat with his head sunk, thinking.

"We're the same age, you and I," went on the other. "We've not yet become such dried-up civil servants as to see everything in terms of personal pique and personal prestige like rival shopkeepers. Time enough for that to happen, and it will happen sure enough if we stick to the job!"

"But what do you want me to do?" Manifassier exclaimed.

"Prevent your chief from handing in his resignation tomorrow, and keep him from doing anything to imperil the agreement. He's a man of intelligence and a man of heart. . . . If you talk to him he'll understand. It's not a question of asking him to be false to his policy or his ideals. Just the reverse. What's he been fighting for all this time if not for a policy of understanding with Germany, an easing up of tension, a policy of peace? I admit that he has a right to be annoyed at the way Monsieur Caillaux has behaved, but he has no right to pretend that Monsieur Caillaux's policy is wrong, or that he has failed to obtain as much as anyone could possibly have obtained without taking the appalling risk of a war—of a war, don't forget, that would involve the whole of Europe!"

Manifassier remained plunged in thought, occasionally exchanging a glance with Courson, who since the beginning of the interview had maintained the silence of a specialist who was present only to be consulted, and had no right to intervene in the discussion unless his opinion was asked.

Manifassier got up and held out his hand to Geoffroy.

"I'll do what I can . . . with the help of Monsieur Courson here, who, though he has said nothing, has thought the more. Whatever the result may be, I should like to say that you have behaved like a gentleman. For your sake I promise to do everything in my power. But I hope, all the same, that you'll give your chief a thorough dressing down—if you're on those terms with him—and tell him that Monsieur Gurau will be even with him yet. If we don't play him a dirty trick tomorrow—and, mind, I can say nothing definite, I give no pledge—it won't be for his sake, but for the sake of the Republic and of Peace. He needn't think we're fools."

GURAU'S STOICISM

From four o'clock that afternoon Manifassier and Courson had been talking to their chief without a break. Now it was getting dark, and no one had thought of turning on the lights. The last of the autumn daylight was fading from the mouldings of Colbert's desk. They had spoken each in turn, sometimes both together, taking the words from one another's mouth, interrupting each other, qualifying each other's statements. Since half past four Gurau had said nothing. He had sat with an expressionless face, giving vent now and then to non-committal phrases such as "Yes, I understand," "I follow you," "You needn't go over that again, I see exactly what you mean," or "Have a cigarette?"

Suddenly Courson and Manifassier noticed a slight change in their chief's face. They realized that he had listened long enough and might have something to say in his turn.

They ceased speaking. Gurau leaned towards the ash-tray, and there was a long pause while with great deliberation he removed the ash from the end of his cigarette.

They got the impression that he was waiting to control his voice before replying, so that when he spoke it should be with clearness and vigour. Then he raised his head. He did not look at them, and when his words came, they were as unemotional as he could make them.

"All right," he said. "I shall not hand in my resignation tomorrow."

SUMMARY

Stephen Bartlett's travel diary; the powers that be in France; conversation with Torchecoul and Maykosen.

Gurau refuses the Ministry of Labour offered to him by Monis. He has an altercation with a conductor on the subway; returns to Monis and accepts the position of Minister of Public Works. A smart dinner-party given by the Comtesse Lambron de Crauze. Gurau sits next to the beautiful Mme Godorp. He finishes the evening with a young creole.

Laulerque renews acquaintance with Margaret-Désideria, who has turned up suddenly in Paris. They discuss the Organization. Laulerque is disturbed by what he discovers about the secret society and by the young woman's attitude. He confesses his uneasiness to Mascot, who gives him discreet advice.

Jerphanion, after re-reading Clanricard's article, is seized with remorse and decides to make overtures to him. He offers to give up Mathilde.

Gurau, with the help of Manifassier, goes through the postmen's records. He receives a visit from a certain Monsieur Courson, one of the senior officials of the Foreign Office. The Ngoko-Sangha agreement; the urgent need of its ratification. Gurau talks the matter over with Caillaux and tells Manifassier what has happened. They discuss plans.

Laulerque pays a visit to the White House, and watches its inhabitants from a place of concealment.

Spring in Paris and the suburbs. The mill of Sannois. Country restaurants on a Sunday morning; what they stand for.—Edmond and Georgette, as the guests of Romuald and Isabelle, celebrate the young ruffian's acquittal.

Roland de Lommérie writes a letter home to his father from Morocco, describing life with the column which is marching to the relief of Fez, and his impressions of the campaign. His enthusiasm and preoccupations.

Gurau and Manifassier, attending the start of the Paris-Madrid air race, are witnesses of the accident which results in the death of Berteaux and leads to a reshuffling of the Government.

A confidential conversation between Mme de Crauze and her daughter, in the course of which Mme Godorp's love for Gurau is revealed and her disappointments discussed.

Gurau is offered the post of Foreign Secretary in Caillaux's Ministry.

In the course of one of Jallez's long walks through Paris we are reintroduced to his innermost thoughts and are informed of the state of his mind in June 1911.

Gurau and Manifassier dine together and draw up a plan of campaign to be observed in their dealings with the Foreign Office. Their first step is to call in Courson. Gurau invites him to make a résumé of the general state of Franco-German relations. Mutual attitude of the two countries in the past. Hanotaux's policy. Delcassé's policy. The perils and possibilities of the moment. Gurau's good intentions. A curt note from Herr von Schoen. Agadir.

Champcenais, while staying at the Zülpichers' château, indulges in silent adoration of Christine Zülpicher. He discusses with the steel-magnate the chances of war, and together they examine the best way of turning the situation to their advantage. The oil-king composes a sonnet to Christa, after which he writes to his wife. At midnight he knocks at Christa's door, and she admits him for a few minutes, much against her will. She punishes his attempts at intimacy. His enjoyment of the punishment.

Manifassier anxiously awaits the upshot of a talk between Gurau and Herr von Schoen. Courson telephones to him. He tells Gurau what Courson has revealed to him about the Prime Minister's direct and secret negotiations with Berlin.

Jerphanion, after successfully passing his examination, takes a holiday in his native village and writes to Jallez, who has also succeeded in getting his degree. His delight at having finished his training, and his meditation on the subject of security. The larger aspects of the question. He invites Jallez to pay a visit to the Haute-Loire. Jallez agrees to come and tells Jerphanion about an evening he has spent with Tellière and Gentilcœur.—Jerphanion and Jallez at a mountain inn.

Geoffroy, one of Caillaux's personal staff, makes certain proposals to Manifassier. Caillaux is worried about Gurau's attitude, and fears that he may offer his resignation. Manifassier, implored by Geoffroy to intervene, relieves his feelings to the latter, but finally yields, and promises to do what he can to persuade Gurau.—Supported by Courson, he succeeds in persuading Gurau, despite his sense of grievance, not to upset Caillaux's policy and wreck the Franco-German agreement by handing in his resignation.

INDEX OF CHARACTERS
Note regarding the use of this INDEX

This Index will figure at the end of every volume, and will be extended as necessary.

Large roman numerals refer to the Book.

Small roman numerals refer to the chapter.

Arabic numerals refer to the page.

If there is *no page reference,* this means that the character takes part in the *whole* of the chapter indicated.

When a chapter or a page is given *in brackets,* this means that the character is involved, but does not take part personally in the action.

EXAMPLES

I, x. Refer to Chapter x, Book I, where the character plays an important role.

I, xviii, 149. Refer to page 149, Book I (Chapter xviii), where the character appears only incidentally.

II, (xi). Refer to Chapter xi, Book II; a chapter which, as a whole, involves the character, though he is not personally present.

II, xv, (391). As above; the character is involved only on page 391.

In the case of important events the reference is preceded by a brief summary of the event.

Proper names extraneous to the action, and intended to remain so, are not included in the Index.

INDEX OF CHARACTERS

(xvii).—The subject of an anonymous letter, VII, (xx).—Returns from a meeting with Jallez; her thoughts, VII, xxi.—Has a scene with her husband, VII, xxii.—Discussed by Jerphanion and Maurice Ezzelin, VII, (xxviii).—Questioned by Jallez, VII, xxxii.—X, xvi, (472-3).

EZZELIN, MAURICE, I, (vi).—Reads the paper, II, i.—II, xx, 448.—Receives an anonymous letter, VII, xx.—VII, xxi, (173).—Has a scene with his wife, VII, xxii.—Goes to see Jallez and is received by Jerphanion, VII, xxviii.—VII, (xxix).—VIII, ii, (321).—VIII, iii, (322).

FAGUET, IX, xxxiv, (270).—IX, xxxvii, (287).

FARMERS, their life, tastes, and habits, VIII, xiv.—VIII, xv.

FONDÈRE, X, xxvi, (550).

FOREST-RANGER OF THE FORÊT D'OTHE, THE, (xx).—V, xxiii, (181, 184-7), 187.

FOREST-RANGER, WIFE OF THE, V, (xx).—V, xxiii, 187.

FORILLON, IX, vi, (55).—IX, vii, (62).

FORT, PAUL, IV, xx.—At the Closerie on Christmas Eve, IV, xxii.—VIII, xii, (429).

FREEMASONRY, IV, x.—V, xxiv, (199).—VII, ii.—VII, vi, (43).—VII, vii, (46-7, 57).—Rothweil's, VII, xviii.—VII, xxiii, (182).—Discussed by Jerpha-

nion and Laulerque, VII, xxvi, (196-8, 200-1).—As Ardansseaux sees it, VII, xxvii.—As Lengnau sees its, VII, xxxi.—Clanricard's first impressions, VII, xxxiii, (297-8).—VIII, i, (311).—VIII, xxv, (533).—IX, v, (50).—IX, vii, (64).—IX, xix, (136).

FRIEND OF GERMAINE BAADER, VIII, xi, 413-21.

FROSINE, IX, xxix, (230).

FRUITERER IN THE RUE DAILLOUD, THE, I, xii.—II, vii.

G—, MADAME, IX, xix.

GAMBAROUX, FIRMIN, VIII, vii, (365).—VIII, xiii, (443, 445-6, 453-4, 456).—Among his friends, VIII, xiv.—His thoughts and preoccupations, VIII, xv.—His first meeting with Mionnet, VIII, xvi.—Their drive together, VIII, xvii.—VIII, xviii, (479, 480).—VIII, xxvi, (540).

GAMBAROUX, MADAME, VIII, xiv, (459).—VIII, xv, (467, 469).

GAMEKEEPERS AT THE WHITE HOUSE, THE, X, x, (420-1).

GENILLÉ, BARON DE, III, x, (115).—III, (xiii).—III, (xv).—III, xviii, (201).—V, xx, (139).—VI, iii, (307).

GENILLÉ, BARONNE DE, III, x, (115).—III, xiii.—III, xiv.—Talks about conjugal beds, III, xv.—VI, xxxi, (528).

GENTILCŒUR, MADAME, V, xxvii, (251).

GENTILCŒUR, and the "perfect

x

INDEX OF CHARACTERS

INDEX OF CHARACTERS

MANIFASSIER, LÉON, the young civil servant, I, (xiv).—II, xx, (449). —III, xvi, (181–2).—As Gurau's secretary guardian-angel, V, xxiv, 193, (194, 204–6).—V, xxv, (217).—IX, xxvii, (209).— Is present at the discussion of the Ngoko-Sangha agreement between Gurau and Courson, X, viii.—Questions Gurau about his interview with Caillaux, X, ix.—Accompanies Gurau to the start of the Paris-Madrid air race, X, xiv.—Reconsiders nominations for the Legion of Honour, X, xv, 459–61.—Helps Gurau map a plan of campaign, X, xvii.—X, xviii.—Is present at the discussion of the Franco-German situation between Gurau and Courson, X, xix.—X, xx.—Is warned by Courson, X, xxv.—Reveals Caillaux's activities to Gurau, X, xxvi.—Geoffroy defends Caillaux to him, X, xxx. —X, xxxi.

MAREIL, HENRY, at the supper given to Germaine Baader, VII, ix.—His origins, his love of France, his nom de plume; his uncertainty about Germaine, VII, x.—VII, (xi).—VIII, xi, (417, 420–1).—Spends a night with Germaine at Celle, VIII, xxiv.—IX, vi, (51–2).—X, iv, (349).

MARGARET-DÉSIDERIA, see KREUZ, MARGARET-DÉSIDERIA.

MARGUSSOLES, MONSIEUR DE, V, ix, (65).—V, xii, (79).—V, xxii.

MARILHAT, Inspector of Police, interrogates Quinette, II, xiii.— Shows him photographs, II, xvi. —Gives him some professional reminiscences, II, xviii.—Is offered his services by Quinette, III, xxi.—Listens to his report on "Social Control," IV, xvi.— Lunches with Quinette in the suburbs and talks to him about the murder in the quarries, VI, xxx.

MARJAURIE, "Number One," orders the "Quel Khon for the Pot," III, iii.—Author of a confidential note on Jerphanion, VII, xviii, (146–8).—VIII, xi, (423).

MARQUIS, II, (xi).—IV, xi, (378). —VII, ix.—VII, xi, (98–9).— VIII, xi, (416).—VIII, xxiv, (524).

MARTINET, X, viii, (400).

MASCOT, receives Laulerque and tells of a secret society, VII, (vii). —VIII, vi, (344, 346, 347).— IX, xx, (140).—Introduces Laulerque to M. Karl, IX, xxii.— IX, xxiii (164–5).—IX, xxxi.— IX, xxxiii.—X, v, (370).—With Laulerque; the mysteries of the Organization, X, vi.

MASSON, JACQUES, X, iv.—X, xv, (454, 455).

MASSON, SIMONE, helps her mother place the dinner guests, X, iv.— Asks her about Mme Godorp's feelings, X, xv.

MAUDUIT, III, xix, (219–21).

MAURRAS, CHARLES, VII, x, (91–2). —VIII, xxi, (501).—IX, xxxvii,

xxv.—Writes to him, II, (vi).
—Is nicer to him than ever, II, x.
—Pays a visit to Allory, who shows himself very gallant, III, xviii.—IV, i, (284).

Monis, offers Gurau the Ministry of Labour, X, ii.—Gives him that of Public Works, X, iii.—X, viii, (397).—Seriously injured at Issy-les-Moulineaux, X, xiv.—X, xv, (458).

Montech, Madame de, VIII, xxi, (500).

Montech, Monsieur de, III, xi.—VIII, v, (329, 342).—VIII, xxi, (500, 502, 503).

Montech, Second Lieutenant de, VIII, xxi, (500).

Montech, Uncle de, VIII, xxi, (500-1, 503).

Montéhus, curses the police, V, xxviii, 270.

Montsauche, Councillor de, IX, xi, (88).—Talks with Mionnet, IX, xviii.—IX, (xix).

Moréas, Jean, IV, xx, (463, 464).—At the Closerie on Christmas Eve, IV, xxii.

Mother in the shack, the young, VI, xxix, (518).—Is visited by Abbé Jeanne, VI, xxxii.

Mun, Albert de, VII, xxiv, (188).—VII, xxv, (189-92).—IX, xxviii, (222).

Münster, de, X, xix, (498-9, 502).

Nephew, Zülpicher's young, X, xxiii.

Nieuwenhove, X, xx, (523).

Occupants of the White House, the, X, x.

Oil-dealers, the, I, (iii).—I, (xiv).—I, (xvi).—Hold a council of war, II, xiv.—II, (xv).—II, xx.—Their arrangement among themselves, III, xiii.—Their role in the past, III, (xvi).—How Gurau pretends to interpret their attitude towards him, IV, xi, (379-80).

Organization, the, Laulerque learns of its existence, VII, (vii).—VII, (viii).—He joins it, VII, (xxvi).—He is sent by it on a mission to Amsterdam, VIII, (vi).—IX, (xx).—He is introduced to an important member of it, IX, (xxii).—The house by the sea, IX, (xxiii).—Its aims and leaders half-revealed, IX, (xxiv).—Laulerque's ideas of it, IX, (xxv).—Laulerque gives a power of attorney for purchase of the White House, IX, (xxxi).—IX, (xxxiii).—Margaret's disquieting confidences, X, (v).—Laulerque and Mascot discuss its mysteries, X, (vi).—The White House and its occupants, X, (x).

Ortegal, IV, xxii.

Oyster-woman in the rue Ramey, the, VI, xxiv.

Painter, the Master, I, viii.—I, xiii.—I, (xx).—IV, ii, (287).

Pal, Maillecottin's, IX, xvii, (116).

Parampuyre, "Ma," VIII, xiv,

INDEX OF CHARACTERS

PENITENT, THE UNKNOWN, approaches Mionnet, V, XVI.—V, XVII, (112).—VIII, xxv, (530).
PERRIN, X, xxv, (546).
PICHON, IX, (VII).—IX, (XXVII). —IX, XXXII, (252–3, 255–6).— X, (VIII).—X, IX, (412–13).—X, XVII, (482).
POINCARÉ, X, IX, (416).
POINSINOT, MADAME, renovates the Sainte-Marthe school, VI, XXIX.
POLICE ORDERLY, THE, II, XVI, 409.
POLLETERON, ABBÉ, VII, XXX, (248).
PORCHERON, X, XXIII, (535).
PRESIDENT OF DEPARTMENTAL TRAMWAYS, THE, negotiates a bond-issue, VI, XIII.
PRESIDENT OF "SOCIAL CONTROL," THE, IV, XVI.
PRESIDENT OF THE FRENCH LOAN AND DISCOUNT CORPORATION, THE, argues with the president of Departmental Tramways, VI, XIII.
PROPRIETRESS OF THE CAFÉ IN THE BOULEVARD DE LA CHAPELLE, THE, VI, VI.
PROVOTAIS, YOUNG, VIII, XIV.— VIII, xv, (469).

QUINETTE, is visited by Juliette, I, VII.—The Herculex belt; irruption of the stranger, I, IX.— Makes inquiries in the neighbourhood, I, XII.—I, XVIII, 149.— Meets the stranger in the rue Saint-Antoine, I, XIX.—Accompanies him to the rue Taillepain, I, XXI.—Reads the report of the crime, II, II.—Takes Leheudry to Saint-Merri's, II, IV.—Under the arches in the rue de Lyon, II, V.—On the scene of the crime, II, VII.—At Sophie Parent's, in the rue Vandamme, II, VIII.— Rents the apartment in the faubourg Saint-Denis, II, IX.—His sleepless night, II, XII.—Goes to see the police superintendent, II, XIII.—II, xv, 405.—Is confronted with the photographs, II, XVI.— Takes Leheudry along the canal, II, XVII.—Listens to the inspector's reminiscences, II, XVIII.— His drowse and anticipatory dreams, II, XIX.—Takes, Leheudry to the gallery in the Bagnolet quarries, II, xx.—His memories since his murder of Leheudry, III, V.—Lives over again his hour of love after the murder, III, VI. —III, XVIII, (212).—Makes an offer to the police to spy on "Social Control," III, XXI.—Attends the "Social Control" meeting, IV, XVI.—Reports on it to the police, IV, XIX.—V, VI, (49). —V, XVIII, (116).—Spends an evening at Estrachard's, V, XXI. —Learns why Leheudry's murder was hushed up, VI, XXX.
QUINGEY, MADAME DE, VIII, VII, (365).—VIII, IX, (391–2).— VIII, XIII, (443, 445–6, 452–3). —VIII, XVIII, (479–80).—Meets Mionnet, VIII, xxv.—Makes a spiritual confidant of him, VIII, XXVI.—VIII, XXVII, (546, 548).— Warns Mionnet of rumours cir-

xxiv

A NOTE ON THE TYPE IN
WHICH THIS BOOK IS SET

This book is set in Granjon, a type named in compliment to ROBERT GRANJON, but neither a copy of a classic face nor an entirely original creation. George W. Jones drew the basic design for this type from classic sources, but deviated from his model to profit by the intervening centuries of experience and progress. This type is based primarily upon the type used by Claude Garamond (1510–61) in his beautiful French books, and more closely resembles Garamond's own than do any of the various modern types that bear his name.

Of Robert Granjon nothing is known before 1545, except that he had begun his career as type-cutter in 1523. The boldest and most original designer of his time, he was one of the first to practise the trade of type-founder apart from that of printer. Between 1549 and 1551 he printed a number of books in Paris, also continuing as type-cutter. By 1557 he was settled in Lyons and had married Antoinette Salamon, whose father, Bernard, was an artist associated with Jean de Tournes. Between 1557 and 1562 Granjon printed about twenty books in types designed by himself, following, after the fashion of the day, the cursive handwriting of the time. These types, usually known as "caractères de civilité," he himself called "lettres françaises," as especially appropriate to his own country. He was granted a monopoly of these types for ten years, but they were soon copied. Granjon appears to have lived in Antwerp for a time, but was at Lyons in 1575 and 1577, and for the next decade at Rome, working for the Vatican and Medici presses, his work consisting largely in cutting exotic types. Towards the end of his life he may have returned to live in Paris, where he died in 1590.

THIS BOOK WAS COMPOSED, PRINTED, AND BOUND BY H. WOLFF, NEW YORK · THE PAPER WAS MADE BY S. D. WARREN CO., BOSTON.